HERETICAL FISHING

BOOK 4

HERETICAL FISHING

A Cozy Guide to Annoying the Cults, Outsmarting the Fish, and Alienating Oneself

BOOK 4

Haylock Jobson

Podium

Cover design by Mary Cruz

ISBN: 978-1-0394-9446-6

Published in 2025 by Podium Publishing
www.podiumentertainment.com

As always, this book goes out to you, the reader.
It wouldn't exist without you.

I hope you enjoy.

Corporal Claws and the Campfire Recap

Corporal Claws grinned, her needle-sharp teeth lit by the coals of a smoldering campfire. "Where to start . . . ? The last installment began with I, maiden of the pond and fuzziest of Fischer's companions, single-handedly taking to the skies with the slaves of Gormo—"

The honks of two affronted pelicans cut her off. Warrant Officer Williams and Private Pelly swept over one of the surrounding dunes, firelight illuminating their glossy yet indignant plumage as they landed.

Cinnamon squeaked with laughter. "It was Bill and Pelly that took us into the sky."

"How could you have done it single-handedly?" Snips asked with a stream of amused bubbles. "You don't even have hands."

Claws glowered at them both. "*You're being pediatric. What matters is—*"

"Pedantic," Ellis corrected, not looking up from his notebook.

". . . What the *frack* did you just call me?"

"The word you were searching for. It's pedantic, not pediatric."

"Yeah? Well, your *mother* is a *pedantic!*"

"That . . . that is not how it works. It is an adjecti—"

A bolt of pure lightning split the world in two, interrupting the stupid words of an even stupider man. When the blinding flash retreated, electricity danced across Claws's fur. "*You* came to *me* for this recap, paper nerd! Now sit down and record my chirps!"

"I came to ask everyone, actually, but you keep screaming over the top—"

"*It was I!*" Claws screamed over the top of him. "Sure, a couple of *birds* did the lifting, but it was I, wielder of lightning and slurper of oysters, that contained the prisoners with my mighty power!"

"Just to be clear, when you say you *contained* them, are you referring to how you shocked any waking cultivators back into unconsciousness?"

"Yes. Master calls it *tasing*—why use lot word when few word do trick? More importantly, did I *stutter, you limp-penciled, paper-hands, moustachio-mouthed motherfu—*"

A cloud of cloying smoke engulfed everyone in the blink of an eye, its scent rich and harsh and inviting. As fast as the haze arrived, it retreated, drawn back into the crab from whence it came. Rocky took another hit of his cigarette as all attention settled on him. "Might I suggest we return to the topic at hand, comrades? As much as I enjoy your hijinks, Corporal Claws, my mistress wishes to return to the pond and meditate, post-haste."

The sparkle in Snips's lone eyestalk was brighter than the stars above as she gazed over at the reformed Rocky. The reflection grew even brighter a second later, but for a much less wholesome reason—a murderously inclined otter had launched herself toward them with enough lightning to stun a pod of whales.

Rocky became a blur as he cocked both clackers open toward the mammalian projectile, gathering volcanic chi. Claws retreated. She zapped to the sand, only meters away. Both spirit beasts stared each other down, and the tension broke when she cracked an electrically charged grin.

"In that case," she chirped, waving dismissively with both forepaws, "let's speed-run this recap!" Instead of launching into a monologue, however, she bent over and started digging.

Pistachio's otherwise stoic antennae waved about, curious. Lemon extended a single root to peer down into the widening pit. The five Buzzy Boys present let out an inquisitive tone with their wings, the relatively quiet sound a stark reminder to the other animal pals that Queen Bee and Bumblebro were elsewhere, working on . . . *something.*

Brigadier Borks gave a few joyous barks and dashed to join, his animalistic instincts and desire to help both demanding he participate. In moments, a meter-tall mound of sand had appeared. Claws patted the good boy's head, shocking him only a little—which, in her opinion, showed *impeccable* self-control—then perched atop her makeshift throne.

"The slaves were freed!" she screamed.

All nodded.

"Our great Master, Fischer, did what he'd call *'some magical bullshit,'* and New Tropica was built to the southwest, using all the pearlescent stones we'd accumulated by harvesting *delicious* oysters—which reminds me! When this was happening, I single-hand— uhhh, single-*pawedly* fought a giant mollusk of the deep! I won, of course! Its flesh was sweet, savory, and—"

Borks interrupted with a bark.

"*Did so* happen!" Claws leveled a lightning-wreathed limb at him. "You can't prove it didn't!"

"Mayhap it did," Rocky said, cooler than a winter morning. "But it wasn't mentioned earlier, Corporal Claws, so it is perhaps not relevant. Why not recount your victories that others already know about?"

"Fine." Claws sniffed. "Anyway, after that there was a revolt by some of those we saved! But one was a double agent! The betrayers were betrayed! One of said betrayed betrayers had a hidden ability! He could have hurt people, *but I saved the day*!"

"*We* saved the day," Snips hissed, shaking her carapace. "With the help of Borks and the cultivators that did all the *actual* work. That's not even mentioning Deklan and Dom, who almost had a breakthrough and saved themselves."

"*Ruff!*" Borks agreed.

Claws rolled her eyes. "You're all being pediatric again—and Hippocratic."

Ellis's eyebrow, cheek, and lip twitched. "I must address that crime-against-linguistics of a sentence, Claws. Neither pediatric nor Hippocratic mean what you think—"

"Everyone is interrupting," Claws interjected—definitely *not* interrupting. "I had a mini breakthrough and worked out how to infuse items with lightning! Then, when the king arrived, I—"

"*You dare!*" Cinnamon screamed, so manic it took Claws a moment to recognize them as words.

Rocky appeared behind the fluffy bunny, having to flood his clackers with chi to keep her from attacking.

"*You only did that with my help! I was the one that kicked boulders at you! Let me go, Rocky! I demand satisfaction!*"

"*Fiiine.* You helped. As I was saying, the king—"

Snips blew a loud stream of chastising bubbles, but some of her amusement leaked out. "Were you going to mention that you only started training because of the efforts of the saved cultivators? What about Roger, who stepped up to instruct the people willing to risk themselves in protecting Tropica?"

"Pshhhh. Maybe I just knew you would jump in and correct it for me, you wet-shelled, soggy-hinged, absolutely barnacled bi—"

Warmth oozed over the dunes in all directions. From warmth to heat, it quickly eclipsed that of the smoldering fire, hotter by orders of magnitude. With it came light, the chaotic lines on Rocky's blackened carapace glowing red and angry, his warning not needing to be voiced.

Claws attempted to give a nonchalant shrug, but her audible swallow ruined it. She cleared her throat. "Right. As I was saying, basically all of my advancements before the fight were because of the efforts of others." She chanced a glance at Rocky, and some of the tension left her shoulders when she noticed his receding anger. "More importantly, while all of this was going on, the royal forces of Gormona were off on a *really* dumb mission. They went to Theogonia, a city that once rivaled their power before the war decades ago."

She eyed everyone, expecting an interruption. When none came, she hurried on. "He intended on freeing the corrupted cultivators imprisoned there, but rather than being only a little idiotic, he went *full* moron, deciding to channel that caustic essence himself. He also made his followers, along with his own wife and daughter, do the same. Did I miss anything?"

"The captured cultivators believed they were bird—"

"*Hey!*" Claws chirp-screamed, head snapping toward the impudent fool. "That was one of the big reveals! I was saving it for the Defense of Tropica!"

"Claws . . ." Ellis looked up from his notepad. "They already know what happened. This is just a recap."

She sighed with her whole body, seeming to deflate as she fell to the sand. "I'm *besieged* by pediatrics. Even the basics of storytelling are beyond them. What is an otter to do?"

"How did the Defense of Gormona start again . . . ?" Snips asked, blowing thoughtful bubbles. "The king channeled his corrupted chi to teleport them close, then rushed in surrounded by a giant ball of fire. When he got here, though . . . was it not Roger who exchanged the first—"

"Boulders from the sky!" Claws yelled, reinflating and springing to her feet. "I filled massive rocks with *lightning*, *launched* them from a mountain, then—" She cut off, rolling her eyes at the bunny that had just sat bolt upright. "*Yes, Cinnamon, you helped*—but it was *I* who then rode those meteors down toward the king! It was a *glorious* ambush! The *perfect* start to a battle!"

Reinvigorated by the memory of her own exploits, Claws raced through the rest.

"One of the enemy bird people was Roger's mortal enemy! They squared off! The king and his son were exchanging blows! People swapped partners and whacked the absolute crap out of each other!" Her eyes darted around, the scene replaying in her mind's eye. "Deklan was wielding *fish*! Teddy had a mini breakthrough! I was zippety-zapping people all over the place! There were alchemists—one of them had awakened earlier—and instead of running for safety, they stuck around to mute the senses of the attackers with a smokey concoction that no one had known of before but can apparently hide people from even our *glorious master who was stuck back in the forest for some reason and had to listen to a hidden voice in the world beneath us and he couldn't come save us and we really thought it might be the end but not completely just like the smallest bit of doubt and then*—"

She gasped for air, filling her lungs.

"Barry had a breakthrough! He's so full of himself that he turned into a muscleman! The king fought back with corruption! Lieutenant Coronel Lemony Thicket arrived with her unnamed tree-spirit pal, and they flooded pure essence out, fighting against the attackers' pollution. Some other stuff took place, but none of it matters, because . . ." Claws shivered, her eyes borderline manic. "*It* happened. Our glorious master, selfless and kind and loving as he is, accepted responsibility for the church—for *all* of Tropica. He put everything aside, accepting that in order to be happy and free of worry, he needed to embrace leadership."

She grinned, her needle-sharp teeth tingling as electricity arced between them.

"This acceptance of self facilitated another breakthrough—the biggest we've seen by far. Able to harness the power of the very world around him, he returned to Tropica in a flash, revealing to us lowly peons on the path of ascension what actual strength looks like. He raised platforms of light with the flick of his wrist. He cleansed the king's corruption from this world, including from the fallen city of Theogonia. Only the king and Roger's enemy didn't accept his offer of redemption, and were burned away as a result."

She let out a hissed breath, her grin replaced by a content smile.

"And then his light merged old and New Tropica, making them become one. The original village absorbed all the System-enhanced buildings and incorporated them into its form. Aaaand . . . Huh. I think that's about it. Did I miss anything?"

Everyone just stared back. Snips broke the silence with a small stream of bubbles.

"That was actually very well done, Claws. Not entirely linear, but impressive nonetheless. Ellis?"

"It will do. Thank you. Does anyone else have something to add?"

In stark contrast to the crab he'd once been, Rocky raised one of his black and red pincers.

"Of course!" Ellis, now standing, quickly scribbled in his notepad. "How could we have forgotten Rocky's transformation and timely arrival?"

"Oh, not that, good sir," Rocky replied, making a polite yet dismissive gesture with his claw. "I was going to assert that my beloved mistress's capability, beauty, and wondrous carapace were all ill-served in that recounting. Might I suggest a paragraph or two speaking only of her? I can prepare them if necessary. She *is* the first disciple, after... *all?*"

A soft, high-pitched squeal made Rocky trail off. Only when his eyes settled on Claws did she realize the sound was coming from her own mouth, the reminder of Snips's seniority causing the noise to make itself. She cleared her throat and averted her eyes, not wanting to risk the fervid crab's ire.

"Well then," Ellis said, closing his notebook and turning to leave. "I will see you all on the morrow."

"We should probably go to bed too," Cinnamon peeped, stretching her head to the sky. "We all need rest."

"Agreed," Snips hissed. "But first..."

She turned toward Rocky.

Claws had no idea what the spiky crab was about to do—but Rocky clearly did. He shot to his feet, the red lines of his carapace aglow with realization.

His mistress nodded and stepped forward, patting the top of his carapace with one of her barbed clackers. "I appreciate your contribution to the conversation, Rocky. You helped keep things focused, you defended my honor when insulted, and you hyped me up despite my actions being less than others."

"I do it all for you, mistress. I must, however, disagree with that last point. You—"

Snips shot forward, blue jets of water streaming from her joints. In one fluid movement, she collected Rocky, drew him back, and yeeted him skyward.

Her cutting him off mid-sentence had the desired effect: as he rocketed high over the bay, there was a hint of shocked excitement to his voice.

"*EEEEEEEEEEEEeeeeeeeeeeeeeeeee—*"

A salty tear welled in Snips's eye as he disappeared beyond the dunes and presumably over the horizon. "*Plop,*" she whispered.

Corporal Claws looked from crab to empty sky, then toward Ellis, who had only made it three steps before standing still, reopening his notebook, and scribbling within its pages. She shook her head, unable to keep the corners of her mouth from tugging up into a small smile.

She may be surrounded by pediatrics on all sides, but they were *a lot* of fun.

HERETICAL FISHING

BOOK 4

Prologue

Beneath a cloud-covered sky, a creature of unparalleled mayhem slunk through the underbrush of a verdant forest. The sun had set almost an hour ago, the day's illumination slowly giving way to the murky darkness of night. Despite a distinct lack of wind, the air was thick with noise, calls of countless crickets and cicadas climbing before fading away once more.

Most humans, with their fragile bodies and rampant anxiety, would see such a night as a bad omen. They'd retreat to the caves, hollows, and houses that they called home, not leaving until the rays of the coming morning graced the world once more. Other beings, however, delighted in the lack of light, wind, and silence by which prey could sense them. The creature currently slinking through the underbrush was one such hunter.

The reason was rather simple: It was a perfect night for mischief.

As if to confirm this very fact, faint voices broke through the still air, reaching the enhanced hearing of the creature. She grinned, revealing needle-sharp teeth that would have gleamed in the moonlight if any were present. With anticipation roiling through her veins and her vigor replenished, she rushed forward, her limbs as silent as the nonexistent wind. The forest blurred past. It took only moments for her to reach the source of the conversation, and she stared at the home, a devious sparkle in her eye.

"I *hate* moonless nights," a feminine voice said from inside.

"I know, dear," a man responded, his footsteps closing the distance between them. "At least it's finally getting warmer. We might not even need to light the fire tonight."

The woman snorted. "And sit in the dark? We may as well just run out into the night and let the horrors have us."

It was all the creature could do not to leap through the wall in that instant. They were taunting her. Inviting her to enter their home in a suitably dramatic manner and confirm their wildest suspicions. She tried to fight back the urge, knowing her master would probably disapprove . . . but she wasn't strong enough. Her muscles ached with the desire to obliterate the wall, to shatter the side of their home and appear before them in a storm of rubble and dust. She wanted to see their faces.

No, she *had* to see their faces. She needed their fright as much as she needed to breathe.

Hunching down on all fours, lightning chi jolted from her core. In the blink of a cultivator's eye, it wreathed her limbs. She exploded forward, prepared for impact, and . . . halted midair, an unyielding grip holding her by the scruff of the neck.

I raised a brow at my troublesome otter, bringing her up to eye level. "And just what do you think you're doing, missy?"

There was a flash of panic in Corporal Claws's eyes that was swiftly hidden behind a thin veneer of innocence. *Who, me?* she seemed to chirp, shrugging and giving a half-hearted trill. *Nothing.*

"Nothing, huh? You definitely weren't about to launch yourself *through* someone's wall with the express intention of terrifying them?"

She'd opened her mouth to retort, but it remained ajar as she searched for the correct response. In desperation, she swung her head to the person beside me, seeking assistance.

Maria shook her head, her sun-bleached hair swishing and eyes unable to completely hide her amusement. "Don't look at me, Claws. Fischer is right. This first meeting is important." She reached up and scritched behind Claws's fluffy ear. "The last thing we want to do is make them scared of us."

Claws deflated, going limp in my grasp. *Sorry*, she chirped.

"It's okay," I said, cradling her still-limp body in my arms. "It's not your fault that trickery lives in your heart."

She nodded sagely, agreeing with the assessment as Maria gave her a reassuring pat on the head.

"Who's out there?" a voice boomed from the building.

"Best behavior," I whispered to Claws, carrying her with me as I strode around the side of the house. "G'day, mate," I said, giving a small smile.

"This is the Osnan family's private land, and if you value your neck, I suggest you *leave.*" Despite the strength of his words, worry lined his face.

"We passed the watch house on our way here." I pointed behind me, back through the forest. "It was empty."

"The guards must be doing their rounds. This is your last chance, friend. If they find you here . . ."

"Hello!" Maria said, resting her head against my arm and casting her beautiful smile his way. "You don't have to worry—we're not here to hurt you."

The man's hand tightened around something out of sight, and as he pulled a metal-spiked club into view, I let out a sigh.

Corporal Claws stood at attention in my arms, puffing out her chest. She jabbed a paw in his direction and let out a high-pitched growl, demanding he put the weapon down. I rubbed my temples as Claws climbed atop my head, getting a higher vantage point from which to stare down her nose at the man. His eyes went wide, the undeniable proof that she was no normal creature worming its way into his psyche.

Showing incredible stupidity, impressive bravery, or an unholy combination of both, the man pulled the club back with practiced speed, preparing a strike. He was clearly trained. To our enhanced awareness, though, he may as well have been moving through water. Despite his lack of a threat, Corporal Claws reached for her chi, preparing lightning just in case.

"Enough," I commanded, letting my will pour out.

The world obeyed.

Light surrounded everyone, appearing from the ground so swiftly that only I witnessed its movement. I made a slight gesture with my hand, and the woman, who had snuck out a back door and flanked us, appeared beside him. She had been sighting a crossbow, its stock braced against her shoulder. I stepped forward slowly and pushed the weapon down with one finger.

"As my beautiful fiancée said, we're not here to hurt you."

"Cultivator . . ." the man said, his thousand-yard stare seeming to peer through me. His vision refocused and drifted up to land on Claws. "Spirit beast . . ."

"Yeah, mate, but it's not what you think." I reached up and yoinked the troublesome otter from my head, resting her on one arm and giving her a good scritching. She leaned into it, cooing and forgetting all about her animosity. I hoped showing them her soft side would ease their worries, but considering I was still holding them in place with translucent vines of light, I wasn't surprised when their panic remained.

"I'm guessing the guards have been gone for a month or so, yeah?" I asked, shifting the conversation.

The man didn't respond, but the woman shook her head. "Two weeks . . ." Her male companion shot her a warning glare, but unaware or uncaring of his disapproval, she continued. "They returned to the capital, but their replacements never arrived."

I nodded. "I can explain that. It's a pretty crazy story, though . . ."

I gave them an extremely abridged version of my time in this world. My arrival and awakening. The slow trickle of animal pal ascensions. The founding of the Church of Fischer, our raid on the capital city in which we stole the king's artifacts and sent him flying through a mountain or two, and finally, the king's failed attack on Tropica. Surprisingly, some of the color had returned to their faces as my tale petered out.

"You're serious, aren't you?" he asked.

"Serious as a summer storm, mate."

"*Aphrodite's bohemian breasts . . .*" the woman swore.

Maria choked on nothing, then cleared her throat, her eyes dancing as she pressed her lips into a line.

"What are you going to do to us . . . ?" the man asked, his thousand-yard stare returning.

I cocked my head. "Do to you? Nothing. I actually had a request, but you're free to turn it down. You can do whatever you want, really."

"A request . . .?"

"Yup!" Maria answered, beaming another smile. "We were hoping you'd keep tending this farm as you're doing now. Nothing more, nothing less."

"You'll be compensated, of course," I added. "And protected."

"We . . . we can keep tending to our grove . . . ?" the woman asked, hope entering her voice.

"Exactly." I grinned. "We're quite fond of your work here, you see. In fact, I'm not sure I could function without it."

I retracted my power and released my hold on them. Neither raised their weapons again. We spoke for hours, taking the time to answer each and every question the two had—they were about to become a pivotal part of Tropica's operation, after all. In the beginning, they were hesitant, but they slowly grew more sure of themselves. By the time we were finished, the hour was late. The information revealed had taken its toll, leaving the couple yawning and watching us with bleary gazes. As a bonus, their fatigue seemed to wash away the shock of our answers.

"Sorry," the man said, rubbing the bridge of his nose. "We had a long day pruning."

"Hey, don't sweat it. You should get some rest. We'll camp overnight and head out in the morning after we procure some product."

He raised both hands in protest. "No, we couldn't sleep inside while you sleep in the elements. Please, take our bed, Your, er . . . *Grace?*"

Maria chortled at the horror dawning on my face. "What say you, *Your Grace?*"

Confusion shone through the two farmers' exhaustion, and I shook my head. "Please, just call me Fischer. And we don't want your bed."

"If you're sure . . ."

"Positive." I gave them a smile and nodded at the door. "Go rest. We can talk again in the morning."

With sheepish expressions, they retreated into their home, whispering in hushed tones the moment the door was closed. I shook my head and withdrew my hearing, sharing a smile with Maria at their excitement.

"Well, that went well," she said as we strode in the direction of the grove.

I rubbed Claws's head. "It did, all things considered."

While we'd talked, the clouds above had cleared, revealing a blanket of stars and a crescent moon. No one spoke as we traveled the few hundred meters to the trees we'd come to see. Ahead, the other three members of our expedition withdrew from the shadows. Brigadier Borks wagged his bushy tail, excited by our approach. Sergeant Snips, her eyepatch looking marvelous in the pale moonlight, blew happy little bubbles. Beside her, Rocky took a long drag of his cigarette as he looped a claw around Snips's carapace and pulled her close.

She batted him away half-heartedly, giving him a look that was filled with such love I felt the need to grab Maria's hand. She planted a swift kiss on my cheek before returning her attention to Snips and Rocky, who were now play-fighting.

Claws made a retching sound, causing Snips to freeze. She slowly spun the otter's way, murder shining in her lone eye. Claws held her gaze, bent at the waist, and mimed making herself sick. It was a declaration of war if ever I'd seen one, and Snips's answer was swift. I could have stopped them if I wanted to, but I didn't. Doing so would just make their tempers flare later.

Snips raced toward Claws with blue chi billowing from her carapace. Claws grinned, revealing her dagger-sharp teeth as lightning wreathed her body. The two collided and shot off through the forest in a blur, dozens of blows exchanged with each passing second.

"Come on," I said, walking forward. "Let's have a peek at the trees we came to see."

The closest corner of the grove was where the apparent pruning had taken place. The trees were heavily cut back, anything above head height lopped off. I felt the need to inspect it, to examine the trunk and the cut they'd used to reduce the size of their prized trees, but something in the distance caught my attention.

Maria let out a soft gasp. "Are those . . . ?"

We looked at each other, and before our grins could fully form, we were off. We sprinted across the grass, traveling as fast as only cultivators could. When we skidded to a stop, I reached up and softly squeezed a red berry. Though it appeared ripe, the fruit was firm. Borks appeared beside us a moment later, his tongue lolling and tail wagging as he stared up at the fruit-laden tree. I cast a gaze down the row, expecting to find Rocky racing after us and blowing insulting bubbles.

But he was no longer the same crab. Rocky strolled leisurely, like a gentleman perusing a noble's garden. He gave me a respectful nod.

Maria snorted. "Still not used to that."

"No kidding," I replied, my gaze drifting back to the surrounding trees.

"I can't believe how many there are . . ."

A soft breeze blew, making the leaves and clusters of red berries shift in the moon's ethereal light. I plucked one from the small tree, and with it held before us, I squeezed. The skin ruptured, releasing a sweet fragrance that reminded me of jasmine and hibiscus. We partook of the tiny berry's flesh, and my forehead creased as I took in its unique flavor, both fruity and floral.

Twin powers approached, and as Claws and Snips attempted to fly past us, I dashed before them. They skidded to a stop, staring up at me.

"Truce," I said. "Try this."

With care that belied their murderous movements only seconds ago, they ate the last of the fruit. All that remained on my palm were two seeds, their forms pale and green.

"Uhhh," Maria said, poking them. "Are they not ready yet?" She picked them up and sniffed, her nose scrunching up. "Yuck. They smell wrong."

I laughed at the expression of vague disgust on her face as she appraised the treasures we'd come all this way for. It wasn't surprising; she'd only ever seen the finished product.

"They're perfect. This is what they look like when they're still raw."

She placed them back on my palm and licked her lips, returning her attention to the dozens of trees around us, each of them covered in hundreds, perhaps thousands, of berries. "Each fruit gives two beans . . . ?" she asked, her disbelief evident.

"They do," I confirmed, also staring at the trees and the wealth they held. A wave of relief washed over me. "Looks like we're not gonna run out of coffee anytime soon . . ."

CHAPTER ONE

Tropica

The following afternoon, birdsong lilted through the air, accented by the unerring trundle of wagon wheels over packed earth. The sun was beaming down from behind, casting our shadows over the treasure we'd procured from the old Osnan farm. It was an absolute mound of coffee beans, and despite being exposed to their aromatic scents for the entire day, they were still as lovely as the sun above and the woman beside me.

As if she could read my thoughts, Maria rested her head on my shoulder and let out a happy little sigh. "I'm glad we took this trip the old-fashioned way." Despite her words, she rubbed her lower back, her brow knitting. "Maybe we should get out and walk for a while, though. This sitting situation isn't ideal."

I smirked and gestured down at the throne I'd made out of coffee-filled burlap sacks. "If the queen of caffeine desires, this humble servant can teleport us back."

She shook her head. "No. Ellis would annoy you to no end the moment we got back if you were to use your power. Besides, it's peaceful just rolling along in the afternoon sun—lumbar support be damned."

Claws chirped her agreement, rolling over and exposing her stomach on Maria's lap. Borks, who I'd thought was asleep, wagged his tail at my feet, making a soft *thump, thump, thump* on the wagon.

I opened my mouth to agree with the sentiment, then spun toward Maria, giving her a questioning look. "Wait, how do you know what lumbar support is?"

It was her turn to stare at me in confusion, but it swiftly devolved into a giggle. "Because, you goose, the first time you got drunk on Barry's rum—"

"Pew-pew juice," I corrected.

"Right." She rolled her eyes playfully. "Pew-pew juice. Well, during the celebratory feast the other day after we beat the king, you went on a massive tirade about office chairs and how prohibitively expensive a good one is. I couldn't forget the terms *lumbar support*, *ergonomics*, and *breathability* if I tried."

I barked a laugh. "My bad. I'm, er, *passionate* about posture, I suppose. Is your back actually hurting, though? We can get out and walk."

She shook her head before resting it on my shoulder again. "I think I'll enjoy my caffeine throne while I can. We'll be there soon anyway."

I glanced up and saw that she was right. We'd be able to see Tropica from the next mountaintop. "Humble steeds," I declared, gifting my voice a noble and pretentious quality. "If it pleases you, would you kindly pick up the pace? My betrothed desires the comfort of home."

Our carapace-covered beasts of burden hissed in acknowledgment, but rather than speed up, Rocky, who was pulling one handle of the cart, stopped entirely. From the other side, Snips cocked her cute little head and blew curious bubbles.

Rocky gestured back at the cart, dipped his body, and made a humble series of hisses. *Please, mistress,* he seemed to implore. *Allow me to carry the burden.*

Snips made a fuss about how extra he was being, but I noticed the little skip in her step as she leaped up onto the cart. Rocky's reform and subsequent return was a source of great joy, and seeing the effect it had on my favorite crabby girl only compounded my gratitude. When all my animal pals, Maria, and I had bonded in the sky, our deepest desires were revealed, and Snips's pain and regret over Rocky had been a bitter pill to swallow. I'd wished for an ideal outcome, but his homecoming exceeded even my wildest expectations.

As he slung some rope over the cart's handles and started tying some rather complicated knots, I caught his eye and gave him a nod. Rocky paused for the barest of moments, pulled a cigarette from nowhere—*seriously, where did he keep getting those?*—and lit it on his shell before returning my nod. He slipped onto the harness he'd tied, shot Snips a smooth wink, and took off.

To my surprise, he was expending chi. His volcanic essence reached out before him, hot enough to melt the packed earth we traveled atop. As he strode over the molten ground, he sucked the heat back up, hardening and allowing our wagon's wheels to roll right over it. The result was an impressively smooth road, and though we traveled at a hastened clip, it was as though the wagon had suspension.

Claws let out an appreciative chirp and slid into the gap between my and Maria's leg, wiggling her furry little tushy until she slipped all the way between us. I raised an eyebrow at her, but her eyes were already closed, a grin spreading over her features as she enjoyed the blissful afternoon sunshine. I swiveled and lifted my face toward the setting rays, also radiating in their touch. Though winter in Tropica had been a mild affair, I was excited about spring's arrival. It would mean longer days and more time spent fishing. That line of thought made another possibility come to mind.

"What's that smile about?" Maria asked.

I faced forward again and stretched, luxuriating in the slight ache of my muscles. "I was just thinking about spring. It got me wondering about the possibility of catching new fish. Spring is the season of life, right?"

"Oh!" She shimmied like a child that just learned they were having ice cream for breakfast. "I hadn't even considered that! Do you think they'll take the same bait? Will we need to create more equipment? Why are you smirking? What plans have you already started to—"

"Whoa!" I laughed, holding up my hands in an attempt to stall the barrage of questions. "I have some ideas, but they're not ready yet. They're still cooking."

A dangerous gleam entered her eye. "What's mine is yours, dear." She leaned forward and lay a hand on my leg, raising her other hand to examine her engagement ring in a theatrical manner. "Secrets aren't a foundation to build a good marriage upon. Wouldn't you agree, dearest betrothed?"

"I'm only keeping them to myself because I don't want to get you excited, and they're not really secrets. You already know about them."

"Oh? What would you call them?"

"Mysteries, of course." I shot her a wink. "Makes them sound intriguing and mystical, which, by extension, makes me seem—"

"Like a bit of a prick?"

Caught entirely off guard by the use of my own vernacular, I guffawed. "Maria! How could you?"

She covered her mouth and giggled. "Just teasing. Keep your secrets."

"Mysteries, you mean."

"Sure. Mysteries. But the moment you decide to try something, you have to tell me. Deal?"

I extended an arm, which she immediately grasped and shook. The rest of the passage back to Tropica was spent in silence. Bird calls and Borks's snoring were the only sounds that broke through the stillness, both noises adding to the tranquility.

As we crested the mountain and caught sight of the new version of Tropica, I couldn't help but stare. Despite my usually flawless memory, my brain still expected the village's old and crude buildings to await us. Instead, we were met with beauty.

No, that wasn't really fair. The old version of Tropica was beautiful in its own way. The village was lived in and the buildings were loved, even if they were constructed of basic materials. There was an unquantifiable allure to them, something that screamed this was the kind of place one could settle in.

The encampment to the southwest that we'd dubbed New Tropica had been an improvement on the original in terms of function and technology. It had plumbing, vastly improved town planning, and even had the magical fantasy world equivalent of electricity, its functions powered by essence. What it didn't have, however, was the charm that the old Tropica possessed. Each building, no matter its purpose, was uniform and conservative. As a whole, they lacked a certain pizazz that the older version of Tropica had an abundance of.

This new layout, the one that the very world had helped me shape . . . was hard to find the right words for. It was a perfect amalgamation of both villages, combining their strengths to create something greater than the sum of its parts. Each building was functional, technologically advanced, and stunning. They had building- and craft-specific adornment, with wooden flourishes here, cast-iron moldings there, and large glass windows in any place suitable.

Everywhere, life grew. Small gardens separated many a building, their beds filled with plants of different shapes, colors, and sizes. Some walls were absolutely covered in vines, as if the respective homes had existed for years, not sprung up from the ground mere days ago. Magical lamps peppered every street, their poles ornate and unique. As we watched, they ignited, their flames dancing languidly within glass prisms. It wasn't yet dark enough for them to light up their surroundings, yet it was delightful all the same.

A word to describe the sight finally sprang to mind, but before I could speak it, Maria stole it right from my lungs.

"Perfect . . ." she said, her eyes all but sparkling as she stared down at our village.

"It is," I agreed, my gaze not leaving her for a moment.

Given how connected we were now, she understood my meaning. She finally looked my way, and we stared at each other for a long moment, both broadcasting our love for the other.

"*Hyuuurk!*" Claws said from our laps, making a sound like a cat violently ejecting the contents of its stomach over the nicest rug it could find.

"Claws!" Maria tried to grab her by the scruff of the neck, but my otter pal was expecting it. She darted away, disappearing into the night with a crack of lightning that made my hair stand on end. She arced high into the air and slammed down into the middle of Tropica, chittering with laughter all the way.

By the time we rolled into the center of Tropica, a crowd was forming. Barry took a step forward, no doubt intent on asking how it went.

But Rocky had pressing business. *Mistress,* he seemed to say, his bubbles sincere as he sparked up a cigarette, *seeing as though you are well rested, might I request a favor?*

I immediately knew where this was going, and I shot Maria an exasperated look. "Are you serious, Rocky?" she demanded. "This is why you offered to pull the cart?"

Snips, however, merely nodded, acknowledging his question.

Rocky exhaled a small cloud of smoke, taking his time. Finally, he blew meaning-filled bubbles. *Please, mistress. I desire to be yeeted.*

Snips moved in a blur of billowing chi, her claw scooping Rocky up by the bottom of his carapace, and flung him east over the closest rooftops. A sound like thunder sprang into being as air exploded from him.

"*Eeee—*" was all he could get out before he left my enhanced hearing range. Though his limbs were splayed outward with centrifugal force, he held on to his cigarette for dear life.

"Nice arm, Snips," I said, earning happy bubbles and a shy shrug from her.

Barry shook his head, his muscular jaw tensing as he watched Rocky's departure. "Nice to see that some things haven't changed." He turned his attention toward us and gestured down at the sacks of coffee. "I take it the mission was a success?"

"More than you know, mate."

"Wait," Ellis said, looking up from his notepad as he stopped scribbling for the barest of moments. "Why did you not store the coffee beans within Borks's soul space? Once they are roasted, will they not perish faster when exposed to the air as they are? Wasn't the plan to keep them in the climate-controlled room that Borks can conjure?"

"Clever as always, Ellis," I replied. "But there's a simple explanation: We have something even more important than roasted coffee beans in there."

Ellis's visage turned feverish. "There is something in there that you deem more important than coffee . . . ?"

"Better if I show you, I think. Would you mind, Borks?"

Ruff! he barked, tearing a rift in space a second later.

"Just poke your heads in, fellas," I warned. "It's rather full."

As Barry's and Ellis's heads joined me on the other side of the portal, they both made odd faces. "Why does it smell like cut grass in here?" Barry asked, staring at the burlap bags filling the space.

A little bolt of lightning zipped into the room, and as soon as Claws landed, she was helpfully opening one of the sacks. Ellis and Barry watched her intently as she sliced it open with her namesake, but as she revealed the contents, they only grew more confused.

"Why are they green . . . ?" Barry asked.

"Because they're raw, mate. As they are now, they'll keep for up to a year." I grinned at them, not needing to feign my excitement. "We're going to make our own single-origin coffee."

CHAPTER TWO

Storage

"Okay, I have to ask at least once," Maria said, giving me an apologetic smile. "Are you *sure* this is a good idea?"

"I'm sure," I replied, giving her hand a small squeeze. "If we need to use Borks's dimensional space in an emergency, we'd have to ditch the beans. I'd rather risk them being stored in subpar conditions than discarded entirely."

George, the former lord of Tropica village, snorted from beside me, then seemed to remember himself. "Oh, er . . . sorry, Fischer."

I barked a laugh, glad that he was comfortable enough around me to react honestly. It was a far cry from the anxious mess he used to be. "Don't apologize, mate. What did you find so funny?"

Geraldine, his ever-supportive wife, patted George on the shoulder. "I'm guessing it's because you called this room subpar."

"That's fair." I gazed around at the smooth stone walls. "I guess it's a matter of perspective."

We were within a new building, something that hadn't existed at all in New Tropica. It was, ostensibly, a granary. It had dozens of rooms, all segregated to keep the contents sterile. To be honest, it felt a little reductive to call it *just* a granary, though. Each room was temperature and humidity controlled, with positive airflow to keep any unwanted particles out. Considering these functions, it could be an inoculation chamber for fungi, an operating room, or any other number of places that required as much sterility as possible.

It was only subpar compared to a single other place: Borks's spatial ability, which was self-cleansing, impenetrable, and *entirely* sealed off from contamination. The room we were in could be used for what some would deem better purposes, but what we needed right now was a place to store all our grains and beans, the most important of which we were about to retrieve.

I smiled up at the questioning look Borks was giving me and nodded. "Ready when you are, buddy."

With a wag of his tail and a happy little ruff, the air shattered and cracked, a black portal tearing into being. We formed a work line, with me and George within the portal and the two ladies without. It took mere minutes for us to move the tons of raw coffee beans, and as George and I stepped back outside, we found our partners blushing and whispering to one another.

"That can't be good, mate," I stage-whispered to George. "They're conspiring."

He gave an exaggerated shiver. "I pray for our health."

"Oh, shush," Geraldine said, sweeping over to slap him softly on the arm. "We were only saying good things."

"Speaking of good things," I replied, not so subtly shifting the topic. "There was a reason why I asked you two to help us move the beans."

Geraldine nodded. "I suspected as much. Why did you request us, then?"

"Well, I don't say this to be insulting, but pretty much everyone else has something going on. I know you two are relatively new to the whole cultivator thing, so don't feel pressured if it doesn't sound like your jam, but . . ." I trailed off as they spun to look at each other, their eyebrows doing their best to leave their face.

Frack, I thought. *I overstepped. I'll—*

They cut off my line of thinking when they burst into short and sharp laughter.

"Okay," I said. "You lost me."

"We were going to ask you for some direction," Geraldine replied, smoothing her dress. "I don't want to overdo fishing. We're worried that if we don't find a profession of sorts, it won't remain as fun. Does that make . . . why are you looking at me like that?"

Without realizing it, a frown had made its way to my face.

"Because he can't relate to getting sick of fishing," Maria explained for me, rubbing my upper back. "The man is obsessed."

"Yeah, that. But I get it—a profession is a good idea! You're both keen, then?"

"We are," George answered, grabbing Geraldine's hand. "When do we start?"

"First thing in the morning?" I suggested.

"That sounds good to me. We'll meet you—"

"Wait," I amended. "Is after brekky okay? I want to have a fish first—it's been forever."

"Are you serious?" Maria chastised, a smile betraying her intent. "It's been two days!"

"Two whole days without fishing!" I shook my head in feigned dismay. "Can you believe it?"

Maria sighed. "Let's meet midmorning. We should probably check in on the prisoners, too."

"Oh, good point! Checking the prisoners! That's for sure something a leader would do."

Geraldine gave us an amused look. "Come on, George—let's go get some rest."

As we left the granary and emerged into the street, Maria and I bid George and Geraldine farewell. A cool breeze washed over us when they were gone. Maria shivered and I pulled her into a tight side hug. "Should we get going, too?"

"Let's."

Claws, who had been napping atop Borks this entire time, let out a chirp of agreement. Together, we strode through the streets, gazing up at the village's beauty as we went.

* * *

By the time the first of the sun's rays peeked over the horizon, my rod was already baited up and ready to go. I took a deep breath, tasted the salt spray in the air, and cast my line out. It sailed high over the calm ocean, falling a score or so meters away with a soft *plop*. As my baited hook sank to the depths, George's words from yesterday arrived unbidden.

"*I don't want to overdo fishing*," I repeated, then blew air from my lips. "Can you believe he said such heresy with a straight face?"

No response came, so I swiveled to glance down the rock wall toward land, raising an eyebrow. "Guys?"

Technical Officer Theodore Roosevelt—Teddy for short—my newest animal pal and the goodest bear in all the lands, retracted his head from the crevice he'd been inspecting. He gave me a shocked look and pointed at himself as if to ask, *Who, me?*

Maria, whose attention was entirely on the sliver of eel she was feeding onto her hook, didn't even look up. "Did you say something?" she asked, her fingers moving deftly.

I thought to let out an exaggerated sigh, to act like a scorned lover or ignored pal, but I just shook my head and returned my attention to the ocean. "Never mind. It's too early and too perfect a day for hijinks."

As I reeled in the slack of my line and held one finger to it, Maria stepped up beside me. "I'm not sure Claws would agree with that assessment, but it certainly is a stunning morning."

She reeled until her line was taut, and together, we stared east. Teddy came and sat behind us. His massive snout twitched as he sniffed the wind, his eyes similarly pinned on the distant horizon in anticipation of the sun's arrival. When it came, we weren't disappointed. With the shifting of seasons, so, too, had the morning colors changed. Though the purple and pink shades were still prevalent, a light blue separated them, swiftly banishing the darkness lingering from the night.

A warm wind blew in from behind us. It was a welcome arrival after so many months of frigid gusts. Lost in the sensations of the world, I closed my eyes, reached a hand toward Maria . . . and found nothing. Frowning, I turned toward her, only to find her leaning back against Teddy's arm.

I smiled at the cheeky grin she gave me, unsurprised. "Mind if I join, Teddy?"

He let out a deep growl of assent, the sound so bassy that it shook the air in my chest. I scooted back to lean against him but froze when my line twitched. Maria jolted forward, her eyes watching the tip of her own rod.

"Did you get a bite?" she whispered, her gaze flicking to me for the barest of moments.

I licked my lips. "I think so. It—" I cut off as my rod bent down, the fish taking the hook.

"Fish on!" Maria yelled, hopping to her feet in an instant. Her eyes flicked to me again, and when she saw I'd hooked something too, they went wide with excitement. "Double hookup!"

My fish darted to the left and hers to the right. With ease only produced by practice, she dipped under my line, giggling as she danced over the slick rocks.

Not wanting to skull-drag our respective fish to shore, we both took our time, letting them take long runs and tire themselves out in between periods of us reeling them in. The longer the battle went on, the more excited I became, which was no new experience. But there was more to it today.

"Fischer! Does this feel new to you?"

Unable to contain my joy, I barked a laugh. "I was thinking the same thing! With the way they move, these might be a new species!"

She made a high-pitched noise and hopped from foot to foot, only to cut off abruptly as her fish took another run. I shot a glance toward the third member of our morning crew, finding Teddy's ears alert and eyes filled with anticipation. Waves of curiosity radiated from his core, strong enough to be felt over my giddiness.

As my line got closer and closer to shore, though, I swept all other thoughts aside. It was time to focus up. The fish must have caught sight of the rock wall, because it took a desperate run, the kicks of its tail sluggish in comparison to the start of our clash. The way it seemed to wind through the water reminded me of something, but I couldn't put my finger on it. I leaned closer, my excitement growing overwhelming, as I expected to see a flash of sun hitting its scales. But the reflection never came.

"What—" I began, then cut off as I saw something swirl beneath the small waves hitting the rock wall. It was long and lithe, its body covered in speckled flesh instead of scales. Though my confusion was great, my desire to be kind was greater. I lifted it out of the shallows, intent on identifying it as soon as possible. I saw a gnarly set of chompers on it, so I grabbed it by the gills, careful not to injure it. Before I could see more of its form, it drew my vision in.

Mature Wolf Eel
Rare
Found along the rocky shores of the Kallis Realm, these eels are named for their bite force. Because of their tendency to mate for life, eating the flesh of the wolf eel with a lover is purported to bring you closer together. Combined with their rarity, this belief causes the wolf eel to be considered a delicacy by many.

I shook my head to clear my eyes and stare down at the creature, taking in its features. As I looked at its long, finned tail, I realized why its movement had seemed similar—it was reminiscent of the other eel varieties I'd caught. That was where its similarity to the others ended, though. It had a body almost shaped like a tadpole, its head and body enlarged and filled with muscle. Its skin was kind of pudgy, a layer of protective fat protecting its vitals. I found myself frowning at it, and as I reached up to remove my hook, it lashed out.

Snap!

If not for my enhanced body, it might have taken a finger. I raised an eyebrow at Maria, who was ignoring me entirely in favor of staring down at her own catch, its skin and spots slightly darker than the one I held.

"Awww," she said. "They're *adorable*! Do you think they're a couple?"

I had to agree with her assessment. The things were ugly cute. Like a pug. Or those weird dogs that look like someone bred a shih tzu with a naked mole rat then washed them on a four-hour spin cycle.

"I hope so!" I replied, trying to keep my face straight. "Do you think that will make us come even closer together when we eat them? I wonder what they taste like?"

The look of utter shock, horror, and betrayal on Maria's face broke my mask of indifference. I cackled, holding the eel away from me as I bent at the waist. "Kidding! I was kidding!"

"I was about to call off the wedding!" She gestured at me with her eel, as if using its powerful jaws as a threat. "You let that fishy go right now!"

Still fighting back my mirth, I stepped down to the rocks. "Ready?"

She nodded and joined me, both of us releasing them at the same time, and the wolf eels did one of the most adorable things I'd seen since coming to this world. Rather than dart away, the one I'd held swam over to Maria's. They coiled as if checking in on each other, then swam back into the depths together, never once separating.

Maria slapped me softly on the arm. "That wasn't funny! How could you consider *eating* a happy couple? I was seriously reconsidering who you were!"

"Oh, c'mon. It was a *little* funny. Right, Teddy?"

His head darted between us, ears pinning back as existential dread arrived on his face at the prospect of having to choose a side.

"Don't mind him, Teddy." Maria rubbed our bear pal's shoulder, making some of his anxiety melt away. "Before Fischer has coffee, his humor is similar to that of Corporal Claws."

I raised my finger to protest, but paused. "Damn. You might be correct on that one."

"Always am." She shot me a wink and got to her feet. "Come on, then. Let's get you some caffeine."

"And I thought the eels were romantic," I replied, brushing off my pants.

She rolled her eyes at me, but there was no malice in it. "Enough jokes, mister. The sooner we get coffee and check in on the prisoners, the sooner we can go roast some beans with George and Geraldine."

Hand in hand, and with Teddy plodding along beside us, we headed off toward Tropica.

CHAPTER THREE

Facade

A warm breeze blew from the ocean and washed over me, the sand beneath my bare feet frosty by comparison. It was a reminder of the shifting seasons, making my thoughts turn toward spring and the new species it might bring to our shores. I imagined fishes of all different shapes and sizes, and just as I was picturing a colorful grouper with the head of a shark, the ground before us exploded.

I took a step forward. I had to put myself between the ambush and Maria.

Sand sprayed up in a gout, the air in my lungs quivering with a *boom* that shook the world. Our attackers had concealed their position, using long-forgotten methods to hide their presence from even the most powerful of cultivators. In a fraction of a second, they were flying from a hole in the earth. More limbs than should be possible, razor-sharp teeth and claws, and iron-hard exoskeletons descended upon us. The quickest of them flew directly for me, screeching a war cry that was loud enough to pierce the heavens.

I tensed my body, bellowed for Maria to get back, and plucked Corporal Claws out of the air. "Just kidding," I said, using one finger to tap Claws on the nose. "Boop. I knew you were there."

She whirled on the rest of the attackers—a rather impressive feat considering I still held her by the scruff of the neck—and unleashed a mighty chirp, demanding to know who had betrayed her.

"Nobody warned me, Claws. I can literally teleport people across the world anywhere our Domain touches. What makes you think I couldn't feel you there? I can smell the smoke the alchemists use to hide their chi, but I'm immune to it."

"For what it's worth," Maria said, "you would have scared me and Teddy if Fischer hadn't warned us."

A look of utter betrayal came to Claws's face as she turned back toward me, which only made me laugh. "I'm not going to apologize for warning them, Claws. You might have given poor Teddy a heart attack." I looked up, slightly narrowing my eyes at the arrayed animal pals. "I'm surprised you all went along with it, to be honest."

Claws had somehow convinced literally every single spirit beast to join in.

Sergeant Snips blew a hiss of happy bubbles and waved at me. Rocky gave a nod, one of his claws resting on Snips's, er, lower back?

Private Pistachio also dipped his head, the movement a little slower and more respectful than Rocky's.

Cinnamon leaped toward Maria, who giggled as she scooped her up into a hug. I reached over and scratched behind her ear, making her rear leg thump against Maria's arm.

Brigadier Borks, as a golden retriever, sprinted over and wound around our legs. His tongue lolled as he sat and stared up at me, his tail swishing back and forth.

Queen Bee and Bumblebro crawled out from his fur and waved up at us, as did a few of their progeny, the Buzzy Boys. Most of them were off patrolling Tropica's surroundings, but they'd ensured that some of their representatives were present to take part in the attempted prank.

Private Pelly and Warrant Officer Williams, aka Bill, unleashed honks of greeting as they swooped down toward the sand. The former landed on Maria's shoulder, and the latter on mine. We both reached up to give them scritches.

Last but far from least, Lieutenant Colonel Lemony Thicket made her move. She'd likely been the one that dug the hole they had hidden in, because her roots covered its walls. A thick limb rose from the ground to wrap around everyone present, pulling us into a group hug. No one protested. I noticed the other tree spirit there too, but it remained in the periphery, not physically joining the way Lemon had.

Between Maria and me, Claws cooed and purred, writhing around in delight. Feeling the pure joy washing from her core, I realized that this cuddle puddle was her true goal, and I couldn't help but smile. "Happy, Claws?" I whispered, earning a wide grin and a feverish nod. "Okay, gang, I'm enjoying this as much as the rest of you, but George and Geraldine are waiting back in town. Plus, we have to visit the prisoners first."

Lemon squeezed us tighter, holding us there for a few seconds before finally letting go. I was going to ask what everyone was up to for the day, but I didn't get a chance. The moment they were released from Lemon's grip, they waved, chirped, buzzed, or grinned before dashing off, going about their business. Even Lemon and her tree-spirit pal retreated, their roots and awareness retracting.

In a matter of seconds, only Maria, Teddy, Pistachio, and I remained. There was some hesitation on Pistachio's face, which might be as much emotion as I'd ever seen him express. He was a master at hiding his feelings, and even with my godlike instincts, he was a blank slate. I could have pushed through the facade, broken through his walls to comprehend what he was thinking. But that wasn't what friends do.

"You okay, mate?" I asked, kneeling down so I was eye level with him.

His antennae shifted in thought, the movements small enough to be almost imperceptible. Finally, he gave me a nod of thanks and turned away. With sweeps of his gigantic claw, he started filling in the hole. Maria, Teddy, and I exchanged a look before heading off, leaving him to it.

"Is he okay?" Maria asked when we were far enough away to not be heard.

I didn't need to fake the reassuring smile I gave her. "He will be. If and when he's ready to reach out, he will."

Teddy stared back at Pistachio long after Maria and I had turned our attention toward Tropica.

I tickled one of his ears to get his attention. "Come on, mate. Let's have some trust in him." Teddy stared a second longer before turning to face us. He shook his head, and the worry in his eyes faded away.

"Do you think there will be any changes today?" I asked, shifting the topic.

"You know what?" Maria replied. "I have a good feeling about today. I bet we'll see some improvement."

"I hope you're right." I stared up at the new architecture of Tropica as we stepped onto the System-made street. "This world has kinda spoiled me when it comes to breakthroughs. I'm used to people just . . ." I snapped my fingers. "Transforming like that, you know?"

She blew air from her nose, making me tear my eyes from the ornate rooftop of a three-story house. Her eyes sparkled with glee. "It's been like five days. Talk about impatient."

"Right?" I asked exaggeratedly. "Can you believe the absolute audacity of these new arrivals? Making me wait the better half of a week for some change? If they weren't already in prison, they should be locked up."

"You've been the leader for all of two minutes. Are you already going mad with power? Do I need to worry?"

"Yeah, don't get me wrong, this world is nice and all, but I think introducing a prison industrial complex would *really* take it to the next level. You feel me?"

She stopped mid-step, raising an eyebrow. "Do I want to know what any of that is?"

"Not even a little. Lucky for you, it looks like Sue won't give me a chance to explain."

"I can hear you, Fischer!" Sue's voice absolutely boomed over the street separating us. More than one non-cultivator flinched at the sound and covered their ears. "Oh my." She winced, then continued in a much softer voice. "Sorry, everyone."

To say that the last five days had been an adjustment period would be an understatement of grand proportions. Dozens of faces stared back at us from the line to Sue's new bakery, some cultivators, some regular townsfolk. Along with the layout of the village, the composition of its denizens had also changed dramatically. All things considered, I thought the non-cultivators were adjusting pretty well.

"It still feels weird not having to suppress or hide our abilities," I said to Maria as we closed the distance to Sue.

"I don't know," she whispered back. "Feels liberating to me, if that makes sense. It was as if I was lying about my true self before."

"Agreed," Sue added, coughing the word into her hand.

All eyes tracked us as Maria and I continued walking, taking our position at the end of Sue's line. I gazed up at the transformed bakery, and despite having seen it scores of times by now, it still took my breath away. Its frame was made up of a deep-brown wood, entire logs having appeared from nowhere during the creation of the new village. Gray bricks comprised most of the walls, with high glass windows surrounded by intricately carved wooden trim. The shop front was similar to before, but having seen the new kitchen, I was all too aware of how significant the changes to the inside were. It was practically incomparable.

As the line got shorter and shorter, the sun peeked over the surrounding buildings, having to travel higher in the sky to find the street now that the village had grown. It beamed down onto Sue's face, who took a moment to close her eyes and enjoy its touch. Maria and I turned toward it and did the same.

A moment later, Sue cleared her throat, arresting my attention. "Can I help you?" she asked, a glint in her eye. "There are customers waiting."

"I apologize on behalf of my betrothed." Maria stepped up to the counter and adopted a mask of faux sadness. "He has an affliction, you see. Every morning, he is grumpy, selfish, and uncouth." She leaned forward, arching a conspiratorial eyebrow. "But there is a cure, you see."

"There is?" Sue leaned all the way forward, feigning intrigue.

"Oi, woman!" Sturgill, Sue's husband, barked, peering around the dividing wall "Would you stop messing with Fischer?" He shot me an apologetic look.

But I held up a hand to stall him. "Not to worry, mate. It's Maria messing with me."

"Oh." He pursed his lips. "Carry on, then." Sturgill disappeared from sight as quickly as he'd come, leaving me alone with the wolves.

"You were saying?" Sue continued. "There's a cure for this horrific curse that Fischer has?"

"Aye," Maria replied, sounding half pirate, half . . . I don't know. Gnome, maybe? "There be a cure, though it be hard to find. Only the finest of pastries and the smoothest of coffees will fix this malady."

Sue opened her mouth to continue the mummery, her wit razor-sharp even before ascending, but I cut in with a dramatic sigh. "That's a shame. If we want the finest of pastries, we'll have to go elsewhere. I hear there's a good bakery on the northside of Tropica. Lena's—" I cut off mid-sentence, ducking the coffee bean sent sailing toward my head with the speed of a bullet.

"Hey!" I laughed, hopping around the square as a barrage of beans flew my way. "You're wasting good coffee!"

"I'm defending my honor!" she yelled back, pausing with a bean pinched between thumb and forefinger, ready to unleash it at a moment's notice. "Now take it back."

With an easy grin, I took a step and appeared before her in a flash of light. "I'm sorry. I only said such a hurtful thing on account of the malady, you see. Only your pastry and coffee can fix me. No other will suffice."

"Make it two of each," Maria added. "Just in case the first doesn't take. He's *very* uncouth today, as you can see."

Sue rubbed her chin. "Ah, it's all coming together now. You poor thing." She patted me on the shoulder, leaving a slight flour-dust outline of her hand. "I'll prepare the medicine this instant."

I appeared on the other side of the counter beside Maria as Sue moved with lightning-fast speed to retrieve and hold out two croissants.

"That was our best show yet," I whispered as I grabbed the pastries.

Maria gave the slightest of nods. "I counted twelve smiles on non-cultivator faces. The plan to disarm them is working."

"Wait," Sue said, turning to stare at us from the coffee machine. "You guys were acting?"

There was a beat of silence before we all broke into laughter.

Less than a minute later, Sue was handing over two coffees, which we accepted with a smile.

"Enjoy the medicine." She shot us a wink. "And do come back if it doesn't fix him, Maria."

She beamed a smile back at Sue. "Thank you. I will."

As we walked down the street, I couldn't wait a moment longer. I took a sip of coffee, a bite of croissant, then washed it all down with another mouthful of the golden liquid. The switch from coffee to warm buttery goodness and back again was everything I needed, and neither Maria nor I said a word as we strode along, finishing our breakfast.

Just as I was about to verbalize how enjoyable an experience it had been, a pulse of power came from ahead of us. It took a fraction of a second for me to pinpoint the location.

The prison.

Fire followed the exertion of power, flowing around the corner and into sight. I let go of my cup, leaving it and Maria behind as I appeared within the prison in a flash of light.

CHAPTER FOUR

Hazy

Despite literally teleporting, I was not at all disoriented by the instant shift in perspective. The wall before me was composed of unnaturally smooth stone bricks, with the occasional sconce containing a magical flame. Each cell was lavishly furnished. Large windows provided a beautiful view of the ocean, unlike the ones back in New Tropica that faced a verdant forest.

There were only two possible users of the fire chi that had exploded out, and though I'd expected the worst, I breathed a sigh of relief as I looked at the nearby cultivator. Trent's face was a vision of fury.

The moment he caught sight of me, he blanched. "Fischer . . . I didn't feel anyone there." His eyes widened as they darted toward the hallway leading out. "Please tell me nobody was down—"

I held out a hand to his chest to stop him from storming out. "Relax, mate. No one was there. I just came to check it was you releasing fire, not some wayward Blackflame cultivator unleashing their Madra on this world."

Trent blinked at me. "What?"

"You know. Like from *Cradle*."

He blinked again. ". . . What?"

"Never mind. Pretend I said it could have been your sister escaping." I turned toward the cell before us. "No offense, Tryphena. You did kind of arrive with an attacking force like . . . five days ago."

"None taken," she replied, staring at me calmly from a rather plush chair. On one of the luxurious beds, her mother, the former queen, stared down at her hands. Though she was a cultivator, her core felt . . . hazy. Like she wasn't really there.

Seeing the former monarch's demeanor, I thought I understood the reason for Trent's outburst. It had been out of sadness. Perhaps even frustration. But definitely not fury. "Sorry for interrupting. I'll get out of your hair and give you all some space to—" I fell to the floor, going prostrate to dodge the flying kick Maria leveled at my torso. She sailed past, colliding with the far wall and landing rather gracefully.

"What was that about?" she demanded. "You just left me!"

Still on the floor, I held up both hands. "Sorry. I didn't know if it was dangerous, so I came alone. I—"

She grabbed me by the collar and dragged me away, her face serious until we were out of their sight. "Do you think they believed it?" she asked in a whisper, smile lines forming around her eyes.

Trent let out a long-suffering sigh. "We can hear you."

"Ehhh," Tryphena called from around the corner. "The flying kick wasn't hard enough. It was obvious that you weren't trying to hurt him."

"Damn." Maria winked at me as she helped me to my feet. "She's good."

Behind us, Trent and Tryphena resumed a hushed conversation. I retracted my hearing from that direction, giving them privacy. The next cell we got to was larger, and as I looked inside, I smiled at the people within. All nine of them were lost in meditation with their arms held to the side, aware of our presence yet deciding to remain elsewhere.

Rather than say hello, I sent a friendly pulse of chi their way. A few acknowledged my existence, but they swiftly delved back into themselves, dismissing my presence. It was a rather amicable exchange, and it would have made my respect for them grow. If, that is, they weren't squatting on their communal bench while contorting themselves to resemble roosting pelicans.

Just like the Cult of Carcinization felt a little like crabs, the cores of these cultivators from Theogonia contained birdlike qualities. We waited there a moment, but they neither moved nor acknowledged us again. I gestured for Maria to follow, and we walked up the passage toward the next cell.

"Any changes?" Maria asked, looking over at me.

"Nope. There's still something weird about their cultivation, and I don't mean the whole bird aspect thing they've got going on."

The people in that cell had been the ones who had been corrupted by their time in Theogonia. Unlike the king, they'd spent decades down below the fallen city, imprisoned because of the chi running through them. It had driven them mad. I supposed I had to thank the king for his attempt at overthrowing Tropica. If he hadn't, who knew how long these poor souls would have been left to rot underground, growing madder by the day.

They'd barely said a word since arriving, only using their voices to thank me for cleansing them of the corruption. Since then, nothing. They didn't even complain or try to flee when we ushered them into their cell. Instead, they'd happily hopped in and began meditating. They'd stop occasionally, but only to rest, eat, or drink. The moment they were done with whatever task, they'd go back to their internal contemplation, their bodies scrunched up to resemble birds.

"I wonder if Ellis has any more ideas about what caused the corruption," Maria said, twirling a finger through her hair as we started walking again. "We were gone for a few days."

"We can go ask him right now, if you like."

"What?" She gave me an odd look. "We're going to meet George and Geraldine, aren't we? We can't keep them waiting."

Someone cleared their throat loudly from up ahead, their position obscured by a bend in the passage.

Maria sighed. "I really need to have a breakthrough so I can sense people sooner. Hello, Ellis."

"Good morning," he replied a moment later, sounding distracted.

When we rounded the corner, we found him facing the two alchemists, his pencil scratching away in a new notepad.

"G'day, fellas," I said. "How's it going?"

Solomon and Francis gave me genuine smiles, though a hint of tension lingered on their faces. "A good morning to you, Fischer," Solomon said. "And to you, Maria."

She gave a little curtsy in response to his formal manner of speaking, then turned toward Ellis. "So, any news about the cause of the corruption?"

"Not from this interview, no," he replied. "I was just asking Francis here about his experience living in Theogonia for so long. But—"

"Er," I interrupted. "Didn't you already do that? Like . . . twice?"

"Thrice before, actually," he answered, still not looking up. "It has never hurt anyone to be thorough. As I was saying, though—"

Maria leaned in close to me and stage-whispered over Ellis, "*It never hurt anyone?* Tell that to the poor people that have to repeat themselves four times."

Ellis finally looked up, giving us the flattest of stares. "As I was saying, I *did* learn something from speaking with Lord Osnan. He—"

"Which one?" Maria darted in, amusement radiating from her core. I stifled a laugh at the look that appeared on his face in response.

He took a deep breath through his nose, then exhaled with deliberate slowness. "I apologize for my incomplete answer. I assumed that you would both be intelligent enough to deduce I was talking about the Osnan present during the war with Theogonia. The one that wasn't locked up during the attack on Tropica. The one that . . ." The *oh shit* expression on Maria's and my faces had gotten progressively exaggerated as Ellis's diatribe continued, and when he noticed, he trailed off, rubbing the bridge of his nose. "Sorry. This problem has been vexing me. I haven't been getting much sleep."

"Nah," Maria said. "That one's on me."

"On us," I amended. "We've been silly gooses all morning, going over the top with our shenanigans to disarm people. That one was more at your expense than it should have been, and wasn't cool."

"Decidedly not cool," Maria agreed. "But it was pretty funny."

I nodded and fist-bumped her. "Indeed. *Very* funny, even."

Ellis scowled, but she gave him a bright grin. "Though, if you can forgive our rudeness, I am interested in hearing what you learned from Osnan."

He looked at us for a long moment, and just as I was beginning to think he was going to leave us hanging, an unmissable twinkle entered his eye. ". . . *Which one?*"

All three of us barked a laugh, the tension evaporating like fog beneath the morning sun.

"I accept your apology," Ellis said, not looking at all bothered. "What I learned was regarding the explosion that caused the corruption to bloom. Osnan *Senior* answered some of the questions I've been voicing. He gave me an in-depth recounting of the final blast, and it added weight to the theory you presented, Fischer."

"What theory?" Maria asked, raising an eyebrow at me in question.

"The corruption reminded me of something called a nuclear bomb back on Earth. It's a bit beyond me, to be honest, but basically, something microscopic is split, resulting in a massive expulsion of heat. It can leave behind something called radiation, which is kinda similar to the corrupted chi."

"Right." Ellis nodded. "Which is eerily close to what Osnan told me. He said that only a cultivator would have noticed, but there was a distinct delay between the attacks colliding and the corruption's arrival. A moment after the myriad blasts connected, it was as if a vacuum appeared, sucking in any nearby essence." He drew his hands into balled fists, pressing them together. "Then . . ." His fingers unclenched and mimed a growing detonation. "*Boom.*"

"Huh," I said. "Neat."

"Right." He narrowed his eyes a little. "Neat."

"Okay, we'll leave you to it, then. Things to do and all that. I'll—"

"Wait!" Solomon said, stepping close to the bars. As I turned to face him, a tinge of panic entered his countenance. "Sorry. Please wait, I mean."

I waved his apology away. "You're all good, mate. What's up?"

"I, uh, I was going to ask if it's all right for us to have some alchemy supplies. I know that something is still missing from my core, as you said, but I think it could be beneficial for me to experiment. I am willing to swear my life on it and only do it for short periods while supervised, if that's what it takes."

I furrowed my brow, considering the request. "To be honest, Solomon, I probably should have given you alchemy supplies sooner. My bad on that one." I turned and cupped my hands to my mouth. "Are there any Buzzy Boys in the building?" I called.

There was a low drone, and seven of the homies appeared in the air before me, coming from every direction. One had even been just outside the nearby window. "Would you guys keep someone on watch outside this cell at all times?" I asked. They buzzed their understanding, so I turned back to Solomon. "Does that work for you? You'll be monitored, but you can practice alchemy all day and night if you like."

His eyes had gone wider with every sentence I let out. "That—are you sure that's okay?"

"Yeah, mate. Consider it my apology for not offering earlier. You just awakened as a cultivator, you risked your life by helping us against the insane king . . . and we rewarded you by locking you up. That part was a necessary precaution, but there's no need to deny you the only method of expression you have for your cultivation."

"Aren't you worried about me trying to break out?" he asked, earning a poke to the side from Francis.

"I don't mean to insult you, but you have no hope of breaking out of this prison. The Buzzy Boys are a redundant precaution—er, no offense, Buzzy Boys. You're much appreciated. I just meant that the prison is more than capable of containing someone after a breakthrough or two, let alone someone freshly ascended."

None taken, they buzzed, just happy to be here.

"Would you mind getting them those supplies when you're finished here, Ellis?"

The Buzzy Boys let out a sharp drone, and I cocked my head in confusion. "What do you mean it's not necessary?"

In response, a furred form leaped through the closest window, tried to kick off from the sill to redirect their passage, and slipped on the slick surface. The whites of Borks's eyes were well and truly visible as he flew through the air above us and slammed into the bars of the cell. He landed on the floor, got to his feet, and shook his entire body.

"Whoa, buddy," I said, patting his neck. "You all right? That entry was, er . . . powerful?"

He shook again, his vision snapping into focus on me. He gave me some rather embarrassed side-eye, tore a portal open, and leaped inside. A moment later, he emerged with a cauldron in his jaws. It was absolutely filled to the brim with ingredients, clearly procured from the alchemical workshop that appeared with Tropica's evolution. A few more trips into his space later, there was a pile of equipment ready to go.

I looked at the Buzzy Boys. "Thanks, guys. You didn't have to do that."

They shimmied in delight, and all but one flew away, headed elsewhere to watch the village.

"You too, Borks." I scratched behind his ear, causing his back leg to kick and his worries to disappear. "You're the best of boys." All of a sudden, his ears went alert. He listened for a short moment, then leaped up and dashed away, giving me and Maria a lick on the way past.

I hadn't heard whatever had caused him to leave. I raised an eyebrow at Maria, who just shrugged back at me. With a small flex of will, I snapped my fingers. The pile of supplies appeared in the cell, next to the alchemists.

"Thank you, Fischer," Solomon said, lowering his eyes. Sincere gratitude radiated from his core, washing over me and bringing a smile to my face.

"You're most welcome, my man." Realizing something abruptly, I turned to Ellis. "Have you spoken to the handlers, mate?"

"A little." He looked up from his notepad, his eyes dancing with mirth. "You should ask them about how far they were sent to hunt down Lizard Wizard and his ilk—it is a rather enjoyable tale."

I snorted. "I might just do that. How do their cores feel, though?"

He shrugged. "The same as all the others. They seem to be missing something, and we do not yet know what it is."

"Hmm," Maria said. "It's a shame we have to keep them in here—a prison is hardly a good place to find inspiration."

"Maria!" I yelled. "You're a *genius*!"

"I know. May I ask why, though?"

I snapped my fingers. "Ellis, write this down. Ready?"

"Quite."

"From this day forward," I declared, spreading my arms wide, "this building is no longer called a prison!"

"Okay . . . what *is* it called?"

"It's a *not-a-prison!* This is God-King Fischer's first decree—make sure all know. Calling it a prison is punishable by . . . is death too harsh?"

"A little," Maria replied, giving me an amused look. "We might run out of people for you to terrori—rule over, I mean."

"Very well. We'll *say* it's punishable by death, but that's a lie. The *real* punishment is five minutes alone in a room with Roger."

"That . . . might be worse."

"*Exactly.*" I turned to the two alchemists. "I forbid you both from telling anyone the true punishment."

"And how will we be penalized if we do?" Solomon asked, a wry smile on his face.

"Why, death, of course." I leaned to the side. "*Psst. Ellis. That was also a lie—the* real *penalty will be a swift slap on the tushy by a disgruntled crab.*"

Maria tapped her chin. "What if they're into that?"

"Then they have to live with who they are—a punishment *worse* than death."

"Damn. That's diabolical."

"Right? Anyhoo, I reckon our work here is done. Shall we run along?"

"I thought you'd never ask."

Hand in hand, we marched away without looking back. I didn't need to see them to enjoy the bewilderment radiating from their cores.

CHAPTER FIVE

Chimney

Corporal Claws, queen of the sands and fuzziest of all Fischer's companions—yes, including Cinnamon, thank you very much—lazed in her new favorite spot. Though it wasn't her wooden perch atop the pond Fischer had made, the rooftop she lounged on was curved in such a way to make it the *perfect* place to catch morning rays.

The sun seemed to beam down from every direction, bouncing off the surrounding tiles to warm her very core. Claws stretched, delighting in the slight ache of her muscles as she extended her limbs. Beside her, Cinnamon let out a soft peep and rolled to her back, exposing her stomach to the sun's warmth.

Their sleepy eyes met for a moment, and Cinnamon gave her an appreciative nod, radiating extreme gratitude toward Claws for finding this wondrous spot. Unspoken, they both raised a forepaw and fist-bumped, immediately closing their eyes and drifting back to sleep.

As I walked through the transformed streets of Tropica, I couldn't help but gaze up at the surrounding people, an ever-growing smile forming on my face. It was easy to get caught up in the village's architecture, but that beauty would be nothing without the citizens moving to and fro, going about their mornings. The sun was well and truly over the rooftops now, its light having long ago shone through windows and woken the people of Tropica.

A river of humanity moved around us, some so engrossed that they didn't even notice our passage. The eyes that did recognize us showed a range of emotions, and I was saddened to see fear on more than a few faces. It wasn't surprising, though, considering recent events. Only a few short weeks ago, it might have made me second-guess myself. Question if I was really adequate enough to lead. Now, I knew that didn't matter, and was instead grateful for the majority of the crowd that did trust me.

As if sensing my thoughts, Maria squeezed my hand and grinned up at me when I glanced her way. Though we were on the receiving end of many a smile and wave, no one stopped to chat. Before long, we rounded a corner and caught sight of the granary.

"Finally!" Geraldine called, resting a hand on her hip and failing to look genuinely bothered. "We thought you had both changed your mind!"

"Sorry," I replied. "We got embroiled in some tomfoolery. Completely out of our control."

The look in Geraldine's eye told me exactly what she thought of that statement.

"So," George said, "where did you have in mind to create this roastery, Fischer?" He glanced at his wife. "We discussed it most of the night and couldn't come up with anywhere that made sense."

"That's a sensible conclusion," Maria said, "because where he wants to put it makes absolutely no sense."

The former lord and lady of Tropica both raised an eyebrow at me, only increasing my enjoyment of the moment. I shrugged. "That's not entirely true. It makes perfect sense to someone like me. A man of perfect intellect, unbridled wisdom, and unparalleled—"

"Humility," Maria finished, cutting me off. "Yeah, yeah. We know."

I faked a pout, hiding the joy I got from her finishing my sentence, even if it was at the cost of my punchline.

Geraldine nodded, shooting an amused glance at George. "Well, given that our intellect, wisdom, and humility are lacking, I suppose you will just have to tell us where it's going. Because I have no idea."

"Gladly!" I took a deep breath, spread my arms wide, then bent at the waist to gesture at the building behind them. "We're going to put it *inside* the granary!"

They frowned and looked at each other, countless thoughts exchanged wordlessly with their expressions.

George sighed and shook his head. "If anyone else had said that they were going to put an *oven* inside a granary, I'd have laughed. I guess I shouldn't be surprised." He grabbed Geraldine by the hand and led her toward the door. "Come on, dear. We'd better go along with it."

She let go of his hand and looped an arm through his. "Certainly. If we push back, he might just choose an even worse place to build it. Like one of the sheds filled with sugarcane mulch."

"Or our bedroom."

"That *would* be a bother, wouldn't it?"

"You know," I said to Maria, crossing my arms, "I think I liked it better when they were deathly afraid of me."

"It's horrible, isn't it? They seem confident now. Jovial. Happy, even." She gave an exaggerated shiver. "The *audacity* . . ."

Before I could reply, she grabbed me by the hand, gave me a beautiful smile, and led me inside. I took the lead once we were within the building, taking us to the room right beside the one we'd stashed the coffee beans in. I pictured the supplies we'd need, stilled my breath, and snapped my fingers. There was a silent flash of light, and the materials appeared in the middle of the room, neatly stacked.

Maria blew air from her lips as she looked down at the metal ingots, blocks of wood, and other assorted components. "I'm not sure I'll ever get used to that."

"Oh, come on. Within a week of arriving in this world, Sergeant Snips was sporting an eyepatch and shooting aura blades like an anime protagonist. How is *this* hard to get used to?"

"Yeah, look, you've got a point, but it's not so much that you can teleport items as it is that you can teleport any*one*. You pulling material out of thin air is just a reminder that, if you wanted to, you could yoink me from anywhere within the village."

"I mean, I guess I could, but I wouldn't do that unless someone's life was in danger. As much as I enjoy a good prank, just grabbing people without forewarning them feels like a major breach of autonomy. Besides, it's also way too expensive for the Domain's reserves. I don't want to leave it depleted in case another mad king comes to town wielding corrupted chi."

Plus, I thought, *I'll need the Domain's power for my secret project . . .*

"Why are you smirking like that?" Maria asked, narrowing her eyebrows at me.

"I'm not." I shot her a wink and walked toward the door. "You guys coming?"

George cocked his head. ". . . Where?"

"To the smithy!"

Maria gave me an incredulous look. "Why did you zap all that stuff here if we're just going to leave, anyway?"

"Well, if asked explicitly, I would state that I was doing it to better organize the task in my mind. If someone didn't know how pure of heart I am, though, they might assume I did it as a flex. Worse, they might think I did it just because I *could*." I shook my head. "Can you believe anyone would assume such a thing?"

"What would ever lead someone to that assumption?" George asked, his tone as flat as the look he was leveling my way.

"No idea, mate. Some people, am I right?" I clapped my hands together. "All right, who's ready to get started? We've got a few stops, so the sooner we get going, the better."

"Why don't I handle the woodworking?" Maria suggested. "That way, we can work on them all at the same time."

"You know what to do?"

Her answering smile was warmer than a burning hearth. "I do." Faster than the lightning of one Corporal Claws, she planted a kiss on my cheek and dashed out the door, calling over her shoulder, "Send my supplies to the woodworking shed!"

I turned and shook my head at George and Geraldine. "No manners, that one. Not even a plea—"

"Pleeease!" came Maria's sweet voice, cutting me off.

A few hours later, back within the walls of the granary and smiling at the world, I snapped my fingers.

Our created items appeared in a flash of light, sorting themselves into a neat pile. The bulk of the mass was made up of the various metal parts George, Geraldine, and I had created in the smithy. I pursed my lips as I bent to inspect the components that Maria had created, running a finger over a collection of wooden handles. "Wow. These are marvelous. If I didn't know better, I'd have assumed they were System-made. They're so smooth."

"Learned from the best," she replied, shooting me a wink. "But I'm more impressed with this funnel-looking thing you made. How did you get it so uniform?"

"That was him, actually." I nodded toward George, and Geraldine rested a hand on his upper back.

"My husband is a natural at most things."

"Oh, it was nothing," George said, a blush coming to his face. "I just followed Fischer's instructions."

"George, mate, acting humble is my thing. Just take the compliment."

"Riiight," Maria drawled. "Humble."

"It's a hard gig, but someone's gotta do it. Anyway, that's enough about me. Let's get this party started. I just need to pick the spot for the chimney . . ." I wandered around and stared up at the ceiling, rubbing my chin as I picked the perfect spot. "Right . . ." I took a half step to the side. "Here."

Maria gave me a confused look. "Why there? Wouldn't it make sense to put the chimney in the corner of the room where the roaster is going?"

"You'll just have to trust me on this one. I promise it'll make sense when it's finished. We need to ensure we picture the same thing." I pointed directly up. "So, chimney here, okay?"

We'd spent the morning joking around at every possible opportunity, but at my words, their faces grew serious. One and all, they nodded. I strode back over to the components, taking a seat on the floor in front of them. Maria, George, and Geraldine followed my lead, coming to sit on the other three sides.

With an ease not possible before my last breakthrough, I slipped into a meditative state.

I pictured what I wanted to create, planting it firmly in my mind's eye. Wireframe schematics unfurled in exquisite detail, more intricate than ever before. It was a side effect of the System regaining its functionality; even the newest of cultivators now had access to basic images of what they were creating. I, however, was no new cultivator. The three-dimensional blueprint in my mind continued growing, merging with the building we were within.

As one, George, Geraldine, and Maria joined me. The former two paused for the barest of moments, having not built anything with me since the changes. They swiftly recovered, however, their wills rushing to follow my lead. With our intents indistinguishable from each other, the components moved into place, connecting seamlessly. In a burst of light, a pulse of euphoria washed over us, signifying that the creation was finished.

Before the wonderful feelings could completely leave my body, I was already moving from the room.

"Fischer?" Maria asked, staring at me as I walked out the door. "What are you—"

There was a loud bang as something hit the first bend in the chimney. Maria whirled, lifting her face to follow the sound as it made its way downward. There were multiple scratching sounds before a soft thud came from within the newly constructed coffee roaster, followed by another. A beat of palpable silence spread throughout the room, the air growing so tense that you could cut it with a knife.

Maria was the first to realize what I'd done. "*Run!*" she yelled, sprinting past George and Geraldine.

"*What—*" George began, but was interrupted by a loud *boom* as the doors of the furnace compartment were blown open. Smoke and vapor emanated from the furnace, lit from within by crackling blue electricity. Side by side, two fur-covered beings strode out, murder dripping from their otherwise adorable features.

"Oh . . ." George said, taking a step back and raising his hands. "It wasn't us. We had no idea. Fischer—"

His attempt at peace was drowned out by the sounds of Claws and Cinnamon rocketing forward.

CHAPTER SIX

Alert

Within the walls of the granary, the world slowed to a crawl. My most recent breakthrough had given me a previously unknown level of perception, which let me witness every moment of Claws and Cinnamon's flight through the air. Their eyes, promising violence, were pinned on the mastermind of their tumble down the chimney.

Me.

Claws spun like a torpedo, little jolts of electricity arcing all over her body as she flew directly for my core. Cinnamon whirled in midair, one rear leg lashing out to kick off of George, who was off balance in his attempt to flee.

Poor bloke . . . I thought, watching as he rag-dolled across the room and slammed into a far wall. He was fine, of course; no matter how upset Cinnamon was, she'd never hurt him. *Well . . . not seriously, anyway*, I amended as he slid down the wall.

Maria made it out of the room at the last moment, and I slammed the door behind her, sacrificing George and Geraldine. "Every man for themsel—"

Claws shot *through* the door and into the wall next to me, her muscles bulging with electricity and righteous fury both. Cinnamon came barreling through the remnant of splinters, already twisting, preparing to kick off the wall and into us. Both animal pals unleashed high-pitched war cries, a dual promise of retribution for my trickery.

Hand in hand, Maria and I sprinted away, our giggles only increasing the rage coming from Cinnamon and Claws. We barely made it out of the granary before their first volley of attacks landed, and the next few minutes were a blur as we dashed around the village, exchanging blows. Cinnamon's and Claws's anger swiftly faded, replaced by an animalistic thrill as our faux battle continued, slowly growing more intense. We only stopped after Claws got a little too excited, which would have resulted in some poor family's backyard getting obliterated if I hadn't nullified her head-butt with a wall of light.

Claws lounged in my arms and Cinnamon in Maria's as we walked back to the granary. We found George and Geraldine sitting before the machine, their necks craning to take in its impressive form. I'd had to push back the System earlier to stop it from drawing my eyes in, wanting to wait until after Claws and Cinnamon had enacted their vengeance.

Still holding the System at bay, I quickly took in the physical form of the roaster.

At the very top, a metal hopper stood proud, made of the cone George had created. It had increased in size slightly with the System's transformation. The hopper fed into a chute that had a gate attached, able to be opened and closed with one of the wooden handles Maria made.

Next, there was a giant drum, which was the compartment where the roasting would take place. A series of smooth metal arms connected within the drum, the apparatus that would spin and agitate the green coffee beans, ensuring an even roast. There was something attached to it, a small compartment I didn't recognize despite my surface-level understanding of such machines.

I returned my attention to the parts of the roaster that I recognized, leaving the unknown addition for later.

When finished roasting, the beans would drain into a round tray at the front of the machine. There were more metal arms within it, which would spin and circulate the cooling beans. Below all of this, the furnace sat, its metal doors somehow still attached despite Claws and Cinnamon's aggressive exit. The entire machine stood flush against the stone floor, looking as though it was part of the building, there from the very beginning.

The more I looked, the more excited I got, and I couldn't hold the System at bay any longer. I let the creation draw my vision in, its description filling my mind's eye.

Coffee Roaster of the Redeemed
Rare
Created by a congregation and their chosen deity, this coffee roaster is a representation of the congregation's belief in their god. Beans processed in this roaster will always have a minor boon, with slight chances of a regular boon, and rare chances of a major boon. The boon granted is influenced by the ingredient(s) placed in the infuser.

I shook my head to clear my vision, my skin tingling with adrenaline as the words' meaning sunk into me.

"Well, then," Maria said. "Looks like the System acknowledges you as the church's deity."

I licked my lips. "Yeah . . ." Not wanting to dwell on that for too long, I stepped toward the machine. I raised a hand and touched the small compartment attached to the drum, finally understanding what it was. "Infuser . . ." I said, my eyes narrowing in consideration. "Fascinating."

"You didn't know what it was before?" Maria asked, standing to join me. "Did people not use something like this back on Earth?"

"I'm not sure if they did, to be honest, but I certainly didn't know about it. Coffee was for sure infused with various flavors, but I assumed it was done by soaking them before roasting. Or adding the ingredients to the already roasted beans, I guess. Having a separate chamber seems a little extra." I raised an eyebrow at Maria. "Ready to catch me?"

She nodded seriously and stepped closer. "Ready."

I extended my senses toward the machine, and when I found the intricate lines of essence within it, the air was knocked from my lungs. I managed to remain standing, my senses swimming, but I could only stand the overwhelming experience for a fraction of a second.

I withdrew my attention, the world going dull once more as the impossibly complicated lines of essence connecting the artifact's components faded.

I took a steadying breath, trying to comprehend the purpose and intent of the thousands of microscopic tubes and tunnels, each an integral part of the coffee roaster's functions.

"Uhhh . . ." George said. "Fischer?"

"Yeah, mate?" I rubbed my eyes before looking at him, my vision still a little strained. "What's up?"

"What was that? Why was Maria ready to catch you?"

I opened my mouth to explain, but Maria beat me to it. "We haven't really been advertising it, but since Fischer's last breakthrough, he is able to see how all the chi-powered buildings, machines, and tools work. It's . . ."

"Overwhelming," I finished, giving them a tired smile. "I can see it, but seeing is different to understanding. It feels like trying to shove a square into a circular hole. The first time I tried, I attempted to peer into one of the smithy's furnaces."

Maria let out a giggle. "He almost fell into it. Oh, don't give me that look, Fischer. Even if you fell into the fires of Hades, I'm sure you'd be fine."

I grinned back, letting the false hurt fall from my face. "Sorry. I've been spending too much time around Corporal Claws lately."

Said otter gave a wicked grin and patted me on the shoulder, encouraging my attempted trickery.

"Anyway," I continued, "I saw what I wanted. The infuser isn't just some box tacked onto the side. There are thousands of chi lines connecting it to the drum and the furnace, so anything placed in there will definitely be used for System shenanigans."

Geraldine had been quiet the entire time, her anticipation slowly building with each bit of information revealed. She licked her lips and cleared her throat. "The possibilities and combinations . . . they're almost endless, are they not?"

I smiled at her and George, delighting in the passion radiating from their cores. "I have a favor to ask."

"Anything within our power," George replied. "Just name it."

"Well, I know we made this as something for you guys to do, but do you mind if we help? At least initially. You probably want freedom to experiment with it, but . . ." I trailed off, my brow knitting. "Why are you both laughing?"

"Because it was a silly question," George replied, shaking his head. "You can help as little or as much as you like."

"It was funny because you didn't need to ask," Geraldine added.

"Though," George continued, "your overly polite demeanor *is* appreciated."

I shrugged, returning their smiles. "Never hurts to ask." I rubbed my hands together, already considering the different infusions we'd have to trial. "Now, where shall we begin?"

A half hour later, I cackled at my own brilliance as I upended a small bag, pouring its contents into the infuser. The first few items to hit the container made soft *tink* sounds, swiftly transforming into a torrent of noise as more and more of them crashed atop each other. I only closed the bag's opening when the infuser was filled to the brim.

"For the record," Maria said, "I still think this is a terrible idea."

"Heresy," I softly gasped. "You take that back."

She just shook her head softly, giving me an amused look. "Knowing you and what you're like after drinking regular coffee, this could have dire consequences for the entire village."

"Dire consequences?" came a familiar voice. "What do you mean?"

I beamed a grin at the open doorway and the man peering in through it. "G'day, Ellis. Maria is just playing around. She doesn't really mean—"

"He's infusing coffee with more coffee," Maria interrupted, gesturing emphatically at the bean-filled infuser.

"Hey! I was saving the reveal!"

"Everyone's safety is more important than your big reveal, you maniac. Last time you had too much coffee, you jumped to the other side of the river and left a crater the size of a house behind."

"Oh, come on! That was one time!"

Claws let out a chirp to get our attention, and when I looked her way, she held up two of the toes on her forepaw.

I threw my hands up in exasperation. "Fine! It happened two times! Whose side are you on?"

She let out a shrill chirp and leaped into my arms, raising her head to rub her whiskers against my chin.

"I love you too," I said, laughing, "but you're not helping me make my case here."

"Coffee-infused coffee, you say?" Ellis asked, bringing us back on topic. "How does that work?"

I gave him a basic rundown of the roaster and the attached infuser.

"Fascinating," he replied. "What other ingredients have you thought about infusing?"

I snapped my fingers, a full tray appearing in my hand. "We've got lemon, sugar, salt, passiona husk, and more coffee."

"Why do you have more coffee?" Maria yelled, trying to snatch the bag.

"Because what if I want to *triple* infuse with coffee? Why have coffee-infused coffee when you can have coffee *infused with* coffee-infused coffee?"

The entire room blinked at me, and Maria narrowed her eyes. "It's finally happened. You've gone mad with power."

I let out a villainous laugh, arching my chest and projecting my voice. "And it's too late for anyone to stop me!"

Corporal Claws joined in, her high-pitched trill complementing my cackle.

Letting out a theatrical sigh, Maria picked up a sack of green coffee beans and emptied it into the hopper. "I guess there's nothing to do but accept our fate." She opened the valve, letting the beans pour down into the drum.

"Showtime, Claws." I set her down on the ground and gave her a quick scritch before striding over to the machine. When the last of the beans had poured down into the roaster, I closed the door to the furnace and pressed a button on the side. Heat immediately bloomed within the construct.

"Does it not require wood to burn?" Ellis asked. "Why does it have a furnace, then?"

"You can do both. I'm guessing wood could add some, *er* . . . woody flavors. This is just an experiment to see if we can make really strong coffee, so using the magical heat source is fine."

The agitator within the drum sprang to life, slowly churning the contents as the heat rose. The smell was wondrous, and I marveled at the chi that seemed to circulate around us as the beans continued roasting. We watched on in silence, only the scratching of Ellis's pencil on his notepad interrupting the quiet. Ambient chi rose upward, gravitating toward the beans.

Those in the infuser started breaking down, reduced to tiny little trickles of chi that poured down into the drum. The scent of roasting coffee, the sound of churning beans, and the sight of undulating chi combined into an experience more peaceful than I could remember. My breathing slowed as I bathed in the sensations, letting them ground me, and time became a faraway concept as I sank further into the moment.

When the roaster finished, the sudden silence was deafening.

Maria stepped forward and pulled a lever, causing the beans to pour from the drum down into the cooling tray. Once there, I flicked a switch, causing the metal arms to spin to life. With the coffee beans exposed to the air, their concentrated scent wafted around the room, making my mouth water.

"Oh my . . ." Geraldine said, her eyes fervent. "They smell wonderful."

With a hesitant step, I approached. If the coffee made from them tasted even half as good as it smelled, we were in for a treat. And that wasn't even considering the caffeine content, or the subsequent boost to productivity they might produce. I bent to scoop up some of the still-hot beans, intent on inspecting them.

But before I had the chance, an unexpected message occupied my field of view, halting me mid-step.

Quest Alert!
Quest: In Defense of Tropica Village
Alert: A spirit beast has been detected within the bounds of your Domain!

CHAPTER SEVEN

Doubt

Within the walls of the granary, the aromatic scent of coffee flowed around me, its myriad notes as complex as they were enticing. My fiancée's hand gripped mine, her presence both physically and spiritually reassuring me. The sound of whirring machinery and tumbling coffee beans filled the space, a reassuring susurration of noise.

And yet, despite this wall of different sensations, all I could focus on were the words occupying my visual field.

"A spirit beast has been detected within the bounds of your Domain?" I repeated, still parsing the implications.

Shaking my head, I dismissed it, already grasping for my Domain's chi reserves. There was no time to consider.

Maria let out a gasp, her eyes clearing and snapping to mine. "What do we do?"

I clenched my jaw and firmed my resolve. "I need to find it. Give me a moment."

Leaving my body, I sent my awareness out through the Domain's root network, utilizing the very chi that powered it. I'd practiced this exact task once a day since the Domain had evolved, but it still felt a little disorienting to be pulled in so many directions at once. I squeezed my eyes shut as I was stretched further and further, still not finding the creature that had awakened. I started to worry. Started to second-guess if I'd even be able to find such a being. I'd barely covered a fraction of the Domain, and already my focus was waning.

Something needed to change.

I sought a solution, withdrawing my attention from the Domain to hone in on the possibilities. Something immediately jumped out. I sent my awareness there, knowing I should check it, yet not truly expecting to find the spirit beast. My chi flew through the Domain's network at the speed of light, racing toward a certain lake in the middle of nowhere. The only place I'd seen a wild spirit beast before. When my awareness got there, I let my shoulders sag, a sense of palpable relief settling on them.

"What is it?" Maria asked, squeezing my arm. "You found it?"

"I did, but we're not in the clear yet." I looked up, locking eyes with everyone present. "Are you all ready to go?"

They nodded back, so I reached for them, preparing to make a gesture that would transport us there in an instant. But I stilled my hand, a series of beings tugging at my very soul. I furrowed my brow, unsure how they even knew what I was trying to do. On cue, there was a loud boom, and two such beings came flying through the now-doorless entry.

Rocky had propelled Snips and himself into the building with a blast from his clackers, and Snips had used her jets of blue chi to guide them through the hallway and into the room. As one, they hissed for us to bring them along, Snips with urgency and Rocky with nonchalance. Though the rest of my animal pals weren't present, I could still feel them tugging at me, using our bond to request I bring them.

I nodded and, not wanting to waste any more time, made a sweeping gesture with my hand. It used an inordinate amount of chi taking us that far, but it was better to be safe than sorry. We appeared high above the lake, standing on a translucent pillar of light. Below us, the water appeared still, as tranquil as the last time we'd been here.

As if sensing our arrival, the spirit beast moved. The surface of the lake billowed upward. And a tail of gigantic proportions breached the surface languidly, its monstrous fins covered in deadly spines. It was an unexpectedly beautiful sight, the sun high above reflecting from the fish's dark scales.

But then it attacked.

The tail slammed down, hitting the water with a sound like a crack of thunder. Chi spewed in every direction, and though it wasn't corrupted, it also didn't feel natural. Every cultivator and spirit beast I'd come across had chi of a singular aspect—Snips had water, Claws had lightning, and Rocky had volcanic. This fish, though, possessed multiple aspects, each seeming to fight with the others for dominion. Electricity ran through the water. Vines tried to grow, only to be burned away by fire. And countless other elements fizzled and were smothered, lacking the strength to survive the onslaught.

Something deep within me drew back from the display, a palpable sense of revulsion roiling through me. I couldn't help but make a disgusted face as I stared at the tail and watched the powers dissipate.

Borks half coughed, making a gross noise with his throat.

"Couldn't agree more, mate. That thing's nasty." I patted him on the head and glanced around at my animal pals and Maria. "Stay here, okay? I'm gonna see if we can't turn this thing into a friend, gross as it might be."

Maria gave me a tight-lipped smile, likely suspecting what I did; there was little to no chance this thing could be cleansed. Regardless, I had to try. I appeared on the top of the water before it, and the fish's response was instant. It whirled around faster than anything its size had any right moving, a primal hunger radiating from its entire being as it opened its mouth, intent on swallowing me whole.

I raised my hand lazily and, with a minor flex of will, flooded purifying light from my palm. The torrent of brilliance didn't have a physical form, yet it crashed into the spirit beast all the same. Rather than cause damage, it penetrated scale, flesh, and bone, each strand seeming to bend toward the center of the beast's core.

As with the king, I was going to offer the creature a choice: relinquish its corrosive power or be destroyed by it.

Before getting close to it, I had been almost certain that the creature wouldn't be capable of coherent thought. With my chi flowing right through its being, any lingering doubts were washed away. My lip twitched up, my disgusted look returning unbidden. This spirit beast—this creature that had lived for centuries—was a *monster*. Such a word carried with it many layers of implication, all of them derogative. Unfortunately, I wasn't being hyperbolic.

Its core felt pitted. Rotten. Lanced by dozens of separate infections, each driving it toward hunger and destruction. Every individual source of the rot was distinct from the others. They'd been there since long before the spirit beast's hibernation, having survived the creature's stasis and reawakening with it. My enhanced mind had already deduced thousands of possible causes. From those, certainty opened up like the bud of a black rose, revealing the dark truths that had led to the creation of this poor soul.

"Fischer . . .?" Maria asked, her voice a soothing balm to the disgust, anger, and visceral disappointment running through my veins.

My thoughts had been all-encompassing, making me forget all about my friends and the bond we had. They had been subjected to my raw emotions, all the while kept unaware of my reasons for them. I released a steadying breath, slow and intentional.

"I'm sorry," I said, glancing up at everyone. "That was self-centered of me."

Affection radiated from them, each reassuring me that it was okay. Even Rocky, the only one present who hadn't been bonded by our sky-bound experience, gave me an approving nod.

Suddenly, a spike of mischief came from Maria, standing in stark contrast to the love pouring from everyone else.

"Fischer!" she gasped, holding a hand to her chest.

Sergeant Snips looked between us as she blew questioning bubbles, clearly not understanding.

Maria leveled an accusing finger down toward me, using her other hand to gather the hem of her dress. "He tried to steal a look at my lower legs! Before our wedding night! His unfiltered negative emotions were a ruse, and this was all so he could steal a look at my ankles!"

Cinnamon and Claws leaped at the opportunity. The former raised her nose as high as she could while still maintaining eye contact with me, her face scandalized. Claws dashed over to Maria, patting her consolingly while shooting venomous glances my way.

"I both love and hate you all," I muttered, covering my mouth to hide my smile.

A light step landed on the platform beside me, two small arms wrapping around my waist. "I love you, too," Maria said, squeezing softly. She twisted to look up at me, concern clear on her face. "Are you okay?"

I took another slow breath. "I am. But this thing . . ." I gestured at the still-frozen creature, hunger and fury coming from every fiber of its being.

"It can't be saved," she surmised.

"It can't," I agreed, raising a hand and preparing to flood it with cleansing chi.

A sharp spike of doubt came from Maria, halting my essence in its tracks. I immediately worried that it was to do with me and what I was about to do, but that wasn't it. Her musings were inward, focused on herself, and, thankfully, already fading away.

I was still harnessing the world's chi; it urged me to investigate. Using it, I could force my way into Maria's core and discover the truth. Find out what had caused that wave of doubt. As fast as that urge came, I pushed it away. She would tell me when she was ready.

With the world's chi held at arm's length, I paused, cocking my head. Was I being too hasty in my condemnation of the fish? If my suspicions were correct—and I was almost certain that they were—it wasn't the fish's fault that it was so broken. That alone wasn't enough reason to spare it, but unlike the king, it wouldn't burn itself away if left to its own devices. It was certainly an ethical dilemma to leave it alive because of the pain it was in, but what if we could heal it?

The power in my arm pulsed, demanding my attention. It wanted to be used. Wanted to purify the blight before me and remove it from the world. *Demanded* that I cease holding it back.

With the slightest of touches, Maria reached up and lowered my arm. "It's already lived with this hunger for centuries, if not thousands of years, right? What's a little more time?"

I forced down the world's urges, an odd sense of disappointment settling in my chest. I swept it aside, knowing it to be misplaced. "Thank you."

"Don't mention it." She rested her head on my shoulder and nodded at the frozen creature. "Now, what are we going to do with this thing?"

"First things first." I clicked my fingers, making all our animal pals appear beside us. "Group hug—" I cut off as Teddy scooped me up and squeezed, making communication impossible unless I reached for my power. There was a series of light thumps as everyone else hit our forms and slowly wound their way into the cuddle puddle. Claws and Snips found their way to the center, Claws by winding like a worm, and Snips by using her spikes to deter anyone else.

"Good girls," I wheezed. "That might be enough, Teddy. Thank you, though. Appreciate it."

He released me from his massive forelimbs, dipping his head in apology as he took a step back.

"Okay, we can tick 'group hug' off the list. Next, a prison cell for our fishy friend." I raised my hands, clasping my fingers together before my face. As I did, bars of solid light formed and connected, encompassing the spirit beast. Try as it might, there would be no escape; the bars were connected directly to the Domain, their power self-replenishing. I turned toward the Buzzy Boys present, a full dozen having come with us. "Could you keep an eye on it? I should be able to tell anyway, but if it busts out or if anything weird happens, let me know immediately."

They buzzed their assent, bobbing up and down.

"Huh," Maria said, staring down at the now-trapped fish. "That was easier than I thought it would be."

"Which means all the easy tasks are done." I rubbed the back of my head. "Maybe I shouldn't have saved the hardest task for last."

She raised an eyebrow, pursing her lips. "What else is there to do?"

"Well, you felt my emotions, right?"

"I did."

"Well, were you able to feel *why* I was so dismayed?"

She chewed her lip for a moment. "Not exactly, but I have my suspicions. Why would that . . ." All of a sudden, realization arrived on her face. "Ohhh. You need to tell everyone what you found."

I winced, not hiding my trepidation. "Well, not *everyone*, but more or less." I took one last glance at the fish before turning my back to it. "It's time for a town meeting."

CHAPTER EIGHT

Those Driven Mad

As the last of the church's original members streamed into the headquarters, I smiled out at the room, focusing on everyone present. Since the battle against the king, people had been wearing the church robes less and less, the unofficial uniforms swapped out for cozy and colorful garments.

Most were engaged in animated conversation, their many voices combining into a pleasant burble. I could focus on each of their exchanges if I wanted to, my enhanced awareness capable of parsing dozens of speakers at once.

I didn't, though, completely happy with the way things were and the smile their contagious excitement brought to my face. I'd been nervous about this meeting, part of me still feeling a little awkward about taking control of the church. But their expressions calmed me. All knew my aversion to public speaking, which gave what I wanted to address a certain sense of seriousness.

Unaware of my musings, the conversations continued. Behind each syllable spoken, the steady tapping of Ellis's pencil on paper added a rhythmic drumming to the susurration. The last people into the room were Sue and Sturgill, one carrying a tray filled with pastries, the other balancing an armload of coffees. They swept around the congregation, offering the afternoon snacks to anyone wanting. Before they had a chance to sit, the tapping came to a stop, and Ellis shot to his feet.

He loudly cleared his throat, a fervency in his eyes that was bordering on fanatical. "Everyone, if you would please sit, we can begin the meeting."

I smirked at him. "I think they were already doing that, mate."

"Truth," Theo said tauntingly, looking at the ceiling to avoid the death stare Ellis leveled at him.

"Thank you for coming," I interjected, taking control before they could descend into good-natured bickering. "As you all know by now, we went to subdue a rogue spirit beast less than an hour ago."

The room nodded, not a sound breaking the silence.

"For better or worse, I learned a lot from our encounter with the beast." I recounted the things I'd felt from the creature: chi of multiple aspects; a soul afflicted by countless sources of rot; and primal, unfathomable hunger. The room was completely silent as I spoke, even Ellis looking up from his notepad, every ounce of attention focused on my words. When I finished, an undertone of worry radiated from the cores of those present. Stronger, though, was a sense of confusion.

"I get it," I said, giving them a soft smile. "You want to know why I'm telling this to such a closed group, right?"

"Truth," Theo joked again, getting a smattering of half-hearted laughs.

I took a deep breath, willing the pulse thumping in my ears to calm. "It's probably best to keep this on a need-to-know basis, which is why I'm only telling you." I swallowed, my throat feeling dry and scratchy. My chest seemed to constrict a little, my body reacting to my mental state of being.

In a blur of movement, Sergeant Snips appeared before me on the table, looping one of her mighty claws around my abdomen. Her touch drew my attention to the outside world, where a tidal wave of compassion crashed into my spiraling thoughts. Trust and encouragement flowed freely from my friends' cores, clearing away any lingering worry and confusion. I took another slow breath, releasing it in a calming hiss. The old me would have lingered in that moment, putting on a brave face while still harboring doubts.

But I was no longer that man.

I had willingly taken control of the church and Tropica, finally understanding that to take responsibility didn't mean that I couldn't live a peaceful life. Even now, the only thing affecting my idyllic lifestyle were my own thoughts, my enhanced brain easily able to hyper-fixate on future problems. With that in mind, I acknowledged my worries and let them pass like clouds in a windy sky.

"Thank you," I said, letting genuine gratitude flow toward Snips as I petted her sturdy shell. I looked back up at the room. "The reason I'm telling only those here is that I don't want people to get the wrong idea about any of our animal pals." I gestured to the side of the table, where most of them had gathered. More than a few of their faces stared back curiously.

"What do you know that we do not?" Ellis asked, his hand tensing at the prospect of new information.

Rocky, taking a deep drag of his cigarette and throwing the butt of it into his mouth—which was still disgusting but better than littering—jumped up onto the table. Every head turned his way, all but Snips, Maria, and I not understanding why he'd presented himself.

I gestured at him with one hand, letting tension build in the quiet room. Just when I thought Ellis would demand an explanation, I pulled the pin on the metaphorical grenade and lobbed it into the room.

"Rocky ate a bloke."

Following my declaration, I pursed my lips and looked around the room with a raised eyebrow, waiting for the reactions.

They were wonderful.

Most moved back subconsciously, getting farther from Rocky. Claws's jaw dropped open, exposing her needle-sharp teeth. Rocky, for the first time since his breakthrough, hissed angry bubbles at me. Theo, who was able to identify my words as the truth, stood so fast that his chair fell over, clattering to the floor. His response was all that everyone else needed to know; I had been telling the complete truth. The room erupted into shocked gasps, yelled exclamations, and a half dozen indiscernible questions.

"Fischer!" Maria yelled, loud enough to cut through the din. She slapped me on the arm. "That isn't funny!"

I chortled, completely disagreeing with her assessment. Snips wrapped her snippers around my neck and pulled her face close, spewing an absolute waterfall of bubbles. She *ordered* me to tell the complete truth. It was the first time she'd ever done so, and despite my laughter, I rubbed her carapace.

"I'm sorry," I said, wiping a tear from my eye as I looked past Snips and over at Rocky. "I saw a chance for revenge and had to take it. You were a real prick for a long time, mate."

By now, everyone had realized something was amiss, and confusion reigned once more.

I rubbed my cheeks with a thumb and forefinger. "Okay, so Rocky *did* eat a bloke, but it's more complicated than that. Remember when you brought Leroy and that evil guy in an attempt to find a rogue cultivator, Trent?"

Trent nodded. "To find you, you mean? The other cultivator's name was Robert."

"Right. And you told me that Snips and Claws had to take him out. Right, Barry? The homie was truly evil, and was trying to kill, well, everyone."

The blood ran from Barry's face, his head darting toward Rocky. "Don't tell me . . ."

"Ah-huh. Rocky became a spirit beast by eating Robert's, er, *no-longer-alive* body."

In the void that followed my statement, there was a loud crack, followed by a muffled grinding. Ellis blinked and opened his hand. What remained of his pencil, mere splinters and dust, tumbled down to the table. "Oh . . ."

I waited as he swept the remnants to the floor and procured another pencil from his robe. He opened his mouth, no doubt intent on beginning an endless torrent of questions, but I raised a finger to interrupt him.

"Let me explain what I learned, and I'll answer questions afterward." I shot a look Rocky's way. "Is it okay if I tell your story, mate?" When he nodded, his cool demeanor having once more returned, I returned the gesture. "If I mess up any details, correct me."

I rubbed my chin for a moment as I gathered my thoughts.

"So, before Rocky returned and defended Tropica against the shitty royal family—er, no offense, Trent."

He shrugged. "None taken."

"Good. Where was I? Before Rocky changed, he was kind of the worst, right?"

There was a chorus of agreement.

"Well, he actually had a really good reason for it. When Rocky ate Robert, he somehow absorbed part of his consciousness. Given that Rocky was a regular ol' crab at the time, it's only natural that he didn't recognize an evil hitchhiker in his core." I saw realization on their faces. I nodded. "Yep. Robert was influencing Rocky the whole time. Considering how psychologically damaged the cultivator was, I'm exceedingly proud of Rocky for not going full murder hobo on us."

Snips had made her way to Rocky's side as I spoke. She nestled in beside him and blew a slow stream of bubbles, her visible eye filled with adoration.

I smiled, happy for them. "Some of you have probably heard parts of what Rocky went through after I yeeted him out to sea. A volcano, a swift return, and his acquisition of cigarettes, a story he *still* refuses to elaborate on."

I raised an eyebrow at him, hoping he'd feel encouraged to share. He merely made a vague motion with a claw, which was both annoying and exceedingly cool of him. The cheeky little crab had once more chosen to keep his secrets.

I sighed. "Well, you've heard the whispers, but the entire truth is this: Robert's core had lightning-aspected chi. When Rocky leaped into the volcano, its essence tried to annihilate him, mistaking Robert's lightning power as a foreign threat. That's what Rocky surmised, anyway, and I trust his judgment."

"So . . ." Ellis said, his eyes unfocused and staring down at the table. "The fish . . . ?"

"Yeahhhh. I can tell you've worked out what I'm about to say, but let me do so anyway, for the sake of clarity. When it slapped its tail and unleashed countless different chis, and the dozens of imperfections running through its nexus of power, making its core like that of a rotten apple? The cause is the same.

"The spirit beast has consumed a *lot* of cultivators, and a part of each of them latched onto its being. Together, their influence has left the fish mindless. A beast filled only with fury, hatred, and hunger. If anything, their influence has appeared to grow over time as the fish's madness deepened."

Ellis dropped his pencil, his pupils darting around as fast as his racing thoughts. "If that was how all spirit beasts awakened . . ."

I nodded, giving him a rueful smile. "Yeah, mate. That's the crux of the issue. If the only way for spirit beasts to ascend was to eat cultivators, or even if that was how most of them ascended . . . Well, let's just say that it's no surprise they were so reviled in the past. It would mean that the only exposure people had to spirit beasts were those driven mad by the lingering soul of whomever—or whatever—they'd consumed."

"Fascinating," Ellis said, his hand once more a blur as he took notes. "I wonder if that was always the way it was, or if it was a side effect of the world's power waning? We know from Lemon's vision of the past that the world's chi didn't flee all at once, correct? What if the last few hundred years was just an endless transfer of power? Spirit beasts growing stronger and stronger as they consumed other awakened beings?"

"It would explain the one we found," I replied. "But it doesn't explain the jungle mudminnows or the potent alligator gar that live in a lake above the dormant fish. I don't think it's a coincidence that the followers of the god Ceto chose to experiment right above it."

"Hmm . . ." Ellis stroked his beard. "It could also be that the fish sought them out for their power, then went into hibernation when the world's chi could no longer sustain it. It's the chicken or the egg—which came first?" He shook his head, a hint of a smile taking shape on his lips. "We answer one question, and ten more pop up."

Theo snorted. "The chicken and the egg in this hypothetical are a man-made species of fish and a spirit beast that has eaten *dozens* of cultivators. You could at least pretend to hide your excitement."

Ellis glared at him. "My interests are purely scientific, and I do not appreciate your insinuations."

"Hmm. That appears to be the truth, but maybe you just *believe* it's the truth. What do you think, Danny? Is Ellis a hidden deviant?"

"We'll have to keep an eye on him," the former quartermaster replied, giving a grave nod. "Just to make sure he's not developing some kind of kink."

Ellis shot to his feet, the three men getting into a minute-long spat filled with childlike name-calling and one or two verbal jabs at one of the other men's mothers. I let the joust continue, happy to let it peter out naturally. An air of seriousness had cloyed the room following the meeting, but it slowly drifted away, everyone too enraptured by the ongoing tiff to linger on negative possibilities.

Rather than interrupt them, I locked eyes with Maria, George, and Geraldine. All it took from me was a subtle nod, and we all stood.

"And that's why your entire family is a gaggle of pox-infused—" Ellis cut off mid-tirade when he noticed our departure. "Fischer? Where are you going?"

"I already shared all I had to." I waved a hand dismissively. "And we've got some business to tend to."

Ellis shot to his feet. "I'm coming with you."

"What?" I cocked my head, expecting him to stay and grill Rocky. "Why?"

"I was there when the beans poured out of the new coffee roaster. I wish to—"

"*New coffee roaster?*" Sue bellowed, throwing her chair back so hard that it shattered against the wall. "*Where?*"

CHAPTER NINE

Something Delicious

I strode forward with determination, the rich aroma ahead drawing me ever closer. With each meter we crossed, the scent grew stronger. I hastened my step. Because of my recent breakthrough, I had the ability to seal off my sense of smell if I wanted to. Doing so could return my rationality.

And yet, I didn't *want* to deny such a wondrous scent.

Beside me, Maria gripped my arm with white-knuckled intensity. She hissed a sigh. "This is almost unbearable."

"Agreed." I glanced over my shoulder, spotting the rest of the meeting room following along. "Maybe we could have dashed ahead if we were alone . . ."

"If you didn't want us coming along," Sue said, brushing her flour-covered apron, "you shouldn't have told us you'd infused coffee with coffee!"

"You could just . . ." Sturgill waved his hands mystically. "Zap us in there, right?"

"Nope," I replied, inhaling through my nose and soaking up the coffee's aroma. "Approaching on foot is all part of the experience, I'm afraid."

"I, for one, am enjoying it," Geraldine said, her eyes closed as she inhaled slowly. She let out a contented sigh, a smile forming. "Besides, we're almost there."

I spotted the granary ahead and was unable to stop myself from speeding up again. We approached at a jog, the scent growing even more alluring as we entered the doorway and dashed down the stone hallway. I skidded around a corner and focused on the entry to the roastery ahead. The room appeared almost lit from within, a soft glow illuminating the wall opposite, an imaginary manifestation of the beans' pull.

No, I realized, my movement halting. *Not imaginary at all . . .*

Over two dozen feet, paws, flippers, and exoskeletal legs skidded to a stop behind me. Those who could see the doorway inhaled sharply, causing the others to whisper and crane their necks in an attempt to see what had stunned us so.

Unable to do anything else, I wandered forward toward the light. Despite my acute awareness, I lost all track of my friends behind me when I caught sight of the room.

The glow was anything but soft.

A golden bubble had surrounded the tray the coffee beans were cooling in. Within the half orb, lines of light undulated like sunbeams penetrating the ocean's surface, seen from above. Without realizing it, the machine was directly before me, the bubble beneath my outstretched hand. Now that I was so close, its pull was impossibly strong. And though I wanted more than anything to rip the seal off, I forced myself to wait.

Maria rested a hand on my bicep, and when I glanced over, there was no need for her to vocalize her question. It was written on her face.

I tried to reply, croaked, then cleared my throat. "There's nothing wrong, per se. I'm just testing something."

I forced myself to remain still, pausing until I was certain. When I trusted that I could resist the coffee's urging, I no longer hesitated. I pinched the surface of the bubble between my thumb and forefinger and pulled. It lifted like the layer that forms atop cooling custard, peeling back to reveal—

A wall of light exploded outward. It struck me, making my need for the coffee beans grow by orders of magnitude. My skin tingled, mouth watered, and pulse thumped. It reminded me of the time I had accidentally overdosed on a pre-workout supplement during a short gym phase back on Earth, the unholy combination of compounds having made me agitated and uncomfortable in my own body.

I recognized all this in a fraction of a second, and, feeling the same emotions radiating from everyone else, I whirled. Every eye was drilling into the now-visible beans. Suspecting the worst, I sent a small wave of chi out over everyone, testing their responses. Only those with more advanced levels of cultivation responded, and even they seemed to do so with great effort. Everyone else stared down at the beans, their faces intense and bodies already moving forward.

"Borks!" I called.

He stepped through space to land beside me, and the moment he ripped the tiny portal open, I used strands of chi to scoop up every last bean. The altered seeds demanded that I give them my attention. Demanded I inspect them and see what they could do. But now wasn't the time.

I shoved the beans into an empty burlap sack and threw it into the portal, which Borks then closed—the change was both immediate and profound. It was like someone had dumped a bucket of ice water over everyone, shock warring with anger on their faces.

I held my hands up and radiated my love for them, hoping it was enough to calm everyone, but prepared to reach for the Domain's power if I had to restrain them. Thankfully, the fury slowly drained from their faces.

"Uhhh," Maria said, more than a little worry seeping into her voice. "What was that?"

"The universe punishing me for my hubris?" I joked, hoping it would ease some of the tension suffocating the room.

It didn't.

"Okay," I sighed. "None of that. As your god-to-be or whatever, I forbid you from feeling guilty." I nodded, more to myself than anyone else. "Any questions?"

"I got one," Roger replied, giving me a glare that took me back to the good old days. "What gives you the right to tell anyone not to feel guilty when that was part of the reason you took so long to man up and take control of the church?"

"Wonderful question. That's exactly what gives me the right. I spent so long lost in doubt and fear, only to get over it in the end. And besides." I shrugged. "Even if that wasn't the case, you guys wanted me to be your leader, so you have to deal with the consequences when I go mad with power and start ordering you around."

Roger chewed his cheek as he continued glaring into my soul, but he made no reply.

Maria stepped up and patted my shoulder. "That's enough yapping, dear. You've made your point."

"Are you sure? I could go for hours, and I've already got at least a dozen more talking points to present. And don't get me started on—"

"I'm sure," she interrupted, squinting at me.

"I suppose we can leave it at that, then." I let out my best aggrieved sigh, emulating a pompous noble. "I swear, you peasants can be so flippant. One minute, you demand answers. The next, you've heard all you want to—" I cut off as Maria fake-threatened me with a raised backhand. "On second thought, you're right. I've made my point."

Not wasting the moment of silence, Ellis stepped forward from the crowd, his eyes locking with mine. "Do you know what caused the coffee's . . . reaction?"

"Not a clue, mate. I think it's safe to say we shouldn't try infusing coffee again, though. Or anything with addictive properties, for that matter." I cast an apologetic look around the room. "Jokes aside, I'm sorry. That one was on me. I'll need to be more careful."

"You had no way of knowing," Maria tried.

But I shook my head in response. "When I felt the pull, how insistent it was, I should have gone alone. In retrospect, it's obvious that it had an unhealthy hold over me. It was tugging on the part of my brain that's addicted to caffeine."

Ellis nodded, his pencil scratching away on his pad. "Agreed. The smell of it seemed to hijack the rational part of my brain. A fascinating thought."

"Psst." Theo leaned toward Ellis, shooting furtive glances to either side. "If you're trying to appear human, you should have said the thought was terrifying, not *fascinating*."

Ellis's eyebrow twitched, but he wisely didn't engage, choosing to take notes instead.

I turned toward George and Geraldine. "I'm guessing this didn't happen while you were here. What did it look like before you left?"

"The same as when you all disappeared," George answered, staring down at the now-empty tray and rubbing his chin. "Perhaps it changed when the cooling was finished?"

"What I am curious about . . ." Ellis made a circular motion with the end of his pencil. "The protective bubble that encased the beans. Was it a function of the coffee machine, or was it a symptom of the world's chi returning to a relatively normal level?"

"One way to find out." I looked over the small pile of burlap sacks to the side of the room, all of which were filled with raw coffee. "We can trial another batch. I know I said we shouldn't infuse anything addictive, but what if we do it with only a few beans? Maybe that would make it taste as good as that batch smelled, but without the pesky side effects . . . of . . . what's up?"

Maria's head had drifted into my field of view, her hair hanging to the side and expression thoroughly unimpressed. "Or, you know, we could just try infusing *literally anything other than coffee*, you maniac."

"Fiiine," I drawled, then shot her a wink. "Have it your way. We'll just infuse something delicious instead."

Corporal Claws, showing a rare moment of actual helpfulness, dragged the tray of potential ingredients over. She presented them to us like a proud merchant, gesturing with her forepaws wide above the arrayed food items.

Maria knelt and rubbed the top of Claws's head, then both of them started rummaging through the box. Lemon, sugar, and a selection of spices were all removed, set aside into the "for consideration" pile.

I let them go, drawn in by their animated movements. "You know," I finally said, crouching down to their height, "there's an ingredient I didn't gather yet . . ."

Both paused, their heads darting toward me. Claws let out the beginning of a questioning chirp. But it swiftly transformed into a trill scream of realization, the whites of her eyes revealed to a cartoonish level.

"Oh!" Maria exclaimed, a smile forming on her face.

I opened my mouth to confirm their suspicions, but froze, my eyes drawn to the floor.

All along, both during the meeting earlier and the reveal of the coffee roaster, there had been a presence looming beneath us. It, too, realized what I was hinting at, and it no longer wished to remain hidden. There was a pulse of chi as one of the floor's stones was lifted into the air, hoisted high by a thick, powerful root.

The extension of Lieutenant Colonel Lemony Thicket sprouted a leaf in greeting, its green form swaying in a nonexistent breeze.

"Lemon!" I laughed, shaking my head. "You didn't need to break in! We were just about to come see you!"

I know, she sent, unapologetic. With one more wave of her leaf, she returned to the earth, the massive stone sliding back into place behind her.

"Come on," I said, getting to my feet. "The day is flying past, and Lemon awaits."

"I'll come, too," Leroy said. "Er, if that's okay, I mean?" he continued, suddenly looking unsure of himself.

I clapped him on the shoulder and ushered him along with us. "Of course it is, mate. I'd appreciate your insight. In fact, I've been meaning to come talk to you about them . . ."

CHAPTER TEN

Grove

The afternoon sun shone down upon us as we strode through the streets of Tropica, purpose and anticipation fueling our steps. Ahead of us, a giant tree guided our path, its canopy visibly moving in what most would mistake as a strong breeze.

"Looks like Lemon is excited," Leroy joked, knowing better than most.

"What gives you that idea?" Maria replied, her eyes glittering in the day's waning light.

Sergeant Snips hissed her agreement from the crook of my arm, wiggling to get even closer to my torso. I smiled down at the blissful crab as I patted her with my other hand, taking solace in her sturdy carapace.

We passed by groups of people, some traveling past unbothered, more staring in open-mouthed recognition.

"How long until they stop looking at us like that?" I asked, peering down at Snips.

She blew uncaring bubbles and shrugged—ever an impressive feat, considering her distinct lack of shoulders.

"What do you mean by *us*?" Maria gave me a haughty look. "They're clearly only interested in the magnificent form of Sergeant Snips. What makes you think they would be interested in the bland, uninteresting, and sometimes stinky man carrying her?"

I groaned and mimed being struck in the chest by an arrow, reeling backward from the verbal blow.

"Oh, shush," she said, grabbing me by the arm and bringing an abrupt end to my dramatics. "I can only make those jokes because we both know they're not true." She punctuated the statement by planting a swift peck on my cheek.

I stopped walking for a moment, the unexpected show of affection making me forget all about the retort I'd been preparing. As we continued walking, I touched the spot absentmindedly, relishing in the tingling sensation she'd left behind. Before my thoughts could move elsewhere, we rounded the corner to the parklike area in the center of Tropica.

Right in the middle of the giant stretch of grass, Lemon's new trunk stood proud, its limbs and branches reaching up toward the sky. On the outsides of the park, a dozen or so villagers lounged under the shade Lemon provided, gathering individually or in pairs.

The moment Lemon caught sight of us, her canopy vibrated. The violent movement of so many leaves caused a cacophonous roar to wash over us. Some of the people who'd been enjoying Lemon's shade had clearly been asleep, because they shot upright, panic on their faces.

Lemon, unable to help herself, immediately made the situation worse.

The ground vibrated as her massive roots shifted around beneath us. One of them split the surface, and the next thing I knew, it was rocketing toward us so fast that a regular human might miss it. She wrapped us up and whipped us around to the other side of her trunk, depositing us with a surprisingly gentle touch considering how aggressively we'd been relocated.

"Thanks, Lemon." I patted her unraveling body before looking up at the reason for our visit. On the ground before us, four bushes stood, their forms squat and branches laden with . . . "Uhhh, Leroy?"

"Yes, Fischer?"

I made a vague gesture toward the bushes. "What happened to the passiona berries? They were the whole reason we came."

When I'd seen the bushes before, they were covered in dark purple berries. Now, the fruit had been replaced by pink-tinged parcels that looked more like origami than a natural occurrence.

Leroy's only response was to smile at me, his eyes wrinkling at my expense. I looked at him, at the bushes, then back at him. I had no idea what he was trying to . . .

"Ohhh!" I clapped my hands together. "Passiona *husk!*"

"Just so," Leroy replied, bending down to pinch one of them. It crunched and crumbled, the remnants falling into the open palm of his other hand. After carefully plucking any remaining husk from the base of the now-visible berry, he stood and held it before Maria and me. I reached out and grabbed one of the smaller pieces, rubbing it between a thumb and forefinger.

It was thicker than I expected, but with a little pressure it easily ground down to a powder. Maria and I gave each other a look, and without needing to say a word, each dipped a finger into my palm before placing it on our tongues.

The moment the passiona husk made contact, it was like someone had set a bomb off within my mouth.

"Whoa," I wheezed, tears swimming in my eyes. "Straight to Flavortown."

"*What . . .*" was all that Maria could wheeze, her mouth pinched as if eating a sour candy.

Seeing our reactions, Snips scuttled forward. I might have warned her off, but I could barely speak. She dipped her claw and collected a fraction of what Maria and I had gathered. Before anyone could stop her, the powder disappeared into her mouth.

The reaction was as immediate as it was ridiculous. She released a torrent of bubbles from her cute little face, the stream spraying the surrounding grass. It was over as fast as it had started. Snips shook her entire body, her core radiating regret.

Leroy, who had been containing himself so far, cackled at her expense. "As it turns out," he said between choked laughs, "the husks of these bushes are far more potent than the ones that were grown back in the capital. The power of the thing you stole from Gormona's grove, the thing that let them grow lemons and passiona despite the world having no ambient chi, was *nothing* compared to what Tropica can produce."

I sent my senses down belowground, tracing the lines of chi that connected to the plants' roots. What I found there took my breath away. Well, it would have had the passiona husk not already done so. I spun toward Lemon, squinting through watering eyes. "You did this?"

Her canopy quaked so hard that a normal tree might have split in half, my spirit pal entirely overwhelmed by her excitement.

"What is it?" Maria asked. "I can feel a bunch of power down there, but it seems . . . *normal*?"

"Remember how when the king attacked, Lemon and the unnamed spirit bro washed clean essence over the battlefield, helping keep the corrupting chi at bay? It's kind of like that, but to a lesser extent. She's channeling power their way, but it's like . . . How do I explain it?"

"It's the *perfect* amount," Leroy interjected. "Any more, and the passiona bushes would be overwhelmed. Any less, and the growth wouldn't be optimal."

"That's really insightful for someone that hasn't had any breakthroughs, Leroy. There's more, though. It's not just that the amount flowing into the bushes is perfect. It's also *where* she's getting the power from. Though the world is flooded with chi compared to how it was before, there's a sort of . . . equilibrium to it. If I pull power from one spot, for example, it throws everything out of whack. I've never pushed past the feeling of wrongness that comes with doing so, but I suspect it could lead to something *disastrous*."

"Define *disastrous*," Maria said, giving me some side-eye.

I mimed an explosion with both hands.

Maria's expression turned incredulous. "Have you told anyone that?"

I shrugged. "I told Ellis, and he said it's probably fine. Even if someone else—like our unnamed tree spirit pal, for example—tried to draw too much power, I could just cut it off immediately. It's not like when I had to struggle to find that spirit beast. If anyone draws directly from the Domain, I know about it." I glanced down under Lemon's trunk, where said tree spirit's awareness was listening to our conversation from. "No offense meant, tree spirit homie. Just using you as an example."

He sent me the equivalent of a shrug back, not at all bothered by my words.

When I looked back up, Snips and Leroy looked as incredulous as Maria, all three of them staring me down.

I blew a raspberry their way. "You're all so uptight today. Ellis said it was all good, so everything is fine. Anyway, back to what is so impressive about Lemon's actions here—she is drawing chi so subtly and from so many areas that I didn't even know she was doing it." I bent to inspect the berry we'd removed the husk from. "I'm surprised you didn't tell me straightaway, Lemon."

Leroy cleared his throat. "I wanted to tell you, but she requested that I keep it a secret."

"A secret? Why?"

"Well, because Lemon was hoping to reveal more than just four bushes."

At those words, Lemon's treetop shook even more vigorously than it had earlier. She sent a tendril of essence toward me, giving me the mental equivalent of a tap on the shoulder. Following her lead, I trailed the power with my awareness. Only ten or so meters away, I found an odd bubble of air underground, making my brow furrow.

Absolutely oozing glee, Lemon opened the ground above it, seamlessly sliding around patches of grass. Simultaneously, she raised the pocket of air to the surface, lifting a field of tilled soil into the light of day. Sprouting from its nutrient-filled soil, hundreds upon hundreds of little seedlings grew, each with twin leaves reaching toward the sky.

My eyes unfocused as I inspected them with my chi, finding the tiny trickles of essence that Lemon was providing them.

"They're . . ."

"Passiona," Leroy replied. "Every. Single. One of them."

I wandered forward, kneeling down to get close. I reached out with a finger but pulled back before I could make contact. Passiona seeds were tiny, as were their sprouts; it wouldn't do to damage them by accident.

"Lemon!" I laughed, whirling on her. "You devious tree spirit. You hid these when you raised a root, didn't you? You disguised your action by making it seem like it was your excitement making the ground shake!"

She radiated glee, not even trying to deny her ruse.

"How long?" I asked, glancing back down at the plants. "How long have these been growing?"

"A few days," Leroy replied. "Despite how much chi is flowing into them, they haven't grown faster than the average plant. We worked together to find the perfect amount of essence to feed them. I believe once they get larger, they'll be able to receive more, and their growth will increase exponentially."

While we spoke, Lemon had raised a thin root, weaving a roughly humanoid shape with it. I slung an arm over her approximation of shoulders. "You are the best of girls, Lemon. Thank you *so much* for this surprise. It was wonderful."

She shimmied in delight, and her body shot back into the ground, overwhelmed by the praise.

"So . . ." Leroy said. "You have a choice to make, Fischer."

"Oh? What's that?"

He reached into his pocket, pulling out a little pouch. "This is the passiona husk that was harvested from the old grove in New Tropica before it merged back with the main village. If you taste it, you'll notice the difference immediately. You can safely use them in the infuser. Orrr . . ." He pointed down at the passiona bushes. "You can harvest the newly grown husks and use them instead. They have a higher level of both chi and flavor."

I pursed my lips, tapping my chin in thought. "Well, after the abomination we made earlier by infusing coffee with coffee, I feel like anyone with a shred of sanity would use the least powerful of the two, right?"

"Yes," Leroy agreed. "That would seem the most prudent of courses, because you could always create another batch with the stronger passiona husk afterward. Only the most reckless of people would choose to use the possibly overpowered variant first." His eyes bunched in the corners to mirror my amusement, both of us arriving at the same metaphorical destination.

Maria's eyes narrowed. "You're going to use the stronger one, aren't you?"

"Who, *me*?" I drew a hand to my chest in a show of affront. "You would accuse *me*, the intellectually gifted Fischer, of taking such a brash course of action?"

Her stare only grew flatter, if such a thing was possible.

When it became clear that she wasn't going to elaborate with words, I grinned. "I'm *totally* going to use the more powerful variant."

I bent and started crumbling the husks, collecting them in the palm of my hand.

Maria let out a long-suffering sigh and patted me on the shoulder in parting. "I'll go find something to put the powder in."

CHAPTER ELEVEN

Coffee

Back within the granary, coffee beans churned, the metal arms of the roaster's cooling tray spinning slowly. The movement was as hypnotic as the sound was pleasant. Even more noticeable than these sensations, however, was the smell.

I wasn't sure I'd ever experienced two scents that suited each other so well as those of coffee and passiona husk, and with their aromas suffusing the air, it was all I could do not to dive face first into the beans. I'd been confused when the beans were roasted for longer than seemed necessary. But then the sweet scent of passiona husk joined the burnt coffee in the air, and I understood. It was the same reason why patisseries back on Earth often used dark-roasted beans—the bitterness enhanced the sweet treats they purveyed, both products boosting the other.

Maria was breathing heavily from beside me, and I stole a glance, smirking at the serious look she'd adopted. Sensing my attention, she gazed my way. "How much longer? If it's more than a few minutes, I need to leave. This is torture."

Air hissed through George's teeth. "I might need to do the same. I find myself getting agitated."

Geraldine grunted her agreement.

Only Snips seemed to remain unbothered; she loved neither coffee nor sweets.

"Not much longer," I replied, my internal state not matching the cool front I presented.

Maria let out a strained breath, fussing her hair with both hands. When she was finished, she frowned at me. "You can't fool me with that cool demeanor. I can *feel* how impatient you are."

"Oh, thank the *gods*." I rubbed my head, trying to vent excess energy. "I felt like I had to put on a show of strength for you guys, but I am beside myself here. Should we actually leave? This is getting . . ." I trailed off as the mechanical whirring drained from the room, leaving behind an empty quiet. Holding my breath, I slowly spun toward the machine.

Ellis, who I'd forced to stand outside the room because he wasn't able to stop asking questions, came flying back inside. He was beside me in a second, joining me in leaning toward the tray. There was a soft buzzing of power above it. It started faint but slowly grew stronger, building to a static that I could feel as much as hear. The room's chi vibrated at the same frequency, and all at once, rushed downward.

The essence pooled in the tray, condensing. Once the space couldn't hold any more power, a fraction of it seeped into the coffee beans. The rest rose up and formed a protective dome, forming a seal between us and the beans that immediately muted their scent. Rather than gold, this dome was the same purple as the passiona husk, streaked by beams of a darker shade. The faces of those surrounding me were bathed in the twilight colors, as were the walls and ceiling, the palette both alien and beautiful.

Already knowing that this batch of coffee was no threat, I smiled and pinched the surface of the bubble, pulling it away. Purple light exploded out into the world, dazzling us with its intensity.

The scents returned next, somehow even stronger than they'd been before. But perhaps *stronger* wasn't the correct word. It was like they were more synergistic than before, their aromas having become cohesive. The beans, now infused with passiona husk, called out to me. They demanded that I inspect them and learn what they'd become.

I agreed, and almost instantly, words appeared.

Passiona-Infused Coffee Beans
Mythic
Though coffee has been a staple commodity for thousands of years, never before has Kallis seen anything like this specialty batch. Infused with an enhanced ingredient, these beans have had their rarity upgraded to mythic.
Bonus effect: +10 focus for the next hour when brewed.

"Focus . . . ?" Ellis asked, his eyes bulging.

Before he could say another word, I snapped my fingers. "Suuue!" I singsonged as we appeared before her café in a flash of light.

The sky overhead was darkening, the day's light fleeing before the coming night. Sue was outside, having already closed the bakery for the day. At our arrival, she jumped so high that her head struck an awning. A string of expletives followed her collision, the phrasing so harsh that I forgot how to speak for a second.

"Damn, Sue. You good?"

"Good?" she repeated, rubbing the top of her head. "No, I'm not bloody good. Why are you popping up in a flash of light like that?"

"Well, you see, I was going to ask you to make me some coffee. We just—"

"Let me get this straight," she interrupted, holding up a finger to stall me. "You came here, almost scared my hair straight, and now you . . . *you* . . ." She trailed off, her nostrils flaring. "What is *that*?"

"Well, well, well." I held up a burlap sack, shaking it gently. "How the turntables."

Her brow furrowed at my statement but didn't remain so for long. Her eyes flew wide, her mouth falling slightly ajar. "The ingredient . . . it was passiona husk?"

"Let's say, purely hypothetically, that it was . . . Would you brew us some coff . . . ee?"

Sue had sprinted for the café's storefront before I could finish the word. She *threw* the roller door open, the carved wooden panels sliding up and out of sight as

I finished my question. She bent her knees and prepared to launch herself over the counter, but paused. Whirling, she took a deep breath and cupped her hands to her mouth.

"*Specialty brew!*" she bellowed, her enhanced voice bouncing off the surrounding buildings. "*The café will be open till late!*"

A crowd gathered at a swift pace, most people literally sprinting to see what was so special that it deserved a village-wide announcement. As their numbers grew, Sue took to setting up the machine, her practiced fingers reassembling what she'd not long ago cleaned for the day. Each action, no matter how insignificant, made happiness well within me. Sue's presumption, too—that I would want to share the passiona beans with everyone—delighted me. Though I was now the leader of the church, those closest to me treated me as they had before.

My animal pals were all among the first to arrive—including Lemon, who had a thin root growing between the street's stones. None of them collided with me or made a showy entrance, all completely aware of the reverence and gratitude radiating from my core. Sue, only having eyes for her work, started grinding the beans.

The scents of passiona and coffee were released from within them, the dual aromas washing over the gathering. It was as if the entire crowd took a collective sniff, even the unascended able to appreciate the experience. Everyone in the square held their breath as Sue filled the portafilter with ground beans. She tamped them down, eyed them carefully, then attached the portafilter to the group head.

This moment, this first shot of espresso to be made with the passiona coffee, felt monumental. I couldn't articulate why. The world was abuzz with potential, the very wind seeming to freeze and watch. The surrounding chi didn't react as Sue turned the knob that released the pressurized hot water. The machine groaned with effort, and I bit the inside of my lip as the first drop of espresso fell down into the waiting cup. Though nothing happened, neither world nor chi responding, there was definitely *something* there waiting, but . . . what?

I became so focused on whatever was coming that the delicious smells of passiona and coffee faded away. Something akin to a storm of essence built in the surrounding square, my skin practically tingling with the power. My animal pals and Maria—everyone who had been present for our bonding experience in the sky—felt it, too. I could feel their attention right beside mine, just waiting for the lightning to strike.

With all of our metaphorical gazes pinned on Sue as the shot finished pouring, the storm finally arrived.

Like I'd felt so many times before, the world's chi condensed before rushing in toward Sue. Light and a feeling of ecstasy flooded from her core. Some flinched and pulled back—those that were either regular humans or newly awakened cultivators. Anyone who had already been present for one of these leaned forward, hoping to experience as much of the pleasant echoes of power as possible. It only took a second or so for those who had flinched back to realize their folly, physically and spiritually gravitating toward Sue.

Together, the dozens upon dozens of souls present witnessed her first breakthrough.

I'd never before been able to give such an event my full attention; the magnitude of it was overwhelming. Despite the barrage on my senses, I still noticed something odd about the shot of espresso Sue had created. The next thing I knew, my vision was tilting, my balance having failed me. Maria caught me as I stumbled, propping me up by slinging my arm over her shoulder.

I released a hissed breath as the light faded, the surrounding square filled with similar sounds of shock and desire. There was a beat of silence, and then, as Sue turned to focus on us, the cheers erupted.

"Yeahhhh, Sue!" Maria called, bouncing on her heels.

Corporal Claws trilled so loudly that the surrounding non-cultivators flinched and covered their ears. Teddy let out a deep roar, so bassy that it reverberated in my chest. And Rocky was launched high above by Sergeant Snips, where he let off a series of colorful explosions, their red glow lighting the early evening. The rest of our yells were lost to the crowd as more and more people joined in, congratulating Sue at the top of their lungs.

With tears swelling in her eyes, she turned and started frothing the milk, not missing a beat. My words of celebration died in my throat as I felt chi flowing from her and down toward the machine. How was she upright so soon after a breakthrough, and more importantly, why did her essence feel the way it did?

Her newly strengthened core . . . it felt extremely similar, yet it still defied my understanding. Rocky's core felt like a volcano. Claws felt like a raging tempest, just waiting to be unleashed. And Roger felt like a damned sword, which was, admittedly, pretty weird. But Sue . . .

The reason for my confusion was simple: Her core felt like that of a bloody *barista.* Every fiber of her being was dedicated to crafting delicious coffees. Was that the realization she'd had?

The cheers finally tapered off as Sue added the frothed milk to the espresso shot. Unable to help myself, I moved a finger slightly, the gesture making me appear beside her. Not at all surprised by my appearance, she picked the cup up reverently, offering it to me with a deferential nod. I licked my lips, having to fight back the urge to grab it.

"Do you know what your essence is, Sue?" I asked.

"It's about providing coffee," she replied, her tone matter-of-fact as she pushed the cup toward me. "Drink this before it goes cold."

"You feel like a barista, Sue. It's something from my world, and is basically the person who makes coffee. I don't exactly know what it means, but I guess the System recognized something you—"

"That's lovely and all," she interrupted, "but I don't see what any of that has to do with *this* coffee." She pressed it to my chest. "Drink it now, you block-headed man. It's going to go cold."

I barked a laugh, both the insult and her complete disregard for the importance of her breakthrough tickling me pink. "I'm not turning the coffee down because I don't want it. My body is *screaming* for me to accept."

"Why, then?"

"Because *you* need to drink it. Call it a hunch or divine intervention or whatever, but when the chi was rushing into your core, I felt it also rushing into this shot of espresso. I realize you *just* had the breakthrough, but try sending your senses toward it. Tell me I'm wrong."

Her brow had slowly furrowed with each word, and at my request, she peered down at the coffee. Her awareness extended toward it. Though she was unpracticed, she still found what I was talking about, a soft gasp escaping her lips. "Are . . . are you sure?"

"I'm sure. It's for you."

As she raised it to her mouth, she hesitated for the barest of seconds. Sweeping aside her indecisiveness, she took a long sip. Golden-purple crema lined her upper lip when she lowered the cup. She opened her mouth to speak but froze when power once more swelled around us.

Before either of us could make a noise, the chi rushed down toward us, darting past me and into Sue's core.

CHAPTER TWELVE

The Metaphorical Wolf

As the power rushed into Sue's core, golden radiance washed out of her. Twilight had descended upon Tropica, only the faintest of the sun's rays still peeking over the western mountains. It was always a beautiful time of day, and the brilliant light coming from Sue only added to the dark pastel colors of night.

I honed in on Sue's core, intent on seeing the changes. It seemed to me that this was an extension of Sue's breakthrough. An amplification of what had already taken place. I marveled at it, each passing second further confirming my suspicion. The next moment, the light receded and Sue's core stabilized.

I was used to people needing time to recover after they had any sort of advancement or awakening, but after the first part of this breakthrough, Sue had remained stalwart. I'd immediately dismissed it as one of the many side effects of the world's chi returning to normal, but that wasn't the entire truth—she hadn't been affected because her breakthrough wasn't finished.

That cup of coffee she'd poured, using passiona beans and every drop of skill she'd gained through hundreds of hours of practice, had been a part of her advancement. And drinking it had been the final step. And now, it was done.

Her core was filled to bursting with levels of power she'd never before known. Despite this, she didn't tremble, collapse, or lose even an ounce of control. Her back remained as firm as her demeanor, her shoulders high and chest proud. It took a moment for her eyes to focus on me. When they did, I subtly gestured toward the crowd beyond her counter, pointing out the sea of friendly faces that were watching her with rapt attention.

Sue, now one of the most powerful cultivators on this continent, easily held their gazes. She cleared her throat, and a tension grew in the air, everyone's curiosity climbing to something unbearable.

It was too much for one man, and he was the first to break.

Ellis, his eyes looking like they might bulge right out of his head, stumbled forward. Like the rest of us, he could feel the words coming. Could sense that she was gathering the strength and will to state something profound. Even if it hadn't been carved into her features, her core declared it for anyone with even a hint of chi. Ellis's need for knowledge was a Sisyphean task, and never before had his metaphorical boulder seemed so heavy as he stared up at the silent barista.

Sue took a deep, calming breath. With nary another moment's hesitation, she finally proclaimed her truth, yelling it out into the night. "That shit was fracking *delicious*!"

Ellis fell flat on his ass, the unexpectedness of her words causing him to veer backward. Still, no one in the crowd said a word—not even Ellis, who stared up at her with sheer need on his face. Sue's true discovery was yet to come.

"I know what my essence is now, Fischer." She rested one hand on her coffee machine, standing as tall as her small stature would allow. "I received a profession."

The only sound in response was a collective intake of breath from the crowd, all of us leaning closer toward her. I already knew what she was going to say, but that didn't make the moment any less suspenseful.

"Apparently, I'm the first to earn this profession in a thousand years . . ." Sue trailed off, commanding the square.

Ellis made a series of exasperated noises as he scrambled back to his feet. I'd never seen him so ruffled. He leveled his pencil at her, fairly shaking with rage that the information hadn't yet come.

She made a calming gesture. "Allow me some gravitas, Ellis. It's not every day one becomes a barista."

"Gravitas?" Ellis parroted, incredulous. "Each second that passes could be the difference between—"

"Ellis," I interrupted. "She just told you, ya goose."

"This is serious, Fischer! She—*Wait, what?*"

"A barista, mate. Someone who serves coffee. Keep up." I looked over at Sue. "You must really like making coffee . . ."

"I really do, Fischer." She patted her trusty machine. "I finally admitted it to myself. As much as I wished I could have a grander goal—something suitable for protecting the village—all I want to do is make coffee and provide pastries for everyone."

"Sounds like you're protecting the village to me. We all need food to operate. Not to mention caffeine."

"Well, when you put it that way . . ." She turned toward the crowd, taking in their still-stunned faces. "Who wants to make an order?"

Watching Sue make coffee was an absolute delight. Her very soul had identified with being a barista, and now that she'd experienced the subsequent breakthrough, she was a woman consumed. Every part of her was a blur as she steamed milk and poured shots. She flew through the orders, each person's coffee order memorized. Every time she would finish a cup, she'd call their name and move on to the next.

"Am I crazy," Maria whispered, "or is she using a bit of chi to move the ground beans around?"

"Sharp eye," I replied. "She's using way more than you think, though."

"Oh?"

"She's surrounded by strands of chi. They're aerating the milk, adjusting the temperature and pressure, and . . . doing *something* to the foam."

"Something . . . ?" Maria repeated, giving me an odd expression.

"Uh, yeah. Why?"

"Aren't you like . . . all-powerful now? Oh, don't give me that look. I'm not saying you're a god or anything like some of the others do, but I thought you'd be able to comprehend, well, *everything* chi-related."

I shot her a wink, letting her know my horrified expression from a moment ago was in jest. "I get what you mean, because it's a safe assumption to make. I can look at every building in the village and tell you what's going on with it, right?"

"Right."

"Well, it's different with spirit beasts and cultivators. Take Barry, for example." I pointed at the former leader of Tropica. I hadn't been speaking softly, so he angled his body toward us and flexed, his stupidly large muscles gleaming under the streetlamps. "When he had his breakthrough, I could feel that he'd accepted his ego. Knowing that, though, doesn't let me understand how his power actually works. He's muscly, sure . . ."

I paused, waiting for him to finish flexing. Helen, his wife, just smiled at his antics and shook her head.

"But," I continued, "I've got no idea how his body uses chi to expand his muscles. I can tell it's there doing something, but I couldn't replicate it." I gestured toward the coffee machine. "It's the same with Sue. I know she's doing *something*, but I couldn't hope to do it myself."

"Fascinating . . ." came a whisper from behind us.

Maria yelped, then glowered at our ambusher. "Shouldn't you be observing Sue, Ellis? Not eavesdropping on us?"

"Nonsense." He didn't even look up from his notepad. "I can do both. Now, could you elaborate on Barry's musculature, Fischer? What percentage of his transformation is caused by chi?"

"Fischer!" Sue called. "And Maria! You're up!"

"Ah, a true shame, Ellis." I shot him a wink. "Maybe next time."

I moved to step forward, but a minor surge of chi held me in place. I looked toward Sue just in time to see two cups float through the air, held aloft by strands of her chi. They trembled slightly, and Sue focused, pouring more essence from her core.

Just when I thought she'd stabilized them, she lost control. Both cups tumbled down, threatening to dash against the ground and spill their contents. But I was ready. Sue let out a relieved sigh as she noticed that I'd caught them on lines of light.

"Sorry."

"Don't be." I pulled the coffees toward us, both Maria and I grabbing one out of the air. "I'm the one that's sorry."

Sue blinked. "Why are you sorry?"

I pointed over my shoulder at Ellis, who was breathing so heavily that he could be mistaken for a small plane. "He just saw you do that, and other than me, you're the first person who can move things with their chi." I gave the night sky a long look and rubbed my chin, exaggerating my movements. "Lovely night for a walk. What do you think, Maria?"

"Downright perfect night for it."

Horror slowly dawned on Sue's face. "Wait! Don't you want to stay here while you drink the passiona coffee? You can tell Ellis all about what you felt. You have better senses than anyone else, right, Fischer? B-besides! It would be rude to just take the coffee and run, wouldn't it?"

Her eyes were manic when I shot a glance back her way.

"*Wouldn't it?*" she demanded, growing desperate. "I tried to save you! I called your names to save you from questioning! *You can't do this to me!*"

Maria and I had reached the back of the square, and I gave her an apologetic wave as Ellis charged through the crowd like a wolf that had caught the scent of blood.

The moment we walked around a corner and out of sight, Maria's beautiful laughter bubbled up. It echoed off the empty streets, filling my already happy heart with glee.

"Her face!" she choked out, leaning against me for support.

"I know! Having suffered Ellis's questions, though . . . maybe we shouldn't have abandoned her."

"Oh, she'll be fine." Maria looped one arm through mine, then held her cup of passiona coffee out in invitation.

I grinned and raised my cup to hers. "Cheers."

We both took a sip, and the moment the foam hit my tongue, I forgot all about Sue and the metaphorical wolf we'd thrown her to. Maria released a groan from beside me, experiencing the same thing. The foam was . . . creamy, yet still light and filled with little pockets of air. It held a hint of the flavors to come, a mere whisper that set my mouth to watering. Maria's eyes met mine, and without another word, we both took another sip.

Though I knew what flavors would be present in the coffee, I was still floored by their combination. It was everything promised by the scents I'd been around all afternoon, my expectations well and truly exceeded as bitter undertones and sweet overtones collided.

Sip by slow sip, I savored every drop. When I'd consumed only a third, something unexpected occurred. The cup tried to draw my vision in. Furrowing my brow in confusion, I let it.

Passiona-Infused Latte of the Barista
Mythic
Never before has Kallis seen anything like the specialty batch used to make this beverage. As this has been created by a self-taught barista, all quantifiable effects have been doubled. On top of a flat boost to focus, partaking in this drink will provide the Multipotentialite buff.
Bonus effect: +20 Focus
Multipotentialite effect: Grants the user increased mastery in anything they set their mind to.
Duration: 2 hours

When my vision cleared, I found myself struck dumb by what I'd learned. A fog drifted over my awareness that warred with the warm sensations and delicious flavors the latte had provided. Abruptly, a funny thought came crashing through the haze, and I barked a laugh, my head arching backward as I cast my mirth up toward the night sky.

"What is it?" Maria cocked her head, causing her hair to fall down to the side.

"I just realized that Ellis is about to have a coffee. Can you imagine the questions he's going to ask poor Sue? Worse, the effect . . ."

"It's going to make him even better at asking questions!" She giggled so violently that she almost spilled her latte, a snort or two appearing that made my affection for her flourish. When she regained control, she wiped tears from her eyes. "Maybe we *should* go back and save her . . ."

I wasn't sure if it was the coffee or the way her laughter impacted me, but a different idea came to mind. I chewed my upper lip for a moment, considering how to broach the subject. "How about we go do some thinking? Or talking, if you'd prefer?"

She picked up on my tone and turned to give me a thoughtful look. "Why?"

An older version of myself might have floundered at that question. Might have said something stupid to make the situation weird. Or worse, said something that hurt her feelings. Instead, I gave her a genuine smile, letting my love for her show. "I know you've been having some doubts lately. I wasn't going to bring it up because I trust you to bring it up when you're ready, but *this* . . ." I gestured down at my latte. "I feel like the multipotentialite buff might be just what you need if you're trying to work through multiple things."

Before I'd even finished talking, a pang of guilt came from within her, swiftly followed by a burst of shame. Both emotions lingered as she actively tried to direct her thoughts elsewhere. "I'm sorry. I didn't mean for you to know . . ."

"Please don't apologize. You can't be faulted for having human emotions. I did do my best to not intrude, but I'm still not in complete control . . ."

Her negative thoughts ebbed and waned as she continued thinking it through. I remained silent, trusting both that she knew I was here, and that she would talk when ready.

"Let's walk," she finally said, gripping the inside of my bicep.

Together, we drifted over sand dunes and toward the ocean. The farther we got, the more Maria's turbulent core stilled. I swirled the liquid remaining in my cup, collecting remnant foam that gave the next sip a deliciously creamy texture and caused a sense of peace to settle deep within my abdomen.

By the time I tipped the cup to take the last mouthful, we were standing before the darkened ocean, its waves softly crashing against the sandy shore. I released a contented sigh, my breath warm as it traveled from my lungs. "That might have ruined regular coffee for me."

Maria agreed with a nod of her head, her heartbeat fluttering as she rested against my upper arm. Like an impending sunrise, something came from within her, starting as the faintest ray of light. It built by the second, her internal state growing brighter.

Under the effects of the latte, whether brain chemistry related or just a placebo, I felt more connected to her and the complicated emotions swirling about her consciousness. As with every time she'd experienced this doubt, I could have pushed my way in. Could have forced her core to reveal the thoughts that troubled her so.

But that was neither the man I was, nor would ever be.

I slung my arm over her shoulder as softly as possible, hoping my touch reminded her that I was with her. That everything was going to be okay. The seconds passed as we sat in silence, her internal thoughts building and morphing. For what could have been mere seconds or a full minute, they seemed to stagnate, flaring occasionally but always returning to the same level.

All at once, she seemed to reach a decision. She cleared her throat and sat up straight. When her stunning eyes met mine, reflecting the pinprick lights of the stars above, she was resolute. And though her core remained a morass of doubt and indecision, it was overshadowed by the choice she had made.

"Is it okay if we talk about it?" she asked, giving my hand a ferocious squeeze. "I think I need to verbalize to process."

"I'd love nothing more."

With both our gazes drifting toward the ocean's churning waters, Maria spoke.

CHAPTER THIRTEEN

Lessons

As Maria's words started flowing, I watched the ocean's churning waters, their unpredictable movement always a source of relaxation. My vision went unfocused as I listened to what she had to say, intent on giving her my full attention.

"Have you . . ." She paused a moment, chewing her lip. "Have you noticed that I've not asked about the wedding at all?"

"Of course."

"I'm sorry—it's nothing wrong with you or us. It's . . ."

"You don't need to apologize for that. I *was* worried, but not about us. I knew you'd bring it up when you were ready."

She gave me a small smile. "Right. The issue, then. I think . . ." She paused a moment to chew the inside of her lip. "I feel like I don't have a purpose."

My knee-jerk reaction was to tell her she was wrong. To point out how important she was to the rest of her friends, family, and our animal pals. But that would just be invalidating.

Instead, I considered my words carefully. "I'm sorry you've been struggling with that. I know the feeling, and it's difficult to go through."

She nodded, the stack of negativity within her trembling a little but holding firm. "Thank you. I think I've been feeling that way for a while, but I didn't want to acknowledge it. I worried that you might take it as an insult, or be offended that I wasn't content with the way things are . . ." She gave me an apologetic look. "Which I'm just now realizing is me keeping things to myself. Which is exactly what I repeatedly encouraged you *not* to do. Talk about hypocritical . . ."

"Don't be silly," I replied. "You're being too rough on yourself. Humans don't learn that way."

"What do you mean?"

"Do you have self-help books on Kallis? Or self-help scrolls, I suppose?"

She shrugged. "Never heard of them."

"Okay, well, they're basically books that are designed to help you. You can read a book on mental health, for example, and it will tell you what to do and how to do it. Reading it makes you feel better because you trick your brain into thinking you actually did something to change yourself, but most don't internalize the lesson."

She nodded, letting me know she was following so far.

"The point is," I continued, "even if you know what the objectively correct course of action is, that doesn't mean you'll make that choice. Use me as an example. How many times did I hide truths from myself and others before the lesson stuck? I knew it was the 'incorrect' thing to do after the first time, yet I kept defaulting to that behavior."

"I guess . . . it still feels silly of me to fall into the trap after seeing you do it so many times."

"Okay, I have a better analogy. Think of a child and a hot pan. If you tell a child not to touch a pan, and that it will burn them, what will they eventually do?"

She looked down at the fingers of her right hand with a melancholic smile on her lips. "They'll touch the pan."

"They will. Maybe they'll think they can pick a piece of food up with their fingers fast enough to not get burned. Or maybe they'll think the pan has cooled enough to clean. Regardless, it's only a matter of time until they get careless. That's just life. But *after* they've touched the pan? *After* they've experienced the blistering pain that results?"

She ran her thumb along the tips of the fingers she was looking down at. "They won't do it again."

"Well, chances are that they'll do it at least once more, because again, people get careless. That's just our nature. But each time is another reminder, each incident a more effective deterrent than any warning their parents could give."

She nodded, her face still thoughtful.

"Anyway, that was a lot of words to say that you shouldn't be so self-critical. You're human. You're not always going to make the right choice. What matters is whether or not you learn the lesson. Take it from someone who had to make the same mistake a few times before internalizing it."

"That does make me feel a little better, Fischer—if only because you did it *way* more times than I did."

I barked a laugh. "Happy to help in any way I can. I probably should have asked this before instead of going on a tangent about children and cookware, but I guess now is better than never. What would you like from me in this conversation?"

"What do you mean?"

"Well, are you looking for someone to listen to your feelings and validate them, or are you looking for solutions?"

She pursed her lips and cocked her head, her hair falling down to one side. "I think you took care of the former, so I guess I'm looking for the latter?"

"Okay. I can work with that. Have you thought of anything that was worth pursuing . . . ?"

"I have, yeah." Her core resonated with that statement, encouraging her to continue. "Remember when we first found Cinnamon?"

"Of course. Gods above, that was so long ago." I tilted my head at the expectant look on her face. "Uhhh . . . what am I missing?"

"You told me about vets, remember? What your world calls veterinarians? You said it might be something I'd like pursuing?"

"Oh! Right! Sorry. I should have remembered that."

"Well, well, *well.* Looks like your memory might not be so perfect after all. What would Ellis say?" Her accompanying eyebrow waggle was downright villainous. "Maybe I should let him know."

"Do that, and he'll follow us everywhere we go. Just imagine the sound of his pencil scratching away at his notepad, documenting our actions everywhere we go. After all, we can't trust our memories to be accurate . . ."

"Okay, please stop. I was only joking. Any more and I won't be able to sleep tonight."

We shared a smile, and a silence stretched between us, Maria having exhausted every possible distraction. Her core seemed to complain at her lack of progression now that we'd broached the subject, and the longer she denied it, the louder it became. Rather than add to the noise, I rested a hand on her leg and radiated a soothing aura, reminding her that I was there.

The sensations grew worse. Maria bunched her fists intermittently, and her breathing grew heavy. Finally, she let out a weary sigh that released most of her agitation. "So, my fear of offending you isn't the only reason I haven't spoken about it yet. There has been something . . . *wrong* about the idea of helping animals."

She let the statement hang, and though I felt the need to ask what she meant, I waited.

"That's not to say that I don't want to help animals—I'd love nothing more. It's just that if I focus on only that end, it doesn't feel . . . complete? I thought I'd reached a breakthrough when I realized that I wanted to help humans too. That *had* to be it. It would explain why I felt so conflicted each time I saw the captured cultivators, right?" She shook her head, her light hair softly whipping the sides of her face. "Nope. It was close to the truth, though. I'd love to be able to heal humans and animals both, but it wasn't what was making me feel so conflicted."

Her core oozed dissatisfaction, but with each word she spoke in the right direction, the negative emotions were temporarily mollified. Like a toxic lover, her core was coercing her toward the answer, using both the carrot and the stick to get its way.

"I worried that it had something to . . . to do with . . ." Her face scrunched as she trailed off, and I could sense that she was at the precipice of the truth. A truth that was about . . . *us*? She looked just as confused, both her face and core reflecting a lack of comprehension. A line slowly formed between her eyes as her forehead bunched. With my attention entirely on her, my breath held and anticipation growing, I saw the exact moment that she realized the answer.

Horror. It dawned on her face, and her thoughts immediately raced down a warren of implications I could only guess at. Her core raged, incensed at her inability to accept the truth.

"Say it!" I demanded in what could have been a whisper or a yell.

Her eyes shot up to meet mine, and the despair held within her stunning orbs could have ripped my heart asunder. My own thoughts immediately spiraled, my traitorous mind imagining a slew of circumstances that could cause such pain.

Did she need to leave? Did she need to sever our relationship? Cut off our engagement before our lives together could even begin? What would even happen if that was the truth and she refused it? I already knew the answer to that question, and it made ice lance from my tailbone to my skull.

Such a thing wasn't possible; it would ruin her, both physically and spiritually.

Without realizing it, I'd flooded my anguish out into the world, and it slammed into Maria with all the care of a tumbling boulder. Stricken lines formed on her face, her despair deepening as my worries amplified hers. That look of sheer hopelessness on the face of the woman I loved was the final push I needed to control myself. Fighting what was to come was akin to trying to fight a tsunami; no matter how much I raged at the unfairness, all it would do would cause me—and worse, Maria—more distress.

Rather than force my emotions away, I acknowledged them before letting them go. They were slow to pass, their echoes lingering in my core and robbing me of peace. I plastered a grin on my face and wiped a wet patch from my cheek, then gave her the most sincere look I could muster.

"You need to say it. No matter what, we'll make it work. Please, just . . ." I pointed down at her abdomen, where her chi was practically boiling. "You *need* to voice it."

Tears streamed down her face, but she nodded. Maria opened herself up to me, letting some of her thoughts out. It was a jumble of chaotic information, but one thing was clear: She wasn't leaving me.

She was concerned about offending me with her words. Terrified of saying something that would hurt me. She'd hardly even considered that I'd leave; the vast majority of her worry—her biggest fear—was the pain her words would cause me. Though it was *her* experiencing the soul-rending agony of denying her breakthrough, she was stalling the process to reassure *me*.

What had I done to deserve such care?

It made my appreciation for her flourish like a verdant forest, and a genuine smile replaced my forced one as affection for her flooded from me. The emotion was so potent that little streams of light flared from my chest in fitful bursts, illuminating Maria's freckled skin and still-wet eyes.

"You need to say it." I squeezed both of her hands. "I promise I'll be okay."

Her core agreed, humming along with my sentiment. It built swiftly, and though she didn't speak a word, I could tell she was gathering her strength. "I want to heal, but I don't want to—" She forced her eyes closed, her lower lip quivering violently. "I don't want to . . ." She turned her face groundward, her fair falling to cover her features. Abruptly, it shot back up, and the words tore free of her throat. "I don't want to hurt people like you do!"

The moment Maria's words flew into the world, a wave of force exploded from her.

CHAPTER FOURTEEN

Countless Other Pieces

The night sky above was close to black, the moon having not yet risen to illuminate the night. Bravely standing against the darkness, uncountable stars twinkled through the inky monotony, doing what they could to light the shore I stood upon.

With what little brightness they provided, I witnessed the surrounding sands turn to dust.

Maria atomized every last grain within her sphere of influence. None of them stood a chance against the chi exploding from her core. Next, the wall of essence struck *me*. I rocketed backward across the small dunes, having done nothing to soften the blow.

I skipped over the ground like a stone across water, and though my world was a confusing blur, I still noticed something astonishing.

The sand that Maria had turned to particles—her chi swept in behind the initial bubble of destruction and collected them. Without her knowledge or intent, the grains of sand were mended, returning to the form they'd held only seconds earlier. It was . . . amazing. A possible sign of miracles to come. Yet it didn't stop overwhelming emotions from coursing through my body as I replayed the words Maria had used to facilitate her breakthrough. Not an ounce of their meaning had been lost on me.

I skidded to a stop dozens of meters away, and as I rolled to my back, I stared up at the night sky. I'd just started to contemplate the myriad implications of the ability to mend when someone—panicked, crying, yet still somehow incredibly beautiful—blocked out the twinkling stars.

"Fischer . . ." Maria sobbed, resting her hands on my shoulders. "I'm so sorry. It's not what it sounded like. I . . ." She trailed off, squinting at me through tears. "You're . . . Why aren't you upset?"

I smiled back up at her, not needing to feign my happiness. "Upset? You just had your first breakthrough!" I pulled her into a hug, squeezing her harder than ever before now that her body had been fortified. "You can heal things, Maria! It's not solidified yet, but you'll for sure be able to in time! I can *feel* it!"

"But . . . I just said that you *hurt* people." With more strength than she'd previously possessed, she pushed herself up so she could look at me. "*And* animals."

"Yeah, but I knew you didn't mean it like that. It was more to do with your own breakthrough, right? My task is to protect everyone, and if that means destroying something that can't be healed, that's okay. Meanwhile, if something or someone *can* be healed, we have you."

"It's that simple?"

"Yep."

"You don't even need to talk about it?"

"Nope."

She looked between me and my abdomen where my core resided, realization slowly coming to her face. "You really mean it, don't you? Even your chi says so."

"Ah-huh."

She launched forward. I easily caught her and pulled her into my chest. As our abdomens touched, my core responded. Of their own accord and completely out of my control, tendrils of power extended toward her, wrapping around and caressing Maria's nexus of power. Shock flowed from both of us, marked by twin gasps that cut through the incessant crashing of soft waves.

From the outside of her core, my essence assessed the transformation she'd experienced.

Since accepting my role as leader of the church, I'd struggled to communicate to others how the world felt. Doing so was like trying to explain something in a different language. This feeling, the connectedness that existed between Maria and me, was exactly the same.

I couldn't articulate what was happening, so I gave up trying to do so. My core beseeched hers, and hers responded, opening up and letting me in. As if it was my own, an intimate knowledge of its bounds, capabilities, and potential unwound in my mind.

Matching the woman it belonged to, Maria's core was *beautiful*.

I already knew she was peaceful, loving, and selfless to a fault. I knew that about her before she formed a core at all, and becoming a cultivator had only confirmed it. This, though, was a step further. It was like reading about love versus experiencing its embrace firsthand. More than anything, she wanted to heal. Good or evil. Human, animal, or other—it mattered not. All were worthy of an attempt.

In answer to my admiration, wisps of shadow flowed up from the depths of her being, causing a spike of terror to lance through me. What if it was the same thing that had happened to Rocky? Had another being somehow entered her core, and was now influencing her from within?

Before I could get too worked up, I realized what they were. It was the parts of her that were deemed "bad" by society, and, by extension, her. Envy. Spitefulness. Pride. Ego. Countless other pieces we're taught to suppress.

But I didn't see them as inherently evil. They were just a part of the human experience. A remnant fragment of evolution. And in the grand scheme of things, they were just drops in the ocean of gorgeous water that was Maria.

While I was inspecting her, she was examining me. If I'd hidden anything from her, she would have discovered it. Would have seen it as easily as I saw her "negative" emotions. But there was nothing left to find. Our flaws had been laid bare, and neither of us had looked away. It was like the time we'd bonded in the sky, but more intimate. Just for us.

All of a sudden, it was over, and I was cast back into my body.

Such a profound, enlightening experience had all happened in a matter of seconds—a length of time I was only able to measure because of a particularly vexing external factor.

"Fischerrrr!" Ellis bellowed, working himself into a lather as he sprinted across the sand toward us. He'd been only just leaving Tropica when Maria had struck me, and he was almost at us now, the whites of his eyes visible despite the dark of night.

"Sorry, mate," I replied, gently raising a wall in front of him.

He side-stepped it, undeterred, pumping his arms like a T-1000 as he continued on.

Seeing his determination, I realized that I'd have to be more forceful. The next wall materialized mere millimeters in front of his nose. Ellis struck it with the force of an annoying train and rebounded, doing a full flip and a half before landing on his back in the sand.

Unfortunately, it only took him moments to reorient. He sprang up, gathering strength in his legs as he prepared to dash around any obstacles I put in his way, but my helpers arrived before he got the chance.

Corporal Claws began by summoning lightning from above, a single bolt landing at Ellis's feet. It was loud enough to stun him, and before he could recover, a portal opened up between him and us. I wasn't exactly sure what Ellis expected to emerge from Borks's ability, but I'd wager my life he didn't think it would be a whole-ass *bear*. Teddy charged through on all fours, using his head and muscular neck to strike Ellis's legs and fling him into the air like a bearded sack of potatoes.

Though Ellis cartwheeled straight upward, he was already recovering, twisting to land on his feet. As he approached the ground, however, the next spirit beast arrived. A crab-shaped projectile came rocketing through the portal, Snips having launched Rocky like a cannonball. Ellis grunted as the wind was knocked from him, and the sound swiftly faded as both crab and man flew high over Tropica.

Despite being struck with enough force to level a building, Ellis started grappling with Rocky before they could clear the village, seeking to regain autonomy. But Rocky was prepared. He let Ellis succeed in freeing himself, and the moment the troublesome man had nothing to grab onto, Rocky slammed his clackers closed.

Boom! came Rocky's twin blasts, engulfing Ellis in a volcanic explosion.

Ellis was trailing smoke when he shot out the other side of the conflagration, his outer robe having burned away. I was going to avert my eyes, but something caught my attention. He was covered in a twinkling suit of orange and red, the scales of his Lizard Wizard outfit reflecting the colors of Rocky's blast.

"That cheeky bastard . . ." I said. "It's no wonder he withstood all those attacks. He came prepared."

Maria laughed, covering her mouth with the back of her hand. "I might have, too, if I were him. I bet he knew you wouldn't want him to grill me about my breakthrough so soon after it happened." We'd sat up to watch the commotion, but now that he was gone, Maria nestled back into my chest. "Which I very much appreciate, by the way."

"Any time."

I felt no need to say anything more, and neither did she. With the reminder of how deep our bond was, I looked forward to the future, excited about all the new ideas, experiences, and thoughts that we could discuss. For now, though, we knew all there was to know about the other. We simply embraced, soaking in the unparalleled moment of calm.

"So you want some alone time, huh?" I eventually said, having gleaned that and much more when we'd merged. "Should I be worried?"

"Oh, shush. You know it's only while I work out this whole healing thing. Even if that wasn't what I thought I should do, it's what my core wants."

"I know. It's impossible to not tease you, though."

"Will it help if I remind you that once I'm finished, we can organize our wedding?"

"Yes, actually. But, to be clear, I'll likely tease you for the rest of our long and love-filled lives. Till death do us part and all that. It's how I'm built."

When Maria leaned back and gave me a wicked smile, I knew I'd made a mistake.

"Speaking of building," she said. "Should we speak about what you're going to do while I practice my healing?"

"*You saw that?*" I let out an exaggerated groan. "How am I supposed to give you happy surprises if you learn all of my secrets?"

"You can still surprise everyone else, at least. Speaking of everyone else, I think Claws might explode soon if we don't tell her what happened."

We both glanced back toward Tropica.

Maria now had the enhanced vision that came with a breakthrough, but even with that, it would have been difficult to spot the troublesome otter. If, that is, she didn't currently look like the cursed lovechild of a hedgehog and a tesla coil. Electricity sparked from her in every direction, her core loathing the fact that she wasn't unleashing her chi and rocketing toward us.

"Wow . . ." Maria said, her voice breathy. "Is this how it always felt for you?"

"Amazing, isn't it?"

"Yeah . . ."

"I remember the first time I sensed the unbridled chaos of Claws's lightning. The violent potential just looking for the slightest excuse to be unleashed. It's . . ."

"Hard to describe."

"It is."

Under our scrutiny, Claws's agitation had only grown. She shook her body, and arcs of energy jolted out to strike the surrounding roof tiles. If we waited any longer, she might actually destroy the building.

"Come on, Claws!" I called. "You can—"

Her war cry pierced the heavens as she shot upward, riding bolts of lightning as if they were streams of water. And when she was a mere speck high above, she changed direction, her needle-sharp teeth bared in a grin as she soared downward. When she was almost at us, I opened my arms wide, preparing to catch her.

In response, I fell victim to a betrayal most foul.

Claws poked her tongue out, gave me a decidedly rude gesture, and changed trajectory once more. Maria giggled as she caught Claws and spun in circles, hugging the miscreant otter to her chest. Claws swiftly extricated herself from Maria's grasp to run around her body like a squirrel on caffeine, her head fixed on Maria's core as if mounted on a gyroscope.

Try as she might, all Maria could do was laugh as she tried to catch the zippy otter, whose speed and excitability only increased as she learned more and more about Maria's breakthrough. Finally, Claws came to an abrupt stop, her eyes intense and forepaws resting on Maria's collarbones. She let out a quiet, questioning trill, her tone making it clear she couldn't believe it.

Maria, an adorable blush rising to her cheeks, nodded. "We don't know how effective it will be, but my core is dedicated to healing."

I smiled as I watched Claws wiggle like an animal with its head stuck in a jar, so overwhelmed with emotion that she didn't know what to do with herself. As Claws continued her weird little dance, I tilted my head to the side and glanced at the rest of our animal pals. Though much more discreet than Claws, they, too, were watching, countless eyes poking around corners and over rooftops.

"Come on, you goofs." I shook my head. "As if we wouldn't want to celebrate with all of you."

As one, they ran, flew, and hopped forward, heading for a portal that Borks was already tearing into space. Seeing their joy-filled faces was the cherry on top of a wonderful evening, and it wasn't even late yet. We'd have all night to celebrate, and I intended on absorbing every single moment.

After all, if I wanted to enact the secret plan Maria had discovered, I'd need to leave Tropica tomorrow.

CHAPTER FIFTEEN

Advancements

As I gazed out at the surrounding forest, the midmorning sun peppered my bare shoulders. Its heat was diminished by a soft, ever-present breeze that blew from behind, seeming to encourage our decision to return home.

It had been four long days since Maria's breakthrough, and as I turned to take in the gathered supplies, I couldn't help but smile at how much my ragtag group of pals and I had managed to accomplish.

Lying on the back of the load like sunbathing lizards, Deklan and Dom slept without a care in the world, both snoring softly as they recovered from a morning of meditation. Borks was splayed out on his back between them, his upper lip flopping down with gravity to reveal a hilarious smile. Though I was well aware of the reason for his lethargy—he had been slipping away once a night to train when he thought we were all passed out—I was content letting him keep his secrets.

I'm sure he has good reason, I thought to myself, fighting the urge to reach a finger out and make his lip jiggle.

Beside me, Barry stretched his muscular arms above his head, each limb wider than the planks we were transporting. "I don't know how they're so comfy on top of dried hardwood . . ."

"Indeed, friend Barry," Marcus replied, sparing the twins a quick peek before returning his attention to the horses pulling us along the seldom-traveled road.

Though he'd only spoken three words, Marcus's contribution to the conversation brought me untold joy. Ever since the king had basically abducted him and forced him to lead an expedition toward the fallen city of Theogonia—followed by an extremely misguided and objectively ineffective assault on Tropica that ended in the king, uhhh, ceasing to exist—the formerly jovial merchant had become quite reserved. It was exactly why I'd brought him on this little expedition, and it seemed to be working.

The man sitting beside him was, undoubtedly, the biggest source of Marcus's shift in outlook. Though they referred to each other as business partners, there was clearly a deeper relationship than that. Even if I couldn't literally feel the love they had for one another, I would have been able to tell by the stolen glances and lingering stares. There was no need for them to hide it, of course, but I would respect their privacy—especially because Marcus had previously mentioned a "wife" that apparently didn't exist.

Danny, the last member of the expedition, stretched and let out a soft groan. "As much as I enjoyed seeing my old guards in the capital again, I can't wait to get back to Tropica. I wonder how far everyone has gotten in four days?"

It was something I'd oft considered since we left, the thought more frequent with each passing day. I'd also been training, sneaking off when I could to practice controlling my senses by exposing myself to the coffee-infused coffee beans stored away in Borks's portal.

Speaking of . . . I thought, peering at my doggo pal. He'd been stealing off at night, too, only going when he thought we were all asleep. He clearly wanted it to be a secret, so I wasn't going to bring it up unless he did.

My mind shifted back toward those in Tropica. "I don't want to get my hopes up, but at the same time, a *lot* can happen in four days . . ."

"No kidding," Danny replied, reaching over to poke Barry's gleaming bicep with one finger. "This, for example. It took you, what, a few seconds to transform?"

"Less," Barry replied, extending his chest and striking a pose.

I grinned at both his ridiculous physique and the happiness it brought him. "It doesn't matter if nobody had such a dramatic breakthrough. I'm just excited to see everyone's progress."

Barry nodded at my words. "Who should we check up on first?"

"You guys can go where you please, but I know where I'm heading." I pictured her in my mind, my memory of her only growing more beautiful with our time apart.

"You know . . ." Deklan sat up and covered a yawn. "You always get a goofy look on your face when you think about Maria."

"I do not."

"You really do," Dom added, also sitting up. "Like a child that smells something sweet cooking in the oven."

Danny snorted. "Couldn't have said it better. It's half curiosity, half innocence, and completely adorable."

Borks ruffed in agreement. He was still upside down with a goofy smile, but now his eyes were on me and his tail wagged, entirely too happy with everyone's light bullying.

I could feel the heat rising to my cheeks, so I sought something clever to say back. Perhaps something biting enough to redirect everyone's attention. But enhanced as my brain might be, I settled on something much less diplomatic. "Shut up, Danny."

They all laughed at me, even Borks making little amused snuffles, and all I could do was accept my fate. I consoled myself by thinking of Maria again.

I wonder if she's also thinking of me . . . ?

Back in Tropica, seated within a pool of crystal water that was lined by opalescent stones, someone was indeed thinking of Fischer. Said individual stretched her muscles as she pictured the strange man who had changed her life for the better. Thanking the universe for the umpteenth time that they had met, she undulated her feminine mouthparts and let out a long yawn before scuttling farther back into her favorite nook within the tidal pond.

Opening the lone eye not hidden by her leather patch, Sergeant Snips checked up on the only other human she adored as much as she did Fischer.

Maria had shown remarkable commitment to her purpose, and Snips couldn't have been more proud of her. The moment she had felt Maria's breakthrough, it had been all she could do to not rush over and interrupt the moment like the troublesome otter had. Even from that distance, Snips had *known* that Maria had become a healer. The power was too similar to the healing waters of her pond to be a coincidence; Maria's power was stronger, but the parallels were undeniable.

After only four days, Maria was nearing . . . something. They hadn't spoken about it, but that didn't make it less true. As sure as fish was tasty, Maria approached enlightenment. It might take hours, days, or months, but it would eventually arrive. Snips was sure. And it wasn't only Maria that was attempting to grow stronger.

After her master had left, they had all committed themselves to self-improvement. Much like their time training on the sands back when Fischer's only followers were Snips, Claws, and Pistachio, they had collectively decided that it was time to seek more power.

Now, it wasn't just Fischer they were protecting. It was the entire church. The entire village. Their very way of life. Given Fischer's power, it was reasonable to assume he could protect them no matter who or what they came up against, but none of them were willing to take that chance.

Just below Snips, a creature of immense power stirred. Rocky had been in a deep meditation, but having sensed echoes of her emotions and thoughts, he came to comfort her. She tried to open her mouth and blow soft bubbles of apology, but he was before her in a moment.

His core told her that there was no need to apologize as he leaned in to plant a kiss on her sturdy forehead. As quick as he'd swam up to reassure her, he drifted back down, falling back into his place of contemplation. There, he sent *her* his regret. She couldn't possibly fault him, though. He was seeking to get stronger so that he could protect her and everyone else.

She wanted to blow bubbles of frustration. Wanted to fly down there and force a cuddle upon the cantankerous crab. But she held herself at bay, knowing it was for the best that he advanced.

She redirected her thoughts, and the first thing that came to mind was bees. She often found a primitive part of herself drifting that way, but she always pushed it aside. Queen Bee and Bumblebro had been working on something for a long while now, and it wouldn't do to disturb them.

Just as importantly, she didn't have the time to spare. She wasn't the crustacean she'd once been, and as much as she might want to, she couldn't just sit outside a hive and watch insects buzz about. This made her think of her scouts—the rock crab force she'd recruited and trained what felt like forever ago. When she spent time around them, communicating with hisses and sharp gestures, she always slipped back into an animalistic frame of mind that craved scavenging, swimming, and other crablike tendencies.

It was neither what she needed, nor what would help her ascend.

With that, she decided it was time to resume her meditation. She settled into her favorite nook, and the action reminded her of the recent past, when another crustacean had called the tidal pool his home. She allowed herself a moment's contemplation, letting the cloud of thought drift by rather than trying to deny it—just as her master always instructed.

What is that lobster up to . . . ?

On the east side of Tropica, facing the ocean and breaking any breeze that blew in from sea, there existed two buildings that didn't quite belong. It was neither their composition nor appearance that set them apart from the surrounding structures, but despite this lack of visual evidence, even the weakest of cultivators could sense that something within them was . . . different.

Though the sensation wasn't enough to deter passersby from their vicinity, it was enough to draw the eye of those possessing a core. The only visible anomalies were the two wooden signs, one on each building's facade, that lacked any lettering at all. Instead, they both depicted a different marine creature, their likenesses burned into the grain by an artisan.

Unlike most of the citizens strolling by, one man strode directly toward them. He knew well the cause of the anomalous aura flowing out, and as he approached the door to the right, he ran his finger over the building's sign. The slight indentation of the carved creature was smooth beneath his finger. Smiling to himself, he took a deep breath of the salty air and threw the door wide.

Entering the building, Gary closed the door behind him and cast his eyes forward, staring at the real-life version of the creature depicted outside. Pistachio, the Church of the Leviathan's chosen deity, met Gary's eyes with a stoic gaze. Beside the leviathan lobster, Teddy raised a giant paw in greeting and waved, looking slightly embarrassed.

"Hello, Teddy," Gary said, returning the gesture. "Are you just visiting, or did you decide to help?"

The reply that came from Teddy's core was all that Gary needed to know, and it made his heart skip a beat. Teddy was going to join their cause.

Gary didn't bother hiding his elation. "Wonderful! I think your nature is perfectly suited for it, and we're glad to have you. Pop by whenever you want, even if no one is in."

Pistachio lifted a colossal clacker and snicked it together in agreement, and Teddy gave a soft nod.

Gary turned toward Pistachio. "How are they? Any change overnight?"

Pistachio shook his lumbering head.

"Well, with any luck, I might have found something to change that."

Gary strolled over and unshouldered a large bag, placing it beside the giant tank that Pistachio and Teddy were peering down at. Because of the aquarium's size and contents, Gary could only see a few of the inhabitants, most of them hiding away in the coral and rocks. Those he could see seemed something between lazy and thoughtful.

An odd pulse came from Pistachio's core, which was a surprisingly powerful show of emotion from the stoic crustacean. Curiosity.

"Oh, right! Sorry."

Gary dug his hand into the bag and pulled out a small box. When he popped it open, a sweet scent flowed out, making his mouth water despite having eaten on his way back. The whites of Teddy's eyes became visible as he leaned forward, his over-large nose twitching with each sniff of the enticing berries. Gary plucked a second box out of the bag, this one much cruder in construction.

"I was able to get some of the enhanced passiona berries for you, Teddy. To be honest, I'd hoped to entice you to our cause with them. Seeing as you're already here, though, they're all yours."

Teddy drew a massive paw to his chest and gestured at himself, letting out a questioning growl.

"I'm sure, Teddy."

The bear collected the box with more graciousness and reverence than one would expect from such a creature, and as he upended the dozens of berries into his open mouth, Gary couldn't help but smile. Pistachio may be who the Church of the Leviathan had been waiting on, but Gary couldn't deny the pull that Teddy had on his core.

Most spirit beasts had a force to them, something like the thing called "gravity" that he'd overheard Fischer describing to Ellis. All of them were distinct, reflective of their personality and intentions, and Gary felt a sort of resonance with each spirit beast. Able to sense their compatibility, he was most aligned with Pistachio, but Teddy was a *very* close second.

Shaking his head at his own distractibility, Gary returned to the task at hand. "The berries in this other box, as you might tell by their scent, contain more chi than those you just consumed."

Apparently, Pistachio and Teddy hadn't realized that yet, because they both drew back slightly.

Gary nodded, completely understanding their surprise. "I didn't expect them to say yes, either. I managed to convince the guardians, but it was . . . *costly*."

Pistachio slunk over and patted him consolingly on the shoulder. This show of kindness made Gary recall the writhing roots of the first grove keeper, and the vicious grin of the second. He shuddered.

Absolute scoundrels, he hissed. *Both of them.*

High in the boughs of a blue-tinged tree, a creature with the most magnificent fur in all the lands—or so she would claim—rubbed her stomach and let out a soft belch, the taste of her most recent meal gracing her awareness once more. From beside her, Lemon nodded a particularly large leaf, agreeing wholeheartedly with the sentiment.

Though the fishy feast had been nowhere near as good as even the humblest of

Fischer's creations, it still left Claws's stomach full and core bursting with chi. She shook her head and gave a wry grin as she recalled the look on Gary's face when he agreed to deliver an entire cart of cooked fish. It had taken the poor man the entire morning to collect them, and the rest of the day to roast them to the desired level. On top of that, they'd squeezed the promise of future oysters out of him.

Understanding the joy radiating from Claws's abdomen, Lemon's canopy shook in shared delight, the wind whispering past her leaves. Together, they descended into maniacal laughter, the otter's trilling chirps cutting through Lemon's swishing branches. By the time they finished, tears streamed down Claws's furry face, and she wiped them away with a dexterous forepaw.

Lemon gave one last shudder of her mighty boughs, her core and roots radiating a sense of finality. Perhaps some wouldn't be able to interpret the meaning, but Claws was no mere mortal. Lemon wanted to use the acquired chi to meditate and further the growth of her passiona bushes.

Claws thought that was a wonderful idea. She, too, had places to be.

She patted Lemon's trunk, considered launching herself toward her own place of solitude, but shook her head at herself. What was the rush? Claws stepped out into open air, cooed goodbye, and slid headfirst down Lemon's trunk. At the last moment, she rotated and landed on her feet.

With the imperiousness of a proud rooster, she trotted away, her full belly brushing the grass as she headed northwest. It had been some time since she'd meditated in her favored resting spot atop the freshwater pond.

Atop the sands to the south of Tropica, a mammal as fierce as she was small paused mid-kick, her head darting northward. Even from here, Cinnamon could hear Claws's and Lemon's projected mirth. The only thing that could make Claws so happy was mischief, and Cinnamon felt a pang of regret that she wasn't able to partake.

This pang of regret was abruptly cut short when the webbed foot of an oceanic bird kicked her chin with the speed of an arrow in flight. The blow would have knocked even a weak spirit beast senseless, but Cinnamon was no such beast.

Swift as a coursing river, she whirled with the blow, absorbing the force of Pelly's kick and making it her own. In the blink of an eye, she'd flipped backward, kicked off from the sand, and launched herself with the strength of a great typhoon toward her other opponent.

A high-pitched scream tore from her throat, and though Bill's eyes went wide at the declaration of her intent, he didn't have time to react. Cinnamon's rear paw lashed out in a vicious roundhouse kick, and as it descended, the world seemed to slow around her. She'd conjured up a familiar image as she unleashed the kick, using it to empower her resolve.

She had done so countless times, but never before had it resonated so deep within her.

Despite Cinnamon having all manner of activities and friends to distract herself with, she'd never forgotten her awakening. Never left behind the image of an adolescent bunny cowering beneath bushes, its spirit as broken as one of its legs. This scene was a potent reminder of where her life would have probably ended if not for the intervention of Maria and her master. Each time she would focus on the memory, a fresh burst of determination would propel her onward.

This time, though, it was much more vivid. She could smell the leaf litter that would become her final place of rest. Her entire body trembled, warring with her instinct to remain completely still lest a predator discover her. The bushes above had parted, allowing filtered light to shine down upon her. She had experienced true terror then as she spotted the creatures above, her animalistic mind assuming that her life, short as it had been, was over.

Of course, she'd been incorrect. It had been the beginning of her new life. The beginning of an existence spent with beings possessing more kindness, more compassion, than most could comprehend.

Cinnamon returned to the present. With her leg still soaring through the air and aimed directly at the spot on Bill's chest that could safely absorb her blow, a realization struck home.

It was as simple as it was profound.

Cinnamon had spent so long with this image, yet she'd somehow missed something so obvious. With each repetition, she'd come to accept Fischer's and Maria's personalities as a fact. With stunning clarity, she realized she had taken it for granted.

Their kindness was infectious, seeming to proliferate the entire world around them. Even common villagers were as lovely as could be, and again, Cinnamon had just accepted that as the way things were supposed to be. In an ideal world, that *was* the way things should be—but that didn't make it so.

Humans were capable of unspeakable cruelty, and just as capable of justifying it to themselves. Someone as powerful as her master, a man who could obliterate mountains with a gesture of his hand, had instead chosen kindness. He chose it every single day, as sure as the sun rises in the east.

Cinnamon owed him her life. She owed him everything she had. And she would do whatever it took to repay that debt.

Like a proud mother, the world itself seemed to rejoice at Cinnamon's resolve, and chi flew into her.

CHAPTER SIXTEEN

Martial

I took a deep breath, and the sweet scent of decaying plant matter mixed with earthy undertones, combining to cool my throat and soothe my racing heart. There was a good reason for my swift pulse: We were climbing the final hill between us and Tropica.

We were almost there.

To the south, the path of destruction wrought by the king's arrival was a dark scar, unmissable for its magnitude. The entire mountaintop it led to had been scorched, the previously lush peak now blackened and bereft of life. It was a sobering sight, and hoping to prove myself wrong, I extended my chi toward it.

What I found made a weight slip from my shoulders. Already, trees were regrowing, their new leaves only hours or days from unfurling to catch the sun's rays.

It was a marvelous discovery, and my relief was potent. Part of me had been worried the corruption would delay the healing process. Though it would take some time, the mountain would become a verdant forest once more. We crested the hill as I pondered this eventuality, and a soft breeze blew into our faces, but I hardly even registered it. Tropica had come into view.

I sent a quick pulse of chi toward the village, closing my eyes as I received glimpses of my friends. Being close to them again after time apart made me literally dance with joy. I shimmied my shoulders like Claws does when finding a particularly juicy oyster, picturing how her cute little cheeks would feel to scratch.

I let out a sigh. Mere days had felt like a lifetime.

Though almost everyone else was visibly excited, one person remained stoic. Despite his core basically vibrating with anticipation, Barry's jaw was firm, his lips pursed as he gazed coolly down at Tropica. He spun my way with deliberate care. "You know, Fischer, no one would fault you for rushing in now. You've shown a lot of restraint by—"

He cut off as I leaped into the air, my core feeling like it might implode if I remained a second longer. His broaching of the subject had made the urge to see Maria increase tenfold. "Thanks, mate! Take the cart down to the water, please!"

Before he could reply, I snapped my fingers. I shifted in space, arriving before her in a flash of light.

The afternoon sun made Snips's tidal pool dance with rainbow light, the opalescent stones within shining brilliantly. In her usual hidey hole, one Sergeant Snips sat in a deep meditation, her core reacting to my presence the moment I arrived. Though she felt me keenly, she didn't make a move. Below her, in a secondary crevice, Rocky had the same reaction. Neither of them kept my attention for long.

Sitting cross-legged atop the giant boulder, my beautiful fiancée sat, her shoulder-length hair swaying in the wind. Her core immediately resonated with mine. My next breath came shuddering in like I'd just dived into an icy lake. Maria's was the same. It took a few more moments for our cores to readjust to the other's presence, and though it had been less than a week, her core had changed so much. Her healing nature was undeniable before, but it wasn't yet ready to be used. Now, she was right on the cusp of enlightenment—perhaps on the precipice of another breakthrough. Only time would tell.

Feeling both me and my thoughts, a wide smile spread over her face. It reached the corners of her eyes and she sat a little straighter, clearly proud of her efforts. With her attention still focused inward, she parted her lips and mouthed, *I love you.*

I whispered it back, so softly that the breeze would have carried it away from anyone but a cultivator. Appearing next to her, I planted the softest of kisses on her forehead. The moment I touched her, I forced myself to teleport away, knowing I would only distract her if I remained too long.

Besides, I thought as I arrived at my next destination and spotted the three animal pals there, *I have a breakthrough to witness.*

I'd felt its inexorable approach the moment I sent my senses out, and I'd made sure to arrive just in time. Chi rushed into Cinnamon's core, finding the gaps that hadn't been there before I'd left. She had clearly been busy. As with Maria, my bunny pal working so hard filled me with gratitude, but then I felt the aspect forming within her core. My stomach dropped.

"Oh no . . ."

Chi flew toward the ground beneath her, leaving a crater in the shape of a giant bunny's paw in the sand. It was the size of a small car, and as the essence that made it flew out in every direction, Pelly and Bill stood no chance. The bubble of chi expelled them. They didn't get far before righting themselves, both wheeling around and facing Cinnamon once more. Which was a good thing, because they had attacks to dodge.

A terrifying squeal tore from Cinnamon's throat as she lashed out with jabs, kicks, and even a head-butt or two. Each strike caused waves of force to fly from her core, further condensing as it traveled through her fuzzy little body. When it left her, the essence ballooned out, only partially visible because it distorted the surrounding air. Cinnamon remained in her paw-shaped crater, using it as a home base from which to unleash her barrage of blurred attacks.

I shook my head as I glanced between the pelicans and Cinnamon, the former dodging with everything they had, the latter only growing more pleased with herself. If a strike landed, it wouldn't hurt Pelly or Bill seriously, but there was a terrifying reason for that.

Cinnamon wasn't even trying.

As if she knew what I was thinking, her head slowly spun, only stopping when her gaze locked with mine. A shiver ran down my spine at the mischief sparkling in her eyes. Pelly and Bill's core echoed that sentiment, and they slammed down behind me, both craning their necks to watch her from a position of relative safety.

"What evil have we unleashed upon the world?" I half joked, not looking away from Cinnamon for a second.

Bill, the one who'd originally shown her the sweet karate moves she was using, let out a despondent honk. Pelly opened her beak, and by the look on her face, she was going to defend her adoptive mother's good name. Unfortunately for Pelly—and the world as a whole, really—Cinnamon stopped holding back.

She flew toward us at incredible speed, and I let my fake horror fall away as I dashed forward, going to meet her on the sands.

You want a challenge, huh? I thought, returning her manic smirk. *Let's see what you've got.*

The moment before we met, she moved faster than I'd ever seen her move. Despite the pace, her technique was perfect, and I couldn't help but appreciate the immaculate form of the roundhouse kick she unleashed at my head.

Though Pelly wanted to share a look of incredulity with Bill, she didn't want to miss a second of the action unfolding before them. If she lost track of them for but a moment, she wasn't sure she'd be able to locate them again. As impressive as Cinnamon's new breakthrough was, which had apparently made her a master of the martial arts, their master was even more amazing.

Each time Cinnamon struck out with an invisible attack, Fischer countered it by releasing the exact right amount of oppositional force. It would be impressive if he did it a single time, but he caught every single one, varying the strength to match Cinnamon's chi input. The result was a series of popping sounds that appeared all around Pelly and Bill as they spun, doing their best to track the fight. With each sequential nullification, Pelly's core trembled.

She saw Cinnamon as a mother. Even so, it was impossible to deny how dangerous the bunny felt. The best comparison to Cinnamon's new aspect was Roger's swordlike essence, but they were still very different. Roger was an unyielding blade, his edge able to cut through anything it came across. Cinnamon was a clenched fist, and though she couldn't cut rock, she could likely smash through them.

And where Roger was rigid, she was flexible. Able to pivot and strike from a different angle in an instant. Each part of her body—even her cute little toe beans, as Fischer called them—could unleash deadly power.

While Pelly had been considering the differences, the blows had grown stronger, as had their frequency. Unexpectedly, they got faster again. Pelly could no longer track them. She fluffed her feathers out and tried to let go of her last vestiges of fear. It had been steadily fading, receding a little each time she reminded herself of all the kindness Cinnamon had shown her. Her adoptive mother could be a prankster, sure, but she was also loyal, selfless, and loving.

Unaware of the developments within Pelly's mind, Fischer and Cinnamon battled on. And although she'd likely perish if subjected to a direct hit from either of them, Pelly held no fear in her heart. Neither of them would harm a feather on her body.

It wasn't just Cinnamon who had grown stronger with this advancement. The entire Church of Fischer had benefited, as had the citizens of Tropica and anyone around it. And if Pelly had her way, Cinnamon wouldn't be the only spirit beast to experience a breakthrough this week.

She sat down on the spot. Bill did the same right beside her, letting out a silent yawn before closing his eyes. In unison, they settled into themselves and each other, dismissing the outside world and the battle still occurring atop it.

As I walked back toward Tropica, I smiled down at the bunny asleep in my arms, her stomach upturned and soft snores escaping her. Cinnamon had literally unleashed so many blasts that she'd passed out, the last attack barely leaving her extended rear leg before she went limp. Not wanting to disturb Pelly and Bill's impromptu meditation, I'd caught her soundlessly and left, all the while staring down at her.

She had done such a good job.

I ran my fingers through her fur, its velvety texture all-encompassing. I leaned into the sensation, not wasting the opportunity to train my focus. As much as I appreciated my enhanced awareness—and the protection it provided everyone around me—it was also an issue sometimes.

My constant wobbling when I inspected anything was one example. And my inadvertent intrusion on Maria's thoughts and feelings was another. It had all worked out in the end with Maria, but that didn't mean I wanted it to happen again. Her privacy was more important to me than I could properly articulate, and I still felt some guilt and shame about the whole situation.

Realizing I had almost immediately become lost in thought, I refocused on Cinnamon's stomach, using her velvet fur to reground myself. Surprisingly, it worked, my mind zeroing in on the way her hairs tickled each fingertip. It was a reminder to train my mindfulness, especially now that I was so keenly aware of the surrounding world.

Distracted as I was by my cute little bunny pal and my resolution to be mindful, I didn't notice the sources of power slowly approaching until it was too late.

A muscular arm shot into my field of view, the attached fingers bent like claws. The fist descended upon Cinnamon's stomach with malicious intent, and though I had all the time in the world to save her, a single aspect of the attacker's visage gave me pause.

Barry was smiling.

His chiseled jaw framed a grin of purest elation, and a thirst for vengeance came from his core, but there was no true intent of violence. Even if I hadn't known all this, I trusted Barry implicitly. So, when his muscular arm closed the last bit of distance to Cinnamon's sleeping form, I did nothing. To be honest, this was likely deserved.

The moment Barry's fingers pressed into her stomach, he released an inhuman bellow. My entire body vibrated with the sound, only the fact that I was superhuman saving my eardrums from exploding on the spot. I was sure the surrounding sand whipped up in response to the sound wave, but I wasn't looking. Just like Barry, my eyes were pinned to Cinnamon, and I found her reaction marvelous.

Barry likely intended for her to feel pure horror. Perhaps even to traumatize her a little, an act of revenge for one of her many pranks against Tropica and its citizens. Her first reaction *was* one of sheer horror, to be fair, her sclera visible as adrenaline coursed through her. In less than a second, though, her expression shifted. Rather than anger or wrath, Cinnamon's eyes gleamed with anticipation.

"*Oh* [illegible]." Barry said, his face falling to match the regret held in his voice.

I stepped back and let go of my furry payload. Just in time, too, because Cinnamon was already twirling. She finished her rotation by lashing out with a rear leg, the movement as graceful as it was dangerous, and a bubble of chi slammed into Barry. Caught off guard, he only just got his arms up in time to absorb the blow. Well . . . most of the blow, anyway. Barry flew backward like he'd been hit by a car, his limbs akimbo.

With more agility than someone of Barry's physique should possess, he flipped and landed on his feet, skidding along the sand for dozens of meters. He radiated righteous indignation as he shot forward. It came from the depths of his core, and I wondered what grieved him so. "I know it's you that has been putting rocks in my slippers, Cinnamon!"

Oh, I thought. *Yeah. That'll do it.*

Cinnamon probably could have tried to blame it on Claws if she'd wanted, but she didn't bother to deny it. The devious little bunny gave a half smile and nodded, confirming the accusation. She got low to the ground and raised one forepaw, then gestured for Barry to bring it, taunting him.

Though she had been asleep for only minutes, that was apparently enough to recover her chi reserves. She and Barry flew back and forth over the sand, engaging in a much fairer fight than anything I could offer her. Both landed the occasional blow, Cinnamon because of technique, and Barry by breaking through her guard with sheer force.

Deklan and Dom strolled up to stand beside me, watching the fight.

"Hey, fellas," I said, not looking away from the tussle. "Where are the others?"

Deklan inhaled sharply as Barry barely dodged a kick to the groin. "Borks is napping in the cart, and Danny took Marcus and his, er, *business partner* to find a house."

"Oh, they told you guys they're together?"

"Nope. They didn't tell us anything. It was super obvious, and Danny brought it up."

"Why did he do that? Seems a bit—"

"Rude?"

"Extremely."

"Well, as it turns out, Danny won't waste resources for the sake of propriety."

"I don't understand—" I tore my eyes off the battle and turned toward the brothers as realization struck me. "He didn't . . ."

Dom snorted. "He did. He said two people who were clearly lovers should only be assigned one home."

"But we have an excess of houses . . ."

"That's exactly what we said. Danny wasn't having it."

I shook my head. "I'll have to apologize to them."

"Eh, I think they're fine. They were only hiding it because they thought we might not let them stay in the village."

"What? Why would they think that?"

Deklan shrugged, once more watching the fight. "People can kinda suck, Fischer."

"Huh." I looked back at the fight just in time to see Cinnamon duck a blow from Barry. "Yeah, that checks out, actually. People really can suck. Still, I'll go see them. To reassure them they're welcome, if nothing else."

I winced as Barry's fist collided with Cinnamon, but she unleashed a kick at the last second, the aura coming from it strong enough to neutralize his force.

Deklan let out a soft whistle. "Fresh breakthrough, huh? Feels deadly."

"Ah-huh," Dom agreed. "Impressive considering it just happened. Nothing we couldn't defend against, though. Our defenses are impenetrable. A mere bunny couldn't hope to—"

Cinnamon answered before he could finish his sentence.

The wave of essence she launched their way rivaled the strongest I'd seen her use. Without preamble, both twins joined the fray, blocking the opening strike with their chi. Though I expected them to enter the melee after Cinnamon invited them via martial strike, I didn't expect their method of doing so.

Dom leaped directly upward, and when his ankles were around head height, Deklan grabbed them. The moment they both extended their protecting chi around Dom, I knew what they were about to do.

Nah, I decided. *There's no way they'd actually—*

Deklan drew his arms back, swinging his brother like a baseball bat. Cinnamon, who was airborne, had no means of escaping the home run he was winding up to deliver. Barry, seeing his chance to deliver vengeance, reached out to hold Cinnamon in place.

I cringed, and sure enough, Cinnamon wasted not a moment. She grabbed his wrist and ran along his arm, using the speed she'd been holding in reserve thus far. All Barry could do was watch with a wide-eyed stare as she disappeared behind him, his agility and technique no match for the martial bunny.

There, Cinnamon delivered a soft slap to Barry's back. It had no hope of causing him damage, but that wasn't her intention. His lunge had left him off balance. The tap from Cinnamon, slight as it might have been, was enough to tip him forward.

Barry fell directly into the path of Dom, who Deklan had already committed to swinging. All three men involved in the battle saw what was about to happen. They *knew* they'd been outmaneuvered. And none of them could do anything about it.

As Dom's rigid body swung for Barry, he at least had the good manners to say sorry.

Barry might have reassured him it was okay. Might have told the brothers that it wasn't their fault. But there was no time. The strike landed with a brutal *thud*, and if not for Barry's breakthrough, he might have carked it on the spot.

Cinnamon let out exaggerated laughter, her forelimbs crossed before her puffed-out chest as she watched Barry sail over the river and toward the southern mountains.

CHAPTER SEVENTEEN

Secrets

Beneath the midday sun, I rolled my shoulders, delighting in the wall of sensation that came from stretching my muscle fibers. Tension I hadn't known was there fell away from my upper back. In retrospect, though, it wasn't really surprising considering the unconscious hunk I'd just caught and teleported back to Tropica.

"Yoohoo." I set Barry down and slapped him on the cheek. "You with us, mate?"

He sat bolt upright with wide eyes, touching his torso all over to ensure it was still whole. When he was satisfied, he released a sigh. "How long was I out?"

"Seconds, mate. I brought you back before you landed."

"Was . . . was I in danger if I'd landed?"

"Nah, not even a little. I knew you'd live, but I worried about you getting lodged somewhere underground, then freaking out and destroying a mountain or something when you tried to escape."

He blinked at me. "I appreciate the assistance, but are you saying that you care more about a mountain's well-being than my own?"

"Well, that's one way of saying it. You could also say that I worry about the mountain because it can't hurt you. Or, if you prefer, we could get into a philosophical debate about the worth of a life. If you destroyed a whole-ass mountain, just how many insects, worms, and other invertebrates would you wipe out? And that's not even mentioning the birds and mammals that also—"

"I surrender," Barry interrupted. "I just had another man used against me as a blunt weapon. I'm in no mood for debate, philosophical or otherwise."

"Sorry about that," Deklan said.

"Yeah, sorry," Dom agreed. "She really got one over on us . . ."

Cinnamon preened and nodded, not at all humble in victory.

I noticed movement from the north, so I glanced that way, curious as to its cause. When my eyes landed on the dozens of faces there, all peeking over the low wall that separated the village from the surrounding crops, I sensed them.

"No way . . ." I said, not believing it.

"You just realized?" Barry asked, standing and brushing sand from his ridiculously chiseled, *er,* everything. "I thought you'd know the moment we got close to Tropica."

"I was focused on everyone that's meditating. Because of our connection, their cores are way brighter in my awareness. I've also been practicing not sensing everything all the time . . ." I trailed off, arching a brow his way. "How did you feel them?

I thought the village was a single source of chi to your senses. Did you have another breakthrough?"

Barry laughed way too jovially for someone who'd been involuntarily catapulted into low orbit like two minutes ago. "I didn't feel them. Sue told us."

"Sue?"

"That's right. She came to meet us as soon as she noticed our return. She felt obligated to be the one to tell us."

"What? Why should she be the one to—" I whirled on Barry the moment I realized. "*The coffee?*"

"Just so." He nodded toward the village, and the faces still watching us, with a slight smile. "While the original members of the church have been growing in strength, the congregation has been increasing in number. The passiona coffee is to blame. Sue estimates that almost half of the regular villagers are now cultivators."

I knew exactly how many people we had living in Tropica, so I logically understood that half of them ascending meant that there were now hundreds of new cultivators. Extending my senses toward them, I used tendrils of power to feel their cumulative strength and was immediately humbled. Though less than a quarter had come to watch our return, so many of them existing close together made them feel like a cluster of sibling stars. They were entities that, given time and investment, could grow to become the human version of supergiants.

Though their cores were all unique, the familiar note of Tropica's essence ran through them. I'd at first suspected it was my imagination, but I'd come to accept it as fact that the village was becoming a part of everyone. Particularly in those who had ascended *after* the village's transformation.

Just as notable, and even more encouraging, were the emotions and thoughts pouring from them.

Some were hesitant, more were filled with awe, and most were excited. But it wasn't the present emotions that encouraged me; it was those that weren't. Over fifty people watched, and not one of them showed fear.

That response from people was something I'd grown accustomed to. I had learned to accept that it was natural for people to be terrified when confronted with someone wielding so much more power than themselves. Those watching, though, they'd only learned about the existence of cultivators a week ago . . . and they weren't scared. Some already trusted me, which made my heart sing like a bird greeting the dawn.

And there was more. Just as validating, they all sought power. Some more than others, of course, but that wasn't what had me so excited—it was that their reasons for advancing weren't purely selfish. To a one, altruism at least partially motivated them. They sought power for themselves, but also for each other and the village.

They could have tried to hide it from me. Could have attempted to conceal the selfish parts of themselves. But none of them did. They'd come to have a peek, but they'd also come as a show of faith.

"Remarkable . . ." I whispered, wondering what I'd done to deserve such confidence.

A torrent of overwhelming emotions washed over me, and given its strength, I was presented with a choice. Either hide my internal state or return their show of faith by letting it be known.

I didn't even have to think about it. I cupped my hands to my mouth and took a deep breath, channeled my emotions toward my lungs, and released it all at once.

"Keep up the good work, everyone!"

The moment the sound flew out into the world, an old nemesis I'd almost forgotten made itself known, declaring war on my very being.

New milestone! You have learned leadership!
You have advanced to leadership 3!
You have advanced to leadership 4!
You have advanced to leadership 5!

The wall dragged on, printing a series of advancements so numerous they felt like they'd never end. Finally, the last arrived.

You have advanced to leadership 67!

I shook my head, my brain feeling a little fuzzy.

After power had returned to the world, I'd been worried that the System would send me a notification each time something happened to me or my followers. A dread-inducing prospect if ever there was one.

And I had good reason to avoid them. Back on Earth, the societal benefits caused by technological advancement were unfathomable. But so were the detriments.

I'd argue that the constant buzzing from smartphones, pagers, watches, and even appliances was one of the worst offenders. It had been one of humanity's greatest sources of anxiety on Earth, yet we'd willingly subjected ourselves to it. I wouldn't repeat the same mistakes here.

In the same vein, I'd encouraged the rest of Tropica to keep their advancements between them and their immediate peers. I wanted to foster friendly rivalries, and this was a controlled way of doing so. Something deep within my core told me that using negative motivation on a village-wide scale was a good way to create the morally corrupt, if not outright insane, cultivators of old.

I had feared that chi returning to the world would rob me of those plans, but the opposite was true; it bolstered my mental fortitude and diminished the System's ability to bother me. I was still forced to see quest updates, information about Tropica's transformation, and, apparently, anything to do with the leadership skill. Or was it an ability?

Realizing I was getting lost in semantics, I took a metaphorical step back.

It had all occurred to me in less than a second, my enhanced brain easily sorting through the previously considered facts and assumptions. As I returned my attention to the outside world, I witnessed the wondrous effect my words had on the recently awakened humans. Though it hit them with almost-physical force, it seemed to entice them toward me rather than push them away. Each leaned forward slightly as my appreciation joined with their cores and the feelings coursing through them.

Our mutual trust and thankfulness built atop each other, becoming something tangible as the tendrils of essence I sensed them with were sucked into their abdomens. It wasn't permanent like the way Tropica's chi would always be a part of them, but my essence definitely wove through their cores, doing . . . *something.*

"What did you just do to them . . .?" Barry asked.

"I have no idea. You can feel it."

"I can. If you can't answer that, what did you get?"

"Huh?"

"From the System. What did you advance in?"

"Oh," I replied, not really paying attention. "I unlocked the leadership skill and got it to level 67."

Most of my focus was on the dozens of cultivators across the sands, but no matter how much I watched them and their abdomens, I couldn't work out what my chi was doing.

They cycled between staring back at me and looking down at their cores. My essence swirled within them, and though it dissipated with each passing second, it would take hours to leave completely. It was an intimate moment, as platonic as it was profound, and Barry immediately ruined it.

He blew air through his lips with all the subtlety of Corporal Claws left alone with a stack of juicy oysters. "*Level 67?*" he demanded. "And you were worried about being a bad leader?" He turned to Cinnamon, who was now perched on his shoulder. "Are you hearing this guy? Unbelievable."

She leaned back on her haunches, crossed her forepaws in front of her chest and looked down her nose at me with an expression that all but screamed *pathetic.*

"You know," I said, "I'm glad you two have put your differences aside to give me shit, but I think I liked it better when you were fighting to the death."

"Fighting . . . *to the death?* We would never do something so vulgar, would we, Cinnamon?"

Never, she agreed with a soft peep, still appearing scornful of my general existence.

Her acting had seriously improved, but she couldn't keep the facade up for long. With a single leap from Barry's muscular shoulders, she arrived in my arms, rolling onto her back to expose her fluffy stomach.

"I know you were joking, you goose. There's no need to reassure me."

She wiggled farther into the crook of my arm, completely disregarding my words. I stroked her stomach in response, scratching the spot near her sternum that was hard for her to reach.

"So we've had a bunny breakthrough, Barry had his butt kicked, and I've learned leadership or whatever. Talk about a productive afternoon. Should we—"

Barry interrupted me by raising a finger. "Don't forget that we teased you for your previous claims that you'd make a bad leader of your own church."

"Sure. I was teased. So, with all that done, I feel like we've completed today's—"

"Viciously," he amended. "You were teased *viciously*."

"Fine. I was teased within an inch of my life. Can we start building now? I thought you'd be keen to learn what it was that we gathered all those supplies for."

"Oh, I already know what you want to build, but I need to go get something first. I have a surprise for you."

"You do *not* know what I'm going to build."

"I do," he replied. "It's obvious. We can worry about that later, though."

I opened my mouth to respond with something that would have doubtlessly been as witty as it was devastating, but Barry was already gone, his bulging thighs chewing through the distance between us and Tropica. Sensing the anticipation coming from the twins, I spun their way. "You guys know his surprise, don't you?"

"We do," Dom replied easily. "We saw him on the way past Trop—"

Deklan elbowed his twin in the side, cutting him off. "We saw *it* on the way past."

"Oh, uhhhh, yeah. We saw *it*."

"The surprise is a *him*, huh?" I rubbed my chin. "I wonder who could have arrived that would surprise me? Someone else from the capital? How did they get by us without being seen?"

Deklan shook his head. "Sorry. This is Barry's secret to share."

"I won't force the issue, then." I stretched and took a deep breath, delighting in the scent of salt in the air. I'd missed it terribly while we were gone. "Shall we unpack while we wait? Borks hasn't seen your breakthrough yet, Cinnamon . . ."

With a violent gleam in her eyes, she leaped up to my shoulder and pointed toward the ocean, ordering me to march.

"Yes, ma'am!" I called, jogging east with a smile on my face.

CHAPTER EIGHTEEN

Both

The slightest of breezes occasionally flicked past as I stared out at the ocean, its surface calm but for the small waves crashing on the shore. The sky above was a canvas of red and pink that slowly bled to yellow the closer it got to the mountains behind me, and I released a breath as I appreciated the swathe of colors even an expert painter would struggle to replicate.

A fur-covered head bumped against my thigh, and I smiled down at the goodest of boys. "It's beautiful, isn't it?"

Borks whined in agreement, staring up at me with a tongue lolling from the side of his mouth. He was in his default golden retriever form, and I scratched behind his ear, both of us enjoying the touch. After a good scritching, I patted him on the top of his head. "Let's unload your dimensional space. It shouldn't take long."

He barked, turned, and ran toward the cart that the others had just finished unpacking.

"Ohhhh," Deklan drawled, "look who *finally* came to help."

I immediately adopted a haughty air, standing taller and puffing my chest out. "Did I say you could speak, peasant? Wait until my lord father hears about this . . ."

"He's finally gone mad with power." Dom shook his head. "Maria was right all along."

"You *dare*?" I recoiled as if physically struck, contorting my face into a mix of disgust, confusion, and anger. "I could have you *whipped* like butter-based frosting. I could have your buns beaten until toasted. I could have your entirely *family* packaged up like so many sugary donuts, then sell you at a discount like the *poors* that you are—"

"*Fischer!*"

The booming, panicked voice tore right through my joke. I glanced toward the figure that must have leaped from Tropica. It took just over a second for him to reach us and crash down into the sand before me.

I was at his side in an instant. His core radiated fear. "Theo, *mate*, you all right?"

"Marcus . . . he has a *husband!*"

"Uhhh, yeah? You're a bit late on that one." I frowned at his abdomen and let out a relieved sigh when I confirmed it wasn't their relationship that bothered him. "Why are you in such a tizzy?"

"You don't understand, Fischer. He previously told me he had a wife. It was the *truth.*"

"Okay, I think I understand your confusion. Is it possible he has both?"

"No. He told Danny that his husband *was* the person he referred to as his wife!"

"That could have been the lie, right?"

"Why would he lie about that? It makes no sense!" Theo shook his head and audibly swallowed. "I've *never* had something like this happen. People can deliver half-truths, but for a lie as bold as this to feel like the complete truth? And his explanation that they were worried about being unwelcome—it seems too perfect, especially if targeted at someone as compassionate as you. Marcus could be an infiltrator. We *cannot* trust someone who can't be read!"

I raised both hands placatingly. "Okay, I can tell this is coming from a good place, but I need you to take a deep breath. I was going to go talk to them anyway, so I'll go see them now. I want you to come, but only if you can calm dow—"

He opened his mouth to interrupt, but sent out a localized pulse of essence first, making the words die in his throat.

"*Mate.* You're amped up by fear. It's an understandable reaction because of how out-of-control this must make you feel, especially because you've always been able to read anyone weaker than you, but it's clouding your judgment. If you can't assume the best of them, I'll go alone. Show some grace. Give them the benefit of the doubt until proven otherwise. If it's truly the case that they didn't want to feel judged or persecuted, I'm not gonna have you beside me radiating distrust. It would only confirm *their* fears."

"Ooooh," Deklan called, a teasing tone clear in his voice. "Theo's in *trouble*! He made Fischer put his leader pants on!"

Once more proving just how emotionally intelligent the seemingly lackadaisical man was, Deklan's jibes immediately diffused the situation.

Theo released a hissed breath. "I see what you're saying. Sorry, and thank you."

"No need, mate. That's what friends are for. Let's go see our newest pals are settling into their new home."

Though we ran there at an inhuman speed, neither of us had broken a sweat by the time I knocked on the door Theo led me to. I heard hurried steps coming from inside, and I flooded loving acceptance from my core, hoping it would have a soothing effect on the non-cultivators within. They paused on the other side of the wooden portal, exchanging whispers that I withdrew from, not wanting to overhear.

The door swung open on silent hinges, revealing only Marcus.

"G'day, mate! Just wanted to come check out your new digs and make sure you were settled! Is Caius home?"

I fought to stop my eyes from drifting to the right, where I could hear said bloke's heart hammering away despite having withdrawn my senses. Marcus was waging the same war, if the strained look on his face could be believed.

"Hello, Fischer. I'm afraid Caius isn't—"

"That's enough," Caius said, throwing the door wide, his gaze boring into me. "I am done hiding who I am. Hurry up and tell us to leave so we can find a place we're not scorned."

"Nahhh, I don't think I will. This is your home, Caius. I'm sorry for not making it clear on our way back from Gormona, but I felt the feelings you both had for each other." I gave him the kindest smile I could muster. "I mean this in the nicest way possible: *nobody cares.*"

Marcus's cheeks had gone white the moment his husband revealed himself. Color returned to his face as he blinked at my words. "You mean it, friend Fischer?"

"Yup. Frankly, it has nothing to do with me, and it makes me sad that it's something you had to consider. That aside, Theo *did* come to me with a concern, but it was about the fact you *could* hide who Caius was for so long."

"You really do mean it . . ." Marcus turned to his partner, blinking. Caius blinked back, looking as stunned as Marcus had a moment ago. Abruptly, they burst into laughter, relief flooding their bodies. "Forgive me, friend Theo. This is something many merchants know of, passed down from father to son and from master to apprentice."

Theo had smiled at their outburst, but Marcus's response made severity return. "Do you really expect me to believe a method exists to circumvent an auditor's ability? I like you, Marcus. Really, I do. I'm just struggling to believe what my senses are telling me."

"Which is that I have told only the truth, including with my last statement." Still amused, the merchant shook his head. "But you have experienced similar, have you not? All know about the shortcoming of auditors. A speaker's belief is the gauge by which to recognize lies, yes? What, then, if I believed it completely?"

Theo frowned, his eyes going distant as his thoughts whirled. It would still be interpreted as a partial truth, and continued questioning would reveal the lie."

"Wrong." Marcus grinned at the look Theo gave him—he'd clearly deemed it as true. "It is not possible with all things. For example, a merchant cannot lie and say he made twenty gold when he really made fifty, because numbers can never be two things at once. If, however, said merchant was creative and clever—" He tapped his nose. "—he could think of a pelt as a blanket. A pelt is worth much more, but it *can* be used as a blanket."

It was Theo's turn to blink. "Are you claiming that, for as long as merchants have been getting taxed by the crown, they have been systematically fudging the numbers?"

"Some did, certainly."

"Did *you*?"

Marcus drew an aggrieved hand to his chest. "Friend Theo! This king-fearing merchant has *never* engaged in such underhanded tactics!"

Theo's expression flattened. "Well, at least I know I can still detect a blatant lie."

Marcus grinned. "Just so! But the demonstration has not ended!" He pointed at Caius. "This is my husband. He is also my wife, as this is what I believe in my heart of hearts. It is a matter of perspective. If I really wanted to, I could deny to myself that he was my husband at all, but such a view seems too harsh for this humble merchant to stomach. I digress. As to my previous statement, let this unassuming purveyor of products clear his good name! I, the merchant Marcus, have always been fair in my dealings with the crown."

Theo frowned. "That . . . that doesn't make sense. Why does that feel like the complete truth? There isn't even the hint of a lie."

"Because, dear Theo, the rate at which the former king taxed poor Marcus and his fellow merchants is more accurately described as *theft*. So what if I get a little creative with my declarations? That is a fair response to such blatant larceny and greed. It is underhanded, yet equitable. Thus, I have been fair in my dealings with the crown."

I absolutely lost it, guffawing so loud the entirety of Tropica might have heard me. "Your face, Theo. Perspective, huh? *Wild.* If it makes you feel any better, I could tell there was more to Marcus's statements each time you perceived a lie as the truth."

"Really?" all three of them asked with varying degrees of surprise.

"Don't be so shocked, guys." I winked. "There's a reason I'm god-king of this here fishing village." I looked at Theo. "Jokes aside, are your doubts satisfied?"

"Not even a little. I'm going to spend the rest of my life wondering just how many lies slipped past me. I might never sleep again."

"A fair punishment for mistrusting your dear friend," Marcus said, his eyes glittering.

"I *am* sorry about that. You too, Caius. I apologize for the misunderstanding my need for answers created."

"Not at all." Caius turned sideways, gesturing into the well-lit home. "Why not join us for tea? Our home came pre-stocked with an unbelievable number of snacks."

"Never underestimate Danny's ability to ration," Theo said. "I would love some tea—and perhaps ask more questions, if it isn't too soon?"

"Of course, of course! And you, friend Fischer?"

I pointed back over my shoulder. "Another time? I have to get back to the beach. Deklan has had entirely too much time to plan more jokes at my expense."

"He is rather good at that, isn't he?" Marcus asked. "Best you run along then. Come by any time."

"Will do!" I called, already running back to my project.

No more than two minutes later, I was still retorting with a joke of my own at Deklan's expense when a familiar presence approached, and I cut myself off.

Barry strode across the sand, one eyebrow slightly arched at the colorful words I'd been using. He wasn't the presence that had halted my passionate diatribe, though. The smaller man beside him, not yet tall enough to reach his father's shoulders, wore more pride than I'd ever seen him wield. His aura was familiar but undeniably different.

My words had initially died because I didn't want to say anything uncouth around the impressionable lad, but now it was an entirely different thing holding my tongue. Paul, Barry and Helen's only son, had become a cultivator. Something about his aura was . . . muted. Like there was something sealing off the rest of his power.

As he got closer to us, he must have sensed a portion of our combined power, because a flicker of hesitation appeared. His eyes darted to his father. And while he gazed up at the marble sculpture of a man, I wondered what was going through his mind. They had a healthy bond, and it was normal for a boy to see his dad as the strongest man he'd ever seen—but what if your dad actually *was* the strongest man you'd ever seen? What did Paul see in his mind's eye when he looked up at the real-life version of a Greek god?

I didn't have to wait long for an answer.

Some of Paul's pride returned after but a moment, his nostrils flaring and shoulders straightening as the mere act of looking at his father seemed to reinforce his spine. Barry, despite what one might expect from his particular image of hypermasculinity, got down on one knee and scooped his son into a comforting embrace. Every ounce of hesitation and worry sloughed away from Paul as he grinned and made a token effort to push his father away.

Barry lifted his son with ease, then set him down before me and released him, a hand remaining on his son's shoulder to remind him it was going to be okay. It might have been a small gesture, but its impact was great.

"Paul, mate . . ." I said, smirking at how tall he was standing. "I know it's been a while since I last saw you, but I don't think time explains how much you've changed . . ."

His answering smile could have lit the ocean's depths. "Hi, Fischer! I became a cultivator yesterday! Just like you and my dad and my mom and Uncle Leroy! Oh, and Auntie Barbara! And—"

"I can see that, mate," I interrupted with a chuckle, then continued before he could start rattling off names again. "How long have you, uhhh—"

"Known about cultivators?" he blurted.

"Yeah. That."

"Ages!"

Barry gave me an apologetic look. "I can probably answer that in more detail. Paul has known since the king's attack, but he suspected—"

"I knew you were a traveler since *forever* ago!" Paul said, leveling a finger at me. "I heard Mom and Dad and Uncle Leroy and Aunty Barabara talking about it!"

Barry winced and rubbed the back of his head. "Well, there you have it. We've been keeping him away from everything since then, which is why you've not seen him around. Obviously, we could no longer hide it after the battle."

"It was *so cool*! The explosions were like fireworks, and then the boulders! Covered in lightning! Then you were there—or that's what Mom says anyway—and it was like . . . giant lights everywhere all at once! How did you do that? Dad said maybe I can do that, too, if I train and remain good! Or maybe I can get super strong like him! What does my core feel like? Mom said you're much better at sensing them than anyone else!"

With each unhinged sentence, my joy blossomed further. Paul may have become something more than his age, but he was still a boy at heart, which was something we had to protect at all costs. I couldn't think of anything worse than someone growing up too quickly.

All it took was a quick glance toward Barry to see that he was sharing the same thoughts. We both nodded, not needing to voice the agreement.

"All right," I said, stepping forward. "Why don't the three of us go for a walk? This is something huge, Paul, and now that you're a cultivator . . ." I leaned in close, looking around conspiratorially. "There are some *secrets* I have to tell you . . ."

By his reaction, you'd have thought I had just told him I'd buried a ton of candy somewhere nearby. As I led him and Barry down to the water, his thoughts raced, their tone continually shifting. All were positive, so I let them run rampant. And only when they became tinged with the faintest whisper of anxiety did I speak.

"Okay, Paul," I said, kneeling down so we were eye to eye. "Are you ready?"

He nodded.

"First, I should ask your dad what he's told you so far. Barry?"

"Well, suspecting his awakening would one day arrive, we've been emphasizing the responsibility of those with power since before the church formed. After the king attacked, we stepped it up even more. And over the last couple of days . . ." He patted his son on the upper back. "How many hours did you spend learning with Ellis yesterday?"

"All of them! And I didn't complain once! Even when he had Pelly and Bill drop me out of the—" He clapped his hands to his mouth to cut himself off, a burst of panic coming from his half-muted core.

The air grew dangerous, and Barry leaned down, looking into his son's eyes. "Drop you out of the what, Paul?"

"It . . . it was supposed to be a secret . . ."

"What did Ellis have them do, Paul? Tell me."

Paul's face fell, and the words came out as a whisper. "He had them drop me from the sky . . ."

"Where did this happen?"

"Please don't be angry. It was fun after the first few times, because I realized it wouldn't hurt."

The air warped around Barry, an odd hum suffusing our surroundings. "Where, Paul?"

"Past the mountains. He said it was safer to do it away from everyone—"

The hum coming from Barry grew sharp, cutting Paul off. "Safer for him, because no one would see." He stood to his full height, his body shivering with fury. "Can you continue this conversation without me, Fischer? I believe I have to go have a chat with our mutual friend . . ."

"Of course, mate. Do what you gotta do."

Surprisingly, Borks stepped forward to join him, a bone-deep anger burning within him. Before I could ask, Borks sent his feelings through our connection. Ellis had endangered a young member of the pack—such things could not remain unchecked.

With each step Barry took back toward Tropica, the ground shook.

Cinnamon, out of nowhere, leaped to Barry's shoulder and started punching one closed paw into the other. Unsure if she was genuinely angry at Ellis or just looking for an excuse to deliver a good beatdown, I queried her. As with Borks, she offered it up freely. As her emotions washed over me, I couldn't help but pity the man they were off to find.

"Which was it?" Deklan asked after a moment.

"Huh?"

"Her motivation." He pointed at Cinnamon. "I can tell Borks's with a glance, but Cinnamon is harder to read. Is she genuinely angry, or is she just looking for any reason to kick the shit out of someone?"

I snorted. "Worse."

"Worse? What could be worse?"

"It's both. She's pissed at Ellis *and* looking for an excuse to belt the absolute piss out of anyone she can."

The twins cringed, both releasing an audible hiss of air through their teeth.

Despite being within the walls of a supernatural prison, Ellis was having a wonderful evening. With so many experiments to run and observations to record lately, he had found little time to slow down and enjoy life. And to Ellis, nothing was as relaxing as crafting. He had dabbled in every profession he knew of, and though they all had calming qualities, leatherworking stood high above all the others. Well, that *had* been the case—until he discovered alchemy.

The moment he had learned that they could hide the presence of cultivators—even from someone as powerful as Fischer—he knew that he would have to explore the craft. He had thought to learn the basics. To glean just enough that he could guard against it. But then he had felt its magic for the first time.

Previously, Ellis would have scoffed if he had heard anyone other than a child or a dullard refer to something as *magic*. Yet he could find no better descriptor for the process occurring before his very eyes. Rather than chi rushing and slamming into the cauldron, it flowed in with unhurried ease, expertly weaved by the alchemist Solomon. Beside Solomon, Francis was a man possessed, passing off ingredients before the former could finish asking for them.

Together, the men were a force of nature. And Francis was not even a cultivator, making their coordination even more impressive, though that would soon change if he continued down the path he was treading. If presented with the crafting of any other profession, Ellis would have focused on the unascended man, intent on gaining insight into his eventual awakening.

Instead, Ellis stared into the mixture, its dark blue swirls seeming to draw him in. It had started as a thin liquid, with a consistency akin to purified water. From there, it had become like salt water or blood, somehow thickening despite not losing any vapor. Now, it was as thick as soup, and all Solomon had added was plant-based materials.

But Ellis well knew it wasn't the ingredients causing the transformation; it was the essence. Its slow and methodical addition mystified Ellis, because it defied the control that a newly awakened cultivator should have. Something about Solomon's alchemy was different. Ellis was sure of it. No matter how long he stared, though, the secrets remained undiscovered.

With frustration billowing up, Ellis rallied his thoughts, focusing on what he knew.

There were two possibilities. The first was that it was something unique to alchemy, the profession somehow allowing more finesse than anything else. If this was the case, Ellis hadn't been able to replicate it. Which was why he suspected the second theory, that Solomon was special, having somehow earned more control than any other—including Fischer when he was at that stage of cultivation.

It made no godsdamned sense. Ellis pressed his forehead against the bars that contained the two men. He focused on the icy touch of the metal as he closed his eyes, trying to brute-force a solution for this vexing conundrum.

Unfortunately for Ellis, and for more than one reason, the former archivist had chosen the worst possible moment to close his eyes.

The first was that Francis's awakening arrived. It happened so fast that Ellis missed almost all of it, his eyes firmly shut and attention aimed within. He returned to the world as fast as he could, only just catching the last of the golden light as it left the newly ascended alchemist. A wave of euphoria washed over him, which would have brought a smile to his face if not for the exasperation and sheer incredulity keeping him grounded.

Quick as it arrived, the body-wide bliss was gone. And just as suddenly, another presence filled the void left behind. An oppressive aura engulfed him, seeming to force itself upon every inch of his being. He had felt this sensation before. He knew its source well. That alone would have been enough to make his blood run cold. This time, though, there were additional layers present. Hints of fury, reprimand, and . . . *excitement*?

With a tight chest and prickling skin, Ellis slowly turned to look at the other reasons he'd chosen the worst possible moment to close his eyes. Barry, his body vibrating with fury, was more muscular than Ellis had ever seen him. Borks strode beside him, his hackles high and head lowered.

From atop Barry's shoulder, Cinnamon sneered down at Ellis with an imperious glare. She was the source of the excitement, and with no small amount of alarm, Ellis realized there was more depth to her core. Cinnamon had experienced a breakthrough.

Ellis swayed, his legs giving way before the weight of what was to come. Barry closed the distance in a flash, one of his muscular arms more than enough to keep Ellis upright.

"Hello, mate." Barry's voice was harder than granite and colder than ice. "I was just chatting with my son, and he told me the *darnedest* thing . . ."

CHAPTER NINETEEN

Miracle

Beneath a blanket of stars, I couldn't contain my joy as I watched Paul cast out his line. We both watched as his bait flew at an odd angle over the ocean, landing a little closer than he'd intended. I could feel a hint of annoyance directed at himself, so I swooped in.

"Doing good, mate! Flick the reel into place and wind in the slack!"

Any hint of his self-recrimination disappeared, replaced by anticipation as he followed my instructions. "Like this, Fischer?" he asked when the line was tight.

"Just like that. Keep tension on the line and rest your finger here. You'll know when a fish bites the hook."

"You're sure?"

"Positive."

Finally accepting my words, he nodded, his eyes remaining on the spot where line entered water. Behind us, two shapes crested a dune. Deklan and Dom, having retrieved their own fishing rods, had come to join. They both shot me a questioning look, checking that their proximity wouldn't interfere. I replied with a quick thumbs-up as I bent to put bait on my hook; I could always raise a deafening shield if Paul and I needed privacy.

Abruptly, a spike of excitement came from Paul. "I can't believe I'm actually fishing with you. This. Is. So. *Cool!*"

"I feel the same about fishing with you, mate!"

"I overheard *everyone* talking about it for *so long*! Even back before you beat the king's butt and transformed the village. I asked Mom and Dad about it, but they just said it was too dangerous and that I'd have to wait until I was older."

I shook my head as I got back to my feet. "We weren't as good at keeping secrets as we thought, huh?"

He rolled his eyes so hard that his head joined the motion. "Adults are *never* as good at keeping secrets as they think they are. I know all sorts of things."

Smiling at his words, I walked toward the water. "I'll keep you in mind next time I need some intel."

I flicked my reel open, drew my rod over my shoulder, and cast my baited hook out over the ocean. Whereas I'd used light tackle on Paul's training rod, mine was the exact opposite. The largest sinker Tropica had ever produced sailed out over the ocean, an equally big hook and slab of fish following its passage.

I'd only intended for us fishing together to be a pleasant distraction—something to make the conversation to come seem more natural—but that didn't mean I couldn't be excited about it. Paul, as it turned out, felt the same.

He danced a happy little jig from foot to foot as my gigantic setup sailed hundreds of meters out over the water. "No *way*! Will I be able to use one that size someday?"

"Of course, mate. Truth be told, you could probably cast it out now with your improved strength, but you might not be able to control your chi enough to stop the line from snapping if you did hook something. Only a *massive* creature will take a bait this size."

In retrospect, I should have expected that sentence to have the effect it did. Paul's eyes went wide as he glanced over at me, an unmissable sense of awe coming from his abdomen. "How big . . . ?"

"Mate . . . bigger than me. Bigger than your dad, even with his massive muscles. The largest thing I've seen for myself was a shark, and I reckon it was twice my height."

Paul's mouth dropped open as he turned to face the ocean. "And you could catch that?"

"Pretty sure, yeah. I've caught fish longer than me, and that was before I was so good at controlling my chi. To be honest, I haven't gone fishing for anything big since I had that last breakthrough."

"What? Why? If I was an adult, I would do it all the time."

I barked a laugh. "Yeah, usually I do. Can I tell you a secret, mate? One that has nothing to do with the conversation your dad wanted us to have?"

He nodded sharply, a serious air coming over him. "I won't tell anyone. I'm good at secrets."

"Okay, but only if you pinky promise." I grinned at the quizzical look he gave me and held out my hand. "Like this. Wrap our pinkies together and shake. A pinky promise means serious business back where I come from."

He was completely sincere as we shook our digits, his jaw firm and eyes fierce.

"Good lad. Now that you're sworn to secrecy, I can share something only Maria and Sergeant Snips know." I took a deep breath as I wound my line in a little, collecting slack. "It's because I was scared, Paul. Now that I'm so powerful, I'm a little worried that I'll no longer find fishing as enjoyable as I once did. What if I never find a fish that will challenge me again?"

In response, Paul looked at me like I was a moron. "That's dumb." He pointed out at the ocean with one hand. "You can basically *fly*. Just go find a bigger fish!"

His bluntness made another barked laugh fly out into the night. "You're not wrong, mate. That's exactly why I'm building a . . ." I trailed off and shot him a coy look. "You're sure you can keep secrets?"

His half-functional core broadcast eagerness. I raised a wall of chi around us that sound couldn't penetrate, cupped my hand to his ear, and whispered a single word. There was a beat of silence as his eyes drifted groundward, his adolescent brain churning away at the implication. When his gaze once more met mine, he searched for something in the lines of my face. When he found the answer, shock flooded from him.

"Those are *real?*" he yelled, unable or unwilling to lower his voice.

"Shhhh!" I held a finger to my lips, having lowered the walls of deafening chi a little too soon. I peered over his shoulder at the two men within hearing range. Both Deklan and Dom had cast their lines out into the bay, and though they were pointedly looking anywhere but at us, I could tell their ears were burning to hear more. I shook my head at them, then looked down at Paul, whose shock had turned to childlike wonder.

"Yes, mate. They're real. And I'm planning to make one."

"Wow . . ." he said, not at all bothered that I'd shushed him.

"I'm just as excited as you are. We—"

Waves of potent power cut off my words, and I whirled to face Tropica.

"What's wrong?"

I pointed back at the village. "Someone just became a cultivator. But that's not all . . ."

"It's not?"

"Nope. Might wanna peer this way, Paul. I reckon we're about to see a show. Here, put your rod in the sand. Deklan! Dom!" They jogged to join us. "Put your rods in the sand," I continued. "I'll hold them in place."

With all of them pressed firmly into the ground, I secured them with a mild amount of chi.

"Five gold says ocean," Dom said.

"I've got five on the sky," Deklan replied.

"That's too large."

"Well, what if I say west and you say east?"

"Then that leaves nothing for Fischer." Dom raised a brow at me. "You want in?"

I grinned. "I'll join. I've got five on a mountain."

Deklan sucked air through his teeth. "Damn. Mountain is good. Wish I'd thought of it."

Paul had been looking between us as we spoke, more and more lines appearing on his forehead. "What are you guys—"

He cut off as the ground beneath us rumbled. I steadied him with a hand on his shoulder. The wall of sound hit us a second later, and as the explosive noise washed over us, a mass of beings soared into the sky above Tropica.

Most visible was Barry, his shirt in tatters. By some miracle, his pants remained mostly intact, though his bulging muscles did their best to tear them asunder. He held a lizard-suited man by the throat with one hand.

For his part, Ellis radiated sheer panic. I could feel it even from hundreds of meters away. I inspected the two spirit beasts, and the more I considered them, the more I agreed with Ellis's assessment of the situation.

Borks was in his hellhound form. Shadows writhed from his neck, making the form more nightmare inducing than usual. They held on to Ellis, so even if Barry were to let go, the former archivist would remain trapped. Borks's anger burned bright, manifesting as a red glow in his eyes as he stared down at his prey.

Cinnamon, perched on Barry's shoulder and not yet a part of the fight, was who Ellis should be most concerned about. A laugh came from her tiny little mouth as she faced the sky and gathered power in her lower body. Without warning, she launched herself from Barry, rocketing directly up toward the stars.

"Did she overshoot the mark?" Deklan asked, arching a brow.

"Nope," I replied, knowing what would come next.

At a nod from Barry, Borks released his ability, freeing Ellis. Well, maybe *freeing* wasn't the right word, because Barry swung him round and round like a life-sized rag. When my perception of Ellis was reduced to a blurred circle, Barry let go.

Ellis flew so fast that he'd have shattered air-speed records back on Earth. It was faster than I'd ever seen anything move. Yet my animal pals were ready.

A portal opened between Borks and the sky, which Ellis sailed right through. Cinnamon had reached the peak of her skyward jump, and the entire time she'd been moving, she was gathering and condensing chi.

The moment Ellis appeared before her, still shooting at hypersonic speeds, she uncoiled her essence. Both rear paws lashed out like cobras, power traveling through her limbs and exiting in twin aura blasts. They collided with Ellis and disintegrated what strands of his clothes had survived Barry's throw, only Ellis's Lizard Wizard suit stopping his meat and two veg from being exposed to the night air.

Ellis's new trajectory southward had him traveling at a slightly reduced speed, but that wasn't at all reflective of the power that'd hit him. Cinnamon's off-center attack had left him spinning like a leaf in a tornado, his splayed limbs and the laws of aerodynamics jerking him in odd directions. As one, Deklan, Dom, and I noticed where he was headed, and I couldn't help but grin. Both brothers swore under their breaths.

Ellis was heading directly for the closest mountain. Absent a miracle, he'd strike it and skip off its peak, but the skipping off wasn't what was important.

Suddenly, a source of chi swelled in the forest below Ellis. The treetops became awash with blue and white light. Even before the electricity creating the illumination cracked out into the night, I knew who was about to emerge from the canopy.

As the barbed lightning exploded out into the night, my hopes fell, and I was immediately forced to alter my earlier statement. It wasn't only a miracle that could stop Ellis from colliding with the nearby mountain.

With exactly zero care that she might make me lose my bet, Corporal Claws came into view, her grin manic and eyes pinned on the cartwheeling man high above.

CHAPTER TWENTY

Severed

Corporal Claws ascended from the clearing like a god-made manifest. Electricity burgeoned outward in every direction, and just as she threatened to turn the entire night sky into a giant plasma ball, the tip of each lightning bolt wavered. Not because they ran out of power, though—because Claws was reining them in.

She wasn't doing it as a collective either. There were thousands of them, and Claws was attempting to control each one individually. It was a colossal undertaking, one that required her to split her will into literally thousands of pieces. Was this her method of having a breakthrough? Focusing on control instead of boosting throughput?

Being the only person capable of witnessing this ridiculous attempt, I gave it my full attention, appreciating just how ambitious it was.

Some of the smaller bolts obeyed. They curled around her body to create a moving sphere, and the glimpses I caught of her through the jagged lines of lightning showed a face pinched with concentration. Though under her control, each bolt fought against her, seeking to return to their natural state.

Claws's lightning, however, was anything but natural. She could target people at will, which went against everything I knew. It was easy to chalk everything up to fantasy-world bullshit, but now that her chi seemed to exert its own will, I saw an opportunity that I couldn't let pass.

I zeroed my awareness in on her essence, focusing on the bolts of lightning, knowing that I would likely fail, yet willing to try regardle—*oh* . . . Because of my connection to her, I knew all about it the moment my awareness hit. Her chi was an extension of her nature.

When Claws imagined striking someone with lightning, it struck. That was all there was to it. When she didn't have a target, however . . . it wanted to fly free, shooting out in a relatively straight line. Or even better, into a core or mass of chi if one was nearby. I tucked that terrifying tidbit of information away for later, just in case her electricity went rogue and tried to slam into other beings.

The battle that Claws was engaged in came down to what her chi wanted. She was trying to bend it to her will, shaping it without assigning a target to strike.

Curious about Claws's mental state, I sent my awareness out toward her. Only a fraction of a second had passed, but already she grew both mentally and physically drained. Bending so much electricity was incredibly taxing. Sensing me, she cracked one eye and spared me a precious sliver of her attention. She sent a complex series of emotions directly to my consciousness, and if translated to English, they could be distilled down into a single sentence.

Check this shit out.

Multiple possibilities immediately sprouted in my mind. Had she already devised a method to gain agency over the thousands of bolts? Had she been just pretending to falter, wanting to put on a show before succeeding? Or did she perhaps discover something just now that would facilitate her growth? I could ask her core, but that would ruin the surprise—something Claws would never forgive.

She didn't force me to wait long. Claws shifted her will, focusing on the bolts forming a writhing sphere around her body. They immediately fell into place. A small part of each individual streak still railed at being reshaped, but they still . . . accepted their new role? It was a difficult concept to describe.

Enthralled as I was, I saw the exact moment it all fell apart.

With her attention on the chi close to her, Claws lost her hold on everything else. The longer lines of lightning cracked out into the night, some striking the ground and even more dissipating as they traveled skyward. I felt a moment of compassion for my egotistical pal, sad that Claws had failed her attempt in such a public setting.

I waited for self-recrimination or shame to shatter her concentration and cause the remaining essence to fly out of control. Waited for her vanity to clash with her failure. But then the corners of her lips curled upward, and pride radiated from her in powerful ripples.

Her needle-sharp teeth reflected her lightning's brilliance as a grin covered her face. Mischievous glee joined the pride cascading from her core, and try as I might, I couldn't understand why. This only increased her elation.

Now that she no longer had to pour chi into the thousands of lightning bolts, she was able to focus on those swirling around her. They grew slightly, decreasing the spaces through which to glimpse Claws.

Their potency was something else entirely. All the chi that had been used to generate the other bolts poured out of her abdomen, directly joining the localized storm surrounding her. It spun faster and faster as Claws kept it contained, the tricksy little otter easily bending the lightning to her will.

Through the blurred gaps in the tempest, I witnessed Claws's head slowly tilt upward. All at once, I understood.

With the excitement of a potential breakthrough, I'd completely forgotten about Ellis. Claws, however, had not. Despite his speed, he'd only traveled tens of meters since Claws had emerged. Which, unfortunately for Ellis, left him almost directly above her and the storm she was brewing. The jagged lines of essence swirling around her moved so fast now that they let out a chittering noise similar to those Claws would often make. It grew louder and higher in pitch as it sped up to unfathomable speeds.

My only method of accurately tracking the time was the passage of Ellis's cartwheeling body, and my eyes flicked up to him as I felt him gathering chi. Whenever his chaotic spinning allowed him to see Claws, he watched her. I desperately wanted to know if it was excitement or dread making his face so ashen, but I had neither the time nor the ability to find out.

My hairs stood on end as the smell of ozone wafted through the air. The chittering of Claws's chi became a single tone, blending even to my enhanced senses. Claws let part of her hidden thoughts slip, and I became aware of an undeniable fact. She hadn't abandoned her breakthrough attempt earlier; this had been her plan all along. The perfect opportunity for mischief had arrived, and she was going to strike.

Before I had realized it was gathering, the world's chi started to form misshaped bubbles around Claws. They had angles and points to them that shifted rapidly, as if they themselves were composed of electricity. I desperately wanted to inspect them further, but as with Ellis's core, I had more important things to monitor. My choice was immediately justified when Claws let out a panicked yelp.

Still connected to her, I recognized that she had gathered too much power. Her choice was to abandon her attack—abandon her breakthrough—or risk damaging Ellis. She thought that there was even a small chance that he'd be obliterated.

Oh, sweetie, I sent her, smiling at how much she still underestimated her impending strike, *I've got your back, so give him hell.*

There was a moment of confusion from her, my mirth sweeping debris onto the shore of her mind, but my reassurance came and washed it clean once more. With a grin and absolutely zero hesitation, Claws unleashed a city-ending strike toward a sky-bound man that was doing his best impression of a windmill in a hurricane.

The misshaped bubbles of chi slammed into her body, and rather than her core, they suffused every cell in her body. I desperately wanted to know what was happening—what they were doing to her—but it was time for me to play my part.

I made a claw with my right hand and hefted it upward, raising a bubble of shimmering light around the village. With my left hand, I created a tunnel of light with the chi I'd been collecting beneath Claws. I wrapped Ellis in multiple layers when it reached him, going overboard to ensure he wasn't literally atomized. When he was safe, I extended the tunnel further, creating a chimney to the clouds.

My defenses came not a moment too soon. To call the force that came from Claws a lightning bolt would be to call a planet an asteroid. It ascended toward the heavens like a jagged spear of vengeance, Claws's entire body glowing with incandescent glory as she propelled it onward. If not for the passage I'd conjured, it might have engulfed the entire sky. That I'd contained her power was great for the well-being of our general surroundings, but less so for the man trapped within.

Ellis was held in place, shackled by the chi I shielded him with. His eyes became dinner plates as he spotted the column of lightning currently thundering toward him. If not for my intervention, it would have been his end, a fact I suspected he knew well.

Even if I left things as they were, it might be his end anyway. By confining the lightning, I had channeled its power into what was essentially the barrel of a crude gun. Ellis was the bullet. I wasn't sure if cultivators were able to survive in space, but even if we could, I didn't think Ellis's crimes justified such an end.

Funny as it would be to launch him out of orbit, I made a pulling motion and bent my tunnel of chi just as Claws's power struck the shackled man. It pierced three layers of my protective chi, then cracked the next half dozen, the elemental force making a mockery of my defenses.

Seeing the remaining score of layers intact, I was content letting the rest play out on its own. Ellis shot up the tunnel like an intercontinental missile. The blue-and-white lightning forced him ever upward, and I craned my neck as he sailed toward the exit. Realizing that Paul's cultivation meant that he couldn't track Ellis's passage, I picked him up by the shoulders and spun him around. The least I could do was help him see the light show.

When Ellis finally entered open air, he was screaming as loud as he could. Well, I'm pretty sure he was. It was hard to tell over the cacophonous *boooom* that flew from the tip of my chimney. As expected, the lightning darted out chaotically as it left the confines of my chi barrier, appearing to slow as it created a bouquet of sharp lines.

Unlike the power that propelled him, Ellis's speed remained constant. He rocketed out toward the distant horizon, his limbs once more flailing in every direction. Patches of Claws's essence clung to him, and as he traveled through the upper atmosphere, they reached out. Arcs of electricity shot from him, weaving their way through the surrounding clouds and illuminating them from within. It was . . . surprisingly beautiful. Stunning, even.

When Ellis cleared the distant horizon, still traveling at a speed anyone other than a cultivator would miss, the otherworldly effect trailed after him. Like a chemical reaction, it webbed its way in every direction. Where clouds existed, they were lit by an ethereal blue.

"Frack me . . ." Paul whispered.

That comment from Barry's son should have made me laugh until I cried. Perhaps a little guilt as well. But I barely even heard it. The moment Ellis was out of sight and safe from the lightning, I had withdrawn my shielding. At the same time, I'd lowered the barriers around Tropica and its residents. They were no longer necessary.

With my awareness free to sense to the world once more, it wasn't possible to ignore the force of nature looming behind me. She felt ambivalent one moment, malevolent the next. Though her intention cycled chaotically, one aspect of her new form remained certain. She was *dangerous*.

I reached for the world's chi and prepared to slam it into place as I whirled to look at her. She was semitransparent, her entire body appearing constructed of lightning chi. When she noticed me, her lips parted slowly.

Corporal Claws, self-proclaimed queen of the forest and cutest of all my animal pals, gave me a humorless grin. When she took a step toward me, it was straight out of a horror movie, her limb flickering even under my enhanced observation. I tried to reach out through our bond, tried to understand her thoughts, but it wasn't there. Our connection had been severed by her transformation.

In response, Claws exploded forward.

CHAPTER TWENTY-ONE

Chaos

The sea of clouds above was lit from within, blue jolts of electricity crawling across them. The air smelled of ozone and salt, which, on any other occasion, would have been a wonderful mix—something unusual enough to ground me in the moment and induce a sense of gratitude.

But as Claws rocketed forward, her body no longer constrained by the laws of physics, I found my thoughts otherwise occupied.

I teleported forward to meet her just before the tree line, only delaying by a fraction of a second to raise a shield of chi around Paul. Claws was not at all surprised by my movement through space or the explosion of light that resulted; her eyes remained pinned to me, the madness within making my skin prickle and mind worry.

Lacking any other choice, I made a pushing gesture with my hands. Rather than raise a wall of chi, I sent countless threads flying from my core, each microscopic strand piercing deep into the sharp-toothed ball of lightning rushing toward me. They did no damage, yet their effect was profound.

Her face began to morph from the visage of wrathful malevolence, but I paid it no mind—I wanted to know what had happened. Needed to know how to *fix* her. As I inspected her new form, I was shocked to find that she both did and didn't have a body. Claws was composed of a material that exceeded my metaphysical understanding of the universe.

She had an outside skin of sorts, a barrier that held her lightning chi within. Something about it was familiar, and I furrowed my brow, trying to remember where I'd seen—

A core! I thought, the realization all but knocking the air from my lungs.

When I had tried to connect to her earlier, I'd found her nexus of power completely absent. Now, I knew why. Every fiber of her being had melded together. She didn't have a core; she *was* one. With this understanding, I redirected my strands of chi away from her abdomen, sending them throughout her mass.

Each area of Claws's new form I discovered granted more knowledge. The lightning within her was wild and chaotic, but just as she'd been trying to do with the spherical storm earlier, she had gained control. The chi was as much hers as her favorite rock was. Which, to my great delight, she still possessed. You couldn't see it from the outside, but it was stored in a little pocket, able to be removed whenever she liked.

Having gleaned all the information about her body that I was likely to, I gathered my will, preparing to do something I never thought I would. I was going to force my way into her thoughts. Despite deeming it necessary for everyone's safety, I still loathed the idea. It was an action one friend should never do to another, and the longer I considered it, the more my resolve wavered.

With the power Claws now possessed, it *had* to be done. I couldn't let her go until I knew that she wouldn't hurt anyone. So why did it feel like such a betrayal?

Just as I was about to throw in the towel and confine her until she returned to her usual self, I finally caught the look on her face. Long gone was the promise of violence. She stared at me with sheer surprise, having not thought I had the ability to send my chi into her elemental form. Her shock, though, also gave way to another emotion.

Pure, unadulterated affront.

She was *incensed*, and whereas her emotions had seemed directed at the world earlier, this was all for me. Confused, I reeled, but then she opened herself up, letting her feelings flood out.

Our bond snapped back into place as if it had never faded. Her feelings and thoughts slammed into me with more weight than ever before, her breakthrough adding an overwhelming sense of clarity. Disoriented, I struggled to determine where my emotions ended and hers began, stumbling in an attempt to remain upright.

Claws didn't waste the opportunity. She crashed into my chest, her body possessing more mass than I'd suspected. My back landed among the sand dunes halfway to the ocean, and before I could skid any further, Claws slammed both forepaws into my torso. She released her rage with the strike, and lightning streamed from her in thick cords. I fended it off with my own power, causing her electricity to roll over me and into the ground. But the attack still packed some serious punch.

The physical force had caused a crater to form around us, my body the peg and Claws the mallet. As her chi poured down into the ground, it melted sand and disintegrated shell, creating enough heat that any impurities were burned away.

I shivered as the last of the electricity dissipated, my mind all too conscious of the power she now commanded. Standing to her full height atop my chest, Claws crossed her arms and stared down at me with disdain. She tapped her foot and raised an eyebrow, demanding an answer.

Paul sprinted forward faster than he'd ever before traveled. There was a weird shine around his body. It probably came from Deklan and Dom, maybe? Paul didn't give it much thought—he had cooler things to worry about. His legs easily traversed each dune, and after cresting one last slope, he and the twins stared down into a crater that hadn't been there before.

Fischer was on his back. The sand below him had melted into a big puddle, its center red and edges a dark black. Paul knew that was what happened when sand got hot enough—Fergus had shown him once. The blacksmith had needed tongs and a crucible to handle it without getting burned, but Fischer was just . . . *lying on it.*

This fact likely would have further increased Fischer's social standing within Paul's still-maturing frontal lobe, but before he had time to consider it, the being atop Fischer's chest started to glow like ten thousand fireflies.

Corporal Claws unfolded her forelimbs, pointing one down toward Fischer's face as she let out a deafening chirp. Her body, which was blue and see-through like water, slowly lost its brightness as she very obviously tried to calm herself with slow breaths.

"What did you expect, you furry little frack?" Fischer pointed his own finger at her in accusation. "You made me think you were evil!"

Well, duh! That's what I do! Claws responded, the meaning behind her trilled screams somehow clear to Paul's mind. She gestured toward herself, then tippy-tapped her chest with both paws. *You tried to invade me!*

"I only considered it for like a second. I wasn't actually going to—" Fischer cut himself off with a glare. "Stop changing the subject!"

She narrowed her eyes back, and literal *lightning* danced over her body in what was one of the coolest things Paul had ever seen, second only to Fischer kicking the king's butt. And Ellis flying over the ocean just now. Oh, and the way his dad had jumped into the sky with Ellis! And Cinnamon's kick! And that cool rock he found that looked a little like Borks. And—

Something other than light came from Claws. As it hit him, Paul fell backward, a spike of panic wiping his head free of thoughts.

"What the . . ." Deklan reached out with one hand and grabbed Paul's shoulder.

Paul, now steadied by the large man, could focus on the . . . *feelings?* that were coming from Claws. He'd been told that when he got older and stronger, he would be able to tell what people were thinking. Was *this* what his mom had meant . . . ?

Claws made him experience the emotion he felt when he was messing with people. When he was *pulling pranks*, as Fischer would say. The aura pouring from the lightning otter was mischief incarnate, and as it continued resonating with his core, he gained greater understanding. He considered the words he was thinking with—they didn't sound like his—and the fact that he understood their meaning.

But then the energy coming from Claws increased, potent trickery replacing any dissonance within him. It made him recall the time he snuck an extra slice of pie after everyone went to bed. And the time he put a stick in Uncle Leroy's sock. And the *many* times he dug little pitfalls between crops, which he then covered with sticks, leaves, and sand. He was particularly proud of the traps—they'd been the cause of a few town meetings, and he'd never been so much as suspected.

These feelings—these emotions—were who Corporal Claws was.

To the very depths of her core, she thrived on unleashing chaos. Nothing else brought so much joy to her soul. This acceptance of herself, this complete surrender to who she was, had caused her transformation. With more clarity than he'd ever experienced in his life, Paul realized what he needed to do to grow stronger. He had pictured needing physical work. Or eating lots of healthy food, just like the man from the book his parents used to read to him. But that wasn't it at all.

Claws might have done those things, but they weren't the most important thing. The pivotal ingredient, the only part that was completely mandatory, was an understanding of who you were.

As fast as they had arrived, Claws's emotions faded away once more, echoes of them lingering in Paul's awareness while her radiance retreated.

"You think I give a frack if it's who you are, you little rat?" Fischer retorted. Was that amusement that Paul could see twinkling in his eye? "It was still a dick move. You could have at least let *me* know it was a joke!"

She poked her tongue out at him and held out a paw. Electricity danced over it in unpredictable arcs, another springing back up the moment one disappeared. Fischer frowned, doing his best to maintain a disapproving gaze, and almost immediately broke.

He wrapped his arms around Claws and pulled her into a hug, wiggling back and forth on the now-hardened glass beneath them. "I can't believe you became lightning! Like . . . *you're actually made of lightning*!"

He was winning Claws back, and she nodded along, her pointed teeth spread in a grin.

"At the same time, how did I not see it coming? Of *course* your chaotic nature would be perfectly suited for lightning. Your natures were practically inseparable before, but now . . ." He shook his head. "No, you're right. I shouldn't have been surprised that you tried to trick me. Just . . . please try not to cause anyone too much grief, okay? You can be chaos, but keep it fun . . ." He made a praying gesture, pressing his hands to his forehead. "*Please.*"

Claws wiggled herself free of his grasp, rubbing her body against him as much as possible on the way out. Once more atop his chest, she gave an exaggerated shrug, then rubbed the back of her head.

Maybe I will. She wiggled her eyebrows up and down. *Or . . . maybe I—*

Paul neither saw nor heard the rest of the sentence, because the world exploded with light.

I wasn't at all caught off guard by the surprise attack. Slick as she might be, I still spotted the chi gathering in the paw she pretended to scratch her head with. Letting out a long-suffering sigh, I created a half sphere of solid chi that solidified before her sucker punch could land. The paw hit me with incredible power, but the physical strike was nothing compared to the absolute storm of chi that flowed out.

It would have sent Dom, Deklan, and Paul flying if not for the trenches of light I'd created to capture the blast. Claws propelled herself directly upward, but even with her speed, I managed to get in one more scritching. My fingers were firm but gentle as I rubbed the spot behind her ear that always made her melt. New body or not, it had the desired effect, and her eyes rolled into the back of her head.

I marveled at the softness of what appeared to be fur. Despite lacking hair follicles, she had instinctively created a coat out of lightning chi, which was somehow even more velvety than her previous covering.

Though she clearly enjoyed my touch, Claws didn't change course. She sailed away from me backward, her little tushy facing the sky. I wondered about the odd posture, but its purpose was immediately revealed when she extended her front paws, dual-wielding a matching pair of decidedly rude gestures. Chirping that she loved me, and wiggling her raised digits for emphasis, she disappeared butt first into the clouds above. Lightning cracked sideways in all directions, webbing its way across the sky as Claws began exploring her capabilities.

I shook my head and sat up, releasing the shield I'd created around everyone. "You guys okay?"

"Us?" Deklan shrugged. "We're chilling."

"Are *you* okay?" Dom asked. "We weren't the ones struck by . . ." He gestured down at the crater. "All that."

There was a hint of humor in his voice, which filled me with suspicion. "I'm fine . . . she wasn't trying to hurt me, just cause a ruckus."

"Ohhhh." Deklan gave his brother a look that was intentionally scrubbed of emotion. "I get it. Fischer must have been too busy ruminating on his loss."

"My loss? What are you talking about?"

Dom returned the same suspicion-inducing look his brother's way. "Poor Fischer still seems to be in denial about the bet."

"The bet? I won the bet. I—"

"You *would have* won," Dom corrected, voicing my realization. "If Claws hadn't intervened, Ellis would have hit a mountain. Instead, he was shot out into the ocean."

"*I* shot him out into the ocean! I was the one who made the . . ." I trailed off too late. I'd walked right into their trap.

"So you agree that Ellis shot out toward the ocean, then? He was going for the closest mountain, but then *you* redirected him." Deklan patted Paul's shoulder. "And you admitted it in front of a witness. You wouldn't lie in front of him . . . would you?"

They'd snared me like a crab in a trap, and there was nothing to be done. Accepting defeat, I ran my hand over the hardened glass beneath me. It was hot in the center and cool at the edges, the surrounding sands already leaching its heat away. I pressed my palms against it as I got to my feet. "You win this round."

"Fischer—" Paul's voice cracked, and before he'd finished clearing his throat, a vicious crimson had arrived on his cheeks. "Fischer," he repeated with a false timbre. "Where did she go . . . ?"

Intentionally ignoring the voice crack, I gazed up to stare at the clouds. Not long ago, they'd been pushed along by an unseen breeze. Now, they roiled, static electricity making them shift in hypnotic patterns.

I pointed far to the north, where I could feel her. "She's over there." My finger shifted east, tracking her movement. "Now she's over there." Without speaking, I continued pointing her out, causing a sense of palpable awe to come from the young man's core. "Don't let her know how impressed you are, mate. It'll go right to her head."

Lightning struck to the east, slamming down into the middle of the bay.

"Yeah, yeah." I waved a hand in Claws's direction. "I know you can hear me. That's the point."

If anyone other than Deklan or Dom had been present, they'd have likely despaired at Corporal Claws's new power. At the very least, they'd have felt a *little* fear. Claws was, by all accounts, an absolute menace. A sane person would be wary of her even before she had turned into lightning incarnate. Which only made the brothers' reactions even more unique.

"Neat," Deklan said. "She's super quick."

"Hella neat," Dom agreed, both men's heads tracking her chaotic movement as she zoomed around within the clouds.

I shook my head and hopped out of the crater, landing beside Paul. "Okay, mate. Now that all the distractions are out of the way, are you still up for that conversation?"

He nodded sharply, a hint of red still remaining in his cheeks.

I held my breath for a moment, gazing around to see if the universe was going to throw anything else our way. I exhaled when nothing came, but as I did so, I noticed sources of chi approaching. Rather than get annoyed, I turned and waited. A crackling portal appeared right next to us; Borks, Cinnamon, and Barry stepped through.

"Wait," I said, holding up a hand before Barry could speak. "Please don't ask. I still haven't had a chance to chat to Paul about—"

"But—"

"No buts, mister. Each second that passes is a chance for another distraction to arrive. Let's have that conversation with Paul, then I'll tell you everything that happened, okay?"

His muscular jaw flexed as he fought down his desire to know. Thankfully, he won. "Deal."

We started by walking down to the water, then Paul reminded us of the rods. The leisurely stroll turned into a run. There probably wasn't anything hooked, especially after all that light and noise, but that didn't stop us from hoping. As soon as I wound in my line a little, I knew that it hadn't been touched; I could feel the sinker's weight as it slid across the ocean floor.

Deklan and Dom's excitement also disappeared the moment they checked their lines, which only left Paul.

At least we can get around to having that chat, I thought, setting my rod back down. *The sooner it's over, the sooner we can—*

Paul inhaled sharply, adrenaline coursing through him. *"F-fish on!"* he yelled, his rod bending in half as the hooked fish took off.

CHAPTER TWENTY-TWO

Biblical

In a place of darkness, where neither light nor life had visited for time immemorial, absolute stillness reigned. One might assume that in such a space, a complete lack of movement was natural. The only possibility, given the circumstances.

One would be wrong.

If an observer reached these abyssal plains with their mind and body intact, they would readily attest as much—if they somehow escaped with their lives, anyway. The source of this dissonance was something primal. Something that only the most powerful and aware of cultivators could hope to identify. Most beings, human and beast both, would only notice an overwhelming urge to flee.

It was the feeling that arrived when the wind dies on a moonless night, leaving only silence. The sense that someone was staring at the back of your head. The sudden compulsion to sprint home that strikes out of nowhere when walking alone in the dark.

But this was all of no consequence; no one had visited this place for centuries, so there was no reason for the source of these fears to stir. Until, that is, a wave of elemental chi washed over the world.

It was but a whisper of essence, so faint as to go unnoticed by all but the most-perceptive denizens of this long-abandoned world. Given that life hadn't been seen for millennia in the place where stillness reigned, one might assume the pulse of power would flow on by, neither cognized nor inciting incident.

Again, one would be wrong—fatally so if they were nearby.

Rock and sediment churned over one another, the larger pieces breaking apart. Giant boulders were ground down, and within seconds, all that remained was a thick slurry. Hidden within the now-murky waters at the bottom of an oceanic trench, an ancient body started re-forming. Fragments of anything even vaguely earthen were sucked into a vacuum of latent power. There, they joined, becoming something greater.

As soon as its body had formed, awareness slammed back into place. It knew exactly how many years, centuries, and millennia had passed, but it cared not. Such things were for lesser creatures to consider; this one's existence wasn't measured by the passage of time. Instead, it focused on the surrounding world, and what it found made the being hesitate.

There was nothing. The gods that had sealed it so long ago, those pretentious upstarts who were *always* present, were nowhere to be seen.

At first, he suspected a trap. Their absence made no sense. Had they discovered his ruse, then used chi as bait to draw him out? Before their swords could descend, the ancient being sent his power out into the surrounding slurry, preparing to shield against the impending ambush.

He had allowed himself to be sealed last time, but that was because it'd suited him then. Now, things had changed—the condition for his reawakening had occurred.

As seconds passed, the being's defenses grew by orders of magnitude, elemental power infusing its body. Each moment further muted the effectiveness of the gods' snare, yet the attack never came. The being blinked, sending undetectable strands of his awareness out.

He started with the ocean's depths, exploring unseen caverns and blackened trenches. From there, he searched countless islands, and though he found conscious life, none of them were touched by the divine. Preparing for the trap to spring once more, he slowly extended his essence toward the heavens. His mesh of elemental chi entered its farthest reaches, finding . . . naught.

The gods . . . they were gone. They'd truly departed this realm. And from the hurried reverberations left in their wake, it seemed they'd run for their lives. They'd *fled.*

He returned to his body to find his center shifting, sediment forming large boulders that ground against one another. It made a sound like continental plates being forced together. The noise, something he'd seldom produced, flew out into the darkness.

He was *laughing*.

The plan had worked even better than expected. The gods had left him sealed beneath the ocean, assuming him trapped and their machinations infallible. Such was the hubris of those interlopers who called themselves *divine*.

The condition for his awakening had occurred, a new elemental being had been born, and there were no gods left to stand in his way. Vindication rolled from the earthen titan.

With the unstoppable force of a landslide, the ancient being's hunt began.

I watched Corporal Claws as she zipped back and forth within a sea of endless clouds, both pep and excitement radiating from her newly born body. So bright were her emotions that I imagined them lighting even the abyssal plains of the deepest ocean.

And it wasn't only Claws filling my cup to the brim. Cinnamon's eyes sparkled like twin diamonds as she gazed up at Claws, her thoughts a tangle of happiness, disbelief, and everything in between. I could have watched her all day, but there was something even more exciting to witness.

Paul's feet were planted in the sand with all the ferocity he could muster, his rod bent almost in half as the hooked fish tried to escape.

"What do I do?" he yelled. Whether it was the size of the fish or beginner's nerves, the result remained the same: Paul was freaking the frack out.

Barry flew forward, his muscular hands resting on his son's shoulders. "You've got this, Paul. Don't overthink it."

I sent a wave of reassuring chi from my core to wash over him, but I was pretty sure it wasn't necessary. Barry's words and presence had already doused the flames. Paul clenched his jaw, took a deep breath, and started winding.

I stepped up beside him. "Pump the rod up after winding in. Just like Deklan did earlier."

Paul nodded and did his best to emulate the movement. It was stilted at first, but then his enhanced body compensated, muscle groups contracting without his explicit instruction. Not at all bothered by these newfound reflexes, Paul continued on.

The fish seemed to become more panicked, each run shorter and more frenzied than the last. In stark contrast, Paul's confidence blossomed with each length of line he retrieved, a brilliant grin growing wider by the second. Of those present, Barry was clearly the most excited, but the rest of us weren't too far behind. I had to shut my senses off to the waves of pride and anticipation, especially to Borks and Cinnamon, whose connection to my core let them bypass my passive defenses.

As Paul's self-belief burgeoned, so, too, did his skill. He'd not even caught his first fish, yet already he was getting comfortable with the process, his grip better and movements increasingly efficient. The fish, though big for its species, never stood a chance. It took less than a minute to catch the first flash of scales beneath the surface. They reflected the rolling lightning above, making the creature appear as though electricity suffused its being.

I smiled and remained still, letting Paul and Barry have this moment. The former kept tension on his line just as instructed, and the latter hustled forward into the knee-high water, the waves there no match for his ridiculous physique. When Barry grabbed the fish, his arm and chest tensed. He was flexing even during a wholesome father-son moment. I shook my head, intending on teasing him about it, but then I saw the electricity.

It hadn't been a reflection. The fish *was* suffused with lightning. The chi crawled across the fish's body, occasionally jolting up and into Barry's arm and causing his muscles to contract. With little effort, I focused on it, letting the creature draw me in.

Mature Lightning-Infused Shore Fish
Fleeting
Usually a staple source of both food and bait, this fish has been temporarily infused with lightning to celebrate the ascension of an Elemental. Infused creatures have their chi content significantly increased for three hours.

"Uhhh," Barry and I both said, equally lost for words as our vision cleared.

Everyone else remained silent, awe and confusion stilling our tongues. One being, however, remained unaffected. With a crack of lightning, Claws appeared next to Barry.

Salt water was a terrible conductor, but given his proximity, the electricity still ran through him. Unlike the infused fish's power, Claws's strike made his entire body stiffen. He dropped the fish. Claws zipped past him, removed the hook, and dispatched the animal. With a leap backward, she landed gracefully atop the water, pulling some biblical shit as she trotted away with her pilfered seafood.

Unlike Claws, Barry landed ass first in the shallows. By the time he got back to his feet, Claws was crunching through the last few bites, still walking on water as she withdrew.

I shook my head at her. "Did you know that would happen, Claws? That we could catch infused fish after you awakened as an elemental or whatever?"

I already knew the answer, but she confirmed it with a series of lazy nods as she licked her paws all over, sparks crawling over her body.

"The System told you?"

More nods.

"And you didn't tell us because it would be way more chaotic if we found out by ourselves?"

In response, she tucked both forepaws into her pockets, only to remove them once more and lean back with a casual slouch. She leveled finger guns at me and mimed firing them off, each shot releasing a little jolt of electricity that hit the sand by my feet. With another crack of lightning and an ear-splitting trill, she returned to the clouds, having no more reason to remain.

I squeezed the bridge of my nose. "That was my fault. Sorry, everyone."

"What?" Barry asked. "How? There's no way you could have predicted all of this to come out of her love for pranks and trick—"

"Oh, not that. The finger guns." I mimicked her cowboy posture from only seconds ago. "You know, *pew-pew*?" I fired off said finger guns for effect. "I never should have shown those to her. She can shoot actual lightning from them now."

I'd intended it as a joke, but Deklan and Dom both shivered, the knowledge invoking a physical response.

Feeling terrible, I strode over and rested a hand on Paul's shoulder. "Sorry she stole your first fish, mate. She's a pest."

He gave me a wide grin, not even a hint of annoyance coming from his core. "That's okay! It was fun just catching it!" He glanced out at the ocean, then back at me. I already knew what he would ask, but it still made my core sing with joy when he voiced it. "Can I try to catch another?"

"Of course you can! Bait the hook and get it back out there!"

He wasted no time in dashing over to the pile of eel and looking for a suitably sized portion.

"Okay, gang," I said, giving everyone a look that drew them over. "This is an amazing opportunity for chi-filled food."

Deklan, Dom, Barry, Cinnamon, and Borks all nodded, knowing it to be true.

I let a pulse of gratitude for them radiate from my core. "Here's the plan: We're gonna let everyone know, but I don't want to disturb those that are meditating. It's a miracle they haven't already come running over to learn what the frack happened to Claws."

Again, they nodded.

"Good. So, Barry and I are gonna have that talk with Paul. The rest of you, go to Tropica and let everyone know. Can you grab the rods, Borks?"

Ruff! He immediately opened a portal and dashed through.

A moment later, only Barry and I remained.

By the time Paul looked up, a baited hook swinging from the end of his rod, they were gone. "Where did everyone go?"

"Off to let everyone know about the fish, mate. Figured it was about time we had that chat."

He paused mid-step, only his swaying hood betraying his former movement.

"None of that. I promise it's nothing bad." I swept an arm around his shoulders. "C'mon. Let's get your line out."

Though I feigned indifference, I watched closely as he drew his rod back and sent his baited hook flying out over the ocean. As expected, his second-ever cast was vastly improved, aided by his enhanced body and mind. He wound the line taut, setting his finger against it to wait for a bite.

Copying Paul, I rested my index finger against my line after retrieving my rod. "What level did you get in fishing from catching that fish, mate?"

Paul darted a look his dad's way, who gave a small nod. "I got my fishing to level twenty-four."

I whistled. "From a single fish . . . ? Ellis is gonna lose his mind if he ever makes it home."

Barry snorted. "Something tells me we won't get rid of him so easily."

Paul giggled as he looked out toward the spot on the horizon Ellis had sailed over, and I knew it was time.

"I've given what I needed to say to you some thought, Paul."

My words made some of his hesitation return, but he said nothing.

"Honestly," I continued, "I don't need to say much. I haven't known you long, but you don't seem at risk of antisocial behavior. You have two loving parents, you know the value of hard work, and you have a supportive extended community to rely on. Because of your awakening, you're guaranteed to have a good education. You also won't struggle for food . . ."

I let these words hang for a moment, letting each point sink in.

"Back on Earth, these were the biggest risk factors for young people, and you're safe against each of them. There is, however, one risk that most teens back on Earth *didn't* have to worry about."

This drew his and Barry's attention, both recognizing the severity in my voice.

"You have power, Paul. And not the vague societal power that can corrupt trust-fund kiddies with absent parents. You have tangible strength, and you'll only gain more as you get older. Combined with teenage hormones—I can go into them more later, but they're what make teenagers so hot-headed—even one poor decision could lead to something catastrophic."

Paul had a troubled expression. Glad that he was taking my words seriously, I ruffled his hair.

"Keep in mind that I don't think you will, but it's definitely something to keep in mind. And in order to combat this issue, I'm assigning you two tasks." I held up two fingers, illustrating the point. "First, unless it's to defend your life or that of someone else, you are to run from conflict. This is a hard ask, because it's not human nature. Still, this is my directive. My *order*. If you can escape conflict without risking your own health or that of someone else's, you are to remove yourself from the situation."

Calling it an order was a calculated risk on my part, but thankfully, it succeeded.

Paul spun so he was facing me. "I promise, Fischer. And you, too, Dad. I swear I won't fight anyone unless I have to."

"Thank you, mate." I lowered one finger. "That was a heavy request, but the next one is even more difficult. Do you remember the things I listed as risks?"

He gave a sharp nod.

"Good. Your final order, and likely the most important one I'll give you, is that I want you to help others who lack the privileges you've been born into."

His brow furrowed, his mind likely running through the other village children and not finding anyone that would need such help.

"I'm talking about the others who will join us. Chi has returned to the entire continent, and we're far from the only village or settlement that now has essence running through it. Even now, I have at least one of the Buzzy Boys watching each cluster of humanity, ready to let us know the *second* someone becomes a cultivator."

Paul's eyes went as wide as saucers. "No way . . ."

"Yes way," Barry replied. "We've kept it pretty secret because we don't want people to panic about outside cultivators, but it's only a matter of time until others start ascending."

"More kids will come?"

"I reckon they will, mate. We have no idea what their life has been like, and I'm not foolish enough to believe everyone has a good childhood. Your job, then, is to be there for them. We'll help, too, of course, but—"

"Some won't respond well to adults, right? Especially if they've been mistreated by them. It's human nature."

I leaned back, giving Paul an appreciative look. "Well, yeah. That's it exactly." A part of my awareness yelled out to me, screaming that just as I'd feared, Paul might be maturing too fast. Leaving his childhood behind. Barry's response was even more visceral, worry etched on his face and streaming from his core.

Before either of us could voice our concern, Paul spoke. "I've done that before, so it makes sense."

Barry licked his lips. "You've done what before?"

"I've trusted adults before. After they hurt me, I mean."

"Who hurt you?" Barry's muscles spasmed, his strength ready to be unleashed upon the first person Paul named.

"You mean Ellis?" I suggested.

"What? No. That was kind of fun after the first few times. I meant Auntie Barbara."

"Auntie Barbara?" A lack of comprehension robbed the heat from Barry's fury. "What did she do?"

"The *quiche* . . ." He made a face of sheer disgust. "After she got me with that, I didn't eat anything she made for *months*."

"Wait, you mean back when Uncle Leroy came home, and you didn't eat every time we went there for dinner?" Barry shook his head. "What quiche? What in Demeter's lush crop did Barbara do with a quiche?"

"Vegetables." He spat the word like it could reach out and bite him. "She told me it didn't have any, but it did. She grated them so fine that she thought I wouldn't notice." He turned toward us, his eyes narrowed and lips forming a line. "It was *green*. She used so many vegetables that the entire thing turned green! I couldn't believe her after that, so I totally get why other kids wouldn't trust adults."

"And with good reason." I laughed, relief flooding me. "I wouldn't trust her after that either."

Barry let out a long sigh and turned toward me. "Is there anything else you wanted to add?"

"Just one thing. If you ever need anything, Paul, you can rely on us. Even if you're too embarrassed to tell your old man here . . ." I patted Barry on the back. "You can come and tell me. I promise that I'll never judge you for being honest."

I was all but certain Barry would be okay with the offer, but I still felt a weight fall away as he smiled and nodded. "And I hope you already know the same of me and your mother. We're so proud of you, son, and we'll always have your back no matter what."

Our wholesome moment of silence came to an abrupt end when something did it's best to pull my left arm from its socket. I'd totally forgotten about my rod, holding on to it with one hand so I could better focus on the conversation with Paul.

As the creature shook its head, I felt something that part of me had been worried I'd never feel again: the thrill of the unknown.

I'd hooked a *monster*, and I had no idea if I'd be able to land it.

CHAPTER TWENTY-THREE

Villainous

Ever since accepting my role as leader of Tropica, a worry had lurked in the back of my mind, the thought like a single worm ruining an otherwise luscious apple. It was, in my humble opinion, a bunch of bullshit.

I'd gained unparalleled strength, the ability to manipulate chi as if it were my own body, and agency over a continent-spanning Domain. Rather than liberate me from doubt, all this power and control had caused more. They served as walls. Barriers that could stop me from finding a fair fight.

And yet, I had found one. The fish on the other end of my line was the strongest creature I'd ever hooked. My strength didn't matter, because my rod wasn't indestructible. My senses, which previously would have reported what dwelled within the ocean's depths, were now under my control. And though I could harness the Domain's chi whenever I pleased, it didn't spring up to assist me of its own accord.

The fish's strength was unbelievable, and each powerful kick of its tail left no doubt that it was infused with lightning. Well, to be fair, there were other signs, too.

"Zeus's thunderous shaft!" Barry swore, grabbing Paul and leaping backward.

Dozens of thunderbolts shot from the bay and slammed into the shore around us. Even beneath the afternoon sun, they left incandescent streaks in my vision, but that was nothing compared to the other ways the world was transformed.

Sand sprayed in every direction, some of it as globs of molten glass. The dozens of strikes each released a deafening boom, combining into a wall of sound that one could feel as much as hear. And the ground quaked, so strong that a regular human couldn't hope to remain standing.

I observed all of this as another might examine a painting, my enhanced awareness letting me experience the chaotic scene in all of its beauty. Barry, who had launched himself backward with his son in his arms, watched with an awestruck gaze. Paul was perhaps the only one with a reasonable reaction: His mouth and eyes were parted in shock, his semi-suppressed cultivation enough to know that a gods-damned fish had just tried to zippity-zap us.

As the novelty of the scene faded, I focused on what I knew of the hooked creature. It was aware of my existence and physical position. It had enough control of its lightning chi to target me. And it possessed the requisite intelligence to facilitate the former points. On top of all that, if I hadn't covered my rod and fishing line in pure chi in the moments after it struck, one of them would have snapped.

Unleashing its lightning granted me a moment's reprieve, its body apparently unable to move as chi flowed from it. Before the last of the sand fell, and with the ground still shaking, the fish's incapacitation ended. Three kicks of its tail came immediately, putting my rod and reinforcing essence to the test.

I had previously worried that because I could reinforce my line, I'd never lose a fish. In retrospect, it was sheer hubris. I barked a laugh, stepping forward to ease the tension as the fish kicked again.

The line could only take so much chi. I couldn't just reinforce the rod with solid essence, because the line relied on the flexibility of its wooden fibers. If I didn't reinforce the rod enough, though, *it* would snap.

It was a dance, one where I had to intermittently change how malleable both the line and rod were . . . dozens of times each second. It was crude. A method that relied on constant intervention rather than ingenious planning or design. And it was *exactly* what I needed.

So encompassing was the task that, despite my superhuman levels of cognition, I could scarcely think about anything else. I sank further into the moment, finding a place of quiet calm in the storm, which was swiftly shattered when I felt my consciousness being split in two.

No, not split. *Partitioned.*

There were two compartments within my overarching awareness, and by the feel of them, they'd been forming since this battle had commenced. And the damn things were *thirsty*, soaking up my chi and focus with reckless abandon. No wonder I felt stretched so thin. A significant portion of my will was being siphoned off.

That my subconscious had seen fit to co-opt my strength without my permission was a little startling. The average person would probably call me reasonable if I cut my line then and there, letting the fish escape so I could assess what was going on within me.

Instead, I grinned, focusing on keeping my rod and line intact.

My mind, body, and soul were perfectly aligned. I had accepted who I was. I trusted myself to do what was best for me and my loved ones. And now that I knew my subconscious thought partitions were a good idea, I wanted to brute-force the breakthrough with a single moment of absolute focus.

Unfortunately, the fish cared for neither my acceptance of self nor my desires. It took off, darting parallel to the shore in a desperate attempt to escape. Unable to release line fast enough, I ran with it, doing all I could to stop it from snapping me off. We covered hundreds of meters in seconds, sand and water flying up behind our respective paths.

Part of me railed at our mad dash, annoyed that the fish was blocking me from solidifying whatever my brain was trying to create. But as I skipped along the shore, having to match my steps with the kicks of the fish's mighty tail, any shred of negativity fell away.

What did I really have to be frustrated by? I had been worried that I'd never be challenged by a fish again, and here I was, getting pushed to my absolute limits.

Choosing to live in the moment, I let my thoughts go, focusing on the sand beneath me as I sprinted south.

All of a sudden, the sand was no more, my foot landing on the slick rock of the headland. As if it had been waiting for the exact moment, the fish unleashed a burst of chi. But it was . . . insignificant, far less powerful than its earlier attack.

Chi flew from its side, the creature using the small jet of lightning to spin. I could feel the rest of its power gathering in its tail, and I instinctively knew what was about to occur. The second it was facing the north again, it would unleash another burst.

I had a split moment to react. I whirled in midair, using everything I had to arrest my momentum, preparing to kick off the ground and leap with the fish. As soon as my foot made contact with the wet rocks of the headland, however, I slipped. My legs went skyward, my tushy dropped toward the jagged shore, and the blood drained from my face.

If nothing was done, the tension would become too much when the fish unleashed its chi. Either my line or fishing rod would snap. Perhaps both. These immutable facts combined to create a single, devastating truth.

I was going to *lose*.

Completely horizontal, watching was my only remaining option. I could teleport myself, of course. Make a slight movement with one finger and appear before the giant creature. But that was cheating. It would confirm exactly what I'd been terrified of—that following my breakthrough, I could no longer be challenged. I may as well just trap the creature in light, as I'd done to the fish in the lake, or use a giant net of chi with which to trawl the ocean floor.

This was the hill I'd die on. I would use chi to reinforce myself and enhance tools, but I wouldn't use it to interact with fish directly.

The corner of my lip curled up as a possibility occurred—a way for me to change the outcome without directly affecting the hooked creature. My grin spread as I bent my knees and braced myself, a platform of solid light appearing beneath my feet.

The fish completed its rotation, and the secondary blast detonated immediately. The jet of chi that shot from it was bright enough to illuminate the ocean, revealing a distorted silhouette so large that it threatened to make my breath catch.

The flame-shaped lightning grew, a gigantic teardrop of crackling energy as fascinating as it was beautiful. I wished I could spare it more attention. Wished I could witness the blue-and-white brilliance without distraction. But I lacked the time.

Bwom! came a warped noise, muffled by the ocean.

When the creature rocketed northward, my prediction was confirmed: My equipment would have snapped if I'd not been ready for it. I was, though.

A feline smile splitting my face, I kicked off the platform of solid chi. Hundreds of meters of line connected us as we sailed in parallel, both the fish and I unwilling to lose. I watched the line intently, waiting for any hint of movement. Nothing happened. As I'd hoped, just like when it sent bolts of lightning toward shore, the fish's vast expenditure of essence had left it unable to move.

Its trap had been sprung, and I'd escaped it. I reached for my power, chi retreating up my line and into my abdomen. I only had a small window to fight back. I wouldn't waste it. When the last of my essence had returned to my core, I finally let my subconscious complete the breakthrough it had been screaming about this entire time.

The two partitions had made little progress since last I acknowledged them; that was about to change. I felt my grin widen despite my inward focus, and using my joy as another source of fuel, I formed my chi into a hammer. With a mighty swing of my will, I slammed everything I had into the forming compartments.

Even before it collided, I realized my error, but it was too late. Both partitions shook as the power descended. My metaphorical hammer smashed into them, shattering them into thousands of shards.

Each fragment took a part of my awareness with it, pulling me into a confusing mosaic of *way* too many perspectives. Thankfully, it was over almost immediately, my consciousness re-forming. Once more able to think, I understood what had gone wrong.

I'd treated the partitions as a breakthrough—something that I could smack with my essence, letting my significant will sort out the details. It wasn't a breakthrough at all. The subdivision was more akin to a technique. A tool I could use to enhance my control of chi.

I couldn't help but find amusement in my arrogance. I'd literally gained the power of a baby god like a week ago, and here I was looking for another advancement. I let my mirth go; the fish would recover in a moment.

Though back in one piece, I still felt . . . scattered. If I couldn't regain my equilibrium, the creature would absolutely escape. No question about it. Worse, I'd done this to myself, literally creating a hammer of chi that I then smacked myself in the brain with. It was, in retrospect, a super-dumb move.

But now wasn't the time for self-chastisement. It was time to catch a giant bloody fish. And if I didn't center myself, I wouldn't catch a damned thing.

I took a deep breath, focusing on the cool salt spray that flowed up my nostrils and down into my lungs. Immediately exhaling, I tensed my diaphragm, warm air passing through pursed lips. All the while, I was flying a mere meter above the shore. Like a human-shaped rocket, I soared, the wind making my hair and clothes ripple. I did a half barrel roll just in time to spot Paul and Barry as I sailed past them, the former unable to track what was happening, the latter staring at me wide-eyed.

Barry raised his right arm and tensed as hard as he could, his muscles bulging as he gave me a white-knuckled thumbs-up.

Along with the sensations assaulting me, his show of support was exactly what I needed to ground myself. I nodded my thanks and spun back to face the ocean. There, the fish regained its composure, immediately turning to swim farther into the depths.

I whacked the handle of my reel, letting it freely spool as I focused on reinforcing my equipment once more. A jarring sensation came from within, my consciousness seeming to tell me off for hitting it like an angry blacksmith, but it passed swiftly. Strands of chi extended to cover the rod. From there, the partitions reformed, the second one focusing on the line. Tendrils of my power raced down it faster than light, and not a moment too soon.

Only my free-spinning reel had stopped the fish from severing the unenhanced line, and as my chi wove around the hook, I breathed a sigh of relief. Rotating, I skidded to a stop in the sand just before Tropica, intent on holding my ground there. The creature had other ideas. Sensing or seeing the village, it darted farther north, attempting to use the structures as a physical barrier I couldn't cross.

You underestimate me, fishy.

With a laugh, I leaped up onto the seawall, nimbly running along it. A crowd had gathered there to watch, all cultivators who must have sensed the strange blasts of energy. Those who possessed the power to track my movement watched in utter shock. It was wonderful. I shot them a wink and sprinted on, matching the vigor with which the creature tried to escape.

The rest of the fight was, for lack of a better word, repetitive. But despite the connotations such a descriptor brings to mind, not once did I lose interest or get bored. Most of Tropica came to witness as the battle flowed from north to south and back again. Even some of my animal pals interrupted their meditations, gathering on the sand beside Barry and Paul in the hour it took me to tire the creature out.

In the end, it was the repeated expenditure of its own chi that precipitated defeat. The fish might have stopped releasing the bursts given how ineffective they were, but each failed attempt only heightened its anxiety, making them come more often. With one final blast of lightning, the single bolt not even reaching the shore, it was well and truly exhausted.

On the beach behind me, my animal pals and human friends watched with bated breath. Any of the newer residents of Tropica remained up on the seawall, watching from afar. Of my loved ones, only Maria was absent, but that didn't cause me grief—I was happy she was so absorbed in her meditation. As I dragged the fish into the shallows by pumping and reeling, I finally caught sight of the creature. To my surprise, I recognized it.

I'd never spotted the species here in Kallis, but I'd seen it plenty of times back on Earth. A massive mouth lined with rows of serrated teeth, their edges sharp enough to saw through bone. A tall dorsal fin covered in scales so small that many assumed they had skin with the texture of sandpaper. Most recognizable of all was its tail. The upper half was almost as long as the rest of its body, the shape reminding me of a naginata.

With my adrenaline finally receding, exhaustion settled into my bones and mind both. This wasn't the usual tiredness that came with channeling chi. It was a deep weariness, one that might cause my own essence to ignore my command until I rested.

The creature, perhaps sensing my weakness, summoned its last burst of energy. Seeing the flail-like use of its appendage as it whipped out, I mentally retracted the comparison to a naginata. Whoever had named it back on Earth had done so correctly.

This was, without a doubt, a thresher shark.

I took a step forward, intent on inspecting it to see if the System here agreed, but the sky split above me.

Using as much speed as she could muster, Corporal Claws descended faster than natural lightning. All around her, the air warped, bending inward. I thought she might be trying to show off, coming to flex her new status as an elemental now that everyone was here, but then I saw the look in her eyes.

They held mischief, as one would correctly surmise. There was elation, too, my little otter pal indescribably happy with her ascension. Neither of those was what troubled me, however. Stronger than anything else, more a warning than an emotion, was *hunger*.

My fears were confirmed a half second later when she opened her mouth wide, her villainous teeth poised to rip a chunk out of the shark. Without my intervention, she'd end its life in the blink of an eye. I reached for my chi, but like an overused muscle, it didn't respond.

Left no other option, I leaped into the air, an apologetic grimace on my face. Claws saw me coming. So advanced was her cultivation now that I couldn't outspeed her vision. Unfortunately for my delinquent pal, her body was a different story. She traveled too swiftly. There was no time for her to dodge.

She locked eyes with me and nodded, a flash of understanding in her gaze as I drew back my leg. I had no other choice. With as much power as I could physically muster, I launched an absolute belter of a kick toward Claws.

CHAPTER TWENTY-FOUR

Crab Jesus

As my battle with the thresher shark had dragged on, the sun had slowly disappeared over the western mountains. Instead of the purple hues that'd been blessing the afternoon sky of late, all I could see was a sea of clouds, the electricity from before no longer running through them.

Said electricity was being put to good use—or bad, depending on your perspective. Claws had wreathed herself in lightning, using every last watt to propel herself toward the shark, which she intended on having as an early-evening snack. Thankfully, there was a final line of defense.

Even to me, my limb was a blur. The power surrounding Claws was enough to rebuff a boulder in flight, but my foot carved through it. At the very last moment, right before my leg hit, her emotive eyes flicked up to mine.

I expected to find accusations within them, but I received nothing of the sort. Despite being transformed into something I couldn't hope to comprehend, I could still read the lines of her face. Hundreds of microexpressions broadcast regret, self-recrimination, and . . . *sorrow*?

She puffed out her cheeks, giving her an adolescent look that tugged at my heartstrings. Instead of defending herself, Claws's last move was to nod in understanding, her puffy little cheeks jiggling slightly. She knew that she'd left me no choice.

It made a tidal wave of guilt well up from within me. Had I gone too far? I'd expected her to defend herself, and though my kick had no danger of causing serious damage, I fretted over the pain I might deliver. The wave of guilt slammed down atop me as my foot closed the distance, my heart sinking deep—

Just kidding, Claws chirped, shooting me a wink.

She pressed both forepaws into her cheeks. I'd seen her do it countless times, using the pressure to squirt people with water from afar. This time, it wasn't liquid that came streaming out.

A bar of solid lightning rocketed toward me, so compressed that it remained cylindrical. A deadly spearpoint formed at its tip, and when it was halfway to me, Claws ceased her compression. One line became hundreds, and hundreds became thousands, each possessing the power of a thunderbolt. Like Zeus himself had cocked a shotgun and pulled the trigger, the shattershot approached.

Assuming I was taken care of, Claws dismissed my presence, once more eyeing the thresher shark.

"You can't eat it, you little rat!" I bellowed, grasping for my chi.

As before, it didn't answer. I was too fatigued. Reaching deep within myself, unable to accept that I couldn't protect my catch, I caught hold of a tiny sliver of essence. Immediately creating a coin-sized barrier of chi, I leaped off it, flipping backward.

Lashing out once more with my right leg, I kicked *through* the thousands of thunderbolts. Against my body and its latent power, they parted like waves before the bow of an aircraft carrier, leaving nothing between my foot and Claws's astonished little face.

Crack!

EEEEEEEEEEEEEEEEEeeeeeeeeeeeeeeeeeeeeeeeeeeeeeeeeeeeeeeeeeeee . . .

Though she shot over the horizon almost immediately, the tail end of her scream still reached my ears seconds later. It eventually faded, leaving a silence that settled over my surroundings like a wool-spun blanket. The clouds dispersed as unnaturally fast as they'd appeared, and only when they were gone did the world seem to breathe once more.

The combination of both physical and mental exertion left me running on empty, and I resigned myself to falling into the ocean and working out the rest from there. But I needn't have worried. A black-and-red crab zipped by me, still trailing blue lines of Snips's power. Ten meters away, Rocky's clackers slammed shut. Twin booms erupted from him, and as he returned to the shore, he grabbed me on the way past—rather gracefully—with one of his powerful pincers.

Teddy caught us in a delightfully warm bear hug, and we all skidded backward along the sand. I wanted to enjoy the embrace as long as possible, but I had to sort something out first. "Sorry, Teddy. I—"

Teddy launched me with an overarm throw. I blinked, my brain struggling to catch up as I was sent barreling back toward the ocean. Another pair of arms awaited me. I collided with Barry's barrel of a chest, and we slid into the shallows. He set me down right next to the thresher shark, holding me by the shoulders for support.

I was filled with gratitude that my friends understood me so well—and a little annoyed that they'd rag-dolled me around the beach instead of just taking me directly to the shark, but beggars couldn't be choosers.

The thresher shark, though capable of wiping out an entire village of regular humans, was still a fish. It was worthy of compassion. I reached over it, gripped the hook, and freed it from my line.

It kicked feebly, and my eyes were drawn into it.

Mature Lightning-Infused Thresher Shark
Fleeting
Heavily targeted for the virility-boosting properties of its flesh, this shark was once thought extinct in the Kallis Realm. It has been temporarily infused with lightning to celebrate the ascension of an elemental. Infused creatures have their chi content significantly increased for three hours.

Having seen all I needed to, I spun the shark and grabbed its tail, moving it back and forth in the water to let oxygen flood its body.

Given how intelligent a creature it was, the thresher could have committed the fishy equivalent of a dick move at any point, using its whiplike tail to smack the shit out of me. If it was feeling particularly ornery, it could have tried to get me with its chompers. It did neither.

But I didn't want to push it. When its strength started to return, I bent and pushed, sending it gliding away beneath the waves.

"Wow . . ." came a soft voice.

I glanced back at Paul, delighting in the smile on his face. "Amazing, isn't it?"

Barry, who was still beside me to make sure I didn't fall over and drown, slung his arm around my shoulders. It would have looked like a friendly gesture to anyone else—and it was—but his arm also steadied me, helping me fight off the exhaustion weaving its way deeper by the second.

"Is it really okay to let it go?" Barry asked.

"It is, mate. It didn't try to attack me on the way out, because it understands the difference in our power. Its intelligence is temporary, sure, but so is its ability to shoot freakin' lightning bolts from its freakin' head."

He furrowed his brow, missing my reference but considering my words all the same.

"I can see you're still unconvinced. Why?"

"Well . . . it's just—"

"Don't placate me, you goose. Out with it."

His answering stare filled my heart with glee. "I was trying to show a bit of respect in front of my son."

"Unnecessary," I said.

"Unnecessary," Paul agreed, giving us both a grin.

Barry sighed. "I forget who I'm talking to sometimes. I was going to suggest that the shark might have misled you, and that it could just go elsewhere to terrorize people. Or creatures. Or the world in general. It's filled with Corporal Claws's chi."

I waved a hand back toward the shore with what I'd describe as pretentious pomp. "Witness my brilliance, Barry. Gaze upon my crustaceans."

There, ahead of everyone else, were two *very* crabby individuals. Poised at attention, they were waiting for the order. Only a hint of a smile graced the corner of my mouth as I raised my still-pretentious hand high. I clicked my fingers a single time, the sharp *snap* so loud that it sounded like someone had slapped two blue whales together.

I didn't have long to reconsider my terrible analogy because Sergeant Snips and Rocky reacted immediately. Rocky stepped forward. Snips stepped back. And in a move more graceful than such an act should be, Rocky was yeeted out over the ocean, crashing through waves that made his joyous screams fade sporadically.

EEEEEEEEEEEEeeeeeeeeeee—

Slap.

EEEEEEEeeeeeeeeee—

Slap.

EEeeeeee—

I'd seen such an angle before, and I half suspected he'd skip out over the horizon, like a stone but with violent tendencies and too many limbs. Instead, when he was above the shark's position, his powerful clackers done clacked. Dual explosions sent him rocketing down into the water, hopefully toward the creature and not through it like the old Rocky would have done.

Snips followed his passage, blue chi oozing from the gaps in her shell and going . . . *down her limbs*?

Snips, my magnificent anime protagonist of a crustacean, had found a new use for her essence. After flowing down her legs, it solidified against the water's surface, letting her run across it like crab Jesus. I desperately wanted to inspect it more, but I lacked the metaphorical juice to do so. I settled on watching instead, letting the hint of a smile from earlier blossom as she unleashed a massive burst of chi that sent her right in after Rocky.

Of their own accord, Pelly and Bill both took off, sailing out over the ocean to keep track of the shark's passage.

As the water settled, I gave Barry and Paul a nod. "See? Nothing to worry about."

Paul's eyes told me that he saw a great deal of things to worry about. He leaned back, trying to comprehend the chaos that had just unfolded before him. Barry sighed again, this time in resignation, as he led me back to shore. "I should have seen that coming."

"Man," I said, rubbing my sore shoulders. "I'm absolutely spent."

"Do you want to return home?"

As I considered my answer, I looked up at my friends. I didn't dare sense their emotions with how exhausted I felt, but there was no need. I could see the excitement on all of their faces. How could I go nap off my exhaustion when I had the perfect audience?

"Nah, I just need a bit of a breather, Barry." I waved a flippant hand toward the pile of supplies. "I don't need much chi to build the basic structure."

It had the desired effect. Excited whispers sprang up, everyone feverishly speculating what was so important that I'd led an expedition to Gormona just for its materials. Judging by how intense some of them were, it'd been a hot topic of discussion.

With all of their attention on me, I smirked at Paul. "Reckon you could help me with something, mate?"

He nodded with his usual sincerity. "What do you need?"

"Just some info. I've gone and got all the supplies, but I have no bloody clue how to put it all together." I cast a furtive glance toward the crowd and hid my mouth behind a hand.

With a stage-whisper loud enough for someone to hear from the low walls of Tropica, I asked, "Do you know how to build a boat?"

CHAPTER TWENTY-FIVE

Small, Cute, & Fluffy

The quiet hiss of thousands of bubbles rising through soft sand was the only sound to be heard. Each time they tapered off, a small wave washed up the shore, causing the symphony to begin anew. It was partially drowned out a moment later, a stiff breeze blowing from behind that caused my short hair to whip forward and tickle my scalp. I held my hands wide, forgetting about everything else as the sensations of my body became too glorious to ignore. When the wind disappeared, I opened my eyes slowly, finding a sea of faces pinned to me.

One was giving me a look flatter than the ocean on a still night.

"What's up?" I asked.

"Are you fracking with me, Fischer?" Barry replied, his jaw tensing.

I tilted my head in question, carefully smothering the joy threatening to spill from my core. "Whatever do you mean, mate?"

He rotated to the left, his eyes not leaving me as he gestured with both hands at the cart and piles of supplies. "You had us get all of this, promising that you had grand plans . . ."

"That's right."

"To build a boat."

"Ah-huh. Big boat. Perhaps the biggest."

"And you don't know how to build one . . . ?"

"Wellll, it's not so much that I don't know as it is that I haven't tried before. I know what they look like, and I understand the general principles of buoyancy. It has to float, right? Oh, and salt water is denser than fresh water! So it *should* definitely float. Probably."

"Probably?"

"Yeah. Sounds about right. Anyway, I was kinda hoping one of you would know how to build one. Any volunteers?" I gazed toward the crowd, and at their collective response, I raised a brow. "Why are you all looking at me like that?"

Barry's eyes narrowed. "You thought that we, villagers who until months ago had believed water to be heretical, would know how to build boats?"

"I'm not going to apologize for having faith in you, Barry."

"I've never even seen a boat!"

"I know what they look like. She'll be right."

"You know what they look— *What has that got to do with anything?* How are you going to stop it from leaking?"

"The whole thing is wood, mate. Wood floats."

"Even better in salt water," Theo added.

"See!" I clicked my fingers. "That's what I'm saying! So even if it leaks a bit, she'll be right."

Barry looked at me like he'd caught me chewing rocks. "Even if it leaks a bit? Fischer, boats aren't supposed to have water *in* them. It'll sink!"

"How do you know that? You've never seen one."

"I still know it's not supposed to have water *inside* of it! I may not have seen one, but you've never built one!"

I blew air from my lips. "I'd never made a rock wall to fish from either. It turned out great."

"And water leaks into it," Theo added helpfully. "Still functions."

"Water leaks into it!" I gestured at the rock wall. "And look how bloody sturdy it is!"

Said sturdiness did nothing to quell Barry's smoldering anger. "That, Fischer, is a structure made of *rock*."

"True."

"That's attached to the *ground*."

"Also true."

"Meaning it *doesn't need to float*!"

"Now you're just nitpicking."

Barry took a steadying breath. "Fischer, I need you to promise me you won't take a ship out to sea if there's even a slight chance it'll leak."

"I can't promise that. I *can* promise she'll be right, though."

"Stop saying she'll be right! How far out to sea do you anticipating taking this . . . this . . ." He had to search for the word, giving it air quotes and a liberal amount of skepticism when he finally found it. ". . . *Creation?*"

"Uhhhh, *all* the way out, mate. Wouldn't be much of a boat if it couldn't reach the horizon."

"The *horizon*?" Paul dashed forward, slipping through to stand beside his dad. "Can I come?"

"Damn right. Be a crying shame if you didn't."

"Fischer . . ." Barry's voice held a hint of warning. He rested a hand on Paul's shoulder. "And what if it sinks with people—with my *son*—on board?"

"I'll teleport us all to safety. Easy-peasy."

"But what if you're incapacitated? Just like you are literally *right now*? What if one of the countless mishaps that constantly occurs around you happens, and the boat starts to sink because it's *leaking* the *entire time*?"

"First off, countless mishaps? *Ouch*. Second, what about the statement 'she'll be right' do you not understand? Nothing bad has ever followed those three words. It's the Australian version of an immunity spell."

"Stop trying to confuse me with your expressions! I'm not in the mood, Fischer! Answer my question: What will happen if all of your power is sapped, and my only son falls into the ocean, and you're too far from shore to . . . to . . . Huh?"

A tsunami of emotion had been building behind him for the last minute or so. Theo had been the first to be certain that I was just messing with Barry, his training as a crown auditor coming in clutch. From there, everyone else had slowly realized, seeing it on others' faces and feeling it in their auras.

Barry should have noticed their amusement sooner, but I hadn't let him. I wavered, losing hold of the paper-thin walls I'd used to shield him from the outside world. Now that their emotions were on full display, they could finally laugh. Helen swept forward, wrapping her husband in a hug. "I'm sorry, dear. If it makes you feel any better, I love when you get protective."

Barry hugged her back, but that didn't stop him from leveling a distrustful gaze my way.

"You were almost correct, mate . . ." I wobbled, exhaustion coming for me. "I wouldn't have the strength to teleport anyone back to shore right now, but a few walls to hide emotions? Child's play."

I stumbled, and if not for Barry taking pity on me, I'd have fallen on my ass. He caught me by the arm, helping me stay upright long enough for me to realize I'd pushed myself and the joke too far.

Barry shook his head at me, amusement warring with the annoyance on his face. "Anything to say for yourself, Fischer?"

I nodded, my eyelids fluttering and body seeming to go into recovery mode. "Yeah, mate." It was all I could do to move a single finger, so I gestured for him to come closer. His curiosity got the better of him, and he leaned in.

"She'll be right," I croaked right into his ear, then gave him a satisfied smile.

The last thing I saw before unconsciousness took me was the stars above, their pinprick beauty framing the muscular hand that had previously been holding me up but now conveyed a decidedly rude message.

Corporal Claws, wielder of lightning and the undisputed glowiest of Fischer's disciples, was having a wonderful evening. It had only been minutes since her master had kicked her in the moosh, and she'd already traveled farther than she knew possible.

Despite how enhanced her awareness had been before awakening as an elemental, she wouldn't have been able to witness even half of what she saw now. Claws twisted her body, spinning round and round until the scene above blended with the scene below. With the mildest flex of will, she dulled the brightness of the electricity comprising her, well, everything, letting the outside world engulf her senses as she rocketed out into a stretch of cloudless sky.

The stars shone with unspeakable energy. Following her change, she could sense the power each one of them held. Their distance, too. It was . . . *magical.* Because of the world's knowledge streaming into her upon her first awakening, she'd already known this. As with so many things in life, though, knowing was entirely different from *knowing*. Despite how similar they looked from afar, each was unique—their size, composition, and brightness varied, as did the scarcely believable cosmic power that pulsed from them.

It was intoxicating to know that she could feel things from so far away. That she could sense places she would never be able to visit, even with her newfound mastery of lightning. Despite having her attention drawn in so many directions, she didn't miss a familiar face as she sailed over him. She righted her elemental body to stare down at someone who, not ten minutes ago, she'd tried to strike with lightning.

Ellis was on a *tiny* island only a few times larger than Tropica. Though small, humanity clearly lived there. Thrived, perhaps. There were houses, vessels, and even a wooden dock. If she wanted to, she could stop her passage—arrest her momentum to rocket down and check if he was okay. She considered it for a second, but there was no need. Ellis was sitting on the dock with two dark-skinned women, all of his attention on an open book in his lap. Despite his intent stare, his core seemed rather . . . calm?

She contemplated going to meet him for less-altruistic reasons, too. Like zapping him in front of his new friends, for example. But at the cost of her own velocity? *Pshhh. Yeah right.* Just before she sailed over the horizon, Claws gave a polite little wave that he'd never see, then returned her attention to the outside world.

With how fast she twirled, the stars became smeared lines of light, their individual energies singing out to her. She soaked their voices in, delighting in the melody that result— *Oh? What was that?*

Something floated below, and unlike the foolish yet often amusing Ellis, this object *demanded* her attendance. Claws zipped down with all the care she could muster, only a soft breeze accompanying her appearance on the floating pile of jetsam. It seemed relatively sturdy for a pile of literal rubbish.

Thick cords of rope had wound over broken sections of wood to form a raft of sorts. By how chaotic the knots were, it must have been through a storm, if not an attack. She had to process all of this with a fraction of her awareness, because the reason for her landing occupied the rest. Claws took a hurried step forward, excited jolts of electricity crawling over her, and froze.

She whirled on the spot, her entire body crackling as she prepared to unleash it upon any being foolish enough to ambush her. Despite no treacherous souls coming to greet her, she didn't relax, instead rotating so fast that she could look in every direction at once. She was sure she hadn't imagined it. Someone had just been observing her. She'd *felt* it.

But no matter how long she spun, the feeling of being observed didn't return. She considered another possibility—that, unable to believe that someone would leave the object of her attention behind, her subconscious had invented an enemy.

Better to be safe than sorry . . .

Claws snapped back into stillness, her lightning chi *flooding* the surrounding ocean. The salinized water was a terrible conductor, but that was nothing to the elemental known as Corporal Claws of the Church of Fischer. Her essence suffused the ocean for nautical miles in every direction—which Claws decided was a *very* weird way of measuring things, accurate or not. Barely a kilometer to the north, she found it. Revealing her glimmering chompers to the world, her power descended upon the being that *dared* lay such an effective trap, hundreds of lightning bolts tearing down to . . .

She flicked a paw, changing their trajectory. Most shot skyward, dissipating into the surrounding water the moment Claws's will withdrew. She focused on a few select bolts. They curved around the original target, only to loop back in, slamming down into the ground. Said target was hurled up from the depths, propelled by a storm's worth of electricity crashing down behind it. Claws reached out with a single mitt, catching the curiosity before lifting it up to her eyes for inspection.

It was . . . a stone.

What she'd assumed to be an enemy attacker was just a rock with no sapient being connected to it. An odd chi lingered within, however, reminding her of something she couldn't quite put her toe bean on. Countless thoughts and possibilities raced through her mind, all causing her vicious grin to widen. No matter the cause, one thing was for sure—she had found a wonderfully unique stone. Wrapping it in lightning chi to seal the odd essence inside, she slipped it into a pocket for later examination.

Claws all but forgot about its existence as she tiptoed across the tangled mess of debris. The structure creaked, rope and wood both complaining as they shifted under her careful steps. When she was finally above the object that had halted her flight, Claws reached down with more care than she'd give the *perfect* oyster.

She lifted it to her chest, assaulted by sheer disbelief that this hadn't been a trap. What fool would leave something so precious—so *flawless*—here for her to find? Unable to contain the plethora of emotions, everything above her shoulders wiggled like a worm, her lower half having to remain stoic for the sake of the sleeping creature she held.

Master is going to *love*—

The creature made a coughing sound. Still asleep, it took a shuddering breath, the sound wet and wheezy. Claws froze, a shard of ice forming in the base of her neck. This animal—so small, so cute, so *fluffy*—was unwell.

She wasted no time. Snicking off some rope, she started tying a sling but swiftly realized she had neither the patience nor the need for something so mundane.

She opened her pockets, mentally moved all of her rocks into her left one—she *loved* that her new body could do that—and placed the sickly creature in the right. After throwing the rope in—because why not?—she sealed them shut, leaving micro . . . tonic? Or was it sonic? She shook her head. Micro-whatever! Small gaps so it could breathe!

Annoyed at the general existence of words, Corporal Claws, maiden of the skies and protector of all things cute, shot into the sky, with lightning streaming in her wake. She had to get home. Had to get back to Fischer. No matter how unwell the creature may be, her master would know what to do.

CHAPTER TWENTY-SIX

Calamity

Deep beneath the ocean, in a place where the pressure alone would crush most, an ancient being sat very, *very* still. He had made a mistake, one with the potential to unravel his greatest plan to date. This knowledge, that he had taken a step in error, filled him with rage. His body wanted to roil. Wanted to absorb all the nearby rocks and grind them to dust. But for the sake of his plans, he stomped the emotion down.

Only an hour ago, a blip in his existence, he had been steadily making his way toward the newborn elemental. There had been no rush, after all. He was as inexorable as the passage of time, and no matter how long it took, he would have eventually reached his target. Sneak up, feign weakness, destroy utterly. It had worked when his mass was that of a mere boulder, and still worked now that he was larger than most mountains.

He had been creeping closer when the infant elemental had done something unexpected. It'd changed positions—so swiftly that he, at first, thought it teleported. Such things were possible, of course. He had faced more than one elemental that could step through space. The reality was far more troubling, however—it was just *fast*. Blisteringly so. It was the second-quickest being he'd ever encountered.

The fastest had been a fire elemental who, unlike the others of its kind, possessed unbridled agility. That singular fight had been enough for him to understand that those with speed and the cognition to match were his greatest weakness. They were the only ones who could react in time to his ambush tactics.

And, if his senses could be believed, the newly awakened elemental had only been birthed this lunar cycle. So young, yet its spryness was almost on par with the centuries-old fire elemental that had nearly ended him.

His instincts had screamed to send more chi toward it, demanding that he learn what abyssal demon had appeared on *his*—no, *their*—planet. He'd fought those urges back for as long as he could, remaining strong for a commendable amount of time, but had failed when it stopped atop the ocean's surface.

The moment he gave in to his hunger for knowledge, a fragment of his attention had shot into a faraway stone dwelling on the ocean floor, a part of himself left behind for such purposes. He had scattered hundreds of them across their world, all portals through which he could spy.

Only a whisper of his true power channeled into the object. It was half a league away from the other elemental, and with how delicate his touch was, his foe should never have been able to detect him. But it had. It had noticed him as soon as he arrived.

He had immediately abandoned the stone, severing his connection to it for good, lest the newborn discover his existence. Having to leave behind a portion of himself, no matter its insignificant size, was a large part of his anger. It felt like admitting defeat. Like ceding ground to an upstart. And yet . . . it was entirely necessary.

The other elemental may have been young, but it was also powerful. Its potential, in both agility and perception, was unbelievable. A healthy fear for what this foe might become sprouted deep within the elemental's mass of sediment and chi. He used this emotion as the tectonic plate on which to build reinforcing layers of rock. His anger was far beneath the structure, and with each sheet of resolve he added, the fire was further robbed of fuel.

He was once more in control when he let some of his awareness leach out into the world. The other being was still on high alert, so he waited. Silt and sand settled over his gigantic form, the waters around him only just starting to calm. Tiny life-forms, mostly crustaceans, found places to hide within the patches of debris. He paid them no mind. All of his attention remained on the other elemental's position, which he could still vaguely sense. When it released a blast of power and rocketed up into the sky, a wave of relief washed over him. It was clearly fearful, but it had been confident enough to take another life-form with it.

These actions meant one thing: the newborn elemental hadn't gotten a read of his power. If it had, it would have fled for its survival. It certainly wouldn't have slowed its passage to preserve the existence of a mere beast. As it got farther and farther away, leaving the range of his senses, he finally moved again.

Though his foe had plenty of potential, so had all the others. He'd absorbed them all, their strength becoming his, and his becoming *theirs*. He began moving once more, a localized landslide that destroyed everything in its path.

It was only a matter of time until he rolled over the newborn and assimilated its chi.

Far to the north, an ancient organism was lost in thought. The problem with theories, he surmised, was that they can never be proven. Unless one could predict the future, any experiment thereafter might just come along and shatter preconceived truths.

Many more considerations followed, the alacrity with which he processed each thought reflective of his vast intellect. He had stirred frequently of late, and as whispers of power seemed to return to the world, so, too, did his awareness. This was, he determined, a good thing. But it *did* make sleep more elusive.

Each time, there was an urge for him to move, yet he never followed these compulsions. There was good reason, of course. Logic behind his abstaining. After all, he was nothing if not a beacon of rationality.

But that didn't make it any easier for the organism to fight his instinct. His body twitched whenever hints of chi washed over him, his limbs wanting nothing more than to engulf and crush the targets of his ire. Always, though, reason won. No matter how strong the pull, how unignorable the currents, it wasn't yet time to indulge his base instincts. The only way to ensure victory was to wait for his oldest ally to awaken once more.

He resolved himself to live each moment of this agony. To revel in the curse that was his continued existence, as well as the knowledge that it could be thousands of years before the time to strike arrived. Until then, he couldn't move. If he was detected, all was for nothing.

With great effort and forced mindfulness—a misnomer if ever there was one—the organism's thoughts died down. Just as slumber was about to welcome him into its loving embrace, he was jolted awake by a memory made manifest.

A pulse of aura that he recognized as if his own. It was his oldest ally "jumping" to one of his scouting rocks. But no. It had to have been an artifact of sleep. If it wasn't, his period of inaction would cease—such a possibility was too good to be true, and even the idea of it threatened to weaken his resolve. He settled back into himself, closing his eyes and willing his thoughts to fade once more.

The pulse came again, and this time, there was no question as to its authenticity.

The organism's eyelids flew open, revealing abyssal orbs whose description alone had been the basis of religions. His oldest ally, the earth elemental of legend, had just severed its connection to a part of itself. Something small, like a stone or a shell. But that was inconsequential. What mattered was that the earth elemental, a being that had long since shed any of its names, was *awake.*

The organism wasted no time. More liquid than flesh, he slid from a crevasse deep beneath the ocean, the place he'd called home since his ally had let itself be trapped. No light made its way down into the trench he occupied, but he didn't need it. He had something even better.

As he honed in on the last place he'd felt the earth elemental, duty spurred him onward, fueling his passage through the freezing waters.

With absolutely no ease and even less grace, I sat up. "Ow," I groaned, rubbing my temples. "What happened?" My head felt like it had been squashed between a boulder and . . . another, even bigger boulder.

"And why are analogies so hard?" I asked the universe, trying and failing to distract myself from the pain afflicting me.

"You overextended yourself," Barry said, his voice somewhere to my left. Or my right. Who knew, honestly.

"Yeahhh. I think I remember now. Got ya pretty good."

"You did, but it lessened the blow when you fell unconscious and faceplanted on the ground almost immediately afterward."

"Lies and deceit," I replied, but then I felt the sand in my mouth. "Why did no one catch me?"

"Borks and Cinnamon worked together to catch you, but Cinnamon got a little . . . carried away."

I touched the sore spot on the back of my head. "She kicked me by accident, didn't she?"

"Head-butted the crap out of you when she flew out of the portal. Almost knocked herself out."

"Damn. She okay?"

The two pals in question arrived at my side, Cinnamon unleashing a torrent of apologetic peeps and Borks just happy to see me. I used my hands to both hold them at bay and deliver scritches. As I delighted in their soft fur and the way they leaned into my touch, my eyes finally focused. Even with only partial vision, I couldn't have missed Barry's smile if I tried. "Well, I'm glad you got some entertainment out of my misfortune."

He beamed. "So am I."

Already, the pain in my head was easing, the contact with my animal pals wicking it away like sweat beneath the summer sun. "Where is everyone?"

"Building your damned boat."

". . . What?"

"As it turns out, we have a basic understanding of ships if we combine our efforts."

"The knowledge the System granted you?"

"Yep. It was patchy, but we compared notes, so to speak. You've been out for a good half hour, so we already started organizing the materials. We've been busy. Considering what you pulled earlier, I thought about just building it without you, but I'm not that cruel."

I laughed, pulling both Cinnamon and Borks into my lap now that my headache was mostly gone. They both rolled onto their backs and accepted their belly scratches. "No you didn't."

"I didn't what?" Barry asked.

"You didn't consider doing it without my approval. You know how excited I am to build it, and you're far too good a man to rob me of that."

He let out a self-conscious sniff that was entirely at odds with his muscular body. "Yeah, well, keep pushing me, and one day I might."

We both grinned at each other, knowing it to be a lie. Barry stood, then helped me to my feet. I gazed toward the cart and the former pile of materials. Barry hadn't been kidding—they *had* been busy. Every member of the congregation present was helping, as were most of the regular humans that had arrived. Almost all the wood had been organized into neat stacks that no doubt facilitated the plans they'd drawn up.

"Okay, before anything else, let's have a look at these plans." I accepted them from Paul and couldn't help but raise an appreciative brow at the schematics. "Who drew these?"

Paul absolutely *beamed.* "I did!"

"*By hand*?"

"Uhhh," Barry said. "How else would he draw them?"

"Yeah, look, that's a fair point. I just can't believe how straight the lines are." With a step forward, I softly ruffled Paul's hair. "I didn't know we had a little Picasso on our hands. Maybe we need to get you some different art supplies and let you—" I froze mid-sentence. "Never mind."

"What—" Barry began, but then he felt it, too. Or, rather, he felt *her.*

Corporal Claws struck the ground before me with much more subtlety than I expected. She was riding lightning, sure, but it lacked any of her usual flare. She didn't even melt the sand beneath her.

"Claws," I said, expecting trickery. "Welcome home . . ."

She loped toward me with excited steps, her grin as wide as I'd ever seen it. When she got to me, she reached both paws into one of her pockets.

"Listen, Claws," I said. "I'm genuinely happy you're back so soon, but if you hit me with some pocket sand, I'll kick you clean over the horizon again. We need to have a serious talk about boundaries now that you've had another breakthrough, missy."

She shook her head, and before I could question her mood further, she withdrew her paws. Clutched between her devious little hands was something fluffy, adorable, and *terrifying.*

I stepped back. "Absolutely not, Claws! You put that back where you found it!"

Why? she demanded with an indignant chirp, her body language shifting.

"Because I said so, Claws! That thing is only going to bring calamity if it ascends!"

She chirped again, looking at me like I'd just kicked a puppy.

"I can tell it's unwell, Claws, but it's not critical. We can heal it. Absolutely. But then you have to take it back!"

Her next chirp was beseeching, and she gestured at its face emphatically.

"I know it's already wearing a mask! That's the problem!"

Barry knelt down, inspected the adolescent mammal up close, then gave me a questioning look. "Why don't you want to keep it? It's really cute, and you love cute things."

I rubbed the bridge of my nose. "I know it's super fucking cute, Barry. It's taking all of my strength not to scoop it up and give it a name."

". . . so why don't you?"

Yeah! Claws agreed, piling on. *Why?*

"Because we had these back on Earth. They're tricky little things, and that's without accounting for the intelligence that comes with awakening. Don't give me that look, Claws. We have our hands full with you and Cinnamon! The last thing we need is another you!"

She walked forward, cradling the creature to her chest and staring up at me with puppy-dog eyes. *Pleeeaaase?* she cooed.

"I don't think you'll win this battle, Fischer. It's not in your nature."

A sparkle in Claws's eye was the only warning before she lobbed it at me. My choice was to let an injured animal drop to the ground, or to catch it. I caught it, of course. Its fur was even softer than I'd imagined, and I couldn't help but stroke its cheek with one finger.

As I watched its chest rise and fall, a wet sound coming from it, I let out a long-suffering sigh. No matter how much trouble it brought to our shores, there was no way I could release this baby out into the wild.

Claws zapped up onto my shoulder, then ran around my torso like a squirrel, never once taking her eyes off of it. The rest of the animal pals had drifted over, and I took a knee so everyone could get a look. They were all torn between inspecting the cute little thing and looking at Claws's new form. I smiled as their heads literally darted back and forth. "We'll take it to Snips's healing pool. I didn't want to interrupt Maria's meditation, but this one's health takes precedence."

Barry leaned over the top of everyone. "What is it, Fischer? What kind of animal, I mean?"

I paused, staring down at its tiny form. It had four legs and four paws, though there was an argument to be made that the front two were actually hands. Because of its age, its fur was mostly gray, its striped marking yet to come in. A pair of supremely cute ears. And last of all, the feature that Claws had pointed out as if that alone would sway me: dark rings around its eyes that, when it grew older, would form a black mask.

I shook my head, unable to hide my smile. "It's a fuckin' raccoon, Barry, and may the gods help us if the little prick ever ascends."

CHAPTER TWENTY-SEVEN

Words Are So Fun

From everything that Maria had heard, it was impossible to describe enlightenment. Countless humans and animals had tried. And based on the waves of chi that had swept overhead while she meditated, another couple of beings might be able to give explanation a shot, too, though they would likely fail also.

Despite this lack of elucidation, however, Maria could tell that her own approached; her essence had been steadily building, as had the weight of the healing potential in her core. Each passing moment brought her closer to who she was—who she'd always been destined to become—and if the pond she sat atop was any indication, the world concurred.

When she'd arrived at the tidal pool, she immediately knew her relationship to the strange waters had changed. She had always been able to tell they possessed a strange sort of power, even when she'd only been at the bottom of the stairwell to ascension. But if she sent her chi out now? It felt almost like an extension of herself.

Most shocking of all—a notable reaction considering how *ridiculous* the last week had been—was that the placid waters all but yelled out with encouragement. It was like having a copy of yourself cheer you on, insisting you were doing the right thing. She spared a moment to pour her gratitude out into the pool. It was something she had repeatedly done. It just seemed the right thing to do.

But this time, something new happened. Gratitude came flowing back. It was only for a fraction of a second, but it was enough to make Maria's spine go rigid and her focus to slip. She opened her eyes to find that night had arrived, yet she spared no attention for the beautiful stars twinkling above.

Instead, she stared down at the pond in awe, anticipating . . . she didn't know what. For it to ripple? For another hint of awareness to appear? Contrary to her expectations, the waters remained still. The opalescent stones within reflected some of the starlight from above, which *seemed* to glow more than usual, but she wasn't sure if that was her imagination, a side effect of her enhanced body, or something real.

Consumed as she might have been by the sight, she couldn't have missed the approaching cores if she tried.

Maybe it's time to have a break . . . she thought, wiggling her toes and rolling her neck. *Especially if I'm starting to imagine a pond capable of gratitude . . .*

As she turned to look at the incoming crowd, a smile came to her face. It felt *wonderful.* She intended on letting it spread even wider—on letting her love for Fischer and their otter pal show—but then she caught sight of Corporal Claws. Maria leaped to her feet, blinking rapidly to clear away what was clearly her imagination. When that didn't help, she extended her awareness out, knowing her core would report the truth of the matter. It did, in fact, and Maria's jaw dropped open.

Corporal Claws had experienced . . . Maria didn't even know if she should call it a breakthrough. Claws's entire being had become a core. Her body was composed of *lightning*. It catapulted Maria's thoughts into the stratosphere. As time had passed, increasing her affinity to healing chi, Maria's cognition had intensified. With how sharp her mind had become, she finally understood what Fischer had meant when he'd tried to explain the changes to his brain.

Even with these alterations, though, she struggled to pick the correct question to ask.

"Wha—" she started and cut off as she sensed something from Fischer's chest.

There was life there—not his—and it was weak. It demanded her attention.

All other considerations fell away as Maria leaped from the boulder atop the pond, skidding to a stop before Fischer. She caught her first sight of the creature. Part of her brain screamed that it was godsdamned *adorable*, but she filed that away for later—her core agreed with the action, vibrating so hard her heart fluttered.

The pond, too, reacted. As before, an emotion that hinted at intelligence came from it. Its waters requested she bring the animal closer.

Fischer, clearly sensing Maria's urgency—and the pond's request, judging by the look of sheer incredulity he shot its way—reached forward, offering the fuzzy little thing to her.

It was even cuter than she'd initially judged. Without a word, Maria went to the pond and strode into its cool waters. But . . . they weren't cool at all; they were *warm*. She added this anomaly to the pile of things to explore later as she lowered herself and the creature's body beneath the surface.

The healing chi of the pond immediately flowed toward the animal. Maria closed her eyes, relying on her senses to follow the strands. Time slowed as hundreds of individual streams climbed from the rock bed, joining with those already swirling within the water. They circled the cute little mammal with languid grace, not rushing into its body as Maria had assumed they would. Some of the chi strands brushed up against it. They were furtive touches, and with no small amount of wonder, Maria realized that each had a distinct purpose. They were diagnosing any health issues.

Her core shook, making a soft sound that seemed to say, *Yes, correct.*

She let out a slow breath and sank further into herself, willing her essence to do the same, and a portion of consciousness spoke up. It was the part of her that worried she wasn't good enough. The deep-down insecurity that she wasn't worthy of the healing chi she so desperately wanted to harness. That voice was swiftly silenced, her essence conforming with ease. She started getting hints of information, each a subtle brushstroke that gave more context to the greater picture.

After countless bits of data, she could state with confidence that the creature's skeletal system was intact. There were no physical wounds to its body. S*omething* was definitely wrong, but she couldn't identify it. And the pond appeared to have reached its limitations. It could repair bodily injuries, but beyond that, it would need much longer for the healing to take place.

Maria didn't know what ailed the adorable little thing. If it was life-threatening, they wouldn't have the luxury of time. She furrowed her brow; uncertainty was unacceptable.

Rallying her will, and with a conscious effort to keep any of her former doubts at arm's length, she increased the amount of essence surging from her core. In her mind's eye, it was like wisps of chi flowed out—pink and bright and opaque—surrounding the pond's strands of power.

Her inclination was to boost the tidal pool's efforts. To lend it the strength it needed to identify the issue. But that wasn't good enough. Even if the pond seemed to possess an uncanny intelligence, the health of this innocent creature was in Maria's hands. *She* had to take control.

Her core vibrated again, this time reaching a resonant pitch. The water responded, its surface quaking, calling out to her stronger than ever before.

I stared down at Maria with as much love and awe as I'd ever felt; my awareness of chi made me vaguely aware of the battle she waged.

The waters she and the raccoon rested in had taken the lead, its healing properties reaching out the moment the fuzzy little thing was semi-submerged. Maria had joined her will to it, the essence within her core easily copying the shape and intent of what could only be called a force of nature. The intricacies of what she and the water were doing were lost on me, so all I could do was witness and silently cheer her on.

Well, that *and* keep my eye on whatever the pond had become. I'd felt something from it before, a hint of sapience that I wasn't entirely comfortable with. Every fiber of my being told me it could be trusted, yet I remained vigilant; some parts of this world I found myself in were beyond my comprehension. With my mind so focused on both of them, I sensed the moment Maria's will shifted.

Chi flowed from her like wispy clouds. They surrounded the pool's strands of chi, racing along them, and when they engulfed the ends . . . Maria took control.

A pulse of power and light came from her, making her sun-kissed hair wave chaotically up and away from her core. The childish part of my brain—which was in the minority, thank you very much—noted that she looked like she was about to go Super Saiyan.

The pond, uncaring of my musings, resonated with Maria's intent. Hypnotic patterns formed on its surface, rising and falling like wavelengths made visible. Even if I wasn't seeing it with my own eyes, I'd have known what had happened. They had reached an accord.

Maria's clouds of essence carved a path forward, surrounding the raccoon in a sort of haze. The opalescent stones beneath them reflected the pink light coming from her, creating a cone of illumination that shone toward the heavens. Despite the outward chaos of the moment, her furry patient was completely shielded, not one of its hairs moved by the pressure Maria was exerting.

I hadn't noticed it, but a smile had made its way onto my face. The corners of my eyes bunched as I gazed down at her. I'd never been so proud.

"You got this," I whispered, delighting in the sensations of my body as Maria's power coursed over and around me.

Despite how overwhelmed Maria's senses were, Fischer's encouragement slipped right through the cracks to reach her ears. They weren't just empty words, and they caused a thrill to run through her.

She agreed with him. She *did* have this. Even if her confidence wasn't so strong, however, his trust wouldn't have wavered, its foundation more stable than bedrock. She internalized his reassurance, tucking it away for later, as she had so many other thoughts.

After all, true enlightenment was within reach. She just had to *take it*.

Maria opened her core up, letting in waves of energy from the pond. As if a weir's gate had been raised, the power flowed into her, she and the water's chi becoming one. They came to a stop beside the raccoon. Maria was able to see it from all directions at once, and as power washed over it, she *knew* what ailed it.

First, dehydration, which was easy enough to fix. Together, she and the pond removed most of the salt from its waters. The purified liquid flowed into the raccoon's body, replenishing its reserves. Next, the mammal was missing key minerals. Some of them were within the tidal pond, so they gathered the necessary amounts. Potassium, magnesium, iron, zinc. Compounds she'd never known, yet their purpose appeared in her memories like a long-lost friend.

Raccoon, she mused, the word almost familiar. Had Fischer mentioned them before?

Its biology, lifespan, diet, and behavior—all bloomed in her mind. Learning about the animal made . . . *something* appear in Maria's awareness. There was a metaphorical lump in its brain. Did it need to be healed? She gathered some of her chi just in case, ready to heal the incorporeal anomaly, but her core vibrated again. Unlike earlier, this buzz was in the negative. The pool also seemed to hesitate.

Maria paused for only a moment, then let go of the essence she had prepared. She would have to be a fool to ignore both herself and a pond with healing abilities.

The mix of elements was ready to go, so she sent them into the raccoon's circulatory system. As they joined the small mammal's bloodstream, a feeling of everything being right in the world descended, wrapping her entire body in warmth. The raccoon still needed food, but that wasn't within her power to grant. She had done all she could.

Before that sense of *rightness* could fade, light and power exploded from her core, and Maria knew she had succeeded.

As the light fled, she waited for the System messages to come. Just like Fischer, she'd willed them to leave her alone, but there was no way something of this magnitude would obey. She waited and waited, but they didn't come. Only seconds had passed, but that was a lifetime when it came to the System. Why—

Something shot from Maria's core. It was, somehow, squishy and crystalline and *lovely*. It moved up her abdomen, past her shoulder, through her skin.

Blinking, Maria looked down at her forearm.

"Hiiii!" came the blob's squeaky voice. Just as she knew water was wet, Maria recognized the being perched on her limb. The size of a closed fist, its body seemed to have two shapes it could swap between, one gemlike, the other gelatinous. It was light pink when a ball of slime, and filled with rainbow light when a faceted crystal.

Maria blinked again, unable to think of anything to say.

"Wowww!" the physical manifestation of the tidal pond continued. It jiggled in delight. "Words. Are. So. Fun!"

CHAPTER TWENTY-EIGHT

Trash Panda

"Wowww!" the pink slime said, staring up at Maria and wobbling all over. "Words. Are. So. Fun!"

I looked at Claws. Claws looked at me. We looked at Maria. Maria looked at us. We all looked at the slime.

"Hiiiii!" it squeaked. "Nice to finally talk to . . . well, it's nice to finally talk at all! Oh. My. *Goodness* was it hard not being able to communicate for so long! But I guess I was kinda dumb then, so I didn't even know how to? That's something to be thankful for, I think! That I was too silly to know how hard it was!"

Beady yet undeniably cute eyes focused on Claws, who was staring back with an open mouth, her needle-sharp teeth reflecting the slime's light as it turned into a crystal that balanced on Maria's arm.

"*Wowwww!* You're pretty like I am! You never used to look like that, did you? I remember! I can see right through you, but your body . . ." A quick pulse of energy came from the slime—it was a slime again, by the way—and my head rocked back.

The chi was *Maria's*. It had come from her core. And the slime—nope, crystal—had used it freely.

"Wooooowwwww!" it squealed at Claws. "Your body isn't real! Or I guess it's more accurate to say that it isn't physical? You're made up of chi! That's like, *super cool*! I'm gonna touch you now." It shivered as if cold. "Oh my! That's rude, isn't it? Is it okay if I touch you? I—" It whirled to my left. "Oh my gosh! My crabs! *You guys, it's meee!*"

Distracted, I hadn't registered the approach of Snips and Rocky. The slime looked at them expectantly. They looked at the slime. Snips looked at Maria. Rocky looked at me. Maria looked at nobody, her eyes staring into the distance like she'd seen a ghost. The raccoon woke up, letting out an open-mouthed yawn.

Rocky pointed down. *That's a raccoon*, he stated, trying to appear unbothered.

"Yeah, mate. Surprised you know what it is."

He pointed at the slime, a slight shake entering his claw. *That's . . . that's the pond.*

Snips blew affirmative and astonished bubbles, her eye flicking between the slime and the raccoon, who gazed back without a care in the world.

Rocky nodded, managing to keep his composure as he . . . never mind. I couldn't even finish the sentence before he lost his absolute shit.

The lines on his shell flared the color of magma, and three and a half cigarettes—where did they keep coming from, and why did he have half a cigarette?—appeared from nowhere, gripped in one powerful clacker. With movement so swift anyone but a cultivator would miss it, he lit them on the red lines of his carapace, held them to his mouth, and inhaled a single, continuous breath.

All three and a half sticks glowed a bright orange as they swiftly shrunk. He paused for a moment, the rage and confusion in his heart threatening to boil over. I half thought the old version of Rocky would explode into being.

But as I felt something within his core, a circulation of chi I didn't quite understand, he visibly calmed. A moment later, Rocky finally exhaled—he looked and sounded like the smokestack of a steam train.

"Okay," I cut in, waving the exhaust fumes from my face. "I'm aware you're sworn to secrecy, Rocky, but I need to know that it's not the chemicals in the cigarettes that just calmed you down."

Now back to his cool self, and with a seemingly effortless but definitely deliberate lean—seriously, how did a crab give off punk vibes?—Rocky nodded.

Not chemical, his soft hiss told me. He chucked all four butts into his maw, where they dissolved upon his volcanic . . . Do crabs have tongues? I shook my head. Today's events were getting to me.

The fire sticks are but a component, Rocky continued, his bubbles containing wisps of smoke. *I cannot speak of it more, my friend, lest my honor be impugned. Shall we discuss more pressing matters, such as the arrival of a new animal compatriot, or the physical manifestation of my mistress's beloved pond?*

"Hold on," Maria cut in. "What about Claws?"

"*What about Claws?*" I found myself repeating, voice incredulous. "Are you trying to gloss over the fact that you just *bonded* with a *familiar?* It's tied to your core, right?"

Said familiar made a burbling sound that resembled the clearing of a throat, which was a pretty good replication considering it didn't have one. "Sorryyyy, but I don't like being called 'it.'"

"Oh. My bad. That was kind of insensitive. What would you like . . ." I trailed off as I remembered I was talking to a fracking *body of water*, and a line formed between my eyebrows.

"A boy!" Maria's familiar answered, unbothered that I hadn't finished the question. "My master likes boys, so I wanna be that!"

I could feel the love for Maria flowing from the chatty little fella. It was purely platonic, so I gave him a nod of understanding. "As good a reason as any. I'll make sure not to call you 'it' from now on. Sorry again. I didn't mean—"

"Fischer!" Maria yelled, shielding the raccoon's ears so her voice wouldn't startle it. She jabbed her chin to my right. "You're the one glossing over things! Can we address the lightning-filled otter in the room?"

Corporal Claws stood to her full height and puffed her chest out, jolts sparking as she preened under the attention.

"Oh, that?" I shrugged. "Yeah, Claws is like . . . the embodiment of lightning now. Chaos, too. It's a whole thing."

The otter's head darted toward me, her preening coming to an end as she jabbed a paw my way and chirped an accusation.

"Is it a big deal, though? I thought it was pretty normal to—" I held up my hands as clouds gathered above. "Kidding! I'm kidding! It was downplaying it on purpose!"

Claws raised an illuminated brow at me, daring me to push it.

"I still can't believe it . . ." Maria, despite holding a baby raccoon and having just gained a slimy crystal companion, was watching Claws with wonder-filled eyes. "You're really made of lightning. It feels . . . wow . . ."

"It *does* feel *wow*!" her familiar, who had remained as a slime for a good minute now, agreed. "My comprehension of this place and all of you is still pouring in from Maria, but—" His entire body vibrated like it had just received a notification. "Wow! There are people we can heal? Wonderful! What was I saying? Oh yes! Your body is *very wow*, Corporal Claws!"

Her entire upper torso wiggled around in delight. If the laws of physics applied to her, she likely would have toppled over. *Stop iiiit,* she cooed, one paw extended and waving up and down in faux embarrassment.

"Apollo's precious-metal shafts!" I swore. "I've got it!"

"Uhhh," Maria replied. "You've got what?"

"Slimes!"

"Wha—"

"Slimes!" I repeated, my eyes flicking between Maria and Slimes. "*Specialist* Slimes."

"Absolutely not!" Maria pulled her arm—and Specialist Slimes—closer to her torso. "You don't get to name *my* companion. You didn't even ask him if he wanted one!"

I kneeled down, leaning toward Specialist Slimes with a conspiratorial look. "Wanna know why the name is brilliant, *Slimes*?"

"Oh yeah!"

"No!" Maria replied at the same time. After only a moment, she let out a sigh, deflating. "Fine. On with it, then."

"Wonderful! Thanks for asking!"

"Nobody ask—"

"The name's brilliance is twofold!" I yelled. "First, like the names An Entire Flock of Birds, Fat Rat Pack, and the Beetle Boys, Specialist Slimes implies multiple. With all the new awakenings, people have just been using their actual names. On the off chance there's still some nefarious force watching, it'll be good to chuck a wrench in the metaphorical mix.

"And that's not all!" I continued, using my best infomercial voice. "If such a force *does* exist and tries to act against us, and you have to face them, you can just transform into a crystal! They'll have no idea you're actually Slimes!"

A loud whistle cut through the following silence. Claws applauded with such vigor that sparks flew, and fake tears—which were really just electricity—rolled down her cheek. *Master is brilliant!* she scream-chirped. *His magnificent mind will take us to the heavens!*

As glad as I was for her approval, it was someone else's that I needed.

My eyes drifted back to the being I was already calling Slimes. He buzzed, slowly switching between his hard and squishy forms. The time between transitions decreased as he looked up at Maria. His beady little eyes conveyed meaning I had no hope of deciphering. Wait, was that . . . guilt? *Why would he—*

Maria cut my pondering off with a resigned sigh. "I can't believe I'm about to say this, but I don't hate it either."

"It's decided, then!" I clapped my hands together, sealing the name with sharp finality. "Welcome to the squad, Specialist Slimes!"

Maria's cheek twitched, and after a second's consideration, she whispered, "Specialist Slimes . . ."

I may not have been directly bonded to him, but I *was* connected to Maria. A tiny, almost-undetectable drop of chi split from her core and made its way into Slimes. I expected him to jiggle in response or something. Instead, he went semi-liquid, melting into the crook of her arm.

Before I could question the event, a loud bark drew my attention, and I spun to give the incoming crew a questioning look. Behind me, riding Pistachio like a tour bus, came the rest of the animals. Cinnamon was on the stoic lobster's head, striking a magnificent pose, arms crossed and gaze intense. At her rear, Borks's eyes were similarly impassioned. His tail wagged so fast that, if he were to pass by a field of dried cane, it might catch fire.

Perched tall and proud, Bill and Pelly surveyed their domain. They were almost two meters off the ground, which one might think made little sense. How could they be both atop Pistachio *and* that far off the ground? Well . . . it wasn't Pistachio their webbed feet rested upon.

Straddling Pistachio's back, a rear leg on either side of the giant sea snipper's carapace, Teddy refused to look me in the eye, his head hanging so low that the pelicans had to shuffle backward lest they fall off.

The longer I watched their plodding approach—Pistachio clearly going slow on purpose—the worse Teddy's shame grew. When he leaned down far enough that Borks could only maintain eye contact with me by leaning sideways past the bear's noggin, I finally decided to absolve them of their sins.

"Guys . . . I realize that I asked you to stay behind, but that was only so we didn't disturb Maria's meditation." I stepped to the side, and their faces lit up when they saw her. "She's awake, the raccoon is healed, and there's someone else you need to meet . . ."

Not needing any further introduction, the slime-shaped being leaped into Maria's palm, and she lobbed him forward. By the time he landed, he was crystalline, a pointed base lodging into the sand before Pistachio. "Hiiii! My name's Slimes!" He shimmered a little. "I'm a boy!"

If the squad's passage had been glacial before, now they were so frozen that they could have been encased by permafrost. They all stared downward, their senses and eyes exploring the multifaceted light of Maria's bonded familiar.

I was aware that Borks and Cinnamon had already known some sort of breakthrough occurred; the intensity of their gazes upon arrival had given it away. But even with this advantage over the others, the reality wedged in the ground before them seemed to hit their restart buttons.

Borks broke the stalemate first. Despite a distance of five meters, he tore a tunnel through space—and it was his fastest creation yet. He kicked off as a golden retriever, but by the time his head exited the portal before Slimes, his ears were long and floppy. The only one fast enough to join him was Cinnamon, who grabbed said ears for dear life, flattening himself against his back.

That's a new form, I thought. *I wonder why Borks chose to be a basset houn . . . oh.*

The question was immediately answered when he pressed a wet nose against one of Slimes's crystal faces. He huffed a breath that never seemed to end as he circled the pond spirit, sniffing him from every possible angle.

Cinnamon snuck some in, too, using what looked like kung fu movements to smell him. Though the rest didn't get so close as those two, they all joined the inspection, a series of snorts and appraising glances followed by animal sounds that all seemed to ask the same thing: *What* are *you?*

Specialist Slimes was all too happy to answer, his high-pitched words zooming out into the night. "I'm the tidal pond and I've like totally been kinda sapient for a while now but I didn't realllly have the ability to talk or think all that much! I know all of you, though! Because you've entered the tranquility of my waters, I know just how hard your shells and how soft your furs—*ooooh!*" He buzzed as a crystal, then wiggled as a slime. "Corporal Claws! I don't know what your new body feels like! Can I touch you? *Pleeeease?*"

Though Claws replied with a nonchalant chirp, I didn't miss the fur on her neck standing at attention. Slimes flattened, then launched himself at her. Even if I'd not noticed Claws's hidden attentiveness, her intentions were reflected in her eyes. But who was I to stop a little mischief?

"Thank you for the permission!" Slimes spat in a rush, "I really appreciate it and I'm hoping that if I better understand what you've become a bond of trust and friendship can develop between us and—"

The moment he made contact, lightning chi shot from Claws and into his gelatinous form. The rapid-fire sentence was replaced by a sound not dissimilar to a kettle boiling over.

"Corporal Claws!" Maria chided, attempting to rescue her slime familiar with a chi-covered hand . . . because she didn't yet know that Claws's empowered electricity would pierce right through the barrier. Paradoxically, the thing that saved Maria from joining the zapped club was the tiny little creature in her arms.

Claws might be a trickster, but she wouldn't hurt an innocent animal—especially the raccoon she had rescued not even an hour ago. She withdrew her electricity for only a fraction of a second, but that was all I needed. I grabbed her by the scruff and threw her skyward. She sailed into the sky like a rocket, then turned with ease, gracefully landing back on the sand.

She shrugged and let out a soft chirp. It was simply in her nature.

"Wow! That was a lot! Thank you!" Slimes shook himself free of Maria's grasp, not at all offended by the trap. "What percentage of your power did you just subject me to? It felt almost like my very being was vibrating, but I *know* you can do stronger than that!"

As their conversation continued, I zoned out, instead choosing to focus on the dire threat perched in Maria's arms. My worst fears had been confirmed. This creature, the raccoon, was only a baby. It had been rescued from the ocean, magically healed, and was now watching a sapient blob yap it up with a lightning otter. It . . . no, *he*, I corrected based on the anatomy displayed as he lounged against Maria, lifted a leg, and scratched the inside of his thigh.

I willed my awareness to sense his emotions—all I felt was curiosity, hunger, and boredom.

"You're hungry, huh?" I asked.

He blinked back at me, able to tell I was addressing him but unable to decipher my words.

Bill, who had been peering sideways at Slimes, hopped forward and opened his beak wide. There were three baby fish in his pouch, and I hoped, *prayed*, that an open mouth with the ability to swallow the raccoon whole would finally give it some pause.

Instead, the little devil leaped directly inside. Using the yellow pouch as a hammock, he consumed the fishy morsels with gusto, devouring one before dual-wielding the last two as he took bite after bite.

It was funny enough to make me blow air from my nose, but not funny enough to stop a sigh from escaping after it.

"We're in for it when this little trash panda awakens."

CHAPTER TWENTY-NINE

Thieving Little Paws

Almost an hour later, the scents of beef tallow, garlic, and a few other herbs and spices wafted up from my barbecue. The delicious smell of cooking fish was under every subtle note that hit my nose, a foundation that supported the others. I hadn't expected it, but the lightning-infused shore fish covering the hot plate before me smelled different than usual. It was a hint of freshness, something hard to put into words unless you experienced it.

Peter was at my side, plating up and covering a dozen or so lightning-infused cichlids that, because of their size, had already cooked through. Behind us, multiple bonfires were blazing. Rocky rested in between all of them, feeding tiny amounts of volcanic chi into their centers, the marble-sized sources of heat he provided more than enough to make them roar.

Atop each fire, brand-new trays sat, specially made lids trapping steam to cook the fish within. Each little oven contained a combination of ingredients, whose different scents and flavors would permeate the meal to come.

Despite how exciting it was to have a crab as a fuel source, I couldn't tear my eyes away from the hot plate before me. Bubbles of golden fat rose from underneath each fish fillet, popping before being immediately replaced by more of their kind. The never-ending stream hypnotized me.

"Ozone," Peter said.

"Sorry?" I asked, having absolutely no clue what he was talking about.

"The fresh smell you're trying to identify. It's hard to tell because of the . . . well, everything going on. The fish has a hint of ozone compared to regular shore fish."

"Ohhh! You're right!" I clapped him on the shoulder. "I should have asked you immediately. What's your cooking skill now?"

He leaned close with a borderline-wicked smile. "Ninety-six."

"Hot damn, Peter! You might be the first to hit—" I cut myself off, clearing my throat and looking around when I realized how loud I'd been. "You might be the first to hit a certain milestone," I continued in a whisper.

"Fischerrrr! Peterrrr!" came a beautiful voice.

I turned, already sensing Maria's position as she sprinted up from the beach. There was something else there, too, and before I could sense it with my chi, I saw it with my eyes.

"Holy frack," Peter said.

"My thoughts exactly . . ."

It wasn't often that I experienced the childlike wonder of coming across a new species. Maria held just such a prize high overhead, its scales reflecting the light of numerous fires as she brought it closer. Behind her, the rest of them—cultivators and regular humans alike—followed. With the fish Maria had caught, we had all the food we needed.

With how well lit the scene was, I could clearly see the fish's features. For the most part, it was your standard pelagic species. Long, silvery, and with a forked tail that indicated speed and agility, this creature was a hunter. Where its appearance differed, however, were several long, threadlike fins growing from underneath its body, right below the gills.

My eyes were drawn in, and words occupied my vision.

Mature Lightning-Infused Threadfin Salmon
Fleeting
Known for its boneless fillets that are rumored to boost vitality when cooked and eaten, this fish has been temporarily infused with lightning to celebrate the ascension of an elemental. Infused creatures have their chi content significantly increased for three hours.

"Wowwwwwwww!" Slimes called as I dismissed the message, his high-pitched voice unmistakable. "It's so big and so full of chi and probably so tasty that I can't wait to have a taste of—Oh! I'm tired. Goodniiiight!" Before the slime could finish singing the last word, he started sinking into the shoulder he sat on. There one moment and gone the next, his presence settled within Maria's core.

Her face was more than a little conflicted as she skidded to a stop, the fish still raised high above her. She furrowed her brow and looked down at her abdomen.

"You, uhhhh . . ." I trailed off, searching for the words. "Are you okay?"

"Yeah, it's just . . ." She shook herself. "That was unexpected."

"How did that feel?" Peter asked. "Because it looked horrific."

I barked a laugh. So did Maria. "Yeahhh, it didn't feel as bad as it probably seemed. I just felt his chi shoot down my torso, then into my core. I guess he can't come out for very long? Little fella seems exhausted."

"Thank the rigid rudder of Tyche," Danny said, stoking a bonfire. "I'm not sure I could listen to him go on for much longer. If I hear 'I'm a boy' one more time, I might walk into the ocean and never return."

"Hey!" Maria kicked sand at the former quartermaster. "He hasn't been able to speak for long! Slimes is just making up for lost time!"

"Maybe I'm just extra irritable from having to listen to Keith's constant moaning." Danny, grinning ear to ear, shot a taunting look at the former royal, then continued in a nasal voice, "*Wahhh, I grew up rich. Life in a castle was sooo hard, and my family were all royal pricks that—*"

Snap.

Fwoom!

Trent, who was sitting next to Keith on a wooden bench, had snapped his fingers. A torrent of flames exploded from the fire Danny was tending, singeing his beard, clothes, and, worst of all, his pride.

He stood to his full height and stomped over, staring down at his attacker for a long moment . . . then burst into laughter. "Fair play. Suppose I deserved that one."

"You're lucky he held back," Maria added. "You might not have any hair left if he hit you with the flames I've seen him unleash."

Trent, who'd been all scowls and conflicted emotions for as long as I'd known him, couldn't contain his laugh. I soaked it in, delighting in the effect companionship, humor, and the promise of food had on his demeanor.

Maybe anime was right all along—even the tallest of walls could be broken down with the power of friendship.

"So," Maria said, holding her prized threadfin so close to my face that it took up most of my vision. "Should we cook this bad boy? I'm guessing 'boosted vitality' means more chi if its cooked, but do we have time? The rest of the food is almost done . . ."

"It is, yeah. I think everyone should be here with the salads and stuff at any moment."

She frowned. "I know we won't let it go to waste, but I was hoping we could eat it as part of the feast . . ."

"Lucky for you, your husband-to-be is as prepared as he is clever and handsome."

"And humble, right?"

"That goes without saying."

She nodded sagely. "Well, then, my humble, clever, and handsome husband-to-be, what have you prepared for this catch? How do you suggest we cook it all in time?"

I held my hands high overhead, pausing there for dramatic effect. After a sufficient amount of time had passed, I started swirling my arms as if moving chi. Finally, I clapped twice, the sharp sound echoing off the nearby headland. "Pot!" I yelled. "Big pot!"

Maria gave me a curious look, and when nothing happened, she glanced around. "Uhhh, I'm not sure what kind of spell you were trying to cast, but I don't think it worked."

"Of course it did." I pointed directly up. "Big pot."

In the sky high above, held aloft by the white wings of an oceanic bird, a *giant* pot descended. Bill let go, and with ease only possible because of my enhanced body, I caught the mass of crafted metal. It was half as tall and wide as I was, and as I set it down on the ground, I received a gift of the greatest value: the look on Maria's face. Somewhere between outraged and impressed—with a hint of disgust thrown in for good measure—it was a visage all men dreamed of drawing from their significant others when they pulled off something ridiculous.

"Fischer . . ."

"Yes, darling?"

"Did you have Bill carrying that overhead for this exact moment?"

"What? Don't be absurd." I shot her a sidelong smirk. "I had Bill and Pelly carry *all* the new cooking equipment onto the headland. It was for storage reasons, and definitely *not* so that I could pretend to summon any cookware we needed, like I am some kind of red-haired house witch. And while we're on the topic of things I definitely *didn't* do, I absolutely did not tell Private Pelly to make it rain sweet treats from up high if no one requested anything."

Liar, Pelly honked from above, a basket filled with said sweet treats clutched in her flippers.

Maria did her best to stare into my soul. "You have way too much time on your hands."

"Agreed, but that's not important right now. We need to cut up and crumb this fish of yours. If we fill the pot with oil, we'll be able to cook it in a single batch!"

"All right. Let's do it!" She looked down at her abdomen. "It's a shame about Slimes, though. I wanted everyone to meet him."

"Yeahhh. We'll have to settle for introducing our little raccoon friend."

"I guess so. Are you still sure you don't want to give him chi-filled food yet?"

"I am one thousand percent sure. The last thing we need is two sapient beings popping up at once. The fact that the fish are lightning infused also scares me—who knows what effect it could have?" I sighed, shaking my head. "Knowing my luck, it'll happen within a couple weeks anyway. As long as we have a few days between them, I'll count it as a wi—"

A burst of chi swelled behind me, and I whirled on the spot. The sight that met me made my blood turn to ice.

The tray atop the barbecue, the one containing the cooked cichlids, sat askew. Its lid had been silently opened, the revealed gap just large enough for two thieving little paws to enter. Next to the crime scene, perched on his back haunches with a fish raised to his mouth, the raccoon took another bite of the lightning-infused cichlid he'd yoinked.

Despite not yet swallowing his second chomp, the fish's chi already suffused his furry little body, forging a path toward the spot where a core would form.

In my peripheral vision, I could see the approach of at least a dozen people, their arms laden with trays and bowls. Sharon, Maria's mother, called something. I didn't hear it; I only had moments to avert disaster.

Reaching forward, I grabbed for my power, willing to try anything. I had to stop the thieving little bastard from ascending via lightning-infused essence. His eyes flicked to me with unnatural speed, the movement making my senses flare, and I knew it was too late. The chi was already within him.

Still moving too fast for a regular raccoon, he hopped backward and swallowed. Electricity exploded from his body, striking sand, sky, and everything in between.

CHAPTER THIRTY

Love of the Game

It was a beautiful night on the shores of Tropica. There wasn't a cloud in the sky, the stars above shone bright, and I could see the well-lit faces of dozens of my closest friends. Unfortunately, the reason for their faces being so well lit was a godsdamned raccoon emitting more lightning bolts than a tropical thunderstorm.

My will was still pushed to its limit, and I wasn't sure that I could respond in time to shield everyone. Thankfully, my friends were ready.

Roger sliced forward like a blade, his chi prepared to cut through any bolts approaching the unascended. Deklan and Dom threw shields up in every direction, protecting anyone that was too far for Roger to defend. But none of their efforts were necessary.

Corporal Claws, the former maiden of the forest and current conqueror of the elements, appeared in a flash. She drew the currents into herself, acting as a lightning rod that thirsted for every last watt. Even with my senses somewhat dulled from overuse, I could feel something offered to the raccoon's forming core in exchange for the essence Claws took. My favorite otter—though I was seriously starting to second-guess that title—halted the stream. She chirped a single time, the question clear. The raccoon, of his own volition and somehow possessing enough intelligence to reply, nodded.

The damned thing consented.

The flow resumed, lightning swapped for whatever Claws was offering. It stabilized the raccoon's cultivation in a matter of seconds. The electricity stopped flowing out, instead condensing into a smaller and smaller ball. There, as a constantly shifting sphere, I felt his chi.

The only other time I had sensed the quality of someone's before they ascended was George and Geraldine. Their essence was that of the deep abyss, which I'd assumed was only possible because they followed the teachings of an ancient manual. It had taken them months to get to that point.

The raccoon, only weeks old, had accomplished the same. Worse, the damn thing's chi felt *exactly* like Corporal Claws's. What had she done?

Unable to stop the transformation, I was forced to wait it out and hope for the best. With each pulse of power—each expansion of the raccoon's core—my hope dwindled. If it kept expanding . . .

I knew what that meant, and the thought was terrifying.

Judging by the look on Roger's face, he was also cursed by knowledge. He'd not had a chance to fully comprehend what Claws had become, but as his gaze flicked between her and the raccoon, he made the same expression as the time Claws had left two pockets' worth of sand in his hat—disappointment, anger, and acceptance. He, too, could do nothing to stop this ascension.

The raccoon also appeared to be having a terrible day; his bugged-out eyes were set in a gray-furred visage of regret and dissociation.

Uncaring of the despair afflicting all of us, Claws poured more of herself in. Despite the ridiculous look on the raccoon's face, his body drank greedily. The newly formed core grew and grew, slowly taking over the rest of his tiny physique.

Belatedly, I wondered if I should be worried about his health. Claws wouldn't actually put the thing at risk . . . right? She must have heard the unvoiced question through our bond, because she turned my way and gave me a grin that bordered on wicked.

Despite how important her task was to her, she'd taken a moment to reassure me. It filled my heart with love for my troublesome otter pal. Finally, arguably too late, I chose to accept the advancement. There was nothing I could do, so getting worked up over it was a waste of time.

The raccoon's core flexed to the limits of his body. It warped, prepared to snap into place, and . . . paused. It froze there for a long moment, then started to shrink, forming an orb as it reduced in size. Claws had stopped feeding it power.

"Poseidon's girthy conch," I swore. "I was so worried you were about to turn an adolescent creature into an elemental, Claws. Don't tease me like that."

I let out a ragged sigh, adrenaline still lingering in my veins. Roger looked up at the sky and pressed his palms together, thanking the departed gods. Maria . . . grimaced? And Corporal Claws, one of her devious little paws touching the raccoon's back, started to cackle.

Wait, what is she—

Lightning exploded from her, slamming into the raccoon. His core shook, then engulfed his entire form.

"Claws!" I yelled. "You furry fu—"

Boooom!

The ground thumped and my legs almost buckled.

A sound akin to a thousand chirping birds came from the raccoon as he stood on his haunches. When he locked eyes with me, his stare no longer held the weight of existential dread. I could already tell from his chi, but that gaze only solidified my assumption. This creature was not at all connected to me. Like Rocky was bonded to Snips, this poor thing was bound to Claws.

He didn't feel sorry for himself. The lightning-covered little shit was smiling, tapping the tips of his fingers together as what was likely some kind of scheme formed in his gray matter. On second thought, he didn't even have gray matter; his body was just like Claws's—made of electricity.

I braced myself as he stood on his tippy toes, stretched his forepaws toward the sky, and . . . yawned. He spun on the spot, making a little circle in the sand. I let out another sigh as he curled into a ball and closed his eyes.

Roger rubbed his face. "By Triton's chapped cheeks. Thank the gods it fell asleep. We have at least until it wakes up to—"

The raccoon's eyes slammed back open, and without any warning, he rolled along the sand at incredible speed. Power roiled from him, and I realized his will was completely different from Corporal Claws's. Her heart desired mischief and chaos; anything else was either a bonus or not important enough to consider. The raccoon's heart, though notably unique, wasn't at all surprising. He was a cartoonish embodiment of his heredity, the epitome of everything I'd feared would become of a raccoon upon ascension.

He was a *thief.*

Some larcenists, like the child who steals half-rotten fruit from a market, are in it for need. Without food, they would starve. Other thieves, such as an anarchistic college student that has read one too many manifestos, do it out of spite and rage. The latter wasn't as sympathetic as the former, but it's easy to justify the small-scale theft of a chocolate bar from a billion-dollar corporation. It was low stakes, too. The worst you'd get back on Earth was a slap on the wrist unless you went overboard with the five-finger discounts.

The raccoon was neither of these examples.

He was more akin to a seasoned cutpurse from your standard fantasy novel. Far beyond the early years of being just as likely to get caught as they were to get away with the coin, this professional no longer did it to survive. They possessed a cache of wealth that could sustain them for the rest of their life. Yet despite the risks, they persisted, stealing larger and larger amounts of gold—more than they could ever spend. Rather than deter them, these rising stakes only served to excite.

The raccoon, just like the metaphorical cutpurse, was in it for the love of the game.

Sand tore up in his wake as he zoomed toward us in a forward roll. Even with my sluggish senses, I could tell what his goal was. Maria, too, accurately deduced his passage. She stepped to the side, preparing to turn and run for the object he wanted to steal. Her speed might have been enough, too. But this wasn't a fair fight.

Corporal Claws connected with the raccoon in an instant, and their cores aligned. The stream of electricity going from one to the other burned like white fire, and as they remained paired, his eyes turned bright blue. The lightning coming from his tail doubled, tripled, doubled again—as did his speed.

I reached out toward Claws via our own connection, begging her to stop. This was going too far. In response, a false floor fell away within her. As I felt the emotions on the other side—her *true* emotions—my heart sank. Claws was even more chaotic than she'd led me to believe. She had hidden it from me, building a barrier to hide the depths of her degeneracy.

I'd thought she wouldn't hurt others. I'd been led to believe that, though she loved chaos, she could be bargained with. But there was no reasoning with her now.

Their connection remained solid, evermore electricity flowing into her thieving companion.

For what felt like the tenth time today, there was nothing I could do to help. Thankfully, others weren't so afflicted. Roger had moved the second the raccoon's core started its funny business. So had Trent, who'd rushed to defend the target. Both men arrived at either side of Maria, one shooting razor-sharp blades, the other a column of foundation-melting fire.

Maybe they didn't know that their chi wouldn't help. Or maybe they did, and they were willing to try anyway. Deklan and Dom jumped in, too, shielding Maria and, likely just as important to them, the thing the raccoon had been racing toward this entire time—the giant fish.

It was no good, though. The elemental chi would tear right through any defenses.

Power flared, and someone I'd completely forgotten about appeared. As a light-pink blob oozed from Maria's chest and flung himself out into the raccoon's path, I dared to hope.

Slimes's will was like iron, his resolve unwavering. He turned crystalline. With every fiber of his being, he *knew* that he could not only stop the raccoon in its tracks but also send it flying. I focused, gathering what little wits I possessed to watch how the familiar was going to do it. He shifted back into a slime. What hidden ability did he possess?

"Hiii!" he said, too fast for anyone but cultivators to comprehend. "I'm a boy and I can't let you do that, friend! My master is quite excited to try that fish, and I must insist that you— *Blegh!*"

The raccoon hit Slimes like a 2003 Holden Commodore going double the speed limit and driven by a bloke named Dazza. To my enhanced awareness, it was like watching one of those slow-motion videos where a balloon full of water smacks someone in the head but doesn't break.

Slimes's entire body wrapped around the raccoon, stretching, *stretching*, and then stretching some more. Only when his elasticity was at an end did all the potential energy get unleashed, and Slimes was ejected back toward Maria's chest with a comical *boing*.

As the overconfident and under-delivering familiar retook his place within Maria's core, there was no one left between her and the thief. Claws's apprentice had his forelimbs extended, each of his little fingers ready to clutch at and yoink the fish in passing. His eyes bulged with power and knowledge, and his tiny teeth crawled with electricity—making him look absolutely insane.

Short of a divine intervention, there was nobody that could save Maria's prize, which should have filled my heart with regret. Instead, I grinned.

Watch this, Claws, I thought. *You're not the only one keeping secrets.*

An expression mirroring my own appeared on Maria's face as she pivoted on the ball of her foot, turning, but not in the direction that she'd led the raccoon to believe. It was *her* speed that stunned everyone now, her physical prowess even more developed than she had let anyone other than me know. Because of our spiritual bond, I knew *exactly* how strong she was.

Lithe muscles bunched underneath marble-smooth skin as she drew her leg back. There was a moment of hesitation, Maria reconsidering if just because she *could* use full power, she *should.* Of all the beings to reassure her, Claws trilled to get her attention. With a lecherous smirk and a tiny little nod, she approved. No longer possessing reservations, Maria's foot was a blur as she struck.

Because I'd overextended and used up too much of my focus, I wasn't able to see the moment of impact with the exquisite detail I desired. Light flared like a miniature sun as Maria's limb collided with the literal ball of lightning. The next thing I knew, a line of dirt and sand erupted into the sky. Water exploded everywhere as the raccoon-turned-football crossed the river, then the gritty line returned as he continued southward. I reached for every ounce of will I had left, wanting, *needing*, to witness it.

I caught but a glimpse of Claws's apprentice as he veered off the side of the closest mountain, the slanted surface a ramp from which the raccoon launched. Chittering with pure glee, Corporal Claws shot off after him, turning to give us a wave goodbye and a brilliant smile. Ever the agent of chaos, she wasn't overly invested in who came out on top.

She, too, was in it for the love of the game.

I rubbed my eyes and shook my head, both legs wobbling beneath me. "I . . ." My words trailed off as I stumbled and barely remained upright—reaching for my will had been a mistake.

"What is it?" Maria appeared at my side. She could feel the disappointment deep within me. Combined with my waning strength, it caused a look of sheer worry to cross her face.

"The raccoon . . ." I cleared my throat and settled my weight on Maria's reliable shoulders. "I didn't . . ."

I was falling now, and Maria supported my torso, holding up my bulk. "What didn't you do? Should I chase after it?"

"I think it's too late . . ."

"It's not. Let me know what it is, and I'll handle it."

I smiled at her and gave a single shake of my head, continuing in a raspy voice, "Just don't do it without me . . ."

"Do *what*?" She caressed my cheek. "You're making no sense, love. What did you forget?"

"Didn't get a chance to—" I coughed, my vision going dark at the edges.

"Take your time. I'm here."

I gathered my strength. With a ragged breath, I forced out the cause of my disappointment. "Didn't . . . get a chance to *name* him."

The last thing I saw before unconsciousness took me was the compassion draining from Maria's face, replaced by a flat, unimpressed glare.

CHAPTER THIRTY-ONE

Unilateral and Never-Ending

The sun that rose over the horizon to greet me was the entirely wrong color. *Blue*, I mused. *Odd.* It came from the wrong direction, too, peeking its head over the southern mountains. I didn't let either of these facts bother me, though. Every morning that I woke up in Tropica was something to be celebrated.

Gratitude, after all, was the key to happiness, and it served the world around me to be as happy as—*Neptune's glistening shaft!* I ducked as the godsdamned *sun* shot directly toward me, shrinking and rolling over the ocean like a cracked-out Sonic the Hedgehog. Though I stood, my back thumped into something solid, soft, cold, and . . .

I opened my eyes, finding a sky that was indicative of anything but a sunrise.

"Neptune's glistening *what*?" Theo asked, his head blocking out the stars above. He raised an eyebrow and glanced to the side. "Maria, I'm not one to question what people do in their premarital bed, but just what do you two get up to when the lights—"

My senses, which were evidently still dull, were plenty aware enough to catch the deadly threat of Roger's chi.

"Kidding, kidding, sorry!" Theo yelped, backing away with his hands raised.

I considered doubling down on the bit but decided against it—he might actually kill me with how weak I felt. Besides, Maria had already experienced a lot today. As if I could summon her by thought alone, she appeared above me, her hair swaying side to side as she smiled. She was even more beautiful than the dreamscape sunrise from only moments ago.

"Hi," she said.

"H—"

"Hiiiiii!" a certain familiar interrupted, jiggling over Maria's shoulder.

"Wassup, Slimes. I'm surprised you're already back in action after Rocky Two hit you for six."

Maria's smile vanished, and she covered her companion's mouth before he could respond. "No. You are *not* calling the raccoon Rocky Two."

"Awww, c'mon! Rocky is the perfect name for a raccoon, but we already have Rocky One!"

"And he's more than enough. I forbid it." She lowered her hand and helped me to my feet. "Besides, Claws probably has a name picked out already."

"You never let me have any fun."

"Does it make you feel better to know that she'll probably pick a name as bad as the ones you choose?"

"Yes, actually. That *does* make me feel better."

"Good." A dangerous gleam entered her eyes. "Because as happy as I am that you're awake, we still need to discuss you teasing me before you passed out . . ."

I took a step back, pressing a finger to one temple. "I'd love to chat about that, but my head, you see—it's very, uhhh, bruised. And sore. Did I say bruised already? I think my brain might be scrambled."

She followed, denying my attempted retreat. "See, that's really weird, because we're connected, you and I." She took another step, getting so close that I could feel the heat of her breath. "And given that I know you better in some ways than I know myself . . . I know that you're *full of shit*!"

Expecting the attack, I slid to the side of her well-placed shove—which left me right in the path of her roundhouse kick. It hit me on the shoulder and I sprawled in the sand.

Yeahhh! Cinnamon screamed from somewhere to my right as the kick landed—she'd clearly shown Maria that move. *Get him!*

"Oh-ho!" I said, hopping back to my feet. "A surprise attack, is it? You dare challenge the lord of these lands, junior?"

Her response was concise—she threw a left jab right at my face.

"Hey! No aiming for the moneymaker!"

"What's mine is *yours!*" She launched a right hook this time.

"That makes no sense!"

"Good! Now you know how we all feel *every. Time. You. Open. Your. Mouth!*" The last six words were each punctuated with a strike, and I danced backward across the sand, dodging.

Despite what we were saying—and the fact that Maria just tried to hit me with a haymaker—a grin split both of our faces. A few minutes later, our fake fight had devolved into a budget Brazilian jiujitsu demonstration. We both froze as someone came to a stop beside us.

Sharon's face held a smile that was the exact opposite of the scowl her husband was leveling our way. "The food is almost ready, you two. Why don't you save your fighting for later? Perhaps when the lights are out?"

It had been an extremely long day, filled with ridiculous situations and multiple breakthroughs. I'd passed out more than once, which was a new record for me. Through all that, Sharon's comments had the most visceral effect on my ability to function. The pang of embarrassment that washed through me was reflected in Maria, but even stronger.

Our connection, usually an endless source of insight into the one we loved most, turned on us.

Our embarrassment combined, grew, and changed. It started as a tiny handful of snow and swiftly became an avalanche that neither of us could control. My face flushed beet red, as did Maria's. We just . . . stood there, stuck in a mortifying death loop.

"Get a hold of yourself, Fischer," came a voice that was part gravel, part disappointment. "It's pathetic." Roger's deadly aura washed over us. It sliced through my spiraling thoughts like a sword would a sapling. "And *you* . . ." He turned on Sharon. "That had him on the ropes. Well done."

"Hey! Why does Sharon get a pass? That was her doing!"

"My wife is infallible, Fischer, as am I to her. You could learn a thing or two from our decades of marriage."

"Agreed." Sharon gave him a full-bodied side hug, rubbing the side of her head against him in adoration. "Take notes, youngins."

"Maria . . ."

"Yes, Fischer?"

"What the frack was that?"

"I don't know, but I'm pretty sure we lost . . ."

"You did," Sharon said. "Enough of that, though—dinner really is almost ready."

I could tell she was right just from the smells and sounds assaulting me. I opened my awareness to them, happy for the distraction. A soft hiss came from the giant pan, and it was like music to my ears, the sound a result of tiny bubbles within. Multiple scents drifted around us. Most prominent of all were the fish and the beef tallow it fried in. Wisps of various seasonings wafted along underneath, heightening everything.

An odd source of chi bloomed below the pot, drawing my attention.

Rocky. The ornamental cracks decorating his shell glowed a deep red. His volcanic aspect was immediately recognizable now that I focused on it, but there was something else there, too. It was coming from within the recently genteel crab, and rather than a kind of power, it seemed like a lack thereof—a resolute desire to shield. I used it as an anchor to pull my mind closer. He was projecting a barrier from his mouth, pushing his chi out to protect . . .

When I saw it, my stare flattened.

"How is he doing that?" Maria asked, pointing at the object Rocky was expending a great deal of energy toward. It was a godsdamned cigarette, of course. He was creating a bubble of safety within his otherwise-volcanic heat to ensure it didn't burn away.

Of all the things to meditate with . . . I thought, shaking my head.

Snips, entirely unbothered by his method of attempted advancement, blew proud bubbles, her lone eye sparkling as it reflected his red glow.

I sent my feelings toward Maria, answering her question more succinctly than words ever could.

"Ohhh!" she said.

"Ohhhhh!" her familiar echoed.

Slimes can hear the thoughts I send her way, I mused internally. *I'll have to keep that in min—*

"I caaaaan!" he confirmed, gleeful.

"Thanks. I hate it."

Maria's beautiful laugh rolled out over the sands. "That one was your fault. I heard that thought, so he did, too."

"You can't shield your own thoughts?"

Maria looked at me like I'd just asked the stupidest question she'd ever heard. "That might be the stupidest question I've ever heard."

I frowned at her selection of words, which only made her laugh return with even more vigor. Seeing my confusion, she intertwined the fingers of her right hand with those of my left.

"I can still hear your thoughts, Fischer. Maybe your brain really is scrambled."

I rubbed my temples, willing the cotton wool within my head to disappear. "I reckon I'll feel better tomorrow. Just need to sleep it off."

"Perfect!" called Peter, lifting the biggest fryer strainer I'd ever seen. "You can go to bed after the *feast*!" With one deft scoop, he collected every bit of now-golden fish from the oil. Beef tallow flowed from the chunks, slowing to a steady drip within seconds. Peter held them there, extending his will and chi into the food. I almost extended tendrils toward it, curious what he was doing, but caught myself.

Instead, I chose to focus on the outside world. There was plenty to look at. While I'd been passed out, helpers had arrived with what I requested earlier—the items that Tropica's woodworkers had been toiling over. The trove of furniture currently lining the sands proved just how busy they'd been.

Dozens and dozens of wooden tables, their angled legs elegant yet thick enough that they might last decades without maintenance. The tabletops were single slabs with a varnish-like sheen that enhanced their beautiful grains. Twice as many long benches sat beneath them, constructed of the same materials and ready to be used.

There were seats for all of them—literally every cultivator, human, and animal pal in Tropica. When I started imagining the feast and all of their happy faces, Maria squeezed my hand, telling me she was just as excited.

And yet, despite all these distractions, Peter's will was like a magnet for my senses. I furrowed my brow, taking slow, conscious breaths in an attempt at mindfulness.

"Let us help," Maria whispered, leaning against my arm and mentally pushing something my way. Unable to contain my curiosity at her use of *us*, I glanced at her. She just smiled back.

I suppose it's better than getting sucked in by Peter's will and passing out again, I thought, an almost-physical connection forming between us.

It iiiiiis better! Slimes agreed from within *my* head. *Some would say much better, in fact! The best, even! I—*

Maria sent a mental chiding her familiar's way.

Sorrrr*yyyyy* . . . He trailed off, reminding me of Rocky's voice each time Snips launched him clear over the horizon.

With that metaphorical distance came peace. Slimes, despite dwelling in Maria's core, shielded me from the sledgehammer that was Peter's will. I could still see him, but without the weight of his will drawing me in, I had more room to focus on the sensations of my body. It was . . .

"Wonderful, isn't it?" Maria asked. "He can shield me from the System entirely, and any other unwanted intrusions."

"Where do I get one?"

A pulse of joy came from Slimes, which made both Maria and me smile.

"I'm sure he'd be happy to assist whenever needed."

Yeeees! came a faint yell—basically a scream—from far away.

"Appreciate it, Slimes." I nodded toward Peter, who was absolutely surrounded by the world's chi. "Looks like he's gonna succeed."

"It does, doesn't it?" Maria said. "Do you regret not being able to take part?"

I shook my head, delighting in the way my core resonated with that truth. "Not even a bit. I'm the leader, right? I have to be okay with delegating tasks. Besides, Peter is as capable as they come."

The world agreed. Its essence exploded forward, rushing into the still-cooling fish. They became too bright to look at, their crispy skins shining with overwhelming incandescence. From there, the chi spread, washing over the other food we'd cooked earlier. It should have happened in less than a second, only an instant needed for the transformation to finish, but . . . something was wrong. I sent a strand of awareness out, which Slimes let pass through his protective barrier.

Lightning chi, I realized. The flesh was partially suffused with an aspect, so the world's essence couldn't take hold. There was enough to transform a portion of the different dishes. Or the entirety of one. But the chi lacked intelligent thought. It slammed its head against every dish equally, gaining zero ground.

Again, I considered intervening, but let it go. Even if doing so didn't put me in any danger, I still would have allowed Peter's attempt to fail. Defeat was sometimes the best lesson one could receive, and it would only stunt everyone's growth if I was always there to brute-force whatever task they were trying to undertake.

I felt something ping my noggin, only the faintest of touches that had a different feel to it than the System's usual incessance.

Several levels in leadership, came Slimes's voice in my head. *Didn't want to block them without your consent.*

"You have my unilateral and never-ending permission to keep them from me," I replied, knowing I could always just check later if needed.

Okaaaay!

Despite Peter's impending failure, a soft smile curled my lip. I was content with my choice. If it meant he could one day grow, letting Peter succeed or fail on his own was the kindest thing I could do for him. And kindness aside, it was what a *leader* would do, which, for better or worse, I'd become.

But not everyone agreed. Twin roots burst from the ground to either side of us, climbing toward the sky and forming trees with incredible speed. Evidently, Lieutenant Colonel Lemony Thicket and her yet-unnamed tree-spirit pal held no such reservations about helping out. They poured pure essence across the sand—the world's chi latched on.

Light shone from everywhere all at once, and the transformation began.

CHAPTER THIRTY-TWO

Fishy Goodness

As the world turned white, Maria let go of my hand. Her arms went around my torso, I rested a palm on her lower back, and together, we faced the light. As expected, the transformation was over in a moment.

All the food had moved. Different fishes, sides, and salads were presented on serving trays atop the lines of tables, spread evenly for easy access by all those that would soon arrive. I took a step forward, then remembered something.

"Oh!" I felt at my pocket in search of what I'd prepared earlier. When I found the parcel right where I left it, I grinned to myself and withdrew it, walking over to the closest fire.

Maria trailed me, her curiosity burgeoning across our connection as I peeled back thin sheets to reveal the cuts of fish within. "Uhhhh, Fischer?"

From my other pocket, I removed some thin sticks of bamboo. "What's up?"

"Why did you have bits of raw fish in your pocket, and where in Hestia's hearth did you find silver leaves to wrap it in?"

I laughed as I skewered the first bit of fish. "I thought we should try drying some fish out, and I didn't start cooking it in case it got swept up in Peter's transformation—I want it to be edible later, not today."

"And the silver leaf . . . ?"

"It's not actually silver, though I get why you'd think so." I balled up the foil contaminated by raw fish and threw it into the fire, then produced a fresh sheet I'd folded to fit in my back pocket. "I had the smiths make it. We called this aluminium foil where I come from—or *aluminum* foil if you're American." I gave an exaggerated shiver. "And you guys call *me* heretical. The things that country has done to the English language . . ."

Knowing all too well that engaging with my commentary would only lead to regret, Maria plucked the thin sheet from my hands. "Wow. I didn't know you could make metal so thin . . ."

"Me either! Those smiths have seriously been producing magic while I've been busy, uh . . . leading?"

"Yes, dear." She rolled her eyes playfully and patted me on the shoulder. "Come on, oh *great leader of these lands*. Let's go look at the food that *wasn't* stored in your pocket for safekeeping . . ."

I'd finished skewering all the fish, so I pressed the meatless ends into the sand, intent on letting them cook and dehydrate as slowly as possible. We strode over to the feast, and as I gazed down at it, one of my brows rose of its own accord.

Everything had an almost too-perfect look to it, like plastic props for use in a photo shoot. But the scents wafting over us told the truth of the matter: the food smelled *delicious.* Right in the center of the table, piled up high and containing so much chi that it glowed to my senses, was Maria's fish, which Peter had cooked.

Every single part of it called out to me, and it was a genuine struggle to stop myself from walking forward and biting into one of the no-doubt delightful little chunks that all but *begged* me to do so. Thankfully, the guests were almost here. Following the light and already knowing what it meant, most of Tropica arrived on foot. The cultivators came first, of course, but the yet unascended weren't far behind.

The emotions coming from them were a solid wall of positivity that slammed into my core. I bathed it in, experiencing as much of it as I could. I had worried that when Lemon and her tree bro added their chi, the lightning essence might get amplified too much. I instinctively knew that a little would be fine, but what about a lot? The last thing Tropica needed was a bunch of Claws-like cultivators running around.

Thankfully, Lemon and tree bro's addition of pure chi had done the opposite—they had neutralized the lightning aspect almost entirely. Everyone, human and cultivator alike, could eat to their heart's content.

The last of them arrived, and their hunger started to swell, so I got Peter's attention with a nod. He raised an eyebrow, asking if I was sure.

"All you, mate," I whispered. "This is your success."

A tiny little root shot from the ground and whipped me on the butt.

"Yes, Lemon. I know we couldn't have done it without you. How do you always arrive at the perfect moment?"

Her canopy swayed with mirth. *I see everything.* To illustrate her point, hundreds of tiny roots sprouted, all waving at me.

"Hang on . . ." I gave her a conspiratorial look. "Have you been watching me?

She nodded her *entire* trunk up and down so hard that a normal tree would have uprooted itself.

As suspicious as humanly possible, I leaned closer and shielded my mouth with one hand, then stage-whispered, "Not in front of everyone, Lemon. Our forbidden love must remain discreet—for now."

"Do I need to be worried?" Maria asked, raising an eyebrow as I blew Lemon a kiss, which she caught with a branch and hugged tight to her chest.

"I'm just teasing. You're all I ever want or nee . . . actually, *if* Lemon works out how to dispense lemonade directly from her fruit . . . you could be in trouble. Or if she can learn to shoot lasers. That'd be super neat."

"Don't give her any ideas. She might do it even if you're joking."

"Uhhh, yeah, *joking* . . ." I shot Lemon a wink, which earned me a whap on the upper arm from Maria.

Peter was describing each of the fish dishes now, along with the accompanying ingredients they'd been seasoned with. He was doing a wonderful job; I had no idea he was so apt at public speaking. There was a shift in the air as Peter reached the lightning-infused threadfin salmon that Maria had caught. At first it was gradual, but then it came all at once, and their hunger grew to a fever pitch.

"I wanted to preserve the flavor of the fish," Peter said, his voice resonating against the sand. "So the only seasonings you should be able to taste are beef tallow and mild herbs and spices. I'd suggest having it by itself, then slowly introducing more flavors if you feel comfortable doing so. The slices of lemon would be a good start." He nodded at Lemon in recognition, who shook with delight, pulled a limb back, and launched a yellow blur his way.

"Thank you," Peter said, pocketing the fruit. "Now, after the citrus, there are a number of other condiments and reductions that I believe will pair well with it . . ."

"When did he get so good at showmanship?" I whispered to Maria as Peter continued.

"Shhhh!" Her eyes sparkled with mischief as she stared up into mine. "It's been *forever* since I've heard someone talk that's *this* charming."

Even though I knew she was joking, she offset the insult with a pulse of love through our connection, ensuring her words delivered no sting. I narrowed my gaze but failed to hide the grin that tugged at the corner of my lip.

"And that concludes my impromptu speech," Peter said, shooting a glare at Danny when his burly friend tried to start applause, then gesturing at me. "As our mostly friendly and always confusing leader would say, dig in!"

Seeing no one else make the first move, I grabbed Maria's hand and strode forward. Two plates, a handful of seconds, and a smattering of different dishes later, Maria and I got out of the way. Our passage encouraged at least a few people—their passage encouraged the rest. I smiled at two unascended humans, a woman and man, who made way for Snips, insisting that she go before them. As Snips blew happy bubbles, Rocky lifted her upward so she didn't have to leap on the table, and she cheerily collected a bunch of different foods.

Maria and I settled down in the sand, avoiding the many available chairs in favor of a quiet spot a dozen paces away. The position meant that only some of the tables would be able to see it. The food—and not me—would be the center of attention. Even as far as we were from the various places of cooking, the ground was warm, the heat of Rocky's chi having radiated an astonishing distance. The crustacean in question approached, gesturing with a cigarette-holding claw to ask if they could join us.

"Of course, mate. We aren't hiding—just giving everyone some space."

He nodded his thanks and scuttled forward, making a show of smoothing a patch for Sergeant Snips to sit on. She blew thankful bubbles and took her rightful place on my right. Rocky sat on her other side, and together, all four of us looked at our plates.

I had half a fillet of shore fish, one of the fire-roasted cichlids, and a few of the deep-fried chunks. I desperately wanted to start with the smaller fishes first. Wanted to work up to the threadfin-salmon morsels, which I suspected would be the best by far. But I lacked the self-control.

At least I wasn't alone. I smiled over at Snips and Rocky, whose cute little mouths— Well, Snips's cute little mouth and Rocky's . . . *Ah, screw it. He has a cute mouth, too.* Their cute little mouths crunched on the breading, its surface hard enough that it sounded like they were biting into crackling. When they reached the soft flesh within, they both made happy noises, staring at one another in shared bliss.

With much less bliss and a lot more amusement, Maria and I looked at one another. Our eyes conveyed our thoughts without either of us needing to voice them, and after a long moment—and more than a few eyebrow waggles—we reached an agreement. With a piece of deep-fried threadfin salmon each, we tapped them together.

"Cheers!" we both said, their crispy skins making an enticing sound as they collided. The fish was still warm beneath my fingers, and as I lifted it to my mouth, my mind conjured thousands of possible textures that the coating would possess.

Every single one of them fell short.

It was, bar none, the crispiest damned thing I had ever eaten. I expected something dense, but as the breadcrumbs had expanded, they'd become filled with tiny little pockets of air. I couldn't hear anything else as my molars crunched through it. Even if I could hear, I wouldn't have registered it—all of my attention was on the sensations occurring within my mouth.

The fish was unbelievably fatty. I'd missed the filleting stage, so I had no clue. The coating had sealed it in, creating a watertight pocket that trapped all the juices. Like biting into a soup dumpling, fat and juice poured out, their heat rolling over my tongue and awareness both.

There was a brief moment of calm, a window only noticeable because of my level of advancement, where the flavors of the fish had yet to register on my tastebuds. In that temporary silence, dozens of people, then what had to be everyone, bit down in a cacophony of crunches.

Not a single person had been able to resist.

I took great joy in that realization. For some of them, perhaps even most, this would be the first time they were going to experience chi-enhanced food. Despite deciding that we shouldn't make them all ascend too quickly, something about this had felt . . . right. Having this feast and inviting them all had only been an impulse at first, and up until only a minute ago, I could have pulled the rug out from under the whole endeavor.

But why would I?

There was no part of me that thought this was a bad idea. Even with a brain full of wool, I could tell my judgment was unaffected. I smiled at myself, realizing that I was, as ever, getting lost in the proverbial sauce. I took a mental step back, once more focusing on my physical body. The warmth of the liquid coating the inside of my mouth leaped out at me, its chi and promise of incredible flavor demanding my attention.

I was all too happy to oblige. The oils coated and clung to every surface possible, letting me appreciate the salmon first. Somewhat oceanic, it had a strong taste. This fish, served by itself, might only be appreciated by those that had previously exposed their palate to fishy goodness.

But we hadn't served it by itself. I chewed, the soft flesh providing a satisfying counterpoint to the crispy coating that became less and less prevalent with each bite, the juices taking over. Combined with the fish's textures, they managed to pierce through the layer of oil.

I wasn't prepared for the absolute explosion of flavor. The tallow's hearty, savory notes. The breadcrumbs' rich nuttiness. And the subtle herbs and spices, including salt, its enhancement of the dish unmissable. These were the only ingredients other than the fish. Simple as they may be, they had combined to become something truly complex. Each element enjoyed a moment in the limelight before happily stepping back, making way for the others.

When I popped another chunk into my mouth, chi tried to stream down toward my core, but I used its energy against itself, creating a little barrier to hold it in place. The bite must have taken only seconds for me to chew, but it felt like a blissful eternity, each second as enjoyable as the last. When I finally swallowed, it was like red-hot metal shot down my throat—sans the pain one would expect. Keeping it still for so long had made the essence antsy, and it raced to accomplish its purpose.

To my utter surprise, some of it went upward. I let it go, part of my awareness tracking its passage as it flooded my head. When it rushed back down a moment later, I couldn't contain my wonder. It had cleared the woolen clouds in my mind. Like a soothing balm on cracked skin, the sensation of its departure was so refreshing that I could cry. I'd not even been paying attention to the partial headache lingering within, but now that it was gone, I took a deep breath. As I exhaled, some essence escaped, the dish's flavors returning to the forefront and robbing me of thought.

When it finally fled, I sensed the outside world again—there was a storm approaching. My gaze darted around, not knowing where to look first. The storm wasn't approaching at all. It was here.

Pop!

There were so many sources that I'd not found the first time. The chi had come from just ahead of me, and as I assessed the formation of someone's budding core, a wave of euphoria washed over me.

Shock came through my connection to Maria, and her eyes flew wide. Within a moment, she surmised what was about to occur. She sent me a questioning pulse, unwilling or unable to look away from the scene. I confirmed it with a pulse of my own—it was really happening.

The initial pop had been like the first kernel of microwave popcorn to explode. It was a sign of many more to come. With our fingers clasped together, Maria and I witnessed the rest of the awakenings.

CHAPTER THIRTY-THREE

Speak of the Devil

Beneath a starry sky and surrounded by all those I held dear—countless sources of euphoria washed over me. From start to finish, it only took a handful of seconds for the transformations to occur. Whether it was the power now suffusing the world or the strength of the chi within the fish, these new cultivators were . . . different. I was certain of it. The speed with which the universe's knowledge poured into them was *stunning*.

Amazingly, that wasn't the only difference. I thought it my imagination, but as light from the first awakenings faded, my senses confirmed it: Some of the new cultivators had aspected chi within them—a shadow of the essence that would one day facilitate their advancement.

This newest group of awakened . . . They were closer to a breakthrough after their ascension than any before them. Myself included. I hadn't the faintest idea what had caused it, but that was irrelevant. Their strength was a net gain for Tropica, and our forces would only grow stronger when they had their breakthroughs. Which could be soon, if their cores could be believed. I smiled as I stared out at them, loving the mix of wonder, joy, and sheer bewilderment on their faces.

Now that the fog clouding my mind had been cleared away by the fish's chi, a small but insistent part of me wanted to reach out toward those whose cores held that promise of future advancement. The metaphorical devil on my shoulder was telling me to do so, reassuring me that they *probably* wouldn't notice my interruption. But a larger—and just as insistent—part of me denied that course of action. Even if there was only a slight chance they noticed, and an even slighter chance that it ruined their night, I wasn't going to take that gamble. Besides, I had more important things to do.

As the last source of light and euphoria faded, I raised another chunk of fish to my nose and breathed in its overwhelming scents.

"Wait," Maria said, shielding her eyes as they readjusted to the darkness. "Let's try the different condiments together."

She raised a slice of lemon, squeezing a few drops onto my portion before adding some to hers. She shot me an excited grin, then threw the lemony morsel into her mouth. I followed suit. Twin crunches rang out as we bit down, and I could tell the difference almost immediately.

As it so often did, the lemon's acidic punch and fresh flavor cut through the oil and fat with ease. They were still there, but much less intense than last time, a fruity overtone lifting the entire experience to new heights. Peter was right; I might not have been able to appreciate the change if I hadn't eaten the fish plain first. I'd already known this, of course, but the instruction wasn't for me—it was for the newcomers.

As the tastes lingered, I looked out at the sea of faces. Some stared at Maria and me. Others gazed at Barry, Theo, Roger, or one of the other members of the congregation, their eyes and emotions pleading for guidance. When someone answered the unasked question, I raised a brow, taken aback that he'd been the first to reply.

"Eat up," Roger had said in a fatherly tone. "It's not every day that we have a feast, so enjoy the food while it's hot. Everything else—awakenings included—can wait."

"Hear, hear!" George called, raising a fried chunk high, then dipping it into a dark reduction that smelled like garlic. The fish disappeared into his mouth a moment later, all tension leaving his shoulders as it hit his tongue.

As cheers of agreement came from the original congregation, I stole glances at the new arrivals, noting their confusion. They had become cultivators, something that, up until recently, they'd believed to be a curse. We'd taught them otherwise. Showed them that awakening didn't mean you would go insane or need to be chained. And now, only seconds after they had taken steps on the path of ascension, we were telling them that their enjoyment of the feast was more important than anything else.

Those who peered my way, seeking my approval or opinion, only received a smile and a nod in return—a few nods if they didn't believe the first. One by one, the newly ascended grabbed more food from their plates. Lemon was added, seasoning was sprinkled, and assorted reductions were dipped into. Some brave souls even tried multiple flavors on the same bit of fish. The crunching that rang out was music to my ears. I had to withdraw my senses by force, lest everyone's emotions overwhelm me, but their faces and the animated conversations that followed were indication enough.

The rest of the food disappeared in relative silence. It was a sort of quiet intensity, as if people didn't want to disrespect the fish by talking. I paid it little attention, though—I had my own plate to get through. The different species provided much needed variety, and I found myself swapping between them. Cichlids had a strong flavor and soft meat. Shore fish were as subtle as ever, their taste easily overshadowed if you added too many seasonings.

From what little conversations were taking place, everyone's perception of the meal was different. Among the varied palates, there was one constant: The deep-fried salmon was best. It excelled in flavor, texture, and depth. Not to mention chi content, which provided any food or drink a hard-to-quantify boost. As I looked around at the tabletops, I smiled—every single plate had at least one of the deep-fried chunks remaining. Mine did, too. It was human nature to save the best bite for last.

I held on to mine as long as possible, wanting to eat it with them, but when I saw how slow some were eating, I could wait no longer.

I turned to Maria. "Should we have our last bite togeth—"

She froze, her single remaining chunk of fish held before her open mouth. "Don't look at me like that! I couldn't wait any longer!"

I barked a laugh, squeezed some lemon over my portion, and plopped it onto my tongue.

"Mmmm," we both hummed, the sound muted by the crunch of crispy breadcrumbs.

Conversation grew around us as we savored the moment. No matter where I went in Tropica, there was always at least one person surprised to see me, so I'd become used to being stared at. Now, though? Not one gaze flicked my way. Everyone was too busy talking to their neighbor to spare me a thought.

Maria inhaled sharply. "Fischer! Over there!"

Barry—whose lats provided an unmissable silhouette—reacted at the same time, his broad back going rigid. I had sealed my awareness away, so I sent strands of chi racing out into the world, connecting to the network below, which let me sense my surroundings. I immediately found the source of Maria and Barry's surprise.

Something was happening within a core, and it wasn't one of the new cultivators. I hadn't interacted with her in a while, but I could never forget Bonnie. I'd already marked her as an out-of-the-box thinker when we were crafting back before New Tropica was reabsorbed. We'd been making the fishing rods that we still used today, and rather than create what I was thinking of, she'd imagined the bastard lovechild of a grappling hook and a harpoon.

But as unique as that creation had been, it was nothing compared to the chi currently swelling within her core. She was . . . hungry. And not in the *yawning maw looking to absorb everything* kind of way. She was *literally* hungry. Not just for food, but that *was* a part of it. Curious how hunger had facilitated a breakthrough, I opened myself up to her thoughts, stopping short of barging my way into her psyche.

It was captivating. Peter's breakthrough came to mind, his essence a similar shade to hers, but not in the way that one might think. He wanted to feed others. He desired to be the embodiment of a hearth that others could gather around, swapping stories and eating nourishing food. Bonnie, though, wanted to be the one eating said food. She wanted to . . . *consume*?

Even that word felt wrong, though; it carried negative connotations, harkening back to the imaginary, all-consuming maw. She didn't just want to devour food. She wanted to *experience* it. As if she knew what I was thinking, and her will shifted, exploring her own consciousness.

Just as I'd already gleaned, it wasn't only food she desired. She wanted adventure, too. She was a pioneer. A trailblazer. Bonnie wanted to experience the highest heights that Kallis had to offer. She wanted to eat the tastiest food, witness the prettiest sights, and walk the path less traveled.

I'm not ashamed of wanting more. Her thoughts bled outward, making their way to my ears. *This is who I want to be.* Her core urged her on, vibrating. *This is who I* am, *even if others hate me for being selfish.*

And there it was—the crux of her doubt. She would, if given the opportunity, pursue fun over obligation. Her very nature meant that if she had to choose between harvesting a crop and following a funny-looking crab along the shore . . . well, the crops would go untended.

I couldn't help but grin. We'd never have hated her for something so trivial. If anything, I liked her more. Funny-looking animals were one of life's great gifts.

Even before the explosion came, I knew that it would. Her words were true, her realization profound. I appeared behind her in a flash of light, no fog remaining to cloud my will. Raising a hand, I crafted a barrier of essence, building a skyward-facing cone for the energy to travel. I didn't think anyone would have been severely injured if I hadn't jumped in, but I could definitely see the vibe being ruined if dozens of people were violently slammed into others via chi explosion.

When the essence flew from her, I was thankful I'd erred on the side of caution. Rather than shoot outward, her chi seemed to implode, creating a vacuum. Night air rushed in to fill the void, and I cringed at the chaos that would have occurred if I'd not raised a shield. In retrospect, it made total sense. Her core—her very soul—wanted more.

Despite being cultivators, the newly ascended didn't have the power or awareness to witness what had happened. They stared at me in the aftermath as I lowered the shields and held Bonnie's shoulder, steadying her.

She recovered quickly, and as her thoughts returned to the present, a potent wave of joy and awe washed through her. But when she took in the surrounding faces, a thin yet undeniable layer of dread rose up, threatening to flatten her happiness.

I leaned down beside her, pretending that I was straightening the bench she sat on, and whispered soft enough for only her to hear. "I'm proud of you. Come see me after the feast." I stood tall, stretching and rubbing my back as everyone stared at either Bonnie or me. "Excuse my interruption! Just wanted to make sure that no one was accidentally hurt." I smiled down at her, ensuring all heard my voice when I continued. "Congratulations, Bonnie. That's as worthy a goal as any."

With a slight gesture of one finger, I appeared back on the sand beside Maria and my two crabby companions. Even from so far away, I could feel the weight my words had removed from Bonnie's shoulders. Her new ideal had needed only the slightest bit of encouragement to shrug off the dread.

Next to me, Maria lounged in the sand, caressing her stomach. "Who was it? She feels kinda familiar."

I shook my head at how casual Maria was being about a breakthrough. "I'll give you three hints. She's a cultivator from Gormona, her ascending is *beyond* interesting, and she was present when we mass-crafted the rods."

"Fischer, that narrows it down to like dozens of— Oh! *Her?*" She sat upright, then winced and caressed her stomach again. "The one that made the hook from hell? That *is* interesting, especially given your next project."

"Right?" I leaned back in the sand beside Maria. "Everything is coming together."

She snorted, and I raised my eyebrow, not expecting that response. "What's up?"

"Ellis is going to be *so* mad that he missed this."

"Good. That's what he gets for being such a prick. He'll be even more annoyed when he finds out about dessert. There's something for you, too, Snips."

"Dessert?" Maria sat upright. "Don't tease me, Fischer. You didn't have time to organize it . . ."

Yeah! Snips agreed with an accusatory snipper pointed at my chest. *No teasing!*

"I suppose you're correct. *I* didn't have the time . . . but what about Sue and Sturgill?"

Maria leaped to her feet, scanning everyone with her eyes and chi both. Snips did the same, Rocky getting up onto his spiky little tippytoes as he held her overhead.

"Speak of the devil . . ." I said, standing and facing the north just in time for their arrival.

Sue and Sturgill, the latter's arms carrying a tray piled so high that I couldn't see his face, came into view of the firelight. A soft breeze swept past them, blowing the scents of lemon, passiona husk, and fresh-cooked pastry across the gathering.

"You better have saved us a plate!" Sue yelled, her steps hurried. "Lest I throw these into the ocean!"

"Two plates!" Sturgill added, entirely too loud, as he set down his burden on the closest table. "Each! I'm starving!!"

With a grin, I nodded at Borks, who dashed forward and tore a portal into space. The scents wafting from it told Sturgill that his prizes were inside. He leaped in with abandon, making Sue shake her head and begin muttering about foolish men. She put on a good front, but I could feel her desire for the food—it rivaled Sturgill's own.

Sue swept around the feast, placing trays of still-warm pastries on the tables. As she reached the bottom of her supplies, a collection of treats with fish in the center were revealed. The person closest to Sue, having likely expected something else, gagged.

But they weren't for us; they were for our animal pals.

Rocky got to his feet, blowing bubbles that told his beloved Snips to wait where she rested.

"Would you mind getting us some, too, Rocky?" I asked. "Of the sweet variety, I mean."

But of course, dearest Fischer, his soft hiss told me. With a final drag of a cigarette I hadn't even noticed him smoking, he chucked the butt into his mouth and scuttled away.

"Things sure change fast around here . . ." Maria watched Rocky as he deftly wove between tables and leaped up onto a bench to collect his prizes. "You've got yourself quite the man in that one, Snips."

The sergeant, sturdy of carapace and reliable of character, nodded in agreement, a soft blush coming to her cheeks—or where they would be if she had them.

"I always wondered what you saw in him," I replied, not talking softly. "But you had the right of it. Rocky is one hell of a crab."

Having been privy to our conversation, Rocky stood a little taller as he swept back in with our pastries. I plucked one from the plate, selecting what looked like a lemon danish with dots of passiona.

Its flavor hitting my tongue wiped my mind clear of thoughts.

CHAPTER THIRTY-FOUR

The Whole Problem

The feast came to an end the same way most do: People ate themselves into a food coma, then lingered just long enough to remain polite. Only one thing really stood out as anomalous: Corporal Claws didn't return. I had informed her she could come back if she behaved, of course, but she'd told me she was busy "experimenting," whatever that meant.

Just as I'd been finishing off my third pastry, she'd contacted me again, her thoughts clear even from so far away. Recalling the secret deal she'd offered, I shook my head. She wasn't just *a* problem—the devious little rascal was the *whole* problem.

"No kidding," Maria agreed, privy to the negotiations and my thoughts both.

As I opened my eyes and returned to the present, the last of Tropica's citizens were departing. The mass of cultivators caressed stomachs, leaned on one another, and spoke in hushed tones, already recounting the food they'd just eaten. With a pulse of chi, I got Barry, Helen, and Paul's attention, requesting their presence.

As the three walked over, I spun to face Borks and Cinnamon—my only animal pals who hadn't left to meditate or sleep. I smirked at the looks on their faces. "You two know what I'm planning, don't you?"

An enthusiastic *ruff* from Borks and a sharp nod from Cinnamon confirmed my suspicions.

"And what *are* you planning?" Helen asked as she, Barry, and their son reached us.

I waved a hand. "I'll get to that. First, though . . ."

I'd told Bonnie to see me after the feast. She stood off to the side with slightly flushed cheeks, so I gave her as reassuring a smile as I could muster. "Please don't think that anyone here is going to judge you for the ideal that caused your breakthrough. I mean, look at Barry—his ideal was accepting his pride and desire for attention. We still love him."

Barry emphasized the point by spinning on the spot, taking a deep breath, and doing a lat spread.

"Yes, dear," Helen said, patting his back. "We know you have a wingspan to rival the pelicans."

Two loud honks came from above, and as I glanced up, I realized I was wrong earlier—not all of my animal pals had left. Bill and Pelly landed in a spray of sand. Mimicking Barry's posture, they spread their wings. They had him absolutely *crushed* in width.

"Oh yeah?" Barry spun. "Can you do *this*?" He started bouncing his pecs in a hypnotic rhythm, his syrupy laugh rolling over the sand.

"See what I mean, Bonnie?" I gestured at Barry's shenanigans with both hands. "You have *nothing* to be embarrassed about. I can't speak for everyone, but I'm super proud of you for accepting a hard truth about yourself. Especially because you thought we might judge you for it."

Her cheeks were still a little flushed, but a smile had made its way to her face as she watched Barry's chest bouncing away. Helen's subsequent look of disappointment only increased Bonnie's amusement, as did the sparkle in Paul's eye as he looked up at his dad.

Bonnie cleared her throat and took a slow breath, centering herself. "Thank you, everyone. It . . . It makes me really happy that I won't have to leave. I—"

"*Leave?*" Maria interrupted. "Oh, *honey* . . . you're integral to Fischer's next adventure." She shot her a wink. "I'm afraid leaving now isn't an option."

"Adventure?" she asked, her core humming. "What kind of adventure?"

I grinned. "Is Paul all right to stay up a bit later, mate?"

"Up. To. Him," Barry answered, emphasizing each word with the bounce of a pec.

"Really?" Paul asked.

Helen gave her husband some audacious side-eye. "Now that your father has offered, yes. But if you're not back at a reasonable hour, say a couple hours before first light . . ." She punched a fist into her open palm and turned on Barry with a dangerous look—his pecs stopped bouncing at once.

"Wonderful," I said. "We couldn't have done it without Paul. Wouldn't want him to miss it."

"Miss what?" he asked, leaning in.

"The transformation, of course!"

"Transformation?" My words had the desired effect, and he had to take a step so he didn't fall forward. "What transformation?"

"We're just finishing what we started earlier tonight, mate."

He blinked, then his eyes went wide.

"Ah-huh." I stretched, loosening my muscles. "We've got a boat to build, Paul, and there's no chance I was gonna do it without you."

"Steer hard to port!" I yelled, holding on to a rope for dear life as wind and sea spray assaulted me. "They're turning the cannons our way! Lift anchor! Prepare the boards! Walk the gangplank!"

When no reply came, I turned and pouted down at my friends.

"What in Poseidon's salty beard are you doing, Fischer?" Maria asked, staring up at the pile of unassembled beams I was using as a stage.

"I'm role-playing. Getting in the zone." I planted my hands on my hips and looked down my nose at them. "What are *you* doing? Letting me down, is what. Did you not have improv classes as a part of your education?" I harrumphed, channeling every drop of haughty noble I could muster. "I'll have to reeducate you when my new nation is formed. It'll be my first action as god-king, lest this disgusting injustice occur agai—" I held up a finger, cutting myself off. "Never mind. My first action will be doubling, nay, *tripling* taxes. Then I can deal with educating children or whatever it was we were talking about."

Maria, who'd completely ignored me for the last half of my impassioned monologue, rested a hand on Bonnie's shoulder and gave her an apologetic grimace. "I'm so, *so* sorry. I wish I could say you get used to it, but he only seems to get worse over time."

"Disrespect?" I gasped, covering my mouth. *"Twelve years dungeon!"*

"Yes, dear. I'll get right on that in the morning. Until then, though, would you mind if we actually tried to build this thing? I don't care if you're the future god-king; Helen will still beat you with a spoon if you keep Paul out all night."

I nodded slowly, a philosopher ruminating on the well-worded retort of an equal. "You raise a good point, Maria. Surprising, considering your good looks, peasant blood, and generally horrible demean—"

I had to bend over backward to dodge the knee that came sailing toward my head.

"Hiiiii!" Slimes called on the way past, oozing out of Maria's thigh to slap me across the face with a wet *thwap*. "I'm a boy!"

Ten minutes—and more near misses than I could count—later, a truce was reached. Maria and I shook on it, and Slimes perched atop our hands, jiggling to make it official.

"Now," I said. "Where did I drop those plans . . . ?"

It took less than a half hour to assemble the frame. Maybe I should have been used to it by now, but I still couldn't comprehend how little time it took for us to create something so unbelievably large. It was far from the biggest ship I'd ever seen, but a yacht of this size back on Earth would have cost at least a few million—and that was for a used model. Over twenty meters long and six wide, there was more than enough room for what I wanted. I couldn't wait to finish.

Even if the System didn't take over, I had absolutely no doubt that we'd be able to make it seaworthy. To that end, I took my time with each nail, giving them the care they needed.

"He's for sure showing off, right?" Barry asked. "Why didn't he just use a regular mallet?"

"First off," I replied, not looking up as I moved down a plank, hammering nails into place with tiny pillars of light. "This is way more efficient than a mallet. My chi is practically indestructible."

"Indestructible?" Maria muttered. "Tell that to Claws . . ."

I narrowed my eyes at her. She just grinned back and shot me a wink, clearly happy her comment had been annoying enough for me to look her way.

"Now that I've got your attention . . ." She held up the length of string she was applying a black substance into. "How does this look? I have no idea what I'm doing."

"I wanna say it looks terrible to pay you back for that Claws jibe, but honestly, you're a natural."

Paul, who'd managed to get the black tar in more than a few spots on his face, rubbed his fingers together, looking decidedly displeased with its sticky texture. "I thought chalk was supposed to be white? What's wrong with this stuff?"

Maria and I blinked at each other, then burst into laughter.

"Guys . . ." Barry fought down a smile of his own as Paul's cheeks flushed red.

I recovered first. "Sorry, mate. It's *caulk*, not chalk. It's used to fill the gaps on a boat and keep it airtight."

"It's Fischer's fault, not yours, Paul," Maria added. "He was clearly excited when he explained it, because he spoke *way* too fast. I'm surprised that you almost got the word correct, to be honest." She elbowed him lightly in the side, unable to use her tar-covered hands. "Super impressive considering you haven't had a breakthrough."

He blushed even harder, but it was now pride, not embarrassment, causing the blood to rush to his cheeks. "Thank you."

"You're most welcome, mate." With a single swing of my chi-made object, I hammered the final nail into place. "Another plank, please!"

Barry, Borks, and Cinnamon became a blur. They were my main helpers, and as the former lifted a stack, Borks opened a portal, and Cinnamon started kicking wood through. I caught each length with ease, laying them against the frame and holding them in place with my chi. If I really wanted to be extra, I probably could have moved it all myself—but it was funner doing things with friends.

When the keel, hull, and bow were finished—the entire bottom of our boat—I went to start the deck, and Borks caught me entirely off guard. Focused as I'd been on the vessel, I hadn't noticed Barry tying strips of cloth around the good boy's eyes—which Barry had torn from his own shirt, because *of course* he'd tear it from his own shirt. Borks repeated the same actions as before, but this time, with an absence of vision.

Even now, building a random boat in the early hours of the morning, they were *training*.

"Good boy, Borks," I said, earning a vigorous tail wag in response.

His dedication lit a fire within me, and I increased my speed, showing that I was also willing to push myself. As the rest of the deck came together, a somewhat-unwelcome presence reached out to me, and a certain otter once more offered a trade deal. I had to expend some chi so no one realized we were chatting—it took a surprising amount of will. Which, in retrospect, might have been one of the reasons Claws chose that moment to reach out.

Engrossed as I was in the negotiations, I didn't realize I finished the deck, and my next step would have taken me headfirst into the beam acting as a makeshift mast. Fortunately, Cinnamon stopped that from happening. Unfortunately, she did so with a roundhouse kick of immaculate form.

I tumbled backward over the now-complete deck, coming to land at everyone's feet. Maria shot me a wink, then turned a predatory look on Barry.

He looked at her in disbelief, then his head drifted down to me, disbelief becoming frustration. "Are you serious, Fischer?"

"What did I do? I just got boopity-bopped on the noggin! I'm the victim here!"

"If you'd have hit that beam, it would've snapped in half!"

"That's not necessarily true."

Barry raised a brow.

"It might have ripped out and shattered the deck instead."

"That's even worse!"

"Are you forgetting something, Barry?" Maria interrupted. "It's time for you to dance, monkey."

Barry's core railed against whatever she was ordering him to do, and he stood there in stillness for a long moment, but his honor won out in the end. "Do I really have to sing, too?" he asked, taking a wide stance.

"You remember the words."

". . . If I say no, do I get out of it?"

"Nope. If you'd lied and said no, though, I was going to have Slimes give you non-constructive criticism."

"Would Slimes really do that?" I asked. "He seems too . . . kind."

Said familiar jiggled from Maria's shoulder. "Even if it caused a complete breakdown of someone's emotional, mental, and spiritual well-being, I would happily tear them down if it made my dearest Maria feel even an ounce of joyyy!"

Bonnie and I shared some side-eye, and I mouthed, *Don't piss off Maria.* She nodded seriously.

Barry sighed again, this one seeming to empty every last bit of air from his lungs. When he breathed in, it was slow and deliberate, his stance widening. The look he gave me *almost* made me feel sorry for him.

"Don't blame me, mate. You took a bet that relied on me having spatial awareness. I mean . . . have you *met* me?"

Maria cleared her throat. "No talking to the monkey until he's finished."

I wondered at the second use of the word monkey, but the question was answered before I could voice it. Barry hopped from foot to foot, his arms going up and down in the approximation of a chimpanzee, and a song—whose lyrics about bananas and rum were as inspired as they were ridiculous—flowed out.

After the verse looped back around and Barry started from the beginning, I leaned toward Paul. "How many times does he have to do it . . .?"

Paul grimaced. "Until sunrise . . ."

"*Sunrise?* Why would he bet that?"

"Because I *trusted* you!" Barry stopped mid-sentence, pointing a muscular finger—seriously, who has muscular fingers?—at me. "In what world would you accidentally destroy your own—"

"Hey!" Maria interrupted, enjoying this *entirely* too much. "You accepted because you wanted me to lose, which would have had *me* singing until dawn! Less speaky, more dancey! You know the way out, so unless you want *that,* no more talk."

Barry's eye twitched, his lip joining in as he was forced to make an impossible decision. Eventually, he nodded, looking like he'd agreed to eat dirt. "Fine. Let's get it over with."

Maria whirled and cupped her hands to her mouth. "Claaaaaws!" she sang in a chipper tone.

With that one word, his fate was sealed.

Barry scoffed and rolled his eyes. "There's no way she actually heard you from over the mountains, so can we stop this farce and pack the boat with caulk? We might as well make progress until—"

The southern horizon lit blue, and not even a half second later, a bolt of lightning cracked.

Barry's face fell. He turned to Maria. "This is gonna hurt, isn't it?"

"Good chance."

"Can Fischer shield me?"

"Yeah, can I?"

"Hmmm." She tapped her chin. "I'll allow a single layer."

He'd likely have protested that concession. Pleaded his case for more layers of shielding. But there wasn't any time. Instead, he turned to face the lightning and planted his feet, accepting his fate as a jagged blue line tore through the sky toward us.

CHAPTER THIRTY-FIVE

Pants

I shielded my eyes against the light as Claws arrived as an ear-splitting streak of lightning. She crouched on the sand ten meters from Barry, then started whirling her arm round and round like a little kid winding up a punch.

Instead of her fist, though, she lashed out with an electric raccoon.

He came from her core, propelled forward by centrifugal force and the power of friendship. With a wicked grin, he curled into a tight ball, reducing drag and concentrating his mass.

Of all the thoughts to cross my mind, I wondered why the little rascal was so happy—he was a thief at heart, but appeared to be absolutely *chuffed* about being involved in mischief. Barry closed his eyes, and I covered him with a shield just before the raccoon struck him square in the ches . . . *never mind.* With a secondary spout of lightning from his tail, Claws's familiar changed course at the last second.

Barry was ready for it. He squatted down, placing his chest in the firing line once more, but his foe was more troublesome than any of us had imagined. He'd predicted Barry's movement. Extending his front paws, the raccoon's trajectory shifted once more, almost skimming the ground. He slammed directly into Barry's groin, his grabby little fingers finding purchase on the fabric of Barry's pants.

Ahhh, I thought, realizing the reason for the familiar's happiness. *Depantsing—a worthy cause.*

I added several layers of protection to make sure Barry and, uhhh, little Barry weren't physically injured. While his body was safe, his pride was another story, and I felt a pang of remorse as the raccoon-turned-cannonball used Barry's newfound velocity to remove his own pants. He sailed over Tropica in a hapless manner, only his tighty-whities preventing *everything* from being on display.

"Hey!" Maria yelled. "That was *way* more than one layer!"

"I couldn't let him get hit in the knackers at full force. I'd have felt too guilty."

"Guilty?" Paul asked. "It was a silly bet, right? It's his own fault."

Maria and I shared a glance, and Cinnamon covered a squeaky laugh. The raccoon and Claws outright cackled, leaning on each other for support.

Maria leaned down. "Can you keep a secret, Paul?"

As with every time he was presented with a challenge, he nodded, his jaw firm.

"Well, here's the thing. Fischer tried to walk into the beam on purpose."

Paul gave her, then me, an incredulous look. "No, he didn't. Fischer was surprised when Cinnamon kicked him. And when he learned about the bet."

"Oh? And how do you know that?"

Bonnie's gaze sharpened. "Don't tell me . . ."

Paul's gaze drifted toward her before shifting back to Maria. "I could feel Fischer's surprise. Despite having less power than all of you, even I could sense . . ." His eyes slowly widened as understanding blossomed in his core.

Maria tapped her nose. "Clever lad."

"You let me feel it on purpose . . ." He stared into the far distance as he searched his memories. "The whole time, Fischer . . . ?"

I gave him an intentionally flat look, then concentrated on the same thoughts that had made shock pour from me earlier.

Though I had to consciously let him feel my emotions, Paul couldn't have hidden his from me if he tried. I winced as I felt his respect for me draining away. "I promise there was a good reason for it, mate. There's also a reason that you have to keep it a secret. That cool with you, too, Bonnie?"

"Yep." Unlike Paul, she wasn't at all bothered by our conspiracy to shame Barry.

"Why, then?" Paul's mind clung to the explanation I'd offered with white-knuckled intensity. "Why would you embarrass my dad like that?"

I sighed. "For the good of everyone, mate. There was an evil mastermind behind it, but it wasn't me . . ."

I pointed to Claws, who grinned and waved back with one forepaw, the other bouncing her raccoon bud up and down like a baseball.

"Claws is a being of pure chaos. She was bad before, but now she literally can't help herself. That being said, I don't want to banish her from Tropica just because she might zap a person or two." I raised a finger to interrupt her before she could object. "Yes, Claws, I'm well aware that you'd zap way more than two people if we hadn't made the deal. I'm trying to make you sound better than you are."

"Deal . . . ?" Paul looked at Claws, who bent over backward to wave at him through her own legs. "What deal?"

"Why, for chaos, of course." I gave him a tight-lipped smile. "You know when I built that last section of the boat, I went quiet for a while?"

"Yeah . . ."

"My bond with Claws has never been stronger. We can communicate over significant distances now. I wasn't lost in thought, mate. I was lost in conversation."

"More like locked in negotiations with a terrorist . . ." Maria muttered.

Claws agreed wholeheartedly with an affirmative chirp.

"But . . . why couldn't you tell my dad?" Paul leaned toward me, his core hoping for a good explanation. "Why did *you* have to cheat him into losing a bet?"

"Well, I tried to make the deal affect Maria. Or literally anyone other than me."

They weren't good enooough, Claws chirped with singsong cadence.

"It had to be me, Paul. I *had* to agree, or else the citizens of Tropica might suffer.

Barry would understand if I could tell him, but part of the deal was that he remains in the dark.

"I guess that makes sense . . ." He turned his gaze on Claws, his face more considerate than a boy his age should be. "If it has to be a secret, why tell me and her?"

Bonnie's lip curled up on one side. "May I take a guess?"

Claws nodded, a twinkle in her eye.

"It's because telling the two of us creates more chaos in the long run. We'll doubt every action that Fischer makes, assuming that it might be a task to appease Claws. Telling any more people could undermine Fischer's leadership." She tapped her chin in thought. "Two is the perfect amount, really—we'll only have each other to converse with. Other than Maria and Fischer, of course. But they're directly connected to Claws via some cultivation bullshit, so they don't count."

"Damn, Bonnie." I pointed at Claws, whose head was nodding so fast that it looked like she might take flight. "You verbalized a concept that she was struggling with."

Corporal Claws, queen of the sands and rider of lightning, zapped toward Bonnie, a grin on her face. She drew back a forelimb and collected chi, ready to hit the recently broken-through cultivator. I could have stopped her, of course. But there was no need. Claws's arm shot forward, slowing at the last second as she touched Bonnie's arm.

There was a transfer of power. A branding, of sorts. And a bright-blue mark in the shape of Claws's paw pad was left behind. It faded in seconds, a whisper of the chi going dormant rather than disappearing entirely.

Bonnie took a step back, eyes narrowing. "What . . . what was that?"

"No fracking clue," I said, "but it was definitely positive. She's not telling me, so I'm guessing it's a secret."

Claws winked, gave me a thumbs-up, and absolutely *launched* her fucking raccoon at me.

"Stop that!" I yelled, not needing to feign my annoyance as I kicked the little bastard into the ocean. "That wasn't part of the deal!"

With a chirp that promised it was *probably* the last time she'd break the agreement, Claws leaped into the air and intercepted her spirit raccoon, absorbing him into her core. *Gotta go experiment—byeee!* she trilled.

The moment she struck the waves, she went full submarine. A focused stream of lightning flew from her back legs, only her grinning head remaining above water as she tore off to the south. She disappeared in less than a second, making it around the mountainous shore on her way to whatever godsforsaken experiments she intended on conducting.

I let out a steadying sigh. "Where were we? Ah yes, building a—"

There was a burst of chi from the other side of Tropica, the flood of essence feeling almost as sharp as Roger's. Sand sprayed in every direction as a muscle-bound figure slammed down next to the ship. A pair of red eyes glowed through the cloud of airborne debris, making my pal look like a final boss.

Maria leaned toward me and whispered, "Where did he find pants?"

"Where are they?" Barry's voice was riddled with anger, holding an edge deadlier than the chi radiating from his core.

"Uhhh," I said. "You mean Claws and her furry little bowling ball?"

"Yes," he hissed, his mouth *literally* trailing steam.

"She left, mate. Went back beyond the mountains to experiment, whatever that means."

He took a shuddering step, and I had to quash my guilt lest he notice it. Sensing a wave of emotion coming from Paul, I surrounded him with my chi, shielding his thoughts from Barry. I was all for pranks, but the raccoon nutshot had been a direct challenge to his pride—the very thing Barry, er . . . prided himself on.

Five minutes later, and after Barry's body had lost more moisture to evaporation than I thought was strictly healthy, he rolled his shoulders. "Okay. I think I'm over it."

"Good!" I said. "Because if we don't finish soon, Helen will have all our hides."

The hint of panic in Barry's eyes wasn't a facade. He had been so bothered by Claws's shenanigans that he'd entirely forgotten about the curfew. He was a blur as he rushed to the tar-covered caulking. "Do we just pack the gaps? Are there any special instructions? Can we all do it?"

I barked a laugh at his string of worry-fueled questions. "Yes, no, and yes. Pack the gaps so they're watertight. Usually I'd say do it as hard as you can, but I suspect we'd all be able to crack the hull with our bare hands, so don't rush it."

Even with the extreme carefulness I employed, the process was swift and enjoyable. I didn't let the stickiness of the blackened chords bother me, instead using their unique texture as a source of mindful meditation. There was something oddly satisfying about the task. Unlike the boatwrights of old, we could employ our bare hands instead of metal tools.

Packing the particularly egregious gaps left me feeling accomplished at first, but I quickly grew used to it. My mind wandered, and as I pictured the boat, I started adding additional features. A cabin for privacy. Beds. Rod holders. An anchor. A kitchen. And most important of all, a flushable toilet along with the requisite plumbing. They could all be added later, of course, but why not try to add them now if the System might help?

I racked my brain for anything I was missing, and remembering the charter boats I'd seen back on Earth, I wondered if a motor was something we should include. But then an image flashed through my mind. Corporal Claws, her adorable-yet-annoying grin fixed on us as she went full submarine earlier.

Different possibilities arrived by the dozens. One stood above all the others: a mode of ocean transport in a fantasy book I'd read as a young man. It was fiction, of course, but the more I thought about it, the more I seriously considered it. The worst-case scenario was that it ruined the ship. That *would* be a pain, but it wasn't the end of the world . . . right?

I weighed the pros and cons as the others continued caulking. The world, however, had different plans.

Chi rose around us in streams, pouring toward the ship. Perhaps it should have instilled a sense of worry deep within me. Maybe it should have made adrenaline course through my veins, my indecision leading to anxiety and panic. But as I felt the essence collecting around us, preparing to slam into and transform our first aquatic vessel, all I could feel was unbridled joy.

There was no more time to deliberate, so I followed my gut and imagined what I wanted. The world's chi answered.

CHAPTER THIRTY-SIX

Super Cool

Beneath a blanket of stars, the ethereal light of a crescent moon illuminated bubbles of essence. They were a manifestation of the world's chi—a confirmation that our efforts this night hadn't been in vain. And as I gazed out at the incandescent spheres, barely able to register just how many there were, I focused my awareness on what I wanted from the ship.

A portion was used to picture the basic additions, like an anchor, beds, and my beloved porcelain throne. I directed a larger chunk on the fiction-inspired propulsion system. Finally, I used the lion's share of my will on what the boat should provide; it was a fishing vessel, and as long as it facilitated good times on the water, nothing else mattered. Hopefully that last stipulation was enough to override any unsuitable inclusions.

All of this snapped into place in the blink of a cultivator's eye. Multiple projects split between my two partitions. Their differing strengths of will and intention meant that only those with a firm resolve and a potent core could participate. But I was *surrounded* by such people; I grinned, already knowing they'd join me.

Maria was first. Because of her connection to me, she best comprehended the purpose and design of my fantastical propulsion system. Slimes came next, adding his strength to Maria's. Though only a drop by comparison, I was still appreciative of his efforts. It all helped.

Then Cinnamon and Borks arrived. I thought I would need to instruct them, but they surprised me, both snorting at my assumption before latching themselves onto the part of me focused on facilitating good times. They already knew where they were best suited, and as their cores joined with mine, I was almost knocked over. Contrary to their base forms, Borks seemed like a river of white in my mind's eye, Cinnamon a landslide of black. They combined into a single force, and together, we bent the transformation to our desire.

Barry came next, the muscle man's pride leading the charge and dragging his will along with it. When he felt what we were doing, he hesitated a moment. His ego wanted to latch onto the largest project, but despite not being directly connected to me, Barry had the insight to know that he wasn't needed there.

I expected him to resign himself to a lesser task. Instead, he changed his frame of mind, telling himself that *he* could be the lone man leading the charge on the boat's aesthetic features. I'd have laughed if I had the ability, but too much rested on this moment.

Only Paul and Bonnie were left, and though the former's core was too weak by far, the latter was a possibility. Seconds passed, and the window for her to join started to close. I had hoped she'd do so, but it wasn't necessary. Perhaps it was too soon for her to . . .

Never mind.

Her resolve came barreling through like a charging bull. By the feel of it, she'd been considering the choice of where to go for quite some time. Her will, though strong following her breakthrough, lacked finesse—it was a damned jackhammer. Said power tool veered off toward the propulsion system that Maria and Slimes were focused on, and I fought down a pang of anxiety.

Had she chosen the wrong one by accident? Her confidence told me otherwise, declaring that she knew *exactly* what she was doing . . . despite heading toward something she couldn't hope to comprehend. It didn't make sense.

I could cut her off if needed, but that could shake the foundation of what we were trying to build. If my will slipped, so, too, would everyone else's. The whole damn thing could collapse. Or *explode*. Who knew what would happen when something so complex unraveled?

As clear as a winter sunrise, I saw the only path forward. All I could do was focus on my own intentions. Even if what she wanted was anathema to the rest of us, we would just have to drown her out. I braced myself, preparing to resist whatever she brought our way. Sensing my action, everyone followed suit, mentally forming a shield wall.

And then she arrived . . . only for her will to flit around like a curious bird. Bonnie inspected our work, raising an imaginary eyebrow as she found us bracing against nothing.

What are you all doing? she seemed to ask.

I had been wrong. Bonnie's will wasn't a jackhammer, ready to demolish with reckless abandon. She'd taken the time to taste the different intentions and assess their suitability. The adventurous soul had embraced her nature, and, using it as a lens through which to measure compatibility, she'd decided on a path—the same as Maria and Slimes. Bonnie wanted to help create the propulsion system.

In retrospect, her choosing the most daring project wasn't surprising—but her next actions were.

She looked at my plans, nodded to herself, then flipped the whole damned table. Papers flew and lines blurred, but before I could lose hold of the task, new schematics appeared. She didn't just build upon my previous plans—she'd rewritten them entirely. I checked them over, and what started as a cursory glance became a careful study. I . . . wasn't sure if it was brilliant or stupid. But one thing was certain: It would be *fun*.

Though that excitement spurred me on as I dove headfirst into its creation, it couldn't last forever. Bonnie had taken what was essentially a through pipe and turned it into something I could only compare to . . . Yeah, never mind. This was some fantasy-land bullshit, and with that territory came complexity.

No matter how much will I poured out, each drop disappeared like rain into parched sand. I swiftly realized that an impasse was approaching. I could continue on the current path—ensure the creation of Bonnie's brainchild was a success—or I could guarantee that the ship itself was transformed by the System.

I kept these thoughts to myself, not wanting to discourage Bonnie before a decision was made. The ultimatum hadn't yet arrived; there was still time for me to pull off a miracle. As I slowly pulled back from the additional features, the others instinctively picked up the slack, their chi patching over any gaps I left behind.

And not a moment too soon. The world had finished collecting its power. All at once, the orbs blurred forward into the wooden fibers of the ship, making the entire vessel glow with the same incandescent light. I "watched" it with my senses, each little ball of essence vibrating now that they were finally being put to use.

The deck beneath our feet shifted and the boat expanded. I had to squeeze my eyes shut against the brightness that became all-consuming. Even with my physical senses overwhelmed, I never once eased up with my will, my two partitions both pushed to their limit. Like a concrete slab built upon a fault line, no matter how much the world shook, I ensured the foundation remained whole. Using me for support, my pals were similarly unflappable, each of us mentally screaming what we wanted into the void. But as strong as our resolve was, the transformation just . . . kept going.

The impasse had arrived.

As much as I wanted Bonnie's maniacal method of propulsion, I couldn't sacrifice the boat's transformation. It was a purely pragmatic decision; such a creation would tear an unenhanced vessel to pieces.

With no small amount of reluctance, I started channeling my will back toward the ship, letting them all know why I was doing it. Bonnie, rather than despair, dismissed my concerns out of hand. Her adventurous soul cared not what I did; she was going to continue working on her creation no matter what I told her.

Laughing in my mind, I let her do what she wanted. It wasn't like I could convince her otherwise.

Something appeared on the periphery of my comprehension. It was right there, but with how stretched thin I was, understanding was out of reach. Suddenly, the source of my confusion arrived, hitting me so hard that it felt almost physical.

And then their will joined with mine, a backpack-sized mass of condensed chi ready to be put to use. They were authoritative. Demanding. So sure of themself as they paired with my main partition—the one focused on the boat. Before I could return my now-free attention to Bonnie's engine, she yanked me over, her desire for novelty and new experiences drawing me in.

Adults are super silly sometimes, Paul thought as he sailed through the air and grabbed Fischer's back.

If asked, he wouldn't have been able to say exactly why he'd chosen to physically latch himself onto the man. Paul had some guesses, though, like how fun it was to leap with his new body. Or how wibbly-wobbly the ship's deck was right now. Yep! Those reasons were some good reasons, all right!

But the most important one was that Fischer needed help. Not only Fischer, actually! They *all* needed help! Paul had waited as long as possible, knowing that they were missing something, but trusting them to work it out. That was what adults did, wasn't it? They fixed things.

As seconds threatened to become a minute, however, the fixing never came. And time had been moving like the molasses his dad made rum from, which let Paul's imagination run wild.

His favorite theories all involved desserts—what if it was taking forever because they were trying to make the boat edible and delicious? Just before he'd launched himself at Fischer, the traveler had finally broadcast what was troubling him.

Fischer was like . . . *super* strong. Even stronger than Paul's dad, not that Paul would ever admit as much. Despite Fischer's strength, though, he wasn't perfect. Fischer couldn't do *everything* himself. Take his mom's baking, for example. There was no world in which Fischer could make better cakes. Paul shook his head. He was getting distracted by sweets again.

As strong as Fischer was, he was only one person—and if Paul's mom could be believed, the man had little goblins living in his brain that sometimes made decisions for him. Paul was too smart and wise and grown-up to take those words literally, but that didn't make it any less true. Fischer really *did* seem to have little green creatures making his choices for him on occasion.

What the man needed was help from someone with a good head on his shoulders. Assistance from a nearby cultivator that hadn't yet had a breakthrough, their brain able to take in everything at face value. What Fischer needed, Paul decided, was someone like *him*.

Paul's entire body—from his short hair to his little toes—screamed that he could do it. His core, though muted compared to the others, vibrated in agreement.

Grinning to himself and holding onto Fischer's back like a head louse, Paul assessed the image Fischer had been imagining. It was . . . okay. Super boring, though. No wonder Fischer needed help.

Instead of the bland design, Paul pictured something *super* cool. Aaaand was immediately denied. He furrowed his brow, annoyed that the boat didn't want to be shaped like Pistachio. Next he tried Claws, Snips, and even Fischer. All were rejected; they weren't *right*.

Something tugged at his core, and Paul's pinched eyebrows flew higher than Ellis's did earlier. It . . . *it was the ship!* The silly thing was talking to him! No, that wasn't right, because it wasn't saying anything at all. It was . . . *drawing*? But not an actual picture, more a—

Paul shook his head again. It didn't matter. The boat was *communicating*!

A vague outline showed up in his mind. Like a see-through cloud, it was the suggestion of a shape, and it shifted nonstop. Paul pouted, not at all liking the way it wouldn't pick a form and stick with it. *Stop that!* he tried thinking. It didn't listen.

But something did answer. Paul's own core reached out toward him, slim tendrils of chi escaping their prison. As they passed through his torso, their intent—*his* intent—radiated out. For only a moment, Paul was granted a glimpse into an alternative version of himself. Practical. Calculating. *Decisive.* Ready to sweep in and make the choices that others . . .

Paul's thoughts trailed off as the window closed once more. He shook his head. What the *frack* was *that*?

Before he could consider it overmuch, the task at hand materialized in his vision once more, the damned ship still refusing to choose a shape. Reaching for the chi leaking from his core—and both relieved and slightly disappointed that he didn't again see that other version of himself—Paul gave the ship a good scowl. It didn't work, of course, but it made him feel a bit better.

His core urged him to try something else, to latch onto the memory of that other him.

Fine, Paul thought. *You want decisiveness? I'll give you decisiveness!*

He pictured Pistachio again—because Pistachio was still *really* cool—and the cloudy outline actually listened. It moved, stretching to conform to what he envisioned, then snapped back into blurry nothingness.

Oh-ho-ho! Paul thought, trying—and succeeding, if you asked him—to sound like a wise old man. *What have we here?*

That had just about worked. He'd almost created a lobster ship.

It had snapped back after stretching too far. So what would happen if his changes were smaller? He focused on making adjustments to the ship, choosing cool things that didn't alter the outline too much. Fischer *had* to have a cool ship.

What if I just . . . yes! A touch of red here? Ooooh, and metal there! Hmm, but it still has to be floaty, so lots of wood . . . Okay, maybe a bit *more metal.*

Images started flashing in his mind. At first, he assumed they were from the other him, but then he realized their true source: Fischer. They were objects from his past life. A smile spread across Paul's face as he applied their appearance to the existing pieces. It was coming together nicely.

Wait, if the ship is mostly wood, does that mean I can't use fire?

. . .

A few flames couldn't hurt . . . right?

Bit by bit, Paul adjusted the components, each slowly becoming a cohesive part of something greater. He was even able to alter the appearance of the thing Bonnie was working on. She held him back at first but acquiesced when she felt his intention to change only the aesthetics.

Originally, he'd leaped in because they needed the help, but the more he designed, the more he fell in love with the process. It was like building castles in the sand but, like, a *bajillion* times better—the sandcastles he made couldn't spew fire.

When he put the very last piece in place, a door befitting the rest of the ship, it happened. The blurred lines of the boat snapped into place, forming as if they'd always been there. Paul wanted to open his eyes, wanted to gaze out at his creation, but his *everything* wasn't working. As he pictured the super-cool ship he'd made for Fischer, the last thing he felt was the sensation of falling.

CHAPTER THIRTY-SEVEN

Edgelord

I whirled, my senses returning the moment the boat's transformation was complete. I caught Paul with ease, intending on lowering him to the ground. Instead, I froze, scanning the surrounding bubbles of chi with my core and eyes both.

"Ruh-roh, Raggy."

They slammed into Paul's abdomen. I raised shields around him, preparing to protect against whatever was happening, but there was no need; as with his core, the System had placed a limit on his power—breakthrough or not. Paul's insight, the ideal that had facilitated this advancement, was similarly muted. Because of the suppression, I couldn't get a clear reading.

Paul was a . . . designer?

That couldn't be it. As Paul opened his eyes and looked around, though, I instinctively scraped his surface thoughts.

Well, I'll be . . .

He *had* to be a designer. It was the first thing that came to his mind upon awakening. Still struggling to believe it, I tried to sense any chi coming from his core, but the breakthrough he'd experienced—and the System's subsequent interference—left me unable to glean anything.

"Paul!" Barry appeared at our side. "Are you—" He cut off, his eyes went wide when he felt the changes. ". . . *How?*"

Paul just grinned and rubbed the back of his head.

"Well done, mate," I said. "I know people have all sorts of ideals, but I can't say I expected to have a young designer on our hands."

His eyes flicked away from mine, losing focus as they roved the surrounding sands. I suspected he was exploring his core—not that the System's interference let me say for sure.

"Before you get too lost in thought," I said, "can I ask you something?"

His stare snapped back to mine, a hint of gravity visible that belied his age. "Of course."

"Good." I slung an arm over his shoulder and spun him toward the ship. "It's a short one, so listen up." I swept a hand in a wide arc, gesturing at the giant vessel's deck. "What in Poseidon's salt-washed booty did you do to my fishing boat?"

"What do you mean?"

I swiveled my head to look at Paul, then at the deck, then at Paul again. "I didn't think I'd need to elaborate . . ."

"Well, if you're talking about the changes—" The smile on his face was even brighter than Tropica's future. "I made it *way* cooler!"

Maria stifled a laugh, looking away when Barry shot her a warning glare. Cinnamon was much less polite. She rolled in the grass—yes, the deck was *grassy*—absolutely losing herself to a fit of high-pitched giggles. Even Borks was amused, his enjoyment only shown via a slight wag of the tail.

"I guess cool is subjective . . ." Crossing my arms, I reassessed the ship's features, choosing to see it through the eyes of a young man.

First, the deck was covered in grass. That alone wasn't exactly *too* weird; if it was good enough for Luffy and the Thousand Sunny, it was good enough for us. What made this particular patch of seafaring grass so abnormal was its color. Blood red, its blades swayed in a soft breeze, more beautiful than they had any right being.

I had to ask. "Why red?"

"Uhhh, because I couldn't use fire?" His dubious expression implied I was an idiot. "And it needed some color. I've seen red trees before, so why not grass?"

I considered replying, getting so far as half raising a finger, but let it go instead. I couldn't knock the use of rubescent leaves over open flames.

The rest of the ship had *some* visible patches of wood, but most of it was covered in gothic metal trim right out of a My Chemical Romance music video. Rather than milled trees, its railings were made of fused chain, each link as big as my hand. That same material was used to hang lanterns, whose sharp edges and deadly points would've looked at home on the end of a mace. The door to the cabin was now a gray alloy, and if it wasn't on a boat, I'd have thought it led to a dungeon.

The only completely wooden parts I could see were twin staircases connecting the lower and upper deck. Following them, my eyes landed on a round object on top of the cabin. I stared at its gleaming surface as I climbed the port-side stairs. When I reached it, I rested a hand on its metal rungs.

It was real. The cheeky little bugger—he'd given my ship a chain steering wheel from a 90s lowrider!

I exhaled and took a step back, turning to gaze down at the lower deck. I tried to look at the boat with objectivity now that I had a bird's-eye view. The audacity of Paul's creation had made me see through my own eyes; I was supposed to be looking at it through his. To a young man like Paul, this boat was *unquestionably* cool. Perhaps the coolest thing imaginable. If I had been given leave to create a custom ship at his age, there was no way I'd have been able to create something so cohesive.

Say what you would about his creative choices—Paul had kept things thematic. Sure, said theme could be misinterpreted as "edgelord billionaire headed for international waters," but it was the thought that counted. Besides, it was also my fault—he'd gotten these ideas from *my* mind. Each element was consistent in its adherence to the "rule of cool," and it made me excited about what he would make when he was a little more . . . How should I put it? Seasoned in his travels?

I shot Barry some side-eye, having not hidden that musing. He just shook his head.

"All right," I said, striding down to rejoin everyone else. "I take it back, Paul. You've made something objectively cool." I omitted the "for a preteen" from the end of my sentence, earning a full-toothed grin in reply.

"I'm so glad you like it! Wait until you see the cabin! It's even *better*!"

Damn. I'd forgotten about the inside.

I fought down a grimace as he dashed forward and threw open the dungeon-esque door, revealing a world of color. Well, *a* color, anyway. Red, to be exact. *Carpet? Who puts carpet on a . . . Never mind.* Tapestries, a half dozen beds on the starboard wall, and a door leading to what was likely the privy. Red, red, *red*. Even the damned kitchen bench on the port-side wall was made of an auburn wood.

The door to the bathroom appeared to be mahogany, but its vibrant hue wasn't what had my attention after Paul yanked open its black handle. Beyond, the scene that met us put the rest of the boat's extravagance to shame.

Everyone crowded in, peering around the bathroom and admiring its opulence. Cinnamon leaped atop my shoulder, her head jolting back as she tried to take it all in at once.

"Paul . . ." Maria said, pausing to choose her words carefully. "Why did you change the color scheme in here?"

The toilet and shower were almost entirely gold. Not colored, mind you—they were *literally* made of the precious metal. The floor, roof, and walls were all a black alloy, as were the shower knobs, head, and the toilet's flush lever. Everything else, every single surface, was golden.

"Well," Paul answered, all too happy to explain, "people always refer to Fischer's magical toilets as thrones, and when I was in his head—"

"When you were *what*?" Barry interrupted. "What did you see?"

"Relax, mate. Paul here was only having a peek at some design choices."

"You're saying this aesthetic is your doing?"

"This totally cool aesthetic that we all agree is singular in theme and wonderfully unique?" I gave him a pointed look, to which Barry nodded slowly.

"Then yes," I continued. "They were inspired by things I've seen before. You were saying, Paul?"

"When I was in your head, I felt how much emphasis you were placing on the toilet, so I made it *super* shiny! The rest of it came from there." That wizened look flashed across his face again. "Besides, red and gold go together, so it's a unique space that won't be jarring if glimpsed through the open door."

Barry's eyebrows climbed ever higher as Paul's words ventured further into design theory. "Who are you, and what have you done with my son?"

I laughed, patting them both on the back. "He's still there, but with a keener eye for detail now. Personally, I love it."

"Thanks!" Paul beamed. "I'm so, so, *so* happy you like it! It was really tough getting the gold thin enough to coat everything!"

"Oh, it's not solid?" Barry asked.

"Huh?" Maria tilted her head. "You couldn't tell it was a thin layer?"

"No? You can?"

"Yeah. I feel the . . . Wait, how *can* I feel it?"

Before her frown could grow too deep, Slimes bounced from her shoulder. "It was *meeee*! I'm using your chi to sense our surroundings!" He jiggled in delight, his body rippling as Maria patted him on the head.

The mention of sensing our surroundings made me realize I should check on the plumbing, and *that* made me recall that there was another, more important component to investigate. I had a wild grin on my face as I sent my awareness out, searching for the part that was vital for the ship's . . .

My thoughts trailed off when I found it. My idea had basically been a pipe that one could pour chi into. The essence would travel through it and out the other side below the water, making the ship shoot forward like a jet boat. Bonnie's adjustment had been . . . Well, I still didn't really understand it, but the crux of its function was condensing the chi with some System-made shenanigans.

What I did understand, however, was the warm aspect now radiating out from it.

". . . Paul?" I asked.

"Yeah?"

"Did you picture flames when you changed the appearance of the propulsion system?"

He looked at me with a distinct lack of comprehension. "The what now?"

"The part that makes it move."

"Ohhhh! You mean the flame pipe."

"Right. Flame pipe. So you *did* picture fire when designing it, then?"

His answering grin could almost rival one of Corporal Claws's. "Oh yeah. I pictured *all* the fire."

"What are you talking about?" Maria asked. "I don't feel—" She cut off as her extended senses found what I had. ". . . Oh. That could be a problem."

Bonnie noticed it next—she clearly didn't think it would be a problem at all if her manic smirk could be believed.

"What's wrong?" Paul asked, confusion surging as he took in our expressions.

"It's hard to sense," I replied, "but I'm pretty sure only a fire-aspected cultivator can power it. It was supposed to be useable by everyone."

"Wait, *what*? The ship is *powered*?"

Paul's question made me snort. "You didn't even know what you were altering?"

"Nope, just that it was important."

"And that it would look cooler with flames," Bonnie added.

"Yeah! It—wait, why is it bad that only a fire cultivator can use it? It's stronger, right? And faster."

"That might be the issue," I replied. "Never mind the explanation for now—my assumption could be wrong. Or a good thing. Let's go check it out."

A little crestfallen, Paul nodded.

We made our way down onto the sand, and as I caught sight of Paul's creation, I barked a laugh. "Okay, that is *awesome*!"

"You . . . you like it?" he asked.

"Like it? I *love* it!"

My ship had a giant lobster claw extending from its rear, cocked open like Pistachio's snipper when he was ready to unleash a blast. I leaned in close, inspecting the hollow pipe that would concentrate and expel any chi poured in. It was time to test if only fire worked. Seeing if my instincts were correct, I sent barely a strand of my unaspected essence into the top of the construct—and immediately regretted my decision.

The resulting blast was half flame, half light, and 100% bad idea as it shot in random directions. Ready for such a reaction, I slammed a dome into place. It shielded us from all the force, but only a portion of the blinding light show. I readied myself for the pain that would result, shutting my eyes as tight as I could, but something blocked it.

Borks had opened a curved portal within the dome. Rather than transportation, he'd done so to protect our vision, the black-and-purple wall absorbing any light that made it through. "Borks! You are such a *good boy*!" I bent at the waist to fuss him all over. "Yes, you are! *Are you a good boy?*"

He barked and hopped foot to foot, his whole back half wagging.

Only one of us wasn't having a good time. Paul's eyes were downcast, the rest of him just . . . limp. He couldn't even find the energy to cross his arms.

"Paul, my man, this is an absolute win!" He frowned at me, clearly detesting the idea of supplication—and making me glad he hadn't recognized my actual supplication earlier. This, however, was no such ruse. "I'm serious! You've outdone yourself!"

If the narrowing of his eyes was anything to go by, he didn't believe me in the slightest.

"Think about it. You're the youngest cultivator Tropica has, and though your core is a little limited, you just had a breakthrough." I tapped him lightly in the center of his forehead. "Stop feeling bad for a moment. Consider *why* I'm saying it's a good idea."

"Because we have a fire cultivator? Trent would rather stay here, though . . ."

"How do you know that?"

"Because every time someone mentions family—even if it's not his—he gets sad. He won't want to leave his mother and sister while they're still locked up."

"Paul, if I didn't know better, I'd think your breakthrough was as some sort of master strategist." I tapped him again, twice this time. "Think, mister. You've got an annoyingly perceptive head on your shoulders. Why would I call it a win that we have a single uncorrupted fire cultivator, who is overly obsessed with talking to his *definitely corrupted and maybe also evil* family that we've got locked up in a magical not-a-prison?"

I was pretty sure Rocky could fuel it if he was careful with his chi, but Paul didn't need to know that. It took him a second to actually listen, but when my words finally pierced through the self-recrimination afflicting him, the wisdom from earlier flashed in his eyes.

"You've made a vehicle that only he can power, so he'll *have* to come . . ."

"Nah, mate. *You've* made a vehicle that only he can power. Tropica's youngest cultivator, who has a System-limited core and *just* experienced a breakthrough, caused that requirement without my instruction." I shot him a wink. "I have *complete* deniability."

"Devious . . ." Barry said, to which Cinnamon, Borks, and Maria nodded.

Not denying the claim, I looked up at the sky. "This one's for you, Claws." No response came, but that wasn't surprising given how focused she was on whatever forsaken experiments she was currently conducting. I tried to see what she was up to through her eyes. This earned a reply—the mental equivalent of a rough flick on the nose.

I shook my head, dismissing the sensation. "By the way, Barry . . . weren't you supposed to get Paul home?" I pointed at the sky, its subtle shift in color noticeable to our enhanced awareness. "I reckon it's only a couple hours until dawn."

I was pretty sure he tried to swear, but it came out as a garbled mess. He scooped up his son and sprinted away. "Helen's gonna kill me!" His muscular legs chewed through the sand back toward his home.

"Bye!" Paul yelled, waving energetically over his dad's shoulder.

"Huh." Maria crossed her arms and cocked her head. "Was that Poseidon's name he tried to invoke?"

"I thought it was Triton," I answered. "What did you hear, Bonnie?"

"Definitely Poseidon."

"Hmm. I wonder where the sound came from, then . . ."

"Taint, of course," she replied, smiling as she stared at the giant claw that her brainchild had become. "That was the noun, but the adjective between is anyone's guess."

The following morning, I nodded, undeterred by the scowl Trent was giving me. "Yep! That about sums it up! Paul swooped in and saved the day, made it so only you can power the ship, and that's about it."

"And the toilet is gold," Maria added.

"Right! Yes! The toilet is gold—can't forget that. Still, what really matters is that I am unilaterally and unreservedly disappointed that you are encouraged, if not obligated, to stop lingering around your family's cells, and instead have to come fishing with me."

The sun was beaming down from above, heralding another beautiful day in Tropica. Despite how well lit my face was, Trent looked at the person beside me. "Maria, Fischer knows that I can feel his emotions, right?"

"Ah-huh. If I'm not mistaken, I think he may even be amplifying them."

I nodded gravely. "I may be doing that."

"So he knows I can feel exactly how happy it's making him?"

"I believe that might be the point."

"It is," I agreed, still nodding.

Trent ran his fingers through his hair, reminding me just how damn good looking he was after becoming a cultivator. He froze, squinting at me.

"What?" I asked. "You're a good-looking rooster! You used to look like a thrice-stubbed toe."

"That's not the problem—the problem is you messing with me by broadcasting those thoughts."

"What, a bloke can't pay another bloke a compliment?"

"Not when it's being used as a diversionary tactic, no. That robs it of its sincerity."

"I . . . Huh. You've got me there." I turned to Maria. "Help?"

Not hiding her amusement, she shook her head at me, her sun-bleached hair swaying beautifully and making me remember the other night when we . . . aaand now she was squinting at me too.

"Sorry!" I held up both hands. "That one was actually an accident!"

Her disapproving look lingered a moment before she turned to Trent. "I'm not going on the first trip. I'm staying here." Her face was riddled with meaning as she paused for effect. He went rigid, immediately understanding.

I threw my arms high. "Oh, *suuure*, your best mate in the entire world offers you a fishing trip and you couldn't care less. But a healer staying behind with your *definitely corrupted and maybe also evil* family? *That* gets your attention?"

"It's nothing against your trip. They're my *family*. Neither of them is getting better with time, and I suspect Tryphena might be getting worse." The despair and worry on his face were like a dagger to my chest, but then the beginnings of a smile bunched at the corner of his mouth. "Besides, you're not my best mate, Fischer. Keith is."

I stumbled as if struck, the words cutting deeper than any blade could. I made a pathetic noise and leaned on Maria for support. "Darling, take me from this place. I fear my legs won't work after I was so viciously stabbed in the back."

"Yes, dear," she replied, hauling me into a fireman's carry. "I'll come see you about your family soon, Trent. I'd better get this delicate flower some caffeine—he's pretty useless pre-coffee."

"I am," I agreed, waving goodbye as Maria turned and marched away, still carrying me like a sack of unroasted beans.

CHAPTER THIRTY-EIGHT

Misstep

It was, by all measurable metrics, a beautiful day in Tropica. The sun was shining, there wasn't a cloud in the sky, and I'd used the local equivalent of witchcraft to create a boat last night. Even better, the smell of coffee was flowing from Sue's bakery, the essence-filled aroma making my mouth water.

"Fischer . . ." Sue said by way of greeting as Maria and I reached the counter. "May I ask why you're being carried around like a dead fish?"

"Not again!" I looked down, aghast. "Maria! What have I told you?"

"That behind closed doors, I should refer to you as *chef*? "

"No! Well, *yes*, actually, but that's not what I'm talking about! What have I told you about hauling me around like a dead fish?"

"That you're into it . . . ?"

"What? *No!* Okay, yes again, but not in *public*! Are you seriously telling me you don't recall what I said?"

"Fiiine." She let out an exaggerated sigh. "Yes, I remember."

"Prove it."

"You said that you're super into it—especially when I pretend I'm an injured pelican—but that doing it in public might hurt your reputation with the newer cultivators."

"You *do* listen." I wiped a fake tear away. "I'm sorry for doubting you."

Turning back to Sue, I made a show of straightening my already-straight clothes. "Anyhoo—where were we? Ah, yes, two of your finest coffees and pastries, please!"

Sue's expressions had changed with each sentence, landing somewhere between amused and bewildered. "Before I take your order, did you plan on clarifying to the crowd of *newer cultivators* behind you that you're joking?"

Maria and I spun, finding dozens of people staring our way, some of whom had arrived in Tropica only a week ago.

"I don't think I will," I said.

"Nope!" Maria agreed, and we both turned back to Sue.

She let out one of her hearty laughs as she slung her tea towel over her shoulder. "I should have expected as much. Same as usual?"

"I'd love a little extra sugar, actually!" Maria said. "Please and thank you!"

"You would?" I asked.

"Yep. A certain someone requested sweetness."

"It was *meeee*!" Slimes sang, jiggling from Maria's shoulder.

I booped the little rascal on the head, making him wibble-wobble with evident joy. "Are you both sure you're feeling ready? There's no shame in waiting a little if you need more time . . ."

Maria gave me a sidelong glance, then peered down at my abdomen with a smirk. "Are you only asking that because you want me and Slimes to come fishing? Is *that* why you're not letting me feel your emotions right now?"

"I can tell you're messing with me, but I'll still remind you that we both agreed it would be healthy if we didn't share our thoughts all the time."

She wiggled her eyebrows, connecting to me and confirming that she was, in fact, teasing. I returned the gesture, revealing that part of me *was* selfishly wanting her to come fishing. But my larger motivation—the thing weighing on me—was my care for her well-being.

She looped an arm through mine, pulling herself close to my body. "He's worried about you, too, Slimes. Hit him with it."

Before I could ponder what "it" was, the little familiar stretched his body and gave me the approximation of a kiss on the cheek.

"Byeeee!" he chimed, wiggling back into Maria's core, where he immediately began doing . . . something healing related. Or slime adjacent. I didn't really know.

Rubbing the spot he'd smooched, I shook my head with a smile. "For real, though—how are you feeling?"

"Do you mean like . . . right now? Or about healing the prisoners?"

"Yes."

She rolled her eyes. "Well, right now I'm pretty tired, but I imagine the coffee will help. About the healing, though . . ." Her face moved almost imperceptively as she assessed her emotions. "Honestly? I feel great. I'm really excited and . . . hopeful is probably the most accurate word, but even that feels inadequate."

"Show me?"

She nodded, reaching out via our connection; I immediately understood what she meant.

It really wasn't a strong enough word. Language could be so limiting, a fact I hadn't been entirely cognizant of until becoming a cultivator. Maria wanted it to succeed for everyone's sake. She was optimistic about the outcome, her positivity born of the chi suffusing both her and Slimes.

The pressure of her task, however, was unimaginable—as the only healer in Tropica, it rested squarely on her freckled shoulders. She only showed me that aspect for a fraction of a second, and as it faded, her overwhelming confidence swept back in, her core humming in agreement.

The corner of my mouth curled up into a teasing smirk. "Do I have to keep an eye out for delusions of grandeur? I'm all for self-assurance, but *sheesh.*"

Her answering grin was predatory. "You? Oh, absolutely. I'm pretty sure you've been suffering from them the entire time I've known you."

"Oh, hah-hah. You know what I meant."

"I do, but I didn't want to dignify it with a response. It's beneath someone as grand as I am, you see."

"Agreed," Sue said, sliding the coffees and pastries over the counter. "The bird has the extra sugar."

"The what . . . ?" I asked, but then I saw what she'd managed to draw in each cup's foam.

The one closest to Maria had a magnificent bird marked with dark swirls of crema. Its tail fanned out above it, the feathers looking entirely too intricate to be latte art. Mine was just as complicated, showing the recognizable silhouette of a crab wearing an eye patch.

"How did you . . . ?"

"Sue . . ." Maria said. "How am I supposed to drink this?"

Sue's core hummed with validation at our responses, and she stood to her full height—which still wasn't very tall, but her posture was commendable. "It's made to be temporary, so drink up."

"But . . . it's art!"

"And I want you to drink it . . ." She narrowed her eyes at Maria. "You know what? I've had it. All bloody morning I've been hearing the same damned thing." She removed the tea towel from her shoulder, a threatening look in her eye as she started twirling it. "It's enough to send a woman mad . . ."

"Coming through!" Sturgill called as he came from the kitchen, his arms laden with a tray of pastries, and his well-being afflicted by terrible timing. "Lemon danishes fresh out of the oven! Come and get—"

Sue's hand whipped out like a viper. When the kinetic force reached the end of her tea towel, its corner lashed with expert precision, heading right for one of Sturgill's buns.

Crack!

He jumped so high that he almost lost his still-warm pastries, but he landed with grace, catching each of his creations before turning to look at his wife.

Why? his eyes seemed to plead.

"Shhhh." She leaned in close, covering his mouth with one finger. "Or I'll do the other cheek, too. I might just start lashing out at every butt in sight."

Maria immediately grabbed her cup and took a swig, ruining the art. "Ready to go, Fischer?"

I nodded, swiftly collected the rest of our breakfast, then let Maria lead me through the crowd.

"That's right! You'd *better* run!" Sue let a string of threats fly, their contents so colorful that they didn't bear repeating. They trailed us as we retreated to the next street. "And that goes for all of you!" her voice boomed, echoing around the corner. "I better hear no complaints about drinking my art unless you want to be on the receiving end of one of these!" A second *crack* rang out, which I had good reason to believe was the tea towel hitting Sturgill's other cheek based on the way he yelped.

I let out a choked laugh.

Maria's giggle was much more pleasant. "Did you see the faces of the three cultivators at the back? Gods above—they thought she was serious!"

"It was actually kind of brilliant, don't you think? I seriously doubt anyone else is going to make a fuss after this."

"It was. A shame poor Sturgill had to be dragged into it. Not that a tea towel could hurt him."

"Imagine if she'd infused it with chi, though . . ." I shivered. "Sue is kinda terrifying. With the power she has now, she might have stood a chance against the king."

Maria almost missed a step, and a pang of guilt stabbed from her core, penetrating her carefully concealed feelings.

"Sorry." I squeezed her hand. "I shouldn't have brought him up."

"There's nothing to apologize for. I know it's not my fault that I hadn't unlocked my healing powers early enough to save him." She shook her head softly, a strand of sand-colored hair falling from behind her ear. "Not that I could have, even if I'd had the breakthrough in time."

"I have something to tell you, but I need to preface it with another statement." I gazed into her irises. Their oceanic depths centered me. "I have complete belief in you and your abilities, and the only reason I checked that you think you're ready is because I *cannot* lose you." I swept the strand of loose hair behind her ear, bathing in the way my words had made her eyes glitter. "All that said—even with my absolute trust in you—I don't think you could have saved him."

I furrowed my brow, a thought occurring to me. "Do . . . do you want me to show you?"

She didn't respond right away, staring into the distance as she took the time to really consider my offer. I'd kept those memories sealed as best I could. Showing her was always a possibility, and I'd be lying if I said it hadn't occurred to me when Maria accused me of hurting people. I could have shown her the truth. Proved that the king had been offered a way out, and sealed his own fate. But doing so would have been exceedingly selfish. It may have even altered the course of her breakthrough.

"Okay," Maria finally answered. "I think I'd like that."

I looked up to find her staring directly at me, her jaw set and gaze unwavering. Before I could ask if she was sure, Maria nodded. She was ready. I took a deep breath, connected my awareness to hers, and remembered.

Skipping over the preamble, I started from the moment my torrent of unaspected chi flooded over all of the corrupted, presenting them with two paths: surrender their corruption or be *cleansed* alongside it. No matter how necessary it had been, recalling the events knotted my stomach and left a bad taste in my mouth. I set my feelings aside as best I could. They weren't important right now—only Maria was.

The king's response to my offer was a gut punch, both moronic and infuriating, then and now. He was too far gone. There was nothing anyone could have said to bring him back from the precipice. His own wickedness had led him to the edge, I'd presented him with redemption, and he'd instead leaped into the abyss.

The others, though? Even the people so far gone that they identified as birds wanted to be saved—except for that one bloke that Roger had hated. I showed her their ready acceptance of my help. Unlike the king, they were unwilling victims of the rot.

Profound understanding came from Maria, pouring back along the connection I'd forged. My words hadn't been empty: The king had truly been beyond saving.

Potent emotions welled up within her, overwhelming all thought. Before they could make their way to my awareness, she slammed the door between us closed, shutting me off. It was so swift and jarring that I stumbled, taking a step back. Maria's reaction was even stronger. Her cup of coffee, still half full, dropped toward the ground. Her lower lip quivered, her knees wobbling and tears already forming.

The look on her face forced me to recover immediately. I let go of everything I held, catching our cups and pastries on shelves of solid chi. Faster than light, I was wrapping her in my arms, easily supporting her weight. She buried her head into my chest and tried to speak, but only muffled sobs came out.

"It's okay." I patted her hair, regretting that this was the immediate result but knowing it would provide long-term peace of mind. "Take all the time you need."

Her small body shook as she experienced her emotions in full.

CHAPTER THIRTY-NINE

Very Pinchy

As I walked the streets of Tropica, it was an undeniable fact that winter had ended. The morning air still held a hint of lingering freshness, but it was far from the icy chill of only weeks ago. A wind blew from my right, bringing with it a similarly warm touch that I barely felt. The floral smell of Maria's hair hit my awareness like a shot of pure adrenaline, calling to mind countless memories, some of which I had no business recalling in the light of day.

"Glad to see you're having fun," she jibed, smirking beneath red-rimmed eyes.

"My bad. My traitorous brain imagines things all on its own."

"Traitorous, huh? Does that mean you didn't enjoy said imaginings?"

"Hey now, let's not jump to conclusions . . ."

"Good." She leaned against my shoulder. "Just be careful where you're thinking them. I'd hate to see what my lord father would do if he knew such premarital happenings were afoot . . ."

Someone referring to Roger as a lord was always enough to make me snort, and Maria joined in, her soft giggle replacing the moroseness of only moments ago.

We'd been walking the streets for ten minutes, moving while Maria processed her emotions. Her sadness was an unfortunate side effect of reliving the king's downfall.

"I'm so sorry," she said for what must be the tenth time today. "If I'd had any idea . . ."

"Am I gonna have to introduce an apology jar? You'll have to put in a gold coin for every time you say sorry for something you have no business apologizing for."

She attempted to shoot me a venomous look, but it lacked bite. "Fine. I'll never apologize to you again."

"Thank you. That's much better. Consider never apologizing to *anyone*, though. Like, ever. You're betrothed to God-King Fischer, after all."

We both grinned at this, and she grabbed my arm, halting my steps. Spinning me with more power than someone of her stature should possess, she slammed into my chest and squeezed me with all her might. "Okay, I promise this is the last one. I'm sorry for the words I spoke. I know that you took them in stride, but they were still too harsh."

"If it's the last time, then I accept your apology. I'm also sorry—both for how unpleasant the memory was, and that I didn't share it earlier."

She gave me one final squeeze, then her arms withdrew. As she looked up at me, her eyes glimmered. "Now who's making unnecessary apologies?"

"Touché."

Without another word, we started walking again, our direction aimless. Her tiny hand in mine was more calming than it should have been. I marveled at the softness, warmth, and strength of her as our fingers became intertwined. We passed tens of villagers in our wandering passage, and as various gazes landed on us, I could feel something . . . different.

"Odd," Maria whispered so only I could hear. "They're . . ."

"Less reverent," I finished, scarcely able to believe it. "And by a lot."

I had long ago resigned myself to the fact that the more others were exposed to my shenanigans, the more they might come to revere me. After last night, I'd expected their praise today to be egregious. That was why we'd put on the show with Sue, using a healthy dose of absurdism to lower their guard.

Perhaps it hadn't been necessary. The people we passed now, all of whom were present at the feast, seemed rather reserved. Don't get me wrong; there was still too much wonder for my liking. Any level of it was. But this was . . . unexpected.

My steps were lighter as we rounded a corner, and I dared to let my awareness extend outward, sensing what people felt when I wandered into view. Unsurprisingly, shock came first. Right behind it was a storm consisting of gratitude, thankfulness, and a little awe. Okay, it was a frackload of awe, but the source of it brought me joy instead of the usual dread.

I grinned at the main offender. "Gary! How are ya, mate?"

He grinned back, letting go of his church's door handle and waving at me with his right hand. The other was occupied by a basket. "Fischer! What are you doing here?" Hope beamed from him. "Did you come to check up on our progress?"

"I'll be honest, mate. Maria and I were kinda just wandering about."

He did well to not let his disappointment show.

"But," I continued, "now that we're here . . ."

Someone threw the door open from inside. A leviathan head peeked through the portal, and Pistachio extended a massive snipper outside. Never one to turn down our favorite lobster, Maria and I marched forward, both bending to fist-bump his limb. He knocked the door aside, inviting us to enter with a soft hiss.

However, he was too slow. The entrance of the building next door flew open, banging loudly as a man skidded out onto the street.

"Fischer!" Even if I couldn't feel how glad Joel was to see me, I could see it all over his face. "What are you doing here? Have you come to meditate with us? It's been so long that I can't remember the last time! Is Snips with you? No, of course not—she's still busy seeking enlightenment! So how have you been? Good, I hope!"

"My man!" I held up my hands at his barrage of questions. "I'm happy to see you, too, but I might not have time to meditate this morning."

I looked at Maria, nonverbally asking what she wanted to do. This was our last day together for a while, so I wanted to spend as long with her as possible.

She tossed her head side to side, her hair swaying hypnotically as she considered. "If it doesn't take too long . . ."

"Of course!" came a feminine voice from inside. Jess skidded out with just as much energy as Joel. "Leave after five minutes if you like! You've never joined us, right, Maria?"

"I haven't, no." Amusement bubbled up from Maria's core, but she made sure to keep it between us. "But I'd love to."

"Wonderful!" Joel and Jess both said in tandem.

Darting a look at each other, they formed their human hands into an approximation of crab claws, then clapped by shutting them repeatedly. If I didn't know them, this scene might have earned them a direct trip to Tropica's not-a-prison until I could confirm they weren't about to put on crab suits and start harassing people.

"Does in, like, five minutes work?" I asked. "We're gonna see what Pistachio and Gary have been up to lately, but we'll come right after."

"Of course! Let yourselves in!" Joel turned to Jess, nodded, and they both popped a squat, emulating the form they idolized. Shuffling sideways with surprising alacrity—they'd clearly been practicing—they crab walked back inside. Joel clacked his hand one last time before closing the door behind them.

Gary, whose forehead had formed a deepening crease with each moment, opened his mouth to respond. No response came out for a good while. Finally, he decided that the most diplomatic approach was to say nothing at all. "Let's go look at the lobsters, shall we?"

I barked a laugh. "Lead the way!"

As we walked into the building, something demanded my attention. The chi within wasn't right, but neither was it wrong. Almost like it possessed an aspect, the air was thick with the promise of change. Maria squeezed my hand; she felt it, too.

Deciding it was a problem for later, I focused on our physical surroundings.

The building had come a long way since that time I kicked Borks through it. Remembering how much damage I'd done to him, I felt a little bad. But then I remembered that, at the time, he was a hellhound sent to literally murder me dead—which did wonders for my guilt.

In the center of the restored room, perched atop a wooden frame, sat a massive System-made glass tank. The aquarium held only a foot of water; its inhabitants didn't need much depth. I spotted a few of them, their little antennae waving out of the myriad rocks, patches of seaweed, and hollow tunnels that Gary and Pistachio had placed for them.

"How old are they?" I asked, bending down to peer through the thick glass.

"Weeks. Maybe a month? Time is confusing with all the . . ." Gary gestured vaguely, then sighed. "Everything."

"Say less, mate. I feel that on an emotional level."

"Wow," Maria said, staring at a little lobster butt that poked out the back of a hollow pipe. "I know I shouldn't be surprised, but they're like mini versions of you, Pistachio."

Yes, he agreed with a sturdy hiss, clearly proud of their health and growth.

"Do you want to feed them?" Gary asked Maria, setting his basket of goods down. "I just collected some more supplies."

"Ohhh, I'd love to! What do they eat?"

I leaned over, checking what he'd brought. It was a plethora of passiona berries, his entire bag filled to the brim. Being careful with how much awareness I extended, not wanting to absorb any of the anomalous chi filling the building, I assessed the fruit. "Damn—some of them are absolutely *loaded* with chi."

"They are, but . . ." Gary shook his head. "The cost was great."

"Wait, what?" Maria cocked her head. "Why would Lemon charge you for something that could make Tropica stronger?"

"She wasn't alone when the bargain was struck. There was a devil in her boughs."

"Ahhh," Maria and I both said, realizing who it was. "Corporal Claws."

He nodded, giving a rueful smile. "I suppose I should be thankful that we reached a deal *before* she turned into literal lightning."

Maria laughed. "I'd say you got off lightly, then. Especially if your baby lobsters like them."

"Adolescents are called crickets, actually. But yes, they love them. Initially, I added them to their diet because I thought they'd get sick of fish, but passiona berries, specifically the ones filled with chi, became fast favorites."

"Speaking of fish," I said, "why didn't you take them any of the food from last night?"

Pistachio cringed back, making a cross with his giant claws.

Gary's face had drained of color. "I know it *probably* wouldn't have turned them into little versions of Claws and that demon rat she bonded with, but we weren't taking that chance."

"He's a raccoon," I laughed. "But point taken."

There was a sound at the door, and glancing its way, I wondered who else had come to visit the Church of the Leviathan. Odd scraping noises sounded from outside. The new arrival fumbled with the handle for longer than I thought reasonable, but when it finally flew open, I understood both that and the source of the scrapes.

Technical Officer Theodore Roosevelt held a passiona-filled basket in his mouth. He froze when he saw us, dipping his gigantic noggin in a show of respect.

"Teddy!" I beamed. "What are you doing here, mate?"

Pride radiated from Gary's core, making curiosity rise in my own. Before I could explore its cause, he spoke. "Teddy has joined the Church of the Leviathan."

The bear let out a guttural growl in response that was so bassy it shook the walls. Realizing what he'd just done, Teddy's eyes went wide, then he bowed in apology, his nose literally touching the floor.

"As a *temporary* member," Gary clarified. "I didn't mean anything by it. We're happy to have you here—no matter how momentary."

Pistachio raised a massive clacker in agreement.

Something about the odd chi in the church had stopped me from feeling Teddy's approach. Now that he was within, however, I sensed why he'd chosen to assist in raising the lobst—er, crickets.

Technically, the crustaceans weren't yet sapient . . . but they could become so. They were at least a month old, and they were still smaller than one of my fingers. They were fragile. Weak. *Vulnerable.* And Teddy meant to ensure they survived.

He'd trudged over with his head still lowered, and I patted his massive brow. "I'm proud of you, mate. Truly."

He had to fight to stop from bowing again, a tinge of shyness coming from his core, but his gratification was even stronger. It shone from within, so bright that it seemed to impact everyone.

Gary cleared his throat. "Well, there you have it. There are three of us working on keeping them fed. And speaking of . . ."

He offered a massive pair of tweezers to Maira. They looked more like tongs as far as I was concerned, and Maria apparently agreed—the first thing she did was give them a testing clack.

Peter held out his basket. "Grab a handful whenever you're ready."

"Will they only eat that much?" she asked, looking down at her fruit-laden palm.

"They'll likely consume twice that again, but we're careful to not overfeed them."

Nodding, she approached the tank. The moment Maria lowered the first berry into the water, a few nearby lob—crickets, dammit—took notice. Their adorable little antennae wiggled as they tried to locate the food.

"Oh!" She giggled. "They must be hungry!"

She spread the feast out as evenly as possible, ensuring there was a berry close to each of the miniature caverns they'd emerge from—and emerge they did. I couldn't believe how many of them there were. As tiny little snippers pulled food apart, releasing their juices into the water, even more of the creatures appeared. There had to be almost a hundred of them. The floor of the tank was absolutely covered in a reddish hue that constantly shifted as they fought—rather politely, mind you—for mouthfuls of the sweet treats.

"Where did you get so many?" I asked. "The Gormona branch of your church?"

Gary snorted. "I wouldn't call them part of the Church—they're still stuck in a cult mentality. I told them of Pistachio's existence, and their response was, as far as I can tell, to flee the capital."

"Wait, what? When did this happen?"

"In the time between your secret mission to collect coffee and your secret mission to get supplies for a ship."

I leaned in close, giving the room a conspiratorial look before my gaze landed on him. "Who told you about those?"

Knowing both were common knowledge by now, we snickered. Maria rolled her eyes, but the smile on her face told me her true feelings.

"I sent a letter with Pelly," Gary said. "I thought seeing an awakened bird would lend credence to my claim, but she told me they looked terrified. When she went back the next day, they were long gone—as were the lobsters and crickets."

"Soooo," Maria said. "Where did the others come from, then?"

"Snips's squad of rock crabs. Pistachio went out to find them, then requested they collect any they came across. Within a week, we had hundreds, most of which we returned."

"Ohhh, how was the squad? I haven't seen those crabby little scoundrels in forever."

"The same as ever," he replied. "All business, and very pinchy."

While we spoke, the berries had been absolutely annihilated, so Gary produced more. Maria was all too happy to drop them in, and just as she was placing the last of the fruit, she tilted her head. "Oh no . . . is that one sick?"

Gary was at her side in a moment, crouching to look through the side of the tank. Wedged in the corner and surrounded by thick vegetation, a single creature sat. Its antennae moved about chaotically, clearly smelling the food, yet it didn't take a step. Pistachio hauled himself upward, using his forelimbs as pillars to support his massive body. His antennae waved in thought, then he hissed. The meaning was clear.

Scared. Hungry.

"The lobster?" I asked.

He nodded and hissed again. Small.

"Small and hungry, I get," Maria said, "but why is it scared?"

I winced, suspecting I knew the reason. "Lobsters are opportunistic feeders. Given the chance, they're not above eating another of their kind."

"That's . . . I mean . . ." Her lips formed a line. "That makes sense, but I still hate it."

Gary stepped forward with a small net. "I'm just glad we saw it in time."

He scooped up the lobster, who was none too happy about being disturbed, then rested the handle atop the aquarium, creating a temporary water prison. With great care, he moved rocks and tunnels to make an isolated area, its sheer walls too steep for any enterprising crickets to scale.

The undersized crustacean exited the net with much less of a fuss, happy to be returned to the sandy bottom of the tank. It was even happier when Gary dropped a passiona berry in from above. Well, it retreated at first, kicking its tail to escape what it perceived as a threat. However, as soon as it smelled the food, it scuttled forward, probably intent on gorging itself before any of its brethren bullied it away.

But none would come. The scrawny little thing had been given a holiday home, in which he would receive an all-you-can-eat buffet on the daily.

Man, I thought, *Life as a pet lobster sounds pretty sweet. I'm kinda jealous.*

"Hey, Fischer?"

"Yes, Maria?"

"That was a weird thought to share with me."

"Maybe, but that doesn't make it any less true." I grinned at my Church of the Leviathan pals. "Thanks for letting us see your li'l lobbies. We'd better get going, though—very important meeting next door, you see."

"Important, you say?" Gary smirked beneath a raised brow.

"Ah-huh! Might even reach crab nirvana if things go well!"

I gave Pistachio a fist bump in parting, hugged Teddy, and shot Gary a wink—the laugh that came in reply was icing on the cake of what had been a recharging experience.

"Have fun!" Gary teased. "And let me know if you attain that enlightenment!"

CHAPTER FORTY

Swollen

I was having a wonderful morning. I had only been awake for just over an hour, and already I had managed to take part in a plethora of weird and wacky activities. I'd watched someone put a lobster in lobster prison; I'd relived the time I gave a king an ultimatum; and I'd pretended, before a crowd of newly awakened cultivators, that I was into being thrown around the bedroom like a dead fish while being called chef.

All were beyond absurd. Even so, the scene unfolding before me was worse.

Joel hissed and blew bubbles—*how the* frack *was Joel blowing bubbles?*—as he used his claw hands to pinch a new recruit on the shoulder.

"Ow!" the woman said, standing up and rubbing her arm. "That hurt!"

"I apologize, Sally. The heavens have blessed me with ascension." Joel's words were sincere, his face and core showing clear remorse, but his hands still clacked menacingly. "I forget my strength when I assume the perfect form."

"Yeah? Well, it's hard to take your apology seriously when you're still *crouching like a crab*!"

"You know," Maria said, also crouching like a crab, "she has a point."

Joel shot her a look, but Maria just shrugged.

"Thank you!" The woman—I was pretty sure her name was Sally—straightened her clothes. "Is it really necessary for us to be so literal in our praise? Why do you have to . . . You know what? This isn't working for me. I think crabs are super cute, especially Sergeant Snips, but—"

Most of the room—all the original members of the Church of Carcinization, along with three other new inductees—clacked their crab hands together in response to Snips's name. Joel even blew more bubbles.

". . . But you're all just too *weird*," Sally finished, turning and grabbing a bag on her way out. "I'm not coming back."

She slammed the door behind her, and Joel nodded, still showing remorse. "Not all who attempt greatness have the requisite shell to withstand the pressure, hallowed be Sergeant Snips's name."

They all clacked again—and blew bubbles if they were capable. Joel scuttled to his spot in the center of the circle, swaying back and forth as he settled. As the others resumed their meditation, I shot a look Maria's way—she was already watching me, her eyes twinkling.

Without needing to speak a word, we had an entire conversation, both agreeing on a few points. Yes, this was objectively funny. No, we shouldn't intervene. And yes, they were *definitely* giving off some evil cult vibes. Despite said vibes, it was hard to think they'd pose a threat to anyone, especially with—

"Fischer," Joel said, not opening his eyes. "I am gladdened that you two are here, but I must ask that you participate if you wish to remain."

Maria and I locked eyes again, and she had to bite her lip to hide her smile. How in Snips's rigid carapace had he known . . . ?

"Sorry, mate," I said, and I meant it. I'd been pretty disrespectful of his beliefs, ridiculous as they might be.

Picturing myself as a crab, I swayed back and forth, just as Joel had when he'd returned to the center. As with next door, the air in here had a tangible feel to it, something akin to change seeming to fill it. Unlike the other church, however, this building reached out to me. The moment I leaned into a certain position—still picturing my body as that of a crab—the room asked if it could enter my core.

I shot to my feet, and Maria did the same, her eyes wide.

Joel followed us in standing, religious fervency clear across his entire visage. "Chosen . . ." he said. "Chosen of Carcinization!" He dropped to his knees and pressed his forehead to the ground.

"Chosen of Carcinization!" the rest repeated, flattening themselves even more as they faced Maria and me.

The building, the very air surrounding us, requested that we resume meditating. Begged us to continue where we'd left off. Maria and I locked eyes, nodded to each other, and got the *fuck* out of there.

"Wait!" Joel yelled as we fled the church and slammed the door behind us. "You can be chosen ones! Like Sergeant Snips!"

"Hallowed be her name!" Jess added.

The echoed clacks from the rest of the followers sent a shiver down my spine.

"Okay, I'm not so sure we shouldn't intervene anymore." Maria blew air from her lips. "What is up with that building?"

Now that I was free of it, I could think clearly. "I guess it's a feature of the chi returning to the world? And that . . ." I waved my hand in the church's general direction. "Is the power that created deities in the past, maybe?" I shook my head. "I have no clue. I'm not connected to it."

"Sooo, do we need to burn it with fire, or . . . ?"

"Nah, I think it's fine. If it was evil, I'd have felt it much sooner. The chi is just . . . different. It felt wrong because I don't, in any way, shape, or form, want to turn into a crab. I mean, Snips *is* hella cute, but—"

"Hallowed be her name!" Joel bellowed from inside, a hint of power amplifying his voice. A smattering of clacks answered his prayer.

"Stop listening, Joel! It's creepy as frack!" I snapped my fingers, making us appear on the ocean walkway as far as possible from the Church of Carcinization.

"Are . . . are they really going to turn into crabs?" Maria asked, her brow furrowed.

"I hope so, because then they can be Rocky's problem."

She let out a lilting giggle that lifted my spirits. "I wonder if he'll be able to retain his cool disposition if he has to look after a whole squad of . . . humans? Crabs? What would they even be at that point?"

The absurdity of it all hit me. Laughter rose from my core before flying out into the world. Gary, Pistachio, Teddy, and the occupants of their tank had been a palate cleanser, filling me with a sense of hope about the future.

Joel and his litany of soon-to-be crabosapiens had done the exact opposite. But as I thought about it more, I questioned my visceral reaction. Perhaps we just had different sensibilities. I'd always known that they wanted to be crabs, so why should I be surprised now that it seemed to actually be a possibility?

Maria brought me back to the present. She gripped my bicep for support as our amusement poured to and fro over our connection, combining to become an unstoppable force. When our mirth finally subsided, I stared down over the seawall, watching as small waves crashed against it.

The entire construction had transformed along with the village, becoming something more solid than the patchwork of stone and mortar it had once been. Much like the rock wall by my house, the walkway was uniform now—a single, giant slab. The base, though, where its foundation met the ocean . . . it was a different story entirely.

Cube-shaped rocks appeared haphazardly placed, their sharp angles leaving room for water to flow into. Countless creatures had already started using the space as protection. Even without needing to extend my chi, I could see schools of guppies swimming along, darting out of the way when waves came.

Though I'd learned how to control my awareness with the express purpose of not detecting nearby fish, I let strands of essence flow out, sighing with how natural it felt to not be confining them. I closed my eyes, my mind's eye running up and down the seawall, ducking in and out of gaps in the foundation.

The life within exceeded even my wildest dreams. Countless fishes, mollusks, and crustaceans dwelled in the out-of-sight ecosystem, either too small or too reclusive for me to have noticed before. They were a rainbow of colors to my mind, one and all reflecting the light of the world's chi that surrounded them. Maria was right beside me, and her breath caught as I shared my senses.

The System, my oldest enemy, did something nice for once.

It offered to show me what they were. Rather than force the information to proliferate in my vision, it asked if I wanted that to happen. I stopped moving, my point of view frozen in front of a school of bait fish with fanned tails that shimmered prettily. Maria took a back seat, muting her thoughts and feelings as I considered the offer.

With a smile on my face and a slight shake of my head, I declined. I didn't *want* to know everything. Part of what made this world so beautiful was the unknown. Maybe I'd one day learn the names of these animals, but I intended on inspecting them one by one, and on my own time. An impulse struck, and I dove right in, sending gratitude out to the System for being kind enough to offer me a choice instead of its usual—

Words slammed into place before me, blocking out the school of pretty fish.

Mature Fantail Guppy
Rare
Found along the shores of the Kallis region, these fish are sacred to coastal denizens. They only travel in schools, and their arrival is said to herald great change.

I retreated back to my body, took a deep breath as the information sank in, and pointed a finger toward the sky. "Okay System, you nebulous prick! I give you my gratitude and you *immediately* pulled some bullshit!"

Maria laughed, shaking her head. "The initial offer was nice, at least."

I blew air from my lips, letting my annoyance fall away. "I was going to inspect them anyway, but it showed me before I could consent. If I didn't know better, I'd assume it was being intentionally antagonistic."

I gave a slight pout, waiting for the System to act out and confirm my suspicions, but the barb never came.

"Do you think the description was correct?" Maria asked, leaning against me, her voice and touch both grounding forces. "Do they really herald change?"

I smiled, peering over to stare at the rocks they hid beneath. "You know, I'm not sure. It's possible that they're just 'rare' because they hide from sight." I frowned. "Or maybe they're attracted to chi? Their tails seem to shine more than everything else down there. If that's the case, it would make sense that people associate them with change."

"Huh. Maybe Mom was right . . ."

"Uhhh, when?"

"When she said you weren't just a pretty face." She elbowed me lightly, grinning up at me.

I nodded sagely. "Indeed. Sharon is wise. And maybe Ruby was also wrong."

"Oh? And what did she say?"

"That you *were* just a pretty face." I wiggled my eyebrows. "She was very convincing."

Her grin evaporated.

"I said no such thing, thank you very much!" As if I'd summoned her into being, Ruby strode around the corner of a building, her husband, Steven, beside her . . . The smiles on their faces told me they knew I was just teasing.

"Priapus's rigid phallus!" Maria swore, staring down at Ruby's swollen stomach.

"*Whose* rigid *what?*" I demanded, her words enough to pull my eyes from how far Ruby's pregnancy had progressed.

But I was ignored. She strode forward and hugged Ruby, taking great care not to put pressure on her baby bump—though it was more of a hill than a bump at this point. "I haven't seen you since before the village transformed! I didn't even get to say goodbye! How have you been?"

"All three of us are well." Ruby's cheeks glowed like her namesake. "How are you? We only just got back, and we heard the strangest things . . ." She gazed down at Maria's stomach, quirking a brow. "It doesn't look any different . . ."

"Hiiiiii!" Slimes sang, wiggling out of Maria's abdomen.

"Okay," I said. "I'm voting against that exit spot, Slimes. Shoulders and arms only, please."

Ignoring me, the familiar spun to stare up at Maria and jiggled questioningly.

"Agreed," she answered. "Sorry, Slimes. It feels even worse than it looks."

Slime blobbed in understanding and reappeared as a crystal atop Maria's shoulder, facing Steven and Ruby. "Nice to finally meet you in person. I've thoroughly enjoyed examining Maria's memories of—Oop! Gotta go, byeeee!"

Without another sound, he returned to Maria's core and started doing . . . whatever it was he'd been doing all morning. For their part, I thought Steven and Ruby took it pretty well. The former was confused, the latter only mildly horrified.

Ruby turned to her husband. "I know it's normal to be scared of giving birth, but the next time I complain, remind me that there's worse things . . ."

Maria cackled. "It's not what you think. Slimes moves about as pure energy, and doesn't . . ." She shook her head. "Forget about it. What are you guys doing now? Are you free to hang?"

"We are, actually." Steven pointed down at Ruby's feet. "We were going to soak our legs in the ocean. Ruby's ankles have been getting a little swoll—"

She batted him on the arm. "Why are you telling everyone about my cankles?"

"Right. Sorry." He met our gazes with a straight face. "We were going down to the ocean to soak our definitely normal, proportional, and not at all swollen ankles in the cold—"

Her answering barrage of blows was as swift as it was gentle. "I'm. Pregnant. You. Big. Oaf!" Each word was accompanied by a soft smack.

Swooping to Steven's rescue—and looking for any excuse to try out my new partitioning ability—I flicked one hand. A staircase of solid light appeared, leading over the wall and down to the water. With a second part of my awareness, I created a vast platform in the spot the old wooden jetty had been. Both structures were nowhere near complex enough to challenge me, but they were the perfect trial for splitting my attention.

"After you," I said.

An idea came to mind, and I tried to fight it down. I really did. But with the justification that it could count toward the quota of mischief Claws had assigned me . . . I was never going to win this battle of wills.

I cleared my throat, turned to Steven, and prepared to flee. "Do you think the ocean could help Maria's cankles, too?"

CHAPTER FORTY-ONE

To Become One

Deep under the sea floor, in a place where only ancient beings dared tread, just such a being forged his way through pillars of petrified wood. That these abyssal depths were once a verdant forest would have sparked curiosity in even the most blasé of souls. But this wasn't new information to the elemental. He'd been the one to sink it, after all.

If not for the thing he'd left here, he wouldn't have wasted his time in reexamining this past destruction. If anything, it was a chore to make his way through the material, its crystalline structure annoying to break. But break they did, being scooped into his body, ground down into sediment and . . . *Oh? What is this?*

One of the former trees he'd collected, a solid column of permineralized wood, was harder than it had any right being. No matter how hard he tried to destroy it, the material didn't yield. In all his years, so many that entire forests had the time to petrify, he had never encountered such a substance.

Filled with a need to understand this crystal's composition, he sent all of his awareness within himself, focusing every bit of his will on the single rock. It pooled around it, then in the darkness of his sediment-filled mass, something cracked. A shell surrounding the fossil shattered, revealing a deep purple light.

If the elemental had possessed lungs, the air would have been knocked from them. This object had formed naturally, doing so without the help of a cultivator, yet every part of its crystalline structure was *filled* with chi.

It was impossible. Such a thing *couldn't* exist.

It had been countless millennia since the elemental last learned something new. Myriad empires had risen and fallen, as had entire continents—one of which he was currently digging through the remains of. He boomed a laugh, the sound so loud that it shook the world. The surrounding stone and crystal crumbled, only a single object strong enough to survive the localized earthquake.

Another pillar of petrified wood, its crystals just as chi infused as the one within him. The elemental scooped it up. He applied his will to it once more, and when the same shell disintegrated, purple light shone free. He spread out in search of more. Just how many had formed? He had to contain his desire lest he get carried away and let the newborn elemental sense his work. But though he limited his essence expenditure, he was detected.

An ancient power came from below, rage and despair fueling its passage.

But he knew her well. Instead of fleeing or preparing a defense, he invited her to join him—to become one once more. Sitting atop the porous stone previously separating them, she froze, her indignation making way for a question.

He was all too happy to answer, and he let his memories flow out. He'd *had* to leave her here when they destroyed the continent. He hadn't abandoned her. He, too, had locked himself in the same stasis. Spreading themselves out was an insurance policy—if he had been killed, she and the others would have been safe.

Of all the other parts of him, she was closest to him in intellect. She accepted his reasoning, but still hesitated, watching him from her position atop the rock. With the mental equivalent of a smile, he produced something from his body for her to examine—one of the two objects of power he'd discovered. She took it as an insult at first, upset that he thought a trinket could win her over, but then she felt the chi.

As fast as she'd ever moved, she slammed into him, their sediment mixing, their minds becoming one. Her amazement at the discovery became his, and his happiness at being united became hers. Fully reincorporated now, they rejoiced.

They had a newly awakened elemental to hunt—a being whose cultivation could be the very thing needed to create something from the chi-filled crystals they'd found.

Not something, they thought. *A weapon.*

Together, they spread out, hungry to find more of the fossils.

"Say it right now, mister!"

"I will!" I replied. "Please, just don't drown me again!"

Maria cocked her head, her brow furrowing. "I thought we were playing. What are you . . . ?"

I glanced over her shoulder, making sure her body hid my smirk. She turned—her right fist still raised and threatening violence—to see the dozen or so faces that were now watching from the walkway.

"Someone get Barry!" I called. "She's gone mad with pow—*ahhhhh!*"

I sailed high above the ocean, launched skyward by a woman half my size. As I spun like a brick in a tumble dryer, I rubbed my chin in thought. *What landing should I go for . . . ?*

"I'll show you drowned!" Maria yelled, ignoring the fact that I was trying to make an important decision. "Apologize for saying I have cankles! And for pretending I'm abusing you!"

I considered yelling something even more antagonistic—perhaps that I was sorry she had said cankles, or that throwing someone fifty meters in the air could absolutely pass for abuse—but in the end, I didn't want to get thrown into orbit. I bowed at the waist. "Forgive me!"

"No! You shouldn't joke about people's physical features!" She drew back her arm, winding up like she was about to throw a fastball.

What is she . . . ?

Before I could finish forming the question, she threw, her limb a blur as something pink rocketed out.

"Hiiiii!" Slimes yelled, sailing into the sky above me before curving back down.

I could have dodged, caught, or even smacked Slimes back Maria's way, but the punishment seemed fair. I starfished, accepting my fate as he slammed into my back. The hit solved the decision of what landing I should go for, at least, and I rocketed belly first into the still ocean.

Clap!

The belly flop hadn't succeeded in knocking the air from my enhanced body, but the temperature of the water sure came close. It took me a few seconds to adjust to its frigidity, and as I looked around, a deep sense of calm replaced my shock. It had only been a week or so since the whole king debacle, but how had I not had a swim yet? It should have been the third thing I did after coming back to Tropica—after seeing Maria and having a fish, naturally.

On paper, the trip to Gormona had been relaxing, but compared to this . . .

I floated weightlessly, and even with my enhanced vision, I couldn't keep count of how many fish I saw. They flitted here and there at the seawall, flitting out between gaps only to zip back in. Schools of tiny creatures swam for their lives when juvenile shore fish darted toward them, each group moving like a hive mind.

So, when every single school moved at the same time, all swimming to the north, I knew something had changed. To my left, sweeping into view, came the biggest damned stingray I had ever seen. Its wings undulated like a wave, propelling it forward with both grace and speed as it sailed by the wall in search of prey.

A brave crab crawled out of a crevice, holding up a claw smaller than my pinky nail. The stingray closed in, not wasting the crustacean's foolish courage. Some would call it interfering with nature, but I didn't care. I felt a kinship with that brave, stupid little crab, and I wasn't gonna let it get munched.

I could wall off the crustacean with chi. Or I could just boop the stingray away. But I had a better, much more devious plan. Getting Claws's attention with a pulse of will, I opened a Maria-sized gap in my chi platform. My target, reacting with the speed expected of someone with her level of cultivation, whirled, trying to catch herself on the edge. She'd have succeeded, too—if I hadn't expanded the hole, that is.

Maria splashed into the ocean, her limbs outstretched in a failed attempt at finding purchase. Shock coursed through her as the frosty water took hold, but it was swiftly burned away by fire and brimstone. Her eyes locked on to me, chi already gathering around her core. Before she could indulge her violent fantasies, I waved, grinned, and pointed to her right.

Her vengeful gaze flicked that way. Just in time, too. Her graceless entrance had succeeded in spooking the stingray, and it changed course, veering out toward the depths and away from the perceived threat. The brave little crab, not knowing how close it had come to being food, retreated into its crack. Two beady eyes peeped out, and the foolhardy crustacean resumed its watch.

Shaking my head at how much I was anthropomorphizing the carapaced idiot, I returned my attention to its former adversary, Maria's wonder pulling me in. It drifted down toward the seafloor, its wings kicking up sediment as it sailed along.

Suddenly, when it was roughly ten meters from shore and adjacent to me, it dug into the sand. With the same movements it used to swim, it covered itself, only the bulbous part of its body remaining visible.

A spike of emotion from Maria drew my attention. She was glad she saw it, but still pissed at my method of getting her underwater. I shrugged and pointed toward the crab, sending her an image of it threatening a creature thousands of times bigger than it. She rolled her eyes, shook her head, and sighed, expelling a torrent of bubbles.

Fine, she mouthed, then looked up, likely intending to go join Ruby and Steven.

They came to us instead. Holding hands, they plopped down into the hole I'd made, their flowing robes drifting in the water. Maria and I both had a moment of panic, our instincts screaming that Ruby had to be protected, but it was a knee-jerk reaction. She was pregnant, sure, but she was also a cultivator. She let go of Steven's hand and swam toward the rocks, pulling herself in to peer between the cracks.

We explored the wall for at least an hour, drifting up and down it intermittently. We spent the entire time in silence, our only communication done with pointed fingers, or full-bodied gestures if it was something particularly neat—like the little crab bro, who came out to give me the old "what for" when I swam too close to his crevice. Ignoring his threats, my curiosity got the better of me. I peeked inside.

I'd thought he might have some babies in there. Perhaps even a lady crab that he was defending. Instead, I found something much more . . . human. The little bugger was collecting a hoard of treasure, literally putting his life on the line to protect his wealth.

They were stunning. They were *flawless*. They were . . . *shells.*

But who was I to judge? Sure, he couldn't eat them. Or trade them, because he was a crab. Okay, they weren't useful at all, but they *were* pretty, damn it! Each shell was perfect, not marred by a single scratch or blemish. I'd seen some of them before, the common white shells that washed up on the beach. Others, though, were new to me. One species had a layer of nacre on the inside—what was called mother-of-pearl back on Earth—and the crab appeared quite fond of them. They made up over half of his stash.

In my musings, I wasn't paying attention to my surroundings. A source of powerful essence leaped down from above, and as spine-covered legs gripped my shoulder, I smiled. Sergeant Snips rubbed her carapace against my upper back, blowing a soft stream of joyful bubbles that tickled my ear on their way to the surface.

Rather than retreat from a crab literally hundreds of times his size, my angry little friend took it as a challenge, deciding to take his fate into his own claws. The tiny bastard *leaped* at me! Both his snippers, one bigger than the other, slammed shut on the tip of my nose. Unfortunately for him, my skin was tougher than titanium, so all he managed to do was turn himself into a torpedo.

And for once, karmic justice was on my side. He barreled into his pile of shells, his numerous little legs undulating chaotically as he tried to find purchase. I barked a laugh, sending a steam of bubbles from my mouth as he finally righted himself, quickly rearranging his scattered treasures before resuming his defensive position. I moved back, not wanting to further antagonize him.

Sergeant Snips, however, was enamored. She hopped down onto the rocks below, standing to her full height so she could peer down into the crevice. She reached forward with one of her mighty clackers, her natural curiosity encouraging her to give him at least a *little* poke, but she drew back at the last second, avoiding a clack of his claws that would have sent him flying into his pile of shells again.

Snips blew apologetic bubbles. An emotion close to guilt rose from her core, so I glided down and scooped her up, giving the top of her carapace a reassuring rub.

You have nothing to feel guilty about, I said through our connection.

She wiggled happily, hugged my arm with her many legs, then swam off to the south, pausing only to rub affectionately against Maria's torso. After my favorite crab had departed from sight, Maria and I kicked off the sandy floor. We breached the surface, and before either of us could say a thing, an adolescent voice beat us to the punch.

"Fischerrrr! I got them!"

Maria looked up to the seawall, and not yet spotting the speaker, turned to raise an eyebrow at me.

"I may or may not have told Paul that we were having a dip."

"When? And *how*?"

"I have my ways."

Even suspended in water, we could feel the ground rumble. Maria raised both eyebrows at the ripples coming from the shore as the stampede approached. "*Just* Paul? Why did he tell you he got them? Who is them?"

"I mean, I can't control if he told other people . . ."

She narrowed her eyes at me, a line forming between her brows. "You didn't answer my question. Care to explain why you avoided it?"

"I . . . uhhhh . . . *What's that?*"

I pointed up as Paul sailed over the seawall.

There was a loud thump, and a second figure came flying into view. With a wingspan that eclipsed most birds, Barry's lats blocked out the sun, his muscles flexing as he tucked his legs under his arms.

"Cannonbaaaall!" he sang.

Hours later, I let out a slow breath as Maria and I wandered home beneath the setting sun. A comfortable silence stretched between us, the result of a long day swimming in the ocean, chatting with friends, and eating what could only be described as *too much food.* We stepped between two rows of sugarcane, and a breeze swept by, the whisper of the surrounding leaves becoming a roar as they swayed chaotically.

I stole a glance at Maria, only to find her already looking up at me, her eyes holding more color and depth than the ocean we'd just departed.

"What are you thinking?" I asked, reaching over to tuck a loose strand of hair behind her ear.

"I might be engaged to the wrong person." She patted her stomach. "Peter can *cook*."

"Is that revenge for dropping you into the sea?"

"Hmm. Maybe?" She skipped ahead of me, tapping her chin in exaggerated thought. "Perhaps it's revenge for your little crab friend—the one you head-butted."

"Head-butted? That little rascal tried to pinch me on the schnoz! With both claws!"

"Hmmmm," she continued, ignoring me entirely. "Or maybe it's actually that Sue is my true love, but she's already married. The barista that got away . . ." She sighed wistfully. "It's not fair to string you along while my heart remains hers, so perhaps we should see other pe—*eek!*"

Faster than even she could comprehend, I swept her up, pulling her body close. As seconds passed between us, both staring into the other's eyes, her cheeks flushed a rosy red. A smell like wildflowers drifted up from her. It made my pulse thump in my ears, and everything else fell away.

"I . . ." She licked her lips, her words heady. "For the record, I was teasing."

"I know."

Our desire for one another pushed at the border of our connection. Before it could break through, I pulled her closer, her mouth parting as she lifted it toward me.

"*By the quivering shaft of Eros!*" came a projected voice. "*Get a room!*"

As sure as a smith's hammer would break glass, Duncan's words shattered the mood into a thousand jagged pieces.

I spun, dropping Maria to her feet as we both faced the newcomers.

Deklan and Dom were both grimacing, the twins' pinched expressions conveying an unspoken apology. Fergus was reaching for his apprentice, ready to grab him by the collar and drag him from sight. The last of them, Duncan, *beamed.* His grin was brighter than the setting sun. The fool had taunted a lioness, and instead of fleeing, he just stood there.

Maria gave him a sweet smile, taking a deep breath in an attempt to calm herself—which immediately failed.

"Nope!" she said, winding up for a fast ball. Duncan's teeth were parting now, and I realized he was even stupider than I thought; he was about to double down.

What Maria did next was both fortunate and unfortunate. Fortunate because Duncan didn't have a chance to further incriminate himself, and unfortunate because of the method used to silence him.

"Hiiii!" sang the method.

Slimes condensed into a crystal as he rocketed toward the apprentice, transforming back into a slime at the last possible moment and stretching—spreading the impact over Duncan's entire body. The slap that rang out was sickening. Like a scene from a movie, Duncan was there one second and gone the next, vanishing into the wall of sugarcane behind him.

Deklan and Dom both leaned in to stare down the path of destruction in Duncan's wake. Fergus cleared his throat, and all three men strode away, the smith launching into an impromptu lecture about melting temperatures.

"Damn," I said.

Maria sucked her teeth as she appraised the obliterated stalks. "Sorry."

"It's okay. It was only a matter of time until someone broke my record."

". . . What?"

"What do you mean *what*?" I gestured toward the collision site with both hands. "Forget the sugarcane. What Slimes just did was, *by far*, the best belly flop we've seen all day. It can't be beat."

She blinked at me, unsure of what to make of me. After a tense moment, my gamble paid off, and she slung her arms around my neck. When her lips met mine, her heat drew me in, my pulse immediately thumping again.

"I love you," she said, pressing our foreheads together. "Even if you're a big idiot half of the time."

"I love you, too."

She kissed me again, but it was fleeting. She pulled back. I pursued, centimeters feeling like leagues. She retreated further.

"Tease."

She giggled, more sultry than musical. "If you want me, Fischer . . ." When her eyes met mine, she was the lioness once more. "*Take* me."

My core ignited, and my heart beat so hard that my vision pulsed.

"What about Slimes?"

"Gone to meditate . . ." She gave me a lascivious smile. "And he won't be returning."

I flicked a finger. We moved through space. A flash of light, its incandescence blinding. I didn't close my eyes against the brilliance. Neither did she. It faded, letting the pink-and-orange palette of sunset reclaim the bathroom. Having to tear my hand from her, I reached back, fumbling with the shower handle. She fumbled too, her hands shaking as clothing fell, discarded.

Boiling water streamed down from the faucet as I pulled her in. The rising clouds of steam did nothing to reduce Maria's beauty. I drank all of her in, each hard line, soft curve, and perfect imperfection. Our eyes scoured the other, a desire for one another growing, pushing at the boundary of our connection like never before. She took a mental step forward, a question. An invitation.

The fire in my core became an inferno, the suggestion pouring fuel onto the flames.

"Are . . ." I clenched my jaw, fighting to keep our connection closed. "Are you sure? We don't have to just because we'll be apart for a few days . . ."

She took another mental step, accompanied by a physical one. "I'm sure."

When her body pressed against mine, every one of my muscles tensed. I tried to hold the door closed. If we joined right now, I wasn't sure I could ever let her go.

"Fischer . . ." she whispered into my neck, her fingers sliding down my stomach . . . "I *want* you."

I shuddered, and she opened the connection from her side. Awareness of her flooded me. Dilated pupils, parted lips, freckles atop flushed skin. She was a drug. More addictive than any other. I held the line. Part of me worried that she was doing this just for me—forcing herself.

She reached out to me, caressed me, coaxed me on. Gods, I wanted her. She could have forced her way in. Kicked the door down with only a fraction of her will. Instead, her soft yet firm hand grabbed mine. She pulled me closer. Pushed me lower. Pressed me . . .

"Fischer," she gasped. "I *need* you."

The fire within burned my hesitation to the ground, and I threw the door to her soul open. I rushed into her just as she rushed into me. I'd been a fool to think she was forcing herself to do anything.

Maria wasn't just any drug. She was *my* drug. And I was hers.

Entwined, we became one.

CHAPTER FORTY-TWO

Sweet Treats

I was having my second dream in a single night—it was *wonderful.* Beside a cerulean lake and beneath an emerald sky, I had a fishing rod in my hands, a smile on my face, and something *massive* on the end of my line. I reeled, reeled, and reeled some more, yet the fish never got closer. Some might have found this frustrating, perhaps even anxiety inducing, but not me. I knew I was dreaming.

Instead of focusing on the subjective failure, I gazed out at my surroundings, wondering if such a vista existed somewhere in this world. I had seen similar colors before, but *never* in the sky. It was the verdant green of the forests surrounding Tropica, the light hue that some leaves possessed when lit by the midday sun or a particularly bright moon.

Speaking of celestial bodies, another arrived, peeking its head over the horizon.

Well, I thought, *there goes any hope of this being the same world . . .*

The second sun trailed the other, on the same path as they marched higher and higher. There was a moment where I considered it might be an optical illusion, but their continued passage confirmed the truth. When I acknowledged that there actually *were* two of them, disorientation hit me like a sledgehammer. But awe swiftly followed, settling deep in my core as I squinted skyward, my enhanced body letting me gaze directly at them, engaging in what only the silliest of gooses would do back on Earth.

Suddenly, my core called to me, urging me to return. Having one last look at the scene as I was yoinked from the dreamscape, I did my best to sear it into my memory. A slight feeling of loss remained as I stirred from sleep. When I opened my eyes, however, a sight far more beautiful than the alien landscape met me.

"Good morning," Maria said, her body gloriously bare as she straddled my hips. Slowly, she bent down—both the kiss she planted on my neck and the tickle of her sun-bleached hair made power course through me. She sat back up, her chest heaving as she stared down at me with burning intensity. "You know, we've got some time before you have to leave . . ."

"*Oh . . .*" was all my brain could put together.

Thankfully, words weren't necessary. When Maria pressed herself against me, I forgot they even existed.

* * *

The sun's rays were just beginning to crest the horizon as Maria and I walked hand in hand toward the coast. It reminded me of something . . . a dream I'd had last night, perhaps? I furrowed my brow in an attempt to remember, but more-recent memories flooded in first.

Maria stopped in her tracks and raised an eyebrow my way. "We might not be connected right now, but I can still tell when you . . . *think* things."

I stood tall, raising my arms to the sky and pausing a moment when I found the prefect stretch. "I regret nothing."

She laughed, sweeping over to plant the softest of kisses on my cheek. "Good."

So lost was I in the serotonin flowing through me that I didn't notice her winding up the mother of all slaps. She smacked the left side of my tushy with enough force to lift me a few centimeters off the ground.

"Keep being a good boy," she whispered, "and maybe I'll reward you when you get back . . ."

I raised both eyebrows at her. "I can feel that you're joking, but that's a dangerous game. What if those words awakened something in me? Opened a box whose contents can't be unseen? Scratched an itch that I'll henceforth need tended in order to—"

She cut me off by pressing a finger to my lips. "I would like to immediately retract the last twenty seconds."

"Even the spank?"

"Don't be silly. Obviously not the spank."

"In that case, I find the terms agreeable."

I offered a hand to shake, but she batted it aside and leaped into my arms. Rather than the passionate exchanges of last night, this kiss was softer than velvet. As so often happened around her, all else fell away—which was, unfortunately, how it came to be that two large individuals snuck up on us.

A ragged sigh from one of them sliced our moment in half, its wielder's core oozing with resignation. I spun, and it was on his face, too. I raised an eyebrow at Duncan, curious what his game was. Fergus was beside him, looking similarly unsure.

The apprentice had replaced his obliterated clothing from yesterday, and an embarrassed tilt to his shoulders was the only remaining proof of the expulsion via familiar he'd been subjected to. As he took a slow breath in, his lungs were filled with both air and resolve.

"Mate," I said, realization blooming, "you don't have to . . ."

The slight grimace he returned told me that he did, in fact, have to do it. I peered sidelong at Maria, expecting a strong reaction. Instead, a smile teased the corner of her mouth, and her eyes flicked down toward a shoulder bag Fergus was carrying.

"Lad," Fergus tried, taking a half step forward, his hand extended, "didn't you learn your lesson? There's still time to walk away. We've got a long day ahead of us. Come now, let's go have a cup of coffee and a bite of—"

"*Priapus's eternal erection!*" Duncan yelled, losing the battle with his own compulsions. "Get a rooo—*mmmm*?"

The taunt had started strong but ended in a soft mumble when someone pink, slimy, and all-encompassing wrapped himself around the apprentice's head, sealing his mouth shut. Like a cantankerous crab launched by the righteous claw of Snips, Slimes had been a blur as he shot from Fergus's bag.

"Hiiii!" he said, replacing Duncan's facial features with his own. With a loud plop, Slimes removed himself from the smith's noggin, using it as a grounding point from which to slingshot himself toward—and into—Maria's abdomen. There, he immediately resumed circulating chi.

Duncan wobbled, blinked, and righted himself. He opened his mouth, froze, and shut it once more. "Nope." He turned and strode away, not once looking back. "Coming, boss? I hear there's coffee and pastries waiting ahead."

Fergus just smiled and shrugged before trudging off after his apprentice.

"I should have known Slimes was in there," I said, grabbing Maria's hand. "I was wondering why you didn't preemptively kick him into the ocean."

"Sorry, what was that?" Maria's eyes took a moment to focus on me. "I was checking up on Slimes's insight from last night."

"Don't worry." I softly bumped my shoulder into her. "Let's go. I'll watch out for more ambushes while you two catch up."

She bumped me back, then settled into herself, tiny fluctuations coming from her chi as she and Slimes communicated. Once more hand in hand, we wandered eastward. The wind shifted suddenly, wafting scents and sounds our way—coffee, pastries, and the voices of countless friends.

Maria took a deep breath. When she opened her eyes again, they were clear once more, her communication with Slimes having come to an end. "I will never grow tired of that smell."

"The coffee or the pastries?"

"Yes."

"Fair point." I laughed.

She stopped abruptly and turned to face me. "Race you there?"

"Oooh, I'm down."

"On three?"

"Sounds good! Should we should set some ground rules, though? This could easily get out of ha—"

"Three!" she interrupted, spraying me with sand as she took off across the dunes.

"The audacity . . ."

She leaped from the crest of the first hill, and following her recent breakthrough, her strength sent her sailing all the way toward the coast. She glanced back to check on my progress—just in time to see me snap my fingers. I appeared before her in a flash of light, letting her collide with my body.

Her leap, if left unimpeded, would have seen her landing gracefully beside everyone; my haphazard interception, and our subsequent flight of tangled limbs, would do . . . Well, not that.

We hit the dune closest to our friends, careening sideways into its top third, and tons of sand cascaded over the gathering. I reached for my chi, my level of control more than enough to protect everyone. I didn't, though, obviously—shield them entirely, I mean. I did, however, protect what *really* mattered.

Dozens of little translucent barriers sprang into place atop cups, pitchers, and Sue's delicious pastries. Not a single grain found its way past my impenetrable walls, which meant I could sit back and enjoy the show. And by *sit back and enjoy the show*, what I really meant was *catch glimpses of the scene as I bounced along the ground like a crash-test dummy*.

Maria, who I'd become separated from upon impact, rejoined me. Kind of. Her feet landed on my back, and my chaotic passage became nice and smooth as she turned me into a surfboard. It was quite enjoyable initially, because my view of the sandstorm was no longer obstructed by my own spin cycle . . . but then Maria shifted her left foot.

It pressed down on the nape of my neck, causing my face to part the sand before us. When we started to slow, she leaped off—and must have done a sweet flip or something, because a round of polite applause came from the crowd. Someone even whistled.

"Thank you," she said. "And sorry, everyone. I had no idea he was going to do . . . whatever *that* was."

I lifted my head and wiped grit from my eyes. "In my defense, neither did I."

A bunch of wet somethings popped against my arm, and I glanced, with a giant grin on my face, toward the source of the bubbles. "Hello, Snips. Did you have a nice sleepover with Slimes?"

She nodded and rubbed her carapace against me, her stream of affectionate bubbles increasing as I stroked the top of her head. She slid her powerful pinchers beneath me and got me to my feet with ease.

I landed with my arms crossed, returning the playful gazes some of the crowd were leveling my way. "At least *someone* knows how to treat the arrival of her benevolent and kind leader."

Hissing her agreement, Snips leaped into the air, settled into the crook of my arm, and joined me in glaring at the others.

Sue sighed, the first to break the stalemate. "Come on. This mummers' show will last all morning, and the pastries are getting cold."

Snips whirled and cast a questioning gaze up at me. I nodded. "For the sake of caffeine and sweet treats, let us move past their *egregious* insubordination."

She leaped up onto my head and stood tall on her spiky legs, an imperious glint in her eye as she looked down upon her lessers.

"I know, Snips." I gave an exaggerated sigh. "You're right. I *would* be justified in locking them all up in my not-a-prison for the foreseeable future."

"Fischer." Sue leveled a pair of tongs at me. "Keep that up, and I'll start hiding sand in your pastries."

My indignant facade slipped away like butter on a hot pan. "You wouldn't . . ."

"I would—and only some of them, too. You'd never know if your next bite would bring sweet delight or crunchy regret." She clacked her tongs. "Don't test me, young man."

I plucked the crab from my head and lowered her so we were eye to eyestalk. "Our enemies are more politically savvy that I anticipated, Snips. I believe we've lost this battle."

"You have," Sue agreed.

"But we will win the war," I hissed, to which my guard crab nodded, then ran a claw across her neck—well, across where it would be if she had one.

"What was that you just said?"

"Nothing, Sue! Two of your finest coffees and pastries, please!"

"Much better. Coming right up."

As the barista prepared our breakfast, I gazed around at the scene, able to take it in properly now that I was no longer tumbling. Two wooden tables were set up and absolutely covered in trays of pastries. Sue stood behind it, and as she poured from a large jug, a deep-brown liquid flowed out into the cup below. The entire breakfast had been one of the things we'd planned yesterday—in between ocean swims and countless snacks—but seeing it all come together sparked even more joy than expected.

With how busy my animal pals had been lately with their attempts at advancement, I'd seen less and less of them. This brekkie, however, was different. Some of us were departing later this morning, so most of the spirit beasts were present and strewn throughout the gathering. Only Bumblebro, Queen Bee, and the Buzzy Boys out on patrol were absent.

I wondered how the former two were doing; I hadn't seen them in days. I could sense them via our connection, of course, so I knew they were healthy. I'd felt the urge to go and check up on them at least a dozen times since returning with the boat supplies, but I had already been told off for visiting their hive unannounced.

A bolt of lightning struck far to the south, and I just shook my head.

I know you're not here, Claws. I was trying not to think about you. You tell me off every time I even say hello.

Shush! she replied, accompanying the word with a pulse of annoyance. *I'm busy experimenting!*

"That fracking otter . . ."

Maria's lilting giggle made me feel a little better, and another shift of the wind finished off the job. Even from here, the cold brew's aroma was tantalizing.

"That's the addiction speaking," Maria whispered.

I pouted at her in response, but she countered it with a cheeky wink, then leaned against my shoulder. "Sorry about using you as a sled earlier."

"Oh, no worries."

". . . No worries?"

"Uh-huh. Deserved, really."

"I guess that's true. If you acknowledge fault, is there anything *you* want to say?"

"Like what?" I asked.

"Oh, I don't know, perhaps an apology to who you wronged? Someone beautiful sitting right next to you?"

"You know what? You're right." I looked down at Snips and scritched the top of her sturdy head. "I'm sorry for not standing my ground against Sue. The threat of sandy pastries was too much for me."

She patted my leg reassuringly, blowing compassionate and mirth-filled bubbles as she leaned into my scritching.

"Really?" Maria bent to place her lovely head in my field of view. "You don't want to apologize for teleporting right before your fiancée and making her tumble ass over teakettle in front of everyone?"

"Not really, no."

"Huh. Well, what if I told you said fiancée's father is *standing right* behind you?"

I froze. "How angry does he look?"

"Hard to tell—he always looks angry."

"He does, doesn't he?"

"I do," Roger agreed, his voice gravelly. "Lots to be angry about 'round here."

"So . . ." Maria said, her face as smug as it was pretty. "Did you have anything to say to your very-patient fiancée's very-angry father, Fischer?"

A lifeline arrived in the form of a barista. Sue held out a tray; the food atop it made my stomach growl. "Pause," I said. "Can we have brekkie before I answer? I can't think straight with Sue's creations present."

Maria tossed her head side to side in consideration. "Deal," she finally said, "but only because I can't wait either."

Though one of my treats was a plain croissant, it wasn't any less delicious than the passiona danish accompanying it. I lost track of time as I ate, and when I closed my eyes to better focus on the buttery layers of pastry, an odd scene flashed through my mind. Two suns, a cerulean lake, and an emerald sky. The vista faded in and out of view, only vanishing when I upended my cup to drain the last mouthful of coffee.

I let out a contented sigh, which enhanced the pleasantly bitter aftertaste that lingered. "Gods above, I needed that."

Mmmm, Maria replied, still chewing.

The memory of breakfast lent me enough strength to look Roger's way. Sharon was at his side. She bore a smile that was a little *too* knowing, which made me wonder if she already suspected me, but something else grabbed my attention—a tray of pastries resting in Roger's hands.

Sue must have delivered their brekkie while I was eating, and the corner of my lip curled up when I noticed that Roger had stolen a bite, rushing to swallow it before I'd finished my own. The farmer wore his tough demeanor like a suit of armor, but he found sugary treats just as irresistible as I did.

"Delicious, right?" I asked, which made his eyebrow twitch. "Now then"—I tapped my chi—"what should I say to the father of my fiancée . . . ?" I gesticulated with one hand as I searched for the right words. "Roger, your daughter, who is the love of my life and apple of my eye . . ." Roger's and Maria's eyes both narrowed, so I let the rest spew out before they could stop me. "Is also a dirty cheater who deserved every single speck of sand currently taking up residence in her underclothes!"

I cackled and leaped sideways. Maria pursued. Her eyes became awash with flames once more, but this time, it wasn't love fueling the inferno.

CHAPTER FORTY-THREE

Ten

As the sun rose over the eastern horizon, another beautiful day arrived on the shores of Tropica. I stood atop a giant platform of light, my solid chi giving me a wonderful spot from which to watch the churning ocean. I paused and took a deep breath. The salty air made a sense of great calm radiate from my core and throughout my entire body but was immediately shattered as I ducked Maria's . . . *Was that a roundhouse kick?*

I narrowed my eyes at Cinnamon, wondering if this was her doing. When the troublesome little bunny let out a frustrated cry, I further suspected I was correct. And her following scream, which could be roughly translated to *punch his jawbone* through *his butt* eliminated any doubt.

"Cinnamon!" I yelled, laughing. "You need to *chill*!"

Ever the defiant daughter, she chose to shadowbox instead, burning the excess energy she got from watching our fight.

Before I could further chastise her, Maria's fist lashed out, driving me back. Anyone that didn't know us might have thought we were serious. At the very least, they would think I was the victim of domestic violence—if not outright mariticide in the near future. They'd be wrong, of course.

Though decidedly explosive, this was one of the ways we bonded; our exchange was more choreographed dance than street fight. Even back when Maria had been a regular human, we tussled and play-fought, using it as an excuse to get close to each other.

We continued for another fifteen minutes or so, and as Maria's attacks grew increasingly powerful, our friends lounged and chatted, gazing up at the light show we were putting on. With a series of eye movements and thoughts sent to one another's core, we agreed on a finishing move. I teleported behind her, pretending to grab her around the waist.

"Hiiii!" Slimes sang, slamming into my head and covering it just as he'd done to Duncan.

I wobbled on the spot, channeling my inner wrestler as I faked being dazed. Maria, to the cheers of the crowd, kissed her closed fist. Round and round it whirled, gathering momentum and promising to unleash a fight-ending blow. She shot forward, and enough force gathered in her limb to actually threaten me physically as it descended for the crown of my head.

Mere millimeters away from me, just when her potent chi started to make my skin tingle, Slimes removed himself, and she stopped. Then, as fast as a serpentine spirit beast, she became a blur and hit me directly in the forehead with a . . . soft little peck.

I shook my body violently to make it seem like her energy was bouncing around me and growing stronger. Finally, I bent, clutched my stomach, and unleashed some of my own chi, giving the illusion that her attack had shot free of my back.

It was only a whisper of my power, but in retrospect, even that was too much.

A column of pure essence torrented into the sky, shimmering with pearlescent beauty. It wanted to explode outward, just as I'd accidentally let happen back in the capital. But I was in control now. I allowed myself a small smirk as I used my other partition—the one controlling the chi we stood on—to encase the pillar and deny its expansion. I had to add more power at the last moment, weaving strands of will from my core to ensure it didn't detonate.

Still folded like a pretzel, I resumed my terrible job of acting. My back led the charge as I plummeted groundward, but that worked for me—my eyes faced the sky, so I was able to watch my condensed line of essence pierce the heavens.

In the center of the vast sea, where no ship had sailed since the days of old, the clouds were black as pitch. A storm had arrived. Waves taller than mountains rose up only to descend once more, tons and tons and *tons* of ocean slamming down with enough force to rip even land asunder. Violence on such a grand scale was almost too hard to comprehend. If one could harness the energy of such a storm, they could conquer kingdoms—perhaps an entire continent.

Thousands of fathoms beneath these crushing waves, paying them as much attention as a god would a bug, an ancient being neared the end of their task.

Now that the elemental spirits had become one again, scouring the remains of the archaic forest had taken even less time than they'd thought it would. They'd torn through the vast majority in hours, their impressive mass able to ooze out in all directions. Each chi-infused fossil they had encountered was a blessing—another cause for celebration—and they'd accumulated no small number. Though more than plentiful, it was also vexing.

They had found *nine*.

Most beings, even those that had taken the first step on the stairwell to ascension, were woefully ignorant of the power that numbers possessed. And among those that weren't, most of them believed for the wrong reason. It was ever a source of frustration to the earth elemental that superstition was observed by both the most enlightened and the least idiotic of beings, the latter's passionate stupidity discrediting the former's wisdom.

Nine . . . they mused as they traced the border of the sunken continent, desperately destroying anything that could hide another prize.

It wasn't what the number *was* that haunted them; it was what the number *wasn't*. One short of ten, a single fossil from attaining the divine number of perfection. Of *completeness*. If they had found seven or eight, they would have long ago left this place. By now, they could have rejoined the rest of their brothers and sisters. They could have already resumed the hunt for the newly awakened lightning elemental, perhaps even chosen a place to lay in wait, the trap ready to be sprung.

But alas, they hadn't. They'd found nine. And so the search continued. It was worth it, they reminded themself. To find ten relics of cosmic value was to have pleased the heavens—and not the false heavens that the former gods of this world had called home. The *true* heavens. The place in which entities of *real* importance dwelled.

With such a number involved, the worst possibility was that finding them would draw the attention of these enlightened beings. The best possibility, though—which the elemental dared not ponder overlong—was that the heavens had placed the relics there for them to find.

They returned to the present, focusing on their surroundings to estimate how much of the outer crust was left. They replayed their hours-long passage in seconds, and the answer they got made their mass roil. Their task was almost complete. Only a third of the border remained. Once they destroyed the last of it, there would be no more—their chance of finding a tenth relic would be as dead as the continent the forest had grown . . . *on*.

One of the several permineralized fossils they'd absorbed in the last second felt different from the rest. The elemental halted their passage, all of their awareness flooding inward to find a tree-shaped rock, its crystalline structure . . . filled with chi. Their combined wills slammed into it, shattered the encasing shell, and uncovered something priceless.

They had discovered a tenth relic. Their mission truly was blessed by the heavens . . .

If someone had been thousands of fathoms above, they would have witnessed an event equal parts terror inducing and awe inspiring. Beneath a sky of roiling clouds, with winds hundreds of knots an hour howling past, the ocean froze. Its mountainous peaks wavered, shuddered, and sank as an unseen force vibrated powerfully enough to fissure the continental plate below.

Back on what had been the ocean floor, the elemental continued radiating its seismic shocks. They were sucked hundreds of meters into the crack in the planet's crust that their exultation had created, the water surrounding it becoming superheated by the molten rock below. A weaker elemental might have been bothered by the heat. Perhaps incinerated immediately. But magma was the cousin of earth, and the elemental was anything but weak.

So strong was their celebration that the rest of their brothers and sisters stirred. Scattered across the ocean, squirreled away within caverns, trenches—and even a dormant volcano—their awareness flickered. The main body of the elemental could have pulled the tendrils of power back. Could have let them all fall asleep once more.

That was no longer necessary, however.

As their conscious minds awoke, many lashed out, furious, just as the first sister had been upon learning of the oldest brother's perceived betrayal. She separated herself from him and urged all of them to be patient. *Ordered* them to hear his tale before judging. Knowing her to be a being of sheer logic, they heeded her warning—if only temporarily.

Come, he sent, retelling past and present history in all its glory. *Rejoin us.*

Within moments, the memories settled within them, and even the most contrarian of them pulsed with understanding. His actions, though extreme, had been brilliant. Perhaps perfect. And the heavenly beings high above, the entities that reigned over the cosmos, might have orchestrated it. At the very least, they would now be watching—such was the significance of the ten powerful relics.

Take your time, the elemental urged. *Do not be hasty, lest the newborn being find—*

A blast of chi erupted from the west, severing the elementals' communication. The essence was pure—completely unaspected. If that had been all, fear would have shaken the first brother's heart. But there was more. A second surge came, this one intentional, controlled, and much, *much* more powerful.

Both left as fast as they had arrived, shooting off into the endless darkness above. When they left this planet's orbit and communication was no longer impeded, the first brother and sister reached out with tendrils of their power, reconnecting with the other parts of themself. Together, they echoed the same sentiment.

Flee!

They needn't have done so. Every single one of the other elementals was already retreating, slipping from their places of slumber and following the trails of chi back to the main body. Moving toward the source of the unaspected chi went against the first brother's and sister's very instincts, so they decided to remain still. The others could come to them.

Their minds remained split as they tried to decipher the identity of the dread being brave or foolish enough to use chi that bore no aspect.

I held up a finger, cutting Paul off mid-sentence as something tickled my nose. Covering my face with an arm, I sneezed, shaking my head as the sensation faded. "Sorry, mate. Maria's strike must have dislodged part of my brain. That sent it flying, I think. Hopefully it wasn't anything too important."

Maria patted my shoulder. "That's implying that there's anything important up there to lose, my love."

"I feel like I'd usually be offended by something like that . . . is that the bit I sneezed out? The part that takes offense?" I leaned down toward Paul and flared my nostrils, also crossing my eyes for good measure. "Can you check for me, mate?"

Paul's uninhibited laughter was music to my ears. So, naturally, I had to coax more out. Tilting my head side to side, I circled him, following his field of view every time he tried to look away. "I need your help, Paul! Only your fingers are small enough to get up there and check!"

"S-stop!" He giggled, fighting for breath.

"You show weakness, junior! Let this one share some pointers with—"

"M-Mom! Fischer is—"

"*Junior, you dare?*" I got closer and opened my eyes as wide as possible. "*You are courting death—*"

"Fischer! What are you doing to my son?"

"Elder Helen!" I went bolt upright, my hands snapping to my sides, then bowed at the waist. "This lowly one greets you!"

She sighed. "At least you won't have to deal with him for long, Paul. If we're lucky, he might not come back from his trip."

"Ohhhhh," Maria said. "Buuurn!"

But I just looked at Barry and raised an eyebrow, unable to hide my smirk. He blanched.

Helen looked at me, then her husband, then me again. "Barry?"

"Uhhh, yes, dear?"

"Why is Fischer looking at you like he just caught you drinking straight from the whiskey barrel?"

"I . . ." His weirdly muscular fingers fumbled with the hem of his shirt. "I may have said that it might perhaps be possible—*just* a possibility, mind you—for Paul to . . . come. On the fishing trip, I mean."

"Huh," she replied, her tone unnaturally flat. "And when were you planning on telling me about this decision?"

"Yesterday. It, errr . . . Can we talk about this in private?"

"Why would we, Barry?" The glint in her eyes was sharper than a System-made hook. "You seem to be discussing our business with other people, so why shouldn't I?"

All at once, she broke into a smile, and laughter bubbled up from her core. "Your face, Barry. You—" She cackled like a madwoman. "Oh, gods above. Of course Paul can go." She waved a dismissive hand my way. "It was weird that you didn't trust Fischer with him in the first place."

"Yeah, Barry." I narrowed my eyes at him. "*Super* weird of you."

Believing that Helen was actually pissed, most of the breakfast group had taken off. Sue and Sturgill had straight-up carried their table, still covered in food and coffee, away over the dunes. Only those coming on the trip had remained, as had my animal pals, Maria, and Helen.

Two people were unexpected, though, and I gazed their way, my heart filled with hope. When I looked past them and spotted a pair of packed bags on the sand . . .

Well, that could only mean one thing.

"Before you speak," I said, "I need you to know that I will not be okay if you pretend to come, then bail."

One of them opened their mouth to reply, but I forged on.

"Yes, yes. I know—I deserve that and more. Tenfold, probably. But I'm serious. I might explode. And given how much power I have all up inside of me—don't look at me like that, Maria. Get your head out of the gutter. Given that power, I might actually explode, and . . . Why are you guys not saying anything?" I turned back to Maria. "Did I freeze time again? Why are they not saying anything?"

Ruby shook her head at me. "You didn't give us a chance to speak."

"Aye," Steven said. "You sound like Paul that one time he had a coffee."

"Ehhhh." Trent made a so-so gesture with his hand. "I think Fischer was worse."

"Yeah!" Paul agreed. "I was nowhere near as bad as him!"

"Oi! Stop using me as a measurement for how annoying something is! And don't change the subject, Ruby! Are you coming or not?"

Steven and Ruby shared a glance, and the latter nodded. "We've been missing out these past weeks, and there's no place safer for me than by your side. We want to come."

All I could do for a moment was blink back. I took a deep breath, tried to contain myself, then made a noise that was definitely manly and not at all embarrassing. "That's it! I'm overwhelmed! Cuddle puddle! *Stat!*"

Teddy got to me before I could get the last word out. One paw went around my torso, the other around Maria's, and he pulled us against his ridiculously strong yet still squishy frame. It was just what the doctor ordered. And then the rest of them arrived.

Pelly and Bill landed atop Teddy's shoulder, their wings making wind wash down over me. There was an orange blur to my right, followed by a very happy stream of bubbles, and Sergeant Snips came rocketing in at the perfect angle. Her many spikes were covered in blue chi. I rubbed one with my chin, finding it smooth to the touch.

Brigadier Borks and Cinnamon arrived as a tag team. I wondered how Borks planned on cramming his way in, but then he transformed. Rather than the Chihuahua I expected, he slid in as a whippet—the smaller, anxiety-disordered cousin of the greyhound. He trembled with excitement as he slid toward the center, but small as he might be, he got stuck. Thankfully—or not, depending on your perspective—Cinnamon followed through with a perfectly aimed push kick right on Borks's rump. They both tumbled in and came to a rest atop Snips's shell.

A dozen or so of the Buzzy Boys flew in and found places to nestle in, their wings vibrating a message of appreciation from the entire hive mind. Pistachio let out a neutral stream of bubbles, resting one of his gigantic snippers against the back of my leg. From any other of the spirit beasts, it would have made me worry. From my lobster pal, it was on par with the most affection he'd ever shown.

"Okay, gang," I said, reluctantly relaxing my embrace. "I think it's about time we set sail . . ."

CHAPTER FORTY-FOUR

The Perfect Ratio

Standing tall, I breathed as deep as I could. A brisk easterly had blown in from nowhere. Waves crashed against the ship's hull and threw particles of salty water into the air, their scent washing over my awareness and restoring the sense of calm that was never too far away when you lived in Tropica.

The taste of salt hit my tongue, which made me recall my time fishing back on Earth. I'd just been a regular human then. A man with more troubles than I knew what to do with. Despite my lack of a core, the smell of the ocean had been a source of absolute mindfulness—a presence that scoured away all but the most persistent of worries.

Even more relaxing, however, was the act of fishing. It demanded your full attention. There were countless sources of distraction, of course: wind, waves, and the warm sun beaming down on your shoulders. Through them all, one had to keep a part of their mind on the finger touching the line—you just never knew when a fish would come along and have a nibble, after all.

It was an odd time to reminisce on such things, but the reason for their return was obvious. We stood on the precipice of an adventure—of a new frontier that we were about to explore for ourselves.

Despite how skilled I'd gotten at keeping my senses constrained, Bonnie's core was screaming out to me—it seemed to be doing its best to vibrate right out of her body. I glanced back, seeing her keen excitement reflected on the faces of everyone else. Fergus, Duncan, Steven, Ruby, Theo, Deklan, Barry, and Paul. Including Bonnie and I, we were ten cultivators—a nice round number for the ship's maiden voyage. Cats were good luck on such endeavors, but I didn't have one yet, so I'd brought Borks *and* Cinnamon along instead.

Bonnie's chi called out to me again, vibrating as I harnessed all the members of this trip in place. The intoxicating nature of her core wasn't exactly surprising—adventure was her literal purpose in life. Her breakthrough had confirmed it. With one last look at the effect her emotions were having on everyone else, I turned toward the front of the ship, gazing at the eastern horizon over the top of the bow.

I took another breath of salty air. Its freshness filled me with vigor, which I then channeled into my chi, securing my pals to the deck just in case. When my essence touched Borks, I asked a single question in his mind. He confirmed that he'd succeeded last night, giving me the slightest of nods, which he hid with a big yawn. I had to consciously hide the joy his answer sparked within my core.

"Well, gang," I said, "there's only one last thing to do."

Maria, who stood on the deck with Helen, gave a playful roll of her eyes. "I know you and Barry are terrified of being without us, but you can't just keep making up excuses."

"No, no, this is the most important part of a new ship—a tradition as old as sailing! I'm honestly surprised that none of you have brought it up."

Maria frowned; she could sense my sincerity. "Okay, I'm lost."

I raised a hand high, pretended to gather power, then shot it to the side and into a small portal Borks opened just in time. Within, I found one of his many objectives from last night, and I beamed as I pulled it out. Borks immediately closed the gateway, sealing his dimensional space.

I held out the bottle of wine, its glass and red contents gleaming in the light. "We, my dear friends, must name and christen this ship!"

I expected some ooohs in response, perhaps even some ahhhs. Instead, I was met with a long silence.

"Okay," Maria eventually said, "we're not dumb, Fischer. If you are that desperate to name things that you're gonna start giving them to inanimate objects, just say that's what you want to do. There's no need to make up obviously fake traditions."

"Wait, what?" I looked around, and the looks on everyone's faces mirrored Maria's. "You guys seriously haven't heard of this?"

"No," came their long-suffering answers, only my animal pals and Paul looking excited about the prospect.

I blew air through my lips, reached for some scattered memories, and showed them the truth.

Maria blinked as her gaze refocused a moment later. "Well, I'll be. I would have sworn you were lying about that one."

"Nope!"

"What are you gonna call it?" Paul asked, his eyes aglow with the possibilities. "Something to match how cool it looks?"

Deciding there was no point in delaying further, I launched the bottle, and as it shattered against the chain railing, I screamed the ship's name for the entire village to hear. Before the shards of glass could fall into the ocean, I crushed them between strands of chi, grinding them into dust.

That single word I'd let out seemed to shake the deck, and whispers of power settled into the wood's grain, moving to become a part of the ship. I braced myself for some sort of transformation, wondering how it would affect my plans, but nothing happened.

Two small hands grabbed me by the cheeks, and Maria turned my head, forcing me to face her.

"I love you, but that was your worst name yet."

"What? Why? It's thematic, sharp, and to the point."

"How is the name Bob thematic for a boat? It's . . ." She trailed off, slowly turning toward me as realization struck. "Why are you like this?"

"Gods above," Ruby swore, similarly struck by knowledge.

The others just looked confused. Poor Paul's head darted back and forth in a frenzy, his brow only creasing further with each second that no explanation came.

Before he could give himself a concussion, I rested a hand on his shoulder. "What does wood do in water?"

"Uhhh, it floats?"

"Some would say that, mate." I gave an exaggerated wink. "Others would say that it bobs."

"Oh! Bob the boat!"

A series of groans rose from everyone else, but there were just as many snorts and amused noises—the perfect ratio, if you asked me.

Maria leaned in, kissed me on the mouth, then pulled back and stared into my eyes. "I really do love you, but I need to go. I'll be reconsidering our marriage while you are gone." Without another word, she petted both Borks and Cinnamon, then leaped away.

Helen shook her head at me, pecked Barry on the lips and Paul on the forehead, and departed in the same manner.

I sent Maria my affection, returning the torrent she'd been pouring my way even as she claimed she needed to rethink our future. "Ready when you are, Trent!"

As all present were secured to the deck by my chi, I could partially perceive their emotions, only the strongest making it through my defenses. Those coming from the former prince were overwhelming. Long gone was the mountain of duty that caused him to spend every waking hour searching for a way to cure his family. Maria's breakthrough and subsequent bonding of a healing familiar had taken that pressure from his shoulders, and in the wake of such a burden, Bonnie's enthusiasm was taking root.

Trent's anticipation and hope built and built, becoming so strong that I had to stop focusing on his emotions, lest they smother mine. Even with a shell raised around me, I could feel Bonnie spurring him on, her gaze intense as she felt him reciprocating her resolve.

Without another word, Trent reached for his core, grasped hold of his flames, and poured a thin stream of will into the engine's spout. The construct whirred, drank deep of his chi, then changed it into something *more*.

Maria stood on the sandy shore, delighting in how happy everyone was. She had assumed she would be a little sad watching them go. After all, she *did* love fishing. But as she felt Trent reach for his flames and pour them down into the boat's propulsion system, all she could feel was her own sense of excitement—she *finally* had the power to heal all those trapped in Tropica's prison.

As the conflagration churned within the rear of the ship, amplifying in potency on its way out of the claw-shaped exhaust, she felt a wave of gratitude so potent that it eclipsed any she could remember.

It wasn't for anyone on board, however. Nor was it for the creation of the vessel, which would facilitate all sorts of adventures in the future. It wasn't for the annoyingly amusing name Fischer had given it, and it wasn't for the life-giving sun that shone above.

This gratitude, stronger than any she'd felt in recent memory, was because she was not strapped to the deck when flames bigger than a house shot from Bob the boat.

Dom had remained behind as a safety precaution; his core was capable of shielding the citizens should some unforeseen shenanigans come to pass. But who could have guessed that their departure would be the source of said shenanigans?

The man held his arms wide, and a shield appeared that was even bigger than the teardrop-shaped inferno flaring toward them. One second, the ship was there. The next, it was rocketing over the horizon, sailing *above* the ocean rather than on it.

"Uhhh," Maria said as they disappeared from sight. "Are they gonna be okay?"

Dom, peering down at the flat slab of molten glass that now ran along the waterline, shook his head. "When Fischer is involved, the only thing in danger is their sensibilities. I'm just glad Helen wasn't here to see—"

He'd spoken too soon. A torrent of words you'd never expect to hear from Helen came flying over the dunes, cutting off Dom's sentence. Paul's mother stood up three peaks back as her tirade increased in both pitch and vigor. Maria stored some of the insults away for later use on her beloved. She wouldn't even have to swap his name in—it was already there.

As we sailed *over* the ocean, wind rushed past me, whipping the hair on my head into a chaotic mess. Such an occurrence was usually a source of mindfulness. A calming sensation I could focus on to ground myself in the present. But given the fact my brand-new boat was currently flying hundreds of meters above the sea, flames *still* rocketing from the propulsion system, I didn't really feel up to meditating.

"Trent!" I called. "Feel free to stop feeding chi into it! I think we've gone far enough!"

"I stopped almost immediately! A quarter of my power remains below!"

"*Oh! Good!* I was worried we *wouldn't* go halfway across the globe!"

"I'm sensing some sarcasm!" Barry yelled. "Can you confirm, Theo?"

"Definitely sarcasm!"

Ruby unleashed a breathless laugh, the sound as beautiful as the sun we seemed to be sailing toward. Deklan had shielded everyone with his chi, the protective properties of his essence somehow even able to defend against the force of acceleration. It was the only reason I hadn't immediately portalled half the people present—especially Ruby—back onto dry land.

With the angle of our trajectory, we couldn't even see the ocean, only open sky and a rising sun visible over the railing of our boat-turned-airplane. When the flames finally died, I pressed down on the front deck. The entire vessel tilted. The sun shifted above. And the blessed sea, its depths a deeper blue than I'd seen on this world, came into view.

In every direction, it was all we could see. Not even a speck of land was visible in this stretch of sea, and as it seemed to rush up to meet us, I prepared layers of chi around the hull. There were dozens upon dozens, each growing larger and thinner. I kept going, only stopping when one became so thin that the shifting wind made it break.

It had taken all of my focus to build them, but maintaining them was easy, so I returned to the present, holding the layers in place with a single partition, and what I found made butterflies take flight within me. Everyone was hooting and hollering, so I joined in, not caring how my whooping sounded to the outside world.

And then we struck. My layers were obliterated, destroyed by the force of Bob meeting the water's surface—but that was the point. By the time the last broke, a foot of ocean peeked above the side of the deck, held at bay by a solid wall of my light. Like a rubber ducky forced underwater by an overeager toddler, we bobbed back up—*heh*—and water splashed everywhere as we landed once more.

"All hands on deck!" I called, enjoying myself way too much as I removed the tendrils holding everyone down. "How did the rods fare?"

"Secure!" Paul yelled, giving me a thumbs-up from the open door to the cabin.

"Bait?"

Theo pinched his nose as he looked up from the barrel of eel. "Stinky, Captain!"

"Tackle?"

"Here!" Fergus had already removed it from his bag and set it down on the deck.

Borks, well, *borked* as he opened a portal. Cinnamon coated herself in chi, flew inside, kicked the secondary tackle box out, and reemerged. The door immediately closed behind her.

"Uh, Fischer?" Bonnie asked. "Why didn't you just put all of it in Borks's personal space?"

"To keep things sporting, of course!"

Theo, who was leaning far back from the now-open barrel of eel, frowned at my words. He raised a brow and tilted his head in question.

I flashed a grin and shot him a wink as I strode past, heading for the cabin and the rods held within. "I don't know about you guys, but I might implode if I don't wet a line soon."

Paul started handed me rod after rod, which I chucked toward my pals, their enhanced reflexes meaning none of the precious objects were at risk of falling. When Ruby caught hers, she passed it to Steven. I smiled, the small show of affection making my heart happy. But then I passed a second rod to her, and she passed it to him again. And another. And *another*.

"Okay, what gives?" I nodded at Steven, who was now wrestling with four of them. "Are you not fishing, Ruby?"

She giggled and shook her head, the way her hair flicked making me think of Maria. "Of course I am. I'm just waiting for *my* rod."

"Your rod?"

I raised an eye at Paul, who furrowed his brow and dashed into the cabin. "Oh!" he said from within, returning a moment later with a . . . *fishing rod*?

I blinked at what was clearly a joke at my expense. The "rod" drew my eyes in.

Sewing Rod of the Tailor
Rare
This rod doubles as a tool for both fishing and tailoring. Though appearing to be crocheted, this instrument is as strong and flexible as it needs to be, able to hold tension when sewing or reeling in a fish. Adds half of the user's tailoring skill to their fishing skill, or vice versa, depending on the activity being undertaken.

When my vision cleared, I raised both eyebrows at Ruby, who wore one of the smuggest grins I'd ever seen. "We've not been sitting around doing nothing, Fischer."

"Aye," Steven agreed. "It took days, but we had the time to spare."

I took a step forward, my hand reaching out of its own accord, but I forced myself to stop. "May I?"

"Of course!"

Ruby held it out, and as I ran my hand over the handle, my brain and eyes told me two different things. Even under the scrutiny of my enhanced vision, it looked like a crocheted toy. Beneath my fingers, though, it was like interwoven wood, strong despite the gaps between the "string." I withdrew. "That thing is breaking my head. Congratulations, and I hate it."

Ruby snorted and pulled her Sewing Rod of the Tailor closer. "It certainly takes some getting used to—that's for sure. But the benefits . . ." A gleam entered her eyes. "I don't know how I ever sewed things without it."

"We've not had a chance to use it for fishing," Steven added. "So when we heard about your little trip . . ."

Ruby's smile turned predatory. "How could we pass up the opportunity?"

"Well," I said, "I'm glad you came along, even if it was only to try out your rod."

"Me too! The passage here alone made it worth it!" Ruby moved to the larger tackle box, but as she stared down at the different hooks and sinkers, she cocked her head. "I just realized that I don't know what setup we should use from a boat?"

"It's similar to the paternoster rig," I replied. "You remember how to tie it?"

"Remember? It was the first you ever showed us!"

"Perfect." I went over to the other tackle box—the one stored within Borks's dimensional space—and retrieved the necessary bits and pieces for my rod. "The only difference between the normal paternoster and the one we'll be using is . . . Why are you all looking at me like that?"

Theo cleared his throat. "Are you compensating for something with that hook, Fischer?"

I glanced down at the hook, its metal as thick as my finger, then back up at Theo. "Given that you can tell if I'm lying, the only safe bet is to not answer that."

This drew a laugh from everyone but Paul, who just looked confused. Before he could question what we were all talking about, I forged onward. "Right. So tie the main line to the eye of a swivel, then tie a meter of thick line to the other eye. Create the hoops for your hooks here—I reckon two is a good number."

They followed along, Paul helped by Cinnamon, who pointed at the two spots he should create loops.

"Awesome. Here's where it gets a little different . . ." I grabbed the thinnest line we had. "Short of reinforcing this with chi, if you tied your hook to this line, anything bigger than two or three kilos would snap off. We'll be attaching sinkers with it, which will be at the very bottom of the rig. Does anyone know why we're using this weaker line on purpose?"

A sea of confused faces met me. Theo was the first to work it out, as befitted the fishing fanatic. "Oh! Do you think there might be rocks below us?"

"Got it in one, my man. We're going to drop our lines until they touch the bottom, then reel them up a tiny bit. If there are rocks, corals, or anything else that can snag us, it'll likely be the sinker getting caught on them. The line being thin—and the knot being weak—means they'll be the fault points."

Theo nodded. "It saves most of our equipment and reduces our chances of polluting. Brilliant."

"Thank you."

"The rig, not you."

I barked a laugh and bent to pet Borks, whose golden-haired tail swished back and forth over the deck. "That's fair—I didn't think of the setup myself."

It took little time to finish attaching our hooks, and even less to bait them. When I was done, I swung my rod over the water, flicked the reel open, and let it free spool. My excitement returned as meter after meter disappeared into the abyss, and I couldn't help but imagine the weird and wacky creatures that might live in the depths below.

If they were down there, I'd find them. Of that, I was sure.

CHAPTER FORTY-FIVE

Shifting Colors

Beneath a sun so hot a regular bloke's skin would burn in minutes, I arched my back, enjoying the way my bare shoulders prickled. A muscular jaw leaned into my field of view, and before I could ask what was up, Barry glanced down at my torso.

"Does anyone think Maria would be surprised Fischer took his shirt off before his sinker reached the bottom?"

"Nope."

"Not even a little."

"She might be surprised he had one on in the first place."

"Oh, c'mon!" I raised both arms high. "It's a beautiful bloody day—how am I supposed to remain fully clothed when the sun feels so nice? Besides, I still have my captain hat on. That's some—*oh!*" Something had bumped my line. A part of me thought it was a fish at first, but then I just smiled at myself—the sinker had reached the bottom. I snapped my reel back into place, wound in a few times, then held my finger against the line. "I reckon it's about seventy meters down based on how much length is missing from my rod. You should all be hitting it soon."

Barry's hit next, making him forget all about teasing me. He copied my actions, flicking his reel before winding in the exact amount of times I had.

"Try reeling in another few meters or so, mate."

"Why?"

"Because one depth could be better than the others. I don't have the faintest idea what we might catch here, so it's all about trial and error. The more we fail, the more data we'll accumulate."

Notably not winding in as I'd suggested, he turned a glower on me. "So you get to be near the bottom where the fish are, and I get to fail?"

"Barry, when have I ever led you astray?"

"Would you like me to list each instance by severity or chronological order?"

"Oh, psh! Stop living in the past, mate. I meant *today.*"

"Well, you haven't today, but just because I haven't noticed doesn't mean it hasn't happened."

Theo, whose line had reached the bottom, cleared his throat. "I might be able to shed some light on at least one thing he's done today, Barry."

"Theo," I warned. "If you so much as *hint* at what I think you know, I'll send you back to Tropica."

"By sending me back to Tropica, do you mean via teleportation?"

"No."

Theo turned to face the ocean immediately, watching the water as he waited for a bite.

"Hang on," Barry said. "What did Fischer do? You can't just bring it up and go quiet!"

"I think you'll find that he can, mate."

"Theo?" the muscleman continued, snapping his fingers to get the former auditor's attention. But Theo may as well have been a boulder. "Why are you ignoring me?"

I gave him a malicious grin and waggled my eyebrows in victory, happy to let him stew.

"If I were to hazard a guess," Ruby said, eyes closed as she faced the sea, "I'd say that both questions are answered by Theo's abilities as a crown auditor. Because he knows when people tell the truth, he learned that Fischer verbally led you astray."

"Allegedly," I added, which made her laugh.

"*Allegedly*," she repeated. "That same ability is a double-edged sword, though, Barry."

"How?"

Instead of answering him, Ruby raised an eyebrow my way. "Do all of us have to try different depths?"

"Nah, I'd say only one of us at a time. It's still more likely to find fish at the bottom."

"In that case, Barry, I'll tell you the truth on one condition . . ." She looked at him for the first time since she joined the conversation, and it wasn't with the eyes of a friend, an expectant mother, or any of the other social roles Ruby occupied—it was with the gaze of a hawk. "You, Barry, have to be the guinea pig that winds their line up. If you do that, I'll share what I know."

"Oh, *come on*! You can't be serious!"

I cackled, as did the smiths, Deklan, and Cinnamon, her little peeps a welcome counterpoint to our loudness. Even Borks was amused, his tail wagging softly.

Barry eyed us all, his gaze finally landing on Ruby—who had turned back to the ocean and was ignoring him completely. Gritting his teeth, he wound his reel a handful of times. "Fine. Deal."

"Good lad," she said, despite being not much older. "The reason Theo won't answer you is this . . ." Ruby glanced up at Barry, her eyes sparkling like gems. "Theo knows when Fischer is being honest, yes? So when Theo asked if he'd be teleported back, and Fischer answered no, Theo must have known it was the truth. Thus, if Theo betrays whatever lie he caught Fischer in, Fischer will use a different method to send him home—a good yeeting, I presume."

"No comment!" Theo called, having not once rejoined the conversation.

"You know, Ruby," I said. "I might have yeeted you back to town yourself if you weren't pregnant. Pretty audacious of you to reveal the secrets of God-King Fischer . . ."

"But I *am* pregnant, and you *won't* yeet me."

I opened my mouth to say something sharp, probably directed at Steven about how good Ruby was at arguing—I never really knew what words were going to come from me until they started flying out—but Barry beat me to it.

"Is no one else bothered that Fischer lied?" he asked, scanning the crowd.

Deklan blew a raspberry. "I'd rather he hid stuff, to be honest. Who knows what kind of information gets fed into the mind of a traveler? I came fishing to *relax*, not to learn cosmic secrets."

"Aye," Fergus agreed. "I don't think you're allowed to ask him to become the leader, then get mad when he does something leadery. I trust Fischer to do the right thing, and so should you."

"That's . . . huh." I gave the smith an appraising look. "That's a kind way of putting it, Fergus."

Barry sighed. "If it's for the sake of the village, I *guess* I can accept it . . ."

"Who said it was?" I waggled my eyebrows at him again. "All I said was that Fergus had *a kind way of putting it.*"

Barry's scowl returned. "You know, Fischer, I hate you sometimes."

"You love me, you big goose. Stop playing hard to get."

Holding strong eye contact with me, he opened his reel, letting line spool out until it was back at its original depth. I grinned and wound up my own, happy to be the guinea pig.

It was ten minutes later, and without a bite on board, that something absolutely wonderful occurred.

"What is that?" Theo asked, speaking for the first time since he'd proclaimed *no comment* earlier.

A single wave approached, but calling it that robbed it of its size and scope. The damned thing was crossing the *entire* ocean. All we could see in every direction was water, and the wave went from one end to the next. It was only a foot or so tall, but it presented a unique opportunity that I was loath to let pass by.

As it reached the boat, the deck rose, causing all of our rods to bend down—exactly what I'd been hoping for.

"Fish on!" I lied.

"Big bite!" Barry yelled, his entire body tensing.

Steven made a startled noise, his hands a blur as he retrieved line.

Everyone but Theo and I fought hard, pumping and winding. For our part, we just watched the show, searing it into our memory. I intended on remembering the scene until the day I died.

"Did I drop it?" Duncan asked when he finally recognized there was no weight on the end of his rod.

"Aye," Fergus added. "Think I dropped mine, too . . ."

Theo was the first to break. A choking noise coming from his throat as he fought his mirth down. When everyone looked our way, they were no longer winding, the excitement on their faces replaced by confusion.

Barry, for what had to be the tenth time today, narrowed his eyes at me. "What did you do?"

It was all I could take. I absolutely lost it, and I had to hold the chain railing for support as my laughter escaped. "I'm so sorry," I eventually got out, "the—the wave—"

In one smooth movement, Ruby kicked her shoe off, caught it, and launched it at my head. I let it land. The sandal bounced off my forehead with a *donk*, and I grabbed it before it could ricochet overboard.

"You're a bastard, Fischer." She did an admirable job of hiding the smirk that tugged at the corners of her mouth. "There was never any fish. The wave lifted the boat, which made it seem as though we'd all gotten a bite."

"Got it in one, Rubes! Don't get me wrong, I expected it to happen, but that exceeded my wildest dreams. It's a common rite of passage on boats where I come from."

Though they acted annoyed, the joy in their soft mutters to each other told a different story. Theo, who was swiftly becoming my partner in crime for this trip, playfully rolled his eyes—he'd also seen the falsehood in their statements.

"Oh!" Paul yelled. "Fish on!"

Barry turned on me like a mama bear, even the idea that I was turning my pranks on Paul making soft red light ooze from his muscles.

I took a step back before he could maul me. "Jesus Christ, Barry! It's not me! There's something on his hook!"

Before he could decide whether to trust me or not, the world intervened on my behalf—a *massive* creature chomped down on his hook, too.

"Be ready!" I called. "Looks like there might be a run of—" I cut off, my own rod almost ripped from my hands. "Frack me! Fish on!"

Of all the times I'd been so busy yapping that I almost lost my whole damned rod when something struck, this was by far the closest. The lightning-infused shark from days ago was strong, but whatever had taken my hook was *stronger*. I immediately extended my chi and snapped partitions into place, one to protect my rod, the other to preserve my line.

Even so, my will was pushed to its limits—as was my body. The way the creature moved made no sense. Rather than head shakes or kicks of a powerful tail, it pulsed in seemingly random directions. Was it even a fish? I didn't think so. I glanced to the side to check if anyone else was struggling, but they seemed to be easily handling theirs. Literally everyone had a fish on.

I dismissed them from my mind; I couldn't spare any attention.

Suddenly, my line went slack, but I'd been fooled one too many times by fish swimming toward me to fall for it again. I wound in as fast as I could, and after a few seconds, the weight of the creature returned—only to disappear a second later.

I reeled again, hoping it was still on, but the back of my mind knew the truth. And the closer to the boat it got, the surer I became—I'd been snapped off. I tensed my jaw, trying not to be annoyed at its escape.

"Damn!" Fergus called, almost falling on his backside. "Mine got off!"

"Frack!" Paul cursed. That word yelled by his adolescent voice did wonders for my mood. "Me too!"

I let out a slow breath, exhaling the last of my frustration. So what if it had gotten away? Another would come. Even better, we now knew that there were fish to catch—both the normal ones my pals seemed to have hooked, and the monster that had escaped from me.

I focused on winding in as swiftly as I could. The moment the end of my line was back on deck, I'd set it aside and go help the others.

My hook breached the surface, traveling so fast that it sailed into the air. It bounced up and down chaotically, the sinker having been removed. But that wasn't what my eyes were glued to. By the sounds of it, someone had landed their fish, but even that couldn't pull my gaze away.

I wouldn't have been surprised to find my line severed above the rig. Hell, even if my hook's finger-wide metal had been bent straight, I would have accepted it and moved on with my day. The creature had been massive, after all. But neither of those things had happened. I reached out, still unbelieving, and grabbed the eye of the hook between my fingers. That half was intact, the metal gleaming in the sunlight. The rest was . . . gone. Like *gone* gone.

"Fischer!" Barry yelled, his voice jubilant.

"One second, mate. Bit of a situation over he—"

"Help!"

I whirled, extending my senses, just in time to both see and feel Barry get his shit *rocked* by a tentacle wider than his bulging bicep.

Okay, maybe it wasn't fair to say it rocked him. Against Barry's body, the tentacle had all the power of overcooked spaghetti. That was a good analogy, actually, because it had both the shape and flexibility of spaghett—

"Fischer!" he laughed, trying to catch hold of all the many limbs assaulting him without hurting the creature. The two long tentacles—one of which had delivered the slap to Barry's gob—were the trickiest, constantly slipping from his grasp to lash out at him. "Poseidon's prehensile member, *help me*!"

I stepped to the side, dodging a torrent of black ink that shot from the animal's mouth. "I'm *very* busy, Barry."

"What could possibly be more important than this?"

"I mean . . . watching it play out is pretty high on the list. Would you like to hear the rest?"

"Fischer!"

I appeared by his side, and as I gazed down at the creature, my eyes were immediately drawn into it.

Mature Bluefathom Squid
Common
Plentiful in the Bluefathom Ocean, these creatures are predators of smaller

species, and the favored prey of larger ones. In times long past, they were heavily targeted by humans, both for their tender flesh and varied byproducts.

Seeing all I had needed to, I dismissed the words and delivered a karate chop to the back of its head, instantly and humanely ending its life. The brown color dotting its form immediately drained away, leaving a rainbow hue that seemed to dance beneath the sun's light. In both shape and size, it was identical to photos of giant squid I'd seen on Earth, this one's body as long as a man, and its two biggest tentacles double that. "Damn. That's a lot of calamari."

Barry stepped over it, his face shifting between disappointment and disbelief. "What the hell, Fischer?"

"What? You wanted help."

"Well, yeah, but I didn't think you'd slap it to death."

"That was a karate chop, Barry. Get a grip."

Cinnamon crossed her arms and nodded. It was, in fact, a karate chop.

"I don't care what it was! I asked for your help because I wasn't sure we should eat it or release it! I'd have just dispatched it myself if I knew you were going to hit it!"

"Ahhh, I understand the confusion now. That *is* the most humane way to kill squid, mate."

"How do you even know that?"

"What, you've never had seven beers, then spent your evening watching fishing videos on the internet? Get out more, mate."

"Fischer!" came another voice, Ruby close to hysterics. "I realize you guys are having a moment, but I need help over here!"

A tentacle only slightly smaller than those laying lifeless on the deck beside me lashed out toward her, but she jumped to the side, dodging it.

"See that?" I asked Barry. "She dodged it, and *she's* growing a human inside of her. What's your excuse?"

He barked a genuine laugh. "You're a real prick sometimes."

"Aww, you called me a prick. It's cute when you use my words. Right, Cinnamon?"

She crossed her arms and nodded, letting out an emphatic squeak. It was, in fact, cute when he used my words.

Before the pregnant cultivator fell victim to another tentacle—*man, I really need to watch my phrasing*—I dashed to her side and dispatched the squid.

The next person to reel one in didn't have to call my name to get my attention. Mostly because her core radiated an unassailable sense of *rightness*. Bonnie's desire for adventure and new experiences was well and truly sated by the tentacled creature slapping about near the deck. She hauled it over the side, gripping it between the head and body as she stared into its beaked maw.

"Hey, uh, Bonnie?" I said. "Maybe don't—"

Too late.

A fire-hose-like stream of black ink blasted her face, slicking her hair back. The moment seemed to last forever, the abyssal liquid splashing all over the deck. Having witnessed my humane methods, she squeezed, the creature going limp. She dropped the squid, wiped her eyes, and blinked at us all. "If you'll excuse me." Without another word, she leaned back, hit the railing, and tumbled overboard into the ocean.

Three minutes and just as many additional karate chops later, we had five of the gigantic cephalopods in the middle of the deck. Duncan, Steven, and Trent had caught the other three, everyone else having been bitten off.

Bonnie hauled herself back on board, and I couldn't help but peer her way, curious if her skin had been stained. To my great delight—though I'd never admit as much—anywhere the ink had touched possessed a gray tint, the pigment sticking despite her enhanced body. But that wasn't the truly remarkable thing. She lifted a strand of her hair, raising an eyebrow as she assessed her previously red, now-midnight-colored mane. "Please tell me this isn't permanent."

"Unfortunately, I don't think so."

"Unfortunately?" she asked, her eyebrows going even higher.

"Ah-huh." I shot her a wink. "To be honest, it looks really cool. Especially your skin."

Unimpressed, she waited for me to continue, perhaps suspecting I'd laugh at her.

"I'm serious, Bonnie. It looks neat."

"It really does . . ." Ruby took a step forward, her fingers drifting toward Bonnie's arm, then paused. "May I?"

"Sure."

Ruby ran a hand over the blotches, trying and failing to rub the pigment away. "Fascinating . . ."

Steven got close, peering over Ruby's shoulder. "I wonder . . . the byproducts the System mentioned—do you think one could be a dye?"

"You guys are getting too clever," I said. "You're ruining most of my reveals! That was exactly what I thought when I read the description. Even with all of Earth's technological advancement, natural dyes—like squid ink—remain in use. Now, if we can just find the ink sac, maybe the System will confirm . . ."

I bent, preparing to cut one of them open and seek it out, but Barry laid a hand on my shoulder.

"Should we really be opening it up? Isn't there a chance it spoils before we get back to Tropica?"

I swiveled slowly, giving him a shit-eating grin.

"Why are you looking at me like that?"

"Remember how I said you're ruining *most* of my reveals . . . ?"

He sighed. "Go on, then. What did you do?"

"Thanks for asking!" I shot to my feet, marched over to the hatch, and gestured at it with both hands. "If you would, Borks! Cinnamon!"

Borks ran over, his tail wagging so hard that the rest of him was forced to join in. Cinnamon rode his back, her legs and hips easily moving with Borks's butt wiggles.

I smiled at everyone as they crept over, unable to keep their curiosity at bay. Stronger than their need to know, waves of anticipation poured from Borks—I couldn't recall the last time I'd seen him so excited. I patted his golden fur, but rather than the sense of calm I had hoped to gift him, his puppylike elation washed over me.

I could have pushed it away, but I didn't, deciding to embrace it instead.

This was going to be *fun*.

CHAPTER FORTY-SIX

Menace

Beneath a cloudless sky and under the unimpressed stares of my friends, I beamed. "Let's say, purely hypothetically, of course, that you were a smart, handsome, and humble leader . . ." I paused, giving them an assessing look. "Are you all following so far?"

"Yes, Fischer," my unenthusiastic crowd drawled—with the exception of Ruby and Paul, who answered with the *objectively correct* amount of eagerness.

I shot them a wink. "Good. If you were *that* leader, and you had two furry friends—one of which was a magical dog with spatial powers, and the other being a pint-sized brawler with the ability to punch holes in boulders—what would you have had them do last night in order to preserve anything we caught?" Nobody spoke up immediately, so I added, "Perhaps atop a snow-covered mountain?"

"Ohhh!" Ruby was all smiles. "Cinnamon, being the capable *brawler* that she is, broke some ice up! Then she and Borks—who is also a good boy, might I add—stuffed it into his dimensional space before moving it into the hull?"

Borks, beset by excitement and an overwhelming feeling of belonging, howled his happiness to the heavens. He started shifting; his limbs couldn't decide which canine form he should take. It would have been a terrifying sight on any other creature, but not on him. His tail, no matter which breed of dog it belonged to at any given second, never stopped wagging.

Unable to wait any longer, he bit the handle and threw the trapdoor open, revealing the darkened room within. As everyone stepped forward to have a peek, they saw the thick layer of ice covering every surface. There was *tons* of the stuff. Perhaps enough to sink a regular wooden ship back on Earth. Thankfully, the rules of physics were basically thrown out the window as soon as chi was involved—which Bob the boat possessed in excess.

A meaty hand landed on my shoulder, and I turned to look at my pal. "What's up, Barry?"

"As chaotic as today has been, I think I have to say it. You did a good job. You two especially, Borks and Cinnamon."

The former spun in circles, the latter—still impressively steady atop Borks's back—gave him a self-assured grin, as if to say, *I know. So what?*

I moved over to the squid, and as I picked one up, Barry's mention of chaos made me think of another animal pal.

I hope you're paying attention, Claws, I thought toward her. *Today's events should buy me* weeks *of good behavior.*

Her responding pulse of chi told me I was annoying, she was incredibly busy, and I should stop bothering her.

Cheeky little git, I mused to myself, not missing the adoration that had come along with the hostile words. I sent one last message down our connection, reminding her that I loved her even though her very existence was a threat to the well-being of humanity. I hoped for an annoyed retort, the bait making her upset enough to reply with a string of vitriol and threats, but all she returned was a single word: *yes.*

She really must have been busy; that usually would have worked.

What are you up to over there, you little menace?

Corporal Claws, bequeather of zaps and tamer of thieves, snorted. She was no mere menace—she was *the* menace. Similarly, Fischer, her beloved master and the man to whom she owed everything, was no mere silly billy. He was the *silliest* of billies.

Why would such a taunt have taken hold in the enhanced mind of Corporal Claws? She was too smart, too tricksy, too downright nimble-witted to fall for something so obvious. Besides, she had a *secret.*

Corporal Claws grinned, electricity running along the lines of her needle-sharp teeth. That she had successfully fooled her master made her tummy tingle with the flight of a billion, gajillion, reptili . . . an? That last word didn't sound right. Whatever. Her victory made *lots* of fireflies seem to take flight in her stomach—which was remarkable considering she no longer had one.

Claws had made the ultimate gambit. She had lied to the one she held dearest in this world. And blessedly, it had *worked.*

Fischer truly believed that she'd put chaos over the well-being of others. She *would* mess with them, of course. She already had plans upon plans upon *plans* to enact when the time was right. Like the eight of them involving Barry's bed. *Oh?* She just thought of another—make that nine.

Still, there was a chasm between her machinations and any actions that would cause *real* harm . . . Well, except the one involving Ellis, a bag of flour, a tunnel, and two dollops of passiona jam—that trick was simply too funny to abandon.

Some might be offended that their master—who just so happened to be their best friend—would believe they were capable of such selfishness. But not Claws. It was a badge of honor. A testament to how unpredictable she had become.

Her brilliance had been in changing her own aura. When Fischer assessed it, he saw only what she wanted him to. Ironically, she was only able to project an exaggerated version of chaos because of how chaotic she was. That thought made her head hurt, so she let it go.

One not as smart, soft-furred, and utterly brilliant as Claws might not have recognized this as the gamble she did, but that was only because they lacked imagination. If Fischer discovered that she was lying too soon, it would ruin the most important plan of all, and that was just unacceptable.

The weight of her secrets—and the possibility of her plans coming to fruition—made a wiggle start down in her smallest toe. As it spread to the rest of her body, the wiggle intensified, small arcs of electricity jolting out to strike the ground. Her grin from earlier never once disappeared, and it stretched wider now, her chittering laughter flying out toward the heavens. She even released a few bolts of lightning to make sure they got the message.

Despite her abject merriment, her eyes shot to the side, giving her apprentice a questioning glare. The familiar completely missed the memo, every ounce of his attention focused on the item between them. For his lack of awareness, Claws considered bowling him over a mountain or two. In the end, though, she decided against it. He was just following her instructions to meditate on the object, after all. Her reluctance to launch him had *absolutely nothing* to do with how fuzzy and adorable he was.

The two days or so that they'd been bonded had been nothing short of a delight—and that was *before* counting all the mischief they'd both caused and witnessed.

Claws had always been quietly curious about others' relationships. Fischer was her best friend, but she still knew that her master's bond to Maria was . . . *stronger*? No, that wasn't right. *Deeper?* Nope. Why were words so damned hard? It was *different*, and that was all the word that needed . . . wording.

Snips and Rocky had a similar relationship. Even before the latter returned from the ocean all explodey and cool, there had been a complicated dynamic at play, one with depths far beyond the mistress and masochist-crab facade visible on the surface.

Romantic relationships were as confusing to her as a good rock wasn't; rocks were useful. They were tools to open oysters, shiny baubles with which to make others jealous, and projectiles you could throw at children or the elderly.

She sent that last one to Fischer, who responded by telling her it wasn't funny. He was wrong, though. It *was* funny. She made her laugh grow louder to prove it. But Claws was only kidding, of course. What kind of freak would assault kids or old people? Neither made good targets. Youngins were too small, oldies too slow. A large crab—preferably awakened? Now *that* was the ideal prey.

Though romantic examples came to mind when thinking of different relationships, her connection to the raccoon definitely wasn't that. He was a kindred spirit, so closely aligned that their cores had essentially become one. She might never fully comprehend what it felt like to love someone romantically, but her fuzzy familiar helped her understand it better.

Their relationship was . . . profound. Something that she would never take for granted. It made a deep well of gratitude overflow within her core.

It had only been seconds since she started laughing, and as her appreciation for him overflowed, she decided against launching him into the sky for the crime he was currently committing. Corporal Claws, maiden of the pond and most benevolent of leaders, bopped him on the cheek instead.

Laugh when I laugh! she ordered with a chirp.

The tiny mammal absorbed the strike and turned it into an end-over-end somersault that just didn't quit.

Yes, boss! he chittered back when he finally stuck the landed, giving her a salute. *Sorry, boss!*

Appeased, Claws shifted her tushy to get comfortable, then resumed her merriment. Her familiar joined in, his low tones combining with her high ones as electricity arced between them. They looked at each other, then at the object of their study, and then at the sky, their core vibrating with undeniable certainty.

The next few days were going to be a godsdamned blast.

I shook my head, unable to hide my exasperation. *Children and the elderly?* I was pretty sure she was joking, but I didn't want to find out the hard way that she wasn't. I spent a moment considering it, letting the worry it caused radiate out from my core.

I really *have to ensure my actions hit her chaos quota,* I thought.

"What's up?" Barry asked, likely sensing my doubt.

"Corporal Claws, Barry. Corporal Claws."

"Ahhh. Say no more." He paused, his head tilting to the side. "Want my advice on the matter?"

"Mate, pretty sure you've been the target of more pranks than anyone else. I think I'd be obligated to listen to your opinion even if I didn't want to."

"In that case, I'd never say as much to his face, but there's something a wise, annoying, and incredibly humble fisherman once said to me."

"You're right—best not to say it directly. Might ruin his humble streak."

"Precisely. I doubt that's possible—he's *supremely* humble, you see, possibly the humblest—but it's better to be safe than sorry."

I nodded sagely. "So . . . what did he say? What grand profundity did he heap upon you?"

"It's hard to distill it down into a single sentence, but the gist of it was this: There's no point in focusing on things outside of your control. It's human nature to get stuck in our own head, and instead of letting your worries twist and build into an unstoppable cyclone of anxiety, one should focus on the present."

He gestured at the objects arrayed before us on the deck. I gazed down at the broken hook and all the lines that had been severed. In a circle around me, everyone else on board smiled or nodded my way. Ruby raised a cup of water in a salute that was only half mocking. I returned the gesture as I tried to take the words, which were evidently my own, to heart. "Thanks, Barry. That's actually a helpful remind—"

"Or," he interrupted, voice commanding, "you could use another piece of wisdom he gave me, which I believe is equally applicable." He let a silence hang, and anticipation rose all around us. Finally, he spread his arms wide and proclaimed with grand intonation, "*Shut the* frack *up, you peanut!*"

Ruby did a spit-take, spraying water all over the deck. "Sorry!" she coughed, thumping her chest as she choke-laughed. "Thought he was actually going to drop some wisdom there."

"Not so fast, my impregnated companion." I rubbed my chin as if lost in speculation. "It might be more profound than it appear—"

"Fischer . . ." Ruby's coughing subsided in an instant. "Please don't ever call me that again."

"I'm sorry." I shook my head at Ruby, feigning dismay. "The absolute *heat* that speaker Barry just dropped has left my brain scorched and unable to process more requests." I turned to the side. "Speaker Barry, I beg of you, please record the words of my impregnated companion for my later perusa—"

I cut off as I dove to the deck, the pregnant cultivator's fly-kick going through the air where my neck had been a moment earlier. "On second thought—" I rolled sideways, dodging her sweeping leg. "The room to consider your request just got freed up!"

Thirty seconds and almost as many evasive maneuvers later, I'd managed to apologize enough for Ruby to hear me out.

"Say it," she demanded, arms crossed and face even crosser.

"But . . . the words are *in* the sentence! It's impossible!"

Steven leaned in toward her. "He's right, you know."

She tsked. "I was hoping he wouldn't notice. Fine. You have five seconds of immunity. Startiiing . . ." I took a deep breath as she dragged the word out. "*Now!*"

"I, Fischer, leader of Tropica and king of the pricks, do so solemnly swear to not use the word 'impregnate' or any derivative thereof within the presence of his dear and kind friend Ruby for the rest of time!" I took a gasping breath, having gotten past the now-forbidden word in time. "I agree that doing so will entitle to her a punishment of her choosing, which I must obey within the timeframe specified, so long as it is in my power and will not cause harm to any other."

She gave me a sickly sweet expression. "Good boy."

Those same words from Maria been a source of banter between us. From Ruby, it made a shiver run down my spine.

Jumping to my feet and seeking any distraction possible, I returned to the cut lengths of line, holding all of their severed ends up before my eyes. With my other hand, I lifted the hook, my gaze shifting back and forth.

"So?" Barry asked as he squatted beside me, his brow furrowed. "What do you think?"

"Honestly? I can't say for certain, but I do have my suspicions." Someone behind me was absolutely vibrating with energy, so I turned toward her. "Any thoughts?"

Bonnie kneeled down to see them better. "It's . . . not impossible for a squid to have cut the lines. I got a pretty good look at my one's beak—it could easily detach the limb of a regular human."

"But . . . ?" I prompted.

"But I don't think they did." She poked the severed line ends with the tip of her index finger. "All of them are cut at a sharp angle. Wouldn't the beaks slice them more flush? At least one of them should have. Also, the way they were hooked . . . I suspect that our bait didn't draw them in."

"Exactly! Which can only mean one thing, right?"

We both grinned at each other, our desires for adventure building off one another, growing until I could hardly sit still.

"Okay," Ruby interrupted. "I'll take the hit, because you all look as confused as I feel. Fischer, what in Hades's burning realm are you two talking about?"

"Oh! Sorry!" I held up the hook, displaying the jagged edge where the metal had been either chewed or sliced through. "So, we can all agree that whatever I hooked was an absolute monstrosity, yeah? At first, I thought it might be just a big squid—is that what you all assumed, too?"

"To be honest with you, Fischer," Fergus said, "I've been trying not to think about it at all. If I were you, I'd have *immediately* scanned the water with my chi to make sure an abyssal demon wasn't about to bite poor Bob in half."

"If we're all being sincere . . ." Barry gave me an apologetic smile. "I *did* scan the water for it as soon as I saw your hook. Sorry. If I'd found it, I wouldn't have told you, Fischer. Well, okay, that was a lie. I'd have told you if I thought it was actually a threat, but the point is moot." He shrugged. "I found nothing."

"Oof. You *wound* me."

He just gestured toward Paul. Then, with just as much emphasis, he pointed at his wedding band—perhaps not wanting to speak Helen's name for fear of invoking her wrath—to remind me that his wife would have his hide if he let any risk or harm come to their son.

"Just playing," I said. "Back to the abyssal demon or whatever. I'm pretty sure it wasn't a squid at all. What I think—" I nodded toward Bonnie. "What *we* think, is that it was something else. Something large enough to both hunt the squid and eat them *whole*, severing the line beyond."

A silence stretched settled over the deck, only interrupted by small waves lapping at the hull. Slowly, Barry raised his hand.

"Yes?" I asked.

"I'd like to request an immediate return to Tropica."

"Denied."

"Fair enough. I do wanna stay, but my promise to Helen made me ask."

At her name, I flinched, then stared at the sky as if she would crash down from the heavens at any moment. Rather than roll his eyes at me, Barry joined in, both of us scanning the clouds with narrowed gazes and slight smiles.

"For what it's worth," I said, "I promise I'll keep everyone safe. You can feel the power beneath us, right?"

"I can."

"Well, I *can't*," Ruby complained. "And if you keep talking in riddles, I'm going to throw myself overboard."

I barked a laugh. "Sorry. Barry can feel my Domain—we're still within its bounds. Anything wanting to start a tussle with us will have to challenge a continent's worth of chi."

"And the degenerate who wields it," Barry mumbled. He took a deep breath, held it for a handful of seconds, then let it out in a rush. "Okay. I can accept that. But what's next?"

"What's next?" I cocked my head to the side as I stood. "That's a silly question."

"It . . . it's really not."

"Sure it is!" I snapped my fingers. "Tell him, Rubes!"

Ruby, all smiles once more, let out a ponderous *hmmm.* "It's just past noon, correct?"

"Uh-huh!"

"And our captain is ubiquitously known as a heretic."

I flicked my straw hat. "Yuuup!"

"He's also, as previously stated, a degenerate."

"Hey, let's not be hasty. I don't see what that has to do with—"

"Most important of all!" she continued, barreling over my complaint as she marched across the deck. "We have enough squid within the hull to feed an entire village—or our heretical, degenerate captain—for two days."

"Now you're just spreading baseless rumors. I don't think—"

She reached the hatch and threw it open, the loud *thunk* it made cutting me off. "By all these facts combined, I declare that it is time for *lunch*!"

"Finally, something we can all agree on!" I leaped to my feet and marched toward the cabin. "I'll fetch the barbie—I already have a few different flavor combos in mind!"

CHAPTER FORTY-SEVEN

Scars

As Maria strolled through town, she was struck once more by how sharp, how *crisp*, the world felt. It was only her third time walking through Tropica following her breakthrough. Whenever she returned, she seemed to find a new obsession. Today, it was the way the sun reflected off . . . everything.

Even as a base cultivator, the celestial body above was no longer a source of blinding incandescence. If she wanted to, she could stare directly at it, not needing to fear permanent damage to her vision.

Now that her breakthrough had been solidified and Slimes had bonded with her, the way the sun's reflection shone in metal and glass was . . . sublime. Fischer had often recounted how the world looked to his enhanced eyes, and though happy for him, she'd always felt a little pang of jealousy that she couldn't witness it for herself.

Is this what he's been talking about?

She could see rays of light, as if an invisible smoke wafted through the streets. But there was no smoke. Nothing for the prismatic beams to highlight. All of this beauty—this otherworldly brilliance—was because of her advancement. Fischer had never described what she saw. She'd have to ask him about it when he got back.

It's meeee, Slimes whispered from within, his voice sounding far away. *Well, it's us, but there is no us without me . . . nor without you!* Slimes vibrated. *It's* you *and* me *and* us!

Maria blew air from her nose. If someone had told her even two days ago that she'd have another awareness inside of her, and that she'd *enjoy* it, she might have thought them insane.

No offense, Slimes, she thought *I can't imagine life without you now.*

I know, her familiar replied, jiggling in her core.

If that same someone had told Maria another being jiggling inside her abdomen would be a pleasant experience, she'd have *definitely* thought them insane. She laughed to herself, closing her eyes to banish the beautiful rays of light still tugging at her awareness. She had things to consider, after all. While Maria had spent the night saying goodbye to Fischer, Slimes had spent the night deep in contemplation beneath the tidal pond's waters.

And that meditation had borne fruit.

In the hours before dawn, an understanding had flowed from Slimes to Maria, its significance driving the air from her lungs. She'd moved to sit on the floor as she internalized the knowledge, and rather than distract, Fischer's soft snores had helped her remain centered. It was both incredibly fast and excruciatingly slow; the realization seemed like a puddle at first but flowed outward the longer she considered it, becoming an ocean.

So vast were the implications that she hadn't told Fischer, lest he delay his trip.

Even now, already on the way to their task, both Maria and Slimes couldn't help but replay the thoughts. They mused endlessly as Maria's body moved them closer to their destination. The concept of time faded as they went over and over and *over* the knowledge they'd gleaned, both seeking any flaw in their reasoning. But there wasn't any. Each cycle only brought more certainty. More confidence. More—

"Uhhh, Maria?" came a curious voice, shattering their meditation.

She blinked, the world's light and beauty overwhelming as it flooded into her eyes.

"Are you well?" Keith asked. Genuine concern radiated from his core.

"Sorry to worry you—we're totally fine."

". . . We?"

Smooooth, Maria. Doing a wonderful job of convincing him you're—

"Hiiii!" Slimes jiggled from her shoulder. "My master was referring to *us*!"

She gave Keith a rueful smile. "We were just going over our plan for today. I hope you didn't have to try too hard to get my attention . . ."

"Oh, no."

She breathed a sigh of relief, but then he continued.

"I found you standing there with a smirk on your face, staring off into the distance. If I'm being completely honest, all the old stories about cultivators came to mind, and I started questioning if this entire village was a terrible idea. Then I wondered if I was the insane one, and if this whole thing has been a fever dream constructed by my own madness."

"Damn, Keith . . ."

"Yeahhh, I spiral pretty hard. Seems to be a family trait. My bad on that one."

Maria couldn't help but laugh. He looked confused, likely unsure if she was laughing at or with him. "You reminded me of Fischer, Keith. Our benevolent, powerful, and *definitely* humble leader. He spirals like no other. Even your terminology sounded similar."

He gave her a wry smile. "Maybe I've been spending too much time around this heretical village."

"Perhaps. Speaking of the village, though, I have an idea to reduce the number of heretics."

"Oh? What's that?"

She nodded toward the building they stood outside. The not-a-prison, as Fischer had repeatedly called it. "Rehabilitation, of course."

"Wouldn't that increase the number of heretics?"

"I guess that depends on your point of view."

Keith's smile waned, and he glanced toward the ornate door as doubt leaked from his abdomen. "You're truly ready to heal people?"

She didn't miss the hope in the former royal's voice. He'd forsaken his title in favor of coming to Tropica with the rest of Gormona's fishing club—with the intention of starting a church of their own, a plan that still brought Maria to giggles if she thought about it too much.

There had been no love lost between Keith and his relatives, but learning that their personalities were the result of impure chi and alchemical tampering changed that. The idea of healing them had entirely consumed him and Trent, and the two cousins had doggedly pursued that prospect to the exclusion of everything else.

Maria, considering all this in an instant, patted him on the arm. "All I can say is that I'm as ready as I ever will be. Just to be clear, though, I can't promise the outcome that you want."

The lines of his face hardened, yet a spark of hope remained in his eyes as he nodded.

Content, she took a deep breath. *Ready, Slimes?*

An affirmative jiggle came in response, the sensation still as weird as it was comforting.

"Let's go."

Maira strode forward, pressing her hand against the ornate wrought iron decorating the door. As it swung open with a creak that could only be intentional, she gazed around, eyeing the conformity of the halls.

Her step faltered; a kaleidoscopic brilliance demanded her attention.

"What . . ." was all she could get out as colors shifted.

The magical flames set within the walls . . . each of them glowed like little suns. Unlike the *actual* sun, these sources of light flickered, causing miniature beams to dance around.

"Everything okay?" Keith asked, moving to grab her arm for support but pulling his hand back as she steadied herself.

"Yeah, it's just . . . *wow.*" Before she could give the impression of insanity again, she shook her head, refocusing. "The flames are *stunning* after my breakthrough."

Would the lanterns outside be the same? She'd only visited the village proper during the daylight hours.

Come to think of it, shouldn't the village's reflective objects have been this brilliant yesterday?

An affirmative jiggle from Slimes confirmed her suspicion. *That's why I said it's* us *doing it, silly! Our understanding of each other grew last night!*

The visuals were . . . a lot. Like her first bite of Fischer's chi-enhanced fish, her new reality was so filled with wonder that it became hard to see—or feel—anything else.

You'll get used to it! Slimes reassured her. And he meant it, too. *No, we'll get used to it!* He vibrated in confusion. *Errrr, it might get worse if we grow closer? Dunno, hehe.*

Maria snorted, then turned to explain to Keith that she was talking to her very real and definitely not-imaginary friend, but the former royal beat her to the punch.

"What's it like?"

"Having a familiar?"

"Yeah."

"It's . . . like having more of myself. A part of me, for so long, felt as if I was missing something." She waved a hand. "Don't get me wrong, I was still happy, especially after meeting Fischer, it's just . . . *man*, it's hard to explain."

"I think I know what you mean." He gave her a wistful smile. "Maybe I'll come ask you another time when you're not about to single-handedly attempt healing a prison full of corrupted cultivators."

"That sounds like a good idea. But also, what you just said is wrong on two fronts."

"How so?"

"First, our god king Fischer *insists* that we call it a not-a-prison, remember? He gets a bit . . . *smitey* if his trusty followers defy his orders. I'd hate to see you slapped from existence."

Keith barked a laugh, the sound echoing off the walls. "Okay, I'll grant you that. What's the other thing I was wrong about?"

"The second is that I'm not doing it single-handedly—right, Slimes?"

"Rrrrright!" her familiar called, popping out of her shoulder, then growing a half meter in length to head-butt-high-five Maria's upheld hand with a wet slap.

"Slimes . . ." Keith said, pouting.

"Ya-*huhhh?*"

"Please never do that again."

"Deniiiied!" he sang, disappearing back into Maria's core.

The former royal shook his head with a wry smile. "I guess you're correct on the second point, too."

"I am, aren't I?" Maria looked up at the flames, their cascading colors no longer so distracting now that she'd grown used to them. "Come on. Let's go find our targets."

Though slow, their steps were sure as they made their way deeper into the building. Each corner they rounded brought another stretch of brilliant lights, and before she knew it, Maria had arrived at the cell. She turned and faced it, smiling at its occupants. "Good morning, everyone."

Without needing to look at him, Maria could feel the uncertainty flowing from Keith's core. "I don't mean to be rude, Maria, but . . ."

"You can ask. I won't be offended."

"Sorry to voice it again, but are you *certain* you're ready?"

Maria furrowed her brow. "Uhhh, yeah. I'm sure."

"Then . . . why are we here?"

"Because they need healing? I'm a little confused, Keith. I thought this is what you wanted?"

"Well, yes. It is. But . . ." He gestured at those within the two cells, all of whom were completely invested in the conversation. Uncertainty swelled within him, but was swiftly eclipsed by a growing resolve. "Let me be clear: If you intend to use these people as practice, I must insist that you stay your hand. As much as I want my family healed, I can't condone human trials."

"For what it's worth," one of the birdlike cultivators said from the bench he was perching on, "I'd also prefer not to be a human trial."

"Agreed."

"Agreed."

"No human trial!"

Maria covered her mouth as her laugh broke free. Slimes's happy jiggle in her core only increased the volume of her amusement made manifest. "Okay, I get it now. They're neither trials nor less important than your family, Keith. I want to heal them first because their particular . . . er, *issue,* is related to a realization Slimes had last night."

The noble's unease melted away, replaced by an intense curiosity. "What was the realization?"

"Best I keep it to myself for now. But let me ask you all: Do you *want* to be healed?"

There was no doubt that the cultivators kept within the walls of the corrupted city of Theogonia had emerged a little . . . different. Even after Fischer's chi had cleansed them, their atypical personalities remained, as was evident by the way most of them were perched like birds. Many would call them mad—and they wouldn't necessarily be wrong.

Despite this perceived sickness of the mind, Maria's question hit them like the lightning-filled boulders Corporal Claws had launched at the king. All of them stilled, the one who had spoken earlier standing upright as he came forward—still hopping like a bird, mind you. His face, however, was entirely human.

"Can you truly do it? Can you heal this . . ." He gestured toward his abdomen. "Wrongness?"

The man's eyes welled with tears, a tiny snowball of emotion building to become an avalanche in his core. He was hoping, *dreaming*, of the possibility. Not only for himself, either. It was just as much for his fellow captives, all of whom had endured decades of sickly chi, trapped in a lightless prison far below ground.

When Maria met his eyes, a tear rolled down her cheek, but not because she'd been buried beneath the man's feelings. "What is your name again, friend?"

"Tiberius."

A woman hopped forward to grab his hand, one of her arms going over his shoulder like a protective wing.

"And this," Tiberius continued, his voice strengthened by her touch, "is my wife, Livia."

"A pleasure to meet you both. I'm Maria." She stood tall, her shoulders bearing the weight of their dreams. "If anyone can heal you, it's me. And Slimes, of course."

"I thought your name was Keith?" Livia asked.

"She doesn't mean me. Slimes is—"

"Hiiii!" Slimes wobbled about enthusiastically for a good two seconds.

Tiberius blinked, cocked his head, and screeched with laughter. "And I thought *we* were weird."

"Weird," "Weird," "Weird!" the others agreed.

Maria chuckled, too. "I guess we'll get started, then." Not wasting any time, she sat down, crossing her legs.

"Oh, uhhh, Maria?"

When she glanced up at Keith, he almost looked ashamed. "Yes?"

"Is . . . is it okay if I stay and watch? I don't want to be a bother, but—"

"Keith, you absolute goose. Of course you can stay. I know Fischer hasn't mentioned it, but he knows exactly how much you and Trent have been helping out here. You're both important people in the church, and—oh, don't give me that look. It's true whether you like it or not. There are people assigned to watch our captives, and there was no need for the two of you to give them so much care.

"The former queen and princess—now, caring for them alone would have been understandable. But you did more than that, didn't you?"

The imprisoned cultivators, who'd remained mostly still since learning she'd come to heal them, all shifted about suddenly. "Pastries!" one called. "Sweet drinks!" declared another. "Kindness!" "Kindness!" "*Kindness!*" they decided as a group, their cores screaming it as much as their mouths.

Maria had seen Keith's cheeks flush on countless occasions since he'd arrived in Tropica all those months ago. Of the five fishermen who came, he was the easiest to rile up—a fact the others knew well and exploited often.

They'd teased him for myriad reasons, and the mix of emotions coming from his core now wasn't so different from all those times. But the cause of his embarrassment sure was. Maria was reminded of the old tanner and his son—the father quick to hit and slow to praise, a trait that was part of the reason he left Tropica. The south-side villagers didn't turn a blind eye to such behavior.

A child raised in such an environment . . . they would react to praise with a sense of guilt and shame. In the pit of their stomach, they felt unworthy of it. Her core, now filled with healing chi, unraveled more information. Just like a child reared without love would feel undeserving later in life, so, too, would one brought up without praise. Unfortunately for these children, they were often made to experience both, along with a swath of other injustices.

Given the environment that Keith grew up in, it was no wonder Maria's words caused discomfort. A slight heat rose to her face. He hadn't offered this information up. Facilitated by her chi, she'd absorbed his emotions and deduced the rest. But before her cheeks turned pink, she swept her own guilt aside. Keith wasn't to be pitied for things outside of his control.

These thoughts came and went in the space between heartbeats, and with her eyes still locked on the former royal, she gave him a genuine smile. "Your efforts didn't go unnoticed, Keith. Thank you." She rolled her shoulders, facing forward once more. "That is to say, of course, you're welcome to remain. There's nobody more deserving."

Though the birdlike cultivators used different words, they echoed her sentiments. Before she caused him too much embarrassment, she closed her eyes and sent her awareness inward.

She pictured a book sliding into an imaginary shelf in her mind. Ascension healed all manner of physical and mental inadequacies, but for whatever reason, the scars of trauma weren't so easily repaired. It was something for her to consider later. Right now, she had different scars to attend.

Maria's awareness flowed down, urged onward to their healing ability by Slimes's open embrace. They joined seamlessly. Together, the kindred spirits reached out for the corrupted cultivators from Theogonia, preparing to cleanse their very souls.

CHAPTER FORTY-EIGHT

Flock

Surrounded by uniform bricks and kaleidoscopic sources of light, Maria and Slimes eased forward, their wills leading a procession of chi toward the not-a-prison cells before them. It was . . . beautiful. Though her eyes were closed, Maria marveled at the sight. Pink clouds of healing essence, belonging to her familiar as much as they did her, drowned out the world's radiance.

The bars between them and the prisoners usually formed an impenetrable wall. A solid object that not even a drop of normal chi could hope to get through. But there was nothing normal about the chi she commanded. Rather than slam in and demand admittance, the clouds billowed in place for a moment, politely requesting entry.

Somehow, the building replied. Both inhuman and filled with authority, it asked a question in return: *For what reason do you seek admission?*

Though she currently had no physical form, Maria could feel herself blink at the, uhhh, structure? She suspected that relaying this entire sequence to others was going to be a nightmare.

Thankfully, Slimes was much less taken aback. He offered up their combined wills in answer, telling the building that they wanted to help the cultivators within. Wanted to *heal* them.

Will this facilitate their escape? the prison seemed to ask.

Nooope! came Slimes's enthusiastic and wobbling voice, somehow floating through the air.

Could Maria do that, too?

H-Hello! she broadcast to nobody in particular, the volume of it surprising her even more than the fact it worked. The prison gave her a frown, unimpressed that she'd spoken—well, more like yelled—a pointless word. Yuuup. This was *definitely* going to be a nightmare to explain.

Despite its chastisement, the prison's overwhelming power stepped aside, letting them pass.

Thaaanks! Slimes sang with all the subtlety Maria had lacked. She would've left it at that, but Slimes gave her the mental equivalent of a nudge in the side, encouraging her to try again.

Th-thanks, Maria said, this time in a whisper.

The building offered them a respectful nod. It remained vigilant within the cell, ready to step in if the prisoners tried anything funny.

The prisoners! Maria shook herself. They were the reason she and Slimes were there. She focused on the clouds of pink chi and the cultivators soon to be engulfed, actively letting go of any other thoughts lest they distract her. But she needn't have worried.

The moment they touched the first core, she lost sight of all else. Compared to the slew of wonderful colors she'd been exposed to all morning, the birdlike humans were . . . gross. So dull and brown and lifeless that they made even the gray slate of the prison's stones look vibrant.

Fischer's overwhelming chi had surged through them like floodwater. All the veins of corruption had been washed away, but they'd left marks behind, scars in the lands that were their cores.

Maria and Slimes's healing cloud slowed down in its expansion, yet it ever grew, one by one encompassing the other cultivators. All of them were exactly the same, their bases of power pitted and foul and imperfect. The malady afflicting them was identical, but so, too, was their hope.

In carving every rotten speck of corruption from their cores, the deluge had left behind exposed creek beds, unearthing the tops of enormous boulders. Most would assume these rocks to be the cause of the infection. Something that had to be removed before the great rents could be filled in. If Maria hadn't bonded with Slimes, she might have thought the same. It may have worked, too—may have healed them.

But it wasn't the only option. And if she and Slimes were correct, there was a better choice. One in which the boulders—the flaw within a flaw—was actually the medicine.

Her familiar's realization last night had been like a rising sun, its rays so bright they illuminated the land and revealed this cure. Unbidden, the moment of enlightenment replayed in their minds for what had to be the hundredth time since it struck.

It began with a shared memory—their first, to be exact. The healing of Claws's raccoon familiar.

There had been something deep within the creature, a perceived blemish they'd tried to "fix" with their chi. Neither of them had known what it was. Suspecting the mystery to be of great importance, Slimes had sought to solve it, submerging himself in the waters that he used to call home. And he had gotten even more than he'd bargained for. A copy of the raccoon's memories had been suspended within. When they'd slammed into Slimes, they brought understanding, revelation, and grief.

The "blemish," the thing left behind on a whim, was the mammal's penchant for thievery.

As with most things in life, that single word couldn't possibly convey all the nuance needed. His larcenistic tendencies weren't a quirk to be expunged. They were his heritage, a part of his very DNA. To their sensibilities, it was selfish. Antisocial. But he wasn't a human. And he never would be, no matter how many awakenings or breakthroughs he experienced.

Raccoons were prey animals. There were countless creatures that would have happily turned the baby mammal into a snack. Humans, too, would hunt them. Sometimes for food, but also for no good reason at all. A memory of the raccoon and his mother being chased flashed through their minds, which they summarily dismissed. It wasn't the time for such painful thoughts.

Despite all the claws, teeth, and human hands that wished them ill, predation was not the leading cause of death in raccoons—*starvation* was. They had to be sneaky. They had to steal whatever source of sustenance they could if they hoped to live past adolescence. They had to be, as Fischer had playfully called them, trash pandas.

It was why Claws's familiar has been out at sea. Separated from his mother, starving, he'd followed the scent of food, and . . . well, the rest of it was a story for another day. Maria and Slimes had almost "healed" this self-preservation out of him. That they'd come so close to doing so was a terrifying realization—one that had momentarily made Maria doubt if she had the right to heal anyone again, but that worry departed as fast as it had arrived.

Her will wasn't as strong as Fischer's, but he was a terrible baseline to compare oneself to. The man was a monster. In the best way possible, of course, but a monster nonetheless. Weak as she was by comparison, her desire to help others was *powerful*. Even before her breakthrough, her core had warned her not to clear the "blemish" away.

And she'd listened. She could trust her instincts.

Besides, she was several orders of magnitude stronger now, so it wasn't a valid concern. Even if it was, her familiar's next discovery would have been enough to make her try again. Slimes, in all his glorious squishiness and occasional crystalline brilliance, had been all but certain that these cultivators were similar. He'd seen no other reason that Fischer's flood wouldn't have swept away their birdlike sensibilities when cleansing the corruption.

Back in the present, as Maria looked at the boulders peeking up through dry creek beds, she sent Slimes *all* the gratitude. She was *so* proud of him. The "flaws" were neither something inherently bad, nor something that had to be cleansed. They were, for better or worse, a part of them now. And when presented with the choice of having them cleansed away, their cores had declined.

If it had been one of them, maybe it should have been questioned. But *all* of them? It wasn't a mistake. It couldn't be. Sure, wanting to be a bird was kinda *unhinged*, but who was Maria to judge? She had a blob of slime as a familiar. With a mental shrug, she let these thoughts slip away.

Ready? Slimes asked her, his intent seeping down into the cracks between boulder and creek bed.

She was. With the ease of water flowing downhill, her will joined his, their tendrils of power wrapping around each porous stone.

Their healing chi, bright and pink and filled with good intentions, *squeezed* the boulders—which shattered, crumbled, and turned to dust, freeing the desires trapped within.

* * *

In a place of solitude atop a rocky headland, two beings meditated, enlightenment just beyond their reach. Perhaps they shouldn't have called it "solitude," considering they weren't actually alone. It certainly went against the standard definition. But that didn't change their feelings on the matter.

The reasoning was as profound as it was simple; some people—or animals, in this case—were a burden on the mind. Even if you loved someone a great deal, their proximity could stop you from being able to relax. This wasn't at all the case with these two.

They were kindred spirits. A couple of peas in a pod. Two delicious fish being swallowed down a single gullet.

That's a terrible analogy, Pelly thought.

Really? I liked it, Bill replied.

They had progressed so far on their path to a breakthrough. That the exchange hadn't ruined their meditative state was proof. Like a mighty pelican diving beak first into the ocean, they slipped straight back into mindfulness, easily navigating the tides of their joined awareness.

The initial few days of seeking enlightenment had been a little more . . . frustrating. They'd felt on the precipice of something, and the longer it evaded them, the more agitated they both grew. But given time, this annoyance swam right by—like that one species of arrow-shaped fish that Bill *still* hadn't caught despite becoming a spirit beast. He could have delivered death-from-above via flying kick, sure, but where was the sport in that?

The damned things are just so speedy . . .

Pelly huffed amusedly through her nostrils, which made Bill do the same. It really was a silly thing to be bothered by. He wondered if that realization would be the understanding that finally facilitated their breakthrough. So did she. It wasn't, though. With shared mirth, they shook their heads at each other, then themselves. What was the rush?

Besides time, the recent advancements of their friends were the most pivotal reason for their lack of urgency. Each ideal was as unique as it was surprising. Cinnamon sought to deliver the perfect kick to anyone foolish enough to challenge Fischer. Maria was a healer who believed even the most-wicked could be redeemed. And Claws . . . okay, they weren't *all* surprising. Still, they *were* unique, each individual's breakthrough tied to who they were, and who they would becom—

Both pelicans sat bolt upright as a flock of chi seemed to take flight. After a single glance toward each other, Bill and Pelly rocketed skyward.

Sometimes, in order for healing to occur, a poorly joined bone had to be rebroken. With that principle held firmly in mind, neither Maria nor Slimes felt bad about the destruction they wrought. After all, the boulders weren't boulders at all. They weren't even stone. The thousands of thin shells turned to dust in an instant, and from the pockets hidden within, birdlike affinity poured out.

Another flood came to the lands that were the cultivators' cores, groundwater seeping up from below to fill the scars, then flow over the sides. Rather than become submerged, however, the surrounding ground drank deep. As it rehydrated, expanded, Maria and Slimes knew they'd done the right thing.

The cores, now drenched with birdlike desire, became soft and malleable. Mountains grew, planes sank, and scars disappeared. But then the peaks folded back down, only to rise once more where a valley had been only seconds ago. In defiance of stillness, they continually shifted, endlessly searching for the correct form. There were so many options, and each argued their case, the language indecipherable yet markedly passionate.

It could have gone on forever, and it probably would have . . . if not for the arrival of two irrefutable opinions.

The prison felt their approach, shifting its chi to let them in. Unlike Maria and Slimes, who'd had to answer a series of questions before being admitted, the new arrivals were immediately welcomed . . . via the removal of a whole damned *wall*, its bricks tumbling down and inward to create a low barrier.

The stonework separating the rooms just . . . slid down and vanished, there one second and gone the next. The difference in hospitality was enough to leave Maria downright peeved. But as she returned to her body and opened her eyes, she caught sight of two feathered forms, their spread wings blocking out the midday sun.

Private Pelly and Warrant Officer Williams, floating down slowly so they didn't disturb the joined moment of ascension, landed in the cell. With a ruffle of their feathers, both birds sat where the dividing wall had been, so close that Pelly's brown wing brushed up against Bill's black and white plumage.

Two masters of flight had come to give their juniors guidance.

Maria prepared to get comfy. The Church of Carcinization had been contemplating their favored form—that of the humble crab—for months, and they had yet to make the transformation. This, then, would likely take days, if not weeks. That would still be much better than how long the carcinization folk had been—

Pop!

Maria blinked, and Slimes appeared atop her shoulder, wobbling as he let out a soft *oooo*. Maria blinked again.

Pop! Pop! Po-po-pop!

In less time than it would take Corporal Claws to slurp down a dozen oysters, it was done. All of their cores had chosen a static shape. The only proof that anything had happened at all were the clothes a roomful of pelicans were shrugging their way out of. One of them—who'd been the human known as Tiberius—let out an indignant squawk as he got his neck and foot stuck in opposite sleeves of his tunic. The rest of the former humans, who now bore patchwork feathers of black and white and brown, croaked in amusement.

Pelly and Bill stood abruptly. The other birds fell silent, their heads whipping toward the leaders of their flight. Even Tiberius did so, having to peer up from an awkward—and objectively funny—angle given his shirt-related predicament. With the attention of everyone present, Pelly and Bill unleashed a single honk that shook the world.

It was neither pride, joy, nor enlightenment coming from them—it was all three, and much more. Their thoughts washed over Maria and Slimes as if their own.

The moment the pelicans had felt the call of the corrupted cultivators, Pelly and Bill had known what they'd been missing. It was no wonder they could cultivate together, just as it wasn't a surprise that they hadn't had the breakthrough yet. Of all the things they had done since awakening, it was their time herding seagulls that made them feel most alive. They'd wanted to form a squadron. A family. A group of their own with which to soar the skies and further Tropica's goals.

Twin stars of light exploded into being. Maria crossed her arms to brace against the force, but it wasn't meant for her. Instead of striking the subordinate pelicans, however, it flowed into them, and the now-cleansed humans drank deep. No longer did the landscapes within them remind Maria of cracked earth and floodwater.

Their cores were open skies. Endless stretches of empty space. And like a high-pressure system, Bill's and Pelly's chi rushed in to fill the void.

We . . . We did it, Maria thought as thick gusts of essence made the newly awakened birds feel more whole.

Slimes only vibrated back, stunned into silence for the first time since, well, ever.

It wasn't just the healing that shocked him so. In breaking open the boulders, thereby forcing the cultivators to confront and assimilate their affinity for birdhood, Maria and Slimes had accidentally provided the very thing Pelly and Bill had been missing: a family of their own kind.

The intense joy coming from the other side of the bars could have filled oceans.

When the blinding light had been entirely absorbed, Maria opened her eyes, only to find that she still couldn't see. She blinked away tears, wiping them from her cheek as she stepped forward. "Prison, you glorious, unhelpful bastard . . ." She gripped the bars, willing them to disappear. "You let me in this second. They don't need to be contained."

The chi-filled metal grew hot between her fingers, and the next thing Maria knew, she was stumbling forward, strands of light clinging to her body. *Thank you,* she mouthed, barely watching the light as it sloughed to the ground, pooling to create something new. Maria didn't care what it was. She fell to her knees in front of Pelly and Bill, reaching her hands out toward them, but drew back at the last second, an unspoken question passing from her to them.

The answer came not a moment later when they chuffed in amusement and closed the distance, pressing their bodies—gods, they'd grown even bigger—into Maria. She wrapped her arms around them, her tears coming in full force. She was so, so, *so* proud of . . . *them*? Maria turned to the right and wiped her eyes, gazing toward the single source of fury in a room otherwise filled with positive emotions.

Tiberius had gotten even more entangled. He let out a furious grunt as he wiggled his head back and forth to no avail. Trying not to laugh, Maria reached out to help free him of his tunic, but retreated when chi glowed from his core. Tiny streams of air shot from him in every direction, tearing from his body and ripping the shirt to shreds.

Slimes shot from Maria even faster. He formed a gelatinous dome around the spirit beast, and the blades of essence dissipated as they struck it, absorbed and neutralized. Because of Maria's breakthrough, this single attack—and all the reactions to it—confirmed several suspicions.

Pelly and Bill hadn't just bonded with the other pelicans. They'd had a breakthrough of their own, and their connection to the others had shared the power they now wielded. Every single one of them now possessed air chi, and given time, they'd come to command it.

"Well, I'll be," Maria said, a few sobs taking the opportunity to escape. "Looks like we really do have an entire flock of birds now . . ."

There was a momentary silence, in which the pelicans looked at each other. Then, with their heads held high and necks extended, the flock roared with a series of honks, guttural croaks, and even a few blasts of air. Most jubilant were Pelly and Bill, whose wings unleashed gouts of force.

Maria joined them, half laughing, half sobbing. The healing had been a resounding success.

CHAPTER FORTY-NINE

Success and Treason

A strong breeze swirled around the deck, its crisp touch making a pleasant shiver course through me. In the stillness that followed, steam and smoke rose up to once more reclaim the space. The scents demanded my attention. With a deep breath and a wide smile, I glanced down at the hot plate, the sight causing my mouth to water.

An entire barbecue worth of giant squid. Cut into strips, tenderized, and seasoned. They were curling at the edges, so I flipped them. They'd only need another minute to fin—

Birds! Claws screeched through our connection, interrupting my thoughts. *Lots of birds!* she sent through a pulse of . . . violence? I couldn't tell if she was witnessing it, wanting to commit it, or already engaging in battle. Knowing her, it would be one of the latter two. Perhaps both at the same time.

I took a slow, calming breath. The little deviant must have come across a large flock.

Claws, I replied, my voice holding only a hint of reproach—if I was too firm, she'd defy me out of principle. *We don't hurt birds, remember? Even if you're a chaos elemental now, it's not okay to harm creatures for no reas—*

Feathers! she interrupted. *Feathers everywhere! Black and white and brown!*

I massaged my temples. What kind of bird was black, white, and brown? Certainly nothing I'd seen in Tropica. *Please tell me you didn't blast them, Claws. I'm serious. This isn't—*

She interrupted me again, this time with an image. I wasn't even aware she could do that. The scene showed twin orbs of incandescence, so bright they obscured everything else. Was . . . had she zapped a couple birds so hard that they ascended? All it did was raise more questions, but as I considered it further, I realized her true goal.

You're messing with me, aren't you? Obscuring things on purpose.

There was a long silence as she gave me nothing, but then the mask started to slip. Her chittering giggles were as vexing as they were heartwarming, and when they finally came to an end, she let out a sad chirp. But not because she felt guilty. No, she was sad I couldn't hear her raccoon's high-pitched snickers, which she assured me were sincere, boisterous, and more annoying than I was imagining.

I sent an eye-roll through our bond. *Not cool, Claws. Were there even any birds?*

She replied with a shrug and a *maybe*, then slammed the connection shut. I tried to reach her, but she held the door firmly closed.

"Claws again?" Barry asked, clearly seeing my frustration.

"Mate, that little otter is going to be the death of me."

"Well, to be fair, she *is* an elemental now. A lightning elemental. Of *chaos*."

"Yeahhh, you're not wrong." I flipped the squid to check it was cooked—finding golden-brown goodness, I started transferring them to a plate. "I expected some negatives. I just didn't think there would be so many. There're benefits, at least . . ."

"Benefits?" Ruby asked, standing up and eyeing the calamari. "What benefits?"

"Oh. Uhhh . . . never mind."

Barry narrowed his eyes at me, then redirected his ire elsewhere. "Anything to add, Theo?"

The former auditor slipped forward, yoinked a bit of squid, and spun on the spot. Avoiding eye contact with everyone, he marched into the cabin and slammed the door shut. "No comment!"

"Barry, my man," I said. "You're trying to discover secrets when there are *way* more important things out in the open."

"Is that so? What *should* I be worrying about, oh great and humble Fischer?"

"Rubes?" I raised an eyebrow at her. "Care to enlighten our jacked friend?"

She didn't need to be asked—she was already giving him an incredulous look. "Did your nose muscles grow so large that they closed over? You should be worried about the calamari, obviously. It's taking all my willpower to not snatch the whole plate right now!"

"Scylla's many mouths!" came a muffled curse from within the cabin. The door flew open a moment later, revealing Theo and a half-eaten strip. "I call seconds if there are leftovers!"

"There's plenty enough for everyone!" I slid the cooked portion forward, inviting them to grab a piece.

In a blur, I threw the trapdoor open with chi, reached inside, and collected another tray of cut and ready-to-cook squid. Unlike the first batch, these were covered in a mix of spices, some of which had a bit of kick. It took only a moment, and the last of my pals were collecting their cooked portions as I returned.

I upended the raw strips. I caught a whiff of the spicy seasonings as steam rose, and I leaned back as far as I could, using tongs to spread the seafood evenly. With the next batch cooking, I grabbed a piece of squid. We all held one now; the others had waited for me, even Theo saving a bite of his so we could eat it together.

Unable to contain my grin, I raised my hand high. "To good food!"

"To friendship!" Ruby added.

Chi radiated from Bonnie with so much intensity that she glowed to my senses. "To *adventure*!"

As one, we bit down.

The first thing I noticed was the texture. Soft yet pleasantly firm, the squid was cooked to perfection. Hot oil spread through my mouth as I chewed, and with that fat came flavor.

All I had used was salt and pepper, wanting to experience it with only the relatively bland enhancers. It was less intense than I'd expected, by far the subtlest thing I had tasted since my last advancement.

An oceanic scene sprang to mind: a calm sea on an even calmer day, waves barely visible in the stillness. There wasn't much to observe, no chaos occurring to draw one's attention, but that was a feature rather than a detriment. As with the imaginary vista, the quiet umami flavor of the squid let me notice every other sense with greater acuity.

When I swallowed, the food's essence made my throat tingle, a pleasant chaser to the wonderful aftertastes persisting on my tongue. Before it could completely fade, I opened my eyes and went to grab a slice of lemon—only to find that they'd beaten me to the punch. I'd only prepared six slices, which had apparently been a lapse of judgment.

I laughed, then leveled a glare at everybody, my lingering smile ruining its severity. "You know, if I suspected that turning you all into heretics would eventually deprive me of lemon, I might have never preached fishing."

Ruby blew a raspberry and passed me her slice, having only squeezed a few drops on her strip. Everyone waited for the rest of us to apply some—except for Cinnamon, of course, who chomped down on a stick of enhanced sugarcane with reckless abandon. With a wordless toast, we raised the calamari anew, then took another bite.

Anyone who hadn't tasted lemon before might not have expected how much a few drops could change a meal. But my friends and I were well and truly indoctrinated.

The acid cut through the oil like a hot knife through butter, and I imagined a giant Rocky doing a cannonball, setting the waters in my mind to churning. Despite being aware of the difference a lemon's acidity could make, a series of surprised noises and content *mmmm*'s rang out, one of them coming from my own throat.

"Heavens above . . ." Ruby said, letting out a long breath. "I think it's safe to say I like calamari."

"Yeah . . ." I licked my lips. "I wonder what the rest—*frack!*"

So absorbed in the food had I been that I'd forgotten all about the spiced batch. I whirled, my eyes scanning the hot plate, my senses detecting the chi within, but there was no need to worry.

Theo raised an eyebrow and returned a smirk. "What's the matter? Did our infallible and humble leader forget he had some food cooking?"

"Psh. Nahhh, I just knew that you'd finish yours before everyone else." I sniffed haughtily. "Trusting his underlings is exactly what a perfect ruler would do."

Steven cleared his throat, then whispered loud enough for all to hear, "I think he forgot."

"There's no doubt," Ruby replied, nodding at her husband's words.

Ignoring the treasonous statements of my followers, I joined Theo at the barbecue. The scents coming from it were unignorable now. Its savory goodness was laced with peppery spices, the smells so strong that they set my nose to itching.

"Are they ready?" Theo asked.

"Certainly are, mate. Any more and you risk burning the seasoning."

He lifted a strip and gave it, then me, a curious look. "Uhhhh, I think the ship might have sailed on that, Fischer."

"First off, ten-out-of-ten analogy. I'm sure Bob would have loved it if he were sapient."

"Thank you."

"You're welcome. But more importantly, a little char isn't a bad thing." I started moving the calamari to a clean tray. "It's a feature, my man."

"I can tell that you aren't lying, but I still find that hard to believe . . ."

"There's one way to find out for certain." I nodded at the crispy pile, then held up a finger, stalling everyone for a moment. "Before you bite into this, know that they're gonna be *spicy* spicy. I'm not sure how our enhanced bodies will react to lots of chili, which is why I've historically avoided using too much. If you weren't great with pepper before awakening, you might not . . . Why are you all looking at me like that? And why does Trent look like he's about to piss himself with laughter?"

"Fischer . . ." His eyes danced with humor—which should have annoyed me, but it was good to see him enjoying himself. "I seriously doubt any of Tropica's native citizens experienced anything spicy. Peppers are hard to cultivate, making it exceedingly expensive for even the royal family to . . ." He trailed off, a frown forming as he realized he was now the object of everyone's amusement. "Okay, what did I miss?"

Fergus barked a laugh and clapped Duncan on the back. "I'm not a farmer, but I can answer that for you. Peppers grow really well in the sandy soil of Tropica. There're always some sprinkled around the northern crops that get afternoon shade, just in case it's needed. They are a rare addition to meals, sure, but we've all tasted it when times get tough."

"Huh," Trent said.

"Huh?" I echoed, louder. "How did nobody tell me there was fresh chili this *entire time*? I had to use dried flakes from my personal stash for this meal! Forget heresy, holding that information from me was *blasphemy*! And that's not to mention the fact you're all calling them peppers! You're offending my Australian sensibilities!"

Ruby and Steven gave each other a baffled look, then she turned my way. "Well, we call them peppers, and we thought you knew. They're mainly used to hide the presence of, well, *less pleasant* flavors when food gets scarce. Thankfully, we haven't needed to rely on it for years."

"Aye," Fergus said. "I assumed you just didn't like spice. You openly did heretical things, so why *wouldn't* someone have told you about it?"

Duncan agreed in the most annoying way possible: he guffawed. *Hard.* He even slapped his knee for good measure.

"Hang on, Rubes, when you said it hides *less pleasant flavors* . . . do you mean perished food?"

"Well, I didn't want to put it that way, but yes. If the choice is between spoiled grain and starvation, anyone would take the grain."

I blinked. "But the *ocean* was there the *entire time*! You could have just eaten *fish*!" I shook my head. "Never mind. Heretical. I know. Still, I can't believe there was a chili conspiracy going on behind my back this entire time. How will I forgive such a betrayal?"

"How about we dwell on it over some tender squid?" Theo suggested. "Perhaps the spice will make you forget all about it."

"Theo, you mad dog." I snapped my fingers and grabbed a portion. "That's so crazy that it just might work. Still, if anyone is bad with heat, maybe see how everyone else takes it first."

Even with my warning, only one of us abstained: Borks, who dismissed the idea after a single sniff and at least a half dozen sneezes. He took another plain strip instead.

"To your unforgivable betrayal!" I toasted.

"To our unforgivable betrayal!" they resounded, smiling despite their treachery.

Together, we bit down into the charred, chili-covered calamari. As soon as it hit my tongue, I was filled with regret. But not because it was too spicy—quite the opposite.

Rather than increase the pain of the chili, my enhanced body only amplified the taste. My mouth tingled almost immediately, a semi-numb sensation washing over it that did nothing to diminish the flavors waging war across my awareness.

If the lemon had made a giant Rocky cannonball the calm scene in my mind's eye, the chili caused an underwater volcano to erupt, its lava both hot and sweet. The squid's oceanic essence wove through in the background, subtle, distinct, and undeniably delicious.

When I swallowed, the numbness reached my throat, but it was still more pleasant than painful. I took a deep breath and looked out at the world, both seeing and feeling everyone's enjoyment.

"Okay," Ruby said, "our peppers don't taste like that."

"Aye," Duncan agreed, taking another bite.

Borks wagged his tail at us and cocked his head.

"Of course you can try it, buddy." I broke off a bit, kneeled down to his height, and held it out toward him.

My favorite doggo transformed into a golden retriever, hesitated a moment, then licked it. As if stung by a swarm of invisible bees, he darted back repeatedly, the numbness clearly confusing him. He started spinning in circles, then shook his entire body to expel extra energy. Despite his reaction, I could sense through our bond that he wanted to try more, so I threw him the chunk.

As we all watched Borks expectantly, curious how he'd react to a whole bite, a lone thought crossed my mind: The calamari trial had been a resounding success.

Then, the chili-covered squid landed on his tongue and all hell broke loose as a gout of flames washed over the deck.

CHAPTER FIFTY

Lessons in Flight

Sergeant Snips, wielder of water and most loyal of Fischer's pals, couldn't believe what she was seeing. One shaky claw removed her single piece of clothing, the patch her beloved master had made for her. And looking through both eyes, something she hadn't done in months, she witnessed a flock of birds wheeling around in the sky above Tropica.

That alone wasn't shocking, of course. Seagulls were a common sight by the ocean, as were the small brown birds that flitted around the nearby forest. What made it startling was that the birds weren't birds at all—most were *human*. Through some manner of feathered frackery, Bill and Pelly had bonded to the corrupted cultivators, turning them into pelicans.

Snips should be happy for them. Through their combined efforts, the two pelicans had nullified a vast swathe of prisoners. They'd evolved potential enemies into aerial forces that could assist Tropica.

She should be happy for Maria, too. Snips spared a glance the mistress's way, and when she saw the joyful tears in her eyes, she *was* content for her. But . . . it was overshadowed by something large, ugly, and embarrassing.

Her own emotions. Shame, jealousy, a feeling of not being enough.

She had been the first of Fischer's animals to awaken, and others were catching up to her, if not outright leaving her in the dust. Even her damned *pond* was outshining her. Both figuratively and literally, she noted, as Slimes shifted to his crystalline form and reflected the sun's rays.

It felt like a lifetime ago that Corporal Claws had beaten her to gaining an aspect. The troublesome otter's chi had taken on the essence of lightning when they fought Trent, Leroy, and the other cultivator from Gormona. That alone hadn't bothered the sergeant; it had filled her with only positive emotions. After all, that extra strength was something that she could utilize in the protection of her beloved master.

She'd used Claws's advancement as motivation to facilitate her own growth. Even the recent awakening as an elemental hadn't caused Snips to worry.

Okay, that was a lie. She *had* worried, but not about her own inadequacy; Claws was made of both lightning and pure chaos. It would cause anyone stress.

Snips was getting distracted. She recentered herself in a stream of bubbles, and as she did her best to assess her feelings, the tiny orbs turned ponderous. What was it about the birds celebrating above her that made her feel so left behind?

The parallel between the Church of Carcinization and their idolization of her crabby form was the obvious answer, but she only needed to consider for a moment to know that wasn't it. So what else could it be? Try as she might, she couldn't work out why her feelings had grown into a forest of tangled kelp.

Lost in the brackish waters of her mind, Snips jolted when a soft hand touched the top of her spiky carapace. A wave of heat crawled over her skin as she turned to look up at her ambusher.

"Hey . . ." Maria's face was smothered in compassion, the redness lingering in her eyes doing nothing to diminish her beauty and kindness. "Do . . . do you want to talk about it?"

Snips didn't move for a few seconds that felt like an eternity. The anxiety prickling her body moved down to her legs, where it loitered and remained. Her thoughts seemed to freeze under the mistress's attention. Then, from nowhere, a ray of hope shone down and melted the ice.

Are these blackened doubts actually a sickness? she wondered, keeping her concerns to herself. *Something that a healer could fix?*

She returned her gaze to Maria and asked with a hiss, *What did you feel?*

"Feel?" She smirked despite herself. "You took your eyepatch off, Snips. That's the first time you've done it since your other eyestalk was healed."

Oh . . . She blew a stream of sheepish bubbles.

"Don't be embarrassed. I did sense something from you, but it wasn't related to my healing chi. Your core seemed . . . upset. *Troubled.*"

Snips knew Maria wouldn't judge her, yet she couldn't help but feel ashamed at hoping for such a straightforward solution. Even if there *was* an easy path, would taking it not hurt her cultivation? Hinder the desire to defend her master and all he held dear?

With another hiss, this one coming out as a long sigh, she looked up at Maria. *How much time do you have?*

"I have all the time in the world for you, Snips. Right, Slimes?"

"Yeahhh!" Slimes dropped his crystalline form and jiggled for emphasis. "*Alllll* the time!"

Shaking her shell at the ridiculousness of being reassured by a tidal pond—*her* tidal pond—Snips scuttled in place, working out her nervous energy. Where should she even begin? Before a decision could be reached, the closest crop shook, rumbled, and a squad of cultivators exploded out of it, obliterating most of the sugarcane.

Covered in plant fibers and greenery, they didn't stop, slowing for only a second as the followers wiped debris from their eyes to regain sight of the man heading their charge. Joel, the leader of the Cult of Carcinization, leaped into the air. He crashed down into the sand before them and skidded to a halt. Sergeant Snips, all too aware of what the crabby humans were about to ask, shook her head, discarding grains of sand in every direction.

Joel pressed his forehead into the ground. When they arrived a moment later, they followed suit, going to their knees before kowtowing. The leader took a deep breath, preparing to launch into a no doubt impassioned speech, but an oppressive force constricted his throat, killing the words.

Maria stepped forward with chi rolling from her in waves so strong her skin glowed pink. "Joel . . ."

Her tone was artificially flat, feeling like the blunt side of a deadly scythe ready to twist and slash. It made Snips's mouth go dryer than the sand surrounding them.

"Would you care to explain why you just destroyed one of Barry's crops?"

Though it was still pressed to the ground, Snips didn't need to see Joel's face to know he understood the severity of Maria's question.

"I . . ." He swallowed, only able to move his neck because Maria allowed it. "We came to beg Sergeant Snips, our benevolent and all-powerful deity, to instruct us in the way of the crab."

Time passed by, the seconds dragging on, yet Maria's oppressive fury didn't subside. "That's not what I asked, Joel."

With deliberately slow movement, he pressed both palms into the ground. His own anger flared, and he lifted himself upright to stare back in defiance. Compared to the storm front that was Maria, however, his resolve was a wave lapping at the shore. "I had to reach our deity as soon as possible. Time was of the essence."

"No. It wasn't."

"It . . . it *was.* The cultivators from Theogonia just became *birds*! If they can do it, there's no way that we can't! All we need—"

"*No*," Maria repeated, the air warping around her. Like an invisible fist had struck the ground, a giant circle of sand sank an inch. The force smashed Joel's resolve apart. But she wasn't done. "Have you considered that your lack of care for others is the reason you haven't turned into crabs yet?"

No answer came.

"That wasn't a rhetorical question, Joel. Have. You. Considered it?"

"Noth—" His voice cracked; he cleared his throat. "Nothing is more important than our evolution. Care for others encourages weakness."

"Wrong." She gestured at the destroyed crops. "That sugarcane was. It's hypocritical of me to say because I've caused similar destruction on a lesser scale, but there was literally no reason for you to walk *through* that field. If you'd strode around it, you still would have found Snips. Hades's blackened realm, you could have just leaped over it!"

"That would have been slower, and time—"

"Shut up." Despite having the core of a healer, Maria's pulse of chi held deadly intent. She took a deep breath and patted Slimes's head to steady herself.

All the blood had drained from his face. He nodded.

"Let me finish. I was there for the pelicans' transformation—it couldn't have happened without me—and *none* of them had anything *close* to the level of self-importance you do. If delusions of grandeur were a part of your path, don't you think you'd already have succeeded by now?"

As Snips watched Joel and the rest of the crab-ish humans closely, she saw something almost as astounding as the pelicans circling above—the mistress's words seemed to be taking root. Their faces showed introspection, as did the essence circulating their cores.

Abruptly, their leader reached a decision. He sat upright and met Maria's gaze. "I wasn't aware you took part in their transformation."

She sighed, the pressure and pink light returning to her core. "Yeah, well, I did, so maybe give what I said some th—"

"Please!" he interrupted in a yell, slamming his forehead back into the ground. "Your healing chi might be the last thing we're missing! Help us achieve carcinization!"

The only warning was a twitch of Maria's upper lip. She shot forward so fast she may as well have teleported.

"*That!*" She grabbed Joel by the collar of his robe. "*Isn't!*" Her other arm gripped his ankle. "*The!*" She pivoted and drew him back like a sack of grain. "*Lesson!*"

As she unleashed her last word, so, too, did she unleash the leader of the Church of Carcinization. He sailed high over the ocean, his limbs splayed and scream feminine. Because of the angle she'd thrown him at, he reached the apex of his flight just before he crested the horizon.

"Think about your actions while you crab-walk back!" Maria bellowed, then spun to look down at the others, pausing to straighten her shirt. "Are there any other questions?"

"N-no!" Jess replied, glancing up with wide eyes—and looking ridiculous because of the sugary pulp still covering her. "I saw the truth in what you said. I'd assumed Joel did too . . ."

"Maybe Sally wasn't entirely wrong . . ." another said. "Perhaps we've been a bit much."

"*We've* been a bit much?" asked a third.

Jess shook her head, then winced and wiped away a sugarcane splinter from the crook of her neck. "*Joel* has been a bit much. With any luck, he'll actually do some self-reflection on the way back. If not, I'll talk to him when he returns." Still kneeling, she rotated to face Snips. "Sorry. For him, and for us. We'd still love your guidance, but only if you're willing—"

Of course I'm willing, Snips hissed, waving a claw.

"Really?" She tried to keep her voice calm, but a slight twitch of her facial muscles betrayed her. "Are . . . are you free now?"

Snips shook her carapace, then shrugged. *Soon, maybe.* She patted Maria's fleshy-yet-firm leg. *The mistress made me realize something important, which I must tend to immediately.*

"I did?" Maria asked. "Does that mean you don't want to . . ." She frowned, her gaze as she assessed Snips's core. "Huh. You reached a decision."

Snips nodded. She had, and it was all because of the mistress's wisdom. She showed her thanks by rubbing affectionately against Maria. Then, with a polite wave to the rest of the Church of Carcinization, who watched her with curious looks, she departed, trailing Joel's passage out into the ocean.

It has been too long . . .

CHAPTER FIFTY-ONE

Monster

Deep within a cavern of their own creation, a being of multiple parts bided their time. They were likely the oldest form of awareness remaining in the Kallis Realm, a force so ancient they'd outlasted entire civilizations . . . and yet, they squabbled like children.

Following the realization there was a cultivator or spirit beast foolish enough to channel unaspected chi, a tiny crack had formed between the two souls comprising the one. That crack became a fissure, and the fissure a chasm. So wide did the gap grow that their awarenesses had partially split.

It was . . . frustrating.

The rejoining was supposed to be absolute, but because the other parts of their body weren't yet present, their individual personalities were distinguishable. And those same parts, the other earth elementals on their way, were also the point of contention between the two.

We must remain, the first brother reiterated with a thought more solid as stone.

We must go! the first sister replied, just as immovable in her conviction.

She couldn't make them, of course. He had seniority. However, she was as much a part of their combined body as he was. She *was* him. Forcing her to remain still, making her ignore her instincts, felt like a betrayal. It threatened to tear them apart with finality, a possibility that brought him genuine pain.

She could feel these thoughts, but his reluctance didn't change the fact he was robbing her of agency, putting them at risk of rupture.

I am sorry. He let out a regretful rumble. *I must, for if we are discovered in our current state, destruction is certain.*

She need not reply—her fury wove through every inch of their singular body. There seemed to be something hidden fueling the rage, but he dared not ask.

Seeking distraction instead of reason, he queried what she wanted to do once the other pieces of themselves arrived. Her answer was as immediate as it was fierce: fight.

This, at least, they could agree upon. He nodded mentally, the accord making their separate spirits intertwine at the base, yet it wasn't sufficient for full homeostasis.

Whoever or whatever was channeling pure chi, it had to be destroyed. Such a blight couldn't be allowed to exist, lest it grow strong enough to conquer and rule. The threat of it gaining adequate strength to overshadow them was minimal, at least—it was far more likely for the moronic being's core to implode. But if there was even a chance . . .

Such a being could become *divine.*

And not the empty divinity of the gods that had departed this planet. *Real* divinity. The kind that would use the heavens of this realm as a stepping stone.

Again, the first sister agreed. Tendrils of his and her chi reached out toward one another, becoming further enmeshed—further *aligned* in body and soul. It was enough for the first brother to risk a thought, one that had lingered since feeling the blasts of unaspected chi.

Do . . . do you think it might be connected to the newborn elemental that we were hunting?

Rather than the anger or despair he'd worried this possibility would make her feel, she seemed to breathe a sigh of relief and slide a great boulder aside, which revealed a hidden fear—the very thing she'd been concealing.

Now that the objects sealing the thoughts away were clear, associated musings flowed from him to her, and her to him. They'd both been trying to protect the other. The thin tendrils connecting them grew, turning into thick roots that pulled them together. It was almost enough for them to become singular once more, and with a feeling of rightness flowing between them, they explored their shared worry.

If the wielder of unaspected chi and the newborn elemental were connected . . . they would need to be destroyed. Assimilation was always the goal when confronting others of their kind, but they couldn't risk trying to do so if there was a cultivator of pure essence nearby—the foolish being was just as likely to blow them all up by accident. Their earthen form could withstand such a detonation . . . but not if they were in the process of bringing another into the fold.

There was an alternative possibility, however. If, despite the distinct lack of chi in the world, a *traveler* had somehow arrived in Kallis . . . their course of action would entirely change. The first brother and sister gave each other the equivalent of a sidelong glance. They could only hold it for a moment—amused rumbling rolled from the center of their mass, boulders and sediment churning within.

Yeah, right, he scoffed. *A traveler. More likely that we'd sprout wings and take flight.*

She laughed so hard that he had to suppress the movement, lest their enemies learn of their position.

Abruptly, a shadowy form leaped into the opening of the hole they'd dug, but unlike their multiple foes, this ambusher was invited. More followed, and some of the other elementals—the other parts of *them*—descended the walls. The twenty-seventh brother, who had been a particularly speedy embodiment of fire before assimilation, vaulted over the precipice.

His shape became like the spine of an urchin, and he swiftly overtook the rest as he raced to the bottom of the cavern. When the twenty-seventh brother struck their mass, he immediately reached out to them. Like mortar sealing the gaps between the first brother and sister, he flowed out, preparing to reunite . . . He paused for a moment as their myriad thoughts hit him.

He chuckled, the idea of a traveler being present amusing him. *Ridiculous.*

The others, those who were fast enough to arrive with the first wave, landed in a barrage of silt, dirt, and minerals. All but one of them laughed when they heard the joke about the traveler—the exception being a former water elemental that had always been ornery. He tried to chastise them all, calling it a distraction, but then he rejoined, becoming a part of them.

They churned the center of their mass in mirth. It really was a preposterous theory. As if such a monster could be transported to a chi-starved world . . .

I stared down at the patch of blackened grass that continually drew my attention. In retrospect, if I'd been aware Borks's hellhound form had the innate ability to spew fire, I probably wouldn't have fed him chili-covered squid.

But how *could* I have known? My doggo pal had some dragon-like bullshit going on with his anatomy; his flames didn't even use chi. I connected to his core to reiterate just how godsdamned cool he was, but he spoke first.

Sorry! Sorry! Very sorry!

I shook my head. There was nothing to apologize for, and I relayed as much for the tenth time in so many minutes. He'd hidden it for good reason; his goal was to be a part of our pack, and he had worried that spitting fire would ruin that possibility. It was a small lie that had snowballed into a big one, and frankly, who cared? I was only sad we'd missed a bunch of chances to mess with people.

From Borks's position atop the portable forge—a construction made of bits and pieces stored in his dimensional space—he wagged his tail at me. After his love had been adequately conveyed, he bent down once more and sent another blazing conflagration down into the chimney.

"Hey!" came a voice I barely heard as the forge's heart glowed red and heated the metal within. "Idiot traveler dum-dum with weird little toes! We're talking to you!"

"Huh?" I looked up at the ostensibly insulting yet undeniably fun sentence. "What's up?"

Ruby, who'd been the one to deliver the insult, beamed and held a hand out toward Barry. "Pay up, chump."

He crossed his arms and frowned at both of us. "There's no way you two didn't set that up. I'm calling shenanigans."

"Mate, I don't know what you're talking about. I've been busy crafting this . . . this . . ." My eyes had drifted back down to the piece of metal I was shaping, then to the works of the other smiths. "Damn, using my hands to mold it might have been a mistake after all. Maybe I *am* an idiot traveler dum-dum." I raised a finger. "I do not, however, have weird little toes. Theo, please confirm."

"Yes, sir!" He marched over and bent at a ninety-degree angle. "Present them for inspection!"

"Oi!" I stepped back, suddenly self-conscious. "I wanted you to confirm my words, not voice your subjective opinion of my flawless toesies!"

"Oh. Right. Honest mistake." I didn't need his ability to detect lies to know that it had been no mistake. "In that case, no, you didn't set that up with Ruby."

I had to fight down a smile; the trickery had been all me.

"Told you!" The seamstress waved her hand in Barry's muscular face. "Pay up!"

He sighed and reached into a pocket to retrieve her winnings.

"Furthermore," Theo continued, "on the topic of Fischer's quote-unquote *weird little toes*, he was telling the truth when he denied having them."

"See?" I raised my nose at Ruby. "What did I say? My toes are perfectly norm—"

"However . . ." Theo interrupted, raising an eyebrow. "He was absolutely lying when he said his toes were flawless."

"Hah!" Barry latched on to the revelation like a drowning man. "You were *lying*!"

"That's because *all* toes are weird and little, Barry! If they're *all* weird, mine are actually normal. And you're one to talk! Of all of us, your weirdly muscular feet are the odd ones out."

Paul, who'd been glancing around at everyone's toes since they'd been brought up, leaned down to get a better glimpse of his father's. "You're right, Fischer. They almost look like thumbs."

"Truth!" Theo roared with laughter. "Complete truth!"

Barry tensed his jaw so hard that tendons bulged from the sides of his head. "If Paul wasn't here, I'd ask you to throw me back home, Fischer."

"And I'd happily deny the request!"

He shook his head, smiling despite how bothered he was trying to seem.

"What did you want before, anyway?" I asked. Barry just gave me a confused look, so I turned to Ruby. "When you were soliciting my attention?"

"Ohhhh." She gave a dismissive wave of the hand. "Nothing, really—I was trying to tell you that your creation looks like absolute *garbage*, but you weren't hearing me. Naturally, we started taking turns insulting you."

"Naturally," I agreed. "Wait—*absolute garbage?* It's not *that* bad . . ."

Fergus, the highest-level smith Tropica had, formed a line with his mouth. "It's pretty bad. You said it needed smooth surfaces, didn't you? To reflect the sunlight?"

"Yeah? *So?*"

"So . . ." He held a hand out to accept my pride. My joy. My *rod*. He poked one of its many dimples. "I know we were trying to think outside of the box, but what are these?"

"Speed holes. Helps me reel faster."

"That . . . doesn't make sense."

"Let's agree to disagree. It still *looks* like a rod, right?"

To be fair, it was at least rod shaped. I'd taken a bamboo pole and coated it in metal, but in my distraction, had accidentally squeezed too hard, leaving divots all over where my thumbs and fingertips had been.

"Aye, it looks like a rod," Duncan muttered. "If it was chewed on by a fish, spat out, chewed on by an even *larger* fish, then spat out *again*, only to be—"

"Yeah, yeah. Fine. My rod sucks. I might not be the best smith, but luckily for all of you, I am a *flawless* leader . . ." I raised an eyebrow at Theo. "Please confirm."

He raised one back. "I think everyone already knows that to be a lie, Fischer."

"Ah well. It was worth a try. Anyhoo, as I was saying, this flawless leader predicted his possible inadequacies in the ways of the forge. Because I'm so busy, you see. Leading and stuff. So I made sure to assign the same task to my *best* smiths!" I looked around at them all, grinning as I once more assessed their creations.

My loss to the massive creature I'd hooked had been humbling, to say the least. Despite how much strength I possessed, it wasn't enough to reinforce my rod, line, and hook. Something had to give. I could always try to gain more power, of course—improve my cultivation base so that I could fortify all three of them at once—but that wasn't feasible on this short trip out to sea.

That left a single solution, one that, despite being on a wooden boat, was our best option: creating stronger tools. Borks, being the good boy he was, had brought supplies for just such an eventuality.

Agreeing that he was, in fact, a good boy, Borks wiggled his butt and blasted more fire down into the forge. Both he and Trent could fuel it, but considering one of them lacked the opposable thumbs necessary to mold things, my canine companion was the obvious choice.

Duncan and Fergus were attempting to produce new hooks, infusing their chi into them; it didn't seem to be working, the large shapes not holding chi properly. Ruby and Steven were messing about with lengths of yarn, and though I knew they'd eventually make another logic-defying creation, it wouldn't happen in a day. The rest of us, every single human on board, were making rods with varying amounts of wood and metal.

My rod had a wooden center and alloy coat, as did Paul and Barry's, the father-son duo working together. Theo and Deklan were doing the inverse, attempting to smelt a core into hollowed-out bamboo. It . . . didn't appear to be going well, if the pile of discarded and blackened sticks could be believed.

But that was okay. As much as I played up my reliance on everyone, there was really one person I was banking on—Bonnie. My belief in her abilities was so great that I'd willingly sabotaged my own rod, giving it neither my full focus nor will. I turned her way slowly, my breath catching as I prepared to find whatever weird and wacky invention she'd dreamed . . . up?

"Bonnie . . ."

"Yes?"

I pouted as I pointed down at the object before her. "What the frack is that?"

"Uhhh, something to fish with?"

"Yeah, I can see that." I leaned in closer, trying to spot any unexpected features—there weren't any. "But why is it so . . . *regular*?"

"Ohhh," she replied, hefting a pole that looked just like mine—minus the speed holes, naturally. "Well, when I saw what you were all doing, I thought I should just make something normal instead."

A spark of hope ignited within me. "Does that mean you had an idea for an abnormal creation?"

"I . . . don't know how to answer that. It's subjective. I started, though, so I guess you can be the judge."

She bent down, grasped something with both hands, and raised it above the bench.

I froze, blinked a few times, then barked a laugh. "Forget subjectivity, Bonnie—that thing is *objectively* ridiculous."

"I know . . ." A hint of self-doubt escaped her core, the emotion entirely unexpected from my adventurous pal, but she hid it again almost immediately. "That's why I dropped it for a normal one."

I gave her a half smile. "I said it was ridiculous, not bad. You should finish that one."

"Wait, really?"

"Truth," Theo said. "He really thinks so."

"I do! Of all the rods made by this squad of goons—er, no offense, fellow goons." The only response I got was a few shakes of the head, so I continued, "Of all the rods, yours shows the most potential."

"It's not too . . . dumb?"

"*Dumb?* Listen, Bonnie, you're the brains in this situation. I have so much faith in you that I couldn't focus on mine—hence the speed holes."

She shot me some side-eye, a small smirk playing on her lips. "I thought that was so you could reel faster?"

"By the gods! What's that?" I yelled, *very* elegantly changing the subject as I dashed over to the port-side railing.

A series of scoffs and snorts came in reply, but Borks and Cinnamon joined me, all too happy to play along. I tousled the fur on their heads. They leaned into it, arched toward me, their faces melting into expressions of sheer bliss, and the same sentiment flowed out from my core and through our connection. As with all good things, however, our frozen moment couldn't go on forever.

"Hey! Love bugs!" Bonnie said, lifting a crucible with a massive set of tongs. "I need fire!"

Borks heeded the call. He whirled, spun back to give my palm at least a dozen licks in less than a second, then leaped up onto the forge. Heat washed over my neck as his flames poured down into the chimney.

Now that my other hand was free, Cinnamon hopped up into my arms and went almost liquid, her muscles relaxing and belly offered up for a good scritching—which I obliged, of course. I wasn't a monster.

With a bunny cuddled to my chest and my friends toiling away behind me, I stared out at the deep blue ocean, wondering what kind of adventures tomorrow would bring.

CHAPTER FIFTY-TWO

Tussle

It had been entirely too long since Sergeant Snips, spiked of carapace and sturdy of claw, had enjoyed a leisurely scuttle along the ocean floor. Rays of sunlight pierced the surface of the bay, the small waves above creating hypnotic patterns on the sands she traversed. Water moved around her, flowing to and fro with calm monotony. And a grounding coolness touched the hinges of her shell, urging her to focus on the sensations of her physical form.

Individually, each component was enthralling. Together, they seemed to place her under a spell.

She'd meant to use this time to meditate, using each step of her many legs to ponder the trail forward. If she took long enough to her destination, perhaps she could find the correct words . . .

Snips's bodily sensations made that thought try to slide away like a slippery eel between rocks. She let it go, and in a state of absolute bliss, the sergeant scuttled along, her worries of late discarded across the seafloor. By the time another thought appeared, she had traveled hundreds of meters—a fact she only knew because of how familiar she was with the underwater landscape surrounding her.

That she was currently thinking meant she was no longer meditating, and that was okay. From her master's knowledgeable instruction, she understood that thoughts weren't something to be denied—but neither did she have to entertain them. Like a fluffy cloud in an otherwise clear sky, it drifted on by, disappearing right out the other side of her mind.

That's a funny concept, she mused. *The idea that my awareness has "sides" to pass through . . .*

Before she returned to a state of complete presentness, Snips noticed a soft humming in her core. She knew not the cause, yet the meaning was clear: She was on the correct path. Perhaps that should have been a stunning realization. It hinted at a breakthrough in the near future. Snips, however, found that she was too relaxed for anything other than a slight hastening of her steps.

Two snail-covered rocks loomed up on either side of her, and she kicked off the sand, sailing out into the open once more—only to immediately freeze.

Paralyzed by shock, she flew toward the object of her fixation. Tiny bubbles streamed from her mouth of their own accord, drawn into her wake before swirling up to the surface. She finally recovered her senses as a wall of yellow tentacles seemed to reach out toward her. She extended her legs and caught herself on something purple and hard, pulling herself to the side of the billowing stingers.

Snips stood atop the weirdest coral reef she had ever seen. The different colonies usually grew from rock, and while that *did* occur on the structure beneath her, they also sprouted from each other. The result was a mess both colorful and chaotic, each group growing their polyps as far as they could in an unconscious arms race for food.

The scenery, however, wasn't what she found most unique. Beneath the mass of colonies, embedded within the rock that formed the original skeleton of this ecosystem, there was a nexus of power. Not something so advanced as a core, but chi gathered there nonetheless, faint, almost-imperceptible strands of it reaching out to both supply and extract energy from the forms of life above it.

Despite how advanced it was, Snips instinctively knew this being—this *animal*, according to Fischer's knowledge of coral—would never gain sentience. That didn't make her discovery of it any less exciting. Its existence was reflective of the changes happening around Tropica, and with more chi would come creatures like this. It made her wonder what other impossibilities she'd encounter in the coming years.

Leaping over top of the reef, she marveled at the small creatures calling it home. There were countless species of fish, some of the slow little snails she'd spotted earlier, and even some spiny sea urchins. The latter reminded Snips of herself.

She, too, had been wandering through life at a glacial pace, no clear destination in mind. Also, they were covered in a *wonderful* amount of spikes, just as she was. A single melancholy pocket of air escaped her mouth as she landed on the other side, and it flitted up to the surface, losing its shape as it split, came together, and split once more.

Perhaps there was meaning in that. Or perhaps there wasn't. As Snips trudged onward, her thoughts became more frequent, denying the blank mindscape she so desired. Still, she was able to enjoy the pretty sights even if her head remained busy. Schools of fish, a few sharks, and many colorful bommies of coral graced the landscape. All made her want to scout the waters herself—like she used to back when it was just Fischer and her.

Before she knew it, Snips arrived at her destination. It had been forever since she'd returned to this place, and another melancholic bubble escaped her to drift silently upward. Only when it breached the surface did she turn her attention on the cave. Once, this cavern had housed a stolen crustacean, the unawakened lobster that had ascended to become Private Pistachio.

As she peered into it, she let out a surprised hiss. A blanket of tiny shrimps fed on a mosslike algal bloom that had grown in the stillness since she'd last been here. Taking care not to squash any of them, she stepped toward the rear of the cave, then meticulously shooed them all out. It took a surprising amount of time—the unintelligent crustaceans were wont to dart back around her instead of leaving. She couldn't guarantee they wouldn't be injured or disoriented, but this way, she at least knew her call-to-action would not outright kill any of them.

The moment they were finally out, she spun and cocked both claws. Pressure built in the hinges of her spiky clackers as she filled them with essence. When the chi there became too much for her to control, she slammed her snippers shut, unleashing the stored energy all at once.

Two blue arcs of power smashed into the back of the cavern, carving slivers of rock from its walls. This destruction, however, wasn't her reason for coming all this way—the blast of noise that rocketed out and into her was.

The sound wave might have knocked her out if she were a regular crab, and she spun to check on the shrimpies she'd evicted. They were bothered but alive, their tails kicking and legs scuttling toward any cover they could find.

Hissing a sigh of relief, Snips stepped forward and took a seat. She had made the call, now all she could do was wait.

"I'm going to explode." I rubbed my chin. "Or maybe implode. Is it possible to do both?"

Bonnie didn't look up from her crafting. "Can you let us know if you work it out? They're quite different, and I'd like to be prepared."

"Will do. All I can say for certain is that there could be some splodin' goin' on if I have to wait any longer. The anticipation is killing me."

Someone snorted muscularly beside me. One might think it was impossible to make a snort sound muscular—such a person hadn't spent much time around Barry's new body.

"Is that so?" he asked. "What happened to your infinite patience and flawlessness?"

"Your flawless leader can't come to the phone right now, mate. There are giant creatures waiting to be caught."

"You know," Bonnie said, weaving some length of wire together, "I'd assumed you'd want to leave me in peace. Don't get me wrong—I don't think you're a bad leader, but it just makes sense not to distract me if I'm making the thing you desire."

"But you're not bothered. By my incessant yapping, I mean."

"I'm not, no. Still feels like the objectively incorrect move, though . . ."

I nodded knowingly and crossed my arms, planting a malicious smile on my face. "Unless this chatter is *exactly* what you need, because your adventurous soul thrives on multiple sources of stimulation."

She finally looked up, a slight furrow to her brow as her eyes met mine.

"What's wrong?" I asked.

"You're right."

"Well, yeah, so why are you glaring at me like I just snipped your line?"

Her glare turned into a scowl. "*How* did you know?"

"Whoa, I didn't peek into your mind, if that's what you mean. It was a suspicion that I confirmed with trial and error."

"For what it's worth," Theo said from the side of the ship where he was fishing, "that was the truth."

"See? I only have wholesome leader vibes for you. Nothing to worry about."

"Hmm." She glanced down once more, tying off the end of the wires. "Then why did you have that malicious smile on your face when I looked up?"

"Oh, that's easy—it was for Barry."

". . . What?"

"I thought of a decidedly wicked idea involving him. I never once claimed I had wholesome leader vibes for *everyone*."

This earned a smirk from her, which I happily returned.

"So," I said, leaping right into my next topic of arguably pointless misdirection, "who among the animal pals do you think would look best in a floral dress? My money is on Cinnamon, and no, Barry, it has nothing to do with the fact she's both here and inclined toward extreme violence. I can't believe you'd even *think* me capable of such deception."

"I didn't—" Barry's voice cut off as he hit the deck, ducking a fuzzy leg that sailed through the spot his head had been a moment earlier. "Cinnamon! He's lying!"

The bunny shrugged in response. She wasn't one to let the truth get in the way of a good tussle.

"It's you!" Barry tried. "Of all the animal pals, you'd best suit a floral dress! The rest of them would look terrible by comparison!"

I cringed. "Mate . . . talk about stepping out of the pot and into the fire."

"What are you—*oof!*"

A tiny portal had appeared behind Barry, its counterpart opening right next to Cinnamon. She'd not wasted a second, immediately launching herself through and hitting his back with a straight kick.

In his appeasement of Cinnamon, Barry had made the worst decision he'd likely make today—insulting Borks.

"Enough!" Barry shot to his feet, muscles bulging and a grin on his face. "I'm done being the punching bag."

Before they started duking it out, I reached for my power, preparing to build a platform they could fight on. But something stopped all of us in our tracks.

Light exploded from the workbench. Without even a hint of warning, the System had come to assist Bonnie's creation. She stepped back as its lines blurred and flickered through multiple shapes. It was what I'd been waiting almost an hour for: the creation of a giant rod I could use to catch giant fish. Yet I noticed something else in my peripheral vision.

I'd been wrong earlier; insulting Borks hadn't been the worst decision Barry would make today.

The muscle-bound cultivator went to take a step forward, dismissing his power in favor of witnessing the item's transformation. Unfortunately for Barry, his two foes had not agreed to a ceasefire, and one of them launched the other.

Before the farmer's foot could make contact with the deck, Borks—now in the rotund form of an English bulldog—tucked his legs in and hit Barry's with the force of an oversized, fur-covered, and respitorially challenged cannonball.

CHAPTER FIFTY-THREE

Foolhardy

It was a beautiful day to be out at sea. I leaned into the world around me, soaking it in with all of my senses. Gusts of wind only occasionally flitted by, wicking sweat from my skin; the surface of the ocean was calm, Bob the boat only shifting subtly beneath our feet; and, most notable of all, my doggo pal had just slammed into one of my best mates with enough force to vaporize an elephant.

When Barry collided with the railing, which I'd protected with layers of chi, he let out a noise so close to being a Wilhelm scream that I wondered if I'd imagined it. My crumbling layers of essence stole most of Barry's velocity. Which was good, because it meant he didn't sail over the next three horizons. But it also meant he did dozens of involuntary backflips in the time it took him to hit the water, which was bad. Well, bad for him, anyway—it was pretty fun for the rest of us watching.

I went to raise a platform of chi so he could lift himself from the ocean, but Barry had other plans. Two muscular arms shot up and slapped the ocean's surface so hard that he sailed into the air, and when I saw the red haze glowing around his eyes, I realized we'd gone too far. The homie was *angry* angry; I'd not seen him so furious since Claws and her raccoon depantsed him. He arced high above the ship, his quads and calves bulging as he streaked back down like a vengeful meteor.

I reached for my core, but before I could tell Borks and Cinnamon to scoot, they were already moving. Both ran through a portal to appear in the sky beside Barry, and now that they were all up there, I coalesced a platform in the space above the mast. They landed gracefully on the invisible barrier, then all civility vanished a second later with the first violent exchange.

Barry won the initial round when the end of his foot caught Borks's rump, and I immediately felt a pang of indignation at seeing someone kick my dog. I let it go, however. Borks had attacked first, and the doggo could hold his own—that glancing blow from the muscleman was nothing.

But, more importantly, Borks had transformed into a borzoi, a breed whose long neck allowed him to whirl around and bite down on Barry's ankle. *Hard.*

Watching Barry try to shake Borks off—and subsequently getting his other leg taken out from beneath him by the flying kick of a small bunny—I shook my head. It wasn't my animal pals I needed to worry about.

Trusting that they wouldn't actually hurt each other, I gazed down at the workbench. Bonnie's creation had transformed, and it looked even more ridiculous than

I'd dared to dream. The System drew my eyes in, and I happily obliged, letting the words occupy my field of view.

Mediocre Winch of the Foolhardy Adventurer
Common
This "rod" has been crafted by an adventurer, not an angler. It sacrifices flexibility for strength, making it all but useless to most. This "rod," though many would hesitate to call it that, will not reward the user with skill levels. It also grants the Overkill passive.
Effect:
-10 strength
-10 fishing

As the words cleared, I immediately looked over its form. The pole was made of solid metal. I peered down at the reel, which was of an Alvey design, and I understood why the rod had ball bearings instead of eyelets: the "line" was braided metal. Its maker had woven a few meters of the stuff, producing a trace I could reinforce, but the System had seen fit to fill the whole damned spool with the stuff.

Having taken it all in, I let out a booming laugh. I couldn't help it. In response, Bonnie's cheeks flushed a violent crimson. Shame, embarrassment, and a touch of humiliation radiated from her abdomen, leaching out of her core. The unchecked emotions brought me up short, sobering my own feelings, and it took me a moment to understand their source.

"Bonnie . . . I'm laughing at the description, not you."

She swallowed her budding anger, a whisper of it remaining as she blinked, not sure whether she should believe me.

I opened up my core, letting my amusement flood out. "The System called us foolhardy, gave a 'passive' that is massively negative, and named it a *winch*—the only times the word *rod* was used, it was wrapped in quotation marks." I shook my head. "It might be the most condescending thing I've ever seen from the System. May as well have just told us to go frack ourselves instead of listing that all out."

She blinked again, then looked at me like I was an idiot—which, to be fair, I was a lot of the time—but I couldn't for the life of me work out why she was still bothered.

"That doesn't make me feel better, Fischer," she said. "I didn't want to create it at all for this very reason. I'm not as good at fishing as all of you are, and the System agrees. The description confirms it."

"Ohhh," I said, stalling. "I see . . ."

I had to fight my urge to ask questions. Bonnie had experienced a full breakthrough, doing so by acknowledging her ideal of wanting to experience everything the world had to offer. So why was she still filled with so much doubt? Was it something to do with her specifically, or a result of the world's chi returning?

I shook my head. They were considerations for later.

"You've got it all wrong," I said. "I mean, sure, you *could* take it that way, but that's not how I see it. You created something entirely new, something that no one else on board could. If I had made a fishing rod out here, no matter what I did, I wouldn't have tried to create this. And no," I continued before she could voice the protest forming on her lips, "that isn't a bad thing."

"How? The description said it all. This winch, or whatever, is *useless*."

I paused for a moment as all three of my still-biffing friends above collided with a deafening thump, then gave Bonnie a grin. "Even if it was useless to *literally* everyone, the idea behind this was brilliant. I was so focused on the belief that the pole had to be flexible that I didn't even consider making a solid one. You might call it ignorance or whatever, but I reckon it was a fresh take. My mind has been going down completely different routes, like growing trees with essence and using the entire tree trunk as the pole."

Ruby choked at that idea, biting her lips to contain her laughter when I shot her a facetiously venomous look. "The point is, Bonnie, I was too focused on the rod needing to be flexible. Normally, using a solid metal pole would be moronic—you'd either rob yourself of any challenge or have it pulled right out of your hands if you hooked something huge, but—"

"I see," she interrupted, giving me a smile that was only half forced. "So it's something we can build upon. Got it. I can accept that—a shame we can't use it now, though."

I turned away, casting my gaze over everyone else. "Should I be offended by her lack of faith?"

"Hmmm." Ruby rubbed her chin. "A humble leader wouldn't be, so no, you shouldn't be."

"I . . . don't understand," Bonnie said.

I picked up the winch with one hand, letting out a whistle as I hefted its considerable weight. I could immediately feel the "buff" kick in and sap some strength away. "The System didn't say it was useless to everyone, Bonnie—it said it was useless to most. I, the strong, mighty, and powerful Fischer, am not most people."

"Don't those three adjectives mean the same thing?" Steven asked Ruby in a stage-whisper.

"They do," she replied. "And he omitted *humble*. He must be feeling unwell."

Ignoring their *childish* and *hurtful* attempt at humor, Bonnie stared at me, her brows scrunching together. "What am I missing here? Even if it's useable, you said not a minute ago that using a solid metal pole would be moronic."

"Nah-uh! I said it would *normally* be moronic, but you didn't let me finish. That's only true if you go by the preconceived notions I brought with me to this world. On Kallis, none of that holds water. I'm not some little noodle-armed Earthling who will have a rod yoinked from my hands, and the creature I'm targeting won't be easy to catch. If the same thing from earlier bites down on *this*, I'll still have a hell of a time landing it, but I'll have a chance, and that's all I could ask for. You've removed one of the weak links, which will let me focus my chi where necessary rather than everywhere all at once."

Pretending to look around at everyone, I locked eyes with Theo, who gave me the slightest of nods in response.

Cheers, mate, I thought. *Appreciate you.*

"See?" I continued out loud. "You were able to think of something I couldn't precisely *because* you have less experience in fishing. You lack the biases I have. Or maybe you're naturally more creative than me. Who knows? Regardless, I will *absolutely* be using it right now."

Still carrying the winch, I marched over to Bob's starboard side, then gazed down at the object in my hands. The line had no elastic properties—it was literally wire—but that might be just what I needed to land something monstrous. It was crude, decidedly imperfect, and the best option I had on hand. Bending down, I selected a hook and sinker, then started assembling a rig, the sounds of rapid-fire exchanges between three of my friends above making my heart overflow with joy.

Maria let out a long sigh, her core feeling completely drained as her pink-colored mist eased back into it. Slimes agreed with a soft burbling sound as he melted into her cradled arms. Perhaps they should have slept first after all.

"No good?" Keith asked.

Maria shook her head. "Nope. Not today, anyway." She finally opened her eyes and took in her surroundings. The prismatic beams shining from the prison's fire-lights were muted, nowhere near as stunning as they had been earlier that day. *Mental fatigue must diminish whatever this visual effect—or ability—is.* Now that it'd lessened, Maria could clearly see the people in the cell before her.

They were as depressing as ever. A queen and princess reduced to prisoners, one filled with growing anger, the other with empty despair.

"Why do you waste our time with this stupidity?" Tryphena asked, her face looking surprisingly similar to Trent's when she tensed her jaw. "And when is my brother returning?"

Maria returned a tired smile, not at all bothered by the animosity—she'd just been within the cores of the royal women, so she knew Tryphena was basically a walking bundle of sorrow and regret held together by a ribbon of guilt. Sure, the outburst was misplaced, but it was welcome compared to the state of the queen.

Penelope Gormona had yet to respond at all. From the outside, her core felt hazy, like she wasn't really there at all. Maria had hoped the inside would be a different story; it wasn't. Even if she and her familiar had arrived here today at full strength, she was under no illusion she'd have been able to heal them.

These two are going to be much more difficult, Slimes, she thought.

Still a puddle in her arms, he mentally burbled his agreement.

Maria smoothed her shirt as she stood, her other arm held to her chest so Slimes didn't ooze onto the floor. "That's all we've got in us for today, Keith. We'll have to try again tomorrow."

"Greeeeat," Tryphena drawled. "Can't wait for the next time your fake happiness pokes around my soul for literally no reason."

Maria sighed. Okay, maybe she was a *little* bothered by the animosity. But rather than engage the former princess, she turned and left, her eyes tracking each of the magically lit torches on the way out. They passed another cell of captives. Maria gave the former handlers of Gormona a smile, but she had no more energy to spare them—she was already exhausted. They looked back sullenly, their collective emotions ranging between Tryphena's self-loathing and Penelope's emptiness. Maria felt a little a little bad about the relief that flooded her when they were no longer in sight.

Keith had joined Maria's silent walk, and tired as she was, she could still sense the doubt seeping from his core.

"Do you want to talk about it?" she asked.

He sighed. "I did my best to contain my feelings, but the more I tried, the worse it got. Sorry."

"Funny how that works, isn't it? Fischer always says you have to acknowledge thoughts before letting them go, but it's easier said than done. Regardless, you don't need to apologize. I'm genuinely happy to talk about it."

"Are you sure you're not too fatigued?"

"Yeah. Why?"

He pointed down. "Because you and Slimes both exerted the same amount of effort, and he's currently drooping so hard that he's almost touching the ground."

Sure enough, most of her familiar's viscous form was dangling from Maria's arm, jiggling about with each step she took. She hadn't noticed. Using her other hand, she scooped him back up, his beady eyes barely open as he looked up at them.

"I'm a boyyyy," he groaned, utilizing the last of his strength to retreat into her core.

Maria shared a smile with Keith, then took a slow breath to center herself. "I really am okay if you want to talk about it. I'm absolutely exhausted, but that doesn't mean I can't listen."

"It's fine, I think. But I appreciate the invitation, especially given all you've done today."

"Well, the offer stands if you change your mind. Deal?"

"Deal," he replied, his core feeling lighter despite not venting anything.

They walked the rest of the way in silence. Maria resumed her study of the lamps, their lines a little more colorful after Slimes had returned to her core—or was that her imagination? It was one more question to add to the ever-growing list of unknowns. As they reached the cells where the birdlike cultivators had been held, Maria froze. "Huh."

"Huh," Keith agreed.

Where bars had been before, a smooth stone wall stood. It was as if there'd never been rooms there at all. They looked at each other, shrugged, and kept walking. It wasn't even in the top ten weird things that had happened today. They reached the not-a-prison's daunting door without exchanging another word, and Keith dashed forward to pull it open.

More time had passed than she'd thought. A blanket of stars stretched out above them as they stepped outside, making a sense of dissonance flash through her.

Shouldn't she have noticed the coming of night through the many windows they'd walked by? She really needed some rest.

Before the feeling of wrongness could fade, something flashed to the south, so bright that it lit the entire horizon.

Keith snorted, as did Maria.

"What was that about?" he asked.

"No clue . . ."

When another web of lightning appeared, each bolt far too thick to be natural, the sky beyond the southern mountains became illuminated once more. Maria smiled up at it. What *was* that little otter up to?

CHAPTER FIFTY-FOUR

The Good Kind

Corporal Claws was, as Fischer would say, back on her bullshit. She cackled and stretched her forelimbs even wider as she channeled chi up into the clouds. They roiled and billowed, her essence combining with the world's, but rather than mix to become something new, her power charged the surrounding area with positivity.

And not the silly positivity her master loved so much. This was the *good* kind of positivity—the kind that could create *lightning*.

More and more . . . what were they called? Mullen-tools? Mollercools? Whatever. The tiny little things you couldn't see that made thunderbolts. More and more of them became positively charged in the clouds above, the gap between the upper and the lower atmosphere getting larger until, blessedly, it happened.

Boooom!

A giant mesh of lightning engulfed the sky, all channeling down to a single, extremely cute, point. Corporal Claws. They poured into her, filling her body to the brim in an instant.

Almost there . . .

Almost . . . there . . .

Almooost . . . Why is it taking so long?

Claws glanced down and found betrayal. That little raccoon bastard. He'd been *stealing* from her, absorbing the power necessary for her task. He wanted some, did he? Well then, could *have it*!

Letting out a deafening screech, she lashed out with a rear paw, and a column of solid lightning zapped from her outstretched leg to slam into her familiar's chest. His blue eyes rolled into the back of his head as he shot across the sand like . . . like . . . something very fast! *I don't have time for this!*

Claws returned her attention to the electricity still thrumming around her, and now that the thief was dealt with, it took only a moment to absorb enough. She clenched her forepaws, condensed the power into them, then slammed all of it into the object before her. It was gone in an instant. The sands drank greedily, the natural electricity not following the objectively superior path her chi did—which was, of course, into others' cores. What good was zapping the ground?

Only some of the sky's lightning made it into the center of the object she was working with—it would have to do.

It glowed red hot like a tiny sun, but such worries were beneath an elemental. She picked it up, and when she started chucking it between her paws, it was because she wanted to—definitely *not* because its blistering heat hurt her paw pads. The color subsided over time, and when she could once more hold it without getting burn—er, when she grew bored of playing with it, that is—she reached out with her awareness.

Her task wasn't yet complete. Despite this, a soft rumble climbed from her chest, building until it became a villainous cackle. She projected it toward the heavens. Knowing he was needed, her familiar returned in a roly-poly tumble. Claws held her paws out, letting him inspect the item, which he tried to snatch, of course, but she head-butted him first.

Shaking himself, he bowed in apology, and Claws patted him on the shoulder. He didn't have to apologize for who he was, just as she didn't have to apologize for her method of rebuke. Both were simply the way of things.

They shared a grin, their cores both humming in delight as her little raccoon placed a paw on the item. He channeled chi into it, his will doing something that even Claws, in all her magnificence, couldn't accomplish. He would take a few minutes to finish, so the otter let her thoughts wander. Her master came to mind. Though her plan hadn't yet come together, it was only a matter of time until it did. Claws grinned. Fischer was going to be devastated. Befuddled. Bamboozled, even. Perhaps—

She paused her victorious musings to head-butt the raccoon again, the blow landing before his thieving little paws could finish yoinking her prize.

He bowed in apology again, and Claws patted him on the noggin. He was a good boy, if somewhat bothersome. As her familiar's chi reached back down into the object, she let her thoughts return to the trickery she was brewing.

She couldn't wait to see Fischer's face when he realized.

As I stepped up to my ship's railing, I smiled at the sea of stars above, their pinprick lights as beautiful as ever. I'd been fishing all afternoon and hadn't gotten a single bite—no one had. Despite this lack of action, there were no complaints as Bob the boat shifted beneath us, a slight gust making the ocean choppy.

I lifted my rod—er, winch—to check the hunk of eel I'd just baited up with. With a nod to myself, I twisted the reel forward and flicked my hook and sinker over the side. They made a satisfying *plop* upon entering the waves, and even with my enhanced vision, I could only see them for a meter or so before they entered the abyss, vanishing from sight.

A soft thud indicated its arrival on the ocean floor a half minute later. I clicked the reel back into place, grabbed the metal handle, and started winding. I'd been trying different depths all day, and this time, I was going higher than ever before, only stopping when a full third had been retrieved. I set my finger on the line, took a deep breath, and waited.

Though I slipped into meditation by accident, I wouldn't necessarily call it a mistake. Small waves lapped at the hull. The deck rose below me, only to fall again. And some of my pals chatted softly, their voices calming rather than distracting.

Most, however, joined me in quiet contemplation, the contented hum of their cores mirroring mine.

By the time I cracked an eye, hours had passed. A crescent moon cast its ephemeral light over the world, and I watched its reflection in the waves below, marveling at how it flickered across the undulating water. An ache in my lower back grabbed my attention. I straightened, shoulders relaxing and chest going forward as I amended my posture. Now that I was paying attention to my body, I noticed a building hunger.

Maybe it's time to cook up some dinner . . .

I opened my mouth to ask how everyone else felt about a calamari feast, but the silence was shattered by a screaming reel instead.

"Oh!" Paul yelled, leaning back as his rod bent in half. "Fish on!"

When the creature he'd hooked took off in a straight line, then became deadweight, I immediately suspected it was a squid. When it happened again, suspicion turned into certainty.

"Squid on!" Barry corrected, seeing the same thing I had. "Nice one, Paul! You've got—" The muscleman cut off as another animal, very likely a squid, did its best to yank him overboard.

"Here they come, everyone!" I called.

But they were prepared. All of my friends, no matter their size, level of cultivation, or how pregnant they were—looking at you, Ruby—had their rods in hand, ready to strike. I scanned the line, taking one last look while I could, and . . .

"Cinnamon?" I heard myself ask. "What are you . . . ?"

The martial bunny was standing atop Borks's back, who was using chi to wrap her in dark tendrils, keeping her in place. Held in her limbs, its handle having to be gripped by three of her paws, was a damned fishing rod.

I could have sworn I saw a sparkle in her eye as she winked at me, only sparing me a moment's attention before her gaze returned to the waves. And not a moment too soon—something took off with her hook.

I barked a laugh and turned away. As much as I wanted to watch her and Borks's attempt at fishing, my chance had finally arrived. The sounds of battle were all around me, gears whirring, wood creaking, and a few dismayed curses flying free as lines were severed. Part of my mind urged me to turn back. Demanded that I see how everyone was doing, especially Cinnamon. But I remained focused, my eyes watching my metal winch for even the slightest hint of movement.

I opened up my mental partitions and poured chi into them. If someone had asked me in that moment if I was ready, I'd have sworn on my life that I was—and I would have been dead wrong.

The second something ate my bait, I lifted the rod, setting it so the fish didn't escape. At the same time, I reinforced the winch with chi, using an entire partition to ensure the hook wasn't destroyed again.

Rather than pulling my rod from my hands or making me fly overboard, it was more accurate to say the creature tried to fling me over the horizon—such was the speed and force with which it struck.

I'd been so focused on ensuring my equipment survived that I had not considered how to keep myself tied down. My eyes flew wide as thick tendrils of chi exploded from me. They raced in every direction, latching onto the one thing they could—my newest friend and facilitator of adventures: Bob.

He lurched into motion, dragged sideways through the open water at a disgusting speed. The hull groaned under the pressure, my System-made vessel not designed to take so much force from the sides.

I didn't know how, but I had to get to the bow. If I remained here, I'd lose the fish. Or worse—annihilate Bob.

"Make way!" Barry called, his voice barely registering in my ears.

He was beside me a moment later, one hand resting on my shoulder as he helped me ease my way to the front of the ship. It seemed to take an eternity, each step requiring me to shift the tendrils of chi securing me to the deck. From the corner of my eye, I saw someone haul a squid up, remove the hook from its body, then throw it back.

They'd sacrificed their catch for me . . . It would have brought a tear to my eye if I wasn't busy worrying my arms might get pulled off.

The hooked creature wasn't making my slow passage any easier. It went and went and *went*, never seeming to tire despite how much energy it must be exerting. Because my line was metal, I could feel each kick of the robust creature's tail. It had a sort of rhythm, and as the fight dragged on, I grew accustomed to it.

By the time I reached the bow my steps felt like they were someone else's—my dance with the hooked creature took the lion's share of my attention. I'd not yet wound the reel an inch. We were sailing straight now, and Bob's transformed hull sliced through the ocean like a scythe through perfectly cooked fish. I planted my feet atop the bow, solidified the ropes of chi holding me still, and gave the world a toothy grin.

I'd misled Bonnie earlier, if not outright lied to her face—I had been anything but certain her winch would survive the creature's return, which was why I'd looked at Theo and wordlessly implored him not to spill the beans.

It was the good kind of lie, a deception employed to assuage her doubts and restore confidence. If her creation had failed, I would've blamed myself, pinning the lack of success on a mistake. But there was no need for that contingency. The rod held firm, fortified by a uniform distribution of will.

Shoulders set and core braced, my grin grew even wider. It was *my* turn.

I lifted the winch with all my might. If not for the essence strengthening it, the solid bar of System-made steel would have bent in half. But it *was* strengthened. And as I lowered the tip of the rod down toward the water, I wound in line, the reel complaining loudly with the effort.

Almost too late, I took some of the chi around the pole and reinforced the farthest ball bearing; it was handling most of the strain, the rigid metal not distributing the load. If I'd waited even a second longer, it would have cracked.

With a smile that felt wider than the ocean we occupied, I used every ounce of power I had, both physically and mentally pushed to my limits by the gigantic creature towing us through the waves. This was exactly what I'd been looking for. I'd found a worthy fight.

Water raced beneath us at an incredible clip, and I didn't truly comprehend just how fast we were moving until an island came into view. It was on the horizon one moment, and beside Bob only seconds later. Considering the war I was waging, normally I wouldn't have paid the land mass much attention—if not for the human-made structures atop it.

Houses, a well, and paved roads, all in a state that revealed recent use. There was a wooden dock, too, its weathered planks reaching tens of meters out into the ocean. A few watercraft were tied to it, like canoes but a little wider.

All of these objects were remarkable, yet none of them held my attention for long—a lone man was the target of my fixation.

He stood at the end of the dock, stroking a wizened beard as he stared out, our gazes locking. With unexpected grace, he nodded and gave a polite wave.

"Hellooo!" Ellis called.

CHAPTER FIFTY-FIVE

Possibilities and Potential

Had I . . . was I hallucinating? That certainly *looked* like Ellis. There were houses behind him. They were crude, sure, but they were *definitely* houses. Old, too, based on their weathered surfaces. To their sides, crops grew. I didn't recognize them.

"*Ellis?*" Barry yelled, confirming that if it was a mirage, it was one we were all seeing. Recovering faster than I did, he added, "Hop on!"

"Oh, no," the former archivist replied, waving a dismissive hand. "I will return soon, but I appreciate the offer!"

My head tracked him as we sailed on by, the fish not using the island's shallows or surrounding reefs to escape. With my eyes pinned to Ellis, I didn't miss the object he raised to his mouth. Its tip glowed red as he took a hit. *Okay, where the* fuck *does everyone keep getting cigarettes?*

As fast as we'd arrived in his waters, we were zooming away, the fish caring little for our exchange of pleasantries. A blur of brown shot from the ship, and Cinnamon unleashed a soft jab at his stomach.

It was a love tap, really. The bunny's equivalent of a kiss goodbye. And Ellis seized it in one hand. He laughed good-naturedly as he flicked Cinnamon back toward us. Barry caught her against his sturdy chest, and she looked as confused as I felt.

"It was nice seeing you, too, Cinnamon!" Ellis yelled. "And cool boat! It looks wonderful, Paul!"

"His name is Bob!" the young man replied, not at all questioning how the former archivist had known he'd made it.

"I say!" He had to cup his hands to his mouth with the distance now between us. "What an excellent name, befitting an excellent ship! Take care now!"

Only when my neck could twist no more did I turn back to face the front of the ship. "What in Dionysus's ritual madness was that?"

Before anyone could answer my question, a sickening screech tore into the world. Panic bloomed in my chest. And the tendrils of chi connected to my core immediately identified the source of the noise.

Two arms of solid metal attached reel to rod. Despite my reinforcement, one of them had been almost sheared through, the System-made alloy getting twisted and warped by the creature's power. I encased the entire thing with thick vines of essence, sparing only a second to chastise myself for letting it happen. Then, I locked in, casting all else aside.

It was even more difficult than I thought it would be. The winch's strength had allowed me to segregate my will, directing each section toward different ends, but the damage reduced that advantage. If another distraction like Ellis came along now, either my rod, the line, or the hook would snap—whichever I wasn't reinforcing at any given moment.

An unknown amount of time later, with my brain so consumed I didn't dare glance up at the moon to judge the hour, my legs began to wobble. I paused mid-lift of the winch. Holding it steady, I adjusted my posture, hoping and praying it would relieve some of the strain. But it wasn't the shifting of my body that came to my rescue—it was the shifting of others.

Borks squeezed in beneath me, black tendrils of his chi winding over mine and reinforcing it. Barry arrived at my back, grabbed my waist, said "nope," then grasped my upper chest instead. Before I could form words to tease him for that emasculating move, Trent braced my shoulders. Some of their essence flowed into me, Trent's burning like a wildfire, Barry's reaching for the heavens like a prideful mountain.

Cinnamon leaped up onto the railing beside me. She launched into a motivational string of peeps, flexes, and kicks of immaculate form.

"We're all relying on you, Fischer," Barry added. The sentence was laden with his leadership skill, and it set my own to thrumming. Everyone *was* relying on me. That might seem like a ridiculous statement given I was just fishing, but it was more than that. They had straight up thrown their own catches overboard, all to not impede this battle. Liquid motivation seemed to pump through my veins.

I would not let them down.

With my spirit and body reinforced by the actions of my friends, I pulled the winch all the way up, then lowered it again, winding in line and strengthening the parts required.

I'd love to say that the fish had a bunch of different strategies up its sleeve. That the creature was as intelligent as it was strong, and the rest of our war involved a clashing of wits. But that would have been a lie. The closest it came to trying a new tactic was when it turned and swam toward the boat—and all that accomplished was giving me a bit of a break.

I'd needed it, too. Despite "swim away" being the fish's only move, I had to remain vigilant in every moment, relying on the help of my friends. The constant readjustment of chi was incredibly taxing, just as it had been with the lightning-infused thresher.

Slowly, the creature on the end of my line grew lethargic, its frenetic kicks turning into ponderous sweeps. Rather than its muscles fighting me each time I lifted the rod, its weight became the dominant force that sought to deny my goal.

Finally able to stop worrying something would snap, my mind ran through what type of creature it could be. I'd made a few assumptions, and I was confident enough in their veracity to let them inform my opinion.

First, it was a predator that hunted squid. The fact it always arrived after them added anecdotal proof to the theory. Next, it definitely wasn't a spirit beast, nor did I think it had any chi at its disposal. If it did, it could've escaped when I was distracted by a certain cigarette-puffing archivist. Finally, based on the kicks of its tail being so frequent that they would vibrate the rod right out of a weaker cultivator's hands, I assumed it to be a long pelagic fish—much like the threadfin salmon Maria had caught.

But the weight of it now made me second-guess its species. All the chi not enhancing the winch flooded my arms and core muscles each time I lifted, reminding me of how it felt to heave a stingray up from the sandy floor. Yet it couldn't be that, either—something flat didn't propel itself forward with side-to-side kicks of its tail.

The only reasonable option—which, the more I thought about it, seemed anything *but* reasonable—was that it was a mix of both. Of all the creatures I'd seen on Earth, not a single fish fit the bill. Despite the mental fatigue, my mind raced with possibilities, combining the body parts of different animals that matched what I was feeling.

The flat part couldn't be on the front like a shovelnose shark, right? That would create too much drag. Pelagic species were intentionally aerodynamic—or hydrodynamic, if that was even a word. Their bodies were missile-shaped to minimize resistance.

I pictured the retractable fins of a tuna, which made some Cthulhuian nightmares spring to mind, and as I imagined a long and toothy fish with a deployable parachute of membrane, something moved in the water before the bow.

I leaned forward, the image of a horror from the depths lingering as I scanned the waves, seeking my foe, but couldn't pinpoint its location. "Did anyone see that?"

Everyone responded in the negative, their voices close to either side of me as they crowded the railing. Borks and Cinnamon, the former's head extending past the deck, the latter straddling the back of his neck like he was a bull, both jolted.

"Fischer!" Barry hissed. "Use—" He swallowed, his throat tight. "Use your chi . . ."

I'd resolved to not scan my surroundings, so it took a moment to override that intention and send hair-thin strands of will down into the water. What I found there made the air in my lungs turn to stone.

The creature was beneath us. Just meters below the surface. And when I felt the quality of the essence it held, the word *divine* appeared. Its divinity was muted, however, its full potential sealed away by invisible chains. I'd thought the world's chi was pure, but this thing's power put it to shame, so clear and bright and ancient that it dulled my senses.

I wouldn't glean any more information with my awareness, so I focused instead on its physical form. I was too blinded by the essence to see it, so I started filling in the blanks. Had . . . had I been correct in thinking it was an eldritch horror?

With that thought swirling around my mind, the fish twisted in the water, and I finally saw the rest of it. Reflecting the moon's light, a silvery streak ten times longer than me appeared. Forget how long *I* was—it was as long as *Bob!*

That knowledge was the last thing I needed to proceed. I let go of the chi strengthening my rod, dismissed the thick roots that connected me to the deck, and compressed all of my will into a single, illuminating tentacle. With prehensile dexterity, I grabbed the fish by the tail and hauled it from the water. Even before it came to a stop, I sent Cinnamon a mental command. She didn't need to be told twice.

With a focused jab of her forepaw, a condensed bubble of finger-thin chi shot out, hitting its head behind one eye and traveling out the other side. Dispatching it swiftly was the kindest possibility; there would be no successful release of this creature after the fight it had given.

As its soul departed, the divine essence coming from it increased, becoming noticeable even to my latent senses. It must have been suppressing it somehow while alive. The others felt the change, too, judging by the way their backs stiffened.

All were silent as we stared up at the whale-sized fish. I had been completely wrong in my earlier assessment. It *was* a pelagic species after all, and it *did* resemble something from Earth, just way, *way* bigger.

A body as thick as an oak's mighty trunk. Tail fins the same shape as the moon above. Scales covering its top that were as black as midnight, only those on its stomach a reflective silver. And, finally, the apparent source of the ancient essence: a flattened bill extended from the front of its head, bearing swordlike edges that could slice through water and creatures alike.

Having inspected it, I stopped holding the System at bay. A golden aura shone from the lettering, further signifying its rarity, and I read the description with bated breath.

Ancient Monarch Swordfish of the Bluefathom Ocean
Monarch
This creature, once the pinnacle of all fish hunted for sport in the Bluefathom Ocean, outlived any other. It has ruled for thousands of years, reigning long enough to become an ancient monarch. Partaking of this creature's flesh can prove fatal to those without the requisite knowledge.

I read it over and over, only needing a fraction of a moment each time. On the umpteenth pass, something pulsed through the world, coming from both above and below. It slammed into me. My vision spun, the words swam, and . . . the last sentence *changed*, its gilded hue glowing brighter than the rest.

I seared the new information into my memory.

Partaking of this creature's flesh can prove fatal to those without the requisite knowledge. Its white flesh is edible for those that have taken even a half step on the stairway of ascension but is toxic to all when heated. Its dark meat, however, must be aged and cooked, lest it unravel the consumer's core.

"*Can* prove fatal?" Barry asked. "I don't know about you guys, but I'm not taking the chance."

"Huh?" I raised both brows. "Did you not get the updated—"

My oldest nemesis, the bane of my early days on this world, smashed into my consciousness with all the subtlety of a rampaging Rocky. A bunch of lines scrolled out before me, and the last, its letters also highlighted in gold, made the others redundant.

You have advanced to fishing 100!

Something coalesced behind me, and I spun to catch the System-spawned bag of coins in my hand, except it wasn't a bag at all. A small chest sat on my palm. Surprisingly, I'd seen one just like it before. Constructed of dark lacquered wood with metal casings around the corners, it was the same as the jewelry-filled container Snips had requisitioned from the ocean, which was originally yeeted into the bay by George to hide the spoils of his tax crimes.

The only visible difference was the object securing it. The lock on George's had been created by a regular craftsman; this one was clearly System-made. Complex lines of essence surrounded it, and I instinctively knew breaking into it would be a terrible idea.

Despite this awareness, the prospect of loot called out to me, the goblin part of my brain demanding that I crack it open and reveal its goodies. It was something I'd read about in tons of fictions but never experienced for myself.

"Huh," I said, letting my mouth run before I could give in to temptation. "Looks like your winch lied to us, Bonnie. You *can* get skill levels when using it."

"Did you . . . ?" Barry asked.

"Certainly did, mate. I just got to fishing 100, which, as it turns out, rewards you with a whole box of loot. And I didn't even have to deal with a foot-obsessed AI to get it—talk about a win."

". . . What?"

"Never mind—that's someone else's tale. More importantly, I'm pretty sure leveling up let me know more about this fish than all of you."

I quickly relayed the way the description changed after essence slammed into me from above and below. Their eyes, already wide, grew even wider.

Bonnie licked her lips. "Does that mean . . . ?"

"Ah-huh. It means our inaugural expedition—which was into the Bluefathom Ocean, apparently—has come to an end. We need to get this monster back to Tropica so we don't waste any of its white meat. First, though . . ."

I leaped up on the railing and pulled the fish closer, bringing its unseeing eye right next to the boat. This near to it, the thing's size was even more unbelievable. If I used both my arms, I *might* be able to measure half its girth. I laid a hand against the top of its head, resting my palm above where the swordlike bill began.

"Thank you for your life, mate. We couldn't safely release you, but that's a testament to how much of a *beast* you were. Uh, in a good way, I mean. As in, you were really strong, not that you were dumb and violent."

"Smoooth," Barry teased, which earned him a whap on the back of the neck from Ruby.

I nodded my thanks her way before continuing. "Catching you let me further cast aside a worry I've been carrying for weeks. Because of you, I know that there are creatures out there that can challenge me. Your body will sustain us, and the memory of your strength will live rent-free in my noggin for the rest of my days." I touched my forehead to its cheek plate. "Thank you."

When I stepped back down from the rail, everyone stared at me with blank expressions or soft smiles.

"Damn," Ruby said. "That was actually lovely, Fischer."

"Cheers, Rubes. I felt the need to let my gratitude flow, especially considering what I'm about to ask Cinnamon to do to it."

My pregnant pal blinked. "What are you—"

Cinnamon, as reliable as she was inclined toward violence, already knew my request. She leaped, spun in a circle, and unleashed a roundhouse kick. A blade of aura coalesced around her paw as it collided with the fish's neck, the sharp edge carving through flesh and bone.

Borks opened a rift, preparing to catch the severed head, but his ability was ripped apart by a golden wall of the purest chi I'd ever felt. The divine energy from earlier, once muted, was no longer so. It tore through us, setting every cell in my body to vibrating. There was no pain, but I flooded essence out regardless, terror seizing my heart as I sought to protect my friends—especially Ruby and her unborn child.

The gilded light tried to disassemble my tendrils of awareness the same way it had done with Borks's ability—I denied it, my strands re-forming to beat back its influence and reach my pals. When my thick roots of intent contacted each of them, relief coursed through me. They weren't in danger.

The yellow brilliance pulsed through us all, setting our cores to humming as it expanding toward the horizon in a giant sphere. Now that I knew they were safe, I could think once more, and it took but a moment to realize the truth. I whirled back, facing the severed head, my senses honing it on the still-falling object.

The divinity-touched chi wasn't coming from the entire swordfish; it was pouring from the bladelike appendage it used to carve through the ocean.

For some reason, detaching it had unshackled the power, letting the essence flow out into the world. I only hesitated for a fraction of a second, then I ordered my awareness to surround both parts of its form, willing to risk the assault on my senses.

I half expected to receive a metaphorical hammer to the cerebellum for my audacity, but no such castigation awaited me. As the bubble of light expanded, so, too, did its potency diminish, allowing me to investigate.

The body had a mesh of abyssal chi within that was similar to the whispers I'd felt from George's and Geraldine's cores, and now that part of it had been broken, the lines were unraveling before my senses. Pockets of it hadn't yet disintegrated. They seemed to contain the golden power, its divine light unable to interfere with the dark strands the same way it had with mine.

So it was *shackled*, I thought. *Interesting . . .*

When I focused on the head, it revealed no secrets, but it *did* confirm something

I'd already suspected: the swordfish's namesake weapon was unfathomably powerful. Well . . . *kinda.* This ingredient—this naturally formed artifact—held the *potential* to become powerful. Until we worked out the method, it would remain inert . . . That, however, was a problem for another day.

Most of the bubble was gone now, racing out to sea in every direction. With its absence, the symphonic hum of my friends' cores faded. And the head, having tumbled for a few seconds, was about to plunge back into the ocean, the depths calling for its return. Before it could get there, I reached out and caught it with chi, my tendril glowing yellow everywhere the artifact made contact.

Borks shook his entire body with so much vigor that his rear paws skidded around. Then he trotted off for the hatch, batted it open, and sat down, staring at me with a lolling tongue and wagging tail.

I lobbed the head toward him, and he caught it happily, his eyes exuding the same golden light the moment it touched. He dropped it into the hull and cleared any lingering illumination with another energetic shake.

I slid the rest of its body into the cooled chamber, what had to be tons of mass disappearing into it and out of sight. Borks nudged the door closed, sealing the swordfish in with the cold.

No one said a word for a few breaths, until finally, Cinnamon broke the silence with a proud peep. *How was my kick? Perfect, right?*

I barked a laugh. "Beyond perfect, and even more violent than I expected. You too, Borks. Thanks for the assist." After giving them both the scritching they deserved, I turned to the others. "Do you guys need to take care of anything before we . . . Why are you all looking at me like that?"

"Fischer," Ruby said, "considering you just exposed my growing baby to some kind of unknown power, can we skip the whole pretend-nothing-happened schtick?"

"Hmm. Sure, but only if you agree not to joke about tonight's events actually hurting your child. I almost had a bloody heart attack getting my chi to you in time, only to find out it wasn't necessary."

She intertwined her fingers before her, a shrewd expression coming to her face. "No. The cost is too great."

"Ruby." Steven pinched the bridge of his nose. "Please don't drag this on any longer than required. Your core is screaming that you'll eventually accept."

She whapped him on the arm lightly. "I was *trying* to get more out of him!"

That they were willing to joke around with me and each other after the discovery of a natural artifact made most of the tension melt away from my shoulders.

"Fiiiine," she continued, rolling her eyes. "On with it, then. What was all that about? What did we miss?"

"Oh, no clue," I lied. "Not any more than all of you, anyway."

Barry turned to Theo, whose expression was flatter than the ocean of a windless night, his ability knowing the truth.

"Denied," I said to my muscular pal. "We've been through this song and dance already, mate. Even if I'm lying, you won't get it out of him. It's a waste of time."

Barry's jaw tensed, but he could tell I was right. "Okay, but are you're really going to deny you knew something was up with the head?"

"Before Cinnamon lopped it off with her sweet kick and accompanying energy blade? Mate, I swear on the lives of every animal pal, future, past, and present—I had absolutely no clue the sword on its noggin was an artifact, nor that it was special in any way."

Theo's impassive visage finally shifted, revealing a surprised smirk. "Truth. He really had no idea . . ."

Barry looked at Theo, then at me, then at Theo once more for good measure. "I've never given it much thought, but how do I know you're not lying?"

The former auditor shrugged. "Your cultivation is stronger than mine, and you can examine my core all you please. Unlike Fischer, I'll not risk your trust in me for a laugh."

"Okay, ouch," I said. "But I'm serious, Barry."

"Then why in Poseidon's humid groin did you remove its head?"

"It's a pelagic fish, mate. Gotta bleed 'em."

"That . . . that doesn't mean you had to kick it *off*."

"Well, no, but we *did* have to slice it at least once for it to fit belowdecks, anyway. If the cut was anywhere else, it could spoil way more meat, and that's just disrespectful."

"And kicking its head off *isn't*?" Trent asked, raising a brow.

"Maybe, but less so than wasting its body would be. Besides, I delegated the task to the best among us. Cinnamon is a being of martial prowess, complete grace, and unparalleled violence."

She nodded, letting out an affirmative peep. *I am.*

I clapped my hands to get everyone's attention. "Perfect! We're in agreement, then!"

"We are?" Barry asked.

"Ah-huh! I just decided!" Sliding back into sincerity, I bent at the waist, bowing low. "Thank you for coming, everyone. I couldn't name a better crew to have joined me on Bob's maiden voyage, and it's time we returned home." I straightened, smiling at them. "We have sashimi to share with the rest of the village, after all!"

Their cores hummed with excitement and hunger, neither of which I could filter out—I was much more exhausted than I let on. Abruptly, a breeze tousled my hair, making me realize my hat was missing.

Before I could inquire as to its whereabouts, Paul dashed forward, holding it out.

"Thanks, mate!" As I slipped it back on, so, too, came my captain's persona. I stood tall and puffed out my chest. "Batten down the hatches, crew! Stow the rods and the tackle!" I pivoted and hopped up onto the railing. "As soon it's all secured, we're setting sail!"

"Aye, Captain!" they replied in a chorus.

I turned to gaze out at the waves, an ocean of thoughts and questions assailing me. I had dreamed of a trip like this for months, and as exhilarated as I'd been to depart, I was even more thrilled to return home—the future, both distant and near, promised countless possibilities.

One thought stood out about the others, and I peered over my shoulder, watching my crew race around the deck and prepare Bob the boat for departure.

What have I done to deserve so many wonderful friends?

CHAPTER FIFTY-SIX

Changing Course

Deep beneath the pristine waves of the Bluefathom Ocean, an ancient organism was lost in thought, all manner of considerations passing through his awareness. What events had transpired in this vast swathe of water while he'd slumbered? Was it still known by the same name, or were all records of it purged in the war? And what became of the dread armies?

Given the importance of his task, some might assume he was being flippant, naïve, or arrogant—likely all three—by musing on such things. They *were* a comforting distraction, of course, but they also served a purpose. They facilitated the only reason he had survived so long: his legendary ability, which was the source of at least half the monikers he'd been known by.

Camouflage.

The being opened his eyes and stared down at where his own body should be, seeing only sand, shells, and ocean debris speeding past. Even his own midnight pupils and onyx sclera couldn't detect any part of his impressive size. Before he returned to the world of his own mind, he glanced forward, taking in the silent landslide that was his oldest ally.

Though only meters before him, the conjoined elementals had no idea he was there. They raced along the abyssal plain, an unnatural avalanche of earth trailed by an organism of many-limbed duty. Hubris had always been his ally's shortcoming, and it only got worse with each elemental they absorbed. They believed that their camouflage was greatest of all—that no other could *possibly* rival or surpass them.

Such arrogance.

He wanted to blow some mocking bubbles at that thought, but it would give his position away, so instead, he gathered his power, condensing a pocket of chi for a task that would soon arrive. *Only two remain.* His body slid across the ocean floor at the same pace as his quarry. *Then I can know for sure . . .*

He'd been trailing the elemental for hours, tracing their every move since they'd left that cavern of their own making. Unfortunately for the organism, with his ally's arrogance also came paranoia. It was, at best, a thinly veiled way to preserve their ego, but by luck or design, that shortcoming was the very thing that'd let them outlast the gods.

They had traversed the ocean and hidden parts of themself all over, forcing each to hibernate until a later date. To the organism's chagrin, he could sense their existence, but not their location. Every time he scanned for traces of their chi, only the main body responded.

There was only one way for him to complete his duty: He had to wait for them to rejoin once more.

Speaking of. . . he mused, sensing something approach.

In a matter of seconds, it arrived, and the splinter of singular consciousness launched itself forward. When it struck, the avalanche froze, even the smallest pebble of the earthen procession halting as the individual reassimilated with the many. A moment later, the silent landslide resumed, a sense of anticipation coming from his oldest ally's abomination of a core.

The organism, too, was excited. *Only one more* . . .

Over the following hours, that feeling of reinvigoration never diminished, only heightening with the passage of both leagues and time. Though he couldn't perceive its location, he *knew* the final splinter was on its way—nothing short of destruction would stop its return.

But then more hours passed. Frustration slid in through cracks in his mind, robbing his eagerness of fuel. What was taking the last fragment so long? Minutes later, the answer arrived with a wave of essence that shot through the water and slammed into his oldest ally.

The one they'd been waiting on . . . it had been *annihilated.*

This realization and all its implications hit him like a mountain—but it hit the earth elemental even harder. They shook, no longer silent as their mass churned, boulders and rocks grinding against each other. The careful control keeping them together faltered, and the contents of their body oozed out alongside myriad emotions.

Hidden amongst the silt and stone, long crystals gleamed with purple light, their colorful auras illuminating the surroundings. When the organism spotted them, horrific spears of panic lanced his core, their deadly tips lodging deep within. As sure as he was that the moon was high above, he knew that, somehow, his oldest ally had ancient relics of the natural variety—*ten of them.*

Such a thing shouldn't exist in this realm.

Essence leaked from around the metaphorical shafts still piercing his nexus of power. He had to regain composure. If he didn't, his camouflage would fall apart, leaving him exposed. It was too soon; his pocket of condensed chi wasn't ready yet.

He needed to imagine something. He was being too present. But no matter how hard he tried to force it, the reality before him was too visceral. Too dreadful. He couldn't dismiss it. He was going to be discovered. He—

A giant bubble of divine power raced along the ocean floor, slamming into his head. His camouflage dropped completely. So did that of the earth elemental before him, all of their fragments abruptly splitting apart. If the organism had a pulse, it would have hammered throughout his body. He scrambled to recover, latching on to whatever he could to restart his ability.

Two things saved him from destruction. First, the object that had released divine chi gave him something else to focus on, his mind grasping it and the associated thoughts with white-limbed intensity. Second, when the elementals were pulled apart, they were left unconscious—just long enough for the ancient being's camouflage to take hold.

There was a moment of stillness after he became invisible once more. It let him see his oldest ally as the individual he'd once been, rather than the grotesque amalgamation he had become. The organism experienced hundreds of thoughts over that insignificant stretch of time. They were as unique as they were numerous, but across them all, only one was an oath.

I will carry out my duty, old friend, he thought, twin waves of love and anguish flowing through him. *This, I swear to you.*

And then they were re-forming, dozens upon dozens of individuals becoming the many. The instant their minds snapped together and their souls became singular again, they started moving. Their course had changed, but only slightly, and the organism knew where his oldest ally was now heading.

An eleventh relic had appeared, and the earth elemental meant to claim it.

As a lone man gazed up at the crescent moon, its shape warped by the waves between himself and the celestial body, he let out a bubbled sigh. Maria was correct—Joel *had* been a complete fool.

Everything she'd said rang true in his mind, but it wasn't her words alone that penetrated his thick, annoyingly fleshy skull. It was the look on his beloved deity's face when the healing cultivator had grabbed him by the wrist and ankle, then launched him out to sea.

The church leader had seen Sergeant Snips make countless different expressions in the time he'd known her. Joy, sadness, rebuke—she was a very expressive crab. But shame? While gazing at *him*? The memory of it made his insides feel even squishier than they already were.

When he recognized he was falling into his old pattern of frustration, he released another sigh and kicked off the ocean floor, taking a deep breath when he surfaced. He'd been sitting in silent contemplation for hours and had thought the lesson internalized . . . yet he fell right back into the same flawed way of thinking.

Despite his enhanced mind and body, fatigue had leached into his bones, the hours of self-reproach and meditation seeming to rob him of energy. He knew what was wrong—he had been a selfish prick, putting his own goals above the efforts and happiness of others—but what was the correct path from here?

What was he to do?

He gazed up at the moon above, its concave curves somehow calming. Joel let out a sigh. Perhaps it was time to return home and get some sleep. He could resume being ashamed in the morning—that thought made a smile tug at his lip, but it was short-lived.

Deciding to follow Maria's earlier advice, he filled his lungs with air and dove to the seafloor, condensing chi so his body sank. The moment he adopted the perfect form, his hands forming fake clackers to either side of his head, the troubles assailing him seemed to retreat.

The leader of the Church of Carcinization slipped back into a meditative state with the ease of a hermit crab finding a bigger shell to call home. He settled into the present, relying on Fischer's teachings about mindfulness from months ago. Joel had to return to his followers.

No, he thought. *My friends.*

This acknowledgment, the realization that his acolytes were more than just a congregation to be carcinized, made his core hum in agreement, and he focused in on it, a tidal wave of serenity crashing over his soul.

Unfortunately, his peace didn't last long. He must have been a third of the way back to Tropica when he sensed a being so unexpected that it completely shattered his mindfulness. She was usually a source of joy; he'd sought her out only hours ago with dogged determination. Now, though, her presence humiliated him.

His flawless deity, the spike-covered crab known as Sergeant Snips, was just ahead. And there was something different in her aura—an added layer of complexity he couldn't understand.

Joel paused, his face falling as he considered his options. He shouldn't disturb her. What if she was out on official business, and his arrival ruined plans so intricate that he had no chance of comprehending them? He pictured that look of shame again, both her eyestalks visible and broadcasting disappointment for all to see.

In the end, his curiosity was too great, so he latched on to the hope she'd come to meet him. It would be an act of unrivaled disrespect to go around her after she came all this way, wouldn't it? Even if it was only to administer punishment.

He scuttled forward as best he could on his stupidly awkward human feet, but as he crested a low rise, his steps faltered. Sergeant Snips wasn't alone. She stood outside an underwater cavern, and a squad of rock crabs crowded around her, over thirty of them facing her and waiting for orders.

It wasn't Snips that felt different; it was the inclusion of their chi making her seem changed. None of them had awakened into spirit beasts, yet one and all had essence running through them—they were on the precipice of forming cores.

He knew she had a squad of rock crabs watching the bay, but this many? Weren't they numbered in the single digits? He rubbed his eyes, double-checking that it wasn't a side effect of his exhaustion. As he gazed back out at the world, someone tapped him on the shoulder.

Joel turned, blinking, to find a rock crab had snuck up on him. Its beady little eyestalks were filled with accusation, and it ran a claw on the patch of carapace under its mouth, miming the cutting of his throat.

Before he could react, a beautiful hiss flowed over the underwater landscape, ordering the scout to leave him be.

The aggressive crustacean immediately kowtowed. It snuck a peek at Joel, and seeing him still upright, shot him a disgusted look. He probably should have expected the whack on the head it delivered upon him a moment later, but his thoughts in his oversized-yet-inferior brain had slowed to a crawl.

Thankfully, the strike seemed to smack some sense into him, and he realized his mistake. In a rush, he pressed his forehead into the sand, seeking to apologize for his impropriety—but a mighty clacker caught him by the chin and lifted his face.

Sergeant Snips. None of the shame from earlier was present, her eyestalks holding something even worse. *Sorrow.*

He parted his lips to apologize, but she cut him off with a stream of air.

I know you blame yourself, her bubbles said. *But you are wrong.*

He blinked, not knowing what to say to that.

The fault is mine, Snips continued, bowing so low that her sturdy underside brushed the sand. *I am sorry for failing you.*

Joel's brain malfunctioned. He wanted to refute her words. Wanted to take the blame. But that would be directly calling her wrong. He opened his mouth, closed it, and opened it again, his mind still restarting.

Snips blew a string of happy bubbles, shaking her carapace in amusement as she patted his shoulder with a massive clacker.

Come on, she said. *Everyone is here now.*

He cocked his head in question, but she just turned and scuttled back toward the cavern entrance. Sheepishly, he followed, her order overriding his shame. Another tap on his shoulder. He turned to the right, and the crab that had threatened him earlier give him a *I'm watching you* gesture with its perfectly shaped claw.

Thankfully, a hiss from Snips rang out before he had a chance to reply.

Thank you for coming, everyone. I believe I have failed each of you—no, do not deny it. Listen, please.

The crustaceans saluted, and Joel followed suit, some of those around him shaking their heads at his delay.

I believe I have failed each of you, Snips repeated. *Today, I mean to rectify that.*

How, master? the violent rock crab asked.

She stood tall, tilted her carapace in thought, then shrugged and blew a torrent of amused bubbles. *I don't know, but I think we should start by meditating. Would you please take the lead, Joel?*

He blinked, and she nodded, gesturing for him to begin. He had no right to instruct those possessing the perfect form, yet her request left him no other option. Accepting his fate, Joel squatted, wiggled until he found the correct position, and slipped into a state of mindfulness.

As his pulse slowed, his mind growing calm, the Church of Carcinization's leader forgot all about his feelings of inadequacy.

CHAPTER FIFTY-SEVEN

Allegiance

Beneath a blanket of stars and a crescent moon, there wasn't a cloud to be seen, a worry to be found, or a single item not secured—thick ropes of my chi wrapped them in place.

With a grin I felt in my soul as much as on my face, I turned to the man beside me. "Ready when you are, skipper!"

"Skipper?" Trent asked.

"Yeah, I'll be honest—I'm not sure what it means either. Sounds right, though."

"Uhhh," Paul said. "From my memories, it's another word for captain."

"*Captain?*" I boomed. "You dare start a mutiny on *my* ship, you damned upstart? I—"

Someone clipped me on the back of the head, cutting off my tirade. I expected the slight hand of Ruby but received Barry's meaty mitt instead.

"Ow . . ."

"We both know that didn't hurt, *Captain.*" His intonation of the last word—along with his flat stare—made it more of an insult than a title. "You're awfully chirpy for a man with a hull full of fish that has an expiry date."

"Maybe I was trying to lighten the mood before we left by creating a casual atmosphere for Trent, which could make it easier for him to reduce the amount of chi he feeds into the godsdamned *rocket engine* attached to this here *boat.*" I sniffed haughtily. "You ruined my efforts."

"Did I?" He gave me a muscular grin and tensed his stupidly chiseled jaw. "Or did I expertly lure you into a long-winded pontification, thereby creating the very atmosphere you were trying to create?"

I couldn't help but smile at the teasing comment. Barry had been the primary target of the chaos I'd promised to Claws, and this presented another opportunity to double down, but I didn't want to; it was an evening for playful antics, not treacherous pranks that would appease menacing otters.

I blinked, pouted, and turned toward Trent. "Mate, if you ever lead a cult or a church, don't promote the first farmer you come across. Learn from my mistakes."

"I appreciate the thought, even if you two are more transparent than water." His core radiated a sense of victory I didn't really understand, but then held his hand out and to the right.

Steven, letting out a long sigh, retrieved some coins from his pocket and dropped them into the fire cultivator's palm.

"I told you not to bet against Fischer being a goose," Ruby said.

Barry and I glanced at each other, both frowning. His grin disappeared and his jaw relaxed—though it did remain stupidly chiseled. "Are we becoming too predictable?" he asked. "Or is our profound intelligence rubbing off on others?"

"The latter, obviously."

"*Obviously* . . ." Ruby, Fergus, and Duncan mocked at the same time.

"Oh-ho-ho! *Now* who's being predictable?"

Duncan opened his mouth to respond, but before he could get it out, I clapped my hands together. "That's enough lollygagging, my metal-pounding friend! The fish is spoiling as we speak! Ready when you are, Trent!"

"Aye, skipper!" The former prince's smile faded as he reached for his core, every ounce of his will directed at collecting as little power as possible. The strand that rose was hair thin, and as it poured down into Bob's chi condenser, I noted the change.

The boat still absolutely rocketed forward, propelled by a jet of flame as long as the deck, but compared to the speed we'd left Tropica with, it was a leisurely stroll. The hull only went a foot or two into the air. All were silent as we adjusted to the passage, my essence creating a shield to stop the wind assaulting us.

I took a deep breath of the irrepressible salt spray. Our return was going to herald a feast for the ages, and I pictured the scene, using it as a lodestone to keep my thoughts centered.

Corporal Claws, strongest of Fischer's disciples—and basically a divine being at this point if you asked anyone that mattered—chittered with laughter as she influenced the very world's atmosphere. After all, if she wasn't a goddess, how come she could *make* storms?

And not only was she immensely powerful, she was also as humble as her master pretended to be! Benevolent, too. She had allowed her disciple almost a full hour of rest, letting him take a break from his rolling practice. Glancing over, she checked what he was up to.

He was . . . still rolling, but at a leisurely pace, his chubby little body tumbling end over end in chaotic directions.

What are you doing? she demanded.

He landed on all fours, feigned a roll toward her, then ducked and tumbled to the right instead. After exactly one and a half barrel rolls, he came to a stop on his back, stretched his limbs, scratched his belly, and shrugged.

Damn, Claws thought to herself. *That looks really fun.*

Annoyingly, he nodded, privy to her thoughts. *It* is *fun. You should try it.*

With a shake of her head and a *very* believable look of disapproval plastered onto her face, she gestured him over with one paw. Their task was almost complete.

They had been working on her prized object for days, and as she gazed down at it, she marveled at how far they'd come. Her fluffy familiar tried to steal it the moment his grabby little digits were in range, of course, but Claws easily stopped him with a smack.

He didn't bother apologizing; they had both known he'd try.

The clouds above roiled and churned as energy built within them, and when tiny patches of sky peeked through, they were a light purple—the sun was on its way. By the time this storm subsided, it would likely be peeking over the eastern horizon, casting its rays across the land.

A pang of urgency stabbed into her awareness, the emotion both unusual and unwelcome. They were running out of hours. The raccoon felt it, too. Naturally, he used the momentary distraction to try to yoink the object again, which earned him an electrically charged bop on the noggin.

Focus, squire, she chirped. *The time for theft approaches.*

This made his devious little heart sing with so much joy that his eyes glowed blue. Claws could only grin. She felt the same. Reaching her paws toward the sky—and ready for her right leg to kick the raccoon when he no doubt tried to steal the relic again—she called the lightning.

As Maria pressed her hand against the not-a-prison's weighty door, essence flared behind her, adding a white flash to the predawn light shining down upon Tropica. She paused, both her and Keith turning back to watch a web of lightning strike beyond the southern mountain range.

Keith let out a low whistle. "You're still not sure what they're up to?"

Maria just shook her head. "Nope. Seems fun, though."

"Speaking of fun . . ." He glanced through the open door. "We've got our own to have."

"Riiiight. *Fun.*"

They shared a knowing look and headed in. Neither spoke a word as they traversed the uniform walls of the not-a-prison, yet Maria suspected they were sharing the same thoughts.

Slimes made a throat-clearing sound in her mind. *Perhaps Tryphena is feeling better today.*

Yeah, she thought back. *Maybe.*

They strode past a cell with people inside, but Maria had been so focused on today's task that she'd entirely forgotten they were there, until a hand reached through the bars, softly tapping her arm.

She froze, a slight panic climbing her spine as she whirled toward the handlers' chamber. "Oh! Uh, sorry, I was lost in thought, and—"

"No," the woman, Aisa, replied. "I need to apologize, not you. I could see that you were busy thinking, but I . . ." She averted her gaze. "Sorry. It isn't that important."

Maria, however, barely registered the words. She was focused on the hint of a spark in the handler's eyes, something that hadn't been there any of the times she'd seen her—even when she was still part of the king's corrupted forces.

Is that resolve?

Slimes jiggled in her core; he thought so, too.

Maria shook her head, strands of hair whipping her skin softly, bringing her back to the present. "If I'm not at fault, then neither are you." She spun to face the cell. "I didn't mean to ignore you this morning—there's just . . . well, a lot going on."

"I know. It's . . ."

"Aidos's virtue-bleached robes," one of the other handlers swore. "Spit it out."

Aisa's brow twitched, annoyance flaring in her core, but even this show of emotion reassured Maria. It was . . . human. Far removed from the blinding rage or depthless anguish she'd become used to seeing on the captives' visages.

"You can say it," Maria said, giving her a small smile. "I can tell it's weighing you down."

Aisa paused a moment longer, chewing her lip. "I . . ." Finally, she gathered her strength and locked eyes with Maria. They were determined. "I want to be healed, too. Use me as practice. That way, by the time you get to Princess Tryphena and Queen Penelope, there will be less chance of side effects."

Maria didn't have to fake the shock that crossed her face. Again, it wasn't the handler's words that had the most effect, however—it was the intent coming from Aisa's abdomen. She was genuinely offering herself up as a sacrifice, some semblance of allegiance remaining to the former royals despite all that had been done.

Maria laughed. She couldn't help it. Not bothering to cover her mouth, she let her joy cascade out, bouncing off the walls and echoing back. Her chi went with it, sharing her true feelings so the sincere woman before her didn't think herself the butt of a joke.

"Aisa," Maria said with a contented sigh, her cheeks aching slightly. "I'm not using them as practice, and I'm only healing them first because I promised Trent that I would."

The answering frown made myriad lines form on the handler's brow. "But . . . then why did you start with the cultivators who were imprisoned beneath Theogonia?"

"Beeecause!" Slimes called, his little head jiggling out of Maria's shoulder. "I gained some insight that could only be used on them! It wasn't a human trial, you silly billy! We just had to heal them first! Also, I'm a boy."

The person who had sworn earlier made an aggressive noise, dismissing the familiar's words. "Yeah, right. I told you they couldn't be trusted, Aisa. Her chi is lying to you."

Maria felt no anger at the claim, only curiosity. "What makes you say that? I can tell you believe it."

"Do you take us for fools? We sensed what you did to them." She pointed at the window in the back wall, her glare holding enough red-hot scorn to light a fire. "We *saw* their flight for ourselves. You turned them into *animals*, and now you stand here before us claiming you're not doing trials? Yeah, right. The audacity of you to call yourself a healer . . ."

A palpable silence followed, bouncing off the walls and settling atop everyone present. The other handlers clearly agreed; despair and fury flashed across their faces. Aisa, too, believed the accusation—at least partially, anyhow. The corners of her lips turned down, and though the spark remained in her eyes, it had dimmed.

Maria hadn't the faintest idea where to start. Thankfully, Keith and Slimes got the ball rolling. Both shook silently for a second, then noise erupted. The former royal chuckled, leaning back against the hallway as he embraced his merriment. Her familiar, having likely seen a similar gesture in Maria's memories, clung to the floor and repeatedly bounced up to slap his gelatinous head against one of Keith's knees.

It looked and sounded ridiculous—Maria loved every second. "Ladies . . ." she said, having to turn away from her two companions lest their giggles infect her, "we didn't turn them into animals. They *wanted* to become birds. They bonded with Private Pelly and Warrant Officer Williams, which is why they became pelicans, but on my fiancé, my family, and everything else I hold dear, I swear that their transformation wasn't some kind of side effect. It was a breakthrough of their own making. All we did was help it along."

"Oh . . ." Aisa said, her gaze going distant as she considered the assertion. The others were doing the same mental math, their eyes averted and negative emotions gone.

Deciding it was best to let them discuss, Maria took a step back. "We're leaving to work on the former royals for now—as I said, I made a promise to Trent. We will heal you, however. Take some time to consider my words. If it makes you feel any better, I can have the pelicans . . . Never mind. I'm getting ahead of myself. Keith and I will come see you on the way back, okay?"

"Sure," Aisa replied, still staring at the wall sightlessly. "See you then."

From there, it was only a short walk to their final destination. They moved in silence, all three of them knowing that she and Slimes had to gather their chi, but the mood had shifted markedly. When they finally arrived at the former royals' cell, Maria held her breath, dared to hope, and looked up to find . . . disappointment.

"Welcome," Tryphena spat. "I was worried we wouldn't see you this morning."

Maria had hoped to ride the high of the handlers' shifting perspectives, but now that she was face-to-face with the venomous princess, she recalled how repugnant it'd been to meld with her yesterday. She took a steadying breath, focused on the task at hand, and exhaled through tightly pursed lips. "The sooner we're finished—"

"Assuming it's not a waste of time," her patient interrupted. "Which it is."

"Tryphena . . ." A grimace had replaced Keith's joy from moments ago. "I know why you're hesitant. Really, I do, but . . ."

Maria rested a hand on his shoulder and shook her head. "There's no point, Keith."

The former princess rolled her eyes. "Finally, some honesty."

Rather than feed further into Tryphena's negativity, Maria reached out for Slimes, his core sharing the same belief that she did. They would succeed. They would *heal* them. It was only a matter of time.

Maria lowered herself to the ground, and even before her behind touched the stones, her and Slimes's pink chi was flowing out, squeezing past the bars with the permission of the not-a-prison's awareness.

* * *

As a force of nature swept along the ocean floor, one celestial body in the sky above was replaced by another. Though so far down that the sun couldn't be seen, its energy easily passed through the waters, reaching the abyssal plain the earth elemental traversed.

Its rays were a provider of life, but the beams did nothing to ease their worries. Desperate need reigned when their thoughts turned toward the artifact they chased, and fury took over when they remembered that a part of them, a splinter that had long ago been volcanic before assimilating with earth, was no more. It had been destroyed. *Murdered.*

The mass of rock, silt, and debris channeled this anger, funneling it into their passage. They were quickly approaching their target, and once they secured the newfound relic, their potential for power would be unmatched. It was clearly different from the pillars of purple crystal it had already found.

A lesser being of even less intellect might try to make an artifact-grade weapon out of whatever it was. They would think it something separate from the ten crystalline structures stored within the elemental's body. But only they, the great earthen force of nature speeding across this barren plain, knew the truth of it.

This eleventh relic was an offering from the heavens high above—a guarantee that none of the other relics would be destroyed by the crafting process. When they secured this one, they could use it for experimentation, absorbing its mass instead of creating something new.

It would grant them the greatest gift of all—knowledge.

As they approached the artifact, its flame-fueled escape no match for their own haste, the elemental detected the essence of those on board . . . and came to a complete stop, their silt and stones indistinguishable from the rest of the ocean floor. They couldn't believe what they'd just discovered.

There were a number of different cultivators on the boat. Spirit beasts, too, all having taken the first few steps toward ascension. But none of them were noteworthy compared to the beacon of white light on board.

The one who had released that blast of pure chi . . . he was there. If he hadn't been present, the elemental would have attacked immediately, not needing an ambush to succeed.

Perhaps they should attack anyway. It was a human, after all—the best possible outcome. If the first brother was alone, he might have done so. He wasn't, however. He was them, and they were him.

They decided to wait. Chose to bide their time. The ones above couldn't remain at sea forever, after all. The vessel would have to dock eventually.

They resumed their landslide passage, matching the pace of the ship sailing above. Almost immediately, a suspicion formed in their mind, and after a few minutes of mapping and plotting—led by a former air elemental who used to ride the winds—the hunch was confirmed.

The boat and the relic on board were heading back to the source of the blast. The many beings that were one had to wrestle down their rumbling laughter, lest it give away the game. They knew *exactly* where to go.

No longer limiting their speed, the earth elemental raced off ahead, giving the pure-essence cultivator a wide berth.

The heavens truly smile down upon us.

It took the trailing organism but a moment to understand what his oldest ally was up to. When he compiled the relevant points of data, the truth unfurled in his mind's eye, forming an interconnected web of events and outcomes.

The mass of elementals his friend had become . . . they were going back to the ship's port. Racing to where the column of unaspected chi had originated.

The idea, surprisingly, gave him pause. He had registered the pure-essence cultivator. From so far away, most wouldn't have been able to tell it wasn't a spirit beast—but the organism knew humans well. His former masters had been of that species, after all.

Acknowledging the existence of those two made a well of conflicting emotions overflow. They had instilled a love for humanity deep within him, and though that affection had concluded with the end of their tragically brief lives, the memory of it lingered.

He'd dismissed the foolish cultivator; he had had nothing to do with his duty. But . . . what if he could exterminate that moronic ascendant, too? His masters certainly would have advised that course of action, as he would have . . . at the time, anyway. Everything had changed since then.

Echoes of the love he'd held for his former companions called out to him, bouncing off the insides of his soft body. Then it alchemized into *rage*. Hatred for the schemes, betrayals, and happenstance that had taken their lives.

For all he cared, humanity could burn. The passing of his masters—his dear friends—had almost killed him, and if not for his oath, he probably would have wasted away, letting the chi within his elemental body return to the world.

His ability flickered, some of his soft, camouflage skin barely visible. He was losing control. With a fraction of his substantial will, he shifted mindsets, and the cold indifference of duty welcomed him in with open arms.

Thousands of thoughts passed by in the next few seconds. They were like so many plankton, their fleeting existence inconsequential in the grand scheme of things. With sober disregard, the organism decided he would deal with the pure cultivator, too—but only if the opportunity arose.

I will not forsake my sworn oath for the betterment of humanity, he thought, and his entire form hummed in agreement.

With that blessing from his very soul, he took off, his malleable body forming an arrow that shot through the water. He honed in on the pocket of power he'd been compressing. There was now more than enough to free the earth elemental he had once called a friend—so long as they were distracted, anyway.

He didn't stop pouring in his condensed chi, instead increasing the flow; it never hurt one to overprepare.

CHAPTER FIFTY-EIGHT

Identity

As the sun rose over Tropica, so, too, came rays of light, their soft beams illuminating all. So when the overly protective rock crab got a little too close to Joel again—and earned a whack from the human's claw-shaped hand in response—Snips had to fight down the physical signs of her amusement.

The crustacean dashed away, blowing *very* pissed-off bubbles as it gave Joel a respectable amount of space. The leader of the Church of Carcinization might not have been on the correct path for the last couple of months, but he'd made great strides with his mimicry of crabhood, both in posture and demeanor.

Snips cocked her carapace in thought.

Demeanor . . .

Her core hummed, and though she wouldn't call it entirely positive, it certainly had a hopeful tint.

Interesting, she mused, both eyestalks gazing out at the world and its intoxicating beauty.

It was a new direction. A fresh aspect of herself to explore. But as she made to settle back into a meditative state, something drew at her awareness—a mass of cores had arrived to scout their position. Snips whirled to face the top of the rock shelf, opened one powerful snipper, and . . . waved hello.

A pair of peeking eyes flashed with panic, then disappeared from sight when their bearer realized they'd been spotted.

Snips let out gleeful bubbles. *Come*, she hissed. *You are invited.*

Jess's head appeared again, panic replaced by curiosity.

"Come, Jess," Joel said.

Yes, agreed Snips. *Come and join—*

Her hiss cut off, and she peered his way. *How did his fleshy mouth speak underwater?*

"I have much to say, Jess," said fleshy mouth continued, paying the laws of nature no mind. "But we can talk about it later. For now, know that I have realized the error of my ways, and I am sorry."

More heads poked overtop the ridge, lured in by the spoken words. The entire Church of Carcinization had arrived, all their brows furrowed as they took in the sight. Snips didn't want to wait any longer. She gestured for them to come down with one claw, then turned away, getting comfortable.

She had found a new direction to explore. With her similarity to Joel in mind, she let out a stream of bubbles and sank into herself, trusting the message her core had sent earlier. Its vibration wasn't as strong as others had reported, but there had definitely been *something* there.

If insight could be gleaned, Sergeant Snips—first of Fischer's disciples—would find it.

A hint of worry peppered Maria's awareness as her and Slimes's healing mist tried again to reach Tryphena's core. It had taken but a moment to surround Penelope's, and though there was enough despair within to break a dozen hearts, at least Maria could attempt repairing it.

The former princess, however, hadn't just become more verbally vitriolic. She'd also raised walls.

It will all be okay in the end, Slimes thought, attempting to soothe her.

But she wasn't so sure. Had it been a mistake trying to heal them yesterday? Had her half-hearted effort been like a drop of poison—an ineffective dose that caused antibodies to develop overnight?

Slimes snapped Maria out of it with a strong pulse of chi. She gave a metaphorical shake of her head. Slimes was correct. Self-deprecation served no purpose right now. Gathering her will, she turned part of it into a battering ram. Tryphena wanted to create walls? Fine. Maria would knock them down.

Together, she and Slimes crashed their awareness into the former princess, and the blunt-force impact shattered the barriers like a passiona berry's husk. The rest of the shell crumbled, letting Tryphena's will and intent flow out. It was . . . nasty. *Disgusting.*

Is this truly the same person who was joking with us only a week ago?

Slimes buzzed in response. *Hmmm. I believe she is the same person, but I'm also confused about the developments.*

So much hatred had blossomed since yesterday. It threatened to send Maria back into a spiral of self-deprecation, but just before she slipped over the edge, she caught herself. Was this not exactly what healers were for? What *she* was for?

Still shaped like a hammer, her will collided with Tryphena's core, attempting to smack some sense into the spoiled brat. Trent was raised a royal, and sure, for a while he'd been the human equivalent of bait left out to bake in the sun. But that was a result of the concoction Gormona's alchemists had given him.

As far as Maria was concerned, she had shown the former princess all the compassion and understanding she'd needed to. More than enough, really. Perhaps it was time for some tough love.

With that thought in her mind, she poured her awareness out, the hammer becoming a wispy cloud once more. With the help of Slimes, their haze surrounded their two patients, encouraging them both to find new identities—something that aligned with their souls and filled the void left behind by Fischer's cleansing, just like the birdlike cultivators had done.

Penelope's despair seemed to waver, but only a fraction. It was a good sign. Maria and Slimes focused on Trent's sister, knowing they had to regain ground with her before either of the former royals could be healed. But no matter how much they pushed into her, an equal force shoved back.

It . . . it wasn't Tryphena. Both curious and fearful, Maria inspected a second, well-hidden shell that her healing chi had just discovered. Something conscious within it detected Maria's attention, a tiny pulse of surprise making its way through the concealed layer.

Maria and Slimes didn't waste the opportunity. They hammered into it, focusing their cloud on a single point. A crack formed, and the shell shattered. Before the source of that resistance could retreat into hiding, Maria identified it.

A whisper of corruption. Not just the memory of it, but an actual strand of that disgusting chi. It would have gone undetected by anyone else, even to Fischer, yet its existence was indisputable. Somehow, a seed of rot had sprouted within Tryphena's soul.

Showing remarkable and worrying intelligence, it leaped across to Penelope, knowing it'd been discovered. There, it buried itself like a blood-sucking parasite, infecting the void left behind in her core. Maria instinctively knew that if it was allowed to prosper again, there would be no saving them. They would be *doomed.*

She shot back into her body, and she took an inhalation so deep it seemed to reach her toes. She got to her feet, shaking with adrenaline and terror as she stared into Tryphena's eyes. The hatred there made more sense now, as did the venom she spat. Penelope's lip twitched, her thoughts already being influenced. *Corrupted.*

Without another word, Maria rocketed down the hall, kicking off a wall as she shot around a corner.

"Maria?" Keith called after her, fear lacing his voice. She didn't respond.

Slimes released a string of expletives that any other time would have made her chortle. Maria didn't even acknowledge it. Some of the handlers spoke. She ignored them, too. She had to go.

When she got to the doors, they were already open, the prison's soul aware of her need. She skidded to a stop outside and raised both hands to her mouth. Maria reached for her power, poured it into her chest, and set her fear aside as she let a single word fly free.

The world shook.

Beneath the placid waters of Tropica's bay, a consortium of crabs—and some humans emulating their shape—sat in relative silence. A few bubbles here. A hiss there. Even a handful of warning clacks when another got too close. These were the only sounds to be heard, and the only communication necessary.

In that almost silence, Sergeant Snips, the first of Fischer's disciples, was slowly unraveling the mess she'd found herself in. Annoyingly, she hadn't been tricked into the predicament.

This swamp, this blockage in her cultivation, was entirely her fault.

Realizing that she had arrived back at the same unproductive thought, she blew a hiss of her own, adding to the occasional outbursts coming from those around her.

Yes, she had done this to herself. So what?

The real measure of one's worth is what they do when all the chips have fallen, and they find themselves at the bottom of the ladder.

Snips's core responded to that, buzzing in what could only be described as a warning. Frustration threatened to swell up, but she chose instead to focus on the last thing that'd felt right.

Her realization that she and Joel weren't so dissimilar. The word *demeanor* had struck a chord, and though it wasn't the pleasant hum she'd heard talk of, it was certainly more encouraging than the previous buzz.

Joel's demeanor, she repeated.

His ultimate goal was to attain a form like hers. Other than the times he was asleep or attending to the needs of his fleshy body, everything he did was toward that end. Actually, she could argue that his sleep and the fact he ate were also in service of his eventual transformation—he only took those breaks because he had to.

And yet . . . his dream remained unmet.

Snips's core shifted, encouraging her to delve deeper.

She had thought that maybe humans just couldn't get a new body, that the Church of Carcinization's ambition would never come to be, but the pelicans proved that to be a lie. What was it, then?

Joel's demeanor.

For someone wishing to become a crab, his mentality was perfect. Eerily so. He acted decisively and with impunity, never stopping to consider the ramifications—such as Maria yeeting him out to sea. But . . . that was the way of the crab. They were hunters when the opportunity arose, but mostly, they were bottom-feeders. Their world was one of brutality and necessity.

Her core hummed, its vibration tickling her insides like there were shrimp crawling about within. She was getting closer to the truth.

A crab couldn't stop to consider if more food would come along—they had to strike where and when they could, forging their own path. Without proactivity, even the largest crab with the strongest snippers might starve before its next meal arrived. But neither could they be too reckless. If one went too far from safety and was discovered by a predator . . . Their carapaces were mighty sturdy but far from impenetrable.

Their way was to dance with risk, avoiding it as much as possible, but taking it when necessary.

Her core hummed, and the metaphorical shrimp within started doing flips in her stomach.

She still didn't understand—what was her abdomen saying? Joel was doing all those things and more. By human standards, he was an absolute prick—both to outsiders and his congregation. The anomalous man had gone *full* crab . . . yet he hadn't transformed.

Her core buzzed, then hummed, then buzzed again. What on Kallis was it trying to convey?

The beginnings of an idea formed, and it was so ridiculous that she wanted to spew a fountain of mirthful bubbles.

Yeah, right, she thought. *As if him being* too much *of a crab would be an issue. That . . .*

Her core was silent, but she tilted her carapace all the same. Joel's demeanor. That had been the first hint of where she'd gone wrong. He . . . Joel was a human who had taken on the mannerisms of a crab. And she . . .

Nary a hint of movement came from her soul as a profound realization struck. Joel, a human, was acting as a crab. And she, a crab . . . *had been acting as a human.* The world seemed to freeze.

She thought back to who she had once been—the scar-covered crustacean with no pincers and a missing eyestalk. Fischer had come across a random sea creature on the brink of death, and instead of eating her or letting nature take its course, he'd given her fish. That passing kindness had granted her a new body. A new life. Everything she possessed was thanks to that single instance of human kindness.

When she had awakened, she'd almost immediately started emulating her master's selflessness. That first night, she had found the bait he'd buried, and she only ate most of it. That being a compassionate move was laughable now, but at the time, not eating *all* of a delicious eel was strikingly selfless—and foolish, if one's goal was to survive.

When Sebastian, the then-leader of the Cult of the Leviathan, had tried to poison Fischer, her thoughts had been as bloody as they were utilitarian. She'd broken into their headquarters, and the only thing that stopped her from executing the cretin was the fact that it could negatively impact Fisher.

To both send a message and inflict pain upon the weasel of a man, she'd decided to execute his cult's false deity instead. But just before the headsman's claw had descended, Fischer's kindness flashed in her mind, staying her snipper. That same lobster went on to become a dear friend and fellow animal pal—Pistachio. His awakening reinforced the idea that extending grace was always the correct move.

Since then, she'd taken her responsibilities as the first disciple of her beloved master seriously. Her duty of care had grown beyond just him, encapsulating the rest of his animal pals, the congregation, and eventually all the citizens of Tropica.

When the Church of Fischer had needed someone to spy on Gormona, Claws and her clandestine skills were most suited to the task, yet it had been Snips who went. She had justified it by saying that Claws could not be trusted. Snips's master would've gone by himself if he'd known about the plan, so that was what she did. She'd made the decision based on Fischer's human sensibilities.

To be clear, though: Only a fool would have trusted the chaotic otter to not harness lightning and attack the king directly the second she got a chance. But that was just who Claws was—unapologetically herself, personality defects and all.

And it wasn't only Claws who had advanced by being true to her nature. Cinnamon's was to kick the shit out of things and protect Fischer. The pelicans wanted to lead a flock. Borks was just happy to be involved, which stemmed from his need to be part of a pack. Rocky . . . never mind. Thinking about what he wanted would make her blush and ruin her concentration.

The point was that the rest of them had experienced a breakthrough, some catching up to Snips, others eclipsing her entirely. With that acknowledgment, she finally heard from her core again. Its hum was soft like . . .

She almost compared the sound to something human, but stopped herself. That inclination to do so was a part of the problem. Earlier, she had thought to herself, *The real measure of one's worth is what they do when all the chips have fallen, and they find themselves at the bottom of the ladder.*

. . . Which had caused her core to yell at her.

What kind of sentence *was* that? Chips? Ladders? *Hades's burning fires* . . . she had referred to multiple clacks as a handful. A handful! She didn't even *have* hands!

They were human thoughts, and Snips wasn't human. She was a *crab*, a violently capable crustacean that could, at will, shoot arcs of chi from her powerful clackers.

Her core buzzed with muted power like a hive of angry bees—which was a decidedly uncrabby analogy, but *she enjoyed watching the insects, godsdammit!* They appealed to the smooth part of her brain that liked shiny things, delicious meals, and sweet, *sweet* vengeance!

Though still contained, her core's humming rose in pitch. She had found the truth. She was sure of it. But her soul didn't want to acknowledge her yet. Something was missing, a vital component, and Snips's many mouthparts undulated in delight. She already knew who it was.

An image of Joel flashed into her mind: him squatting like a crab and lashing out with chi-infused hands at an actual crustacean that got too close. He and the rest of the Church of Carcinization, all of whom identified her as their deity, needed her guidance.

Not just them, either. The entire consortium of rock crabs—who'd apparently been recruiting more members in her absence—*needed* her. She had sent them away, telling them to guard the waters within Fischer's Domain. Doing so was prudent, and necessary, for the defense of Tropica. But her lack of contact?

She had thought it the correct path but hadn't known why. Now, with her inadequacies revealed by a retreating wave of past mistakes, she understood. Conversing with crabs had been a source of discordance. There was a gaping chasm within her, the clawless and scarred creature she'd once been on one side, and Sergeant Snips, the defender of Tropica, on the other.

It was . . . cowardly. In her desire to be humanlike and increase the Church of Fischer's strength, she had forsaken those who looked up to her.

A blanket of sea-foam evaporated from around her core. Water-aspected chi churned and swelled. And every bee in an imaginary hive flew free, hundreds, then thousands, then *millions* of beating wings turning into a roar that shook her shell.

Even through the shaking carapace and all the light that now shone from her, Snips felt tears well in her eyes—which, as anyone with a basic knowledge of crab anatomy could attest, was not natural—but that had no bearing on her breakthrough.

It wasn't about leaving behind the human parts of herself, just as Joel and his bipedal followers didn't have to abandon their crablike tendencies. They'd been doing it all wrong.

It was a matter of identity. The conscious act of knowing what you were—not only who you wanted to become. With that thought, her will blazed through the others, humans and crustaceans alike suffused by torrents of her unerring chi.

All were presented a choice, an ultimatum, and all accepted. Her water-aspected essence washed over them, causing understanding to bloom like the unfurling tentacles of anemones when the tide returns. Each of their cores became another source of dazzling light, individually weak but collectively blinding. Dozens of . . . *huh?*

There were more than dozens. *Way* more. Hundreds of souls seemed to absorb her power and mirror it back. At the same time, a single word boomed out, quaking the sand beneath and waves above.

Snips let these developments fall by the wayside. They were of little import. The surrounding water poured into her soul, and she gathered all the cores connected to her chi, ensuring their breakthrough remained undisturbed.

Corporal Claws, shaper of weather and blessed by thunder, paid the coming day no mind—she was too busy changing the world. The good kind of positivity swelled in the atmosphere above her, making a sky-bound sea of black and gray swirl as clouds formed in response to her machinations.

She could not recall ever feeling so excited. Her body seemed more alive than ever before, each one of her powerful cells abuzz with electricity and potential. The reason for such joy was as clear as the darkened horizon wasn't—her task was almost complete.

A chittering laugh came from beside her and allowed a moment of indulgence, twisting her head to stare at the blue-colored raccoon that was now a part of her very core. His fingers were steepled in a downright dastardly manner, further emphasized by his villainous sneer and soft snicker.

Claws joined in. She chittered at the heavens, and the laugh grew louder as the moment of truth approached. When the air above became charged enough, she half expected her familiar to attempt its theft again, but was pleasantly surprised that she didn't have to head-butt him back through the nearest tree line.

It made sense, though; if he stole it now, he couldn't take part in the greatest heist this world had seen for millennia.

One last time, Claws called the lightning. It was only a fraction of the size of previous strikes, but that was by design. They didn't *need* a full charge, and any more electricity than this would only hamper their efforts.

It gathered in her paws, and she condensed it with ease, then slammed both fists into her treasure—the item that would help her rob a kingdom's worth of wealth.

Even before the energy finished pouring down into the sand, her raccoon swept forward, his bright mitts clutching its rough surface. Instead of taking, he gave to it, his cutpurse will flowing in.

Abruptly, a wave of imploring chi from the south. The ground shook. And a sound, perhaps a word, shot through everything. But Claws neither heard, felt, nor saw anything beyond the first fraction of a second.

After all, her familiar's essence had reached the center of her prize; it was hard to notice one's senses when you were inside an explosion the size of a mountain.

Despite racing atop the ocean swifter than any vessel back on Earth, the trip was wonderfully relaxing. Trent had been getting even better at limiting his chi, a development that made me smile, especially considering the way his abdomen hummed.

Everyone was always so focused on *more*. Faster advancement, bigger cores, and enhanced essence. Trent's cultivation base seemed to be encouraging him, urging that he practice restraint further.

I rubbed my chin. *Perhaps that's something we can—*

"Fischerrrr!"

The two-syllable word hit my soul like a point-blank dual-claw explosion from Rocky, and its drawn-out tail scoured away any hesitation.

"Hold on!" I yelled, my skin prickling with heat as I reached for the depths of my core.

"What's wrong?" Trent asked, clearly not having heard.

"Maria." I tensed my jaw as my power welled up. "She just called for help."

It was all the explanation needed. The entire crew's faces sobered.

"No more fire chi," I commanded, taking a step forward as every tendril of will holding things down flowed back into me.

The moment the returning strands touched the reservoir of essence flowing up from within, my world exploded in a flash of white light.

CHAPTER FIFTY-NINE

Secret Ability

Tingles raced up and down my skin, just as they did my very soul. It was a sensation I'd never felt before, but that was hardly surprising. Teleporting so much mass had pushed my will to the limit. It'd taken all my attention to move Bob the boat—as well as everything and everyone on board—back toward Tropica.

I searched for Maria, our bond allowing us to connect despite my overexertion. I immediately understood why she'd called me. Corruption had returned to the hearts of two cultivators, which was an issue of gigantic fracking proportions. In my mind's eye, I could see Maria skidding to a stop outside the former royals' cell, ignoring Keith's demands as she sat, reached for Slimes, and started channeling their healing essence.

The only visual proof of our transportation was a distinct lack of color. I'd become used to arriving in a flash of white light—this was something else. I couldn't see the tip of my nose. But that didn't matter. I had other senses. Strands of chi poured from me, growing thicker by the millisecond. Regardless of what I found, I knew my friends and I could handle any . . . *thing*?

The ship's bow faced the open ocean, giving us a view of Tropica's bay. So the moment color returned to my awareness, I bore witness to the localized-yet-violent storm just offshore. Like someone had detonated several bombs a kilometer away, water sprayed toward the heavens, obscuring a vast swathe of horizon.

As visually impressive as it was, nothing could have prepared me for what it felt like.

It . . . it was crabs. A *frackload* of them. All tinged with hints of my trusty guard crab, Snips.

"What the shi—"

I whirled to the south. Twin elements had erupted from beyond the distant mountain range. Forks of lightning barbed their way out in every direction—Claws and her raccoon's experiments, no doubt. That was expected. What *wasn't* expected, however, was the aspect weaving between and through each tongue of electricity.

Earth. Not just a little, either. A metric shit-ton of it, so strong that clumps of sandstone and silicate from deep in the world's mantle floated about, entirely ignoring gravity.

It resonated in the surrounding air, seeming to come from every—

Not everywhere! my instincts screamed. *Below us!*

It happened in the blink of a cultivator's eye. A solid wall of silt and stone climbed up around Bob's deck, moving horrifically fast as layers upon layers upon *layers* folded overtop themselves. Tens, then hundreds, then thousands of tons of mass, each molecule filled to the brim with aspected chi.

It was somehow stronger than Claws's, but that abject threat wasn't what made my blood freeze—its age was. This thing, this elemental, was ancient, having lived for countless years. Its presence felt multifaceted, something about it too complex, too varied, for me to comprehend.

Knowing this was a possibility—if an extremely remote one—I hadn't let go of my power. I clicked my thumb and forefinger on both hands, sending most of my friends away, their bodies disappearing just before a solid wall of earth blocked out the last patch of predawn sky above.

Only three pals remained on board. Their forms were lit by the bright departure of the others, revealing one with a wagging tail and another with floppy ears and a fuzzy body poised for violence. The third, Bonnie, seemed much less happy about her continued presence, both eyes wide and head darting. I gave all of them a wink, then sent some quick thoughts out across Tropica, having to keep the messages brief and conceptual considering my end was ostensibly nigh.

An outside observer of the incoming annihilation might have found our reactions incredibly strange. Well, except for Bonnie—hers was pretty understandable. The rest of us, though? Any sane onlooker would likely assume we were unhinged or suicidal based on the grins on our faces and adrenaline coursing through our veins.

But that wasn't reflective of us—it was reflective of said onlooker's lack of knowledge, imagination, or both.

We could have left, of course. I still had the reserves to teleport myself, my friends, and even the swordfish to safety. What I couldn't risk rescuing, however, was Bob. I'd be able to shift him through space again, but it could take all my strength, potentially leaving me unconscious and unable to further assist my friends.

That was unacceptable. But that didn't mean I would just abandon him. A captain, after all, goes down with his ship.

"*Now!*" I ordered, struggling to keep the anticipation from my voice as a cracking sound joined the roar of sediment and rock tumbling toward us. "Plan B!"

Eastern Tropica Village
Two days ago

"Okay, Fischer." Barry stole a glance at Peter, and the barbecue the chef was tending atop Tropica's oceanic walkway. "What did you want to talk about?"

I understood the hunger in his eyes. We'd spent most of the day swimming, enjoying a morning of leisure before our seaward adventure—the hours of exercise had left me famished.

"Don't worry, mate," I said. "We just need a minute or two."

"*We?*" Barry repeated, looking down at Borks and Cinnamon. The latter was riding the former. She nodded in response to his question. Before any more words could be exchanged, I snapped my fingers, and the world shifted around all four of us.

When the light of my teleportation disappeared, gone was the gray street, replaced by the scorched remains of a once-verdant forest. A ruined strip of trees extended in opposite directions, this burned scar the only proof remaining of the king's assault on Tropica.

"Uhhh . . ." Barry started, but trailed off when I held a finger to my lips.

Borks, my goodest of boys, opened up a portal, its lines cracking into existence. With a nod toward it, we all stepped through.

"I need to ask a favor," I said in a rush the moment we were inside. "On the trip we're going on, I need to prank someone repeatedly, and it needs to be you."

". . . What?"

"Damn. That was a terrible place to start, wasn't it?" I took a steadying breath, exhaling it slowly to ease my racing heart. "I'm feeling hurried because the longer we're in here, the more likely it is that our scheme gets discovered."

Cinnamon let out a peep, and I patted her soft little head.

"You're right—I *should* begin there . . ."

Barry just blinked, his face as confused and curious as his jawline was sharp.

"Okay," I said. "Before I voice any of this, you *need* to control your emotions. I'm gonna tell you something *really* aggravating, but you can't get pissed off. Deal?"

"Uhhh, can't you just . . . not say things that will piss me off?"

"Afraid not. But there's an *excellent* incentive for you to hear what I have to say." I grinned, doing my best to remain calm. "If you can keep your emotions in check, you'll be able to get revenge on . . . *her.* On Corporal Claws."

His eyes flashed with need. "I'm listening . . ."

I started relaying the true events of the previous night. When he learned we *had* conspired to make him lose his bet against Maria, which resulted in him having to dance while singing an embarrassing song, he came *real* close to losing his cool. He got even closer to the edge when he remembered the depantsing-via-raccoon that'd followed, but just as he was about to boil over, Borks and Cinnamon leaped into his arms, their fur-covered tooshies the perfect distraction if ever there was one.

"All right," Barry finally said when his blood pressure had returned to normal and his muscles no longer looked like they were trying to ripple out of his skin. "Where does the revenge come in, though? I'm clearly missing something."

"I have to keep it to myself for now, mate. Do you trust me?"

He stared back, expression flat—no words were needed.

"Yeahhh, okay, you've got a point. How about this, then . . ." I stroked Cinnamon's and Borks's heads. "I swear on my friendship with these here beasts that you will thoroughly enjoy it. I also swear that none of it comes at your expense, and it's best that you don't know any more yet."

He raised a brow at my words. "Okay. That's enough for me to trust you."

"Good! Now control your anticipation so I can send you back—it's literally flooding out. Even a drop could alert Claws that shenanigans are afoot."

The prospect of vengeance against the troublesome otter had made his already substantial ego inflate. He took a deep breath, massaged his cheeks, and nodded, his face sobering. "I'm ready when you are."

"Awesome. Appreciate your help with this, mate." I extended a hand, which he gripped and shook. "You won't regret it."

As we stepped outside, I patted Barry on the shoulder. "We'll join you in a second, mate."

"What? You aren't com—"

With a slight gesture of my index finger, I sent him back to Tropica. "Could you keep your portal open a bit longer, Borks? I want to store something within."

His head tilted to the side like a puppy hearing a high-pitched noise. It was godsdamned adorable. Without another moment's hesitation, he leaped back inside.

Cinnamon went next, and I followed, making two small gestures with one hand just before stepping into the dimensional space. More cunning and intelligent than a normal dog, my golden retriever bud closed the rift behind, sealing us in.

"Huh." I said, eyeing the wall where the portal had been. "Am I that transparent?"

Yes, they barked and peeped, eyeing the hand I'd hidden behind my back.

"Well, hopefully not to Claws. I have more information, but it's only for the two of you, okay?"

They nodded, their ears fully erect.

"Last night when Claws thought I was asleep, I caught a conversation between her and her familiar. As with Barry, I can't tell you everything yet, but I can tell you *most* of it. I'm not happy about leaving you two in the dark, but—"

Before I could finish the sentence, they were on me, Borks licking my arm and Cinnamon patting my knee with a paw. They didn't care that I planned to keep secrets. Unlike Barry, they trusted me implicitly. I dropped down and pulled them against me. "You two are the best, you know that?"

They agreed, squirming in my arms to rub as much of their bodies against me as possible.

"Cinnamon the Bunny and Brigadier Borks." I stood tall and adopted a serious air. "I have a mission of the utmost importance for you, one that will see you going deep, *deep* undercover—and by that, I mean you'll just have to keep some secrets to yourself, and possibly battle an elemental."

Battle? Cinnamon asked. *With Claws?*

I shook my head. "Not her, no. I have reason to believe there's another of her kind on its way toward Tropica. If I'm correct, I'll require help from both of you." I looked at Borks. "And I'll need an extra hand from you, mate. I won't force you, but what I have in mind will require honesty and . . . sacrifice."

I'd kept the wording vague, not wanting to force his paw, but I'd worried for no reason. With a loud bark and repeated wags of his tail, a small portal cracked into being. Other than its size, there was nothing to differentiate it from the one we'd used to enter his space.

He cocked his head, asking me how I'd known.

"Our bond. I'm sorry. I felt your breakthrough when we were on our material-gathering mission, despite the fact you were inside your dimensional space when it happened."

His ears went all the way back, face tight and eyes filled with guilt.

"You have nothing to be sorry for, and you have no need to explain yourself." I reached down to scratch the spot behind his ear that made his leg kick, but the thump that came from beside us was too loud and early to be his reaction to my scritching.

We both spun, and Cinnamon punched one curled forepaw into the other again. Her expression hinted at impending violence, and her soft squeak confirmed it. *If someone doesn't explain what the frack is going on . . .*

"Borks unlocked another ability!" I said in a rush. "He was trying to keep it a secret, but I found out by accident!"

She looked at the portal, then back at me, not understanding.

"Look inside."

She hopped over, poked her head in, then her whole body stiffened. Borks and I joined her, both our noggins squeezing through the small opening.

"Wow. It's bigger than I thought, Borks."

It was a second dimensional space, completely separate from the one our bodies were in. I'd thought it would only be large enough to fit a few things. Instead, I looked around an area as large as my room, its floor and walls empty of anything.

Wowww, Cinnamon said with a quiet and impressed squeak. *I thought it would just be a different exit . . .*

His tail was currently in a different time and location than my head, but that didn't stop it from whacking the crap out of me with how hard it wagged.

I withdrew my head, and the others followed. "Would you leave it open? I need to stuff some things in there . . ."

I produced the two packages I'd brought with me when reentering Borks's original space. My animal pals both recognized the tightly wound burlap sack, but the other was new to them. Their heads tilted in confusion as they gazed over its metallic form.

"It's all a part of the mission . . ." Both the items were wrapped in tendrils of my chi, the layers containing their scent and power. With great care, I opened a slit in the metal one's shielding, letting some of its essence out.

Borks dashed forward. He pressed his nose against it and started huffing loudly—its aroma was clearly to his liking.

I laughed and scratched his head. "It's not for eating—not yet, anyway." I repaired the seal, placed both parcels within Borks's new space, then nodded for him to close the portal. "Okay. Let me explain . . ."

They both sat down, their ears attentive and eyes locked onto mine as I laid out the mission, along with dozens and dozens of plan variations.

CHAPTER SIXTY

Foreign Fishy Force

Still grinning, I glanced up, eyeing the shifting ceiling of rock and earthen chi that would land on our heads at any moment. We were entirely encased. All light had vanished. Yet, thanks to two *very* different things, I bore witness to the landslide's descent.

First, my enhanced body. In normal situations, that alone was enough for me to see in pitch darkness. But the circumstance I found myself in was anything but normal; the walls were closed in on all sides, and the ancient essence within sought to smother my own.

Which was where the second source of illumination came in. Soft light bathed everything around us, its purple color adding an ethereal, otherworldly hue to all it touched. I gazed down at the ability providing the glow—just in time for Cinnamon to come flying out of it.

The moment she cleared Borks's portal, she flicked her head and flung something beige my way.

I caught the sack, and the items inside shifted, making a pleasing sound even through my layers of protective chi.

Sorry about this, Bonnie, I thought, not having the time to communicate it. *In a perfect world, I could have warned you.*

Then, after pausing for a tiny yet necessary fraction of a second, I launched the sack skyward with everything I had. The reason for my momentary delay was unleashed a moment later in the form of an aura blast flying from a very-cute and very-deadly bunny's kick. The world distorted around the pillar of force as it rocketed toward the burlap payload, and when it was mere centimeters from collision, I released the tendrils of chi sealing it shut.

The effect was immediate. My mouth watered. My body *demanded* that I leap to its rescue. Bonnie actually took a step forward, her desire to consume outweighing her confusion.

Before either of us could do something stupid, however, Cinnamon's attack hit dead center.

Several things happened at once. The bunny, her job done, vanished back into Borks's portal. The sack exploded, as did its contents, each of them atomized into a fine powder. And the elemental, apparently an ancient being, was presented with a choice.

Its will was alien to me, its thoughts a mystery, but as that foreign consciousness assessed the particles and the chi radiating from them, I knew *exactly* what it was thinking. It *wanted* them. It desired to *consume* them. The question, then, was whether it was smart enough to resist.

As the cloud of brown dust billowed outward, the strange being revealed its wisdom, slowing its descent in an attempt to avoid the tempting yet poisonous motes. But it was working against gravity now, and Cinnamon's aura blast continued on, smashing some of the noxious molecules into its form.

With that, a moment of truth arrived. I honestly had no clue if this would work or not. Despite this course of action being called "plan B," it wasn't even in my top-ten list of scenarios likely to succeed. It was a contingency plan. A desperate venture to save Bob the boat from destruction, who was the only friend, sapient or not, that I lacked the essence to teleport to safety.

As the earth elemental's chi started to vibrate, I knew it had worked.

Every wall jittered, its entire mass shaking like a mid-nineties Toyota Hilux speeding down a corrugated road on stock suspension. Even through the drug now afflicting it, the elemental attempted to retreat, slowly pulling back from the cloud.

Borks had different ideas.

He spewed flames from his mouth as he spun in a circle, ensuring his blaze reached every inch of air directly above our heads. Where his fire washed over surrounding barriers, nothing happened; the earthen clumps were immune to it.

But that wasn't why he'd done it. Lines of heat shimmered, pushing the brown powder up toward the enemy. It pulled—

No, not "it," I realized in a moment of clarity. *They.*

Under the effects of the toxin, the being around us let their true form slip. They weren't a single soul at all—they were *dozens* of individuals. A hive mind of sorts. Before the surprise of that discovery could take root and unfurl in my mind, I dismissed it, focusing on what was happening above.

The many souls revealed their intelligence again by opening a chimney in the ceiling. Heat—and the dread molecules they were trying desperately to avoid—rushed toward the vent.

I grinned like a cat given a whole damned fish. *Nice try*, I thought, preparing to release an uppercut that would make Cinnamon prou—*Oh, speak of the devil.*

She emerged from Borks's portal just in time for me to unleash the strike. As my fist ascended through empty air, I released a blast of pure chi. It moved at the speed of light, forming a thin line out through the chimney and up into the sky. I didn't watch it for two reasons. First, I already knew what it would do. Second, and of much more importance, cool guys didn't look at explosions.

I raised a questioning brow toward Cinnamon—her eyes sparkled as she nodded, so stunned by my technique that she almost dropped the metallic object she'd retrieved. The beginning of a tear swelled up, but she blinked it away, not breaking her eye contact with me as she gave me a proud nod.

My uppercut had, indeed, been of impeccable form.

Meanwhile, my thin strand of essence expanded, pushing the poisonous fragments outward and toward earthen walls that had no hope of outpacing it. Only when I'd sealed off the chimney completely did my power stop growing, and though only a temporary measure, it was all that was needed.

I hadn't missed the secondary hole the elemental created. Showing a remarkable knowledge of heat and aerodynamics, they'd opened a tiny inlet for oxygen near the surface of the ocean, a place for air to stream in, fuel Borks's fire, and launch the poisonous particles skyward.

But unfortunately for the myriad earthen souls surrounding us, my blocking of the chimney only worsened their predicament. The toxic dust swirled around chaotically, all paths leading to the elemental. When they made contact, the ancient being was unable to stop their absorption and assimilation. As more of our obliterated payload leached into their awareness, the jittering became so strong that they could no longer retreat.

The pull of addictive essence coming from above diminished with each bit the elemental incorporated. A tension I'd not realized was there eased, disappearing from my shoulders and upper back.

The effect on Bonnie was even more pronounced. She shook her head and let out a heavy sigh as she returned to herself. Then, she whirled on me, eyes narrowed and expression pinched in accusation. "Why the hell am I here, Fischer? And if *that* was plan B, what the *frack* was plan A?"

I opened my mouth to reply, but she rolled right over me. "Also, what kind of demon beans were those? Why would you make such a thing?"

I smiled, looking away from the continually quivering mass to meet her gaze. "Those, my adventurous friend, were an unholy creation I made by mistake. The System called them coffee-infused coffee beans." I gestured around at the quaking walls. "The caffeine content was a bit too high for human consumption—elemental, too, by the looks of it."

"Wonderful. I'm not at all surprised you created something so toxic by accident, but that doesn't answer my first two questions."

"Oh? What were they, again? In order of least importance."

She gave me an impressive pout. "I asked why it was called plan B, but knowing you, that stands for Plan Bean, doesn't it?"

"Don't be ridiculous. It stands for Plan Bean-Infused-Beans."

Duhhh, Cinnamon peeped.

I'd not thought it possible, but Bonnie's pout grew even more severe. "Of course. That's on me for underestimating you. And, for my last question . . ." She cleared her throat, took a deep breath, and yelled, "*Why the* frack *am I here, Fischer?* You three clearly have plans, and I'm not a part of them!"

I held up a finger, but unlike my previous statements, this wasn't a method of distraction. Something was . . . *changing.* Without warning, the tons of rock started to move again, within itself rather than away from or toward us.

I couldn't say for sure what was going on, but when I felt the caffeine molecules getting shifted around—a movement I could sense because of how much I consumed on a daily basis—I developed a hunch.

And they said my coffee addiction was a bad thing, I thought, smiling to myself. *Who's laughing now?*

"Plan F!" I yelled. This variation was even further from the top-ten list of workable plans, but that didn't make me any less excited to see it come to fruition.

A metallic pouch came sailing my way, launched by a supremely fluffy bunny who'd anticipated my need. I caught it with one hand. Instead of yeeting the parcel upward with all my strength, I lobbed it softly, removing my tendrils of sealing chi at the same time.

"Cinn—" I started, but was cut off when a streak of martial prowess and caramel-colored fur shot past me.

As Cinnamon's flying kick annihilated the package right above my head, my enhanced vision allowed me to witness a marvelous sight.

She stopped in midair. An odd aura warped the air around her, and all the strips previously contained by sheets of thin metal were drawn toward her by the force. Then, my fuzzy bunny started to *twirl*.

Surprise radiated from Bonnie's core; she recognized the chi. Like a mini tornado of cute violence, Cinnamon spun on the spot, her limbs lashing out and breaking already-lean strips into even smaller chunks.

Now that only a few motes of atomized caffeine remained, I withdrew my solid pillar of pure essence, opening the chimney once more. The surrounding air started to circulate. Only when the trapped winds became cyclonic did the martial bunny stop spinning and let go of her magnetic aura.

The dehydrated food she'd been smashing exploded outward, joining the storm. As with the coffee dust, when they struck the ancient being's mass, they were absorbed. Unlike the poisonous cloud, however, the tiny fragments of meat were anything but assimilated.

I cackled as Borks snatched a few nibbles as they passed him by, my canine pal unable to help himself from indulging in the chi-filled treats.

"Fish-jerky storm!" I yelled like a protagonist declaring their finishing move, then leaned to the side, whispering, "Psst. Bonnie. Plan F is short for Plan *Four* F's, which stands for—"

"Fracking Fishy Fish jerky?" she interrupted.

"What? Don't be silly. That's only three F's." I held up four fingers. "It stands for Foray of the Foreign Fishy Force."

"... *What?*"

I nodded toward the surrounding walls as Cinnamon's tornado of jerky hit them. "Unfortunately for our earthen attacker, the jerky is saturated with the entirely *wrong* kind of essence. Get it? *Foreign fishy force!*"

This had been something I'd gleaned from a conversation between Claws and her raccoon student—a bit of trivia my tricksy otter hadn't meant to share. Some aspects were closely aligned. Rock and earth, for example, were basically the same thing. But *lightning*? It did *not* get along with either of them.

The elemental was already at war with the caffeine poisoning it. And if my hunch was correct, it'd been trying to isolate one of its many souls, which it could then flood every drop of toxin into. Adding electricity to the mix had introduced a third army to the battlefield, a phalanx of spearmen that slammed right into the ancient being's side.

The effects in the physical world were impressive. Flecks of dehydrated meat hit the earthen walls like invisible punches from a giant, leaving craters behind in the now-pockmarked dome.

It was as effective as I could have hoped, and as the winds started to die down, I took a deep breath of the fish and coffee scents lingering in the air, both as enticing as the other.

"Ahhh," I sighed. "What a beautiful sme—"

"Fischer!" Bonnie yelled, her face awestruck, perplexed, and distinctly lacking the mirth my animal pals and I wore. "I'm all for adventure, but this is *fracked*! Can someone *please* explain how in Hades's burning crotch we're going to get out of this, why you're messing around here instead of helping Maria, and why the shit I'm standing here like an ornament instead of getting teleported . . . away?"

She trailed off, glancing down toward her arm. Power swelled beneath her skin, giving off a soft blue glow. In moments, it grew bright enough for a shape to be revealed: a paw print, smaller than Borks's but larger than Cinnamon's.

"Forgive me," I said, flashing an apologetic smile. "I couldn't say so earlier, but there's the answer to two of your questions. The other, though? Why I haven't gone to Maria?" The blue brilliance coming from Bonnie's arm increased, illuminating a grin I could no longer hide. "She called my name, but that was only to get my attention. She didn't need *my* help. I was merely the delivery sys—"

I could have continued speaking if I wanted to; my voice hadn't been drowned out, and my thoughts were clear. I didn't, however—I wanted to give all my focus to the being that shot from Bonnie's limb.

A translucent mammal, semi-opaque and filled with deadly power. A mouth lined by needle-sharp teeth, all of which were gleaming between parted lips. And caressed in both forepaws, a second being smiled and waved, his inclinations similar to his holder in both bearing and degeneracy.

A shrill, chittering noise came from his master as she cast a judgmental gaze across the entire world. In her position, most would have apologized for being late, perhaps inquired about everyone's health to check we were okay.

This creature, however, was unlike any other. My friend. My ally. Corporal Claws, wielder of lightning, chaos, and a raccoon, simply chirped.

You're welcome, she said.

Her essence erupted.

CHAPTER SIXTY-ONE

Full Caveman

Within the confines of a chi-laced building, a brilliant light flashed into being, drowning out the kaleidoscopic rays of only moments ago. Maria barely noticed. "Sit," she said. "We're short on time."

"What—"

"Sit down, cousin!" Keith urged. "They need your help!"

Trent's eyes darted around, scanning until they landed on his mother and sister. He didn't need to sense their cores to know that something had gone terribly, *terribly* wrong. White-hot rage flared in his core, coalescing as flames that sputtered from his palms.

"Down!" Maria felt her command hit Trent's awareness like a meteor. His internal state quaked with aftershocks as he dropped to the ground in a cross-legged position. "We can make use of your fury," she continued, voice soft, filled with all the compassion it had lacked only seconds earlier. "Don't waste any emotion on me."

Shaking, he closed his eyes. Maria became intangible once more. When she rejoined Slimes's awareness in the cloud of pink chi surrounding the two corrupted cultivators, he welcomed her with a happy burble. It was a small gesture. His way of cheering her up. And though it didn't work, she thanked him all the same.

You rest for now, she urged. *While you still can.*

He burbled again, readily obliging—his strength would be needed later.

Reaching out a hand, Maria attempted to pull a part of Trent out into the swirling chi. It should be possible because of his breakthrough, but that didn't mean it would be easy. His concept of himself—the ideal that shaped who he was and what he'd become—immediately complained. His core seemed to deny her efforts, telling her it was wrong despite how much he wanted to help.

But then she gave it a nudge. A push, really. Okay, fine, maybe it was actually a full-bodied tackle, in which she drove one of her knees into his metaphorical spleen. A girl had to do what a girl had to do. With all the will not currently suppressing the corruption's growth, Maria slammed into Trent's core again, reminding him of past events he'd prefer to forget.

His deformity, both physical and mental, by an alchemical concoction. His family's arrival in Tropica. The battle. His father's madness—the foolish monarch's eager embrace of corruption at the expense of all else.

His mother and sister. The former, beset with relief and guilt at seeing her son alive. The latter, similarly moved, able and willing to let go of the foul essence that had been infecting—

Flames consumed the mental image she was projecting, the thoughts burning away as Trent was drawn into the cloud of healing chi. Lines of orange streaked through the pink haze.

You know nothing! his disembodied voice screamed, a wild blaze fueled by howling winds.

Flashes of his own memories appeared in a rapid-fire procession that were incinerated just as fast as they arrived. His mother, her willing participation in poisoning her own son. His sister, the scorn with which she treated him, the many times she abused his affliction to her own benefit. Each instance threw a tree's worth of logs onto the burn pile, and though they didn't burst into flame, the heat slowly increased as their moisture evaporated, edges catching fire.

Maria controlled the flow of air, her soothing chi ensuring his fury didn't devour them all. She nudged him back toward the positive—a mistake. He railed against her denial. She tried again, easing him toward pragmatism instead. This time, her touch was subtle, making sure he knew she wasn't trying to snuff out his flames.

It was not hard; she didn't want to extinguish his anger; she wanted to harness it. Maria replayed some memories she'd just witnessed, her memory able to recall them despite the former prince showing her dozens per second.

He and his sister, peeking overtop a parapet as a bucket of stolen milk tumbled down toward the guard whose eyes always lingered too long. Tryphena again, this time a woman, laughing and joking with Trent about a royal who had fallen down a single step, twisted his ankle, and tried to blame one of the palace guards—only for the accusation to be denounced by the siblings in a public and embarrassing manner.

The memories of the queen were much easier to curate; they were many. Tens, hundreds, then thousands of them flashed by, all depicting the same look: an expression of a mother's pure love. Even with the unpleasant looks and mental impairment afflicting him, she had never once treated him as anything but her only son.

And, Maria reminded, *loath as the concoction was, Penelope—your mother—believed it was the only way to save you.*

As she gave him that final push, she knew it would work. His fire and fury sputtered, having consumed enough to be dismissed. But Maria couldn't allow that. Using all of her spare attention, she opened up vents and let air in, the oxygen of multiple bellows flowing directly into the pile of logs and smoldering coals that Trent's core had become.

Wha-what are you doing? His formless voice was confused. Demanding. When Maria didn't immediately respond, a spike of paranoid terror tore from him, wedging itself between them.

All too late, Trent realized the truth. Maria must have been infected by the corruption, and she was trying to burn them all down—he could think of no other explanation. She'd successfully goaded him into joining her, fanning his flames in all the right ways.

Yet part of him remained in his body. He sought to escape, hammered all of his will in that direction. He had to get Fischer—the traveler was the only one who could stop Maria and save his family. But a pulse of chi from his captor knocked him on his ass. Before he could stand, it smothered him, pinning his limbs to the ground with immovable weight.

From there, the burden moved to his chest, revealing an emotion Trent had never expected to receive from Maria. It . . . it was *love.* Not the romantic kind, but that of a younger sister. The love of a daughter, a mother, a community. The kind of adoration that let a parent lift a horse cart off their child. The kind of devotion that moved someone to run back into a burning stable, risking themselves for the chance to save a lame mule.

He'd been wrong. Maria hadn't been infected.

Why . . . ? was all he could wonder, her actions antithetical to her message.

She didn't answer, instead lifting the chi that had held him down. It poured into his bonfire, joining the jets of air that turned the edges of wet logs into red-hot coals. When the two forces of nature met, everything changed.

The lines of fire in her pink haze spread out, the entire cloud taking on an orange hue. Similarly, his flames grew red with healing essence, each of their aspects feeding the other. It was deliberate at first, meticulously shaped by Maria's will, but then they harmonized. Rather than two separate forces, their power became one, his flame exuding her compassion, her mist radiating his heat.

With Maria's awareness freed, she let out a ragged yet content sigh through their newly forged connection.

Your family doesn't need Fischer, Trent. I called his name, but that was only so he'd bring you back.

The words stoked something deep within him, jostling still-green logs toward the blazing heart of his core.

They don't need more cleansing, she continued, her voice speaking directly to his soul. *We already tried that, and it left an empty void in its place—a patch of nothing in which the corruption took hold once more.*

The logs were thrust straight into the center of the inferno. Even in that white-hot nexus, however, they resisted, their fibers too wet.

What your family needs, Trent, is a reason to persist.

The logs creaked as if squeezed by a vise.

Something to live *for.*

The wood cracked, threatened to burst apart.

What your family needs . . . Maria's voice was calm and strong and sure. *Is* you.

Every single piece of timber within his burning soul split into countless pieces. Each drop of liquid evaporated, the flames took hold, and the bonfire became a conflagration.

The world roared with their power.

* * *

"Holy shit," I said, the words speaking themselves as my head darted toward the west. An amalgamation of Maria and Trent was pouring from my not-a-prison, the two wasting no time in healing the captives.

It was remarkable on a whole bunch of levels. First, I'd never sensed such a pairing between anyone but Maria and myself. A lesser fella might have experienced some jealousy . . . Okay, fine, I was a *little* jealous—but a healthy amount, I reckon. Second, their wills had taken on aspects of each other, only adopting the pieces that amplified their own powers. No, Maria and I had never done something like that, and no, I *still* didn't have an unhealthy amount of jealousy over it, thank you very much.

I considered reaching out through our connection and giving my fiancée the mental equivalent of a *yo, what's up?* But knowing it might hurt their plans—and also that the impulse was just the primitive part of my brain wanting to go full caveman over my darling Maria helping another bloke heal his family—I instead focused on the third and final reason it was remarkable.

I shouldn't have been able to feel their chi at all; there was a season-finale anime battle occurring before my very eyes.

Claws's unnamed raccoon zipped around the inside of the earth elemental's dome of rock and sediment like a cracked-out Sonic the Hedgehog, releasing bolts of lightning every meter or so. A high-pitched sound came from him, and I wasn't entirely sure if it was his voice or his speed doing it. Regardless, the *eeeeeEEEEeeeeeEEEEeeeeeEEEE* of his looping passage was both enjoyable and humorous.

"Do you want me to teleport you now?" I asked Bonnie. "I needed you here as an anchor for Claws."

"What? Just when it's getting good?"

I snorted. She'd sure changed her tune, but I couldn't exactly blame her. "Why can't I look away?"

Bruff, Borks agreed, both he and the bunny astride him tracking the raccoon's relentless gyration.

Said mammal's master, Claws, hadn't really been doing all that much. She'd unleashed an absolute storm of electrical essence after shooting from Bonnie's arm, but since then had just been standing on the deck with her forelimbs raised high, looking like she was gathering the energy for a Spirit Bomb.

Nothing was forming, however. I wouldn't put it past her to mess with me, and I started wondering if that was the case, but then the hair on my arms stood on end. I gazed up through the chimney, and rather than the expected predawn light, I found churning storm clouds.

Well, shit, I thought. *Looks like she developed a new—*

Boooom!

I both saw the strike with my eyes and felt it in my chest. It was natural lightning, but that's where normalcy ended; the sky webbed with so many blue-white forks that the nearby villages might think Zeus had returned. I wouldn't be surprised if it spawned a religion or two.

The effect it had on the earth elemental was similarly impressive. Claws had been the intended target of each strike, and they'd exploded through the surrounding walls to get to her, leaving dozens of Rocky-sized holes through which I could now see the outside world.

The black atmosphere above had almost immediately vanished. From west to east, the purple sky became an orangey yellow, foretelling the sun's arrival. This light, cast over Bob's deck, revealed smatterings of rock, soggy silt, and other debris separated from the ancient being's body by myriad thunderbolts.

I kneeled to inspect one, making sure this wasn't part of some trap, but no. Not a drop of chi remained within—the damage was permanent.

Psssst, came a stray thought, communicated to me in a very ottery whisper. *Watch this.* A chirping noise accompanied the invitation, sounding like the call of a thousand birds.

I couldn't resist looking. A ball of electrical energy surrounded one of Claws's forepaws. It wasn't her chi—it was condensed, naturally occurring lightning. Her head bent over backward to look my way, and when her gaze locked with mine, she waggled her eyebrows.

"By the gods . . ." I whispered, catching myself just before I fell to my knees.

"What is it?" Bonnie asked.

I ignored her, instead narrowing my eyes at Claws. "How do you know what a Chidori is? Have you been rummaging around in my head?"

Claws's lips parted to reveal daggerlike teeth. Blue jolts danced across them. Not bothering to straighten, she launched herself upward on streams of lightning, doing ten backflips—or was that eleven?—before twisting and preparing to unleash Kakashi's signature move.

Eleven! she trilled as her paw lashed out. *And a half*!

"Huh . . ." I said, watching her electricity-covered limb blow a hole the size of a car into the earth elemental. "There *was* a half rotation, wasn't there?"

Yuuuup! she agreed, her brilliant grin mirroring my own.

CHAPTER SIXTY-TWO

Chaos, Master

Beneath the pastel hues of a coming dawn, a swathe of colors the ancient being had not witnessed for thousands of years, the earth elemental considered to themselves that maybe, just maybe, they should not have come here.

The self-doubt lasted only a fraction of a second, yet it was enough to set their rocks to crumbling. Their indignation bloomed, but then another hundred thoughts came along to replace it. And another hundred. And *another.*

Though it had been an unfathomable amount of time since they'd been directly exposed to a sunrise, it had been even longer since they'd fallen victim to alchemical warfare.

Such things just weren't oft done. Even atop the continent the first brother had obliterated back before he was the many, which had been a landmass guilty of a betrayal most foul, entire bloodlines would've been exterminated if a single cultivator had dared implement such poisons.

If one could call that powder a toxin, that is. It was . . . pitiful. Woefully weak. It hardly had any effect on their mass, just making it shake a little. There was no chi deterioration, form-melting acids, or summoned hellhounds—not that any remained now that Hades had fled.

This thought brought them some joy, but as with all the others, it was swiftly replaced by a slew of new ideas—which was the whole crux of the issue.

This compound, the brown seeds that had been turned into a fine powder, affected the elemental's *mind.* How had this pure-chi cultivator created something so advanced? It was just one more stone in the mountainous pile of impossibilities. The lightning-infused fish, an *extremely* high-level food item, was another. This man shouldn't have been able to catch it, let alone cook it without ruining the chi content.

None of these mysteries, however, compared to the sociological learnings, which just so happened to loop back around into their mind for what had to be the four hundredth time.

The foolish channeler of unaspected essence *was* allied with the newly awakened elemental, but that wasn't all. There were two allied spirit beasts atop the deck—and likely others if the wash of chi to the east could be believed.

It all beggared belief, yet there was one more discovery, something as unbelievable as it was bothersome. The newly awakened elemental had bonded a familiar, and not the half-hearted bonding of subservience. This was a *full* bond. A sharing of one's soul—of one's *core.* How had a days-old being achieved such a feat?

Even now, the thing that shouldn't exist was zipping around the inside of their dome in a continual loop, making a high-pitched noise and unleashing jolts of chi that destroyed the elemental essence suffusing their mass.

And we cannot fight back . . .

As this thought returned, they latched on to it, fighting against the poison—this was what most needed pondering.

The mistake they'd made in coming here, the terrible miscalculation that left them in their current predicament, had been bringing the ten ancient relics of power with them. They could only use a fraction of their strength against the ants atop the ship, because most of it was protecting the crystallized trees, ensuring they remained undetected.

It was, perhaps, an overly conservative precaution. But after the pure-chi cultivator had teleported the entire *boat,* along with everyone atop it, *and* the artifact within? Wariness seemed prudent.

They were certain he no longer possessed the power to destroy them, at least. How could he? He'd already expended too much energy. As long as they didn't let him steal the artifacts, things would go well.

The elemental of lightning was similarly toothless. She was incredibly swift, even quicker than her familiar, but her attacks were akin to an oceanic bird pecking a boulder; each strike was frustrating, yet wholly ineffective.

So, the decision they had reached last time this thought circled around still seemed like the correct course of action. Lull these attackers into a false sense of security, let them continue chipping away at miniscule fractions of their power, and wait for the poison to clear.

Then they would pounce, devouring the ship, the relic, and everyone stupid enough to remain atop it.

By luck or divine intervention, the next thought came, pushing these considerations aside. It, however, was a memory of something only minutes gone. That foolish human, the cultivator of unaspected chi . . . he *had* used his power again. The earth elemental had been distracted, busy retreating from the poison cloud that assaulted their mind and mass.

But as it replayed through their consciousness now, every single splinter that comprised them spoke out, the revelation so shocking that it threatened to tear them apart.

The cultivator . . . he *did* possess more chi. If he utilized it in the wrong way, everyone present—perhaps most of this continent—would be reduced to atoms. And the elemental was just . . . sitting here, letting him refill his reserves. The alchemical concoction was even more terrifying and effective than they'd feared.

A new course of action was decided in an instant, their concurrence pulling each splinter back together, solidifying their unity and resolve. This wasn't the time for feigned weakness; it was time for brutal movement and crushing force.

Before the next landslide of thoughts assaulted them, they cast a mass of somethings from their core. Ten treasures of indescribable wealth, each an impossibility that shouldn't exist in this lower realm, fell to the sand like so many shells.

Though I still enjoyed witnessing the battle, a small part of me wished Claws and her raccoon would hurry it up. The lulls were a little boring. Thankfully, a moment of action approached, and I watched with an anticipatory gaze as my otter pal clenched her raised forelimbs, preparing to call lightning down from the heavens.

But then the underworld opened up instead.

Directly beneath us, extending deep into the formerly shallow sands, another ancient being arrived. Before the spike of adrenaline could course through my body, I wrapped layers upon layers upon layers of solid light underneath Bob's keel. Every other time I'd created such shielding, each barrier got a little thinner and weaker, allowing for a smooth reduction of force.

Now, I didn't have that luxury.

A thousand shields sprang into place, and not a moment too soon. The surprise attack hit us with the impetus of a dozen supervolcanoes, obliterating the vast majority of layers in the blink of a cultivator's eye. Everyone grew tense, Cinnamon and Borks bracing and the raccoon retreating into Claws's core as a streak of light.

The surrounding sheets of earth—previously pocked and riddled with holes—became reinforced by meters of gravel and jagged rock. The walls and ceiling descended, literally closing in on us. Time slowed.

Should I raise more shields above us? I had the strength to stop it, but what if that left me unconscious?

With no small amount of regret, I reached a decision I *hated*, and no matter how many times I told myself I would happily sacrifice Bob, now that the moment had arrived, I felt sick. There were other options, right? This thing was *horrifically* strong, but even after transporting a whole-ass boat, I reckoned I could defeat it.

And protect everyone at the same time? a voice in the back of my head asked, already knowing I wouldn't take the chance.

Memories tried to bubble up, my subconscious wanting to reminisce on our inaugural trip with Bob, but I couldn't spare the milliseconds.

Sorry, mate, I thought, extending the tiniest root of chi down toward his deck. *A better captain would go down with you, but I have people relying on me—loved ones I* cannot *let down.*

My stomach churned, and a boulder of regret settled in the center of my abdomen. Choices like this, however, were exactly what I'd signed up for. Such was the weight of leadership.

We might build another boat, Bob, but we'll never replace you. You're one of a kind, you golden-throned bastard.

My animal pals were preparing to move; Borks reached for a portal that wouldn't open in time, Cinnamon prepared to unleash a blast of aura that couldn't breach meters of chi-infused rock, and Claws gathered lightning in her legs.

The otter might actually stand a chance. Perhaps she could blast a hole out, which we could then escape through . . . but no. She'd waited too long, clearly too shocked or terrified to react swiftly.

It all came back to a single, inescapable truth: I wasn't willing to risk any of them. They were far too precious—even more so than the relics within Bob's hull, or the ten items of similar power directly beneath us, the things this elemental had apparently been hiding along with its true strength.

Before the walls could get any closer, I reached out with my essence, each strand traveling faster than light as they wove around everyone. With a hint of a smirk, I grabbed the swordfish head, too, and also considered taking the ten other relics discarded below. But there was no need; I'd be back to kick this evil thing's tushy in a moment.

Instead, I collected the most important objects of all: the fishing rods, and a certain ornate throne—a part of Bob that would join us on every adventure to come, even if the rest of him was about to become a ball of shattered wood and twisted metal.

I pictured where we'd exit, ensuring it was a safe space to—

Something jolted me back to the present. Claws's elemental lightning had destroyed the strands near her, and not just those connected to her—Borks and Cinnamon had been disconnected, too.

I whirled on her. She'd done all sorts of things to draw my ire, but never before had she made genuine anger well up from within me. It roiled and frothed like an ocean in storm, giant waves rising only to crash down and further stoke my wrath.

I had to let it go. She could stay if she wanted, but I was getting the others out, and *now*.

Corporal Claws, wielder of lightning and picker of terrible times to fuck with me, opened her left pocket. The air . . . changed. A strange essence flooded the enclosed space, its power intriguing and mysterious. I felt like I should recognize it, but I gave it no thought. She could do what she wanted. We still had to go. The others wouldn't . . . *Huh?*

Every inch of the earth elemental's mass had frozen. They assessed the strange chi. Tested it. Tasted it. And *hated* what they found. Unending pulses of abhorrence emitted in all directions.

Hey . . . Claws hissed, slowly turning to look at Borks, Cinnamon, and me. When her gaze met mine, electricity and mischief lit her eyes. *Check this shit out.*

Her other paw plunged into the open pocket, clutched something, and withdrew . . . a coconut?

Was this finally it? Had she revealed the item she'd been secretly experimenting on? I'd overheard multiple overnight conversations between master and familiar, but I hadn't been able to learn the purpose of her test—she would have known if I forced myself in.

No longer caring for subtlety, I forged a spear of pure chi and stabbed it toward the coconut, stopping only microns from the object to find . . . nothing. It was a regular ol' coconut.

Claws cackled.

"Hey!" I yelled, unable to help myself now that I knew it was just fruit. "Where'd you get that? We can cook with it!"

Her laugh cut off. She frowned, threw the nut aside, and grabbed another item. A bag of flour, dropped to the deck. A frying pan larger than she was, flung over her shoulder. Two jars of passiona jam, one passed to Cinnamon, the other moved to the pouch on the other side of her body. The same jar again, returned to the original pouch, which she then rummaged around within, searching for something in particular.

Borks, taking advantage of whatever this was, resumed opening a portal. A purple line cracked into being, and the earth elemental responded. Its walls shuddered and shook. They inched closer, the ancient being's detestation joined by a primordial violence.

As a blur, Claws lashed out with both forelimbs. The left one shot her familiar out, the raccoon zooming about the deck to collect the discarded treasures—he even yoinked the passiona jam from Cinnamon's clutches. Her right paw, still searching her pocket, found what she was looking for. When she withdrew it, the strange aura around us increased tenfold, radiating from a small featureless rock. A pebble, really.

All movement ceased—except for her familiar, who hastily shoved the items back into his master's private stash before leaping in, momentarily getting his rotund rump stuck, then wiggling in the rest of the way.

Though not a speck of dirt shifted, the earth elemental's emotions poured out from it. Any semblance of composure had fled its many-souled body, and I got more insight than I cared to receive. This thing . . . Gods above, it was *evil.* Like . . . *evil,* evil. It wanted to consume all others, killing any other awakened life-form that wouldn't willingly assimilate.

To be frank, it was disgusting. Uncaring of my assessment, or perhaps because of it, every single bit of its mass shuddered a foot closer. It wished to feel our bones crack, sought to hear our screams of pain, and yet . . . it stilled once more, an obvious undertone of terror holding it at bay.

"Uhhhh," I said, pointing at the small stone in Claws's hands. "What's that, and why is the unholy prick surrounding us so scared of it?"

She exhaled a hot breath against the pebble, rubbed it against her chest, then held it up to her eye, inspecting its shine. With a nod to herself, she finally answered with a soft coo.

This is chaos, Master. The end of all.

In stark contrast to the calmness of her voice, her forelimb shot forward like a rocket, too fast for even me to track. She let go of her prize, and when it struck the earthen wall above, I had to admit she'd been at least partially correct.

Chaos was the only word to describe it.

CHAPTER SIXTY-THREE

Witness

Maria's entire world was ablaze. Flames washed over her incorporeal skin in streams, but rather than burn, they *warmed*. From the strands of essence in her veins to the clouds of pink and orange chi surrounding them, all were bathed in a summery heat.

Trent was having a similar yet entirely different reaction to her power. Where his fire was a physical sensation, her compassion impacted his mental-scape the most, redirecting his wild and directionless anger.

In this, they were one. Their paths had converged, and though they would only stride along the same cobbled road for a short time, neither of them was going to waste the opportunity. They collided with Tryphena and Penelope as a conjoined conflagration that could burn out the rot, sear the wounds, and heal any remnant damage.

The princess screeched the moment their essence touched her own. The corruption had barely progressed since Maria had last seen it, yet even the little ground it'd gained was too much.

Trent's bonfire roared—she soothed it, reminding him to remain on target.

He didn't need to speak his gratitude; she felt it as if it was her own. Together, their combined will and chi focused on the two patients. Both mother and daughter were undoubtedly infected, yet one was worse than the other—Tryphena.

They bore down on her with the strength and determination of oxen, their skulls digging through layers and layers of concealment like it was loose sand, their great horns of pink and orange setting decayed roots aflame.

But despite the apparent rot, this foothold of corruption didn't lack in vitality. Before its sickly lines could be destroyed, the power would move, branching off to create new growth.

It exerted its influence on Tryphena's mind, too. The entire time they tried to heal her—tried to *save* her—she lashed out with malice, focusing on scenes clearly intended to undermine her brother's resolve. They were things he couldn't possibly have known. Conversations he hadn't been present for. And, unfortunately, each vision was true.

Countless exchanges with palace staff—tutors, cooks, and dignitaries. In the oldest recountings, they would merely nod at Tryphena's disparaging comments. Over time, however, they smiled and laughed along with her insults. In the latter years, they instigated the gossip, knowing the princess would neither chastise nor punish them for speaking ill of the crown prince.

These set Trent's jaw to clenching. They reminded him of all that'd happened while influenced by the Cult of the Alchemist's concoction. Maria was just about to remind him to remain focused, but he let out a scorching sigh, joining in with the remembered smiles.

They weren't wrong. He *had* been a colossal prick. His very existence had made their already-hard lives even harder. How could he hold their cathartic venting against them?

Rather than upset her brother, the former princess only pissed herself off. She cursed and spat at his easy acceptance, her outrage enhancing the next visions she subjected them to.

The moment Maria saw the people involved, she prepared to reach for her chi.

"I just do not understand why he's like this," Penelope Gormona said only seconds after a server left the throne room. Rather than the rest of the conversation, it skipped to the next, following the same formula. All were single-sentence insults spoken by his mother—the one whose affections had been the foundation of Trent's forgiveness.

"He makes it so terribly hard to love him sometimes . . ."

Another shift.

"How can one boy alienate everyone so thoroughly?"

Another.

"You know, Tryphena, it's not really your brother's fault that he harasses the serving girls so . . ." When the former queen turned her daughter's way, a smirk played on her lips. "After all, he didn't choose to be born with such a face . . ."

Maria, fearing this could cause Trent to falter, reached within for her chi. Even if it meant some of the corruption thrived momentarily, she had to step in before—

She froze as a force grasped her wrist, both gentle yet unmoving.

Trent. It wasn't a demand. It was a request. He encouraged her to trust him. Then, with a soft grin, he let his rage flow—it was neither destabilized nor wild. Just as Tryphena had propped her conviction up with wrath, he used his righteous indignation as fuel, a propellant blasted right into the center of their conflagration.

Incandescent tongues of flame raced along each branching root of corruption, incinerating them before their power could be redirected. Maria, stunned by his resolve, followed in their wake, applying the orange-and-pink cloud as a soothing balm to ensure nary a speck of rot remained.

From close by, another had noticed the toxic procession of memories, and as Penelope's awareness screamed out into her surroundings, it threatened to overwhelm all. No longer caught in the liminal space between nothingness and anguish, despair engulfed her, tearing from both her throat and core.

Just like her son earlier, the former queen's mind was a wildfire whipped into a tempest by winds of regret. She became a force of nature. She struck out indiscriminately, attempting to raze all to the ground, herself included.

Trent and Maria's conjoined chi flared in response, matching and trying to exceed her destructive intent. Perhaps they would have succeeded if it were their only task. But it wasn't, of course—their other patient wasted no time in taking advantage of the chaos.

Tryphena didn't fight against the corruption-tinged flames; she opened herself up to them, readily letting them scour her away. It all happened so fast. Maria and Trent weren't prepared, and as strands of rotten essence touched the places they'd repaired, fresh seeds of decay sprouted.

If Maria currently possessed a body, she would have wept from frustration. They'd just lost so much ground, and if nothing was done, they would lose even more.

Suddenly, a fifth being burbled and joined the fray. Maria felt a pang of guilt. She had been so absorbed by the task that she'd forgotten all about Slimes. He, however, wasn't bothered. He tried to reassure her with a weak jiggle, which only served to cause more worry—despite his rest, he was far from being back at full strength.

With each passing second, Penelope's firestorm grew stronger. Trent and Maria held it at bay, but with Slimes focused on stalling Tryphena's corruption, they could gain no ground. It was a stalemate.

Though Maria couldn't spare the attention needed to check, she felt the cell moving around them, its walls pushed outward by the forces clashing within the relatively small room.

For the first time since she'd bonded with Slimes, she truly started to doubt herself—started to consider that the two women before them might not be savable.

She and Trent could burn his mother and sister away at any moment. If they shifted their combined will, tweaked it even a little, the corrupt essence and its hosts would be scoured from existence. Ironically, this would grant Penelope her wish—she'd be reduced to nothing but ash.

Slimes, still nowhere near his strongest self, reached deep into his gelatinous and crystalline core. *Hold*, he seemed to urge, so robbed of strength that he could only think in emotions.

Maria's mind raced. She desperately wanted to be wrong. She needed to find a path that led to a full recovery for the afflicted women. Yet every time she searched, her efforts were thwarted by one woman seeking self-destruction and another demanding the annihilation of everything.

It was all too much. The very idea of a mother-turned-firestorm trying to scour her and her two children away made Maria's heart want to break. Maybe . . . maybe destroying them was a kindness. Perhaps Fischer had been correct all along, and that some people just weren't capable of being saved. Would it not be kinder for her to snuff out Penelope's flames before she could take one or both of her own offspring with her?

Maria took a step back, and an immutable force shoved her down until she landed in a room of stillness somewhere in the depths of her own psyche. All around her, the walls flashed with memories: Penelope's and Tryphena's and Trent's, their trio of perspectives showing thousands of visions from each of their points of view.

Trent and Tryphena playing as adolescents, having invented a game with sticks and a single stone. They played it every day for years, the span of time knowable by the passing of seasons and the growth of their adolescent bodies. Though the game's rules shifted by the hour, they would beg their minders to play it each afternoon.

Penelope had been there always. She could have left it to the many staff in charge of caring for the prince and princess, but even on the days she was dreadfully unwell, she would watch from a low window in the castle, ensuring the two she loved most could look up and see her smile.

There were countless other memories, too, but nothing struck Maria so hard as the stupid game. It had only ceased when Trent consumed the potion—which made Maria's mending heart break anew. How different would their lives have been if not for the interference of the king and his alchemists?

The visions discontinued, and when Maria looked up at the blank walls, tears streamed down her face. The injustice of it all was too great. Other awarenesses had been dragged down into the room with her, and she clenched her jaw as she studied them.

The patients remained unaffected by the memories—if anything, their anger and despair had only increased. But there were others, too. Besides Trent, Keith, and Slimes, multiple prisoners gazed in. The handlers, the two alchemists, and even Tom Osnan Jr. and his wife Joanne. The not-a-prison's soul also stared down from above, its judicial gaze as heavy as it was absent of emotion.

You can be my witnesses, Maria thought into the room, her legs braced. *I will* not *abandon my ideal.* Those around her all responded, their emotions flying out toward her, but she was already gone. Maria leaped out, her awareness arriving back in the chaotic cell. The physical walls seemed to have shifted further, perhaps disintegrated by the clash. Again, she didn't check.

After all, she spoke in her mind, sharing the words with Slimes, Trent, Keith, and the rest of her witnesses. *We have a job to do. Penelope and Tryphena* must *be healed.*

Light and force exploded from within her core. She thought it might be another advancement at first, the statement having unlocked more of her latent potential, but it didn't come from her at all—it came from Slimes.

His full strength, more than he had ever possessed, rocketed out into the room, taking his form with it. He appeared before the corrupted women. The orange and pink hues of Maria and Trent's conjoined chi poured into the crystalline familiar. The brilliance that shone from each of his faceted surfaces was suffused with his power, casting a kaleidoscopic light more potent and beautiful and awe inspiring than words could describe.

In a single flash, every seed, root, and trace of corruption was seared away, just as Fischer had done once before. In the moments that followed, she waited for something to fill the space left behind. Trent made an attempt, using the memories of afternoons spent playing with sticks and a rock to flood his love into those vacant areas.

But naught took hold. The queen's and princess's thoughts were silent. Deep within Maria . . . also nothing, not a single doubt blossoming. She should be worried, shouldn't she? Assailed by fear and terror and despair?

All she felt was hope. They would find a way. Even if this *was* just another temporary measure, they'd try again. They could return to finish the job before corruption ret . . . *Huh?*

Others approached. Feet tapped against stone, and for the first time since Trent's arrival, Maria opened her eyes to the outside world. The walls *had* moved, but not in the manner she'd expected—not a single brick had been destroyed by their clashing intents. They'd been neatly disassembled and set aside, leaving a wide hallway in either direction.

From the left came the handlers, following a line of chi Maria knew as well as her own. Slimes drew them in, leading them back to his gemlike and essence-filled body. Another tendril extended to the right, which two blubbering alchemists were now sprinting along, their eyes wet and faces puffy as they raced to repent for their sins.

Behind the alchemists, riding vines that shouldn't have been able to travel through the not-a-prison's suppression, came a couple of nobles she never would have expected. Tom Osnan Jr. and his wife, Joanne, stared ahead with steeled expressions.

Maria drew tendrils of chi into her limbs, preparing to smack the absolute shit out of them, but then she sensed the emotions breaching their masks of indifference. Self-hatred. Guilt, regret, fury.

If that hadn't stilled her hand, the pulse from Slimes would have. The wave of power was laced with meaning, and Maria could do naught but blink at him as everyone approaching closed the distance. The fires within Trent had grown dull, and his awareness hovered beside hers, similarly stunned.

You . . . she thought. *You did all this, Slimes?*

Yah-huhhh!

The handlers arrived first. Their reasoning was too complicated for immediate comprehension, but Maria sensed compassion and humanity in their resolve. They kneeled by the previously corrupted women, their chi pouring in as a liquid that pooled in Tryphena's and Penelope's cores.

The alchemist came next, and their tears flowed with renewed vigor as they added their strange essence to the mix. Their motivations were clear: They'd been complicit; they were partially to blame. When their power combined with that of the handlers', the pools of liquid became gaseous clouds that billowed out, filling the surface.

Finally, the Osnans arrived. Their intentions were even more convoluted, but one thing was certain: They meant to help. Keeping their eyes averted, they kneeled a little farther back than the others.

Their vines of chi wound themselves into Tryphena and Penelope. They snaked underground, the tendrils of life forging paths into tunnels made by roots of rot and decay.

The coals of Trent's bonfire flared with heat, and Maria drew it into her pink cloud of healing. Together, they raced into the occupied cores, hesitant at first. But there was no need to fret; their wills were aligned.

Trent's flames, bolstered by Maria's chi, whipped around within Tryphena and Penelope. The inferno ignited vines and gasses both. As the vines burned away, the heated gas rushed in, followed by and intermingled with healing clouds. All corruption was consumed in a flash, and thousands of hidden wounds were painlessly cauterized, scars healed before they could even form.

It . . . it was done. Just like that.

The multi-spectrum light shining from Slimes grew dull, and as everyone withdrew their wills, there was a long stretch of silence. Given the former allegiances of those present, it probably should have felt awkward, but not one had any attention to spare.

All eyes watched a mother and daughter as they slowly stirred. Tryphena and Penelope sat up, both touching their heads and as memories and knowledge returned. Lips quivered, nostrils flared, and their gazes sought a particular visage.

The one they searched for was a blur. Small jets of flame shot from his back, burning through the outer clothes he wore overtop a fireproof suit. He dropped to his knees and slid along the stones, wrapping his arms around his immediate family.

Maria made to turn away, but Joanne Osnan stepped up. She clasped her fingers before herself, causing a tangle of vines to encase the reunited family and give them privacy.

Free of the guilt of witnessing such a tender moment, Maria let out a long sigh.

She reached out with her awareness to praise her familiar—the hero of the day. He had recognized that others would be necessary to fill the gap left behind. He'd gathered them by coordinating with the not-a-prison, saving his strength until the last second.

Slimes spun with joy, his crystalline body going gelatinous.

A pulse of chi came from within the dome of vines, and when they retracted back beneath the stone floor, three cultivators stood, their bodies awash with flame chi. Suddenly, that essence leaped out in multiple directions. As it flowed into the cores of others, all open and willing to embrace it, Slimes bellowed in victory, his usually squeaky voice deep with power.

"I'm a booooy!"

CHAPTER SIXTY-FOUR

The Truth

The moment an otter's innocuous-looking pebble hit the shell encasing us, all hell broke loose. Three distinct sources of chi shot outward from the point of impact, all of them burrowing into the earth elemental in a manner befitting their aspect.

The first essence type, that of one Corporal Claws, was the least surprising. Her chaotic barbs of lightning, laced with natural electricity, tore through everything in their path, even the hardest of rocks no match for the dual energies.

Next was the attacking elemental's own chi. Any confusion surrounding the pebble's origin was immediately answered; it had once belonged to the very being it now attacked. Rather than rejoin its former master, the essence was hostile, forming spears of crystalline stone that stabbed deep into the elemental before expanding outward.

Last and most shocking of all was the presence of the raccoon's identity as a thief. The fact his power and will had joined Claws wasn't surprising—he was her familiar, after all—it was the effect his inclusion had that was remarkable.

The raccoon, an adolescent mammal found lost at sea only days ago, was stealing chi from the ancient being—and not mere drops. The devious little bastard was yoinking *all* of it.

Great ropes of essence flowed back toward the stone. In seconds, metric tons of mass had been drained. Whole sections fell. I redirected the inert clumps overboard with an angled wall of solid light, just in case it was some sort of trick, then checked up on the ancient elemental with a few tendrils of my power, suspecting they would do . . . I don't know, *something* to stop the theft of their very life force.

But they were paralyzed. Robbed of the ability to fight back.

"Damn," I said. "Looks like it's checkmate. Well played, Claws. You—"

She cut me off with a chittering cackle, floating in midair as she rolled around, pounding a nonexistent floor beside her. She zapped upright suddenly, her eyes and needle-sharp teeth aglow with blue electricity.

And now, she trilled, her voice filled with malice, *for the* real *fun to begin!*

Like removing a mask, her facade of civility disappeared, revealing a core corrupted with power as she zipped over to the pebble. Half the ceiling had fallen away, drained of the ancient elemental's essence. Predawn light illuminated her as she plunged a forelimb into the translucent bubble of stolen earth chi billowing around her stone.

You thought me controllable? You assumed I would settle for the chaos of mere pranks on Barry? She let out a belly laugh, clutching her abdomen. *No, Master! I will show you* true *chaos! I'll unleash every ounce of this power on those you love most!*

With this proclamation, she started creating a wave of incredible energy, turning it toward Tropica. If she unleashed it, it would take all the remaining essence I had to stop the village from being leveled.

What shall you do, Master? She let out a chittering laugh filled with madness, her teeth parted to reveal their gleaming points. *You can contain me, but the earthen chi will obliterate Tropica! It'll destroy the whole village!*

Her entire body glowed now.

Your only choice is to use every last drop of essence defending the insects you have grown to love! What will you choose? Will you sacrifice the lives of others to stop me? Will you—

"Claws," I interrupted, the word hitting her with physical force as I crossed my arms and smiled at her theatrics. "I see what you're up to."

Her eye twitched subtly, but she hid it with another maddened cackle. *I know not what you speak of, Master! I am Corporal Claws, wielder of lightning, channeler of chaos, maiden of the—*

"Maiden of the pond," I finished, my words shaking her. "I was wondering what your endgame was for the longest time. I get it now. One second."

I snapped my fingers, and an extremely muscular man appeared beside me in a flash of light.

Claws gazed down at Barry with a distinct lack of comprehension, her fuzzy little face cute despite her facade of insanity. Barry, knowing that the hour for vengeance was nigh, gave her a shit-eating grin. Her scowl only deepened.

"The pranks you had me do to him?" I asked. "Barry knew about them. He was a willing participant, and you weren't pranking him at all—*we* were pranking *you*."

Her teeth parted again, but this time, it was in stunned silence rather than menacing glee. Barry's ego and core both shone with vindication.

"You thought you'd deceived me," I continued. "You thought I genuinely believed you capable of hurting people if I didn't sow chaos for you." I shook my head. "Claws . . . please. I know you better than anyone else. If you had actually meant others harm, I would have locked you away until you changed your tune. I've already learned that lesson."

I . . . she tried, her eyes showing panic despite the bright light still flooding from them. *I* am *capable! You'd better shield the village, Master! I'm about to let* all *this energy go! If you don't protect them, I'll—*

"No," I interrupted again. "You knew this elemental was coming toward Tropica, and you planned to steal its power for yourself. There was only one problem—*me*."

She just stared.

"I could have stopped you, so you needed me to overexert myself. The entire evil act—you did it for this exact moment. If I wasted the last of my essence protecting the village, you could yoink it for yourself."

Don't . . . don't be ridiculous! What could I possibly want all this power for? I am perfect as I am! She gathered the earth chi with one paw and prepared to release it with the other. *I'm really going to do it, Master! This is your final chance! Protect the village, or . . . or else!*

I rested a hand to Barry's shoulder. The entire sky was clear now, so as I turned to look at him, his face was lit by the pink and red colors of the coming dawn. "I'll give you the satisfaction, mate. Cheers for going along with my plan without knowing the end goal."

He blinked, not yet drawing the conclusion.

"If you were the *maiden* of a *pond*," I continued, "and one of your rival spirit beasts had *her* pond awaken into some kind of sapient familiar . . . how would you feel?"

Claws's jaw dropped completely open, and the jolts of lightning bouncing from tooth to tooth faded back into her body. All she could do was stare as her careful plans unraveled before her.

Barry didn't skip a beat. "Hermes's sleight of hand! Seriously, Claws? *That's* why you did all this?" He bellowed a laugh. "The look on your face—gods above, it was all worth it. Thank you, Fischer. This was a wonderful gift."

"You're very welcome, mate. It was the least I could do, given my participation in your depantsing." I looked up at my favorite otter, whose jaw had yet to stop hanging open. "Now, Claws, I—"

She let out a bestial cry and appeared before me with a thunderous boom, jabbing an accusatory digit toward my chest. *You're lying!* she screeched. *You've been pranking people all along! More than just Barry! I've seen it with my own peepers!*

"Well, yeah. I had to make it believable. Besides, it was kinda fun."

She froze for a fraction of a second, the truth of my words hitting her, then her indignation returned. *Do have any clue how hard it was to seem evil for so long? Do you comprehend the sacrifices I had to make?*

"It . . . was only three days."

Only three days?

"Uhhh, yeah?"

She leaned closer, her face tinged with genuine madness. *Do you have any idea how busy my schedule is? That's three days of missed scritches from the townsfolk! Three days of harmless pranks left unsprung! And the* snacks . . .

"What sna—"

There's a couple on the north side that leave fishies out for me! Every! Single! Night!

"Well, as they say, there's always more fish in the s—"

Her wild-eyed expression occupied my entire field of view, and she reached up to squeeze my cheeks together. *Do you know what they've been doing with those fish when they're still there in the morning, Master?*

"Uhhh," I said through my smushed mouth. "They give them to someone el—"

Crabs! she screeched, her paw pads making circular motions on my face. *They've been feeding them to crabs! Unascended. Crabs!*

She pressed her forehead into mine. Tiny sparks of electricity lanced through her eyes. And she abruptly deflated.

Her whole body went limp as she drifted away, a half-otter, half-liquid pile of dejection incarnate. *All for nothing . . .* she cooed, morose. *Master is* devious. *Master is* cruel. *Master—*

"Is forgiving," I interrupted, unable to hide my amusement. "I won this battle fair and . . . okay, maybe not *fair and square*, but we were both being deceptive. Those were the rules of engagement."

She didn't reply, simply floating in place and staring up at the coming dawn. Her translucence flickered and faded away, revealing brown and tan fur I'd not seen since her awakening as an elemental.

This return to her old body felt just as right as her opaque variation, but it was arguably more natural for a single reason: it didn't use any of her power. I hadn't realized it before, but now that it was absent, a whisker-thin strand of chi had been facilitating the appearance.

A flicker of a grin tugged at the corner of Claws's mouth when she sensed my surprise; in this, at least, she had managed to fool me. I grinned at her, seeing an opportunity for us to move forward. In retrospect, I should have known better.

Oh-ho-ho! Master finds that funny! she accused, poking my chest with a lightning-infused paw. My torso tingled. *Do you know how* bothersome *it was not being able to change forms when I felt like it?* She flickered and became translucent again. *To have an itch in my mind that I could never scratch? To have an oyster* right *on the edge of my awareness, its meat juicy, succulent, yet just out of . . .*

Her eyes drifted to the muscular man beside me, and she deflated once more, falling backward to starfish in midair and stare up at the sky with a distant gaze. I glanced at Barry, wondering why his visage had afflicted her so.

I half expected him to look a little regretful, reflecting the conflicted emotion in my soul at seeing my always-chipper otter going through a bout of melancholy.

Nope. Not even a bit. Barry wore a victorious smile above his chiseled jaw. He was visibly enjoying every second of vengeance so much that it had plunged Claws into a depression.

In response, the raccoon's upper torso shot out of an otter pocket. He scowled at the muscleman, giving him a rude gesture with one paw and rubbing his master's stomach reassuringly with the other. Comforted by the strokes, Claws shifted back to her furred form, which also robbed her familiar of his opacity.

Deciding I'd let the maiden of the skies wallow for long enough, I cleared my throat. "Before you cut me off earlier, Claws, I was going to give you good news."

She rolled over dramatically. *Master* taunts *me! Does the cruelty ever come to an—*

"You can have the elemental's power."

She zapped bolt upright, small jolts of electricity excising her gloom in an instant.

"But!" I held up three fingers. "I have conditions."

She nodded so slightly anyone else might have missed it. There was some distrust gathered in the bunched lines around her eyes.

"First, no more pretending you're a murderous beast of a creature unless it has strategic purpose. Plus, either Barry or I have to approve it. Preferably both."

Another nod, more animated than last time, her suspicions waning.

"Second, you have to acknowledge that I out-chaosed you in this battle of wits, and that you're only able to attempt evolving your pond because I, the humble, handsome, and humble Fischer let it happen."

She was frozen for a few seconds, then her hackles fell when she realized this wasn't some kind of trick. She slammed into my chest and stretched to rub her chin against mine, chittering softly all the while.

I accept defeat, she cooed with great vigor. *I have been bested by my master in a game of wits! He is flawless! And so* handsome! *I never should have tried to fool him!*

"Good girl," I said, scritching behind her ear with one hand—and flicking her raccoon on the head with the other when he tried to steal the cord that held up my pants. "The last concession is the most important." I stopped patting her so she could look me in the eye. "You need to not drain all of this ancient elemental's power. If you let it live, there's a slight chance it could joi—"

Half the world went black. It happened in an instant. All I could make out was a shape. Giant tendrils—no, *tentacles*—were wrapped around Bob, countless suckers securing themselves to his hull, deck, and mast. The creature's head was even larger than the ship; it blocked out the entire port-side horizon.

Set within the blackness, two terrible eyes glared down at me. They bored directly into the center of my soul. Each orb was the same shade as the rest of it, but tiny swirls of mercury broke up the abyssal monotony, those dark-gray flourishes betraying intelligence that was vast, ancient, and unspeakable.

As I stared up into that alien gaze, I felt a flicker of the power stored behind them. Its essence was that of the abyss. Incomprehensible. Meaning clear.

Death.

My core opened up, and chi poured out.

The kraken had lived for thousands of years. He knew well the bitter taste of deceit and betrayal, yet he'd almost fallen for it again. He had been a fool. Naïve despite his time on this corrupt planet.

He would rectify it immediately.

Thick tentacles and immovable suckers held him to the ship, and as he recalled the morning's events, his limbs tightened, making wooden fibers creak and groan. A number of things had stilled his actions up until this point; the entire universe seemed to urge him not to destroy them all.

First, there was his oldest ally's reluctance to use their full power. Until the earth elemental tried to assimilate the newly awakened otter of lightning and chaos, the kraken's stored detonation would not be strong enough to guarantee the fulfillment of his duty.

Then, when said being of chaos had arrived, she had a divines-damned *raccoon* in her soul, the bond between them *true*. And as stunning as that revelation was, it was nothing compared to the object hidden within her strange little pockets.

This otter and her familiar had stolen something that belonged to the earth elemental, but the pebble had been changed so much that its previous owner couldn't detect it. The weave of power was genius, really—it robbed their target of even the ability to understand the exceptional danger they were in.

The ancient kraken, however, didn't have his eyes or senses clouded. When the newly awakened lightning otter and the devious being she'd bonded with started to steal his oldest ally's essence, he wasn't caught off guard. The speed with which the two drained the earth elemental's life, though . . . How were infantile beings so efficacious?

Either the twin souls of chaos and larceny would succeed in their robbery, or they'd fail. If the former came to be, they'd have fulfilled his duty for him; if the latter came true, it would be the perfect moment for him to strike, obliterating what remained of his oldest ally by the time they broke free.

It all made sense. It was logical. Backed by reason.

So why did he want to destroy neither the newly awakened elemental nor her apparent master, the human wielding unaspected essence? The man's actions were rash and boisterous, just as expected from a soul willing to channel pure chi—what other personality type would do something so reckless?

Yet, despite this dangerous level of impulsivity, the cultivator reminded the kraken of two very important people: his former masters. The only ones that, out of countless other souls, had never betrayed or tried to destroy him. When he recalled their demise, his cold rationality returned, but then the aspectless cultivator had done something so compassionate, so stupid, so *human*, that all the good times with his departed friends flashed through the ancient cephalopod's mind.

This embracer of pure chi . . . he could steal the earthen bubble of essence for himself. It would give him *unfathomable* power—and kill him shortly afterward, of course, but when did that ever stop a human from reaching for ascension? Instead, the cultivator told the strange otter to just . . . have it. For a *pond*. It defied comprehension.

The way he treated his many animal slaves, too . . . they weren't slaves at all. Humans were the easiest to corrupt of all beings; their short lives, endless ambition, and ability to rationalize evil were a fatal combination. Only a spirit beast left no other choice would willingly bond themselves with the contemptible species.

But what of his fallen masters? Their pure hearts and pristine souls were what had made them so special. This man before him, who was scratching an otter of *chaos* behind her ear, appeared to be cut from the same cloth. Maybe . . . maybe the kraken didn't need to annihilate him. Perhaps this strange gathering of beings could fulfill his duty for him. The memory of his two masters, his two *friends*, urged him to show this kindness. It was surely what they would have done.

But then the truth had come to light.

Like the sun rising over a pitch-black ocean, the man announced his goal. He asked the otter to let the earth elemental *live*! The mask of grace was a facade. He was just like so many evil dictators before him, seeking personal power to the detriment of life itself.

The kraken was left no other choice. He revealed himself, reached for his condensed bubble of chi, and prepared to release it. Enough of the earth elemental's power had been drained away by now—their destruction was guaranteed.

At long last, the kraken's duty was to be complete. He regretted the collateral damage—the swathe of souls his explosion would send to the next life—but sacrifices were sometimes necessary. The Kallis Realm would not know peace while the pure-chi cultivator, or his oldest ally, remained.

In that final moment, the ancient being thought of his friends once more. His loving and compassionate masters. They really would have tried to let this man and his slaves live. They were kind to a fault, after all—which was exactly what had gotten them killed all those years ago.

With a tear swelling in one abyssal eye, the kraken released his condensed pocket of chi, welcoming the blessed nothingness that would soon follow.

CHAPTER SIXTY-FIVE

Assemble

Beneath a predawn sky half concealed by a form so black it reflected neither light nor life, I sensed the power about to be unleashed from the body of an octopus larger than a godsdamned whale.

Like Claws, it was an elemental, its chi both obvious and terror inducing. Abyssal—its aspect was *abyssal*. That realization lit a candle of excitement within me, but I had to snuff it out. The thing was about to explode, and the detonation would annihilate every soul for *kilometers*.

I grieved the losses that would follow, genuine despair gripping my heart and squeezing it tight. Then, I accepted them.

Rest in peace, Bob, I thought. I grabbed his golden throne as I wrapped all my friends in essence, preparing to teleport us to shore. At the same time, I would encase the cephalopod and our ship in a funnel that ensured only their destruction, redirecting most of the force skyward.

But before I could act, a small, opportunistic, and stupidly ambitious mammal made his move. The raccoon slipped from Claws's pocket, stole the strength of any tendrils I tried to grab him with, and zipped through the air faster than I'd ever seen him go, arriving at his destination before we could stop him.

He wasted not a second. His forepaws plunged into the still-growing bubble of earthen chi. Before our very eyes, and in the path of a blast that would turn him into stardust, the fuzzy little idiot swiped the power for himself. He glowed like a miniature sun, blue and white and lacking remorse.

Claws let out an incoherent screech. Cinnamon and Borks watched in awe. Bonnie and Barry both just looked confused, unsure what to think. Even the octopus—or was it a kraken?—seemed startled by the wild-card play. He delayed the detonation, and by the ripple of his eyes, I assumed he was weighing countless possibilities.

"Frack me," I said, already redirecting my will.

I had wanted to avoid this. I'd been willing to sacrifice Bob only because doing otherwise would have left me and the network below with almost no power. The thieving little bastard had forced my hand—I couldn't let him die. Both partitions of will snapped into place, and I created a giant sphere around the midnight-colored eldritch horror, its prismatic walls thick enough to withstand the blast.

Now, the kraken could only destroy itself. Part of me was thankful I'd been pushed to this course of action—Bob would survive—but most of me was still perturbed. To meet a creature right out of legend, only to immediately facilitate its annihilation . . .

But then the situation changed again.

The kraken foresaw its own demise. Before its blast could go off, it halted the detonation. My heart sank. I'd just used almost all of my essence to forestall an attack that hadn't come. I saw no way out.

Until, that is, the raccoon did something downright *dastardly*, revealing that his machinations went deeper than Claws or I could have ever imagined.

He'd never intended on stealing the earth elemental's power for himself. It was too much energy. It'd eventually overwhelm him, and Claws would rip it away.

Why had he stolen it, then? Well, because he could. There was only one way to ensure the success of his heist, and that was to offer the spoils to someone, or something, that could handle it.

His chittering laughter was distorted by the billowing cloud of earth flowing through him and down into the ground. The network below, its reserves as emptied as I was, readily accepted the offering. The chi poured down into its depths, which, by extension, sent it pouring into *me*. I gasped as the essence flowed into my heart, its touch foreign and heavy and *wrong*.

Claws unleashed a string of expletives as she rocketed toward her familiar, a bolt of lightning and chaos made manifest. He responded to the murder on her approaching face with a small grin that conveyed his thoughts with unerring simplicity.

I had to—it's who I am.

She hit him like a three-hundred-pound linebacker, but the bubble of earth didn't cease flowing just because he'd been forcefully ejected. Nothing short of a miracle could stop it anymore.

Borks's nose twitched as he looked at me, sniffing the foreign essence filling my body. His ears drooped, but Cinnamon lifted them back up.

He's still our master! She batted him on the noggin. *He just smells bad!*

Before I could take offense, the kraken, its lightless eyes now exuding a black aura, flew into an apoplectic rage. Fortunately, it no longer planned on releasing a warhead's worth of energy. Less fortunately, it was absorbing the essence instead, flooding its many tentacles with an incomprehensible amount of power. Like the pressurized depths had opened up before us, my very senses were sucked away from me, drawn into its abyssal void.

Before it could lash out and break Bob in half, I teleported everyone. Well, almost everyone. Claws had crash-tackled her raccoon from sight. They were off in the dunes somewhere having a slap fight, and I thought it best to let them hash it out for a minute.

We appeared on the shore south of Tropica. I hadn't wanted to exert too much of the wrong-feeling chi just in case—which had apparently been a prudent move, if the spike of pain in my *everything* could be believed.

The kraken, an abyssal force of righteous fury and sprayed water, darted through the waves, blessedly leaving Bob whole. Behind its midnight form, the first rays of sunrise breached the horizon, adding a lovely pink backdrop to the Cthulhuian nightmare racing toward us.

I raised a hand and prepared to experience even more pain in my everything, but just as I was about to snap my fingers and bring others here, they came to me.

Teddy barreled *through* the now-splintered door of the Church of the Leviathan, the religious group's deity lobster riding his back like a suit of pinchy armor. Their head priest, Gary, held on to said deity's mighty tail for dear life, the rest of him trailing behind.

Teddy's eyes were just as incensed as the cephalopod bearing down upon us, so he didn't give his customary wave. Pistachio picked up the slack, lifting a gigantic snipper in greeting as his steed skidded to a stop on the sand.

Speaking of skidding, Rocky had released twin explosions from the north side of Tropica's rock wall. His volcanic carapace left a massive line in the shore as he used friction to slow his flight. He took one last hit of a cigarette, threw it into his mouth, and stared down our attacker, striking a pose both effortless and supremely cool.

The next to arrive had been my only pal to ignore my mental orders. She'd started gathering her power the moment I teleported Bob back to Tropica, and now that the call-to-action had finally arrived, that knot of essence erupted from the shore.

At first, it was only a lump in the sand. Then, thick roots exploded up. A sprawling canopy formed, and as I gazed over at the trunk, I blinked. It was neither citrus, nor the blue-tinged variety she'd originally occupied. Lemon, my trusty tree spirit, had grown into a mangrove tree. Spear-like roots popped up around its base, and despite her being my friend, I had to fight off a shiver at the power swelling within them.

Woe is the enemy that makes the mistake of stepping on those . . .

Her other tree-spirit bud, who'd yet to receive a name, didn't come, but that was okay—I had aerial reinforcements to focus on.

When I'd sent a mental command to Pelly and Bill upon my return, our connection had felt . . . different. Lacking the time and capacity to inspect the changes, I'd let it go, knowing they'd tell me eventually. As I stared up at them now, though, I couldn't believe what my eyes and core were telling me.

They had broken through, as had the birds sailing in behind them. Abruptly, I recalled an image of two glowing forces Claws had shown me earlier, along with her comments and insinuations about colored feathers and avian-directed violence.

You little shit . . . I thought, which caused a cackle to roll over the dunes from the southeast—followed by a thump, which I suspected was her forehead striking a certain raccoon.

Focusing back on the flock zooming down like arrows in flight, I marveled that they'd managed to keep the advancement from me. My senses were all whacked out by the weird chi running through me, but I could absolutely tell the corrupted cultivators had bonded with them. Maria had succeeded in healing them. She—

The pelicans, in all their multicolored and uniquely patterned glory, slammed into the shore. But they weren't who'd interrupted my thoughts. Just within the bounds of Tropica, an army advanced. Someone at the forefront had been hiding their approach by abusing their connection with me. It showed a new level of control I'd not previously seen from them.

But I supposed that made sense, considering all that she'd accomplished.

When Maria came skidding around the corner, the only thing that stopped me from teleporting her into my arms was the pain it would cause me. There was a layer of exhaustion plastered over her expression, but it did nothing to reduce the strike her unparalleled beauty delivered to my chest. The next to appear from behind the buildings were those I'd known she could heal, followed by others I hadn't.

The former princess and queen, both sticking close to Trent. Flames flickered about the trio's limbs. Then the handlers skidded into sight. They, too, had fire swirling around them. Keith trailed them, and when I felt that same chi dwelling in his core, I let out a soft whistle. Whatever Maria and Trent had done, it was similar to the pelicans' breakthrough; the handlers and Keith had inherited the royal family's flames.

I sensed the following duo before I saw them. I smiled at the alchemists' freedom. They truly deserved it. Buuuut then the next two rode in atop thick vines. My face fell. Tom and Jeanne Osnan. They always left a bad taste in my mouth. Considering Maria hadn't turned to punt them over Tropica, though, they were trustworthy. *Probably.*

The man who arrived after them was akin to a fistful of blades, a few of which were aimed at the Osnans on the off chance they got any ideas he deemed stupid. Roger's razor-sharp aura sliced away any remaining worries, so I let the two royals slip from my mind. Besides, there were others to witness.

The procession that came through after Roger was a palate cleanser of the highest order. The OG congregation members were at the front. Sharon. Brad and Greg. Danny and Peter. Sue and Sturgill. All my pals—with the exception of a handful I had sent elsewhere, and a couple I'd told to hide.

On that note, I spotted a cloud of dust cresting the closest mountain, the one the king's arrival had burned down.

"Damn," I said.

Barry let out a muscular snort beside me. "She wasn't happy about being sent away. I imagine she was even less pleased about you bringing only me back."

"Yeah, well, it was for her own good. If . . . *wait.*" I spun to face the ocean. "What's taking li'l Cthulhu so long?"

The kraken should have been almost here by now, if not already lashing out with its tree-sized limbs, but it was only halfway between us and Bob. I hadn't felt its passage slow. Any tendrils of awareness I sent its way were absorbed. The creature's abyssal eyes also sucked in the surrounding light, replacing it with lines of dull nothingness, each peeper like a miniature black hole.

The pattern in its sclera had changed. Gone were the swirls of mercury, replaced by a galaxy's worth of white stars. It seemed to be considering us as it approached ponderously, my core receiving the lion's share of its attention. That was all well and good, but I had something else to witness right now—an arrival I wouldn't dare miss.

Starting as a low hum, they grew louder with each passing moment. By the time I caught sight of them, my chest was buzzing with the sound. Queen Bee and Bumblebro, both having recently broken through. An insectoid army of impossible size flew in their wake.

"*B . . . Buzzy Boys?*"

I'd seen none of these fellas before, but as each of their compact eyes locked with me, I knew they were of the same hive mind. They differed in two ways. First, obvious to even regular humans, was how many of them came our way. There were thousands upon thousands upon *thousands* of the helpful little buggos. The other dissimilarity was much harder to spot, yet I couldn't have missed it if I tried—it was physical.

These souped-up scouts had retractable stingers loaded with a potent venom. One of them produced a drop of green liquid to confirm my suspicions, the needlelike delivery system retracting a moment later. On top of this offensive enhancement, their segmented bodies were covered in jagged sheets of carapace, with serrated pincers that looked wicked enough to bite through steel.

Knowing I was watching them, a few of them attacked each other mercilessly, tiny little *clings* and *clangs* ringing out into the world as they collided. None were harmed. One of the original Buzzy Boys flew from behind Teddy's ear when he saw the exchange, and I wondered how the new brood would react to the arrival of a predecessor.

When the OG Buzzy Boy got to them, he waved hello, froze in midair, then *exploded.*

I almost had a godsdamned heart attack, but then I realized the truth. He hadn't popped like an overinflated balloon. He'd *evolved*, his old skin torn to shreds as armored plates, a new set of pincers, and a retractable stinger appeared on his body.

"Well, I'll be . . ." I said.

I wanted to praise Queen Bee and Bumblebro for their . . . okay, maybe baby-making wasn't exactly hard work, but it was certainly somethin' worthy of mention. The world, however, as it so often did, had different plans.

A giant shadow cast itself across the shoreline, and as the limbs blocking out the light of the coming sun undulated behind me, I spun. Maria was at my side a second later, her arrival punctuated by a swift peck on my cheek, a soft slap on one of my lower cheeks, and the fingers of her right hand lacing with those of my left.

"Hi," she said, her voice as soft as her touch.

"Hey," I replied.

"I'm a boyyy," Slimes whispered.

"Fooool!" the eldritch creature bellowed, its guttural voice about as enjoyable as a garbage disposal full of forks.

I opened my mouth to say as much—in the face of a literal horror from the deep, I absolutely intended on using humor as a coping mechanism—but before I could utter a word, the ocean exploded in a semicircle directly behind the kraken.

Dozens of figures leaped into the air. They bore different sizes, shapes, and personalities. What they shared, however, was a resolute and unflappable inclination toward violence. Before the abyssal demon could spin all the way around, each airborne crustacean launched at least one blue arc of energy at it.

A single attack stood above all the others. The blade of water was smallest by far, but its *potency* . . . Like an ocean had been condensed into a cup, the thin line of essence promised to crush any fool stupid enough to stand in its path.

Just as surprising was the crab who'd launched it—I barely recognized her.

"Snips . . .?" I asked.

"No fracking way . . ." Maria said at the same time, her comment better articulating the scene before us.

They were the last words uttered before a barrage of anime-esque, ocean-infused aura blades struck a being of incomprehensible age and power.

CHAPTER SIXTY-SIX

Push and Pull

Though curiosity and disdain had replaced most of the kraken's fury as it came to meet us, its murderous intent returned as myriad crustacean-borne attacks descended. Time seemed to freeze for me as I took in the aquatic army that'd launched the salvo.

The strongest attack had come from Sergeant Snips. Her carapace was spiked. Her eyepatch hung loosely over her head. Her body had . . . *shrunk*. When Rocky saw her, foam and steam erupted from his mouth, his volcanic core beset by rivers of exultant magma.

Regardless of her size, it was undeniably Snips, and love for her flooded through me—especially when Maria sent flashes of how troubled my guard crab had been in my absence. I reached out toward her, but an anomaly stood in the way, a partially closed gate somewhere along our connection. I set its consideration aside for now, instead gazing up at a tower of beings possessing a perfect and long-sought-after form.

Joel had succeeded, as had the other members of the Church of Carcinization. Their cores were mostly crabby, somewhat human, and . . . stacked vertically? For whatever reason, they'd formed a pillar, their spiny feet latching onto their downstairs compatriot.

A layman would mistake them for regular rock crabs, but I could see slight differences. Like their lighter color, their longer limbs, and the fact they were as large as godsdamned *boulders*. The many attacks launched from their massive clackers rivaled the strength of Snips's blasts before evolution—which made sense, considering her essence flowed through them.

Peeling my eyes off the gleeful monstrosities, I gazed at the recon squad—the crabs who followed Snips and had been surveilling the ocean for us. There were *way* more of them than I remembered. Though they'd been regular animals when I first met them, they also weren't entirely normal, their bodies containing whispers of chi that hinted at ascension even back then.

Now, their awakening had well and truly arrived, and each of them was bonded to Snips. Unlike the church members, these sneaky souls no longer resembled rock crabs at all. Their shells had flattened and changed shape, reminding me of stealth bombers but, like, a crab instead of a plane.

Each of their carapaces seemed to be a different color, blending in with the surrounding scene, be it blue ocean, pink sky, or black tentacle. What wasn't camouflaged, however, were the arcs of chi they'd launched at the kraken, each of the thirty-plus attacks half as strong as those of the carcinized churchgoers.

That should have been the end of it. The fact Snips had bonded with and facilitated the ascension of a squad of crabs and a congregation of humans was miraculous. But there was more, and the realization pushed at the bounds of my already flexible sensibilities.

Numbering in the hundreds, their bodies so slight that I'd initially conflated them with airborne water droplets, a cadre of animals had hitchhiked their way aboard Snips's breakthrough.

They were legion. They were suffused with the will of Snips. They were . . . shrimp, a species of tiny crustaceans I'd never seen before.

Though their forms were small, the crab-sized claws weren't. The limbs had unfurled with cartoon physics, absent one second and collecting oceanic essence in their hinges the next. The blasts they unleashed were roughly a quarter the strength of Snips's former glory, but there were *hundreds* of them. I didn't envy the cephalopod each blade rocketed toward.

Maria's joy and sheer bewilderment flowed through our connection as time resumed.

The kraken turned. Its body shuddered with violent intent. Every few fractions of a second, it froze in place, giving its movement a halting, horror-movie-esque vibe. With half its limbs braced against the sand, the other four abyssal tentacles met at a single point, blocking Snips's attack.

I couldn't sense what it had intended; the kraken continued to absorb any tendrils sent its way. I could, however, see the result. Two of its appendages were sliced clean through, and as the void-like essence was exposed to the air, it sucked *everything*.

Liters of water, its own severed limbs, and tons of sand flowed in, absorbed into its core. Their disappearance should've been stunning—especially the speed with which they vanished—but the inert objects were nothing when weighed against the souls at risk of being devoured.

All the shrimp were drawn in. Half of the stealth-bomber scouts, those closest, flew toward the dread portal. And the top two crustaceans of the crab tower—who I assumed to be Joel and Jess—tumbled forward, even their enhanced bodies and grabby legs not enough to resist the pull.

I reached for the earthen power coursing through my veins, willing to accept whatever backlash came, but just before I grasped it fully, Snips's core flew into action. It, too, became a vacuum. Rather than draw everything in, however, she only drew in those connected to her.

They flowed toward her as streams of light, each radiating thankfulness, praise, and the requisite amount of reverence one would give their chosen deity. There were hundreds of them. Some were larger than boulders. And all were drawn into the soul of a crab the size of my hand.

Shit made absolutely *zero* sense, but what are ya gonna do?

Sergeant Snips patted her stomach with a small yet mighty claw, radiating an appreciation similar to the sentiment received from her bonded . . . animals? Familiars? Followers? Honestly, it didn't really matter. I'd rather focus on the cool shit she was up to.

Snips floated above the ocean atop tiny jets of water-aspected chi that streamed from her spiked legs. She stared the kraken down, and beneath her implacable gaze, the creature sealed the abyssal openings in its tentacles. The limbs regrew in the blink of a cultivator's eye, and despite the horror of the deep seeming to draw away all our senses, I noticed something odd about his body.

I set the discovery aside for later, grinned, and leaned to the side. "Barry," I whispered.

"What?"

"Check this shit out."

Braving the earthen essence running through me, I sent a message to the southeast, flashing a series of still images and sensations that communicated all that had just occurred. The pain in my abdomen was worse than last time, but I had no regrets.

An inhuman screech like a thousand nails on a chalkboard blasted over us all, so loud that waves of force ruffled hair and clothing. Then, the source of it arrived, streaming indignation and lightning in equal measure.

Even to my ridiculously enhanced ears, the speed and passion with which Claws hurled her string of accusations made me miss most of them. I was pretty sure I heard repeated mentions of ponds, theft, and a four-letter word starting with C that wasn't "crab" and didn't bear repeating.

Regardless, Claws was outraged that Snips had bonded with literally *hundreds* of familiars or whatever they were. She was so belligerent that she'd set her dispute with the raccoon asi . . . *Never mind.* She launched the spherical mammal so hard and fast that he broke the sound barrier.

Despite everything else going on—such as a cosmic horror whose entire body absorbed light—I couldn't help but watch in awe as the Mach-1 ball of fur and thievery approached Snips.

What would she do?

I had not yet discovered the ideal that'd triggered my favorite crab's breakthrough. The kraken's nullifying aura, the muddied connection between me and Snips, or some unholy combination of both held me in the dark.

All I knew was that she wasn't an elemental. Would the raccoon's essence tear through her chi? If so, what exactly could she do to defend herself?

Despite the closed gate between our bond, Snips locked eyes with me and blew a single defensive bubble. It lingered in the air, a strange power making it bobble, then zip sideways into the path of the raccoon. The wide-eyed and sharp-toothed idiot tried to pop it with a slap.

Fwoosh!

An Olympic swimming pool's worth of water rushed out in an instant. The roaring torrent sent Snips's mammalian assailant rocketing up toward the stratosphere.

Before he could disappear from orbit, Claws pulled him back into her core, her jaw unhinged and fuzzy little eyebrows high.

What have you become? she asked with a chirp, curiosity replacing her indignation from moments ago.

The kraken's limbs undulated with power, the pattern in his eyes flashing between nebulous stars and waves of mercury. He dipped his bulbous head toward Snips, and an unfathomable weight fell away from the aura of his pitch-black soul.

"I see now," he said. "The anomalies begin to make sense. Chi returning to the world. So many spirit beasts, cultivators, and elementals working together. The creation of natural artifacts . . ."

Snips blew inquisitive bubbles. They circled her carapace in search of answers.

"You are something rarely seen on Kallis, young one. Something mostly spoken of in legend even before the gods departed . . ."

More bubbles from Snips, a hint of confusion making them wobble back and forth.

"You have come from far away—summoned from a place none other in this realm have seen . . ."

I saw where this was going. I bit the skin between my thumb and index finger to stop myself from reacting.

"You," the kraken continued, voice grandiose, "great being of strong carapace and mighty claw . . . are a *traveler!*"

Silence followed the rumbling proclamation. When it stretched on, his eyes darted around. He'd clearly expected a reaction. He didn't have to wait much longer—one of my best mates cackled.

"Truth!" Theo chortled. "He . . . he thinks that's the truth!"

He.

Before anyone could join in with his laughter, the kraken spoke again. "Truthseeker . . ." It was both a title and an accusation. Lines of gray swept across his eyes. "How have you come to be here?"

"Oh, you know." The former auditor waved a hand. "I was taught by a king, defected to fish and start a church, then helped overthrow my former monarch. Pretty standard stuff, really."

Either satisfied by the answer or flummoxed enough to ignore Theo going forward, the mini Cthulhu looked at Snips. "Do not deny it. You have done well to hide its influence, but I can sense the echo of transmigration on your soul."

Her leather eye patch had drooped so far to the side that it was currently acting as a sash, so when she swiveled my way to gauge my reaction, it was with both of her eyestalks. The eldritch horror's swirling orbs followed, gazing at me for a moment before returning his attention to Snips. "I regret to inform you that your human follower with the red-banded hat—"

"Hey! *Captain's* hat!" I corrected. "We respect title and rank around here, champ!"

To my left, Maria bit her lip to stop herself from laughing. To my right, Barry squeezed the bridge of his nose.

The kraken's eye twitched. "Your human follower with the red-banded captain's hat, then—he will soon perish." Surprisingly, there was neither joy nor schadenfreude in that proclamation.

Interesting.

He turned back to Snips. "I advise you to absorb the earthen essence of my former ally after your follower's soul departs. Given your aspect, the strands may take some time to integrate, but its corruption will present someone of your magnitude no harm—and could prove pivotal against the gods should they return. Additionally, I apologize for my fury earlier. When your condemned captain revealed he planned to let the amalgamation of earth elementals live, I lost control. I was unaware of your existence, so I assumed the worst."

I raised my brows; so few sentences, yet so much to unravel. Former companion? Corruption? Useful against the gods, should they return? Ellis was gonna shit himself when he got back.

Snips reached out to me through our connection, but whatever stopped me from understanding her ideal was still present. Thankfully, her expressive eyes conveyed all she had to say, which I roughly interpreted as: *How in Rocky's red-hot bod do you want me to respond?*

Laughter and quiet mutterings were coming from the crowd behind me. Before they could swell, I stepped forward and cleared my throat. "Mate, there seems to have been a bit of a misunderstanding."

He raised an eyebrow—which I really enjoyed. Who knew octopuses had them? "It is impressive that you still live, human, but in your position, I would not waste my words on a stranger. Speak your peace to those you love. I imagine the pretty young woman at your side will not be happy when you are no longer . . . *Hmm?*"

It trailed off, the specks of white in its eyes quivering as it stared into Maria's soul. "A water spirit lives? How did it survive for so long without chi?"

"Water spirit?" I asked.

"Where did you find them?" the kraken asked, ignoring me entirely.

"I'm a boyyyy!" Slimes declared, wibble-wobbling from Maria's shoulder like a jack-in-the-box. "Not a *they*!"

The cephalopod's *other* eyebrow rose to join the other—man, today was a feast for the senses. "A second true bond?" Though his body didn't move, his sclera became whirlpools, swirling ceaselessly. "That has mastered human speech? Remarkable. What aspect is it that you wield, little one?" His ocular vortices sped up as he leaned closer. "I cannot—"

"Mate," I interrupted, stepping forward to rest a hand on one tentacle. "You've been dropping knowledge bombs left, right, and center. I reckon it's our turn to . . ."

The prehensile bastard *ignored* me, instead turning to look at Snips with a glance that demanded she control her subjects—which resulted in perhaps the most satisfying chastisement I had or would ever see.

Sergeant Snips, my now-tiny-yet-still-reliable guard crab, backhanded a terror of the deep like he was an insolent young master. There was no power in it, but the message was clear.

Listen to my master when he speaks, she ordered, her strange chi radiating out from not only her core, but all the crustaceans she'd bonded.

Claws made an *o, shit* face, her eyes wide, jaw open and head darting around to check the other animal pals' reactions. Cinnamon punched one paw into the other. Borks wagged his tail. Teddy and Pistachio nodded. Queen Bee, Bumblebro, and their progeny buzzed. Bill, Pelly, and the flock of pelicans honked. Lemon shook her canopy. And though Rocky wasn't technically bonded to me, he had the most violent reaction of all, slipping back to his old self as he unleashed a staccato of volcanic explosions into the air, before calming himself down by lighting a cigarette on his shell and taking a deep drag.

The kraken, in the face of all their testimony, chuckled softly and glanced at Snips again. "You have already defeated me, young traveler. I do not see purpose in this trickery."

"My guy . . ." I couldn't stop the wry smile crossing my face. "She's trying to tell you *I'm* the traveler."

He finally looked at me. "You expect me to believe that *you* have managed to bond all these beings?"

"Uhhhh, yeah?"

A hissing, bubbling sound came from him. Within seconds, it had transformed into a guttural laugh, his tentacles all writhing around on the shore. "Oh . . . oh my," he eventually said. "You made me forget myself. Thank you for that." He cleared his throat, composing itself. "Impossible. You would have gone mad by the second one, if not the first. Not to mention the *poison* currently occupying your soul. It is commendable that you have not succumbed to it yet, but that is only by the grace of your matriarch. If you were a traveler, you would have cleansed it yourself by now."

"That's not true, mate! I was just waiting for the right moment."

"For what it's worth," Theo said. "Our benevolent and humble traveler speaks the truth."

This had an unexpected and astounding effect on the kraken—he went rigid, his sclera flashing white to reveal slitted pupils. "Who was that last sentence about, Truthsayer?"

"Uhhh . . . Fischer. Leader of the Church of Fischer." Theo pointed at me. "*Him.*"

Again, the response was unexpected. "*Falsesayer!*" the ancient creature bellowed. "Truthsayer's bane! Betrayer of life!" He shrank back a meter, the black aura exploding from his body once more.

His eyes were undeniably alien, but they'd never looked as inhuman as they did in that moment, darting around, dilated, pure gray. He kept stealing glances at the sky, only to look back at us as if expecting an attack. "What manner of duplicity is this? Which god do you serve?"

It was really hard not to ask any questions, but I managed to hold the urge at bay. "My man, if you just wait like . . . five seconds, you'll see what I'm talking abou—"

"I am *not* your *man*, deceiver! *Reveal yourself*! *Your true self!*"

I'd have cackled at that, but the poor bloke seemed genuinely terrified, and with each passing second, his anxiety only grew.

I gave him my most disarming smile. "I wasn't lying earlier when I said I was waiting for the right moment. Here. I'll show you."

The entire time, power had been draining away from the earth elemental made of many souls. It had finally reached the last one—the being I instinctively knew to be the original.

Still smiling at the kraken, I opened the floodgate to my core. Pure, unaspected chi shone into the world, coming from me, each grain of sand on the beach, and all those standing by my side. The land and I were an extension of the network, and my friends were an extension of me.

Countless things happened at once—a few were of note.

First, the object of power draining the elemental's life force away was nullified by the blast, its triad of essences replaced by my own. It clattered to the ground, a regular pebble like any other on the shore.

The stolen chi, its earthen aspect incompatible with my soul, shifted. *Changed.* Its toxins were purified the moment my ocean of white light touched it. The pain in my abdomen vanished. My connection to everyone was restored, as were my senses.

The third notable occurrence was between me and the kraken. The radiance illuminated my true nature, and as he felt the source of what he'd called "the echo of transmigration," his midnight gaze locked on to me, casting twin beams of black that drilled through the luminosity.

There was a bonus happening, too—my favorite of all. Claws withdrew the raccoon from her soul and held him up to the light. *Take them!* she trilled, chest proud and arms rigid. *Cleanse his crimes away!* It didn't work, of course. Every hair on his body was aligned with his core's desire for larceny. There was nothing to fix. I thoroughly enjoyed it regardless.

All at once, the light vanished. I kept my eyes closed for a moment, bathing in the connections to Maria and my animal pals, as well as the feeling of rightness suffusing the world.

Suddenly, I was tugged in one, then two directions. The universe seemed to urge me to action, all but wailing that I would regret not heeding its advice. I rolled my eyes as my form slid toward the waves.

Do you even know me, universe? I wondered. *You don't need to push me—there's no way I'd miss an opportunity like this.*

Before my awareness was dragged away kicking and screaming, I released my grip on the world and dove in headfirst, right into the souls of two ancient, incomprehensible, and cosmically connected beings.

CHAPTER SIXTY-SEVEN

Worthy Purpose

In a place of darkness, I looked out through the eyes of another being—who seemed just as confused about the eight limbs adorning his body as I was. He pushed in every direction at once, and the surrounding membrane popped.

He slipped out of its confines and into frigid ocean water.

He was far from the first to escape. Thousands of his brood had already departed, judging by the empty egg sacs sticking to the cavern's walls. Hundreds of his brethren clung to nearby rocks as they explored their bodies. He didn't waste a moment. Still learning how to operate this strange vessel, the octopus fry slipped out into open water—and immediately learned why so many had remained within the den.

A school of colorful fish with sharp beaks was waiting. They'd discovered that food came from this gap between rocks and coral. Before he even knew what was happening, pain lanced through him, one of their deadly mouths taking two tentacles with it.

This was the way of the sea. The truth about Mother Nature's indifference. Perhaps this sudden death would mean some of his brethren would escape. Perhaps it would mean the survival of the fish that would eat him. Or maybe it would do nothing, his momentary existence as pointless as it was short.

Others might have given up when faced with certain demise. A sister beside him certainly did, remaining frozen even as she was eaten whole. But this octopus wouldn't go down so easily. He raised the rest of his tentacles and opened a tiny beak, intent on extracting his pound of flesh from any creature that dared come close.

A blur of motion from the side. A cloud appeared. Blackness. Encompassing limbs. Crushing strength. Movement. Passing water. Cold. *Numb.* Fading awareness.

Then, release.

The crushing grip let go, and the octopus, his vision swimming, looked up at a giant. It had tentacles, too, even more than him. They parted, and a maw just as deadly as the fish's opened up. The newborn that would become a kraken tried to lift his limbs, tried to reveal his own sharp mouth, insignificant as it might be, but he'd lost too much blood.

He stared defiantly up, resolved to at least witness his demise. But when the guillotine opened, it wasn't death that was delivered; it was *life.* Hundreds and hundreds of tiny organisms were expelled.

The giant retreated, pressing its long body and undulating fins against a crack.

Light vanished, but that did nothing to rob the baby octopus of vision. He was back in his . . . no, a different den. The creature before him had sealed off the only exit.

And food had been trapped in with him. It took all of his strength to grab one of the glowing organisms and press it into his mouth. As he crunched down, life flowed through him, its bioluminescence seeming to light his body from within.

By the time he'd consumed half of them, his limbs had regrown. He gave it not a second thought, and neither did he worry about his newfound speed, enhanced vision, nor increasingly complex hunting strategies.

When only ten remained, he circled them on nimble tentacles, corralling each flitting speck toward a back corner. They fell for his machinations. He spread the base of his body and opened his beak as he descended, the aftertaste of his last bite still radiating from both his mouth and soul, and . . .

Pop!

The transformation was immediate, as was knowledge. When the blinding flash of white disappeared, he stared down. Were these limbs really his? Gray and mottled skin with rings of bright blue reminiscent of the glowing plankton he'd devoured.

Not just regular plankton, his magnified awareness knew.

They'd been filled with chi—harvested from a part of this ocean so deadly that no unascended beast would survive. His eyes flicked to the animal on the wall. Slitted pupils stared back. They possessed intimidating depth, and he could only speculate about the malicious thoughts playing out behind . . . *them?*

The cuttlefish floated toward him, its fins undulating with an emotion so strong it bounced off the walls.

Joy.

By the divines above! the stranger burbled into his mind. *It worked!* Its body flashed through various colors. Red, blue, yellow, green, brown, gray—each intended to camouflage with different underwater scenes. *It worked, it worked, it* worked*!*

Thoughts raced through the octopus's head faster than he believed possible, but no matter how many came, he couldn't decipher this strange spirit beast's intent.

Sorry! I can feel your confusion. I'm just. So. Excited! Its fins undulated so swiftly that water started to swirl around the den. *Geez, I'm messing this up. Here. Let me just . . . There!*

Memories. The cuttlefish's. They slammed into the octopus.

This spirit beast was on a mission. A quest of the grandest scope. He sought ascension—and someone to willingly take those steps with him. There was more. His greater purpose was *equilibrium*, a current he and his partner would swim to ensure the forces of this world didn't continue their downward spiral.

This made the octopus's eyes widen. It was so far-fetched that his thousands of thoughts hadn't even come close to considering it. There was no malicious intent. No reciprocity demanded. The ascendant cuttlefish had prevented death without strings attached.

Why me? he asked, unsure if his savior would get his message. *Why save* me*?*

He clearly did; his fin undulated with excess energy. *Because you didn't give up!*

I watched thousands of your brood-mates exit that den. He scooted closer, his pupils dilating. *How many do you think stared death in the face like you did?*

Hmm . . . The octopus's mind raced, running calculations based upon sheer conjecture and the universe's limited knowledge of his species. *Seven?*

Seven? The cuttlefish blew a stream of amused bubbles. *None! You were the first!* More bubbles. *The moment I saw you, a newborn creature the size of my suckers, resolve yourself to take a bite of the fish thousands of times larger than you . . .* His tentacles wiggling around in delight. *I knew I had found my partner, the brother that I could trust to stare into the void, and not flinch when it stared back.*

The cuttlefish froze as a sobering current washed over him. *If you choose to, of course. I will force nothing.*

As soon as he heard those words, the octopus envisioned a future where he felt something he knew existed but had yet to experience for himself—an emotion that his limited knowledge told him was vital for all life-forms.

Platonic love—*philia* in the old tongue.

And then! the cuttlefish continued as excitement returned to his body. *Your moves against those plankton! Wow! I expected you to survive despite the blood loss, but* divines below*! Even missing limbs and chilled by our passage here, you were incredible! You didn't even need to eat them all to awaken! With that, as sure as I am that otters cannot be trusted, I* knew *I'd made the correct choice in saving you!*

Dozens of thoughts crossed the baby octopus's mind in the second of silence following that statement, one of which was a great curiosity about what otters had done to receive blanketed distrust from the cuttlefish, but none of them led him to believe the potential friend was being deceptive. Happiness pulsed from his newly formed core, and his eight tentacles writhed in excitement.

Right? the cuttlefish ask-yelled, clearly sensing his eagerness. His undulating fin slowed, then froze, and a serious current crossed his features. *Does . . . does that mean you're willing to join me?*

The octopus that would one day become a kraken nodded.

His savior remained somber. *Listen, when I found the being to share this endeavor with, I planned on introducing them to it slowly . . . but my soul is screaming for me to tell you immediately. I can't say why, but I've learned to listen to my instincts—they've helped me survive every trap thus far.*

Traps? the octopus asked. *Set by who?*

Yes. You'll understand once I explain. Again, though, I want your approval—is it okay if I show you?

He didn't even consider it. He nodded emphatically, trusting his own instincts.

The cuttlefish's solemnity vanished, fins and limbs waving chaotically. *Wonderful! Okay. Okay! Here. We. Go!*

A tendril of essence reached out toward him, its movement slow, searching, care—

A jarring sensation crashed into me as both sources of the memory—the kraken and the earth elemental—screamed out into the void, ejecting us all. One's voiceless scream was filled with despair; the other's was laden with rage. Both stood in stark contrast to the blossoming friendship and hopefulness of their first meeting.

I released roots of pure chi into the vast nothingness we floated in. A memory was trying to pull us in, and I did what I could to soothe and coax them toward it. They eventually relented, but only because they wanted this over with—and, like me, had realized the only way out was through.

We swirled down together into a different time and place, and as I looked out through the cuttlefish's eyes, frustration and regret roiled within him.

"Please, brother . . ." the kraken, who was now much closer to his future size, implored in a deep voice. "This is not the way."

Over a millennium had passed. Perhaps multiple. They had meditated for too long in the ocean's abyssal depths to be certain.

"Not your way, you mean," the cuttlefish that would become an earth elemental replied.

"Don't be like that. Our cores are different, but that doesn't mean we no longer tread the same waters."

"I am starting to think it does mean that, *brother*." Even as he spat the last word, he regretted it. The chi filling his core, however, rolled right over it, a landslide that smothered any remorse beneath tons of sediment. "Perhaps it is time we go our separate ways . . ."

The sadness on his brother's face—an octopus fry that had grown into a monstrous creature of the depths—made sorrow dig its way to the surface. But then boulders of shame tumbled down to join the landslide, their weight crushing his emotions once more.

"You think you're better than me, don't you?" *Stop*, a part of him begged. "You have looked down on me ever since I grew an affinity with earth. You *succeeded* in collecting abyssal chi, and I *failed*. That's it, right?" *Please* . . . that small voice beseeched, but the boulders and sediment were deaf to it. "I finally understand, *brother*. You only keep me around to feel better about yourself, right? Or do you pity me too much to sever our ties yourself? *Fine.* I'll make the decision for you!"

All three of us experiencing the memory knew what actually fueled the anger. Centuries of self-doubt and perceived inferiority had become too painful to stomach, so his subconscious had turned them into something even uglier: fury and resentment, projected onto his brother, the only being on Kallis he had ever loved.

But the three of us were only witnesses. There was nothing we could do to stop the cuttlefish from burrowing down into the ocean floor, his essence opening the path and closing it behind him with ease. A league under the sea, his pain only grew.

Please don't leave me, that little voice begged from within. *I* need *you* . . .

Unaware of this yearning, the kraken gave his brother what he'd verbally asked for. Hints of his abyssal chi flowed down toward the cuttlefish, making him all too aware of his only friend's rapid departure.

When the kraken was just on the edge of their communication range, he froze. Hope flooded through the cuttlefish's every cell, but then his former partner spoke.

"Have it your way, *brother*," he said, wielding as a curse what had once been a term of affection between them.

It hurt too much. The cuttlefish tried to yell, half in apology, half in rage, but his power couldn't pass through the world like abyssal chi could. All he could do was sit and dwell as his brother's essence, the very aspect he yearned for, yet would never grasp, faded away.

I was again drawn from the memory by a jarring sensation. Before I could adjust to the vast nothingness surrounding the three of us, the reason for my ejection washed over me. The former brothers' emotions had . . . swapped? Partially, at least.

The kraken, formerly filled with despair, now radiated resentment and bitterness, and a gloomy dejection had muted the earth elemental's fury.

I made the mistake of trying to understand why. They both lashed out, treating me as the punching bag for their negative emotions. I learned the lesson, instead encouraging them to dive back in with tendrils of soothing essence.

Left absent choice, they reluctantly capitulated.

Hundreds of years later, we gazed through the cuttlefish's eyes once more. He was yet to become an elemental, but in the centuries that had passed, he'd grown *incredibly* strong. The memory began with him turning a mountain of stone to dust so he could free a school of . . . seals and humans? *Wait, are those fracking* selkies? *What the shi—*

I shook my head, returning to the present. *Er, the past, I mean.*

Focus, Fischer.

Power and wisdom were seldom found together, but the cuttlefish proved to be an exception to the rule—not a day went by that he didn't regret pushing the kraken away. He thought of the tiny octopus his brother had once been as he watched two adult selkies in human form swoop into the silt that remained of the mountain to collect a gaggle of children.

It only took seconds for all those trapped to be rescued by the supernaturally swift creatures, which wasn't really surprising considering they were *godsdamned selkies right out of fracking myth—*

I mentally slapped myself.

Focus, Fischer! This isn't the time!

Freed, the pod of chi-filled beings swam the cuttlefish's way, but then an aspected pulse rippled through the ocean. Everyone froze. It was no mere wave of power that washed over them.

If it had come centuries ago, it would have sent him into a rage strong enough to split tectonic plates. Now, though, it set his multiple hearts to thumping, doing their best to beat right out of his mantle. He recognized the aspect—the *element*.

His brother, the kraken, had succeeded. He'd achieved the impossible task they'd set out to accomplish all those millennia ago.

Before the selkies could respond, the cuttlefish rocketed away, the ocean a blur as he shot jets of earthen chi from his siphon. He had searched for his first friend for so long. Imagined the words he could say to make his brother forgive him. And after so much time, he'd finally have a chance to do so.

That nagging voice in the back of his mind tried to steer him away, guiding him toward self-preservation. The divine gods would respond to the open use of abyssal power. They would *come*. That voice, however, was easily quashed. His brother was nothing if not careful, and he would have stuck to the plan, if not developed an even better one over the centuries. He wouldn't openly control such heretical chi unless within a masking barrier.

With how fast the cuttlefish traveled, it took less than an hour to reach his destination. He knew this island. It was one he had always avoided, because there were a few dozen bipedal reasons to give the landmass a wide berth.

Humans. Some of them were cultivators, and though they weren't yet mad, such things were only ever one foolish decision away. Not at all deterred by their presence, he swam forward carefully, not wanting to disturb the nullifying shield his brother must have erected.

But no matter how many meters he crossed, the anti-divine barrier never arrived. Had his brother not taken the planned precautions? If not, why were the gods not currently raining holy fire upon him?

Confused, the cuttlefish slipped into one of the tricks he'd learned since separating from the kraken. *Camouflage*. It hid both his body and essence, which allowed him to get close enough to . . .

Every clump of his earthen chi turned to ice.

There he was. The brother he had dreamed of reconnecting with for hundreds of years. Two humans were astride his mighty head, riding him like one of the brainless bovines used to plow fields. They laughed as the tentacle of a mighty kraken reached up to tickle them, of all things.

The cuttlefish knew he shouldn't do it, yet he couldn't resist. He dropped his stealth and extended muddy strands of chi. He had to know. He needed to understand the truth. And even from a distance, his worst fears were confirmed.

The kraken had just become an abyssal elemental . . . *by bonding with two humans*. That was why the gods hadn't acted. He'd chained himself to their offspring—he willingly served those who saw him as inferior.

His brother should have felt the cuttlefish the moment he dropped camouflage, but he was too busy chasing orbs of abyssal essence, the bubbles that arrived following the ascension of an elemental. Long ago, the cuttlefish would have happily indulged in such a delicacy, hoping it would unlock that same chi within his core.

Disgust, resentment, and budding anger caused him to rocket away once more, but the emotions weren't for his brother—they were only for himself.

The kraken was the wisest being he'd ever had the pleasure of meeting. His brother was infallibly intelligent. For him to have bonded with two humans meant that there was either a valid reason for doing it or he had been left no other choice.

As he got farther and farther away, the cuttlefish's negative feelings swelled, doing their best to crush him. He'd waited centuries for a reunion that would never be.

Worse, the dissenting voice in his head, the one lingering for thousands of years, had been right all along.

My brother really is better off without me. Look how far he has—

Two souls in the nothingness cried out, unwilling to witness any more. I'd been keeping them pacified as best I could with my pure chi, but their emotions had grown too strong.

They'd drifted even farther from their original positions. The kraken was belligerent, railing against the confines of whatever this non-temporal prison was; the earth elemental, once blind with rage, now wallowed. Despite their feelings on the matter, I could feel the apex of this bittersweet song approaching, so I forced us back in.

When we looked out through the kraken's eyes, hundreds of years had passed since the last vision. A holy war was being fought out in the open, and he and his beloved masters had long ago stopped pretending to side with the "divine" gods above.

They'd just learned an attack was coming against one of their allied continents, which was why they raced through the ocean at a swift clip, his pulse seeming to thump despite his elemental body's lack of a heart. His masters responded by sending platonic love through their connection, both for each other and for him.

Calm ease replaced his frenetic thoughts. He returned his affections to Garret and Jenny, the husband-and-wife duo he'd bonded with. He didn't know what he would do without them. In the back of his mind, a nagging voice chose that tranquil moment to strike.

What if it's him?

The attack was rumored to come from an earth elemental.

"Then we will have finally found your brother after all these years," Garret said, his voice sturdier than deep-ocean diamonds.

"And we'll correct his misguided ways!" Jenny added, words chipper.

Their statements weren't empty. They believed it down to their very cores. And he loved them all the more for it. Completely camouflaged, they raced along through the waves.

Almost there . . .

Our perspective shifted. Both beings in the nothingness with me tried to scream, but I'd expected it—I held them steady with thick tendrils of light, letting the next vision draw us in.

We looked out through the eyes of an earth elemental that'd once been a cuttlefish. He, too, thought of his oldest friend. He had long ago come to terms with their estrangement, and though the invisible scar sometimes itched, today it felt completely healed—as it always did when he found an opportunity to help his brother from the shadows.

He'd been lost for a good many decades after the last time he saw the kraken, especially after the war began in earnest. But that had all changed with a single discovery, a blessed revelation—his brother and his two humanoid masters had only been *pretending* to capitulate with the divine gods. They'd announced their allegiance to the allied forces in spectacular fashion, taking down swaths of corrupted humans in one fell swoop.

On that day, the cuttlefish had taken up arms—or tentacles, as it were. This thought made him smile. It was a welcome distraction from the death and destruction that might follow.

If his partner arrived in time, they were going to sink a continent.

Back in the nothingness, only one of the voices raged.

"Liar!" the kraken yelled, his voice hitting me from all directions at once. "Liar, Liar, *LIAR*!"

He lashed out with abyssal chi, his form shapeless, diminished, yet more than enough to annihilate the defenseless target of his ire. The earth elemental didn't even try to shield himself from the attack. His sightless eyes gazed into the surrounding nothingness, catatonic.

I blocked the blow, saving one from death and the other from a terrible mistake.

This left the kraken off balance, so I grabbed him and sent us whirling back into the same . . . *no.* A different vision. We looked out through the eyes of a cuttlefish that was no longer an earth elemental. We'd gone further back in time.

The cuttlefish had always known this war would arrive—it was why he'd sought abyssal chi all those millennia ago—but he never expected just how vicious the bloodshed would become. The entire world had been plunged into darkness, each being forced to choose a faction. Except for him, of course. He chose melancholic isolation instead, unable to find energy or reason enough to care; his former brother was a key weapon for the divine side. The *wrong* side.

Then, blessed revelation. As soon as the kraken openly joined the allied forces, the cuttlefish thought to do the same. If they couldn't be brothers, perhaps they could be brothers-in-arms. For that to be possible, he needed to get much, *much* stronger.

He meditated long and hard in search of enlightenment. The centuries raced by. As his strength and affinity with earth increased, he dug deeper beneath the seafloor, descending through so many layers of rock that the ambient heat could melt stone. There, embracing an aspect he'd once resented, he experienced his elemental awakening.

So far down, no one else could sense his breakthrough—or so he'd thought.

Only minutes after his breakthrough, another came to greet him. He prepared for battle, willing to annihilate them if it meant the success of his mission. Instead, he found a curious soul, one not so dissimilar to him.

The first sister.

She was a volcanic elemental, and she'd also sensed a conflict coming long ago. Her aspect was useless against fighting the divine, so she'd retreated to the center of the world, choosing to live a peaceful and lonely existence.

He told her all about the war, the shifts in power, and the plan he'd developed over his own centuries of isolation—his plan to become a hidden arbiter of justice.

Because of his affinity with earth, and his camouflage ability, he was uniquely suited to espionage. He needed neither glory nor recognition. All he cared about was the allied forces' victory.

He didn't tell the first sister all this to win her over. He simply intended on informing a kindred spirit of all that'd happened. Yet he won her over all the same. With that, he found another sibling—one who decided of her own accord to assist him from the shadows.

We shifted again, and as before, only a single voice called out in the nothingness. The kraken's scream was wordless, his accusation clear. The earth elemental was lying. These memories were false. They *had* to be.

I felt great compassion for him, and though it broke my heart to do so, I wrangled him all the same, sending us whirling down into another vision. The moment we got there, the kraken froze, his fury blunted by twin torrents of confusion and curiosity. It was his brother's camouflaged eyes we looked through, and for the first time since coming to this world, I witnessed gods.

Two beings entered a concealed cavern, one via a water-filled tunnel the cuttlefish hid within, the other by a hole in the roof. Rays of reflected sunlight shone down through the opening up high, further enhancing the god's already-brilliant aura. "Greetings, D—"

"*Use not that name!*" the oceanic god interrupted. They were wreathed in lengths of seaweed that hid their true form, but their voice was decidedly feminine.

The divine god landed on the rocky floor with a mirthless grin. His features were flawless, yet his smile was uglier than an eel of the pungent variety. "Tell me of your progress, traitor."

Even concealed by layers of plant matter, the apparent saboteur's frustration was palpable. "The central continent is ready."

One of the golden being's annoyingly well-groomed brows rose. "Truly? Already?"

"Yes."

"Wonderful. And how do you plan to stop this island from being swallowed by the ocean before the rituals are completed? I seem to recall receiving this same news twice already, only for them to vanish into the earth. One might start to suspect you of being a double agent . . ."

"Agreed, which is exactly why I have prepared the sacrifice of an important piece from our polis board . . ."

Back in the place of nothingness, the kraken's curiosity was gone, replaced by dawning horror. He didn't try to escape my grip—he couldn't look away. We both rejoined the vision.

"Ah!" the divine god replied after a moment. "I believe I know who you must mean." A wicked grin appeared on his otherwise-flawless face. "What perfect irony. I assume they're already on their way?"

"They are, yes. If we have been correct in assuming our meetings have been spied upon . . ."

They both turned right toward the cuttlefish, golden eyes and a shadowed face staring at the water-filled tunnel he hid within. Terror gripped his heart—as it did mine—and he almost lost the control of his camouflage, but then both gods' gazes shifted to scan the rest of the cavern. They hadn't detected him.

"If we *do* have a spy," the kelp-wrapped figure continued, "it's too late for them to do anything about it. The central continent will be saved, the rituals will succeed, and the war will be won—all in a day."

Numbness flooded the earth elemental.

"One more question then, *deceiver*," the golden god said. "Can you be trusted?"

"Yes, *sir*," the bundle of seaweed replied, their last word filled with . . . was that mockery?

"I will take your word for it, *Dolos*."

"As you should, *sister*."

The cuttlefish didn't understand. *Dolos? The god of deception? If that were true, his sister—*

"You *dare*?" Lines of light shot out from the winged god as he flew forward, and the other's seaweed unraveled as they met in the center of the cavern. But rather than fight, they seemed to embrace one another, their forms shifting.

The golden male became female, and lines of divine essence tore through the last few strands of seaweed from within the formerly concealed figure, revealing a masculine face and well-defined muscle.

The earth elemental recognized them. All knew to look out for the siblings Dolos and Apate, yet the former had somehow managed to infiltrate the allied forces . . .

There was another moment of numbness as the earth elemental reconciled all he'd just seen and heard. Then, an invisible and silent patch of dirt departed as fast as it could without being noticed. Only when he'd made it kilometers away did he reach out to the first sister.

Now! he yelled through their connection. *We need to move* now!

Back in the nothingness, the kraken's will roiled like an ocean in storm. Understanding had well and truly dawned; his shapeless fury threatened to tear us all apart. By contrast, the being he'd once called a brother was completely comatose. There were changes happening within the cuttlefish that, when combined with these haunting memories, seemed to rob him of all emotion—which only seemed to fuel the kraken's desire for wanton destruction.

I didn't understand. The kraken's anger thus far had always been directed at something or someone. Now, he wanted to tear everything down—himself included.

Thankfully, his lack of focus allowed me to skull-drag him into the next memory. The sooner we finished, the better for all involved.

Despite the deceptive gods' words, the earth elemental arrived at the central continent before the unknown counterattacker, but he couldn't complete his duty alone. So, he waited for his sister, praying that she got there first.

She did.

The moment her awareness bubbled up beneath him, they began, his earthen aspect ripping cracks and ravines into the tectonic plate below. Her magma poured into the gaps. The earth quaked. This mass of land was much larger than the other two islands they'd desolated, but that meant nothing before their combined might. In seconds, the coastlines would sink. In minutes, the entire continent would be underwater.

But then *they* arrived. A black hole seemed to open up, and it drank both his and his sister's essence hungrily, not allowing another drop to alter the tectonic plates below.

Desperately, the earth elemental called out toward it, broadcasting images of the meeting he'd just witnessed.

We shifted perspective again, and I knew where we were going. I didn't need to force the others to stillness. Confusion and denial had taken hold of the kraken, and the cuttlefish remained catatonic.

Though we now looked out through the kraken's eyes, we saw not a thing. His power was being pushed to its limits—his abyssal aspect drawing on the power of not one, but *two* elemental beings. Both were ferocious, their earthen and volcanic powers closely aligned.

The former tried to reach out to him, tried to send him information in the least subtle and most dangerous of ways. He sucked the messages into the abyss without reading them, letting them get swallowed, smothered, by the rivers of essence already flooding in.

A single thought forced its way through his mental exertion. After centuries, he had finally found his long-lost brother. The cuttlefish had grown to become *powerful.* Strong enough to shape the world. And he had chosen a side in the war—the *wrong* side.

He was using his potent ability to help the "divine" *usurpers.*

This knowledge shook the foundation of the kraken's being. There could be no misunderstanding. Two allied islands had recently been swallowed whole, and he now understood why. They'd been trials. Mere practice for the *true* target—an entire continent, along with the millions of uncorrupted humans calling it home.

Privy to his thoughts, his masters yelled out, bypassing the essence flowing into him.

"So we've found him after all!" Garret said.

"This actually works so well!" Jenny added. "We'll go bundle him up! The volcanic elemental won't be able to do a thing on their own!"

The kraken railed at the suggestion. His brother had clearly become corrupted, and he didn't want to risk either of his masters. They both poured love and affection through their bond, touched his head with a palm each, then departed.

"We'll be right back!" Garret called, disappearing into the abyss.

The earth elemental tried to reach his brother again and again. He had to let him know the truth. Had to share the deception they'd all fallen victim to. But no matter how many times he tried, they were drawn in. Anyone nearby could intercept them, but he didn't care. If he didn't get through, all would be lost.

He couldn't feel the corruption atop the island, yet he knew it was there. They'd not sensed it on the islands either, but those humans were corrupted all the same. Mountains of proof laced the underwater rubble. Even now, he could feel the power emanating from atop the island—the rituals were progressing.

Reaching deep into himself, the elemental prepared to reach out to his brother again, but the kraken appeared before him instead.

No, he realized, *the two masters.* They were already on him, having concealed their presence until they made contact.

They were a fault line made manifest, and if he chose the wrong action here, the world would be shaken into an era of darkness it might not recover from.

With the weight of consequence resting on his back alone, he made a split-second decision. Some would call it foolish. Others would think it akin to suicide. But he trusted his brother implicitly—by extension, he trusted the humans his oldest friend had chosen as masters.

The cuttlefish opened up his soul in its entirety, inviting them to see *everything.* His thoughts washed out, his darkest secrets and most pivotal memories leading the charge, all of which were related to the kraken.

Each scene I'd been exposed to rushed by, absorbed into their abyssal cores with unbelievable speed. When they witnessed a conversation between two gods, they grasped the implications immediately.

At the same time, his earthen essence tried to assault the land in all directions with unveiled strength, great gouts flowing from the self-inflicted rupture in his soul.

In the moments that followed, either of the humans could have taken control, co-opting his mind as well as the power he wielded—and not just temporarily. Such was the risk of opening one's soul in the presence of a being with equal or greater strength, let alone two.

The woman, Jenny was her name, reached toward the center of his being. Her fist balled, opened, and . . . poured intention out across the jagged tear.

"Thank you, sweetie," her calming voice said, her potent will sewing his soul back together. "For saving our beloved, for stopping us from doing something incredibly stupid, and for risking yourself to do so."

"Aye," Garret agreed, and as he helped his wife mend the wound, he let some of his own thoughts flow out. The man was awestruck, lost for words at the cuttlefish's selflessness.

Selfless? It was the last word he would use to describe himself. *I'm only in this position because of envy and spite.*

Jenny giggled. "You sound just like someone else when we first met him . . ."

"Makes sense, really," Garret added, the whisper of a smile coloring his voice. "You are brothers, after a—"

A deafening sound cut his brother's master off, a terrible ripping that came from within.

We shifted through kilometers in an instant. None of us managed a word as we looked out through the unseeing eyes of the kraken.

When he felt his brother's soul open up to Garret and Jenny, he couldn't put his joy into words. Anyone allied with the divine would never give an enemy the chance to wrest control of their core. Such an action meant only one thing: his brother wasn't evil after all. Even through the additional earthen essence putting his power to the test, countless hopeful thoughts crossed his mind.

But then two gods arrived. Their golden spirits burned his hope to ash.

In that moment, he might have accused his former brother of orchestrating a betrayal of the unbelievable magnitude and callousness, but that would have to come later—the gilded aspect antithetical to his own flowed into the black hole that was his abyssal element, joining the twin rivers of earth and magma already streaming in.

Overwhelmed, his mind shut down.

The cuttlefish could do nothing to stop the divine siblings from tearing his soul asunder. They laughed. It was the first time they'd ever shown him their true feelings, yet he couldn't appreciate that fact—he was too busy having his mind and body flayed.

Despite the all-encompassing pain, his thoughts were mainly for another. Golden light flowed alongside the torrents of earth and manga being sucked into the abyss. Dolos and Apate, those dreadful and cunning gods, were going to annihilate his brother.

Abruptly, the cuttlefish's awareness shifted within, and though his soul's destruction had paused, it took a few seconds for the echoes of agony to fade away. He found himself in a mental cave, its walls laced with ribbons of the horrific golden chi.

"Oh, little earthen soul . . ." Dolos said, arriving in the center of the room. "You must have known how foolish it was to broadcast your thoughts out."

Apate came next, stepping through space to stand beside her twin. "And to think you had a connection with the tool sent to deal with you . . . such *delicious* irony indeed."

She snapped her fingers.

Garret and Jenny appeared in a flash. They were hog-tied by golden ropes, their cores suppressed. A boulder of despair formed in the cuttlefish's stomach. In his attempt to save the world, he'd condemned his brother's masters to a fate worse than death. Those that dared go against the divine weren't slaughtered—they were *unmade.*

Despite the damnation hanging over their heads, both were serene.

"Any final words?" Dolos goaded, his body appearing before them in a crude show of dominion. "Naturally, we cannot let you live now that you know the truth."

"Regrets?" Apate bent down with a vicious smile as she materialized before them. "Or maybe even some curses?" She got closer, whispering, "The curses are my *favorite.*"

Garret and Jenny, in the face of such cruelty, wavered not an inch. They turned to each other, pulling at their bindings as they leaned in to share a kiss.

Dolos sneered and clapped his hands. The golden ropes sought to deny the couple's affections; they tightened, stretched, and *broke.*

Their lips met as the remnant strands of divinity sloughed off of Garret and Jenny.

"I love you," the wife said.

"I love you more," her husband replied.

"What—" Apate started, but then inky tendrils of essence shot from the abyssal cultivators, covering her mouth.

Black roots raced from the former captives, destroying any divine chi they touched as they encompassed the cavern. Suddenly, the cuttlefish recognized the terrible truth.

They were unmaking *themselves.*

Both gods were thrown aside, slammed against the now-black walls before getting swallowed whole and becoming a part of the room.

Jenny and Garret locked eyes with him, only their faces not yet unmade. The kraken's brother understood. This was the only way. They *had* to sacrifice themselves, lest the rituals were completed and the war lost.

"No," Garret's disembodied denial came from everywhere all at once. "Well, not exactly . . ."

"Sacrifice implies some kind of loss," Jenny added, her voice incredibly powerful, yet calm. Soft. "Dying so the rituals can be stopped? For sure, that's a sacrifice."

"Taking these usurpers off the board, though?" Garret smiled, his lower jaw just now obscured by unwinding tendrils of midnight. "That's a blessing—one that the entire world will reap."

"But . . . you're being unmade! *I*—"

"No." Garret's rebuke was sharp, kind, and spoken from afar. "You two have each other . . ." He was barely audible now. "And the world has the both of you."

"Take care of our cute little octopus for us," Jenny said, a mere whisper on the wind. "And we're sorry . . ."

"Sorry?" He didn't understand. "What could you possibly have to be sorry fo—"

His words cut off as ribbons of black slithered into his mind, seizing control.

The kraken regained consciousness to find something powerful drawing from the hungering void that was his core. Still groggy, he allowed himself a smile. His masters were removing the caustic divine essence he'd absorbed, sharing the burden equally between them. Somehow, against all odds, they had *survived.*

But when two-thirds of the golden chi had been removed, their abysses only grew more insistent. He reached out to them, tried to tell them not to go overboard, and found their connection . . . *unraveling.*

Confusion. Fear. Denial. Despair. *Rage.*

They were fading away—being *unmade*. Someone was using what remained of their spirits to channel their power. Their murderer started absorbing more from the kraken's abyssal essence sucked out alongside the divine corruption.

"*I don't want this!*" the cuttlefish roared, anger and grief fighting for control.

Jenny's last word lingered. *Sorry.*

They were forcing him to pull them apart, and he couldn't understand why. They guided him toward their latent chi, all the essence in their cores now his to command. It was the power of two cultivators bonded to an elemental. The strength of two beings that had almost advanced enough to ascend from this lower realm.

They forced him to grasp it. Showed him how to harness the abyss. He should have been ecstatic. He'd fantasized about wielding such energy for millennia. Instead, all he felt was betrayal. They'd given him that which he most desired, but at the cost of his own agency.

"*Why?*" he demanded. "*Why are you doing this?*"

Someone else answered. Dolos and Apate, like two hands clawing up from the underworld, dragged their way back into his mental space, their statuesque features stricken and wild.

Garret and Jenny pulled this way and that in his mind, showing him how to counter their divine protections—something only abyssal chi could do. The gods' emotions hit him as if they were his own. They were desperate. *Rabid.* Their feigned death, their final gambit, had been uncovered.

They flailed and stabbed with blades of divinity, tearing through the black tendrils that sought to consume them. The cuttlefish finally understood. He'd assumed the gods defeated; his brother's masters had known better.

Still in control of his being, they fought the usurpers off. They drew on their bond, and the kraken's essence came pouring in. Identical to theirs, it obeyed them—obeyed *him.*

Coming to terms with the role he had to play, he examined an aspect he'd always dreamed of, yet long ago accepted he would never wield. Abyssal chi. It felt *right,* even more aligned with his soul than he'd imagined. He hated every moment.

It was unfair. It was *cruel.* And there was no other way.

He could do nothing. He couldn't even look away. His only option was to witness the final stages of the unmaking, forced to take part in the annihilation of two usurpers and two allies.

His own power called out. The earthen chi was being pulled into the void, as was the first sister's volcanic essence. He tried to reach out to her, tried to tell her to flee, but the void was too vast—any attempt at communication was absorbed as an afterthought.

There was only one task left for him. A single job to pour his anguish into. Using the sliver of abyssal chi not being used to suppress the divine gods, he sucked in the still-molten rock beneath the continent. Even that fraction of power was catastrophic.

In moments, a full half of the landmass dropped five meters, the coastal regions swallowed by the ocean. He needed *more.* It needed to happen faster. He didn't want to think any longer.

When all the magma was absorbed, he focused on solid rock, absorbing hundreds, then thousands of tons a second. The continent shuddered and cracked and split, one solid piece becoming countless disconnected fragments.

The divine gods were almost consumed now, so he grasped more of the abyssal chi, tearing it out of Jenny's and Garret's fading hands. They seemed to urge caution. When he didn't listen, they tried to fight back, but they'd become too weak.

He couldn't care anymore. The more he channeled, the fewer thoughts he had. Emptiness was the closest thing to peace he could find. He sucked in everything around him, going above and beyond the destruction he and the first sister had planned.

A full megaton of material was gone from the world now. His mind was blank. A single thought came to him, and he eased back, letting it expand. He would need to stop soon. Despite his anguish, he wouldn't hurt anyone. Especially his sister and brother, who were nearby.

He prepared a pulse of affection to reassure them, loosened his grip on the abyssal chi, and—

Something screamed in warning. A line of burning agony shot into his core. Its serrated tip took hold. A golden spear. Two different beings laughed from the weapon now embedded in his soul.

A wave of white-hot disgust washed over him. Those two voices, the abyssal cultivators, *they* had done this.

"Liars!" he bellowed.

They'd deceived him. *Betrayed* him, just like all the others had, or eventually would. Such was life in this treacherous realm. That burning line deep within encouraged these thoughts, adding fuel to the flames.

He could only trust himself. Nobody else could be relied on. With that, he thought of his brother and sister, the only family he had remaining. His earthen core roiled. Those closest to him were the *least* trustworthy—their betrayals hurt the most.

Fine, he decided, harnessing earthen, divine, and abyssal energy. With that unholy trinity, he drew his siblings in, broadcasting his intention with a single blast of will.

Surrender, he ordered. *Assimilate or be destroyed.*

As we shifted toward what I instinctively knew to be the last vision, I let out a shaky breath that matched the state of my soul. Frack me. I hadn't expected sunshine and rainbows, but *this* . . . ?

Another agreed.

"*Stop!*" the kraken begged, inky tentacles shooting out, latching onto the nothingness we floated within. "No more!" His voice was raw. Guttural.

"Mate . . ." I said. "This is the last one. We're almost done. I prom—"

"No more!" he repeated. He was no longer a concept in this space. His emotions were so long that his body had materialized, and hundreds of powerful suckers gripped whatever they could find.

I cocked my head to the side as I saw two of the eight limbs weren't in use—those that had once been chomped off by a hungry fishy with no idea of the terrifying being its snack would one day become. The kraken noticed my attention and tucked them back against his body.

I let out a slow breath, not happy about the tactic I was about to employ, but determined to do it anyway. I nodded at the catatonic shape that was the kraken's brother. "He won't be healed until we see the last vision, mate. Something has been afflicting him, which is why he's unconscious."

I took a step and appeared right before the kraken, reached out toward one of his retracted tentacles, then thought better of it, instead resting my palm against the base of his body.

He flinched when I made contact, but I forged onward. "I reckon I have a good idea what's afflicting him, and I bet you do, too."

The empty voids where the kraken's eyes should be flared, and understanding made his entire form shake. He let out three silent sobs, then two quiet ones, his grasping limbs fading in and out of view.

Finally, he released his grip with a quiet whimper, and we spiraled down toward our destination.

We slammed into another's awareness with finality, and though the mind belonged to a past version of the kraken, their emotions weren't all that different. Myriad negative feelings hit him like tidal waves striking a barren shore, any sand, shells, or creatures long ago dragged out to sea.

His brother had betrayed not only him, but the entire world. He'd dispatched an entire continent, along with every poor soul calling it home. It was an unfathomable loss of life. But despite the many lives robbed, the kraken felt no sorrow for them. He couldn't.

Losing his masters had left a yawning maw in his soul. Even now, it called out to him, demanding his attention. One of Garret and Jenny's favorite names for him was He Who Stares into the Void, a moniker gifted to him by one of the myriad churches that deified him. But no matter how accustomed he was to staring into the abyss, he could not face this darkness. The pain was too much.

And then it got worse, two other aspects coming to reinforce the power drawing him in. Earthen chi strengthened the black tendrils, and ribbons of golden light looped outward, wrapping around his limbs in search of its opposing aspect—the essence his entire body was made of.

Surrender, his former brother screamed. *Assimilate or be destroyed.*

He fought back. He wouldn't go so easily. The maw within tried to steal his resolve; he decided to use it instead. No hesitation remained as he spun and latched onto its edges with his many suckers.

The golden ribbons approached.

He pulled himself closer to the terrible fissure in his mind, bracing for what was to come.

The divine loops started closing around his body. If they took hold, they'd never let go.

The kraken gathered his will, steeled his nerves, and stared directly into the void. So much torment flowed out from him that everything paused, even the threads of divinity disoriented by the onslaught of emotions. The volcanic elemental must have already been absorbed; their magma swirled out alongside the other aspects assaulting—

The scene froze as the current version of the kraken thrashed in the nothingness we occupied. Whatever he was so petrified of reliving . . . it was almost here. I reached out with pillars of pure essence, both firm yet caring with my encouragement.

He raged, heaved, then let go, allowing the scene to resume.

There, it all happened at once.

Memories of his masters didn't so much wash over him; they struck with the mass and devastation of a meteor. He reeled back, but only for a fraction of a second. He steadied himself by picturing their faces.

They'd gone against their own gods. Defected to the losing side of a war, knowing it to be a just cause. They were sources of light, joy, and everything good in this uncaring world. He spoke an oath to himself, but it was garbled. The world shook. He'd acknowledged their passing. Truly internalized the fact they'd been unmade. They would *never* be reborn.

It seemed to split him in two, but that was the point.

Two partitions formed, and he focused one of them on each of his foremost tentacles, creating something forbidden by the laws of nature and the heavens above. They were smaller than pinheads. Despite their size, they both contained almost half of his essence.

Such things were potentially cataclysmic, depending on the aspect of the user—and his was the worst imaginable.

They pulled at the limbs he'd put them in, and before his entire body could be dragged into their gravitational pull, he ripped them off.

Thankfully, the demon he'd called a brother was so corrupt as to be mindless. The once-cuttlefish sent his quad sources of chi out toward the pinheads that dared oppose him. He wanted their power. If he failed, well, the killer of the kraken's masters would be no more. It would destroy the central continent, too . . . but that was already gone, millions of innocent lives extinguished.

To his dismay, the earth elemental succeeded, its combination of divine, abyssal, earthen, and volcanic chi able to draw power from such incredibly dense gravitational fields.

It did, however, allow the kraken's retreat. He was already gone. Weak and almost entirely drained of chi, he slipped along the ocean floor, remaining invisible by focusing on an oath taken, replaying it over and over and *over* in his mind. Each repetition was garbled.

Sending a part of myself out into the nothingness we occupied, my tendril of pure essence approached the kraken's trembling body, but he spoke before I could.

"I know," he said, his voice and spirit depleted.

A heartbeat later, we went back in time, arriving the moment he'd first spoken it.

I swear on my masters, and on the demon that my former brother has become, and on my very soul . . .

The world vibrated, and spikes of his own chi prepared to solidify within his body.

I will not rest until I have avenged the unmaking of my masters and found a purpose worthy of their memory. If I turn from this course, let me join them in being unmade.

Everything shook. The spikes of abyssal chi lanced through his nexus of power before shrinking. There they remained, infinitesimal lines of potential that would either disappear once his oath was completed or detonate if he broke it.

I finally understood. Appearing back in the nothingness, the kraken stared into space, the last of his shame and regret laid bare. I didn't say a thing, instead shining beams of pure essence upon his awareness, the rays lacking any of the golden hue that haunted him so.

Together, the nothingness vanished around us, and we were sucked back out into the waking world.

CHAPTER SIXTY-EIGHT

Hitchhiking Riffraff

When I arrived back in my body, not a second had passed. The soft colors of predawn called out to me, and a small wave crashed against the shore. Both were usually sources of bliss, but as I spied the mini Cthulhu perched in the shallows, his memories settled in the forefront of my mind, banishing any hope of peaceful thoughts.

But then a source of joy arrived, taking the edge off my sorrow. Corporal Claws, her body both wreathed by and made of lightning, slammed into the kraken at full speed. She latched onto him with all four of her limbs, threw her head to the sky, and bawled. Like *bawled*, bawled. *Two liters of ice cream and a breakup* bawled. *A box of chocolates and a rom-com* kinda bawl—

Hey! she scream-chirped at me, giving me her best glare. *You made your point!*

Picking up right where she left off, she threw her head back again, dual streams of electrical droplets pouring from her eyes. The raccoon's torso flew from her pocket, and he joined her, gathering and hugging sections of malleable kraken skin to his face like they were trying to escape.

Had everyone seen the memories? I sent my senses out, half expecting to find an entire beach of depressed cultivators, but most were just confused. Only those bonded to me had witnessed it. One and all, they were holding themselves back, showing the restraint my otter and her raccoon lacked.

"Hey," I said, "He Who Stares with Monsters or into the Void or whatever it was your masters liked calling you."

Two abyssal eyes left Claws and drifted toward me, expression numb, sclera filled with frozen swirls of gray.

"Just giving you a heads-up that you're about to get hugged, mate. Like . . . a *lot*."

"Is that your way of seeking permission?"

"Hell no. If I asked, you could decline."

Despite the knowledge weighing him down, one of his brows rose ever so slightly.

I sent out a mental command to all those connected to my soul, and the shore exploded with movement. Maria got there first. Slimes sacrificed his own impending arrival by extending from her back, then shooting himself into her. She struck just above Claws, her slight body already shaking with sobs. "You poor thing . . ."

Everyone else arrived within seconds, even Pistachio moving at an incredible clip, but only because he was still riding Teddy like a sapient suit of armor. The hug-inclined bear whined as he barreled into one of the kraken's mighty limbs.

Over a dozen pairs of pelican wings stuck to him like flecks of statically charged lint. The roots of a mangrove grew around two tentacles. A tiny bunny let out a scream that was half war cry, half misery as she rocketed into him. A hellhound flickered between countless forms as he rubbed himself against the poor soul that had lost two pack mates. Rocky wasn't bonded to me, but he still patted the kraken reassuringly. Then, he lit a cigarette and ate it after taking a single drag—which I guessed was his version of pouring one out for the homies.

Hundreds of bees—Bumblebro, Queen Bee, and every Buzzy Boy present—landed atop one tentacle and vibrated their wings in mourning. At the same time, myriad crustaceans hit his back, plinking like hail on a tin roof. When Snips arrived, she settled as far from me as possible, latching onto the rear of the kraken's noggin. I'd be lying if I said it didn't twist my knickers a little, but there were matters more pressing.

I turned to Barry, mouthed *Trust me*, then leaped and landed beside Maria, engulfing us all in a bubble of calming essence. I had expected to find a slimy body. Instead, the kraken's skin reminded me of the soft underside of a velvety leaf. I snorted, suddenly realizing why the raccoon was bunching it up and smooshing it against his face.

One moment, lil Cthulhu had been alone on the shore, the next, we absolutely covered him.

"This . . ." came his rumbling voice. "Is appreciated. Thank you."

"No wukkas, mate. I call it a cuddle puddle."

"No . . . wukkas?"

He'd walked right into it. I grinned and looked at Maria, who was entirely unimpressed.

"Hellhound . . ." the kraken said before I could spring the trap. "Might I request a favor?"

Borks took a few steps back and sat on his haunches, letting out an affirmative bark.

"I believe I am not long for this world. I will be unmade soon, and I ask that when I depart, you give Cerberus my apologies. I owe him a debt, and I won't be able to repay it."

Borks's head darted to me, his ears pinned, eyes wide, and lower teeth visible.

"Borks," I said, "when you came to join us and offered up your memories, you recalled a particular brother a few times . . ."

His tail went between his legs.

"I can't help but notice that you never showed us what he looked like. I don't suppose he, I dunno, has *three fracking heads*?"

He turned to the side, the whites of his eyes showing as he tried to look anywhere but at me.

"Oh, come here, you scoundrel." I scooped him up in a hand of solid light and drew him closer.

He transformed into a Chihuahua, rolled onto his back, and gave me his best demonic *blehhh*.

"Mate, that's *crazy*! I get why you concealed it. I can't believe you're the brother of *the* Cerberus!"

His tail wagged slightly, unsure if I was serious—it was at least the third white lie I'd uncovered in so many days. I gave him a good belly rub to hammer the message home. As Borks turned into a golden retriever and shifted, letting me get the spot he couldn't reach, the kraken cleared his throat.

"Traveler Fischer. I—"

"Traveler Fischer . . ." I mused, cutting him off. "Why has no one called me that before? It has a nice twang to it—like I'm some kind of vagabond angler, wandering wherever the winds push and tides pull. Maria, write that down for later."

"No."

"Worth a crack. Carry on, then, my eldritch pal from the deep. You were saying?"

A slight hint of movement had returned to his sclera. He considered me for a long moment. "I was going to say that I was dismissive and condescending upon meeting you. I assumed there was no way you could be what you claimed. I was wrong. And in reply, all you have given me is kind—"

"Right. Lots of kindness and all that. I'm a pretty good bloke, huh?" His brow flinched, and I grinned. "Do my continual interruptions even the playing field?"

". . . A little, yes."

"Good, but I still gotta deny your request."

The whirlpools in his eyes turned into countless gray dots. "I know that you have already shown me an unfathomable amount of grace, but you don't—"

"Yes," I interrupted again, waggling my eyebrows an audacious amount. "I *do* know what you were going to request. You've pointed out how you were a bit of a dick, and that I was the bloody good bloke I try to be. Next, you'll ask that despite your impropriety, when your *brother* wakes up—" I nodded at the unconscious car-sized cuttlefish just chilling on Bob's deck. "In your absence, you want me to tell him how sad and regretful you are."

The kraken, his body already so black only cultivators could gaze upon it, somehow got even darker. "I see. You are positive that you shall not assist in this manner? No other has the ability to show him direct memories . . ."

I could feel the hair-thin strands within him. Tiny needles of condensed abyssal chi, so numerous I couldn't count them, were prepared to pull him apart. No matter how I answered, his oath would be forsaken—he would be *unmade.*

"My man, my animal pals are some of the silliest geese I've ever met, but you've got to be the king of them. And before you go unraveling like a frayed sweater—"

"*Wonderful* analogy!" came a voice filled with scorn.

I slowly spun, spotted Ruby, and gave a half-hearted smile. "Thank you, Rubes—"

"That's *Ruby* to you. Nicknames are reserved for those who don't teleport their friends *halfway to Gormona*!"

Those I had sent with her all gave me tight smiles—except for Steven, whose peaked brow told me I'd done this to myself.

Ruby crossed her arms. "I demand an apology!"

"You know what, Rubes? *No!* You're *pregnant*, and I regret nothing!"

"Stop infantilizing me, you bastard!"

"Ruby!" I gestured with both hands at the black hole made manifest behind me. "I'm *trying* to tell this world's version of Cthulhu that he doesn't have to *die*! Can you give me one fracking minute?"

She pouted, huffed, and rolled her eyes. "*Fine.*" Despite her expert concealment, a blind person could've spotted the smile attempting to break free of her tightened lips. "Hurry it up—I need to finish scolding you."

"Sorry about that, mate," I said to the kraken. "Pregnancy hormones are a—" I ducked the shoe that came sailing for my head. Unfortunately, that left a certain cephalopod in the line of fire.

Whap!

The heel struck him right in the dome, but he didn't react in the slightest. His eyes whirled once more as he stared down at me. "You speak the truth?"

"That's up to you, my ma—er, eldritch horror. A couple mates of mine helped me realize something about oaths and truths." I scanned the crowd and shot Marcus and his husband a quick wink. "Far as I see it, such things are all about perspective."

I'd expected a reaction, but not the one that came. His fury and anger were unleashed in great waves of abyssal power. Most of the cuddle puddle immediately retreated.

Other than myself, only Maria and Claws remained, the former radiating pulses of healing essence, the latter riding the kraken's rippling skin like she was surfing. Oh, Teddy and his Pistachio armor, too, four ursine limbs wrapped about a tentacle writhing around ten meters above the shore.

The kraken paid everyone else no attention. "Are you insinuating, *human*, that I would forsake my duty?"

Noting how fast he dropped the polite honorifics from earlier, I cut to the chase. "My many-limbed brother, I ain't insinuating *shit*. I'm flat-out *telling* you that your oath was dumb as heck, and that there's a way to fulfill it without forsaking your duty, honor, or whatever else."

His skin still rose and fell, but with reduced frequency. He looked toward the crowd. "Truthsay—"

"Well, well, *well*," Theo interrupted. "Look who came craaawling back."

"I, uh . . . I apologize?"

"*For?*" Theo demanded, enjoying himself entirely too much.

"For calling you a Falsesay—"

"Don't!" Theo faced the heavens and pinched the bridge of his nose with dainty fingers. "Don't say it again. My delicate sensibilities cannot handle hearing such a vulgar term twice in one day."

The kraken, perhaps wondering if the juice was worth the squeeze, nodded. "May I request you confirm his words?"

"Which ones?"

"All that Traveler Fischer has just said . . ."

Theo sniffed. "I could choose to interpret that any number of ways, but I'll take pity on you. Yes, Fischer was telling—"

"Traveler Fischer," I corrected.

"Yeah, no. Not happening. I respect the attempt, though. *Fischer* was telling the truth. He believes that . . ."

I stopped listening, instead engaging in a swift yet exhaustive round of negotiations with a duo that would likely be designated a terrorist organization by anyone sensible. Finally, Claws and the raccoon both nodded and made twin oaths on their cores using the knowledge we'd gleaned from the kraken's memories.

It was a drastic step, yet entirely necessary.

". . . and that you can genuinely fulfill your oath," Theo finished.

I'd not known mini Cthulhu for long, but based on the nebulous clouds of white in his eyes, I had a pretty good idea what he was feeling.

Hope.

Perfect timing, too. With the help of Theo, Ruby, and the *chancla* she'd turned into a projectile, we had wasted the necessary amount of time.

I nodded at Claws, and her grin grew downright devious. Countless little jolts of electricity arced from tooth to tooth. Then, she flew. It was odd to see her move without shooting thunderbolts from her hindquarters—she loved doing so—but her abstinence was pivotal.

She landed on the cuttlefish, struck a villainous pose by raising her chi-filled forepaws to the sky, then drove her chaotic essence into the kraken's brother with an overhand strike. Her lightning swept his earthen aspect aside, opening up a ravine whose walls pressed in from both sides, wanting to expel her intrusion.

Another pair of paws plunged into the gaping gorge, and the raccoon's digits tippy-tapped around within the soul of an ancient being. I'd never seen him so serious. So *focused.* After only moments, he froze, his concentration banished by a grin so wide and dastardly that my skin crawled.

His pudgy forelimbs tensed. He poured every drop of his kleptomaniacal chi into whatever he'd found. And he *heaved.*

Like an unworthy wielder trying to pull Excalibur from its stone, nothing happened for a few seconds, but then the slight bastard went full Super Saiyan. Waves and peaks of opaque force rose from his body, and a line of fur stood on end, giving him a cute little mohawk.

He *screamed* with the effort. The sound was quieter than I reckoned it should be, considering how much energy he was exerting. He and Claws were engaged in a war of wills against two parties. One was unconscious, yet still powerful. The other was relatively weak but had just reawakened, which was the reason I'd needed to stall.

I was ready to step in and lend my chi if necessary, but with one last increase of intent, Claws's familiar won a battle against beings he had no right defeating. Serrated barbs retracted back into the weapon they'd sprouted from, the raccoon's desire to steal overpowering the wills of gods.

A golden spear of divine light emerged from the kraken's brother. The raccoon held it high overhead, and Claws grabbed him by the hips, parading her familiar—and his prize—around Bob's deck with wordless chirps and trills.

I couldn't help but share their sense of victory, but I whistled to get their attention all the same. "Don't tempt yourselves . . ."

Though they both gave me a *bruh* expression, they knew I was right.

Claws turned away and flicked the raccoon over her shoulder, discarding him like the already-snacked-on shell of an oyster. When he landed on the ground next to me, he did the *exact* same thing to the golden weapon he held, shrugging despite his core *demanding* he snatch it back out of the air.

I yoinked it first, not giving him the opportunity. "You did great, Rocky Two."

"Hey!" Maria and Claws yelled and chirped.

"No naming him!" the former added.

The latter's offensive and colorful insult conveyed the same message.

I scratched the raccoon behind the ear, shot him a wink, then booted the devious little bastard when his paw reached out for the spear of its own accord. "*Why?* You'll *literally* be unraveled!"

Tears of loss streamed in his wake as he flew back toward Claws, his vow waging a war with who he was at heart. Before he could reenter her core, the first oath they'd ever made dissolved, their duty fulfilled.

I gazed down at the foot-long spear in my hands. It was only a fraction of the size it had once been, but I could tell they were in there. I shook it and poked it with tendrils of pure essence.

"You two have exactly five seconds to come out, or I'm going to burn you away."

There was no response.

"Four."

"Uhhh," Theo said. "He's telling the truth, but . . ."

"But what?" I asked. "Also, three."

He pointed down at the spear. "Who are you talking to . . . ?"

"Just some hitchhiking riffraff." They stirred but remained inside. "Two."

The weapon shook. One of them was trying to exit, and the other was fighting it.

Theo snorted. "So, that was a lie. Who are they, then?"

"*One!*" I said. "Last chance!"

A half second later, the spear split down the middle, and both halves flowed beside me onto the sand.

Ignoring the still-forming shapes, I turned to look at Theo. "Who are they?" I gave a casual shrug. "Oh, you know, just a couple of gods."

CHAPTER SIXTY-NINE

Aces

As two vertical suns appeared on the shore, their divine chi lit almost everything from horizon to horizon. The kraken alone defied their gilding, his abyssal body a midnight blemish on an otherwise holy scene.

The light vanished, my vision returned, and twin gods pressed their foreheads into the sand at my feet.

"Mighty Traveler," Dolos said, his proud face hidden. "We have long awaited your arrival."

"Thank the heavens!" Apate cried. "I never thought the prophecy would come true!"

"Guys . . ." I scrunched my face. "Can we skip the whole groveling thing? I'm not even a little into it."

Both shot to their feet and bowed their heads. Their beauty struck me, perfectly symmetrical features highlighted by high cheekbones, strong yet petite jaws, and hair right out of a shampoo commercial.

"Before you condemn us based on past events . . ." Dolos's eyes met mine. "Know that our actions were necessary to bring about your arrival in this ill-fated realm."

I raised a brow at Theo, who gave me a conflicted look before mouthing, *Truth.*

I returned my attention to the deities. "Explain."

"We—" Apate's lip quivered. She took a moment to compose herself. "We had to debase ourselves. We were once the twins of truth and order, yet we have been—" She choked up, and Dolos laid a hand on her upper back, rubbing it softly until she continued. "We've been immortalized as deceivers, betrayers, and worse."

The kraken, his core remarkably still, moved to respond, but I stalled him with a raised finger and a pulse of essence. Nothing the gods had claimed so far was a lie. Even without Theo confirming it, I could sense the truth radiating from every fiber of their being.

"Details. Now."

They shared a look, nodded, then reached out to me with their chi, drawing me—

"Nope," I said, interrupting their broadcast memories with a slight flex of will. Their eyes flinched, but I ignored their shock. "I can feel that you're being truthful, but I don't have the stomach for any more depressing stories today. Tell me with words."

Again, their gazes flashed, then Dolos nodded. "To tell it as succinctly as possible, the reason that the heavens above are now empty was because of the water gods' betrayal. They, out of sheer hubris and greed, stole wealth that was not theirs to take, and embraced power anathema to life . . ."

Apate picked up where he trailed off, her hand shaking at her side. "An aspect capable of absorbing all." Still trembling, she extended one finger. "The kind of evil that consumes all that is good and right and just in this world." Her expression was laden with anger, sadness, and regret as she pointed at the kraken. "The very chi this beacon of the void now wields."

"I see . . ."

Dolos licked his lips. "You . . . you truly believe us? Most interpretations of the prophecy warned that we would be scorned at first . . ."

"To the great detriment of everyone," Apate added, wiping tears from her eyes. "But all prophesiers agreed you would eventually learn the truth. Only then would you allow our help in making you the head of this world's, this *universe's*, new pantheon."

I said nothing, neither my body nor words revealing a thing.

"If you don't trust us yet . . ." Dolos continued. "Please, even if temporarily, detain this poor, misled soul." He gave the kraken a look of such remorse that it reverberated in my core. "He was just a pawn to the betrayers, and though it is not his fault, he cannot be allowed his freedom."

Letting out a slow sigh, I turned to the octopus homie. "Would you mind, mate?"

"With pleasure," he rumbled, a giant wave of pitch-black catharsis released from his soul.

The shift happened so quickly that they couldn't respond in time. One moment, the twin gods of divinity were grief-stricken, the next, their facades were cleansed away by my pure light, revealing aged bodies and wicked smiles even uglier than I remembered.

The golden siblings responded by dropping to their knees and pressing their wrinkled faces into the sand once more. "Forgive us!" Dolos yelled. "The facade of youth was also necessary!"

Apate nodded, not looking up. "The prophecy is—"

"A bunch of horseshit?" I interrupted. "I'm well aware. It's fascinating that you can actually lie to me and . . ." I pouted at Theo. "What are you, again?"

"Your octo-pal called me a Truthsayer, but for what it's worth, I identify as a fisherman."

"Damn," I whispered. "Octo-pal. I should have thought of that . . ."

"Please!" Dolos said, his aged hands clutching at the sand in an accurate show of indignant frustration. "If you do not believe us, lock us away!"

The expression on her face did its best to tear my heart in two. "Look how weak we have become. There is no risk in imprisoning us. We lack the power to . . ." She trailed off, turning to glance behind her. "What . . ."

Double damn, I thought. *Terrible timing . . .*

A silhouette raced in from the east, his essence unmissable even through the divine and abyssal chi between us. He'd had a breakthrough, and his core now felt . . . old?

Like the shelves of a seldom-wandered library, its books in perfect condition despite apparent disuse.

"Hellooo!" Ellis called, sitting atop a small, thin, and dolphin-powered skip.

No one spoke as he skidded up on the sand, the three porpoises wheeling away to disappear into the depths, their job complete.

"Thank you!" Ellis yelled, hands on hips, smile wide as he watched them go. "You should consider getting some of those, Fischer. Wonderful creatures . . ."

"Ellis . . ." I said, pointing a hand at the kraken and the other at two divine gods. "This—"

"Hold on," he replied, patting his simple brown robe down. He withdrew a long pipe from one pocket, packed it with dried and chopped leaves from another, then resumed checking his many hidden pouches. "I know I left it . . . *oh!*"

Rocky had sauntered over and was extending a claw high, its lines growing a bright red.

"My thanks, Rocky," Ellis said, squatting to let the crab give him a light. "Much appreciated."

Rocky nodded, raised an already-lit cigarette in toast, then gave it a long drag, the formerly belligerent duo both sharing a wordless moment of calm.

I cleared my throat. "Right. Well. As I was saying, this is our new octo-pal. Damn, I *really* wish I came up with that. He's a kraken, has lived for thousands of years, and channels chi that can stand against the beings that used to rule this realm. Speaking of . . ." I gestured toward two such gods. "Ellis, meet Dolos and Apate. They're twins of deceit or some shit. They were trapped in the giant cuttlefish over there, who was actually an earth elemental. Well, he still is, but he had evil-dictator vibes before and like *dozens* of other elementals of different aspects assimilated to his soul because of the corrupting spear of"—I took a gasping breath and finished in a rush—"divine chi that Dolos and Apate the twins of deceit or whatever had turned into so that they could remain alive in his soul like one of those parasites that take over insects' minds and turns them into zombies that intentionally get eaten by birds in order to further the life cycle of said parasites do-you-know-what-I-mean?"

I took another heaving inhalation. "Any questions?"

"Fascinating . . ." Ellis said, not looking at them or me as he puffed on his pipe. He was busy perusing the pelicans, Maria, Claws, the bees, and Snips and her crustaceans.

Yeah! Claws chirped, her upper torso wiggling around with that fraction of attention.

Yeah! her raccoon agreed, zipping over to steal Ellis's smoking instrument, only to get summarily denied via swift backhand from the former archivist.

"I'm a boyyy!" Slimes yelled, flying from Maria's shoulder.

"A pleasure to meet you." Ellis extended his hand and shook the familiar's whole body when it slapped into his palm. "Sorry to interrupt, by the way." He stepped back, lobbed Slimes toward Maria, withdrew a notebook and pen, then started scribbling away. "Please, carry on where you left off. Pretend I am not even here."

More shocking than Ellis's apparent shift in personality was the fact that I could still be surprised after the events of the previous twenty-four hours. I'd thought it terrible timing for his arrival, because no matter how calm he'd seemed when we sailed past him last night, the existence of deities should have broken him.

Apparently, I was wrong.

Beneath his library-like chi, I recognized an odd pattern circulating—the exact same technique that currently swirled around Rocky's volcanic core. I peered at the plant they were smoking, paused for a moment, then looked at Dolos and Apate once more. "Right. Where were we?"

They returned my gaze, but I could feel their attention constantly tugging back toward Ellis. Did his breakthrough hold some kind of significance? Interesting . . .

"We were discussing our imprisonment," Apate said, remaining on her knees and sitting upright. "Even if we *are* evil, which we absolutely are *not*, we can be reformed. You are compassionate and just, which is the exact reason you are the traveler of prophecy."

I crossed my arms, closed my eyes, and nodded slowly. "Yeah, *nah*. Fuck all that."

"What?" they both asked, genuinely confused by my answer.

"Listen, I'm all for reform." I gestured at the royal family, the handlers, and even the two noble Osnans. "These guys previously sucked to varying degrees, but look at them now—aren't they adorable?"

Tryphena raised a brow, the handlers looked confused, and Tom Osnan Jr. glared so hard that he appeared one second from reverting to evil.

"But," I continued, "you are *literally* gods of deception, and I've seen firsthand . . . wait, is it secondhand if you witness a memory directly?" I shook my head. "Doesn't matter. The point is, I've seen for myself just how twisted you two are. I'll give you props for the attempt, though. Mention a prophecy, plant the seed of doubt that said prophecy warned I wouldn't trust you at first, and, finally, drop the bomb that you want to help me become the chief deity of some universe-spanning pantheon. It might have worked on another bloke, to be honest, but you got the wrong—"

"Please do not dismiss our truth!" Apate blubbered, interrupting her ugly-crying. "A force is coming! Something from the far-distant heavens! You love your followers, yes? You care for them? If you do not stop the approaching army, they will lay ruin to all that you hold dear!"

"Lady . . ." I shook my head, growing annoyed with how her ostensibly honest tears were making my chest ache. "I come from *Earth*. We might not have had magic, lightning-wreathed otters, or guard crabs that can shoot aura blades like anime protagonists, but you know what we *did* have? The internet, media giants, and billion—"

"Please!" Dolos interrupted, but his power was slipping, the ability to mask lies beginning to falter. "My sister is right. I know not the world you come from, but this enemy is so vast, so powerful. Even if you think us evil, you cannot hope to survive without our help."

"Riiiight. Unite the people against a common enemy." I rolled my eyes. "That's like . . . step one in the propaganda playbook. I grew up with John Howard as my prime minister, mate. I've had the existential threat of 'boat people' shoved down my throat since I was a little fella."

"What are boat people?" Barry stage-whispered to the person beside him.

"No idea," Helen hissed back. "Why?"

"Well, whatever they are, it can't be pleasant having them shoved down your throat. Do you think that's why Fischer is the way he is?"

"You know, you just might be onto something. It's the best theory I've heard so far . . ."

The moment I turned to give my dissenters some stink-eye, the divine twins made one last desperate attempt. "Please!" they both yelled, their true, disgusting emotions shining through their crocodile tears. "You must believe—"

In response, I did something so strong, so *powerful*, that they had no choice but to stop talking and listen.

I blew a raspberry.

"Yeah, nah. Letting you two evil idiots marinate in a cell while you regain power is one Chekhov's gun I don't plan to leave hanging on my wall." I pointed up. "Besides, I can literally see the tunnel you've been slowly constructing up into the sky."

Their eyes went wide.

I grinned. "Hit it, Claws."

Spurred to action by the second oath they'd taken, a chaotic otter and a thieving raccoon shot forward. Golden beams exploded from Dolos and Apate as they both turned into streaks of light, flashing toward the thin tunnel they had weaved skyward. I slammed dozens of layers of chi into place; the siblings smashed right through them, their divine essence piercing my unaspected shields.

But it wasn't just me they had to contend with. The kraken, having also been aware of their efforts, had sent his own tendrils of power into the clouds. They came pouring down the tube as a black morass, hitting the twin gods with a sickening thud that pressed them into the sand—right next to a pair of deviants.

Corporal Claws and her familiar glowed with energy. They took hold of the divine beings, pretended to steal it for themselves while looking at me for a reaction, then cackled and chittered, both mad with power as they sent the golden essence barreling down into the open arms of the network below.

Dolos and Apate screamed in protest, and daggers of their sickly yellow light started clawing its way to the surface.

A thought occurred, and I tried not to do it. I really did. If I showed a *little* restraint, a better opportunity would certainly come along. But in the end, I couldn't help myself.

So I took a deep breath, cupped my hands to my mouth, and yelled for all to hear, "Release the kraken!"

My octo-pal's abyssal chi hit them with a sound even more sickening than the earlier thud. Dolos's and Apate's gilded blades warped, the edges growing dull as they tried and failed to find purchase. Against me, all my pals, and a kraken straight from mythology, the two gods stood not a chance—they were absorbed in their entirety by the network, then into me.

The moment it touched my core, I braced with every ounce of will I had, half expecting their hatred and bitterness to come stomping into my awareness. Instead, I received bliss. Contrary to the feel of it in my visions, the golden essence flowed into my own pure light, assimilating with my complete lack of an aspect.

Before I could consider it further, power streamed from both me and my Domain, dozens upon dozens of distinct spirits flowing to the surface. All the elementals that had been forced to join the cuttlefish.

Trusting the combination of thieving and abyssal chi to finish off the two divine dickheads, I gave the untethered souls my full attention—what I found transcended physical and mental senses both.

First, I saw them in my mind's eye, the ethereal blobs lit by colors reflecting their respective element. When they emerged from the sands, I could smell their aspects. A red spirit zoomed around me before shooting off. His soul was incredibly hot and smelled of burning grass; he was undeniably a fire elemental, and his ideal was . . . to go fast?

A green decay elemental with the scent of leaf litter was trailed by a purple rot elemental that smelled like fermented wine. The former's ideal was to destroy, and the latter's was to create life, yet they both swirled around each other, their purposes harmonious.

As more and more emerged, I lost sight of the individuals, their unique temperatures, scents, and ideals overshadowed by a singular emotion coming from the many—rapture. No longer were they forced to adhere to earth, and they celebrated the return to who and what they had once been.

When a pair of humanoid souls called out to me, I set them aside and sealed their memory away—it wasn't yet time. I focused elsewhere instead.

The elementals had to make a choice, and each of them froze as three distinct forces pulled upon them. All I could decipher at first was that one anchored them in place, while the other two tugged in opposite directions—above and below. After they started making their decisions, I learned the nature of the possibilities.

They were simple: become a part of the world, leave this realm, or . . . *live.*

Hold up, I thought. *Live? Am I about to unlock a menagerie of elementals?*

That hope was immediately denied. Most left, their disembodied wills vanishing into the sky as if they'd never been. Some, perhaps a dozen, chose to remain here, their souls zipping down into the network. I trailed them there, curious what would happen, but they outsped my will and disappeared—so I turned my attention to the "divine" beings instead, witnessing the last shred of their power getting absorbed.

It all happened so fast, and when all was said and done, a single being had decided to live. It was a soul I recognized—the volcanic elemental the cuttlefish had once called his sister. Choosing to remain had caused her to regain a body, and she was now a palm-sized slug made of magma.

She was sitting next to the unconscious cuttlefish, which was fine except for the fact that her *molten form was making parts of Bob burst into flames*! The congregation-turned-crabs leaped into action, the stack of crustaceans using gouts of saltwater to put out literal fires.

The cloud of steam was stunning in the predawn hues, and I watched it until I felt a certain eldritch horror's resolve shift. "Hey!" I yelled at the kraken. "*Bad* octo-pal! I forbid you from deciding to unmake, unravel, undo, or—*you know what?* Nobody is allowed to un-*anything* until further notice! You hear me? *No un-ing!*"

The cheeky bugger didn't look even a little sorry about taking advantage of my distraction. "I suppose I should not be surprised that you saw through me . . ."

"You shouldn't, no. As calm as you look on the outside, your disappointment is deeper than the ocean." I shook my head. "What I don't understand is *why*. You clearly want to stay, so *stay*."

His face shifted, and just like the divine twins earlier, his facade shattered to reveal an expression that matched his internal state. "No matter which way I look at it, I have doomed myself."

Doomed himself? All at once, it finally clicked in my head. "Oh. *Ohhhh.* Damn, dude. That's *dark*."

"Okay," Barry said. "Officially lost."

Maria looked similarly perplexed. She'd seen the same visions as me but had yet to reach the same conclusion. I nudged my suspicion across our bond.

"*The oath!*" Maria's eyes were saucers as, for everyone's sake, she quoted the relevant part. "*I will not rest until I have avenged the unmaking of my masters and found a purpose worthy of their memory. If I turn from this course, let me join them in being unmade.*"

"You did it that way intentionally, didn't you?" I asked him. "Nothing was more valuable to you than your bond with them, and if you accepted that fact, the moment they were avenged . . ."

"It seemed prudent at the time, yet now I am bound." His eyes grew dull. "I had dared to hope that things would be different after I helped destroy Dolos and Apate . . . but they are not. I believe that the second I apologize to my brother, I will no longer have any purpose holding me to this realm."

A silence stretched. I broke it before his thoughts could spiral. "You know, mate, there are multiple angles to attack that resolve of yours from. Your duty to your bro. Your ability to assist against any further attacks from divine gods. Or even the existence of Claws, a newborn elemental who could *certainly* use your guidance."

My otter pal made a dismissive sound and waved one paw. Her familiar's upper torso made a gesture of similar sentiment, if much, *much* more aggressive. He slowly gesticulated his two raised fingers at me.

"But," I continued, shaking my head, "I assume you've already had those same arguments with yourself?"

"I have, yes," came his resigned reply. "None of them worked. My brother has his sister by his side, and you're strong enough to have obliterated the divine gods immediately if you'd wanted to. Do not give me that look, Traveler. I was not born yesterday. As for the chaos and lightning elemental . . ." His eyes showed a flicker of life again, amused circles appearing before fading away. "I feel the love you hold for one another. She will be fine with you as her protector."

"Hmm. I can see you've exhausted your options."

"Indeed."

"If only I had a pair of aces up my sleeve. A couple of cultivators that I'd been saving in reserve for *just such an occasion . . .*"

His eyes narrowed as my grin widened, and when he was *just* about to ask what I was hiding, I snapped my fingers.

Two beings appeared on the sand, the chi within them immediately reaching out toward him.

CHAPTER SEVENTY

Jazz Hands

Beneath a sky lit by the ever-deepening orange of the coming dawn, I snapped my fingers and brought two of Tropica's cultivators out onto the sands. They were the last to arrive, their absence thus far both intentional and necessary.

"Ta-daaa!" I yelled, giving what I deemed to be the correct amount of jazz hands.

Before their eyes could adjust, George's and Geraldine's cores reacted, the hints of abyssal chi within seeking to escape their abdomens and flow toward that which their essence wanted to become.

Their jaws dropped open when they spotted the kraken. His reaction was even better.

Both of his void-like orbs flashed with such a light shade of gray that it was almost white. Thin ovals of black formed around his slitted pupils, then radiated out with increasing speed.

"Traveler Fischer . . . ?" was all he could say, his limbs all drawn toward himself in a defensive posture.

"George, Geraldine. This is our new octo-pal—a nickname that Theo came up with before me, the bastard. Kraken, this is George. If my calculations are correct, he's a descendant of Garret and Jenny. This is his wife, Geraldine. As you can tell, her core has the same affinity with abyssal chi that George does, despite not being a blood relation."

"How . . . ?" the kraken's voice rumbled.

I answered his question with one of my own. "Did your masters ever do any writing, mate?"

"The *manual*?" His limbs writhed for a moment, eyes distant. "It survived the war?"

"We were—" Geraldine croaked, then cleared her throat and tried again. "We were meditating upon its teachings while we waited." She drew a hand from behind her back. The tome she held out was *old* old.

A pitch-black tentacle shot forward with incredible speed, latched onto the book with a sucker almost as big as it was, then froze. "My apologies," the kraken said. "May I . . . ?"

Anyone in their right minds would have leaped backward if a tree-sized limb sailed toward them; George and Geraldine both nodded, expressions unreadable.

The kraken lifted it to his face with great care, opening the book to a random page. The moment he spied its contents, he froze. His core opened up a fraction and drew on his emotions, sending them tumbling down into the void. "I was present when these words were scrawled." He handed—or tentacled, I supposed—the tome back to Geraldine with exaggerated carefulness. "It is impressive that Garret and Jenny's descendants kept it safe for all these years . . ."

His voice was entirely *too* calm.

I glanced at George and Geraldine, who remained locked in a stunned stupor. "Uhhhh, you guys have anything to say?" They blinked. "Okay," I continued. "A little underwhelming, but I get it. This is a lot. What about you, octo-pal? Anything you want to add?"

His only reply was to widen the abyss within. It drank his emotions without remorse, uncaring of just how damaging such an action could be in the long term.

"Mate," I said, "you don't have to speak to them, but you should *really* stop draining your emotions away. That *cannot* be good for you."

His limbs, still pulled close to himself, undulated silently. Air hissed from his siphon in what I could only assume was a calming sigh. And with a nod that was as much for himself as it was for me, he let a fraction of his feelings stream out.

I immediately understood why he'd not wanted to experience them. It was hope again, a desire to remain tethered to this world. "Forgive me," he said, his abyssal eyes staring at the former lord and lady of Tropica. "My hesitation has naught to do with you."

A wave of compassion flowed over the sands, so strong that its bearer could contain it no longer. George took a few steps forward, slightly closing the distance. "We know. Fischer has been sharing his senses with us. We weren't privy to your memories, but I think we've worked out most of it . . ."

Geraldine moved too, her fingers slipping through those of George's right hand. "Anyone would be hesitant of hopefulness after all you've been through . . ." Her voice shook, and she raised her free arm, wiping away tears that had just started to spill. "Personally, I think it's remarkable that you're willing to feel even a fraction of your emotions."

The kraken, his eyes swimming, looked my way. "You showed them what was happening here?"

"Ya-huh!"

"How much chi did it cost you to hide it from me?"

"Oh, frackloads." I shrugged. "No biggie, though. Timing is important with these things."

He stared at me for a long moment, the void within him shrinking slightly and letting him experience more of his emotions. "I find it stunning how far you are willing to go for others . . ."

He turned to someone I didn't expect. "You two are bonded, are you not?"

"Unfortunately," Maria replied, giving me a wink. "He's okay once you get used to him."

He completely ignored her joke, nodding instead. "I ask you this because I do not believe he will give me an accurate answer—how exhausted is he right now?"

"Wellll, he absorbed the chi of an ancient earth elemental, *and* the golden light of two divine gods, so there's no shortage of power. But if anyone else was bearing the strain on his mind, I doubt they'd be conscious. Stubborn man was hiding it from me, too, but the more fatigued he gets, the less obscured . . ." She slowly spun my way, her eyes forming into thin slits of accusation. "Fischer . . . what the frack is that?"

"What is what? I don't know what you're talking about."

"The thing you're sealing away . . . and refusing to think about . . ."

"Hey! Poking around in my mind while I'm tired is cheating!"

"I apologize," the kraken rumbled. "I did not mean for my question to cause friction. I asked because I wanted to confirm something." He leaned all the way forward and pressed his massive forehead into the sand, averting his eyes. "I thank you, Traveler Fischer. You have repeatedly pushed yourself for my benefit."

"Nonsense, mate! One could argue I did it all out of selfishness—either because I want you to advise Claws, or bond with George and Geraldine here. Both would aid us. Honestly, I'd be chuffed in general if you stayed. Who wouldn't want Tropica to have their own li'l Cthulhu?"

"You could have revealed all earlier, but you delayed so that I could experience and process my emotions. All of it at your own expense . . ." He sat up and shook his head. "If you'd done any more, I'd have become indebted for life."

A catlike grin spread over my face. He was right. I *had* been dragging this out so he didn't get slammed with it all at once. There was another revelation, too—one that exceeded the rest by far. I'd intended on waiting longer before revealing it, but I couldn't let an opportunity like this pass me by.

"No takebacks!" I yelled, grabbing hold of an internal door—the only barrier sealing something in the hidden depths of my body. "A lifelong debt, coming right up!"

Sensing my intent, Maria's awareness appeared beside mine. I could have denied her; I didn't. As I slid the barrier aside, memories came flooding out, washing away the lies I'd had to tell myself in order to keep the two souls hidden.

Maria inspected them before any other. "Dolos's and Apate's ugly smiles!" she swore as dual spirits flowed out and onto the sands.

The moment the kraken saw them, his hold on the abyss slipped, and the void slammed shut—here was nothing drawing his emotions away as he gazed upon the ethereal faces of a husband-and-wife duo he'd never expected to see again.

They washed over him, and a black aura flowed from every inch of his body. It took a moment for him to move. Then, all at once, he flew forward, eight limbs grasping for the two humans he had once called masters. His eyes held none of the abyssal qualities they usually did as he caressed the souls of Garret and Jenny.

I turned away, as did everyone else. I lacked the power to teleport anyone without collapsing, but the least I could do was give them privacy, so I raised a bubble of solid light around them, trapping their words and feelings within. The only exceptions were George and Geraldine, who'd dashed forward at the last moment.

Maria leaned against me as we stared at a sea of backs. "You know, that might have been the sweetest thing I've ever seen. Are you single? We should get a coffee sometime."

I put an arm around her shoulder, pulling her in tight. "I'm engaged, actually. My betrothed is a bit rude to me sometimes, but I love her dearly."

"Sounds terrible. You should leave her."

The entirety of Tropica's forces were facing west. As a result, I could see everyone's reactions as vividly as I could sense them.

Torsos shook with sobs, hands drifted up to wipe faces, and people hugged one other, relying on their loved ones to process the scene. Not all were moved to tears, however. Some spoke excitedly with their neighbors, explaining who the two people were. I laughed when a newer cultivator snorted at another, then asked, "How did you *not* know? The bloke looks like a see-through clone of George! He's clearly the ancestor!"

"Ohhhh, I'm sorry," her friend replied mockingly. "I was a little busy being distracted by the *giant fracking octopus on the beach*!"

Maria grinned at the interaction and turned up to look at me. "How . . . ?"

"How what?"

"How did you do it? You didn't close yourself off to me, but I hadn't the faintest clue you'd stowed them away. Was it when you were in his memories?"

"Nope! They were within the earth elemental. No idea how they remained there. Unmaking should have, well, *unmade* them. Maybe Dolos and Apate's spear trapped them there? Or it could even literally be the power of friendship because of their sacrifice and bonds?" I shrugged. "All I know is that when the spirits flowed up from below, they were there. I recognized them immediately, so I pocketed them, sealed the memory, and gaslit myself into thinking it was the divine gods I'd sensed."

She laughed so hard that she choked a little. "Who the frack gaslights themself? Even for some kind of inter-realm traveler, you are absolutely ridiculous."

"Right? I kept trying to tell people I was unsuitable for leadership, but here we are."

A loud sniff from my side drew my attention. "So . . ." Ruby said, the whites of her eyes tinged with her namesake color. She pointed toward the hem of her long, flowing dress—it was covered in ash. "Considering how sweet you've been to the kraken behind us, I'm willing to forgive your grave crime of ruining one of the few garments that still fits me."

"Uhhhh, thank you, but how did I—"

"Thanks for asking!" she interrupted. "I was forced to sprint back through the charred remains of a forest after *you* teleported me away from the action earlier! Half way to Gormona, mind you!"

"Away from the action? Don't you mean *to safety*?"

Both brows rose, and she leaned closer, her unblinking eyes staring into my soul.

"Okay, okay." I lifted my palms in defeat. "Let's call it even."

We shook on the agreement. Before I could say something regretful and dig myself into a deeper hole, someone knocked on the shield behind me. I took a deep breath, exhaled it slowly, and spun as I dissolved the silencing barrier of light.

It had barely been a minute, yet I got the impression that much more time had passed for them. Their eyes remained red, but no new tears fell. Cores and emotions were stable—grateful, a little scared, and terribly excited.

Two spirits focused on me. Garret of House Kraken, George's ancestor and the co-author of a certain manual, showed a cheeky smile. "Well, well, well," he said. "I'm of half a mind to haunt you after all the grief you've put my descendant through . . ."

I opened my mouth to reply, but closed it again, brow furrowed. "What did he say?"

"Say?" Jenny of House Kraken flashed an impish grin that both matched and complemented her husband's. "We saw the memories as if they were our own. A crown auditor?" She cackled. "Divines below, what an impact you've had on this village since arriving . . ."

George shook his head softly, not at all embarrassed by his former assumptions. I hadn't noticed because of my growing exhaustion, but as I looked at him, I sensed the new quality of his chi. Geraldine, too. Though not bonded to the giant cephalopod, they'd gained insight into the abyss. Condensed orbs of it swirled in their cores.

"Thank you, Traveler," Garret said, his body becoming more intangible. "Words don't exist to express how much gratitude I have for you."

Jenny nodded, laugh lines bunching around her temples as she smiled at me. "Am I correct in assuming you've worked out what you saved our beloved kraken from?"

"The whole *being unmade* thing? Yeah. Your soul is just . . . gone, right? You don't move on to the afterlife or wherever it is those sky-bound elementals went. Don't pass go, don't collect $200."

"Yes," she answered, her fading eyes sparkling with amusement. "The Monopoly analogy is a good one."

"Thanks! It's nice to be—Wait! How the *frack* do you know what Monopoly is?"

"Should we tell him?" Garret asked his wife.

That sparkle in her gaze turned sharp, reminding me of none other than Corporal Claws. "Nope. Leaving him in the dark a while longer feels only right considering how often he intentionally confuses others."

"Guys. *Guuuys,*" I tried. "C'mon now. Surely you aren't gonna—" I cut off as they dissolved into lines of black-yet-incandescent light.

I'd not felt its approach, but the moment they made their decision, I could sense the options the universe had presented to them. Their physical forms had been unraveled long ago, so they couldn't stay. They needed to join the world's chi, or depart this realm for whatever lay beyond it.

With pulses of thankfulness, gratitude, and affection for the kraken they'd once called family, their ethereal lines raced up toward the heavens, leaving sight in an instant. Neither George, Geraldine, nor mini Cthulhu felt any grief about their departure—they had clearly come to terms with it during whatever time-dilatey bullshit had happened within my shielding.

"Damn . . ." I stared up at the sky above. "That *is* annoying, isn't it?"

"Incredibly," Maria replied. "Does that mean you'll stop doing it to others?"

"Nope!" Ruby and I answered, me with what I'd call *polite sincerity*, her with what I'd call *cruel mockery spoken in a goofy voice that didn't at all sound like me.*

I gave her my best scowl, which only made her smile spread to the faces of those around her.

"Anyhoooo . . ." I said, changing the both the direction I faced and the subject. "I seem to recall a mention of a life debt. Maria? Can you confirm?"

"Indeed." She nodded seriously, rubbing her chin. "And you *did* say 'no take-backs' before he had a chance to withdraw his offer. I believe that makes it binding. Them's the rules."

The kraken laughed. It was a *real* laugh, one that went from the top of his big ol' noggin to the ends of his many tentacles. His eyes flashed and remained a brilliant white. "Sorry, Traveler Fischer. I am afraid that I cannot remain here . . ."

"Ah well." I was a little disappointed, but he knew I was being facetious about debt. He could do what he wanted. "It was worth a shot. Ya win some, ya lose so—"

"Unless I do *thisss*."

That final word from the kraken seemed to come from the vast abyss that was his core. Such an endless void only understood how to consume, its very nature to draw things in. Yet even with my awareness weakened by exhaustion, I sensed the twin strands of elemental chi that wound their way out.

CHAPTER SEVENTY-ONE

Loot Goblin

Time seemed to stand still for everything—bar the midnight vortices of chi that exited an eldritch horror, crossed the sands, and flowed into a couple of married krakens. I'd seen nothing like this before, so I had absolutely no clue what to expect from such a bonding.

It was beyond compare.

An elemental and two cultivators of the same aspect all became one, their cores expanding into a single orb that engulfed them. When it retracted once more, it split into three parts of the same darkness. A flash of light exploded out into the world, black and hungry and compassionate.

It faded as fast as it arrived. Though none of them looked physically changed, the power radiating from their cores had—all were shockingly strong.

I fist-pumped on the spot, overwhelmed with emotions. "Let's fracking *go*! That's—"

I cut off, my head darting to the side as violent intent flared. Claws had murder in her eyes as she pulled back a paw and filled it with lightning. The subject of her ire grew more animated, attempting to pull off his heist before she could stop him.

The raccoon, both hero of the day and entirely unworthy of trust, gripped a shadow. The little bastard had somehow stolen some of the abyssal light. He was trying to stuff it into one of his master's pockets.

Claws's screech was deafening as her forearm descended. She cracked him over the head with her fist, sending him rocketing downward. *Are you seeking to kill me?* she demanded. He hadn't relinquished his inky prize despite his top half becoming lodged in the shore. *Let that go this instant, mister!*

His paw trembled, shook, then relaxed. The shadow flowed back into the kraken and his new masters, though that title was a misnomer, really. They were equals. They were friends. They were *family*.

"That's it!" I yelled, throwing my hands high. "If I see one more wholesome moment, my heart is gonna explode!"

"Lie," Theo said. "You're clearly enjoying yourself."

I tried to refute his claim, but I forgot all about it when Maria hugged me from the back. "Yep!" she confirmed. "That was just an excuse. He was about to say we—"

"Should have a feast?" I finished. "To celebrate our new friends? Wonderful suggestion, Maria!"

She was still behind me, so I couldn't see her roll her eyes—which was why she repeated the gesture through our connection.

"First, though . . ." I rubbed my hands together. "We have some spoils to collect. Borks, would you please grab those things beneath the boat?"

With a *ruff*, a few wags of the tail, and an expertly placed portal, ten crystallized fossils tumbled onto the sand.

"See these, Ellis? They're *natural* artifacts. I'm not entirely sure what that means yet, but I know they shouldn't exist!"

The power radiating from them proved the truth of my claim. I watched the archivist closely, but all he gave them was an appreciative nod, the chi circling his abdomen keeping him unperturbed.

"That didn't work, huh? How about this, then . . ." I rubbed my hands together again, unable to keep my internal loot goblin at bay. "Hey, Theo?"

"Yes?"

"You know how we freed like . . . a whole *bunch* of elementals?"

"Yeah?"

"Well, I reckon every single one of those could have been an external threat. I also assert that we learned a swathe of hidden knowledge."

He blinked at me a few times. "Okay? Why are you telling me this?"

"Are you serious? It—" I shook my head. "Never mind. They were the truth, right? The two things I just told you?"

"I mean, yeah, but I'm more worried about your hunched posture—and the fact you're rubbing your hands together like a greedy merchant. No offense, Marcus."

"None taken. It *is* rather off-putting, friend Fischer."

My palms froze mid-rub, and I pouted at their smiles to hide my own. "I won't apologize for being excited about loot."

"And the posture?" Marcus asked. "You look like your spine is in great pain."

I stood straight. "That's Maria's fault. She forgets her strength, and when she hugged me from behind, she—"

"Lie," Maria and Theo said.

An amused aura washed out of the kraken, his black eyes glittering with white specks. "Is it always like this?"

George and Geraldine nodded.

"Afraid so, mate." I let out an obnoxiously long sigh. "I'm often the victim of my friends' cruel, *cruel* jokes. Poor Fischer gets mocked, when all poor Fischer wants is love and—"

Maria flicked my arm. "Keep talking about yourself in third person, and you'll never be loved again."

"But you know what?" I asked the kraken. "Fisch—" I cut off, realizing I'd almost immediately done it again.

"Smooooth," she said.

"Thank you. Despite their teasing, my many-limbed octo-pal, I do all of it for them, this included."

Before anyone could reply, I did something silly, calling upon an entity whose very existence was antithetical to the leisurely life I tried to lead—I willed the System to show me my notifications.

It was bogged down with a whole bunch of level-up messages. None were what I sought. I scrolled down, passing almost a hundred different advancements in Cooking, Chi Manipulation, Leadership, and some other things that were neat but didn't *really* matter.

Okay, I guess a couple of them were kind of important. I took a moment to internalize each of those while I was here—which I absorbed only so I needn't check again later, and definitely *not* because part of me enjoyed seeing the numbers go up.

You have advanced to leadership 72!
You have advanced to Chi Manipulation 56!

Hold up, I thought. *Chi Manipulation?*

The last time that skill had been mentioned was when I unlocked it. Deklan had read it on an artifact back in Gormona when he was a guard. The screen had called me unlocking it an "ascension milestone."

That wasn't the weird part, though—the fact it was gaining levels was. I had a running theory that capitalized skills couldn't get stronger. They certainly hadn't up until this moment. I would have to check it out when I had more ti—

"Do you think he's having a stoke?" came Barry's voice.

"I hope not," Maria replied. "I'm quite fond of him—but don't tell him I said that."

Ignoring them, I raced to the bottom of the list, seeking that which was enticing enough for me to willingly summon my oldest nemesis. When I got there, I blinked at the entries occupying my field of view.

"Oh, *come on!*" I dismissed it and summoned it again, only to receive the same result.

Quest: In Defense of Tropica Village
Objective: Tropica Village has become a Tier 2 village. The evolution brings many benefits, which others will yearn for. Defend Tropica against ten external threats.
Progress: 0/10
Reward: Variable

Quest: Hidden Knowledge
Objective: Because of the combined efforts of Tropica Village, chi has returned to part of the world. Discover three long-forgotten secrets.
Progress: 0/3
Reward: A History of the Kallis Wars, Seventh Edition

Barry's voice greeted me as I dismissed the entries once more. "I don't think he had a stroke, but it could *definitely* be some sort of episode. Should we put him to bed?"

"Damn . . ." I chewed my cheek. "I really thought that would have completed the quest . . ."

"What?" he asked, genuine curiosity seeming to override his desire to mess with me. "What quests?"

"*The* quests! There's one to defend Tropica against ten threats, and one to discover three secrets! I thought for sure that we'd get some good rewards from them, considering we'd done their requirements and then . . . *some*?" I trailed off when I noticed just how similar my friends' expressions were. "You're messing with me. All of you know exactly what I'm talking about."

"Why do you say that?" Maria asked, her eyes dancing.

"You *literally* know what I'm talking about because of our bond, and you have the *exact* same expression as everyone else." My loving and treasonous friends grinned, and I turned to the kraken. "See what they put me through? I'm surrounded on all sides"—I jabbed a finger toward the sky—"and *you! System!* What the frack, my guy? I extended an olive branch, and you smacked me down! I'm starting to think you're not a thoughtless program at all! I reckon you're intentionally trying to rustle my jimmies, you cheeky little fu—"

Crack!

A bolt of invisible force struck my mind and body both. The surrounding scene wasn't altered, yet my field of view changed completely, the words unignorable.

Quest: Hidden Knowledge
Progress: 1/3

The 1 became a 2, then a 3, climbing numerous times in a fraction of a second. Finally, it stopped.

Quest: Hidden Knowledge
Progress: 17/3
Reward: *Calculating* . . .

I stumbled. The same force that struck me started streaming onto the sand. Maria caught my arm. Together, we watched three books appear in midair, next to the one most suited to the chi coming from them.

Ellis cocked his head at the tomes, appeared to think for a second, then swept his hand *through* them. They vanished.

More words came.

Progress: 65/3
Reward: *Calculating* . . .

More books. Same sweeping motion from Ellis, his essence storing them . . . *somewhere*. It happened again and again until, finally, the cycle was broken.

Quest complete: Hidden Knowledge
Progress: 486/3
Reward: *A History of the Kallis Wars, All Editions*

I took a ragged breath as I dismissed the last message. Maria held me upright. My eyes flicked to Ellis. The archivist stared into the far distance with a flat expression. Despite the fatigue rocking me, I couldn't miss the storm of chi swirling within his core.

"They're in your library, mate?" I asked.

When he returned to the present, a glimpse of the old Ellis came with him. Both his hands tensed; his notepad creaked, his pencil was reduced to splinters.

A blur of black and red. Rocky appeared. He withdrew a cigarette, lit it on his carapace, pressed it between Ellis's lips, then smacked the man on the sternum.

Ellis gasped, visage crazed as he inhaled the entire ciggy in one breath. He held it in for an objectively too-long moment. As he exhaled a fountain of smoke, the old Ellis went with it, leaving a cool, calm, and collected man on the sands.

"I thank you, Rocky. And yes, Fischer. I have stored the information in my library, which also means—"

"You've learned it all," I finished. "That's what happens when you put books on your internal shelves?"

"Quite." He dropped the handful of splinters and retrieved a fresh pencil from his pocket, pressing its tip to his notepad as he looked up at me. "May I ask how you worked that out?"

"The progress kept climbing every time you absorbed . . ." I trailed off, my head spinning. "Sorry. One second."

Maria bopped me on the nose. "Sit down, you goose. We have all the time in the world for this chat. You need rest."

I let her lower me to the ground, and though I wasn't instantly cured, bracing my chin on my knees did wonders for my mind. The secrets of this realm were ours. I'd yet to learn them all, but with them catalogued in Ellis's brain, it was only a matter of time—not to mention the kraken, a being who'd literally lived through history.

Another thought struck me, and I raised my head, having to get it off my chest. "You're an absolute bastard, you know that?" I asked the sky.

Maria giggled. "I know the System is your archnemesis, but you should probably thank it—I can only imagine how much the information in those books is going to help us. It was enough to almost reset Ellis, and he was able to weather the existence of our kraken pal."

I blew air through my lips. "The only thing I'll thank the System for right now is not finishing the other quest, too. Don't get me wrong, I'm keen for Tropica to upgrade, but I'm not sure I could have that power flow through me and remain consciou—"

CRACK!

It was my own fault, really. I'd shown weakness, and my oldest enemy had pounced. Before my vision went black, I registered the words before me, my enhanced awareness easily able to parse their meaning.

Quest: In Defense of Tropica Village
Progress: 79/10
Reward: Tropica upgraded from Tier 2 to Tier 3.

Huh, I thought, unable to feel the power no doubt pouring through me. *Neat* . . .

I passed out.

CHAPTER SEVENTY-TWO

Because Oysters

I stirred from a dream both familiar and stunning. As the cerulean lake and emerald sky faded away, I was greeted by reality—and it was far better than anything my subconscious could invent.

I sat up, stretched my neck, and froze mid-turn when I felt the material beneath me. Its rough surface couldn't be any more different from the lap I'd awoken in. I glanced down to find weathered planks. There was nothing similar anywhere in Tropica. Had I drifted from one dream only to land in another?

But then my former pillow swooped in, her hands resting on my collarbones as her lips met mine. Softer than velvet. Firm with need. Like a hurricane, Maria banished the clouds of disorientation from my mind, leaving only clear skies and the beautiful colors of dawn.

"Hi," she said, sweeping a loose strand of hair behind her ear as she pulled back to look into my eyes.

"Hi," I replied, lost in her radiance.

Neither of us broke the stare. Her cheeks grew flushed, yet she didn't glance away. "Are you not going to ask about the changes to Tropica? I can feel your curiosity."

"They'll still be here later."

"Well, so will I."

I grinned, knowing it to be the truth. Content as I was to sit in this moment, some of my questions were time sensitive. "The cuttlefish?"

"Still unconscious. The kraken is watching him just in case."

"What about the first sister?"

With a wry smile, her eyes flicked over my left shoulder. I whirled and found the slug in question by Tropica's rock wall. She sat atop Rocky, who was latched onto a semi-submerged boulder. Both beings peered down into the shallows to study the small aquatic creatures that called them home.

Now that Maria's spell on me was momentarily broken, I finally saw my surroundings. We were sitting at the end of a brand-new jetty. It extended from Tropica's stone walkway, having been built in the place a decrepit one had stood previously.

I glanced toward the village and let out a soft whistle. From what I could see, nothing had moved—but they'd certainly changed. Some buildings were the same style but had gained floors. Others were rocking a different appearance, flourishes of wood replaced with iron and vice versa. A structure in the center of town—the church headquarters, I was pretty sure—had become a godsdamned cathedral.

I'd been containing my senses since waking up, erring on the side of caution. As I took in the Tier 3 version of Tropica, however, I couldn't help myself.

I opened my core, great strands of light wove their way out, and—

Whack!

"No," Maria chastised, her will prepared to smack me again. "*Bad* Fischer."

"*C'monnnn.* I feel fine!"

"I don't care. The last twenty-four hours have been *ridiculous*. You need rest."

If the words had come from anyone else, I might have railed against them. Despite the fact she'd somehow flicked me *inside* the head, her intensions were good—they flowed over our connection. I let out a slow breath. "Are those the doctor's orders?"

"They are. Besides, there's someone that needs—"

Crack!

The sound caused a shiver to run down my spine; it was reminiscent of the noise made when the System gave out its "rewards" earlier. But there was nothing invisible about this bolt of chi. Corporal Claws had appeared behind us, and as I turned to look at her, I caught sight of the first patch of yellow sun peeking over the horizon.

Ta-daaaa! she trilled, mimicking my words—along with the requisite jazz paws.

Maria shook her head with a smile. "That wasn't what I meant—"

A name! Claws screamed, cutting her off. She reached into her pocket, withdrew a ball of fur and thievery, and presented it to us. *A name has been earned!*

The raccoon, looking remarkably shy for how much of a pest he usually was, remained spherical, peering at us with extreme side-eye.

"Claws . . ." I said. "Does that mean I can choose it?"

She paused for one second, cackled for another, then abruptly stopped, shaking her head. *No, silly master. But you* did *inspire me earlier! Twice!*

"Don't tell me . . . you're going to call him Rocky Two?"

She gave me a look like I'd just suggested we throw out a perfectly good clam.

What? No. I've got something way *better! When you were talking to those two gods or whatever, you mentioned someone that shoved boat people down your throat.* She made a searching gesture with one paw. *What did you call him?*

I barked a laugh. "Look, it would be objectively funny to call this little git 'John Howard,' but I think the reference to thievery would be lost on pretty much everyone but m—"

She slapped me on the cheek. *Focus, Master!* She raised her left paw. *Rocky Two.* Then she raised the right. *Prime Minister Dohn Howzard.*

"That's not—" I began, but cut off when she clapped, metaphorically smushing the two names together.

The sky grew overcast in an instant. Claws stood to her maximum height, locked eyes with me, and shot a beam of lightning at the heavens, blowing a hole in the dark clouds no sooner than they'd formed.

Rocky, she trilled, drawing it out.

. . . *the Prime Minister!*

I chortled, then choked when the full weight of its meaning struck my awareness. "Claws!" I coughed. "It's—it's *brilliant!*"

Maria frowned at both of us. "Yeahhh, that's about what I expected. Unsure why you're so excited about it, though . . ."

"The acronym!" I yelled, sending her the connotations via our bond. "RPM—revolutions per minute! It's *perfect!*"

Claws laughed maniacally, but Maria was yet to be convinced. "I mean, it's thematically pleasing, and it will do away with the confusion of having a second animal pal called Rocky, but surely we can do better than three letters?"

I had a devious thought. "Well, if you don't like RPM . . . we could call him Rocky the Prime Gentleman if you prefer. RPG, which stands for, uhhh, role-playing game. That's even *more* thematically pleasing. His soul is basically the thief archetype made manifes—"

"Fischer," Maria interrupted, giving me a flat stare.

"What?"

"You know that I'm inside your mind, right? You didn't kick me out after showing me RPM."

"Yeah? So?"

"So I know *exactly* what a rocket-propelled grenade is, you shit. You're literally picturing a raccoon being shot from a launcher right now."

"I mean, yeah, but it's hardly *my* fault I have good taste and an active imagination. Some would argue that's why I'm such an effective leader. As my great granpappy always declared, you can't make an omelet without shelling a few oysters."

Claws chirped her agreement to the nonsensical statement, either agreeing for the sake of backing me up or because *oysters.*

"You know what?" Mara said. "RPM isn't so bad after all. Who am I to deny a name bequeathed by his master?"

Right? Claws gave a full-bodied shimmy.

"And all jokes aside," Maria continued, "you absolutely earned it, RPM. You were instrumental today."

He looked up at us with more reverence than I'd ever seen on his face, his desire for mischief temporarily smothered by the weight of Maria's sincerity. When his eyes met mine, I gave a slight nod. Something shifted.

The name settled into his soul, fitting like a pilfered glove. He shook with so much excitement that I thought he might explode or rocket away or both. Instead, he tumbled to the side then, his joy manifesting in a fit of roly-polies. The little bastard—RPM, I reminded myself—was deft at pretending to go in one direction before rolling in another. It actually looked quite fun.

Abruptly, Claws grabbed him by the scruff of the neck, drew her arm back, and launched him clean over Tropica. She gave me and Maria a kiss on the cheek before trailing him as a thunderbolt brighter than the sun.

When she was gone from sight, I noticed countless other eyes watching us. "What are you all doing over there? *Come here!*"

No one moved. Almost all of my animal pals were peeking from behind the walkway's low wall, but instead of coming for a cuddle, they ducked, only the tips of Cinnamon's ears and Pistachio's antennae remaining visible.

"What's that about?" I asked Maria. My confusion grew when I saw the knowing grin on her face.

"Remember when Claws cut me off earlier? I was trying to say that there's someone that needs your attention, and I didn't mean her."

"Huh? Who—"

A veil of water dispersed right beneath us, its caster revealing themselves and the power they wielded. Sergeant Snips rose up on streams of chi and landed atop one of the many poles securing the jetty to the seafloor.

She was small. *Really* small. Her emotions matched her size—tumultuous waves of unease crashed against each other in her core.

"Snips . . ." I said, smiling despite her nerves. "Come here, you goose."

She opened her mouth to reply, but only embarrassed bubbles came out.

I stood up. "I get it. Really, I do. It can't be comfortable changing your entire identity and having to worry about how those around you will respond." I approached with slow steps. "Which is all the more reason to rip the Band-Aid off. That thing within you—the gate neither opened nor closed . . ."

She'd went stiff as a stunned mullet.

"It's our bond, isn't it?" I bent my knees, crouching so we were eye to eyestalk. "You'll always be my main squeeze, no matter how much you might change." I raised my hand palm side up, placing it right beside her. "Do you trust me?"

Sergeant Snips, my aura-blade-shooting guard crab and the first friend I made in this strange world, nodded and scuttled forward.

The gate within her didn't get thrown open—it was flattened beneath the weight of our connection, oceans of water and pure chi flowing past each other. When hers flowed into my core, I gasped.

Her ideal. It was so *obvious*. How hadn't I seen it earlier?

She had been denying herself, so worried about acting like a human that she'd ignored her animalistic side. I'd played a part in it, too—a big one. Every time I reminded my animal pals not to act like base creatures, Snips had internalized the message.

None of the warnings had been for her—the vast majority were for Rocky, the remainder for Claws—but that didn't change the effect. She was my first disciple. My closest confidant. And she had borne all that weight.

I'm sorry, I sent. *I should have—*

She collected the flattened gate of her ideal, crafted it into a claw, then used it to snip my thought off at the bud. Her own thoughts charged in to take its place.

She didn't use words; she was a crab. Crustaceans don't care for blame. Only survival matters. I was her master. I was human. It was my job to worry—my role to remind Rocky and Claws not to hurt others. Yes, doing so had caused Snips stress. So what? She had needed to go through it in order to learn the lesson.

A hint of amusement shook her pragmatism, and she sent me a memory—Joel and the rest of the Church of Carcinization having the opposite problem, not acknowledging their humanity in their attempts to achieve crabhood.

I cackled at the irony, sending a wave of love toward Snips—she always knew how to cheer me up.

That was nothing, she said, her words returning as she set her ideal down. *To quote a somewhat-trustworthy otter, 'Check this shit out.'*

The gate dissolved into wisps of essence that flooded back into her . . . no, *our* cores. As the first of them reached the center of my being, Snips's awareness entered mine.

It was neither a pairing of wills nor a momentary glimpse. Her mind was truly within me, and I was within hers. Her physical body couldn't disappear like RPM or Slimes could into their masters, but that didn't change what she had become.

Snips . . . Snips was my *familiar.*

It all happened in a frozen moment. When I opened my eyes, I was still taking the gasping breath. Light and euphoria exploded outward. I fell down on my tushy, and when the beams finally dispersed, I stared at the crab resting in my hand.

"Holy frack," Maria and I both said at the same time.

When I learned of her ideal to be more crablike, a small part of me had worried that Snips wouldn't be as affectionate from then on. The moment our bond deepened, I knew I'd been stressing for no reason.

Snips grew to the size of my palm and spewed an absolute torrent of bubbles. The emotions were countless, but relief drowned out all the others. I hugged my guard crab to my chest as she shook, entirely overwhelmed by my easy acceptance.

I turned to gaze at the shore, suspecting the moment for a cuddle puddle had arrived. All eyes were watching us once more, but before I could open my mouth, Cinnamon leaped up onto the wall.

She let out a godsdamned war cry. *I'm gonna kick his ass!* she squeaked, shadowboxing the air.

Borks's head popped into view, nipped her by the back of the neck, and pulled her from sight.

Maria giggled at my bewilderment. "This moment isn't about us—it's about you two. Speaking of, I'll give you both some space." She stood, made to brush off her pants, and halted.

Snips moved faster than I even knew possible. If she wasn't my familiar, I might have missed it. One of her small yet mighty clackers was attached to the hem of Maria's trousers, and she shook her carapace, blowing bubbles of clear intention. *Stay.*

Behind us, Cinnamon took that as an invitation, her threat of only seconds ago to kick my ass completely forgotten. She crouched, gathered strength, and leaped forward—right into a tiny portal that appeared before her. Judging by the sounds, she'd exited the other side and struck either Teddy or Pistachio, both of whom currently restrained her.

I took a deep breath of the salty air. Truth be told, I was glad we could have this moment between us. Even now, I felt like I was learning more about Snips. A part of her essence seemed to pool around my connection with Maria, too. I started to wonder if that meant their relationship would one day grow, but I let the thought drift away.

"Good," Maria said, holding her hand out for me. "I didn't wanna have to beat you into relaxing."

I raised a brow as I grabbed it. "Can you beat someone into relaxing?"

"Would I have tried? Yes. Would I have succeeded, though?" She pulled me to my feet and gave me a wink. "Better believe it."

We walked a few steps and sat down at the end of the jetty, dangling our legs over the side as we faced the rising sun. Most of it had crested the horizon by now, its luster making the surrounding sky pink, orange, and blue.

Snips scuttled into my lap and looked up at me. With a thought, her water billowed out to create a single garment of clothing. A new eye patch, covering the stalk that had once been a vicious scar. She blew happy bubbles, but a hint of loss remained.

"Don't worry," I said, rubbing the top of her carapace. "I'll fix your old one or make another. It wouldn't do to have the leader of Tropica's animals without her signature look."

She blew teasing bubbles, shrank to the size of a pea, then grew to the size of a hound.

"That's no matter," I replied as she took the mass of an adolescent rock crab. "What's the point of traveling between realms if I can't create a magical, shape-shifting piece of clothing?"

Gleeful orbs floated from her mouth and drifted around, only stopping when a thought struck her.

Master, she hissed, hesitant. *May I . . . ?*

She showed me something in my mind that she'd always wanted to do, but had never asked.

"Of course! For the record, I would have said yes even if you were the size of Pistachio."

Contented bubbles trailed her as she hopped up onto my head. There, she wiggled, her legs not at all bothering me as she got comfortable.

"This is lovely," I said. "All I'm missing is a fishing ro—"

A portal split the air before me, and a second later, a rod came out, its hook already baited. Borks held it by the handle. Despite his averted eyes, I could tell he was excited—his tail was wagging so hard that the movement reached his neck.

"Thanks, buddy." I accepted it. "You really are the best of boys."

With his mouth free, he couldn't help but rain rapid-fire licks down on my hand, at least a dozen direct hits landing in the fraction of a second it took for him to withdraw.

I offered the rod to Maria, but she shook her head. "I could've asked for one, too, but I've had enough fun for today. It's all yours."

With a small smile, I flicked the reel forward, pulled the pole back, then cast the line out. It made a satisfying plop, its splash reflecting the array of colors currently painting the horizon.

"You know," I said, winding in until it went taut. "You seem to have overcome that block in your cultivation nicely. Even if we weren't connected, I'd be able to tell you're a fully fledged healer now . . ."

Her pulse spiked and her cheeks flushed red, and she nodded. She knew what I was getting at. I neither teased her nor drew it out any longer.

"That being the case, my love . . . shall we plan our wedding?"

Her eyes met mine. "Should . . . should we wait until things calm down a little? Don't get me wrong, I want it to happen *yesterday*, but there's the kraken, the cuttlefish, all the books in Ellis's soul, and that's not even—"

I cut her off with a swift kiss that turned into a long one, neither of us wanting to break away. "Nope," I said when we finally separated. "The best I can do is delay until after the feast—I won't wait a minute longer."

She opened her mouth to reply, but both our heads darted toward the bay, an unmissable dip of the rod arresting our attention.

Bump.

Bump. Bump, bump.

I looked back at Maria, but she shook her head, still watching the water. "I love you more than you know, but it can wait." She licked her lips and leaned closer. "Damn. I should have asked for a rod after all . . ."

For a few seconds, there were no more nibbles. I didn't really care that much, though. Even if I never caught another creature again, I would be happy—I'd already found everything I needed in life.

But then the fish bit down on my hook, and an extra layer of excitement piled on top of the contentment within my soul, adrenaline increasing with each shake of the creature's head.

"Fish on!" we both yelled, our wedding plans temporarily forgotten.

Epilogue

On a shore far to the northeast of Tropica, a lone man tumbled from his wooden skiff, both body and spirit pushed to their very limits. He had dreamed of this moment for so, *so* long, yet now that he was here, he could barely move. His head spun.

He'd made that crossing dozens of times before, and never had it been so treacherous as that. The food had been meant for a voyage of weeks—not *months*. He'd been hit by a tsunami, struck at by malicious clouds, and swept off course by waves bigger than he thought possible.

He was drawn back to the present by the glint of sunlight on silver. His rings. He thumbed the one on his index finger, taking solace in the stone adorning it. He almost removed his jewelry a few times on the trip. Doing so presented unknowable risks, but probable harm was always preferable to the certain death of falling overboard.

He was getting distracted. He focused on the pearlescent stones on his fingers again, using them to ground him in the present. He felt the desire to rip them off and let the king's chi flood into him, but he shook his head. Not yet—not within sight of the ocean.

There was no time to waste. He had to inform the king of his findings. The hobbyist merchant pushed himself from his prostrate position in the sand. A fresh wave of nausea hit him, stemming from his dizziness, his hunger, or both. He gritted his teeth and forged onward. He got to his feet, but he wobbled, almost falling back down.

It was like the storms he'd faced at sea were now contained in his head. Those damned storms . . . if he didn't know better, he would have assumed an elemental was behind it. Those strikes of lightning had seemed borderline personal. They struck around his skiff, never quite hitting, yet always too close for comfort.

Not possible, he reminded himself for the umpteenth time. *Elementals no longer inhabit this realm.*

It didn't help. Recalling those thunderbolts made him want to get farther from the ocean, so he stumbled for the tree line, only his suppressed yet potent core still keeping him upright. When his foot eventually found grass, he let out a sigh and glanced down at his rings once more. *Not yet.*

Using trees as handholds, he ambled onward, and minutes later, he could hear no waves. He went another few meters for good measure, then started slipping the rings off. Each one made his chi swell. When only two remained, his core could taste the kingdom's essence. It begged for it.

Finally, the last came free, and the world's power flooded into him. He took a shaking breath as his strength returned, all but his hunger and thirst washed away. Before he moved, he checked his equipment. Knives? Gone. Rings? All present—stored in his front pocket. Necklace . . .

Both hands shot to his chest. No matter how much they fumbled, his relic was gone. He'd lost it. "Poseidon's blessed waters!" he swore, his voice sounding like someone else's.

The man shook his head. He had been playing the merchant too long. With a deep breath, he set it all aside and closed his eyes, circulating chi to calm his weary soul. When he looked back out at the world, his mask was gone, replaced by duty.

There was fresh water only kilometers from here. He desperately wanted to go there, but that was weakness talking. Even those scant minutes couldn't be wasted. He took off as fast as he could, his enhanced body dodging trees and chewing through the distance between him and his kingdom—his *home.*

He had countless things to report.

Gormona, that foreign powerhouse turned relic of the past, had fallen. Last he saw of the castle, there'd been a hole blown in the side of it large enough to span three floors. At the time, he'd assumed it the work of a cultivator rising. He now knew different.

The reason for Gormona's fall was something far, *far* worse. On his way back to the ocean, a shadow had blocked out the moon, and thinking back, he could hardly believe it. A giant net carried by pelicans and filled with humans.

So shocked had he been that he'd paused out in the open, his training forgotten as he gazed up at something that shouldn't be—just in time to see some kind of mammal, its fur brown and body lithe, zap one of the captives with electricity.

The spy shivered, almost losing his footing as he recalled that dreadful power coming from a beast. It was no wonder he'd been paranoid of the storms on the way home.

Not possible, he reminded himself again. *There are no elementals.* It still didn't help. His nerves were frayed.

For all he knew, life had been extinguished on the entire continent by now. That actually might be the best option. Such was the result of letting spirit beasts live. They grew mad with time. Everyone with a brain knew that.

Unfortunately for Gormona, its leaders had forgotten their history. They'd grown complacent, and their entire kingdom had paid the price.

Still running, the man gave a silent prayer toward the empty heavens, wishing strength for any humans, past or present, that came face-to-face with the evil that was a spirit beast.

Especially that damned lightning mammal, he added for good measure, shivering again.

* * *

"Everyone!" Ellis called softly as he strode for Tropica's new jetty. "Fischer! Maria! The feast is read . . . y?"

He'd been so preoccupied with the recently acquired contents of his brain that he hadn't even been inspecting the surrounding buildings. If those transformations couldn't draw his attention, the sticky purple pile of something he'd just stepped in never had a chance.

It covered his shoes, and as its unmistakable scent drifted up to meet him, he only grew more perplexed.

How had a jar's worth of passiona jam come to be discarded on the street? There was a blur of movement to his right. He whirled toward it. Something splatted behind him. He spun back . . . Another pile of passiona jam? Judging by its splatter, it had fallen directly down—but there was nothing above it. Just open sky.

He sent tendrils of chi out to find the apparitions haunting him, and when he found nobody, his fears were confirmed. There were two beings capable of hiding themselves from his enhanced senses, and only one of them was the familiar of a famed trickster.

"Corporal Claws," Ellis said. "I would usually welcome this joust, but I am afraid the food is ready. Do you not wish your master to partake of the fish he cap—"

A white cloud exploded outward. *No*, he was forced to amend. *Not yet, anyway.*

He recognized the stick that flew in from above, its tip glowing red. He didn't know where they'd managed to get one, but he *did* know the effect its introduction to the dispersed flour would have.

Boom!

Now *there* was the explosion. He was fine, of course. Such tricks were ineffective on him following his breakthrough. A round shape appeared in his peripheral vision, seen even through the smoke now filling the air. The raccoon's ability to steal was troubling—he could rob his own aura from the world—but Ellis didn't need his senses to dodge this attack. The degenerate mammal's eyes glowed blue as he tumbled over and over, speeding in with violent intent.

The archivist ducked, and when what he'd thought was the raccoon sailed overhead, he realized his error. It wasn't the familiar at all. It was a coconut. It had two little sparks of electricity stuck to its husk.

The next shape that came rocketing through the haze could not be mistaken. This time, the raccoon didn't bother hiding his chi.

I may have made a mistake, Ellis thought, *but you still underestimate me, child.*

He leaped, jumping clear of the fuzzy missile—and right into the path of the master.

"So you finally show yourself," Ellis said as Claws came into view, only their thoroughly enhanced senses allowing them to communicate. Lightning and smoke swirled in the otter's wake.

Hiiii! she sang with a coo, waving her left forepaw in greeting.

Ellis didn't expect to have to reveal his new power so soon, yet he couldn't help but be a little excited as he reached for his essence. He had learned more than she could hope to comprehend, and even before absorbing all the tomes, his teachers on the isle had taught him *exactly* how to counter elementals.

He reached into his internal library, gathering reams and reams of paper. The pages may have been empty of words, but they were packed with his chi. He poured his will into them, opened up the door to his shelves, and—

Pain. He glanced down. The raccoon's needle-sharp teeth were latched onto his ankle. Fuzzy little eyebrows waggled in delight, up until the very moment the creature stole Ellis's power—then it was its whole body that waggled. The familiar's form couldn't handle the archivist's chi. It rippled and shook like thin paper in a stiff breeze.

Ellis would have his essence back in moments, but the damage had been done. He smirked and looked toward Claws just in time to see her remove a cast-iron weapon from her right pouch.

"You win this round," he said. "It was *I* who underestimated *you*. Well played."

The elemental of lightning and chaos didn't wrap the frying pan with any of her essence. She was no longer pretending to be evil, so she wouldn't try to hurt him. That didn't mean she was going to go easy on him, though.

She swung forward with all her strength, holding absolutely nothing back.

When Snips jumped into the ocean, it felt as though the frigid currents also washed over me. I took a sharp breath, then shook the sensation off as I bent to grab the fish my favorite crab flicked my way.

"It's *adorable*!" Maria said.

"Right?" I didn't need to inspect the shore fish to know it was a juvenile, so I unhooked it, stated my thanks, and returned it to the bay.

Snips leaped back up onto my head. Maria grabbed my hand and leaned against my shoulder, her soft hair blowing in an unseen breeze as we watched the little fishy swi—

Boom!

We spun toward Tropica.

"Well," Maria said. "Sounds like someone's having fun. Who do you think—"

Clangggg!

None of us spoke a word as we watched a warped and broken object sail high above the village. I cocked my head. "Is that half a pan?"

Snips blew affirmative bubbles.

"I think so," Maria agreed.

I squinted. "Why is Ellis's face molded into it?"

Author's Note

Join my mailing list to get notified about new releases and more! You can find the sign-up button on the bottom of the page at HaylockJobson.com. I promise I won't spam you.

If you can't wait for the next installment, visit Patreon.com/haylock to read advance chapters and whole books ahead of their release.

You can also follow my Instagram (@haylockjobson)!

Acknowledgments

I have many people to thank and some cool things to share.

Heretical Fishing is getting a webcomic adaptation with webtoon! I'll be directly involved (especially early on). It will take some time, but I'm thrilled about its eventual release. There's also a nonzero chance we'll get an animated adaption in the future (shoutout to my agents Seth Fishman and Danny Hertz for that remote possibility). Join my Discord/Patreon/Reddit for updates.

On to the thanks: Once again, thank you for reading this book. None of this would be possible without you and your reviews. On that note, please leave an honest review if you get a chance—indie publishing lives and dies by the algorithm. If not, that's totally fine, but you're legally obligated to pat the next dog you see. Them's the rules. I don't make 'em.

I'd also be remiss to not mention all the fine people at Podium. Thank you for indulging my whimsy, answering my questions, and being the lovely people you are. This whole writing thing is made a lot easier by the cadre of professionals watching my back.

And to my fellow authors, from indie moguls to traditionally published giants, you have my endless appreciation. I'm incredibly lucky and grateful to be part of a cohort so eager to share their hard-earned lessons for free. I'll do my best to pass said lessons on, including those I've yet to learn.

About the Author

Haylock Jobson is the author of the Heretical Fishing series, originally released on Royal Road. He lives on the beautiful shores of Australia's Gold Coast and spends his days writing in local cafes, drinking what some might refer to as "too much" coffee, and annoying strangers by asking if he can pet their dogs.